Book 1 in the DI Spearing and DS Devlin series

Foreword

I never subscribed to the philosophy that you are what you were you can always escape to what you perceive may be a better life, but you cannot escape the beginning or the end.

Paul Hughes 2016

Copyright ©Paul Hughes 2016.

The right of Paul Hughes to be identified as the author of this work has been asserted by him in accordance with the Copyright, Designs and Patents Act 1988.

All rights reserved. No part of this publication may be reproduced, stored in a retrieval system, or transmitted, in any form or by any means, electronic, mechanical, photocopying, recording, or otherwise, without the prior permission of the copyright owner.

All the characters in this book are pure fiction and any resemblance to actual persons, living or dead, is purely coincidental. Many of the events described did happen and some of the mentioned London gangs were for real.

The story is in some parts is based on actual true facts. However in places to enhance the storyline I have used some author's poetic licence.

Kindle ISBN 9781520740560

Book 1 in the DI Spearing and DS Devlin series

With thanks

To my many friends and family who were in the UK sixties groups, plus friends in the police. They all gave me the background for these novels.

This book was re-edited plus a new cover added and partially reformatted before being re published in April 2019.

New Covers design April 2019 by Richie Cumberlidge at MoreVisual Ltd

Book 1 in the DI Spearing and DS Devlin series

Contents

PROLOGUE	IV
CHAPTER 01 - THE SET UP	1
CHAPTER 02 - ANDY SPEARING	12
CHAPTER 03 - ALIAS 'THE FOX'	21
CHAPTER 04 - KEVIN DEVLIN	35
CHAPTER 05 - THE KILLINGS	41
CHAPTER 06 – DAY ONE	46
CHAPTER 07 - THE FIRST CASE SCENE	55
CHAPTER 08 - OLD CHUMS	74
CHAPTER 09 - HELPING POLICE	79
CHAPTER 10 - JUDITH CLEMENTS	106
CHAPTER 11 - NIGEL AND DAVID	118
CHAPTER 12 - DCI FLASH HARRY	129
CHAPTER 13 - ARRESTS	134
CHAPTER 14 - THE STING	142
CHAPTER 15- TIMELY	145
CHAPTER 16 - OUT OF CONTROL	161
CHAPTER 17 - PIECES FALLING INTO PLACE	171
CHAPTER 18 - GETTING IN PLACE	187
CHAPTER 19- THE HIT SQUAD	199
CHAPTER 20 - BREAKING UP IS SO HARD TO DO	211
CHAPTER 21 - DAY OF RECKONING	215
CHAPTER 22 - HEARTBREAK	245
CHAPTER 23 - THE RAPE CASE	269
CHAPTER 24 – CLOSURE	277
CHAPTER 25 - MI5 CONSPIRACY?	281
CHAPTER 26 - PAYBACK TIME	293
CHAPTER 27- TIMES THEY ARE A CHANGING	309
CHAPTER 28 – PURSUITS	316
CHAPTER 29 – CONCLUSIONS	336
EPILOGUE	377
ABOUT THE AUTHOR	**384**

Prologue

For some, the nineteen-sixties in 'swinging' London, England was their halycon days, a wild amd wonderful long party time. For so many others it was no more than an era of depravity with; murders, rapes of both girls and boys, assassinations, suicides and corruption. in every walk of life.

The late fifties and throughout the sixties saw the release of young men and women from their parents' bondage. Freedom brought its own set of problems many of which were fuelled by the floods of illegal drugs provided by the criminal gangs and legal cheap booze provided by the then emerging UK supermarkets. It was widespread across all areas of the UK society.

No area was left untainted, from the so-called UK Establishment, including the Upper Classes, Politicians, the Police, MI5 and MI6. Then there were the avant-garde people; actors, poets, painters, the sixties so called 'Beat Groups' and the Disc Jockeys most of whom had little talent who were only just about able to put a vinyl disc on a turntable - They were all treated by fans as Gods. It went all the way down through the middle and lower classes.

As a result, many of the depravity scandals were being covered up, some so deep they are only now coming to light fifty plus years later.

In nineteen sixty-seven Sir Mark Wright was the Commissioner for the London Metropolitan Police, known throughout the world as simply 'The Met.' This of course includes New Scotland Yard and the famous, soon to become the infamous, 'Flying Squad' – known in London cockney rhyming slang as 'The Sweeney Todd.' As Commissioner, Sir Mark was responsible for policing and maintaining law and order in the Greater London area.

The vast depravity problems, that the police were supposed to address, were not helped by the nineteen sixties media constantly publishing stories and pictures of detectives and members of 'The Flying Squad' apparently canoodling with known criminals in their Soho clubs, or in their London East End pubs. It has become a standard cartoon joke watching the fifties or sixties films and television programmes with the police in their shining black Wolseley Model 6/110 police cars, blue lights flashing, and chasing criminals down back streets and into country roads. The cartoon headline usually stating something like; "They are late again for opening time in the gang's clubs and pubs."

The standard excuse being used by some very bent copper's, is this is the 'modern way' for collecting information from their 'Snitches' on criminal activities. The usual response was – "What Snitch in their right mind would openly inform on criminals in their own clubs and pubs?" There was seldom a reply to that question.

Sir Mark Wright knew that he had to tackle the depravity raging across London's society, but as a priority; he knew he had to first address the problem of corruption within the police force. He was not naïve and did realise the physical dangers to himself and to the creditability of his beloved London Metropolitan Police force, because the corruption was so deep within the foundations. With corruption, the policemen's and operative's deep pockets were being lined with 'dirty' money. When huge amounts of money is involved on both sides of the law and with some of the biggest names in the underworld on the other side, including the American Mafia who were then trying to get a foothold in the UK underworld, the response to investigations was always going to be violent. How violent it would be he had no idea, or perhaps he would never have started.

Sir Mark knew the red danger signals were there, and being the extraordinary competent manager that he was, he put processes into place, all agreed with his political boss, John Fairley - the Home Secretary. John Fairley was one of the few politicians with rare foresight. The processes put in place were to ensure the guilty would suffer, but 'The Met' would not be tainted or at least collateral damage would be minimised.

Already with the help of John Fairley some months previously Sir Mark had begun covert investigations into the personal finances of many of 'The Mets' detectives, including NSY and 'The Flying Squad.' The initial results were startling and had confirmed his worst fears. He had to tread very carefully and get all of his ducks in a row; otherwise they could easily run and cover up.

Ironically it was the delays to ensure he had all the corrupt ones in a bag that resulted in the media unfairly labelling Sir Mark as rather inept. In fact, for those in the know, the opposite was the truth. At what he did, he was probably the most competent policeman in the force. He was never a front-line policeman. He was an expert manager of people and most importantly he knew how to play the politics and the politicians, a very big part of being 'The Commissioner.'

Sir Mark had somehow managed to procure from his political masters the funding to produce the first major modernisation of 'The Met.' For fifty years. They had just moved into their iconic brand new purpose built NSY office block in Broadway, Victoria S.W.1. This time the press and media had grudgingly given praise to the modernisation, but quite rightly panned the horrific architects' office block design.

Now Sir Mark had moved into phase two of the modernisation plans by obtaining more funding from his political masters. This time it was the funding to hire civilian expertise in modern management techniques like; the new-fangled computers being introduced across the world in nineteen sixty-seven. Also, forensic scientists, accountants who were specialists in fraud detection with money laundering and lawyers to ensure the detectives had water tight cases. Then he started scouring the country for highly qualified young policemen with university qualifications in subjects like criminology and psychology. Sir Mark had already realised that promoting PC Plod to the level of his incompetence was no longer acceptable in a modern police force.Inevitably the old hands in the 'The Met' soon sarcastically labelled the new qualified civilian expertise and the highly qualified young police officers as the 'Trained Brains.'

One of the 'Trained Brains' being introduced was Detective Sergeant Kevin Devlin. He was plucked from the Glasgow police. He was one of the original young Glasgow 'hard men' from 'The Gorbals' of the fifties, but he had gone on to make good. He had somehow managed to get a bursary for a major scholarship from Cambridge University and had gained an honours degree in one of the new courses in Criminology. There followed another bursary for a major scholarship from Keele University and he had again gained an honours degree in Psychology. He was an extremely fit twenty-seven-year-old who also had black belts in Karate and Taekwondo. Kevin Devlin was a rare mix for a policeman those days, having both muscle and brains.

Sir Mark tried to match up the new 'brains' with the best of his existing experienced NSY staff doing his utmost to make sure they were not tainted with the depravity brush. In his wisdom, Sir Mark teamed up his old friend Detective Inspector Andy Spearing with the young Kevin Devlin. Andy Spearing had helped Sir Mark on his way up..

Kevin Devlin and Andy Spearing was not a match made in heaven, they were as different as chalk and cheese, but this pairing turned out to be a minor miracle.

Book 1 in the DI Spearing and DS Devlin series

Andy Spearing was a sultry Yorkshire man, one of the old schools of detectives who had no real qualifications and relied on informants, gut feelings, native cunning and the lucky breaks in cases, which of course did not always happen.

Andy Spearing was now getting on to veteran status with twenty plus years' service as a detective in 'The Met.' He was attached to the serious crimes squad. He was also a veteran of the Burma campaign as a Sergeant in World War Two, during which he had been 'mentioned in despatches,' before being wounded in the jungle. He had, and still suffers from malaria; he was finally medically discharged in late nineteen forty-five. In his prime he had been a very hard man, but now, having suffered from an unwanted acrimonious divorce after nearly thirty years of marriage and having to deal daily, with bent bosses in NSY, many of whom were on the take big time, he had hit the drink. He was rapidly drifting into obscurity. As had often been said by many, having run out of fuel, DI Spearing was now running on alcohol fumes.

Even Sir Mark was beginning to run out of patience, but somehow Andy Spearing was still the best detective in the squad, with the best past and present record of arrests and successful prosecutions.

The real Andy Spearing, when he could stand up, had a very dry sense of humour. In cities like London and across the world, most policemen and people involved in crime scenes, all deal with extraordinary bloody violence and murder on a near daily basis. They must develop a personal safety valve, which is usually a black sense of humour and Andy Spearing was no exception.

One of Andy Spearings remaining ambitions was to capture the assassin known simply as 'The Fox.' The chase by Andy Spearing had been going on for twenty plus years without success.

'The Fox' was another very 'hard man,' although not known at the time, he was also a world war two veteran. He had been one of the elite SAS who had effectively done a disappearing trick when he was also medically discharged close to VE day in nineteen forty-five.

'The Fox' was feared throughout the London underworld. This was not only because of his murderous expertise, but also his strange moral code; He only killed criminals when he was convinced by irrefutable evidence that they deserve to die. There were a lot of them in the London gangs who were in panic mode!

So, Sir Mark Wrights' undeclared covert war against depravity across the UK society and against corruption, both inside 'The Met' and outside across the UK Society was launched. In July nineteen sixty-seven it was the beginning, but who knows how it was going to end? Indeed, if an end could ever be declared in such a conflict

Book 1 in the DI Spearing and DS Devlin series

Chapter 01 - The Set Up

I suppose the real beginning of my working life in London kick started that lovely Monday morning the seventeenth of July in nineteen sixty-seven. I was sitting in the sparse, but very functional meeting room, where they held press conferences at New Scotland Yard in central London S.W.1. This was of course the new headquarters of the London Metropolitan Police. It had just been opened earlier that year and although it became iconic through films and television it was - still is - an awful office block structure, typical of the horrific sixties architects designs for cheap British office blocks and homes.

In the centre of a raised platform behind a long table sat no less than Sir Mark Wright, the Commissioner for the Metropolitan Police, who I only recognized from press cuttings and television interviews. Although I suppose in his mid-fifties he was still an imposing and impressive figure of a man at six feet three, a full head of black hair, but with streaks of grey showing through at his temples, which gave him that distinguished look. He was dressed in his white uniform dress shirt and tie, his black uniform trousers, but without his hat, or jacket. There was a microphone placed on the table in front of him.

Sir Mark was flanked on the raised platform by two men and a woman on his right and to his left three men; all had microphones placed on the table in front of them. The woman was probably in her early thirties, but all the men were, I guessed, reaching for middle age with one exception - One of the men looked more like in his late fifties with a world-weary face. His body language made it clear he was here by order and not by choice. It was a face and body language that I was going to get to know very well in a short space of time.

All the men I remember were dressed in white shirts with dark ties and different dark coloured suit trousers.

The woman was wearing a white see-through blouse and a visible white slip underneath covering a white bra, the shoulder straps of which were clearly visible. Around her neck, she wore one of those black cravats like silk scarfs. She wore a tight fitting black skirt cut to just above her knees, but showing under the table a shapely pair of legs covered by black stockings. For a twenty-seven years old heterosexual young man with leaping hormones, the sight of a woman in black stockings and see-through blouse was still a bit of a turn on. I suddenly noticed her smiling at me with that knowing look and I blushed before averting my eyes.

One of the many other peculiar things I noticed that morning was that all of the platform men's hair styles, very dated with the swept back fifties 'my Dads' look, short back and sides, no acknowledgement there to the sixties Beatles mop top hairstyle, or even the rockers fifties swept back look and plastered down with Brylcreem. Except for Sir Mark, all the other men were overweight, had pasty skins and world-weary eyes. The woman though had a Mary Quant hair style, very fashionable at the time and had a twinkle in her eyes. She had a very trim figure and tanned face. I could see that if I ever fancied an older woman then she would fit the bill, if you will excuse the obvious pun.

Opposite the platform sat five young men, including myself and a woman. We were all in or about our mid- twenties. We had all been briefed that someone important was coming to the meeting and all but one of the men were dressed in our best suits, shirts and tie. The outstanding exception being one guy of about twenty-five, with red hair and a'la musketeer red droopy moustache and a red goatee beard. He was dressed in jeans, white baseball shoes, a whitish/grey cotton shirt with a collar and breast pocket.

The girl also appeared to be in her mid- twenties and she was dressed in what appeared to be a figure hugging Marks and Sparks supplied black woman's business suit, with tight trousers and black high heels. She was good looking with a trim petite figure, but not immediately strikingly beautiful because of her rather large nose. Jewish I thought, only because of the nose and her black hair. Not a fantastic looker, but she had something, a certain sexual attraction and a lot of redeeming features, which I only noticed later when I get to really know her.

Most of the young men on my side of the table, with two exceptions had the Beatles mop top hairstyle. We thought, and most people felt at the time, our hair was ridiculously long for 'real' men, but it was the fashion. In retrospect, it was just over the shirt collar. It would be seen nowadays as no more than overdue for a haircut by a couple of weeks.

"Good morning ladies and gentlemen" Sir Marks voice boomed out over the microphone set in front of him and he signalled to the back of the room to turn down the volume. He continued; "For those who do not know this leathered old face by now, I am Sir Mark Wright, the Commissioner of the Metropolitan Police. As you may already know, I am the boss for the whole of London Met. In other words, as our Yankee friends like to say, the buck stops here, as far as London policing goes!"
Sir Mark smiled at his little joke. There were obligatory smiles all round.

He continued; "Now the reasons for our little get together this morning" He paused for effect before adding; "We recently moved into these lovely new offices from our old offices on the embankment, which is also rather confusingly still called New Scotland Yard, but I will leave you to read the reasons why in our history department. There were two main reasons for our move here in Broadway - Number one was that the old Embankment buildings were cramped and Number two; it was inadequate for a modern police force."

"However," Sir Mark continued looking at each one of us in turn before going on; "In parallel with this move to S.W. 1, I decided in preparation for the massive tasks facing all police forces across the world in the next fifty years, to also move our police working methods towards the next century. One of these moves was to bring in young new bloods, all of whom have been taught in the very latest techniques in their chosen careers, which we do believe will help 'The London Met' in our equivalent multi-disciplines. Hence you young people opposite me are here today. I hope you will be the forerunners of many to join 'The Met' to help to solve crimes in many areas using modern technology and practices."

Sir Mark again held a long pregnant pause, looking directly at each of us with a quizzical, almost challenging, stare and held each of us in turn with eye to eye contact. It was a rather embarrassing silence which made me for one feel very uncomfortable.

Sir Mark then smiled and looked to his left and his right before adding; "Now let me get this started by introducing each person on the platform and they will identify their opposite number among you with whom they will be working very closely as a mentor during the next year, possibly years. Let me also add, you may be attached to the person identified today, but you may also, from time to time, be expected to help in other areas when your expertise may be requested. Okay - let us start with ladies first and you Miss Kay Turner." Sir Mark pointed to my rather sexy older lady with the black stockings.

"Good morning Ladies and Gentlemen" Kay Turner spoke with a rather sexy, but a definite transatlantic accent. "As Sir Mark pointed out, I am Kay Turner. I am a civilian and I am primarily responsible for 'The London Mets' information and communications, which now also includes the computerization of police criminal records, including the payroll. This may be mundane for some, but to most police men and women it is vital that we get the payroll right week in and week out." She smiled friendly enough and appeared very self-assured.

"However," She continued smiling quickly at each of us in turn. "Our new main task is to centrally computerize criminal records, including fingerprints, for use by police forces across the UK. As you can possibly imagine this is a very formidable task and could alone take up to five years. To this end we have purchased, from my fellow Americans, the latest IBM 360 Model 50 Mainframe computers, which are housed in the Computer Rooms within the basement of this building. These Mainframes will house all the required records in a very secure room and eventually entry will only be given on a pre-signed pass from the Chief Super for Communications. Right, the man I am to mentor and to assist me in the computerization is Charlie Wynne – If you would like to identify yourself Charlie please and tell us a little about yourself and your own personal ambitions" Kay Turner smiled and looked directly at the geek sitting next to me who shyly put up his hand.

Charlie had jet black hair, rather scruffy in 'The Beatles' mop style, but it was unfashionable greasy hair and he wore those thick black horn rimmed glasses. He was probably everybody's idea of a scientific geek.

"Hi, I am Charlie Wynne" He said in a weak voice, sounded a little American but a definite hint of a northern lad, not quite a Geordie accent, but maybe around the Middlesbrough, or Sunderland areas. I remember thinking at that time; he obviously spends his time talking to computers and not to fellow human beings. That instant analysis was later to be spot on, although I eventually managed to get him out of his shell.

"Hi, well" - Charlie repeated hesitantly. "Like Miss Turner I am a civilian – I cannot afford to live on a policemen's pay" Charlie paused for effect (I noticed smiles all round, even the Chief had to smile) and then Charlie continued now sounding a little more confident; "I started studying computer science in Houston, America in the early sixties. My Dad took an engineering job there when he joined the Manned Space Centre based in Houston. My ambition is to be in at the start of a large computerization programme in the UK, which this is and to follow on as computers become smaller. They are already much smaller, as my Dad and I saw in the Gemini space programmes. Already the Yanks in the space programme have computers small enough to go on their work desks and there is a fifty-nine-pound guidance computer mounted on board in the consoles of the Gemini space ships." Charlie's voice sounded as though we would or should be impressed, but he did not get a response from us morons. At the time, we probably thought a hard disc, was a problem with the back. Charlie was obviously taken aback by the non-reaction and simply, with some hesitation added; "I appreciate the chance to join this programme." Charlie's voice trailed off in the rather embarrassed tone of an immature young man.

"Good! Right" Sir Mark broke in and again took control. "Our next one on the platform is Detective Inspector Tony Raeburn. "Tony" He said turning to his right to the man sitting next to Kay Turner.

"Right - I am responsible for the Fraud Squad, investigating fraud and money laundering in the UK and on an international scale" Tony Raeburn's voice was the old forties and fifties posh BBC announcer's voice, but carried a sense of self-mocking humour. "Not the easiest of tasks I can tell you, this requires high levels of expertise in business management, accountancy and the many methods of money laundering. I am not admitting to anything governor, but we do need a lot of expertise in this area, if we are ever going to catch these people with their hands in the money trough" Raeburn smiled broadly. "Oh, yes and the man I shall be mentoring is Nigel Worthington – if you would identify yourself Nigel?"

"That is I" A guy dressed in a blue pinstriped, very expensive, almost certainly 'Savile Row' suit, with matching blue breast pocket handkerchief hanging loosely with a blue striped tie and white stiff collar shirt. In nineteen sixty-seven he had a very dated appearance for a young man of around twenty-five or six. He was also one of the exceptions to 'The Beatles' mop style haircut and had wavy jet black hair swept straight back from the forehead. I remember thinking at the time I bet he was one of the shiny black shoes brigade and most definitely a 'Hoorah Henry' type, complete with the required stiff upper class BBC Home Counties accent. He was, I wrongly guessed at the time, most certainly one of the upper classes born with silver spoon in his mouth. He was in fact a 'wannabe upper class,' who never quite made it.

I remember taking an almost instant dislike to Nigel Worthington, just a gut reaction which I went with throughout my life and almost always it served me very well. I thought there appeared to be similar reaction from the others in the room.

"Like Charlie and Kay I am a civilian for the same reasons as Charlie" Our Hoorah Nigel gave a little smirk, but there was no response from anyone. He continued; I read Mathematics at Oxford," He just about managing not to blurt out 'of course' after Oxford, but instead added a slight sneer to his facial expression, which again did not go down well with little old me and maybe a few of the others judging by the look on their faces.

"I later of course went on to study accountancy and I particularly specialized in fraud in UK and international businesses" Nigel said and his sneer on his face reappeared.

"Why did you specialize on fraud in particular Nigel?" Tony Raeburn threw out the question like a comedians feed line, but with a knowing smile. He so obviously already knew the answer.

"Well basically Tony, my initial interest was due to my father's business losing several millions in pounds' sterling. This was in an African gold or diamond mining scam" Nigel paused for effect, looking around some of the others faces, so obviously making the point that his father's business could afford to have lost several millions in pounds' sterling. That turned out to be a fraudulent statement. He then added; "Then of course there was the recent fraud case with Frank Abagnale who managed to pass dud cheques worth millions of dollars and even managed to pass off as a pilot with Pan Am. It honestly fascinates me how huge corporations can get taken in and I think it will be hugely interesting to set about catching these thieves." Nigel managed to sound enthusiastic, but in a 'jolly hockey sticks' kind of way.

Tony Raeburn interjected with a smile; "Yes, well, what we all must remember, despite the public apparent fascination, and at times admiration with these con men and women, it is a fact that in the eyes of the law these are criminals. They in fact rob businesses and ordinary, everyday people of millions of pounds every year. In the case of ordinary people, they steal their life savings and sometimes leave them destitute. However, my department is more concerned with more complex fraud carried out by businesses in the UK and on an international basis and deals with scams with these new Barclay credit cards and things like that." Tony Raeburn's' genial put down of Nigel apparently went unnoticed or ignored.

"Yes, quite so Tony, quite so" Sir Mark smiled knowingly at Tony, but ignoring 'hoorah Henry' Nigel who did not look too pleased. Sir Mark continued; "Right – let us continue with – on my left Detective Inspector Jonathan Bright – Jonathan". Sir Mark nodded to the man directly on his left.

"Yes – my department is the Drugs Squad. As these nineteen-sixties have progressed with the open challenges to the law by leading pop groups such as 'The Beatles' and 'The Rolling Stones' advocating the use of soft drugs such as marijuana, leading millions of their young fans down a rocky road to hard drugs, our job has become an almost impossible task".

Jonathan Bright looked around for effect, particularly at we younger people on the opposite side of the platform and then continued; "It is a fact – already proven in USA - that the majority of people who start with the so called 'soft' drugs invariably finish up on hard drugs which, if they are lucky, messes up the rest of their lives. However, for many unlucky ones it finishes their lives in double quick time. I believe that these pop groups of today will have a lot to answer for in the next few years. With the use of soft drugs becoming an epidemic, there is no doubt that there will very shortly be further epidemics of deaths from hard drugs such as heroin etc. Not only among the pop stars, but also across our young population and there is no choice in this evil - it will cut across all classes from high society down to the streets low life. Anyway, enough of my preaching. the man I am to mentor is Adrian Porterhouse – Adrian if you would identify yourself and perhaps inform us why you are dressed the way you are today?" DI Bright smiled benevolently towards our young musketeer friend in blue jeans.

"Hi, I am Adrian Porterhouse," The musketeer had a quiet voice with a Birmingham England accent, commonly known as a 'Brummie.' Adrian continued; "The reason I am not dressed in a suit is that these are my working clothes" Adrian continued pointing at his jeans and shoes. "I work the streets, the dark corners, the places where suits will never be seen except on undertakers. The only time you will see me in a suit is births, deaths and marriages and normally in my business it will usually be for deaths." Adrian paused a little over dramatically for effect and then continued; "You will probably never see me in this office again unless it is an emergency, I hope any of you seeing me on the streets will pretend not to recognize me, or make it look like an approach for a drugs deal."

"Tell me Adrian" One of the other men on the platform who had not yet been introduced broke into the conversation. He was the one with the bad body language who later turned out to be DI Andy Spearing. He then continued; "Tell me – what experience do you have in the drugs field Adrian? DI Spearing had what sounded like a Yorkshire accent.

"Unlike the others, I do not have a university degrees' sir. I have lived in the streets of Birmingham since I was a nipper and I got my experience in drugs the hard way. I will say no more than that on the grounds it might incriminate me." Adrian smiled shyly and most of the audience laughed. Adrian continued, "So I know the rules, the barons and the drugs laws like the back of my hand sir" Adrian gave a slight smile with a twitch of his eyes"

"Right – let us move on – and - since you have already asked a question we will move on to you Andy – Detective Inspector Andy Spearing" Sir Mark gave an affectionate smile to suggest they may be old friends, which as it turned out they had been for many years.

Andy Spearing replied disgruntedly with a definte Yorkshire accent; "Yes sir. I am attached to 'The Mets' murder and serious crimes squad and not 'The Flying Squad,' which I daresay most of you have heard of at one time or another in your short life time."

I remember thinking at the time he obviously does not want to be associated with 'The Flying Squad,' but it was not till later that I understood why he was divorcing himself from what everyone thought was the elite squad.

Andy Spearing continued in his very gruff manner, so obviously not wanting to be there; "Mostly we work the Greater London area, or as it sometimes known 'The Home Counties' DI Spearing looked around the room with an impassive expression on his face. "However, even today we still occasionally get requests for assistance from other forces across the UK for our expertise." DI Spearing did not smile, only making the point that 'The Met' is the elite force. "Anyway, the man" - DI Spearing emphasized 'man' in a very sarcastic, almost questioning way – before he added; "The 'man' reporting to me is Detective Sergeant Kevin Devlin – If you would identify yourself please".

I was still seething because of DI Spearing's introduction, which in my opinion fundamentally attacked all of us sitting opposite the platform. I then suddenly realized he was calling my name so I stated; "Hello, I am DS Kevin Devlin" I replied in a more sullen voice that I had intended, but then I thought what the heck, I hope he gets the message and so I continued in the same manner, but slowly in order that my Scottish accent was clearly understood. - It was a lesson I had learned from one of my tutors at Cambridge University. - I then started my monologue; "I read Criminology at Cambridge University and qualified with honours." I could not resist a quick sneering glance at Nigel Worthington. I then continued; "And then later I followed up with psychology, a three-year course at Keele University and I somehow got honours from there as well." I tried to keep my face impassive and continued; "I decided to move to 'The Met' because I felt I would be able to put both qualifications to best use here in London" I stopped short and looked directly with eye contact to Andy Spearing and half expected his response and was not disappointed.

"Tell me DS Devlin – how do you think you are going to resolve crimes with these text book qualifications and so little experience?" DI Spearing asked, again with the same sarcastic manner.

"I would say Sir - , I do not expect to be resolving serious crimes on my own soon, but rather I hope that I will be able to help you with some of the large number of unsolved cases on the books at the present time?" I instinctively knew I should not have resorted to counter punching, but this guy was trying it on and my old Celt temper was rising and then I thought that maybe that is exactly what he wanted.

Andy Spearing was the first to avert his eyes, but his face was reddish and he looked and sounded very angry. "So, I ask again, can you explain how, with your lack of experience and with only text book theories; how do you expect to help DS Devlin?" Andy Spearing asked the question with a spiteful tone.

I just shook my head and then replied; "I thought I just answered that question Detective Inspector. Regarding your apparent assertion that I may lack some - what you would call 'on the job' experience. - I don't think I said I have a lack of experience sir." I replied evenly, trying so hard to keep my temper in check before adding; "I spent my formative years in the fifties on the streets – Like Adrian, but I was in the east end of Glasgow, to be exact in 'The Gorbals'. I can say I probably saw more dead or mutilated people, including children, in my pre-teens and in my teens on those streets that you have seen in your whole time in the force. In Glasgow at that time and even today, you either learned to survive, or you do not live to have memories. I believe there were more slashed, beat up, or dead bodies every day in Glasgow than any other city in the UK during the fifties".

DI Spearing face was still reddish and again looked very angry and asked with a spiteful tone; "So I ask yet again."

"Excuse me Sir but I had not yet finished my précis sir--" I blurted out with a tone of indignation. I remember thinking to myself at the time, this is the man I have to work with for the next year or so and it is not the best of starts.

Book 1 in the DI Spearing and DS Devlin series

I then added, acting cool, which I was far from and said; "After I had passed the psychology course I re-joined the city of Glasgow police at twenty-four and joined their serious crimes squad where I helped on many cases from murder to armed robbery. There were so many cases to work on. I was recommended for this job at 'The Met' by the Central Glasgow Police City Chief Inspector Ian Johnstone himself - He is also the Divisional Commander and well respected across the UK. So in answer to your question DI Spearing - 'Yes' - I have experience on the streets and in the police and I like to think I was so well thought of for my work I was recommended for this job by the Glasgow Chief Inspector himself." I smiled for the first time as I finished and there was a pregnant pause.

Sir Mark suddenly butted in; "Rightly said DS Devlin- so DI - This is not an interview for the job! DS Devlin has already passed, so let us move on." Sir Mark smiling tried to calmly defuse the situation. He continued; "So, let us now move on and it is over to Doctor John Harvey."

DI Spearing looked furiously at both me and Sir Mark.

'Good morning ladies and gentlemen" Doctor Harvey had a friendly, round jovial face, a broad smile and a deep baritone voice. He was around three stones overweight and thinning on top, a real roly-poly friendly type character and he continued; "I am also a civilian, but I am afraid a lowly paid civil servant! Doctor Harvey just smiled, but barely paused for effect, before continuing; "I was attached to the British Academy of Forensic Science when I was contacted by Sir Mark and offered this position as Head of Forensics in New Scotland Yard. I came to Forensic Science via my previous life in Pathology and Biology. As you are all probably aware, nowadays Forensics is usually first on all crime scenes before handing over to the detectives."

There was a loud resentful sniff from DI Spearing which he tried to cover up with a consequential cough.

Doctor Harvey just smiled and nodded towards DI Spearing and continued with a sarcastic tone to his voice; "As DI Spearing has just indicated, with the older detectives we in forensics are not always welcome, but I am afraid today that is the way it has to be!" There were several knowing smiles and nervous titters from most of the audience and DI Spearing again looked furious, but this time said nothing. Doctor Harvey continued with a smile and added: "Anyway, with all types of crime soaring, it looks like I at least have a job for life!"

Doctor Healey then looked directly at DI Spearing who stared blankly straight back.

Doctor Harvey held a short pause and continued still smiling. "As most police detectives are aware, the investigations into suspicious deaths, and murder cases, often depend on results in the first forty-eight hours. So, Sir Mark has recognized this need and has somehow manoeuvred this very welcome change (Doctor Harvey turned and smiled warmly towards Sir Mark) and then continued; "A change for me and for placing Forensic Science at the forefront of New Scotland Yard investigations and this should be an immediate boost to police investigations in the Greater London area." Doctor Harvey swept his right hand in an arc to emphasize the large area.

There was a tangible atmosphere between Davd Harvey and Andy Spearing.

This was long before DNA analysis was perfected and I remember thinking at the time how clever these people were in finding minute particles of materials which assisted in associating it to people, places and time.

"Oh and by the way" Doctor Harvey suddenly added almost as an afterthought. "The man I am to mentor is David Arkwright – David as you are the only man left unidentified."

"Yes sir - thank you so much" David Arkwright wore dark 'Buddy Holly' type spectacles, jet black Beatles style haircut and a droopy Mexican style moustache, but no beard. He was a good-looking guy, but for some reason I guessed the glasses were only to give him an academic appearance. He continued; "First may I say it is an honour to be chosen to work with such an imminent Forensic Scientist as you Doctor Harvey" David Arkwright's opening remark, also in a deep baritone voice with a home counties accent could have easily been interpreted as crawling, but I must admit, unlike the twit Nigel, he did sound very sincere.

Doctor Harvey just smiled benevolently and nodded before replying. "Always a good thing for ones' ego to have ones' work recognized, especially by the next generation." Doctor Harvey was obviously delighted, purring like the proverbial cat.

"And I am sure Sir by many future generations your work will be recognized as also pioneering." David Arkwright smiled, this time it was very close to the crawling stage, but he must have realized it and quickly moved on. "Anyway, I must admit I have never wanted to do anything else, but Forensics since I was a teenager. I was fascinated by the science, not the blood and guts – As a kid I used to faint with the sight of blood, even just dissecting frogs in the science class and I would keel over!" David Arkwright shook his head and laughed at the thought and at himself, which I instantly liked. David continued, "Anyway I eventually got over that and have been assisting in all sorts of crime scenes on sudden deaths, in the London home-counties area for the past five years. I am also a civil servant and not a policeman, but like Kevin I was recommended to apply for this post and here I am just raring to go!" David Arkwright sounded enthusiastic, unlike the obvious falseness from Nigel Worthington.

"Well said David. I must say I agree about Doctor Harvey with his impressive pioneering work" Sir Mark smiled and nodded to Doctor Harvey with a sincere expression written across his face and then said; "Now we move towards our final new blood – I hope you do not faint at the expression David?" Sir Mark laughed at his own little joke, but was dutifully joined by the audience.

"Last, but certainly not least, is Joseph Lyall QC - Joseph" Sir Mark nodded to the middle-aged man with thick black hair swept straight back and a very straight parting on the left. He was furthest from Sir Mark on the left side of the platform.

"Hello – I am Joseph Lyall one of many Queens Counsellors and I work for the DPP – for the uninitiated that is the Director of Public Prosecutions. My main task is to prepare cases based on the evidence presented by the police, or other such forces, for example MI5, for the Crown Prosecution Service to consider if there is a case to answer and if it is a possible to win the case."

Joseph Lyall smiled slyly, his middle of the road voice very steady, not at all snobbish, but full of confidence. He had obviously done this sort of thing so many times before in open courts it was not a problem and he continued, "Yes and in case you are wondering, in most cases, part of this consideration by the CPS is the costs, which can at times be millions and have to be considered against the odds of a successful prosecution. So yes, like it or not, it has happened many times that a person we all thought as guilty as sin has walked free, because the odds of proving the guilt in an open court was way too high, based on the evidence in hand. Not a nice feeling I can tell you, but that is one of the realities and the frustrations of criminal law these days in the 'swinging' sixties. Anyway, without further ado the woman I am to mentor is Judith Clements, who incidentally is another of Sir Mark's new blood. Judith will report to the DPP through me, but under Sir Marks' new initiative Judith will be based here at New Scotland Yard as a coordinator. Her primary objective will be to assist the police and detectives on serious crimes only, by ensuring that the evidence is collected within the criminal law guidelines, therefore helping to ensure more successful prosecutions in the future. Judith----" Joseph Lyall nodded towards the one remaining unidentified young woman on the other side of the platform.

Judith Clements looked about twenty-five, but she was the one dressed so conservatively in one of those dark blue women's business suits, straight from a mail order catalogue, or Marks and Sparks. She had on a prim and proper dark blue blouse puffed up at the neck. Her black shining hair was severely pulled back from the front and put into a bun behind her head, very school - Mamish, but it did show off her fine, facial, high bone structure. She had dark brown, almost black, large eyes which darted around the whole audience.

I then noticed she also had a neat and tidy body hidden under the tight-fitting women's business suit.

"Good morning Sir, Ladies and Gentlemen. My name is Judith Clements. I read criminal law at Cambridge University and qualified with honours. Afterwards I joined a private law firm 'Clements and Beckman' within the City of London Law Society at Grays Inn."

Judith Clements voice was self-assured, but sort of monotone, matching her bored looking face. She was wearing those ridiculously large brown framed spectacles, which she wore only while reading from some notes placed on the table in front of her. The spectacles looked like they were worn only for affect and she looked and sounded the essence of boring and then more boring.

Judith continued "My prime reason for applying for the DPP was really – well I got rather cheesed off having to represent people who I knew were guilty, but I assisted in getting them off because of a technicality which nowadays is the first thing defence counsels look for. So, I applied and thankfully got this position. Like most of the others I am a civil servant working for the Crown Prosecution Office!" Judith Clements finished removing the ridiculous spectacles and gave us all a brilliant smile, which immediately transformed her from boring to beautiful.

"Tell me Joseph," Andy Spearing again interrupted and turned towards Joseph Lyall: "Tell me- will young Judith Clements here be deciding on which cases can go to the DPP?" DI Spearing asked with a quizzical look on his face.

I for one could see immediately where this was going and this time I had to agree with Andy Spearing's suspicious mind, but I looked at Judith Clements and she was positively seething.

"No - that is not what I said Andy. Judith's main job will be to ensure that the police follow the criminal law guidelines and have as watertight a case as is possible." Joseph Lyall's reply betrayed more than a little irritation.

"So, what you are saying Joseph – and correct me if I am wrong – but if young Miss Clements here does not agree we have a watertight case, or in her eyes we may have bent some of the guidelines, then we may not even reach the DPP." Andy Spearing certainly did not miss any targets he aimed for and did not mind taking any resulting flak.

"Oh, come on Andy. This thing is in its infancy and it is has to be given a fair chance" Joseph Lyall looked towards Sir Mark who did not respond.

"Oh, come on yourself Joseph. You know very well in the very recent past we have had a difficult time jumping through loops with some of your people and lost a lot of time and effort. We then had no alternative other than go over their heads and get to you before going on to win the cases. – How do you think that this, probably much less experienced, young woman will not be doing the same sort of thing?" DI Spearing had a certain amount of venom in his voice and the protruding muscles in his neck suggested real deep down anger.

Sir Mark looked bemused, but as a former policeman he obviously sympathized with Andy Spearing and so allowed the discussion to go on, at least for a bit.

"Oh, yes Andy, perhaps your memory is becoming selective in your old age. I am sure you are aware that the number of failures because of interference by the police far outweighs the wins and as a result there was a huge cost to the tax payer." Joseph Lyall sarcastically retorted, but without venom.

"I am surprised at you Joseph. As you are no doubt also aware, over the last two years because of your so-called police 'interference' we managed to persuade your department to successfully prosecute six more people who would have walked free along with the other ten you refused to move on. That is your department's problem Joseph; you consider costs to be more important than the law." Andy Spearing certainly knew how to send his arrows straight to the heart, a typical no nonsense Yorkshire man.

Joseph Lyall could only splutter and his face turned bright red and Judith Clément's was crimson and she looked about to retort.

"Right I think that is enough now. I am sure Judith now realizes the fine lines she will be treading and the rest of you now know that it is not only about putting a case together, but making sure it is watertight and within the laws guidelines, not to mention the politics." Sir Mark smiled and nodded to Andy Spearing.

Sir Mark then continued; "Now before we go on to more pleasant things. Let me tell you all and make you all very aware. This initiative, in bringing in new young blood who have been into modern techniques, or in tools like these new-fangled computer things and matching them up to our best Detective Inspectors, or our top Heads of Disciplines, is vitally important, not only for the future of The London Metropolitan Police, but also for the fight against the crime gangs. This is a fight against the widespread depravity and corruption that we have all been reading and hearing about across the UK. So, let us not go into this with our heads buried in our own careers. This is a war that we all must win internally and externally." Sir Mark paused for dramatic effect with an impassioned look on his face.

Andy Spearing interrupted the Chief with what amounted to be an aside, or perhaps more accurately, a snide remark; "It is very noticeable sir - that out of the six new starters only two are actually policemen! – Is that the way we are going?"

Sir Mark chose to completely disregard Andy Spearings remarks and he simply continued in a pleasant manner; "Yes Andy - Now onto the aforementioned more pleasant things. First, thank you all for your attendance today and for turning up for the job. Second, to mark this most auspicious occasion, I have provided a few glasses of wine and snacks at the back of the room so as you can all get to know each other before our young people's official start tomorrow. By the way, I doubt if you will ever again have an 'official' drink in these offices, so make the most of it." Sir Mark smiled and nodded.

They all came down from the raised platform and headed towards the tables with the goodies.

Almost immediately I noticed DI Spearing catch Sir Mark and strained my ears to catch their conversation.

"I am sorry sir, but I have a very important meet with an informant on a current murder case. I must go to. I will catch up later." Andy Spearing muttered keeping his voice as quiet as possible.

Sir Mark looked aghast and quietly replied; "I am sorry Andy, but no! I did tell all of you to keep this morning free and there are no exceptions. So please meet with DS Devlin now and discuss future arrangements starting with tomorrow!"

Sir Mark turned away and walked towards Joseph Lyall who was already in conversation with Judith Clements over glasses of wine in both their hands.

Andy Spearing turned away his face a mask of anger. He caught my eye, nodded and said to me; "I will catch up with you in the morning." He just turned in the opposite direction and walked straight out the door marked 'Exit'.

I noticed Sir Mark catch DI Spearing exit in the corner of his eye and watched him slowly shake his head. I remember thinking my DI Spearing thinks he is a law unto himself and on that point alone I was proved right on many future occasions. It was easy then to understand why Andy Spearing had stayed only a DI for so long, despite his impressive success record.

So, I was right there at the beginning in July nineteen sixty-seven at what had just been described by Sir Mark Wright as a war. There was no way anyone could tell how it would end. In addition, it appeared I was lumbered with the most obnoxious DI in New Scotland Yard.

Book 1 in the DI Spearing and DS Devlin series

Chapter 02 - Andy Spearing

On leaving the reception at New Scotland Yard, Andy Spearing jumped on the 'new' Victoria Line tube at Sloane Square and headed for Oxford Circus.

As he travelled on the tube, which was crammed with the sixties tourists, mostly searching to see anything, from her majesty the Queen at Buckingham Palace, to Carnaby Street where somehow, they had a forlorn hope that they would catch sight of 'The Beatles,' or other such sixties beat groups. Of course, the tube was also packed with the usual every day disgruntled Londoners trying to go about their daily business among the massive throngs of human and animal flesh that the sixties 'swinging' in London now attracted.

As the tube train hurtled noisily through the London underground tunnels Andy's mind reflected on the reception and on Sir Mark Wright. Andy did recognise that Sir Mark's introduction of new expertise and unaffected younger people, or 'young blood' as he had called them, were only the first moves to get the London Met Police from the bowels of corruption that was an everyday occurrence. In his opinion it had been that way since the nineteen forties when he joined 'The Met, but it had now become a lot worse. It was no longer small time corruption.

Although Sir Mark had appeared unable to do anything about the corruption or the East End mobsters who had their fingers in all of these pies, he now appeared to be moving at last towards a cleansing offensive.

It made Andy laugh when he heard the good old British middle and upper classes 'tut-tut' about their American cousins and the corruption in the USA police. He had so often heard it; "No my dear, that sort of thing could never happen here in Great Britain." Andy just smiled, knowing from personal experience over many years that the Brits could teach their American police cousins how to extort top dollar from even the top criminals.

Andy had noticed that Sir Mark had very carefully chosen and selected probably the six cleanest people to act as mentors to the six green recruits. Andy knew that breaking the corruption in 'The Met' could be impossible, even for Sir Mark.

Although respective governments would not even admit it existed, the widespread corruption and graft within the London Met Police, the governments MI5 and MI6 and the Establishment had probably started during and certainly immediately following World War Two.

The men and women returning to Great Britain along with the then ex-army Sergeant Andy Spearing in nineteen forty-five and early forty-six were weary, battle hardened and by now very cynical troops. They had faced the wrath of the Germans and the Japanese and had somehow survived.

Andy himself had been trained to kill as a near eighteen-year-old in nineteen thirty-nine by his beloved Yorkshire regiment. He was sent out in thirty-nine to the Far East and fought his way through many battles, retreats and counter-strikes against the Japanese and had the medals to prove it, including having been 'mentioned in despatches'. Eventually he made sergeant during the Burma campaign against the Japanese from nineteen forty-three to forty-five. He had been badly wounded in nineteen-forty-five and suffering from malaria had been shipped back to Britain.

The soldiers all came back to the laughter and joy of V-E Day (Victory in Europe) and a few months later came V-E-J Day (Victory in Japan), then along came reality.

They all found large parts of the UK, and in particular London, were demolished and needed re-building, but there was no money left in the Governments kitty after the devastation of the wars in Europe and Asia.

In fact, Britain had to start repaying the massive loans they had received from America to help win the war and so the government launched into one of the most difficult austerity programs in history. Rationing of basic essentials like food continued in nineteen forty-five and some was set to continue into the fifties. The country was stagnant and bankrupt. Through the following years, the question of who won the war had often occurred to Andy as 'conscience' money was poured freely by the Americans into Japan and Germany, yet Britain was strapped by our former American allies with hideous debts and huge interest rates.

The returning soldiers, male and female, also found large parts of the inner cities being controlled by criminal mobsters, who had managed, mostly through bribes, to avoid call up to the armed forces and had built up empires using brute force, murder and protection rackets, not to mention drugs and forced prostitution of girls and boys. The girls and boys had no protection, because brothers and fathers were off fighting wars and dying for their country. This was the most galling thing of all, the rubbish many of the returning troops found and their disillusionment was almost tangible.

So, repercussions by the masses were quick and decisive. Winston Churchill was blown away at the nineteen forty-five elections and Clement Atlee, the Labour Party leader, was swept to power with a landslide victory.

The Labour Party's promise to have full employment was not too difficult to realize. Due to deaths and injuries of millions of young men in the war, there were more jobs than people to fill them. So, immigrants were brought in to try to get the country moving, but because of the economic situation pay was low, no matter if you were a 'white collar' worker, or a labourer.

The Labour Party under Clement Atlee also brought in the hallowed British National Health Service and nationalized major industries like coal mining and public utilities.

There then followed in nineteen forty-seven, one of the worst winters on record. Roads were blocked with snow for months on end with few tools available to clear them. Coal supplies to power stations, already short because of the war, could not get through and so there were power cuts, industry was closed so many times over the winter months and ordinary people were again dying, not from the war this time, but from the severe cold and starvation.

Men and women, who only a few months ago had proudly served their countries and somehow helped to win a world-war, were now forced to stand and watch their own people and families dying from hunger, exposure and lack of adequate winter clothes, all because they simply did not have the money to buy anything.

Of course, the Government got the blame for all these things going wrong, including the weather and disillusionment again set in. It was probably for this reason that Clement Atlee never received acknowledgement for his great work and it was not until years later, that some of the top academics in the country, not the working man or the Labour Party, voted Clement Atlee as the greatest British Prime-minister of the twentieth century, even beating Winston Churchill and Maggie Thatcher.

Against this background of disillusionment in nineteen forty-seven the London Met Police had to desperately try to recruit people to re-establish some resemblance of law and order. This was done against the background of government cuts due to the economic situation and the bad winter. Because people were desperate just to try to feed and clothe their families, the wages offered, not only in the London Met Police, but also across industry in the UK, were kept intentionally low, barely enough to survive on.

In London, the shortage of housing and basic essentials due to the ravages of the war meant that it was even more expensive to live there than anywhere else, but in those days no employers could afford London 'living' allowances as they were eventually called. The working men and women, many war widows, just had to accept whatever they were offered and either find a second job, or find ways to make extra money from their existing jobs. Sometimes many had to do all three and then he or she was only seen by their families on Sundays. Even then many had to do overtime to make the ends meet.

So, the seeds of corruption and graft in the London Met Police, Government officials, and politicians, services like MI5 and across the public, were sewn and grew for at least the next twenty-five years. For many it went on throughout their lives. For some it still goes on today. Andy himself had not been totally clean, especially when the kids were growing up, times had been extremely hard in the late forties, not that anybody ever found out, or had noticed. He and his DI Tommy Thomson always known as TT, had limited their little side earnings to a once only scam worth twenty thousand pounds – a lot of money in the late nineteen-forties – Andys share bought him the family home outright in Harpenden in the then rural Hertfordshire. This was the same home which was about to be sold from under him due to his acrimonious divorce.

The scam had cost one of the nicest of the mobsters, namely Joseph Bolger, who ran a gang who became known as 'The Quiet Firm,' based in London's East End. Joseph Bolger insisted on keeping himself and his people on very low profiles, away from the public glare, never looking for publicity and mostly overlooked by police, unlike 'The Hammond's' and 'The Christie's, hence the nick-name 'The Quiet Firm.' Although he knew who had ripped him off, rather than cause any fuss with the two policemen involved, Joseph Bolger had written it off to experience. This earned the respect of the then Andy and in fact through the years they became friends and Bolger had helped as an unpaid informant on several cases.

It still cut deep into Andy that Joseph Bolger had disappeared into thin air a month or so back and he – Andy - despite all his intense efforts, had not got a whiff of what happened. Of course, there were rumours that it was 'The Hammond's,' or 'The Christie's,' but Andy did not buy into either of these theories. Both heavy firms were too reliant on Joseph's firm to supply the drugs chain.

Joseph, or at least his number two John Palmer had contacts world-wide, from Afghanistan to deepest South America and if the rival mobs had rubbed out Joseph, it would be like shooting themselves in the foot, but it was not like that sort of thing had not happened in the past. Also, there had been strong rumours around that Joseph was now trying to entice the American Mafia to take over his drugs portfolio much to the annoyance of the heavy mobs. If that was true, then it would change the balance and cause some real gang wars.

Still, Andy thought Joseph was too intelligent to try something like that; he must have known the repercussions would be violent. Yet there had been rumours of a rift between Joseph and John Palmer, his number two, and some said the real business brain behind 'The Quiet Firm.' Apparently, the rift was all about their involvement in the drugs scene, which Joseph despised.

Andy was hoping his informant this afternoon would give him a lead as to where he was, or what had happened to, Joseph Bolger.

As Andy alighted from the tube his mind clicked back to the present. He decided to walk down from Oxford Circus, along Regent Street, across Piccadilly Circus and turned into Wardour Street. Because of Sir Mark's reception, he was late and was hurrying along heading for 'The Ship' pub and his meeting with his informant. Andy never referred to his informants as snitches, or 'snouts.' He always thought like murder is murder, homicide and snitches are probably Americanisms, so why should we revert to the slang? "Like he is a Psycho" – no he is not, he is a Psychopath, but Andy chose to ignore the fact the word was derived from Russia in the nineteenth century and did not come from America, although he thought maybe 'Psycho' derived from there.

Andy knew that they laughed at him behind his back in the Murder Squad at New Scotland Yard, "good old Andy" he had overheard them many times without them knowing it. "He still lives in the past; he will probably die reading about history." It was mostly derisory, because those saying it were usually on the take; well most of them were at it - all on the golden handshakes. Apparently, Andy was the idiot who stayed clean. Andy just smiled and thought 'Little do they know' as JC was reported as having once said.

The names they called him did not bother him at all. It was the fact that he was only forty-six and did not feel like an old man, though he had to admit the years had not been good to him, especially when he occasionally took more than a glance in the mirror. He was looking more like in his middle fifties. His excuse was it had not been an easy life. There had been the war, which of course had taken its toll on all, never mind a seventeen-year-old kid as he was when he joined up. The war for him had started with months of combat training with The Yorkshire Regiment at Catterick Garrison and then he was shipped out to the Far East. As he had remembered earlier he finished in the jungles of Burma, badly wounded in nineteen forty-five and, suffering from malaria, he was shipped home.

After spending months in a hospital in Portsmouth in nineteen forty-five and another few months in convalescence back home in Yorkshire till the spring of forty-six, he moved down to London with the idea of joining the police. It did not happen due to the economics of the time, there was no recruitment.

It was not until nineteen forty-six when they finally started to recruit in London, that he got his toe in the door of New Scotland Yard, which at that time was situated on Victoria Embankment not far from Downing Street and the Ministry of Defence. They were desperately short of people due to the war dead or injured and were taking on anybody who could walk and think straight; just as long as they were a minimum of six feet which you had to be in those days, or you did not get accepted.

Andy just about qualified and was grateful for the job. As ex-army, he was used to taking and carrying out orders and he could handle himself in a brawl, so with the lack of any quality competition he quickly rose in the ranks to sergeant. Then old Commander McIntyre, a rough and ready ex-paratrooper from Scotland suggested he took his detective exams. It was a struggle for Andy Spearing who was never an academic, but he found that, even that early on, his old gut reactions got him through the exams and the practical. So, he squeezed into 'The Flying Squad.' He did not like 'The Flying Squad' who thought themselves as a bunch of elitists. Somehow, he talked himself, again with the help of his old Commander McIntyre, into the murder and serious crimes squad.

The lack of academic qualifications always made Andy feel inferior for the rest of his working life, but it never stopped him from becoming one of the best detectives in the business. However, he was never going to be comfortable when he came up to these young graduates who were now beginning to flood New Scotland Yard.

During the early days as a Detective Sergeant there were too many late nights in the bars smoking and drinking too much. Walking or hanging around the streets of London in all weathers, knocking doors in the middle of the night. No wonder he had lost his wife, but that was only part of the divorce story which had turned Andy into a bitter man and now a heavy drinker.

The main reasons for the divorce, which had started two years ago and was only now coming to conclusion, he had never told anyone. He could never face up to it, her long running affair that he had known about for years and with a close relative. Worse than that were the downright lies she had told about him to his and her families, including their children that was unforgivable. He still saw her occasionally mainly because of the grandkids, but the bitterness and the booze were slowly destroying him, though he knew it. Just as he knew, like all great generals, there was much to be learned from previous battles and a good policeman (never a copper!) always learned from his previous battles with criminals.

The young ones did not see that, like this new graduate introduced this morning. What was his name? Andy pondered as he caught sight of 'The Ship' pub in Wardour Street at number one hundred and sixteen on the corner just as he passed the famous rock and blues club known worldwide as 'The Marquee Club' at number ninety. Some of the great British names in rock and blues, including 'The Rolling Stones', Rod Stewart, Led Zeppelin and Cream with Eric Clapton, Jack Bruce and Ginger Baker, all had played this venue at the beginning of their careers behind those doors. Andy may look and feel old, but he knew that much, particularly about 'Cream' one of his favourite English groups, simply because he loved to listen to the blues – modern - or the 'real' stuff from Mississippi and the deep south of America.

Oh yes! It was 'DS Kevin Devlin' - Andy suddenly remembered. Just another of Sir Mark's graduates who has been led to believe that he can read all these theories in criminology and psychology books at university and then come in to change the real policeman's lot.

Young Devlin stood up for himself very well though, Andy thought to himself, at least he did not let me walk all over him and he did manage to kick my bollocks at least once. Andy always gave his kind of praise, where praise was due, but then he thought with a grin, that is just the openers my boy; wait till I serve you some of my special googlies. Then we will see if you still come back for more.

Still, Andy thought, Sir Mark had made good points and certainly some of these old detectives in the squad, himself included, had to get their fat asses in gear and use more modern techniques to catch today's criminals. Mind you the majority did not want to catch certain criminals, or for you to catch them, lots of conflicts of interest in there, as they say in the politics show. Some would call it corruption or graft, but hey ho most of it was all down to the low wages paid to catch serious criminals. They – the criminals - had millions to throw around to ensure a trouble-free life, well to at least ensure certain policemen kept their distance and let them know if anything was going down.

It did not matter what they all thought in the squad, good old Andy would use anything and anybody to catch his criminals, make no mistake, including any modern techniques if that was also necessary. Doctor Harvey can think and say what he likes, but Andy was more than glad to use anything just as long as they delivered the goods.

Like now, this Les Hall who Andy was going to meet, a real low life, probably got up to a lot more than some of the criminals who Andy caught. However, he was an informant and in those days good policemen depended on their sources and had to either pay good money from the New Scotland Yard slush fund for the information, or alternatively, sometimes one had to arrange for fellow policemen to call off the hounds on their informant. All done very nicely with a nod and a wink here and there and soon all was sorted. Les Hall was always about money, he was too slimy a customer to get caught, usually slithering into the darkness before the lights hit. Andy did not like having to pay Hall, or any of his type, but it was a necessary evil, if you could not get an informant into the right place at the right time, you were a nowhere man. Despite what people saw on the TV shows, books, or the movies, the undercover man practically never happened. In real life, whenever an organisation managed to get an undercover man or woman in place, they usually eventually turned up dead, or simply disappeared.

In nineteen sixty-seven, 'The Ship' pub was an okay place to meet your informant. Although it was close to Soho and a lot of criminals hung around the area, the real criminals hung out in their own Soho Clubs, or were out in the East End of London. 'The Ship' was still an old-fashioned pub with a mixture of people coming in for drinks. People connected with the film industry, because Wardour Street housed a lot of film company's offices and it was just around the corner from Denmark Street, which was known as Britain's Tin Pan Alley and it housed the British music publishing industry. So, you could see all types in 'The Ship', from the white collar and tie brigade to the long-haired hippie's and groups dropping in for a drink before going to 'The Marquee' and other smaller clubs like 'The La Chasse,' close by at number one hundred. So, in those days in 'The Ship' you did not look out of place no matter how you were dressed. More often than not, there were all sorts of personalities in 'The Ship' supping a traditional beer, or two, including the famous British comedian Tommy Cooper, whose humour Andy loved. Another one was the film star Kenneth More and lots of famous faces in the British sixties beat groups.

The good thing about 'The Ship' was its bright lighting, so you could see everybody in there. If you noticed anybody you wished to avoid seeing you with somebody else, for example an informant, you only had to quickly back out Andy did a quick look round, but did not see any criminal faces he recognized until he saw the low life Les Hall in the far corner at the end of the old horseshoe wooden bar.

Les Hall was a small wiry runt of a man, about thirtyish. Today, he was unusually dressed very smartly for him in one of those Beatles grey striped suits with no collar, multi coloured fish tie, silk shirt and polished black shoes. Another quick glance around confirmed no suspicious faces, so Andy went quickly over to Halls table and sat down.

"So how are you Les?" Andy put out his hand for shaking pretending for the benefit of any audience to be a friend. "What can I get you?" Andy added in a friendly way.

"A pint of best bitter 'Andy' (he foolishly over-emphasized 'Andy') - and then added; "Without the acid please" Les replied in his London cockney accent and added a weak smile.

"Acid costs too much extra for the likes of you Les" Andy replied with barely a smile.

"Hey – are you guys getting spaced out tonight man?" A big six foot plus guy with reddish long hair tied back in a ponytail, no doubt a hippie complete with flowered shirt, necklace beads and pink trousers, broke into the conversation from the bar, obviously ear wigging conversations.

Andy knew from his friends in the drugs squad that 'Acid' was a cover name used by hippies for a drug also known as LSD, which caused horrendous illusions in the mind, sometimes making people totally insane and led some to unintended suicide.

"No man." Andy replied and added sourly; "Not enough room to space out tonight – Man!"

The hippie gave him a quizzical look, but then decided he still wanted to sound cool, perhaps he did not have the latest hip talk. "Yeah man – know what you mean man. You gotta get the right room man" The hippie murmured and turned quickly away to re-join others at the bar. Andy just smiled and shook his head.

"What the hell was that weirdo on about?" Les asked.

"Well if you really don't know Les, you are better off not knowing. Just forget it and I will get you that drink. Move over to that table in the corner – it is quieter there"

Andy pointed.

"Wanting to have a quiet feel in the corner with your little mate then?" The same Hippie again, this time he was trying to be funny.

"Listen mate. If you don't keep that big nose of yours out of it, you will suddenly find it broken in several places." Andy replied matter of fact and with just enough menace.

"Sorry man. Just having a bit of fun" The hippie answered as though he had not recognized the threat.

"I'm not, so shut it tight" Andy replied staring straight into his eyes and brushed him aside to get to the bar. The others quickly turned away as though they had not seen, or heard nothing.

Andy just smiled and caught Bill the landlords' attention and ordered a pint of best bitter for Les and decided on a pint of Stella Artois lager for himself. Lager was becoming the big drink in the UK at the time and Andy enjoyed the occasional pint in the summer months, though Stella was extra strong and was becoming known as 'The Wife Beater' beer.

Andy carried the two pints and headed straight for the hippie, forcing him to move aside with a grunt.

"You are looking well-dressed tonight Les. - A special occasion, is it?" Andy asked politely as he sat down.

"Well you know Mr – err - Andy – Don't get up the west end very often these days. So, thought I would make a night of it. I will be meeting up with my girl in Leicester Square a bit later. Catch a meal and a film. I thought it would be nice change for her." Les replied with his usual somehow sleazy voice.

"First time for everything I suppose" Andy replied dryly with a smile.

"I am good to Susan Mr – err – Andy" Les just smiled without any rancour.

"Yeah, I suppose it beats 'The Pigs Whistle' in Elephant and Castle and fish and chips for after." Andy's dry sarcasm went over the head of Les.

"She does all right from me. I mean we are getting married next month" Les replied defensively.

"Up the spout, is she?" Andy asked with his usual cheeky smile.

"Yeah – well - anyway - how did you know?" Les asked almost naively.

"Call it an educated guess Les! I am a detective you know. How come I did not get an invite then?" Andy replied and smiled his cheeky grin.

"I don't think you would go down too well with some of the mob who will be there Andy." Les replied with a matter of fact tone to his voice, perfectly serious.

"Yeah I suppose you are right about that Les. Anyway, what have you got for me?" Andy smiled as he replied and moving the conversation swiftly onto what they were there for.

"Not a lot really Mr – err Andy." Les sounded shaky and unsure.

"I hope you have not trailed me, yourself and pregnant Susan up the West End just to tell me you got nothing?" Andy intentionally sounded real mad.

"Naw I didn't say that – Andy – All I am saying is everyone is keeping very quiet about this guy Andy. He is one very professional man. Nobody has seen him. He works under a nom de plume 'The Fox' or something, but nobody seems to know him. He is deadly Mr – Andy – I mean he has never missed a target yet. Also, the word is that anybody who happened to get anywhere near to him has soon been found dead." Les was full of words, but no information.

"Quit stalling Les. Have you got something or not?" Andy sounded as if he had enough.

"Well the word around is that he is doing contracts for both sides. I mean not only us, but also contracting for your lot. That is why nobody is talking man. Everybody is shit scared not knowing where it is going to come from man." Les did genuinely sound scared.

"What do you mean he contracts for us?" Andy asked with an incredulous tone.

"Don't know and that is the truth Mister – eh Andy, but the word is somebody on your side is hiring him, regular like, taking out some bad guys, at least in their eyes they are bad guys. The East End mobs don't know who, but they are hitting targets for whatever reason, that is what is happening man" Les voice was low and edgy.

"I have had enough of that guy over there giving me this 'man' stuff without you starting it too Les". Andy replied icily and decided to put on some pressure. "Now what you have given me is worth sod all, it just adds to the rumours. Now by Wednesday I want to know how to contact this guy and a name to go along with this nom de plume. That is worth big money to me, but I need the info by then or sooner. Do you savvy?" Andy just pointed a finger at Les who shook his head.

"I will if I can Andy, but I aint putting my life on the line for nobody. How much is it worth to you?" Les asked, his greedy little eyes showing he was interested at a price.

"Two hundred quid on receipt of good info which leads to us getting our hands on him" Andy replied.

"Three hundred and no strings attached. I will get the name and the contact." Les was getting down to his business.

"You will get two hundred and fifty quid in cash and not a penny more. In here Wednesday - by thirteen hundred hours sharp, or you phone if you find out anything earlier. If you feed duff info Les I will have you on a knocked-up charge and put you away for five big ones. You comprehend? Now get out of here before I change my mind." Andy waved his left hand as a sign of dismissal and Les swallowed his pint in a one movement and moved out real quick.

"Thirteen hundred hours?" Les asked puzzled.

"One o'clock lunch time" Andy sighed as he replied realizing he had reverted to army time and Les did not have a clue, he was lucky if he could tell the time.

Andy watched him rush out the pub and sat for a minute to muse while he finished his pint. How the hell did that low life get a hold of information that our lot was involved in this? Oh well, another problem for another day, time to catch up with other low life tonight.

Another club, more drinks, more smoking, more low life, more stones to turn over and find more worms. Maybe another ten hours or so to go, if he was lucky, then home to the lonely Buckingham Palace Road flat, a ten-minute walk from New Scotland Yard. It would be the usual drunken restless sleep and back in tomorrow. Start the whole sorry cycle back over again.

Was it worth it? Broken marriage from that cow Betty, although not his fault, at least not in his eyes, kids Andy Junior and Rose now aged twenty-seven and twenty-four respectively with grandchildren who hardly even know him.

Many of the bosses at New Scotland Yard were as bent as corkscrews and the bottom line was they did not want you collaring any of their mobs who subsidized their living standards. Dealing everyday with scum like Les Hall and at the end of the day there were small rewards for breaking up your life.

He also occasionally used prostitutes, but never used any who did not owe him and most, like Sophie the Sphinx and Tiger the Alley Cat, had in the last few years become friends. At least as friendly as the girls are ever likely to get with a policeman.

He was not proud of having to do that, but he always paid the going rate afterwards and never accepted a freebie, for him that was somehow important. It was the case that after the bitter break up with Betty he could not, or did not, trust
women and he pretended he did not have the time to develop any meaningful relationships.

Andy knew he had no intention of paying Les two hundred and fifty quid; he would never get it authorized. But he had to give the donkey the carrot to think it was worth his while.

Andy thought; why would anyone risk their life for only two hundred and fifty quid? Is that all they thought their life was worth? Then again, how much did he think his marriage and kids were worth? He just threw it all away for nothing without a fight, or for -oh yes - a job, a policeman's lot at that.

Funny old life we all lead at different levels he thought as he got up and went out into the warm sunny July afternoon, the sunshine hurting his eyes and showing his pasty complexion as he emerged from the pub. With his mind wandering around his lifestyle he did not notice the long-haired hippie keeping an eye on him and following at a good distance behind.

Chapter 03 - Alias 'The Fox'

The day of Sir Mark Wrights declaration of war against corruption and depravity, Sam Aldridge, alias the assassin known as 'The Fox,' had already carried out a daylight reconnaissance from a hundred yards on his next target.

In the evening dusk Sam was now sneaking from behind the nine feet high boundary wall which was supposed to protect the targets huge Victorian country mansion, named without too much imagination as 'Palmers Place.' It was owned by John Palmer, number two to Joseph Bolger, the head of 'The Quiet Firm,' one of London's big crime gangs.

The property was surrounded by about five acres of very green land and positioned on the outskirts of Weybridge in Surrey. This was in the middle of the so called 'stock brokers belt', about thirty miles from the city of London, England. The whole area had the smell of money, old and new. Whoever said crime did not pay was obviously lying.

Sam had spotted several small plantations of trees, some oak, spruce and pine dotted around the fifteen-bedroom mansion, which also had stables running along the east walls behind the house. There were beautiful manicured gardens complete with tennis courts and an outdoor swimming pool facing south, entered from a patio with the most massive patio doors that Sam had ever seen. He had selected the small plantation facing the south side and the swimming pool for his observation post.

He had noticed a fox entering its lair in the trees the previous evening as dusk fell and decided to make use of the burrow. It appeared to him to be appropriate for the man with the nom de plume of 'The Fox' under which he operated his lucrative and deadly business.

Sam hid in the trees and the thick shrubs inside the boundary walls at the side of the main gates which were opened throughout the day and only electronically closed at night. Not much security then Sam thought, must be relying on the two heavies, both of whom had already appeared to be your average thick and non-observant bodyguards. Just yesterday when Sam accidentally came upon a family of pheasants in the undergrowth they all shot out running fast towards the mansion. Neither one of the heavies could be bothered to walk over and investigate. Sam had automatically dropped to the ground, but had very little cover other than a few trees and some undergrowth.

The intuitive evasive action by Sam was bred into him through his SAS training in nineteen forty-two as a young twenty-one-year-old during world war two in the Isle of Wight and in the beautiful, but hard west highland glens of Scotland, especially during winter training. Now forty-six he was still as fit as ever, perhaps not as quick, but he had not forgotten any part of his training and experiences. He was a large six foot three inches' man with solid, developed and gym maintained muscles across his whole body.

He could not understand any self-respecting so called 'bodyguard' to not at least walk over to check out what had scared the pheasants, yes probably one of the silliest of birds, but the silly bird does not break cover for no reason. Again, that was all part of his training with the SAS; failure to notice and investigate something like that could cost you and your mate's lives. Anyway, at the time Sam was grateful for their carelessness and quickly reverse crawled from the spot and managed to get behind some large oak trees. At the same time Sam was thinking, with a slow smile, if they had come across he could easily have taken both of them out without a problem, but that would have generated other problems.

Now dusk was settling in and Sam, just as he always did since those SAS operations in world war two, used loose rich soil from the undergrowth to blacken up his face, ears, neck, both of his hands and prepared to move out towards the plantation with the fox lair. Today he was disguised and wore the red wig, with a false red goatee beard. He had used this disguise on another job, but nobody had reported any sightings, so it was unlikely there would be any connection.

He wore a black turtle neck sweater, black trousers, black stretch rubber gloves and black rubber soled ex-army boots for silent walking and running.

At last darkness settled and Sam made a sprint in the darkest of the shadows, no hesitation - get there as quickly as possible and get back under cover, just as he had been trained all those years ago.

Making as little noise as possible, he passed through the small plantation he had selected and reached the foxes' lair. He acted as quickly as he could and increased the size of the burrow to enable most of his big frame to settle in.He then picked up a lot of loose branches from around the spruce and pine trees and went into the burrow and covered himself with the branches forming an interleafed roof, although he still had visibility of the mansion.

Sam then began to sort the bits and pieces he had brought with him to last the thirty plus hours or so he had to endure before making the entry. He knew his target John Palmer was not due back to the mansion until late afternoon tomorrow, so it would be in the early hours of Wednesday morning before he could possibly make the direct final move.

He had brought with him a couple of cans of cold meat, several small bottles of water and bars of his favourite plain chocolate. He laid out his equipment; a pair of the latest ex-military night vision binoculars and goggles which were ultra-expensive in those days – but both essential for this type of surveillance and operation. Second; a standard semi-automatic Walter PPK 7.65 mm gun, complete with a Bern's - Hall Triple Draw holster. There was a silencer in the kit bag and spare cartridges. More than sufficient Sam thought to control any situation here. Third; a lethally sharp six-inch knife, his favourite night weapon from his SAS days within a collapsible sheaf, complete with a leather band to enable it to be tied onto a leg or arm. Sam preferred to tie it on his left arm for quick pull in emergencies and throwing from his steady right hand. Fourth; a black pen light and last but not least, a set of key picks capable of opening the most difficult of doors, at least when they were in the hands of old Sam. He smiled contentedly as he knew he had all he needed to complete this job.

No smokes on this job, too much of a giveaway, no matter how careful you thought you were, in open country you could see one drag from miles, or catch the smell on the lightest of winds. Another of the lessons learned during the war.

Now followed the usual long wait, hidden away like an animal, he had to stay alert, but in this game the wait can be boring and tiresome. This was the time to lightly snooze or perhaps reflect on your life. Again, the training came to the fore, like so many ex-army types he could use this time to doze, but the senses antennae were always switched on for the least unusual sound.

His mind almost immediately started to wander and, like in so many of these waiting periods, he began to conjecture about what might have happened if he had done this, or that, at those big junctures in his life.

Sam was born in the city hospital in Islington London. So, having been born within the sound of Bow Bells he was entitled to be known as a cockney. His real birth name was Pete Kirkham. The family were poor, even by the depressive London East End standards during the nineteen twenties and the depression of the nineteen-thirties. They lived in the poorest areas of the East End; often doing midnight flits because they could not pay even the meagre rents, so the family would hop around the East End boroughs.

Sam, or Pete as he was known back then, joined the army at seventeen years old in nineteen thirty-seven as a full time soldier.

Pete was an ultra-fit hard young man of twenty-three in nineteen forty-four as world war two drew to its conclusion. The name Pete Kirkham, it seemed to Sam was from his dark and distant past and not really him. As a sergeant with the SAS Pete was operating far behind enemy lines around Arnhem during the debacle of an offensive, code named 'Operation Market Garden', with the objective to lay a breach across the Rhine and get into the heart of Germany during the September of forty-four before the winter set-in. Pete had, in his own mind, renamed the operation 'Remembrance Garden'. He had either lost most of his mates and officers, or a few of the others had been so seriously injured they had been carted back home to England in pieces. Probably they would never be put back together again, at least not in their heads.

'Operation Market Garden' had been a major defeat for the allies with horrendous heavy casualties just at a point when it looked like they were about to win the European war they were forced into humiliating retreat. Questions were being asked of General Dwight D. Eisenhower and Monty on that sortie.

Pete alias Sam, alias 'The Fox' remembered it as if it was yesterday as he fought his way back to the British lines, somehow with super luck, getting there in one piece with only scratches and bruises. It was back then he made his mind up. Even then, at only twenty-three, his mind was crystal clear on the subject.

He had only one trade and that was the one with the British Army, in the name of the SAS. They had taught him how to kill people quickly, effectively and then to get the hell back out. He decided then and there after this war, if he had ever to put his life on the line again, then it would be for real money. As he saw it, no country or creed should put their people through this for a few shillings per day, while the real villains sat back in their palaces way out of any danger.

At that low point during the war he then remembered the infamous words of USA General George Patton during World War Two; *"The object of war is not to die for your country, but to make the other bastard die for his."*

Pete decided to live by these words until he could extract himself from that bloody war. However, soon worse was to follow the 'Remembrance Garden' fiasco. It was only a few months later, during December nineteen forty-four in bitterly cold weather with lots of snow drifting around, the German offensive, led by a mass army of tanks, swept towards Antwerp and there followed the 'Battle of the Bulge', although that was eventually turned around, but not without more heavy casualties.

In parallel with the 'Battle of the Bulge' the Germans continued to counter attack at Arnhem and it was during one of these skirmishes that Pete saw his opportunity to lay out his grand plan for his future. His six man SAS patrol were returning from a reconnaissance sortie and strolling across a clearing between tree plantations. Suddenly they were caught by incoming heavy artillery fire. Pete was luckily on the far-right flank and heard the unmistakable shells whining noise first and shouted; "Cover" as he dived towards a fallen tree about two yards to his right. The shells exploded in the middle of the others, blowing them to pieces, heads, arms and legs flying separately through the smoke and fire.

Pete cracked his head on a branch of the fallen tree as he splattered into the other side seeking some protection, but with the additional force of the blast propelling him he went out like a light bulb.

It was getting towards dusk when Pete finally awakened. He was totally deaf and bleeding from his left ear, his hair was matted in blood and a piece of shrapnel was lodged in his left shoulder, but it was lodged in such a way that he did not have much blood loss from it, at least for the moment. He noticed his uniform was singed and in tatters. He warily looked around, no sign of the enemy, it must have happened a few hours ago as it was now getting on for dusk.

He then saw the crater where the shells had exploded about ten yards to his left. He crawled over the rough ground, just in case the Germans were still watching. Always cautious, never assume because it is quiet, basic training which had stood him in good stead ever since. He reached the crater and began to make out the body parts up to twenty feet from where the shells had landed. He saw a torso with a neck, but no head. Another had no arms and both legs were cut off, one at the knee and the other at the groin. He then saw the tags around the neck on the second corpse; 'Anthony Blanford' it said, the only possible way he could ever be identified was his tags. "Poor sod, a nice guy, brilliant soldier. Boom your dead Tony" Pete spoke like a deaf man, because he could not hear his own voice.

He looked around the crater; he knew he was in utter shock. It looked like everybody else had simply disintegrated. These were the remains of his mates, but only bits and pieces like fingers, a few arms, parts of unrecognizable burned out skulls and little else remained, but some of their metal identity tags were lying around. He was bewildered and mumbling something to himself. He then crawled around trying to pick up the tags, but he now remembered they were so hot they had burned his hands. So, he searched around until he found a piece of an old jacket covered in blood and used that to collect the tags. It was then he saw his opportunity and dropped his own tags with the others. In his mental state, he was not sure how to play it yet, but then he thought play it by ear and see what happens.

He crawled out of the crater in the darkening gloom and when he made sure all was clear he stood up, pointed his nose in the general direction of the British lines. He started his long wobbly walk which he estimated to be seven miles or so, but it was right through enemy territory. His bloody cotton parcel containing the dog tags in one hand and his rifle slung across his good right shoulder.

It was only after a few miles his vision started getting hazy, he felt the shrapnel in his left shoulder coming loose and his warm blood weeping down his arm and across his chest. He thought, this is not good, not good at all, feeling too light headed, need water. He suddenly thought he saw movement to his right, then stumbled over something on the ground, fell over and smacked the ground hard with his head.

He awoke with someone shaking his good shoulder and throwing water over his face. "You okay soldier?" The man was a Lieutenant in the Argyle and Sutherland Highlanders, but with a very posh BBC home-counties accent. It always seemed peculiar to him, an Argyle and Southern Highlander speaking with a posh BBC accent. Pete pointed to his ears trying to communicate he could not hear and in his peculiar, deaf man voice murmured "Hit with shells. All blasted to smithereens" As he tried to hand over the tags he collapsed again.

Pete could feel, what turned out later to be the ten-man Argyle and Sutherland Highlanders squad, man-handling him onto a crude stretcher and then injecting him with what must have been a high dose of morphine. Although the road back was rough and taken on the march with Pete bouncing like he was on a trampoline, he hardly felt a thing. At least until they reached the field hospital and the morphine had started to wear off when the pains in his shoulder and head became excruciating. Then the Doctor appeared in a white coat covered in somebody else's blood and shone a pen light straight into the left eye of Pete causing him to blink. "How are you feeling soldier?"

The doctor asked the stupid question, but Pete could not hear and again signalled he was deaf. "Ah not to worry too much about that old boy – it will probably rectify itself in a couple of days as long as your ear drums have not been burst, the doctor added almost cheerfully.

"Can you give me something for the bloody pain in my ear and my shoulder you fucking idiot" Pete blurted out in his peculiar deaf man voice.

"Of course, of course," The doctor replied with cool detachment and looked amused while loading up the needle. "What is your name soldier? You did not have on any tags." The doctor seemed oblivious to the fact that Pete could not hear.

Pete again signalled he could not hear, although he could now hear someone talking to him like he was under water in a pool. "Just give me the fucking morphine" Pete shouted in his peculiar deaf man voice and felt the doctor almost jump up and the needle going in deep. Probably deeper than it needed to, the doctor's revenge for rudeness, but two minutes later Pete was back floating on a cloud without a care in the world.

Suddenly, Sam was awakened with a start from his dreaming recital; there was a breaking twig in the undergrowth directly behind his position in the burrow at Palmers Place, it woke him like a reveille call. He tensed up holding his breath, waited for the next sound and then it was something touching his back. He whirled around, at the same time yanking his knife from the sheath and thrusting it upwards. It caught the fox on the point of its nose; it let out a howl and bolted out of the trees towards the boundary wall. Unlike common belief, the fox is a timid animal unless it is hunting in a pack like wolves which seldom happens. Sam smiled and shook his head in disbelief before quickly re-covering himself with the branches and settling back into the lair.

With nothing to do for the next twenty or so hours it was not long before his mind again started wandering off to those fateful days towards the end of world war two.

Sam was soon back as Pete in the middle of the war; as Pete awoke in what he thought was the next day, but in the event, it was more like forty-seven hours later. He awoke with a very pretty nurse, with the most beautiful big brown eyes, looking into his pale blue eyes. "Ah you are awake at last soldier" The nurse said with what appeared to be a genuine smile. Pete suddenly realised he could hear again at least in his right ear.

"Yes Miss. Where am I - in heaven?" Pete asked with the best smile he could muster."No I am afraid you are nearer hell soldier. You are in a field hospital near Arnhem. What is your name soldier? Your tags are missing!" The Nurse now looked radiant. It was at this point that Pete made the decision that changed the rest of his life.

"I don't know Nurse. I don't remember a thing. I don't know why I am here – at Arnhem you say?" Pete mumbled almost incoherently.

"Ah don't worry soldier, it often happens when you are caught in direct shell fire. Amnesia we call it." She added without explanation.

"Amnesia - What is that?" Pete asked, sounding confused.

"Oh, just memory loss – It often happens with shell explosions and traumas like you have just been through." She explained simply.

"What trauma? Shelling? - What is this about shelling?" Pete asked innocently and added, "I don't remember any of it nurse" he lied.

"That is common too. When some people suffer trauma like you, their brain just tries to bury it and forget about it." She replied lightly not showing any concern.

Pete of course could remember almost everything except when he was out cold and afterwards when he had been filled with morphine, but now he was going down a path to what he envisaged as freedom, his release to pursue his own life.

"I don't remember any of it nurse. Not a thing. What is your name?" Pete asked as innocently as he could sound.

"I am Nurse Ashbury soldier. As I say, don't worry about it. We have fixed up your shoulder and your head wound. You may have some pain for some weeks and headaches, but you, in all probability, will recover your memory. However, you probably have a burst eardrum which may take some time to heal and between that and the head wounds your balance will be not so good for a time. The good news is you are going back to Old Blighty in the morning." She gave that radiant smile again.

"Really nurse?" Pete asked and smiled back, "I am going to miss you long-time Nurse Ashbury" Pete give her his best sexy look.

"Well at least soldier, you have not forgotten how to flirt with a girl have you?" Nurse Ashbury retorted with a laugh.

"Like riding a bike Nurse Ashbury - Once mastered never forgotten!" Pete laughed and then started coughing which brought on acute pain. "Oh shit!" He gasped and grasped his head.

"Perhaps the next time soldier you will remember the pain that flirting can sometimes cause." Nurse Ashbury smiled serenely, apparently knowing the innuendo. She then gave him an injection in his arm, inserting the needle quite hard as she smiled and walked off just leaving Pete wincing in pain from what he thought was every part of his body, then the morphine kicked in again and it was back to the happy land.

The next thing Pete knew he was being carted into a 'Red Cross' ambulance along with two other unconscious soldiers on stretchers. They drove off almost instantly and hit a rough old road and he instantly recognized the vehicle had no springs left and he reckoned the driver was hitting every bump. Every bruise in his body was shooting pains for what seemed hundreds of miles, but was probably only thirty or forty before finally he was again man handled in a stretcher onto some old rust bucket of a ship.

Then, as he was re-filled with morphine, he noticed the other two stretcher cases having their faces covered and taken away. Poor bastards he thought to himself as he turned away and almost instantly went to sleep. He remembered waking just as he was being carried off the ship in Portsmouth harbour along with the walking and the stretchered wounded. Then there were the covered dead, from the army, navy, air force and civilians. It felt a little bit like Dunkirk in nineteen forty all over again.

The next awakening for Pete was when he found himself in a clean, comfortable bed – another pretty nurse checking his pulse. The hospital was full of injured and dying servicemen from the European and Japanese Asian war theatres and it later turned out to be the old Queen Alexandra Hospital in Cosham in Portsmouth overlooking Port Solvent.

"How are you today soldier?" The good-looking nurse with the label 'Nurse Alison' asked cheerfully as they all seemed to do when dealing with all sorts of horrifically injured and sometimes severely burned men.

"All the better for seeing you Nurse Alison" Pete answered with a cocky grin.

"Oh, I see - another big bad wolf. We seem to see your type from time to time." Nurse Alison smiled and was friendly enough.

"Better be careful Nursey, or this bad wolf will huff and puff and blow your house down" Pete retorted with a big frown.

"My Oh my - What big ears you have Mr Wolf" Nurse Alison laughingly continued with the fairy tale.

"All- the- better- to hear you with Nurse Alison" Pete replied.

Just then the Sister, an Amazon of a woman at about six feet tall and two to three feet broad came onto the open ward and shouted towards Pete; "Well soldier it looks like at least your hearing has recovered. Pity your brain is still scrambled"

Nurse Alison was reading the chart she had lifted from a hook on the bottom of the bed and smiled.

Pete ignored the Sister and nodded to Nurse Alison and said; "Yes, it is a pity we cannot have everything sorted in the big bad wolf nurse" Pete replied with a wink and a nod.

"Yes, but we will have to try our best – I think you are more a Mr Fox?" Nurse Alison blushed slightly as she replied.

"So, your name is Fox is it soldier?" The massive sister just broke into the conversation, much to Pete's annoyance.

Pete replied; "Fraid not Sis – too bruised in my head yet" and added his best 'Cheeky Charlie' smile.

"I am afraid you will have to refer to me as Sister Thomas soldier. Otherwise I will be authorizing these nurses to give you a bed bath and let them see, as I did, just how small a fox you really are!" Sister Thomas wheeled away from Pete with an evil grin.

Pete stared after her, livid, his face bright red amid titters all around the ward; practically everyone had heard and Sister Thomas had made sure they heard. Obviously not everybody was unconscious.

So, unbeknown to all the others, the nom de plume of 'The Fox' was born that day in Portsmouth and stayed as Pete's, alias Sam's, business name for the rest of his working life.

It was a few weeks later that a Doctor Woods, a renowned Neuroscientist, visited the ward and had consultations with several of the men with head injuries, including Pete.

"How are you this morning soldier?" Doctor Woods asked politely as he pushed his dark framed national health glasses, which were very loose and badly needing adjustment. He shoved the glasses back up onto the bridge of his nose before continuing as he looked into Petes' eyes with a bright pen light; "Have you had any recollections of your previous life yet soldier?"

"No Doc – nothing other than hearing some shells coming in and then getting thrown like a rag doll across a field" Pete lied as he remembered everything and who he was.

"Yes, it is typical of your sort of injury soldier. Your brain is badly bruised and of course you have a perforated ear drum, all of which is making you unbalanced. It may take a year or two before you are anywhere near to being fit to go in again. So, I am afraid on these grounds I am going to have to give you a medical discharge. At least you will have a chance of surviving this war, if you can avoid these Doodlebugs which are hammering into London."

"Doodlebugs?" Pete asked.

"Unmanned guided weapons – The Germans have been blasting them on London since June when you lot invaded on June 6th" Doctor Woods replied in a matter of fact way.

"Can't we stop them?" Pete asked.

"Well we have been managing to shoot a lot of them down before they get there, but apparently, it is very difficult. Anyway, I have got to get around everybody this morning. Obviously, we cannot discharge you without a name, so we have given you the name of Sam Aldridge and an age of twenty-five. - You will be given papers and the usual discharge monies, passports, ration card, identity card and clothes etc. It is up to you, when your memory returns, to have your records amended and get back any monies due. You will be released in the morning." Doctor Woods stood up and went to move off.

"So that is it! – Thrown out on the scrap heap - a useless piece of shit now" Pete only pretended the anger, but part of it he felt for real.

"No not at all soldier." Doctor Woods replied reassuringly with his best bedside manner. "I am sure that, as soon as you are well and remember who you are, you will get back to where you were with no problem. The army takes care of its own soldier, it will eventually find out who you are I am sure. It is just chaos at the moment with so many missing, so many badly injured, it is practically impossible to identify so many."

"So, what am I supposed to do now?" Pete asked but already plans were forming in his mind.

"Take a good long holiday by the sea soldier. Spend the time to recuperate, recharge the batteries. I would suggest Brighton or Bournemouth – somewhere the Germans are not attacking. Stay away from London; it is still getting hit more than most! Anyway, good luck 'Sam Aldridge!" Doctor Woods offered his hand and a ready smile.

"Yeah thanks Doc". Pete replied with a touch of sarcasm and shook his hand. He knew he had to go to London to catch the action. London was his home. Pete thought post-war Britain would be run as usual from London and you just have to be in there from the restart. There was nowhere to be but London for a man of action, not in his kind of killing world. In any case, he was not as unwell as he had pretended.

So, Sam Aldridge was born from the ashes of the shells. Another new name, which he liked, and decided was good enough to stick with for the records, but for work he would become infamous as 'The Fox.' He liked the nom de plume of 'The Fox.'

It was the very next day that 'Sam' set off by train from Portsmouth station for London and for fame and fortune. He felt good, although a little unsteady on his feet. He knew his strength was returning after the month in hospital.

In the morning, after breakfast of double everything - eggs, bacon, sausage and fried bread, in a little cafe situated behind the famous Lyons Tea House in Piccadilly, Sam went for a stroll through Soho looking for the clubs. He thought to himself so no shortage of food or naughty clubs then, provided you have the money.

He knew the clubs were often run by the London underworld, but with thousands of wild and foot loose soldiers, sailors and air force, plus USA and European forces, all out for a good time while on leave from the horrors of war. The clubs had real problems keeping their customers in order. Not only that, but also keeping their hands of the girls, at least in public, and until they had paid the going rate.

All of this chaos was within a two-mile radius of Leicester Square and all these forces were 'he-men' or 'macho men' as they are better known these days, they were now used to kill, or be killed. All in competition with each other, all challenging for the best women, the most to drink, fighting for respect, squabbling, gambling and all the while the Doodlebugs fell all around just adding to the general chaos. Sam knew by instinct this was the place to start to make a living and a reputation for the future.

Later that evening, dressed in a navy lounge suit, white shirt and royal blue tie with a 'Windsor' knot, he went into the first of the places he had selected – the dark and dingy 'Hoofers Bar' – this one he had selected during the day advertising wine, women dancers and song with 'happy hours' of cheap booze. The scantily clad girls were 'dancing,' if it could be called dancing, to one of the Glen Miller Orchestra big forties hits 'In the Mood'.

Sam knew from previous experience that in London and particularly in London's Soho, 'cheap booze' means half the usual price, which was extortionate in the first place and always caused trouble. Add to that, the competition for women, the booze and the whole macho men thing, there will always be trouble. Sam knew he could handle most of it so went in with the intention of being hired and moving upwards.

He was directed to a double table led by a torch, it was almost essential to see the way; it was so dark and dingy. A waitress with high bop, bleached blonde hair, dressed in a skimpy bra top with short black and white skirt; it was all very daring for nineteen forty-five. She just sauntered over. "What are you drinking Mister? She asked in a cockney accent.

"Bottled water" Sam replied with a broad smile.

"Are you sure about that?" She asked and when Sam nodded, she said; "OK by me" as she again sauntered off towards the cloakroom grabbing a glass from the bar on the way over. Sam just knew she was filling the glass from the cloakroom tap water and she came back within a couple of minutes and handed him the glass of water.

"I asked for bottled water" Sam stated loudly enough to be heard across the room.

"We got none Mister. We are in a war you know. You are lucky to get clean water in this place" The waitress went to turn away. Sam took a mouthful and spat it out across the table.

"This is filthy London tap water. It tastes of the sewers" Sam shouted at the waitress. "How much is this shit?" He screamed, wanting to draw attention.

"That shit costs a bob a time Mister, so I would not be wasting it if I were you" The waitress retorted in a sarcastic way, with a smile. The audience laughed.

"Get me the manager – NOW!" Sam demanded loudly. The waitress did not have to move since two middle aged heavies suddenly appeared out of the gloom. Both were vastly overweight, both about six feet, with huge shoulders and necks hidden below layers of fat covering chins and the back of their necks.

"You would like to see the manager sir?" One of the heavies asked ever so politely, but with a distinct London east end accent.

"I certainly would" Sam replied standing up to his full six foot three and looking down on the two heavies.

"If you would follow me through the back to the office sir" The polite heavy pointed in the direction of a door in a dark corner of the room.

"Certainly" Sam replied again loudly, knowing what they were going to try as soon as they got out of the room, but he followed them like he was a naive tourist.

As soon as they had exited the room the polite heavy tried to snatch Sam's right arm. Just as the other heavy tried to grab his left arm, Sam shot out his right elbow with all the force he could muster and caught the polite heavy with an enormous blow straight on the solar plexus. As the man doubled up Sam brought his right knee up and smashed it into the bridge of the polite heavies' nose, disintegrating it with blood spurting out like a fountain. He quickly followed up with a karate chop behind the guys left ear and he hit the ground real hard and lay still.

The other heavy stared in disbelief and before he could react Sam flung a stiff left forearm straight across the bridge of his nose, which appeared to disintegrate like his mates. As he staggered back Sam brought his left knee up hard and fast into the guys' groin and as he doubled over Sam gave another karate chop, this time with his left hand just behind the ear and the other slumped down and was out cold.

"Bravo, bravo" A man's voice with a posh London accent came from the shadows with the accompanied noise of slow hand-clapping. "Ok you have passed your own arranged audition. Now what do you do for an encore?" The man emerged from the shadows with a gun in his right hand and a cigar in his left.

"Unless you intend to use that gun and die this minute I suggest you drop it" Sam answered in a low, but very assured voice.

"Are you bluffing I wonder?" The man asked with a cynical smile.

"There is only one way to find out and if you do you will be dead" Sam replied without taking his eyes of the man. It was always the eyes that told Sam if a guy was going to take it on.

The man dropped his eyes and let the gun drop to the floor. "Well - were you bluffing?" The man asked with a quizzical smile.

In a blur of sudden movement, a knife flew out of Sam's hand and missed the man's left cheek by a couple of inches and pierced into a wooden panel behind the man.

"My Oh my - you are very good" The man smiled and looked down at his gun.

"And if you make a move towards that gun of yours my other knife will be through your heart before you move six inches." Sam looked hard straight into the eyes of the man, but this time Sam was bluffing, no knife, but there was always the gun in his back waistband.

"I believe you. I believe! Let us talk." The man waved his left arm nonchalantly. "Those two look out of it. You have not killed them, have you?" he asked, but not appearing to be too bothered either way.

"No but in the morning, they may feel as though they are dead" Sam smiled as he replied. "Best turn them on their side in case they are sick in their needed beauty sleep." Sam bent down as he spoke and turned them both over onto their side.

"Hi, I am Joe Cole, the supposed 'owner' of Athis establishment. Who are you?" He sounded almost rueful as he offered his hand with a near friendly smile.

"I am Sam Aldridge - I am a nobody! I am just trying to pick up a living after being at war for five years." Sam sounded equally rueful as he shook Joe Cole's hand.

"You may not know it lad, but you have just turned over a couple of heavies from one of the east ends heaviest mob families" Joe Cole nodded towards the two limps.

"They are not yours then?" Sam asked quizzically as he walked over past Joe Cole and pulled his knife from the wood panelling. It had been wedged into the wood by about three inches. Sam slipped it back into the sheaf on his left arm.

"Nope, they belong to the Dickenson mob – Richard, or tricky Dicky as we all unofficially know him behind his back. These two assholes work for him. And by the way, when tricky Dicky finds out what happened to his heavies, you my friend will need to be handy with more than your fists and a knife" Joe Cole replied with rancour.

"You are paying protection then?" Sam asked matter of fact ignoring the tricky Dicky threat.

"You could call it that, but I call it extortion. Fifty per cent of everything we take, every single night. - Not bad returns for sticking a couple of thickos into your business eh? Joe Cole was obviously a very bitter man.

"How much do they take out?" Sam asked trying to sound not too interested.

"Seven grand a week and that is the minimum, depends how the girls do." Joe Coles face registered hatred.

"That is a lot of money for nineteen forty-six; especially with this war on. Still it leaves you one hundred and fifty grand per year. Not a bad little earner for this dump" Sam replied and smiled his best cocky little smile.

"Not on your Nellie laddie" Joe Cole retorted. "I have all the expenses of running this place, so I finish up with half that – if I am lucky" Joe added. "Anyway, what do you want? What was your little demo in aid of?" Joe looked and sounded amused.

"First I want ten grand and I will get you shot of tricky Dicky. Second, I want five hundred a week to stop any other tricky dicky getting in on the act and I will keep this place in order. No more trouble with customers shouting about filthy water or running amok in your office. Of course, that is provided you don't still try to sell that shit water!" Sam just smiled and added; "Now then - how about it Mr Cole?" Sam just smiled his best cheeky smile and opened his arms.

"You are joking aint you?" Joe Cole sounded upset.

Sam replied; "I never joke about money! Think about it Mr Cole! – In just four weeks' takings you will have paid me off for good for the money you would still be paying tricky Dicky for the rest of your life. For five hundred a week you are guaranteed you will never have to be paying out seven grand per week and then some to anyone ever again. So, you become a rich man, I have a nice reasonable earner every week and it is happy all round."

"What are you going to do? Kill him?" Joe Cole asked the question outright while probably knowing the answer.

"Me? No way. I don't kill people except for King and Country, or if they try to kill me. No, I know plenty of professional people who will kill clean for five thousand, which I would pay and the rest is mine" Sam lied again knowing full well he, or at least 'The Fox,' would have to handle it himself.

"How do I know you can handle it and you are not going to come back for more? If you cannot handle it, will it all blow up in my face? I mean these guys don't give anybody a second chance you know it is a deadly game" Joe Cole for the first time did sound scared.

"Look Mr Cole, it will be professionally taken care of and nobody will know who did the hit, but I will be here at five hundred a week starting tonight to make sure nobody else moves in. I can assure you that I will be happy with my share and I aint going to want anything more" Sam simply nodded as he finished.

"So, you will never want more?" Joe Cole sounded more assured.

"Not unless it is all going so well that you decide to give me a bonus at Christmas, or something and that I will gladly accept" Sam just smiled.

"OK you got a deal" Joe Cole smiled and again offered his hand.

"Right, I expect five hundred right now and I will start immediately. The ten thousand I expect by midnight tonight in cash and no traceable bills or counterfeit." Sam just smiled and took his hand.

"Hey Sam, the banks don't open till 9-30 in the morning. I cannot---" Joe Cole stammered slightly and Sam cut into the conversation.

"One other thing Mr Cole you will have to remember about me from now on. A bit of a warning really, I do not like my clients lying to me, or lying about me. If you are putting all this money through a bank then you are a prize idiot. I know you are a clever man, as I am. So please no more bullshit. Get out and get the ten grand from your wall safe, or wherever it is hidden and be back here by midnight. - Savvy? Sam's voice carried just the right amount of threat.

"Yeah OK I guess I can do that, if you can keep an eye on the place for me." Joe Cole replied quietly.

"No problem Mr Cole. Take it as part of my five hundred a week wages starting tonight. By the way, where is the tricky Dicky HQ? " Sam nodded and started to turn away to re-enter the club.

"You are ex-army aint you? - HQ and all that sort of thing?" Joe Cole started, but seeing the anger in Sam's face he immediately changed tact. "He is down in the docklands at Southwark. 'The Birds Cage' is his club. It is because the birds all dance in a cage with whips and all that Marquis De Sade torture gear around. If you ask me the birds are so rough he should use the cage to keep them locked up." Joe Cole laughed at his little joke.

"OK I will see you here at midnight." Sam nodded again and walked into the club.

"Did not think I would see you walking out of there mate. If you got your money back get some for me, this booze is watered." A youngster in an RAF Flight Lieutenant's uniform had one of the club's girls, obviously reluctantly, sitting on his lap with his hands all over her as he loudly shouted across the club room.

Sam turned around and walked over to the table. The youngster had three of his RAF mates sprawled around the table all drinking beer and laughing At least two of them looking nervous as Sam came over. Sam went to the side of the youngster and put his fingers on his collar bone and added a little pressure.

Sam then bent over and talked quietly, but with threat, in the youngsters left ear. "Now my young friend - Flight Lieutenant I see - I fight my own battles - and before I lay you out like the other two buffoons back there, I suggest you put the lady down. You know the rules - no touching the ladies until you pay and then it is only if the lady wants you."

"Ladies – What fucking ladies are you talking about?" The youngster leered, not displaying much common sense. Sam tightened his fingers grip on the collar bone.

The youngster screamed. "My mates will" – He cut off as Sam increased the pain.

"Now – now –I do not usually give a second warning to anyone my boy. But since you are fellow servicemen - I am sure your nice friends here do not want to finish up as hospital cases during their leave – Now do you boys?" Sam's voice was full of venom as he looked directly at the other three.

They did not want to know and shook their heads.

"Now release the girl and then you can get on with your evening sir." Sam added and nodded towards the girl.

"I have had enough of this crappy place anyway" the youngster announced petulantly. Never the less he released the girl and went to stand up, but Sam put more pressure on the young mans' collar bone and forced him to sit back down. "Now then sir, let us see you settle the bill and it will be an extra twenty quid for accosting the lady."

"Twenty quid you must be joking!" The youngster was gasping with the pain as he said it.

"I just said to the manager here – I never joke about money or the Ladies sir" Sam replied with a friendly smile.

The waitress came over with the bill. The youngster looked at it and sorted out thirty pounds from his wallet and muttered "Four pounds for seven glasses of beer and twenty quid for extortion."

"Extortion? What extortion? You very kindly gave a very generous tip sir, because you agreed you had accosted one of our ladies and saved us the problem of calling in the police. That is very kind of you sir. Thank you." Sam gave another of his cheeky grins.

"But I just gave you Ten pounds for a four pounds' bill. Where is my change?" The youngster almost wailed.

"Don't you remember sir? You agreed to a very generous tip for all the trouble you caused."

Sam replied and snarled. "Now get out before I really loss my temper and let our ladies loose on you."

The youngster stumbled out and shouted something back from the door when he was sure he was away.

Sam handed the waitress ten pounds with the bill and beckoned the involved lady over.

"What is your name love?" Sam asked her. "Sandra" She replied without adding her surname.

"Well Sandra - This is for you" Sam handed her the twenty pounds. And remember the next time a punter lays their hands on you before you agree to anything; just scream blue, bloody murder and I will sort him out." Sam flashed his most friendly smile.

"Thanks Mister?" She hesitated.

"Sam will do. Like play it again Sam in Casablanca. OK?" Sam replied and gave her his best sexy look.

"Yeah sure honey - that was real nice work. Anyway, thanks for that – I got more for him touching me than I would have got for spending a horrible night with him." Sandra had a nice smile.

Sam turned away and noted Joe Cole had been standing in the doorway to his office and had taken the whole scene in. He simply nodded as if to say well done and walked out of the club.

The rest of the night in the club was boisterous, but nobody got too far out of line at least not after Sam had a quiet word here and there. About eleven thirty Joe Cole returned and nodded to Sam to join him in the office.

The two bouncers were just beginning to stir in the corridor, having breathing difficulties with their broken noses. Joe and Sam went past the pair and went into the office. Joe snapped on the light.

"OK here is the lot – ten thousand and five hundred for this week. I only hope I have invested wisely in you, or I will be in a right pickle" Joe Cole did sound shaky and concerned.

"Don't worry Mr Cole. You have never made a better or safer investment. By this time tomorrow my man will have taken care of your problem and you will be free and easy." Sam sounded confident and he was nonchalant, knowing full well it was himself who would be taking care of the business that night.

So, it was the beginning of Sam's lucrative and deadly business starting in December nineteen forty-four.

Suddenly Sam's retrospective reverie was interrupted by a set of headlights flashing across his hideout lair. It was the headlights of a brand new nineteen sixty-seven Rolls Phantom V coming down the driveway heading for the mansion. It was John Palmer's roller; he had arrived back a day earlier than expected. Just as well Sam had done all the reconnaissance and had settled in position early, always good to be in the right position at the right time.

The roller was driven by another heavy guy, probably bodyguard number three, whom Sam had been expecting, but this one appeared to be more alert. As he alighted he glanced all around, even appearing to look directly at the plantation where the lair hid Sam from view. He opened the offside passenger door to allow John Palmer to alight.

Sam, for the first time had a gut reaction, feeling a little uncomfortable with this and there and then decided to play it as safe as possible. He had always found it best to act on gut reactions.

The lights from the mansion showed the car to be two-tone, with a silver body and a dark probably navy hood and roof. John Palmer was dressed in a very smart dark grey business with white shirt and matching dark grey tie. He too looked all around and Sam was convinced he also had a brief but definite glance at the plantation where Sam was hidden before quickly averting his eyes. Of course, it could be a bit of a coincidence, but Sam no longer believed in coincidences, even if it may all be down to imagination.

The two kids came out from the mansion Mary Rose, the thirteen-year old daughter and turning as pretty a teenager as Sam had seen in a long time, with jet black long hair and big brown eyes, dressed in a brightly coloured summer mini-skirt which showed off a nice pair of pins. Sam thought it was just as well they cannot jail you for thinking about it with underage girls. These days they are young beautiful women.

Mary Rose was followed by Bobby Palmer aged twelve, the son with 'The Beatles' mop hair style. He was dressed in jeans and a white T Shirt on a very thin frame as he emerged from the mansion. He had the same dark looks as his sister, with similar big brown eyes.

They were both shouting; "Hi Daddy". They were followed by the dutiful and beautiful wife Sarah, dressed in a white turtle necked tight fitting nylon sweater, which accented her small, but pronounced breasts and she too wore the customary sixties blue jeans with high heeled boots.

The reason Sam had all their names and knew the faces was he had been given all the details on foolscap sheets of paper with photos attached, by the people who had hired him as 'The Fox.' Although he did not know them, they also did not know him, other than as 'The Fox.' At least that was the theory. Sam recognised the clients report style; he had worked for them before on a few jobs, always full details on the target, this time including a lot of family details, most unusual.

The family all hugged each other and went into the mansion followed by the driver cum **bodyguard.**

It was only ten o'clock in the evening and Sam settled down for a long night. With the unexpected early arrival of the target action time had now to be moved twenty-four hours earlier than he had originally planned. The action was scheduled for three in the morning, just like old times. All the best SAS raids came when the enemy would be in their deepest sleep and just before dawn. Hit hard and fast and get out before the cock crowed.

The instructions Sam read were to make this look like a burglary gone wrong, but he knew with six people, plus possibly a couple of servants in the mansion, that was a tall order. Sam knew this was going to be a difficult one and for some unknown reason he had an uneasy feeling right from the start. However, that was why it was big bucks, fifty grand up front with a promised bonus if it went to plan.

The money was getting to be less important now, he no longer needed more.

After all the killings since nineteen forty-five, the money had simply poured in, but the truth was all he needed it now was for the kicks. He was the best, he knew it, those who hired him all knew it, and the adrenalin kicks were massive. As far as he knew the police still did not have a clue who he was, or even linked him to the killings.

He was the master, the cunning fox. He thought of himself as the ultimate killing machine, trained by the army and now paid princely sums to get rid of scum. One of his many, strange rules was he only killed scum who deserved to die. He demanded that his hirers proved the targets were scum and John Palmer appeared to be no exception, lovely family or not.

So, let the same old waiting game begin. This time though, there was a strange gut feeling with this one which Sam did not like one little bit. For the first time in a long-time Sam did not feel confident how this one would end.

Book 1 in the DI Spearing and DS Devlin series

Chapter 04 - Kevin Devlin

I decided not to hang around today for Sir Mark Wright's once only wine drinking reception in New Scotland Yard. It was an easy decision since my so-called mentor, namely DI Andy Spearing, had made that quick exit before the reception even began. Basically, at this stage, there was nobody for me to converse with, except for Sir Mark himself and being a very busy Commissioner of London police; he also made a quick feint for the same exit door as DI Spearing.

In any case the fact that I am one of the few Scotsmen, who do not actually enjoy a drink, even if it is free, meant that I was off at the first opportunity. I do have the occasional wine with a meal, but basically, I have spent my life looking after my body, which I often refer to as 'my temple'.

Thinking about looking after my body, I made for Buckingham Palace Road and walked all the way up to the Victoria Palace Theatre. Around the corner from the theatre was Andy's Gym, which I had joined a couple of weeks ago when I came down from Scotland. I decided on a couple of hour's session before heading for my digs.

In nineteen sixty-seven there were no flash gyms with swimming pools, saunas, power bikes etc. All the gyms were basically slimy, old, dirty rooms with a lot of work weights and then some more weights and possibly, if we were lucky, a hard work mat or two and a punch bag with skipping ropes. The gyms were usually run by somebody who had once competed in Mr UK, or if was a bit more special it may be run, or owned, by an ex contender for Mr Universe. The owners generally gave personal sessions at no extra cost, but it was all about building muscles and unlike nowadays not for general fitness.

The gyms back then mostly stank of stale sweat, old jock straps, sweaty socks and soiled trainers. There were seldom any shower facilities, so everybody just had to head for home, or to their digs, sweating from everywhere.. Not many UK homes or digs had showers back then; most, at the time, only had communal baths. Then again landlords in digs did not like their residents using too much water from the expensive heated water supply, so many, believe it or not, had a rule - only one bath per week per tenant.

On the basis, back then 'real' men did not wear deodorants, or aftershave (that was like perfume for girls, sissies, or old queens and 'poofters' now known as gays!) and unless one did not mind a reputation as having a pong, there was no alternative other than to go down the local swimming baths (not yet called pools!). There, if they were 'modern,' you could usually get a shower, otherwise for the older traditional swimming baths you had to pay extra and get a hot tub, but periodically all the down and outs used these places and there was no telling what you could pick up and bring home. Still, there was swimming afterwards, or for some dirty blighters before showering or having a hot tub, so again you did not know what you could pick up – only thank God for the chlorine! Anyway, eventually I stopped swimming and only had the shower, or the hot tub bath.

Most girls could not stand those smells in the gyms, so other than lesbian bruisers; one seldom saw any tottie around.

Anyway, I had picked Andy's Gym only because it was on the way to, or back from New Scotland Yard. It was also straight across the road to the 'new' Victoria Tube Underground Station opened earlier that year, which linked me to Kings Cross and then by over ground rail to Palmers Green Station. I had decided to live around the Palmers Green area in north London when I moved from Scotland to start the New Scotland Yard job. The main reason for choosing Palmers Green being I had a cousin and a few Scottish friends around the area that I could meet up with on occasions, but I soon discovered my unwieldy working hours and life in gyms and martial arts meant it was a rare occurrence to set up any meet. So once again I was mostly on my own, the loner that I did not mind.

In Southgate Technical College they held evening classes in karate. The Southgate College was only about a mile or so walking distance from my digs in a shared house in Old Park Road, around the corner from Palmers Green railway station on Alderman's Hill. So, I also managed to keep up my karate, which I was anxious to do as I had already reached Black Belt Hachi or 8th Dan, which for a twenty-six year old was quite advanced towards the top Ju Dan or 10th Dan, my ultimate objective.

I was also into Taekwondo and had already reached 7th Dan, which was the first master's level, but I had not contacted anyone in the London area who could take me on to the 9th Dan, this was the Grand Master. I was hoping to meet up with a fellow Scotsman during the following week who knew of someone coming to live in London in the next few weeks who may able to take me on to the top grade which was a long way to go.

As I had mentioned earlier at Sir Mark Wright's New Scotland Yard reception, I was brought up in 'The Gorbals' in the East End of Glasgow. The housing was mostly nineteenth century tenements built for Catholic workmen coming from Ireland, or the Scottish Highland Clearances.

Most of the tenements were now in a state of decay from the nineteen forties onwards and in one of the hardest, most depressive areas in the city.

The thing was in 'The Gorbals' from a very young age you had to learn how to take of yourself and I suppose it was then I learned to be a street fighter. If you allowed yourself to be bullied at school, this usually spilled over into the streets at night where we all ran free until ten o'clock or so. Then there was always the Kids Gangs and quickly followed then by the Teenagers Gangs and you graduated from there into the criminal gangs. As I say, I managed to steer clear of the gangs and was always a loner, even from my own family who typically, like most Scottish families, all got on with their own lives and friends until something went wrong in the family.

There were a few reasons why I drifted into being a loner. The first was, when I was nine years old, our Mum just got up one morning, walked out to go the shops and never came back, leaving us six kids with a part time drunken Dad, who then rapidly became a full time drunken skunk. We kids heard the reason that Dad hit the bottle so hard was he found out that Mum, who I remember was still a good looking woman in her early forties, had gone off with one of the local hard men - Fran Donnelly. Dad knew there was no way he could tangle with Donnelly so he just hid under the bottles. Although only nine years old I took my Dad fearing this hard man into my little brain and I had started learning Karate at Gallagher's Gym, a flea pit near the 'Barrowland Ballroom' and just around the corner from 'The Barras Market.' In the Barras where at that time you could buy almost anything you happened to be looking for, legal or hooky gear, it was all available if you knew where to look. I had it in my little mind that one day with my karate I would sort Fran Donnelly out good and proper.

By eleven years old I was already a recognised street fighter taking on, and usually beating the hell out of sixteen years old kids. They knew not to mess with me! I was then known as 'a wee hard man.' That was no mean feat for a wee boy in the Gorbals.

I then started the gym work when I was eleven years of age, only to get up my body strength and fitness for the Karate. At that time in Scotland, nobody seemed to worry too much about what ten years old and upwards was getting into. I remember being tall for my age and getting very fit and strong through my gym work. I started at eleven years old playing football, Scotland's national sport. I played with Saint Lukes School in 'The Gorbals' and then I went for trials with Scotland schoolboys. I travelled all over Glasgow into some rough areas on my own and many a time I had to do a runner from local gangs from Kirkintilloch, Bearsden and Paisley. Although I could fight, even then I knew against a gang it was better to retreat and live to fight another day.

I don't think, even to this day, any of my family knew I had successful trials for Scotland schoolboys, but had to turn down going on for further coaching, because I had no more time available and the family just did not have the money. In any case, it clashed with my karate and gym nights, which at that time was more important to me. Maybe a big missed opportunity, but I knew it just could not happen.

At twelve years old I added my fourth sport taekwondo, which with karate made me think about my body and take care of myself. I was already five feet ten and more than capable of beating the shit out of the older guys.

To pay for all of this I began buying and selling anything and everything using 'The Barrowland' Market where a mates' dad had a stall and allowed me to sell bits and pieces on Saturday and Sunday mornings. I was quite the entrepreneur, making more money in two days than most men earned in a week.

With Karate, Taekwondo, Street Fighting and my weight training fitness routine, plus six feet of solid muscle, I had the physique by sixteen to now become known as 'a big hard man.'

My Dad then developed a heart problem on top of the drinking when all six of us kids were young, so we lived from hand to mouth until all the sisters and brothers left school. I was the eldest brother and my sister Ann was ahead of me.

In Glasgow families were not dragged up, but we certainly learned to grow up fast and we were expected to be independent from an early age. I don't remember anything like parent's school nights, or them having any checks on our education, other than the end of term report cards which we usually conveniently forgot to bring home and forged our parent's signature. The parents usually forgot and just left the teachers to get on with it.

Most of the fathers in 'The Gorbals' worked in manual labour jobs and as I said earlier were mostly descendants of either the Scottish highland clearances, or the Irish potato farm labourer's people who came over to Glasgow and Liverpool during the Irish potato famine in the eighteen forties and fifties. However, although lowly labourer's it was amazing how well read the majority were and with a drink or two they could talk at length on most subjects. It must have been something to do with working outdoors all day back in Ireland or in the Scotlands highlands, but when they were young the majority educated themselves by reading throughout the long cold winters when they had no money, or inclination to go out. That is, except for the traditional Friday night for the men's drinking night and Sunday mornings to church, Catholic or Protestant.

Few of the wives worked in those days and except for the Sunday church they were left at home in the tenements looking after the kids and making friends, or enemies, with their neighbours.

Still, something about the Scottish education system just worked and has gone on working for generations through those desperate years with high unemployment. From a small country like Scotland with a population at any time of between only four and five million, the Scots produced people like Alexander Fleming who discovered Penicillin and were known worldwide for great engineers like James Watt who perfected the steam engine. Not to mention Alexander Graham Bell who invented the telephone, or how about John Logie Baird, the inventor of the worlds first practical television and the first colour tube for television.

The list goes on and on, but my own very favourite Scotsman, my hero, was Andrew Carnegie, not because of any invention, but because of the legacy he left for future generations to America, Canada, United Kingdom and many other countries. Andrew Carnegie made his millions in America in the steel industry in the late nineteenth century and in today's money terms was said to be worth a cool $325.3 Billion. He sold up his empire and went on to devote the remainder of his life to large-scale philanthropy, with special emphasis on the welfare of working men, including building and funding in all these countries; local libraries, education in schools and scientific research. Not to mention a devotion to achieving world peace, obviously not one of his most successful projects. Without Carnegies millions, it is highly unlikely that the working man in any of these countries would have been educated by the end of the twentieth century and some of the wonderful inventions of the twentieth century may never have happened. After all, respective governments in all of these countries, over hundreds of years up to that point had never gone out of their way to educate, or take care of the working man. So, the term "You must be as rich as Carnegie" was born at the beginning of the twentieth century.

That is enough of my ravings on my favourite Scotsman.

The second reason I suppose I naturally drifted into being a bit of a loner was after my first girlfriend and first love Theresa Owen moved with her family to Corby, when much of the steelworks moved from Motherwell in Lanarkshire where they all worked, down to Northamptonshire. As far as I knew Northamptonshire was somewhere in the English countryside. Eventually Northampton became better known as the birthplace of Princess Di but that was way off in the future.

Somehow, I got enough schooling to get the Lowers and then, low and behold, I only went and got five Highers in the Scottish education system. That gave me enough to go on to a university place, the first in our family to ever manage this amazing feat. I then had a real stroke of luck when I managed somehow, through the Glasgow police, to win a scholarship to the University of Cambridge at the Institute of Criminology, which had only recently been founded by Sir Leon Radzinowicz in nineteen fifty-nine. Because of the money restrictions I had to work my way through university, so I continued to be a loner through that phase of my life.

Why criminology? Well I suppose it started back then when I was seven or eight roaming the back streets of 'The Gorbals'. No kid, no matter the age, should be allowed to see what I and my contemporaries saw back then in the fifties. There were the razor gangs of course who regularly appeared on the scene and cut people up for whatever obscure reason they had to justify their horrendous acts and they just left their victims in the street dying, or at best massively disfigured for the rest of their lives. Either way it left massive scars on us kid's memories. Then there were the addicts, not only the druggies, but especially the alcoholics, the meth drinkers, the weirdo's and then the poorest of the poor unemployed, just begging and sleeping real rough on the cold mean streets of Glasgow.

As far as the police were concerned 'The Gorbals' was the pits, not a place to be on a beat, or for detectives knocking doors on their own. There was always the pretence of police investigations into victims in 'The Gorbals,' but most of the cases were almost instantly shelved in the cold files as unsolved, unless of course somebody from outside 'The Gorbals' was hit, but even then, it depended how important their family was. If they were working class families, then they were not far behind 'The Gorbals' victims in hitting the cold case unsolved files. We who lived in 'The Gorbals' tenements, all knew not to expect much from the police and we were seldom surprised. Watching all this going on, almost daily, soon instilled in me, at a very young age, a sense of injustice and so gradually there came the strong will to eventually be able to do something about it, how, what and when? - I was still too young to know enough.

Of course, there were the ordinary good working guys trying to scrape a living to support their large families within the tenements, but with high unemployment and little from the welfare state, many had already drifted into being no hopers, most never stood much of a chance in the first place.

It was one of the teachers at Saint Lukes school, a Miss Tierney, a lovely middle aged little lady of five feet nothing, who tried so hard to really make a crowd of hard boiled street wise city kids to understand about life. Anyway, one day she started to try to teach us about sociology. Most of the class of nine year olds could not even pronounce the word until she spelt out the pronunciation from the dictionary; "so-ci-ol-ogy". However, when she went on to talk about social problems and how it could be related to crime, then we nearly all, except of course the usual thickos, understood very well where she was coming from, what it was all about. Only then did we start to recognise what was really happening in 'The Gorbals.'

For my part, even at that young age, with the help of Miss Tierney, I put together the social problems in 'The Gorbals' with crime and depravity. Then I knew what I wanted to do with my life, it was so simple and clear to me. I wanted to study crime, the criminal's minds, but even then, I realised it was not all about social problems, some of the wickedest criminals in history did not come from anti-social backgrounds. However, initially all I wanted to do was catch the criminals in 'The Gorbals' and show the people that the police did care about them in the same way as any other citizen. I did not begin to understand the problems that being a policeman and living in 'The Gorbals' would bring to me, all that was to come much later.

Still, all of this gave me the goals to set my targets, to make something of my life, which is probably why I did so well at the Lower and Higher exams. By then I knew that crime investigation could be studied under something called Criminology which came from America and then to go on to also qualify as a Psychologist, which was my real beginning to seek to understand the criminal's mind and bring them to face justice.

My God, I had been bitten by a big bug of idealism, probably watching too much of 'The Untouchables,' an American television series with Elliot Ness at the time. I knew if a kid from 'The Gorbals' or 'Drumchapel' said something like that to me back then I would probably not be able to hide my laughter. The naivety of youth allowed me to ignore the mountains that were in front of me and I just sort of skirted round them and came out the other side - somehow about where I wanted to be.

Being six feet, good looking and a muscular, I did not have to be a complete loner and I got my fair share of the best of the girls in Glasgow, then particularly at Cambridge and this I hoped would be carried on in London. However, using my newly acquired psychology skills, I reckoned it went back to my mother and my first love Theresa, probably having disappeared so suddenly out of my life, I could never see myself ever being able to fully trust another woman or girl again. Of course, I soon realised that, like a lot of psychologists' suggestions, this was a lot of bollocks. When I finally met my next love in my late twenties my whole attitude changed, but things in life also change so quickly. It is funny how, when things go wrong, people usually revert to type and go back into whatever shell they were in to hide from hurting.

I finally got to Andy's Gym at Victoria and set about the boring daily routine to keep 'my temple' in shape. As usual my mind drifted to the events of the day as I switched to auto with the weights and exercises.

One thing I knew for sure was DI Andy Spearing was going to be giving me a hard time. This was not going to be an easy ride. I reckoned he had some sort of chip a mile high on his shoulder and he was going to be acting the hard man right from the start. I smiled at my thought. If he thought he was tough, he ought to go and work with the Glasgow police like I did after university. The Glasgow police were not only tough, they were like oak trees, we reckoned they could only be cut down by electric saws and even then, they would probably have to replace the steel blades!

So, I thought, okay DI Andy Spearing, come right on and that is exactly what he did - big time! That was all to start the very next day.

As usual I finished in the gym and dry towelled off the sweat, changed back to my office suit and took the Victoria Line to Kings Cross and then the overland train to Palmers Green.

Luckily, it was my night for a bath, but even that went wrong and it was a cold-water bath, because somebody else had jumped in before I got back. Time to find my own place I thought. Then the lights went out, the meter needed money and I did not have a penny of change, so that was the clincher; it was time to move on and I decided, well maybe, to move into town nearer work.

I had an early night and started my plan on how to handle DI Andy Spearing. What a waste of time my little plan turned out to be.

Book 1 in the DI Spearing and DS Devlin series

Chapter 05 - The Killings

At ten fifty-five the lights came on in the stairway within the 'Palmers Place' mansion near Weybridge in Surrey and they were soon followed by three bedroom lights on the first floor.

Sam alias 'The Fox' quickly drilled his night binoculars on the bedroom windows and saw young Bobby pulling his curtains closed, quickly followed by the one next door as Mary Rose closed her curtains. A couple of minutes later the beautiful wife Sarah went to her window overlooking the swimming pool and pulled her curtains. No sign of John Palmer in the bedroom.

Sam swung his binoculars back downstairs and spotted John Palmer making for the stairway while the two bouncers went towards the rear of the house. The number one bouncer went off in the direction of the spare room beside the office, turning off the lounge light as he went.

Sam thought to himself, still a long night to go, need to be doing something to keep alert to any change in the house until it is time to hit.

To keep his mind active and on the alert Sam settled down in his burrow covered by the tree branches to read once again the dossier on John Palmer. The reasons Sam had accepted the contract were all right there. The judge had decided he was guilty as charged and there was no appeal, the death sentence had been passed to Sam to execute at a cost of a fifty grand plus a bonus.

Sam read all about John Palmer, how on the surface he was the apparent shining light of a typical London east end kid done good. From time to time he was also paraded as such by bent politicians who were actually on 'The Quiet Firms' payroll.

From the back streets squalor of the East End docks in the thirties, John Palmer clawed his way through the roughest schools, where some of the toughest kids in the east end became known as his mates.

One Joseph Bolger, a name that Sam immediately recognised from a previous contract, became John Palmer's best friend throughout their schooldays. John Palmer had pulled his friend through school, teaching him to read and write more than the teachers ever could or would.

Joseph was the son of Joseph Bolger, a world war one USA soldier who had lived on in England after the Great War 1914-1918. He had an affair with Joseph's mum Alice Rigley an original East Ender born within the sound of Bow Bells, but when Joseph Junior came along, the father Joseph Senior had done a quick exit back to New York, never to be heard from again.

Joseph had, almost as soon as he was old enough, became a petty criminal with his own mob in the East End docklands area.

Early in his criminal career as a youth Joseph Bolger, being the son of an American, had with John Palmers help, learned a great deal about how the American Mafia operated. The Mafia set-up what appeared to be legal businesses so as they could launder their illegal monies. Businesses like the Las Vegas Casinos, Restaurants, Trucking, Builders, Union's and so on, all with large cash flows going through them with untraceable amounts of ready cash.

As far as discipline within the Mafia families or rivals were concerned, it was all mostly done by hired professionals with little associations to the families. Joseph had also studied people like the famous gangster Al Capone in the nineteen-thityies and likened him to 'The Hammonds' and 'The Christies' from London's east end, where apparently, executions and severe beatings were carried in the public domain, often in front of witnesses who were left alive to later testify. They also did not cover their illegal earnings in any way, instead relying on 'the bookkeepers' who invariably, when caught, would turn states evidence to get lighter sentences for themselves. In the thirties, Al Capone had become a liability in making too much noise and had performed too many public assassinations, and then got himself caught with a basic mistake of incorrect bookkeeping and tax evasion. What a plonker!

Joseph instinctively knew that it was a stupid way to do business and to have all this crap going down in your own backyard was asking for big time trouble there and then, or later in life. So again, with the help of his life- long school friend John Palmer, he started legal businesses and hidden accounts. He opened several very fashionable casinos in London's Mayfair, with night clubs and set-up illegal bookmakers' offices across London. Bookmakers and betting outside of horse racing on the courses, or football pools betting, were not legal until nineteen sixty, therefore up until then they were a great source of income for the gangs. Then came a chain of quick food restaurants, all businesses with high cash flow turnovers.

Joseph Bolger soon became known as one of the most enlightened gang leaders in the UK, although he had mostly taken advice from John Palmer.

So, Joseph's criminal businesses were set-up with the motto; 'Quietly, so quietly, catch the monkeys' and the 'Quiet Firm' was born way back in the nineteen-forties before the other big gangs came along.

Joseph's 'Quiet Firm,' with John Palmers astute guidance, soon got clear of their back yard in the East End and following the cash flow businesses they then bought into, using some muscle, several Import and Export business. It started with legitimate fancy goods from the Far East and then America, including records of the 'new' rock and roll and blues artistes, most of which were just not available in the UK during the nineteen fifties and early sixties while the country was still recovering from the ravages of war. It did not take long for the legitimate trade, which made good, but never big money, to become a very good cover for illegal trade in everything from guns, to a slave trade in prostitutes.

Joseph Bolger's 'Quiet Firm' monies soon set-up John Palmer with a legitimate large East End Accountants company registered as 'Palmers Associates.' They were extra plush offices in East Ham, especially for someone apparently starting out, but not many knew where the money was coming from.

'Palmer Associates were officially the accountants for the legitimate companies owned by Joseph Bolger's 'Quiet Firm.' In the background, he also covered the books for the illicit operations and for the management of the money laundering. Everyone thought John Palmer was now the real powerhouse who knew every detail about the total operation. Following the legalization, in nineteen sixty, of the bookmakers in off course betting, it was John Palmer who led the firm into the drugs business using the Far East contacts and then setting up contacts within Latin America, Columbia, Peru, Bolivia and Holland.

Joseph Bolger gradually became only the figurehead who did not need to get his hands dirty, only to be there representing the heavy team and, because they were not in competition with any of the other firms and did not run any protection rackets, there was little for Joseph to do.

Although huge profits were rolling in, the rumours began to spread around that Joseph Bolger was not happy in dealing with drugs, which he hated with a vengeance and with his new minor roles. Soon there were more rumours of rows between Joseph and John Palmer about everything and everybody.

Suddenly, Joseph started talks with the American Mafia about sub-contracting the drugs operations. This resulted in another massive row with John Palmer who had built-up the drugs trade from nothing to a £100 million a year turnover in the mid nineteen sixties and it was getting bigger by the day as the hippies and the 'in crowds' led the 'swinging' generation to the drugs troughs.

Somebody leaked the news, without naming any names, of the American Mafia's planned invasion of the UK rackets. Suddenly 'The Hammond's and 'The Christie's firms, with The Liverpool and the Glasgow mobs were all up in arms. They were quickly followed by practically every bent policemen and politician in the country. The media followed and then Westminster woke up to the danger. A stranger lot of bedfellows you could not find and probably would never find again.

Soon everyone was trying to find out who was introducing The Mafia into the UK and it did not take too much longer for the finger of suspicion to point to Joseph Bolger. Almost immediately, just a few weeks ago, Joseph Bolger appeared to do a runner and has not been heard of since.

Sam thought nobody knows, except me and my customer thought Sam, if Joseph Bolger had engineered his own 'disappearance', or if somebody put out a contract on him, maybe 'The Christie's or 'The Hammond's. Alternatively, any one of the many bent police or politicians could have been responsible for the contract, but it is again a rumour that his old-school friend John Palmer used the opportunity to officially take over the 'Quiet Firm.' He certainly sent out the message that with Joseph Bolger's disappearance any prior agreements with Joseph Bolger, although none were known at this time, were cancelled. This has certainly upset the American Mafia who no longer had a toe hold in the UK rackets and it could just as easily have been them who ordered the contract. Sam had a passing thought just hoping that this job was not for the Mafia; he did not want to get involved with that mob, no way.

So, the little evidence there is, certainly points to John Palmer, now running the biggest drug operation ever in the history of UK, which is sentencing thousands of Britain's young to a lifetime of hell and almost certain early deaths. His organisation, although he blamed Joseph Bolger, was responsible for trying to bring in the American Mafia, which would be catastrophic for the UK rackets.

The dossier then went on to provide details of John Palmer's location, family and heavies working at the mansion.

Sam thought to himself, a very comprehensive dossier from this customer. He thought he recognised the style of the document, he had worked for this lot before, but although he suspected who they were, he could not be sure. He tried to be anonymous to his customers and he thought his customers were, on the whole, anonymous to him; that is how he wanted it to remain. Usually he could make an educated guess who he was working for, but he had been proven wrong on several occasions through the years.

One thing that he thought he did know; it was not the same customer as for the previous Joseph Bolger contract. They wanted him alive for information and he knew who 'they' were because after dropping Bolger off – alive and well - he had then followed them back to their workplace. It could be they were laying down a false trail, which they were more than capable of doing with their background.

Sam again felt that uneasy feeling about this contract. It had come too soon after the Joseph Bolger contract and he smelt a rat. He had also heard rumours on the grapevine of DI Spearing, from the serious crimes squad, investigating Joseph Bolger's disappearance. Unusual for them to bother too much about one of the gang leaders disappearing Sam thought. DI Spearing must be one of the few straight ones, not in the gang's back pockets. Of course, there were the usual snitches feeding him with information that would have to be taken care off when he got back to London.

In normal circumstances, this uneasy feeling would have been enough for him to pull out of the contract, but he thought he knew this customer and they had been one of the biggest on his books and he had never failed them over the years. So, it had to be done, he repeated his earlier thoughts, big risk for big bucks.

Sam thought some more. This could start a gang war and perhaps that is what it was all about? It may be as simple as that. Let us start gang wars and watch the fall-out, take over when there is an opportunity. That would certainly work for 'The Mafia.' Then again, the two main men out of commission from one of the main gangs, if not the most important gang, it blows the whole lot wide open and none of the gang's benefit. So, it must be police or MI5? Sam thought again, so why am I feeling so uneasy about this? This could be a set-up that is why and he was being led like a sheep to the wolf. As per the boy's scout's motto 'Be Prepared' and go in expecting the worst.

He suddenly noticed the time at 02-40 it was time to move in.

Sam started by putting his knife into the quick button release sheaf and tied it low down under the right sleeve of his black turtle neck sweater. He then placed the Walter PPK fitted with a silencer in the small of his back under his black leather belt. He then picked up the tools in a black leather bag which would enable him to break into the mansion. He took a few deep breaths which always tended to settle his nerves, but not this time, he was on the edge.

He slid backwards out of the lair and very slowly raised himself up to a crouch position. He then walked very slowly, still crouching, through the trees making sure he did not trip over roots or create any noise by snapping any twigs on the ground. Once on the lawn, he sprinted for the corner of the mansion nearest the side door entrance. He made it, a little breathless, but easily blended into the darkness beside the door.

It took two minutes to pick the old-style lock and quietly he slid into the dark interior corridor. His eyes were already adjusted to the dark and he opened the first door on the left which was a huge modernized kitchen. He closed the door and moved to the next door on the right, a downstairs shower and toilet. He quietly closed the door and moved onto the next door on the left which led to a small corridor with a door at either side.

He opened the door on the right, a bedroom with useless bodyguard number one, sleeping soundly and snoring. He gently closed the door then noticed the key on the outside and locked it, any delaying tactics always good, but unlikely that guy would hear an earthquake.

He then opened the door on the left and found useless bodyguard number two again sleeping soundly, but not snoring. Again, the key was on the outside so he locked it and moved on.

Back in the main corridor, he saw a light from a room with an open door just past the stairs and he could hear someone apparently speaking on the telephone. He took out the Walther PPK from his back and held it down his right thigh. He moved towards the door and slid through the gap and a piece of cold steel was pushed into his left temple. Another Walther PPK fitted with a silencer, held by the more alert bodyguard number three.

"Drop the piece or you drop right there." Bodyguard number three spat the words with a deep menacing voice.

"Well now we would not want that, now would we?" Sam replied with a confident voice seeing John Palmer sitting at a desk with yet another Walther PPK and fitted silencer pointed straight at him. Sam dropped his gun and his tool bag with a clatter onto a tiled floor and took a step away from them.

"Well, welcome Mr Fox. We thought you would never get here. You army types are so predictable. Waiting till the dead of night, which is always just before dawn with you lot." John Palmer smiled confidently his white teeth showing against a tanned face with dark pepper and salt hair. He was still a good-looking guy in his sixties dressed casually in jeans and white T shirt.

"You were expecting me then?" Sam asked causally.

"You should check out your customers. They are more bent than a corkscrew!" Palmer was still smiling as he added; "To tell you the truth Mr Fox we thought you would be a bigger challenge, given your reputation." John Palmer smiled graciously again showing those white teeth.

"You don't know much of my reputation Mr Palmer." Sam replied.

"I am sure you are right Mr Fox, but right now your reputation appears to be in tatters. Search him Tony" John Palmer was arrogant.

Tony put his Walter PPK in his belt and stepped over, but got himself between John Palmer and Sam. That was a very big and fatal mistake; the one Sam had been waiting for.

"Tony, you bloody idiot! -" John Palmer screamed what was to be his last words on earth, but he never got a chance to finish his sentence. Billy went to turn to look back at John Palmer. The knife appeared in the right hand of Sam and in one swift movement he slashed Billy's throat from ear to ear. The blood spurted out like a burst oil well as Sam flung himself to the right and threw the knife straight and true into John Palmers heart. As he fell forwards the gun went off with a pop quite harmlessly into the desk.

"My- Oh my - Mr Palmer you did underestimate me. Not even a vest. Normal service resumed. - I guess my reputation is fully restored don't you think?" Sam smiled and went over and felt John Palmer for a pulse. There was none, so he removed his knife cleaned it thoroughly on John Palmers T shirt and put it back in the sheaf on his right arm.

He then retrieved his gun from the floor, put it back in his belt and lifted his tool bag.

He noticed the huge blood pool under Tony the bodyguards' body. It looked like his body was already drained of blood. It never ceased to amaze Sam how quick the body drains from the jugular vein. He quickly made up his mind to escape through the window so he went over and had a quick look around out and went out just as dawn was starting to break.

As he was leaving through the window, unbeknown to him, he was seen from the end of the mansion by the local poacher - a gypsy road traveller - who was coming from the estates river where he had caught, at least poached - a few salmon for tomorrow's dinner.

Sam headed back to the trees and the fox lair. He picked up all his rubbish, stuffed it all in his tool bag and sprinted out the gate. He looked at his watch; total time from leaving the lair to coming back was twenty minutes and two men dead, one of them an idiot, a casualty of war. It was time to beat a hasty retreat and get out of here. Must stop using these army phrases Sam thought as he went out the gates.

Book 1 in the DI Spearing and DS Devlin series

Chapter 06 – Day One

I decided to get into New Scotland Yard early for my first full day on the job as Detective Sergeant Kevin Devlin on Tuesday morning the eighteenth of July in nineteen sixty-seven. There were two reasons for being there by seven o'clock. First, being a natural born nosey person, I wanted to nose around DI Andy Spearing's desk before he arrived and see if I could find out what he was currently working on; always better to know as much as possible in advance. The second reason was to look around the office and get a feel for the layout for the important things, like the coffee machine and canteen. Good coffee and food were always the most important things to me if I was to survive.

I signed in at the reception desk printing my name and signing the book. I was given a Temporary Pass key by the pretty young receptionist. I gave her my flashing, most friendly smile and she responded by smiling sweetly and blushing, almost an acknowledgement that she liked me. She had big boobies hidden behind a tight-fitting pink V neck sweater and beautiful long blonde hair. A trim figure, I could not see her legs or anything below the twenty-four-inch tiny waist. "You are cleared to go in DS Devlin" she said with a sweet sexy voice.

"Why thank you Sandra" I read her name from the name pad pined just above her left breast and gave her my biggest expansive smile as I turned to go to the lifts. I thought yes, I would not mind a word later with little Sandra, maybe at lunch time.

As I walked through the entrance hall towards the lifts I suddenly felt someone on my right shoulder and glancing sideways there was that smarmy pounce from yesterday Nigel Worthington, the fraud squad guy, most appropriate for him I thought. He was dressed exactly as he was yesterday, same or duplicate suit, shirt, tie and black, shiny shoes. His hair was plastered down with that awful Brylcreem hair cream which had gone out of fashion with our generation from the early sixties since the rockers went out of fashion. Then there was the smell of Brute aftershave, it was overpowering another 'no- no' in the nineteen sixty-seven fashion stakes.

"Well hello – Kevin our criminologist, isn't it?" Nigel had that smarmy grin on his face again.

"Yes – Nigel – the fraud - isn't it?" I replied intentionally leaving out the squad.

Nigel looked flustered unsure if I had intended what I had just said and replied; "Yes – 'The Fraud Squad'---" Nigel replied unable to hide the annoyance in his voice.

"Oh yes of course. Sorry! - I have not woken yet. Need that first injection of caffeine!" I said and put on my most disarming smile. As expected it was ignored.

We both went into the elevator and I pressed the button for Floor 3 and noted Nigel hitting the Floor 10 button. I thought, did you ever notice that in most office blocks, the accountants always appear in the higher echelons of the company, while we mere plebs, who do the day to day work, are down in the lower levels?

"Always pays to be early especially your first day on the job." Nigel smarmy Worthington smiled ever so slightly, that sort of false way.

"Especially if you are feeling bum licking good, but it does makes your breath smell does it not?" I said it without a smile.

"You think yourself a bit of a comedian, do you?" Nigel asked in a hostile way I thought." That is not very funny." He added.

"That is sad Nigel 'old boy'. I am just trying to keep it light. Peace man!" I again added my disarming smile accompanied by the Churchill V sign, in reverse of course.

"Not remotely funny" Nigel smirked.

"It does depend on you having a sense of humour of course." I replied with a sly smile as I stepped out of the lift at the third floor. Nigel's face was bright red, but he could not manage a retort before the lift door closed. I decided I now had made enemy number two, not bad going for my second day.

I made my way along the corridor and entered the open plan offices. I saw the Notice Board with a plan of the desks and checked that I was still allocated the same desk directly opposite DI Spearing which I had been told about yesterday. There I was, sure enough, about forty - five degrees from the Notice Board. Then I saw some envelopes addressed to different people fixed to the Notice Board with pins. Obviously, messages left for people who were out of the office.

I noticed a signing in and out register for people on this floor. There were five others already signed in and it was still only 07.05. I signed in and went over to my desk, which was clear except for new stationery – Bic ballpoint pens, pencils, the statutory policemen's notebook and an A4 lined pad. I pocketed the notebook and a couple of pens in my inside jacket pocket then hung it on the back of my chair; there were no coat hangers around.

I looked around for the all important coffee machine and noticed one of those awful, six feet high machines in the far corner with three middle age looking guys standing around supping from those equally awful plastic cups. Oh well those machines threw out gut wrenching stuff labelled as coffee; still better than nothing. I made my way over to the machine.

"Hi, I am Tony Booth- I am in the serious crimes burglary squad" Tony offered his handshake. He had a mop of blondish hair, about thirtyish around six feet, fit looking in a body builder's sort of way, with a pleasant, smiling face and offered his hand. He was dressed in an expensive looking light weight grey suit, crisp white shirt, grey silk tie and shiny black shoes.

"Hi, I am Kevin Devlin also in serious crimes on the murder and assassinations reporting to DI Spearing." I smiled and shook his hand.

"You poor bastard – what did you do wrong at the interview?" Tony laughed as he said it.

"He is that bad then? I got the impression he was a surly introvert, but that is my first impression," I replied as I went over to get a cup of gut wrenching stuff labelled as coffee.

"Surly and introvert are probably understatements and could only apply when he is sober. That aint very often these days. Still he is probably the best detective in the building, but the way he is going he is heading for the old heave ho." Tony smiled and winked as though I would understand.

"And here was I thinking I was joining the elite police force in Britain. At least up until I walked in the door yesterday." I smiled and that brought a laugh from the others.

Another of the guys, salt and pepper black hair came over and offered his hand. "Jack Thomson, I am in the same squad as you, but I am allocated to DI Sanderson to try and tie something on the bigger East End gangs and pull them in. A near impossible task with some of our bosses!" Jack's voice trailed off like he felt he had said something he should have not said. He was dressed in a more conventional and much less expensive blue lightweight suit, white shirt and dark blue plain tie and he added; "Andy is not that bad really - just going through a bad patch at home just now." Jack added with a slight shake of his head as he shook my hand.

"Honestly Jack, this bad spell has gone on for over two years. His liver must be pickled by now." Tony again with a smile and all three, plus myself, again laughed. Tony was obviously the wise ass in this group.

"He is still one of the best irrespective of the boozing." Jack said, rather defensively

"Bill Brown" The third guy with reddish hair, high blood pressure face and a slight Scottish, probably one time Edinburgh accent, offered his handshake. He too was dressed in an expensive brown suit, high polished brown shoes, crisp white stylish shirt and silk brown tie. Gold rings left and right hand and solid gold watch. "I am in the prostitution catch squad, females and males these days, seedy old world." He smiled, but did not appear to be genuine.

I shook his limp cold sweaty hand. "You don't blend into the environment with your dress gear then?" I replied with my manly smile.

"Yeah well actually I do. I get taken for a punter most of the time by the new faces, but I am known to the old hands so it does not really matter with them!" Bill Brown was curt in his reply.

"I thought we did not bother so much with the prostitutes these days? I said flatly as I was fast getting into a winding up mood.

"Well we still try to put the wind up the new faces, but they just keep coming. We always can use the old hands for information, because they don't like being booked no more." Bill Brown replied with a wink and a nod.

"Yes, well I suppose that is better than arresting the stars and business men who are actually the real culprits? I just came out with it, both feet in as usual.

"I suppose you are one of the chiefs new 'Trained Brains' then? All brain and no job knowledge, is it?" Tony Booth again the joker.

"Probably better than job knowledge, but no brain wouldn't you say?" I retorted again knowing full well I was once again creating at least another two new enemies. Not bad going for a new starter, four new enemies in my first two days.

"More like 'Trained Bairns' if you ask me." Bill Brown answered in his surly way and we all laughed, me included.

"Well I had better get this 'Trained Brain' into gear before I shit my nappy" I laughed as I said it and they all joined in the laugh as I turned away and headed back towards my desk with the remains of the poison in my plastic cup. It looked like that had defused a potentially confrontational situation.

I checked the watch, 07-30 already and then I looked over to DI Spearings desk and saw six large buff files neatly piled in an in-tray on the left side. I walked around and picked the top one titled 'Joseph Bolgers' disappearance on June 26th 1967,' a current case I thought, so took it back to my desk and sat down to read it and bring myself up to scratch.

The top of first page was typed and detailed the facts of the disappearance. "Joseph Bolger the head of a long-established London East End Gang known as 'The Quiet Firm' had disappeared on 26th June 1967. His wife reported him missing on the 27th June 1967. In the right column of the page someone, presumably DI Spearing, had written in pencil; *'Unusual for gang to involve the police so soon.'*

The case has been allocated to DI Andy Spearing on 27th June 1967. There followed a hand written itemized list of actions taken with questions, answers or comments again in the right-hand column.

Interviewed Joan Bolger, the wife, on 27th June 1967. Appeared genuinely distressed. Appears a solid marriage lasted 22 years to date. She appears a bit naïve re the business. JB got a call at 7 pm on 26th June said he had to suddenly go out on business- Joan does not know where or with whom. Then in the right-hand column was written; *'Checked phone call – public phone box in Westminster borough, so not traceable.'*

Talked to John Palmer of Palmer Associates on the 27th June – the accountant's for 'The Quiet Firm.' - Thought to be number two in the gang and the brains. Pushed the gang into the drugs trade late fifties/early sixties. JB does not like the drugs trade. JP said he did not know anything until Joan phoned on the 27th saying JB had not come home. Advised her to wait for a few days, but she would have none of it. Gut feeling JP may know more than he is saying? Then in the right-hand column was written; *'Need to get in contact with informant see what they are hearing on this. Dead end at moment.'*

Informant on 15th July tells me there was a big row between JP and JB who it is thought is trying to sell out the drugs trade to 'The Mafia' – Not good news could cause repercussions across the UK. Means all the gangs could be looking to take JB out – 'The Hammond's' 'The Christie's,' Glasgow, Liverpool or Birmingham mobs? Also look at JP a possibility? If JP was trying to pull out of any deal, then 'The Mafia' could be out to get both JB and JP? Need to go see JP, but tell DI Harry Lawler to keep an eye out in Royal Tunbridge Wells and let me know if anything happens. JP lives outside Tunbridge Wells.

Cold trail. Set up another meet with informant on Monday 3rd July to pressure. Nothing from any other source.

Monday 17th July met informant in Soho in afternoon. The word is there and he seems sure, the disappearance of JB is down to 'The Fox' yet again. Disturbing news is that our lot supposedly using him as well as the gangs. Could be a police vigilante group? MI5? Everybody appears to be scared because they do not know if it is another gang, The Mafia, JP, or our lot?

Don't like the sound of all this, it could all go tits up. Pressure on informant for more information, promised reward of £250 (Not paying that much!). The slush fund will not pay that much for information on a known criminal disappearing, different if it was a lord, or a pop star or such like. Gave him till Wednesday 19th July to come with a name or valuable information.

    That was the last entry in the file so I went around to DI Spearings desk and left it on top of the pile in the same place.

    My thoughts were; First, it was strange that DI Spearing is using the gang's wives first name, very familiar? Second, he seems to be very disturbed, regarding the disappearance of a known criminal. Why? Usually, it is a given that at some time these gang members disappear and most are never heard of again. The bottom of the sea or a concrete grave in the foundations of some new building is the usual presumed places, where they are never found. So why is JB causing our DI Spearing so much heartache? It does seem very strange.

    The phone on DI Spearings desk suddenly rang loudly breaking my meagre thought process and I lifted the receiver.

    "This is DI Spearings phone. Detective Sergeant Devlin speaking – Can I help?" I said in a monotone voice.

    "Telephone operator here sergeant." A sweet girlie voice said. "I have a message for DI Spearing, is he in yet?"

    "He is not to my knowledge, unless he is under his desk." I replied with a laugh.

    "That is quite possible, knowing DI Spearing DS. Could you have a look?" she replied with a hearty laugh.

    "No - I can definitely confirm DI Spearing is not under the desk. Is that Sandra?" I was smiling my most expansive smile as I said it, although she could not see.

    "Why yes, it is. Good to know you remembered after all this time. Almost an hour since you came in. Kevin, is it? Sandra replied with another hearty laugh.

    "To quote the famous song – How could I ever forget one as beautiful as you? You want to give me a message Sandra?" I was into my smoothie act again.

    "Don't remember the song before my time! No, we are not allowed Kevin. I will have a message sent up to him straight away and have it pinned to the board." Sandras' voice was getting sexier by the second.

"Perhaps you just inspired me to write the lyric." I lied.

"You certainly have the Gaelic charm no doubt about that." Sandra laughed but hung up, just as I was getting into my stride.

I watched the notice board for anyone coming up. Saw some security guard type person arrive ten minutes later and pin a message. I waited till he had gone, picked up my notebook and pen and wandered over. Quickly found the open envelope addressed to DI Spearing pulled the pin and had a quick read of the inserted note:

'Message for DI Andy Spearing received 8am on the 17th July 1967. From DI Harry Lawler, at Guildford Surrey Police Station, re your request to keep a wary eye out on JP. Reported breaking and entry at JP's mansion, also reported dead bodies. Just on my way there now with a team. Care to join me since you are tying into the JB case?'

A-Ah I thought some more problems for our bedevilled DI Spearing. I quickly re-inserted the note into the envelope and re-attached it to the Notice Board with the original pin. I moved back over to my desk looking at my watch which told me it was 08-15, still no sign of DI Spearing, should have been here for 8 a.m. Time for another cup of the gut wrenching stuff, could not make up my mind yet if it was an alkaloid stimulant or a laxative. The next half hour will tell the tale. At 08-45 I got the first part of the answer as I rushed to the toilet.

Just after 09-00 there was the wondrous sight of DI Spearing wandering across the office. He was unshaven and was wearing the same suit as yesterday, but crumpled. It was same shirt etc. He sat down opposite me and the wave of stale alcohol hit me like an incoming tide.

"A hard day's night then was it sir?" I asked with a ruthful tone and a little smile.

"Been working all night" DI Spearing surprisingly replied, but with his usual dour tone.

"Park bench was it then with a bottle in one hand?" I knew I was pushing it again, but what the hell!

I swear he almost did smile; maybe the booze was still having an effect. "Almost, but it was a night club leather seat and a few too many beers." DI Spearing replied almost cheerfully, the booze was hanging on in there.

"Anyway, do you smell the booze then at that distance?" He asked as he opened his desk drawer and pulled out wet shaving gear, toothbrush, toothpaste, and soap with a dirty looking white bath towel. Obviously used to living out of the office.

"Put it this way sir, if I was a smoker I would be wary about lighting up a ciggy at this distance" I replied.

This time he did laugh, maybe he did have a sense of humour after all; well down below that dour surly Yorkshire exterior. "Yeah well I am going down the locker room get washed and changed be back in half an hour if anybody comes looking for me." DI Spearing put together some sort of hand sign and wandered off carrying his toiletries in his massive hands.

I remembered about the message, but decided to forget about it for now. Anyway, I thought, he couldn't go anywhere in his present state.

Almost exactly on the half hour DI Spearing reappeared in a different, well pressed dark grey suit, clean shaven, hair combed, brilliant white shirt and dark plain grey tie and polished black shoes. The only giveaway was the red eyes.

"Hello, you will be Mr Hyde then?" I asked with a smile.

"DI Spearing to you laddie. The monster has returned." He said it with a smile.

"Yeah it was the eyes that gave you away." I retorted. "Did you see the message on the board for you?" I asked politely.

"What board?" He asked in his gruff voice ignoring my jibe at his eyes.

"That board over there with the booking in and out record that you are supposed to complete on entering and leaving!" I pointed to the board.

"Oh, that board. Don't worry about signing in and out on that thing laddie, nobody bothers," he said as he walked over to the board.

He returned from the notice board still reading the message I had read earlier. He immediately lifted the phone and asked for Guildford Surrey Police station. On reply he stated he was DI Andy Spearing from the Serious Crimes Squad and asked to be patched through to DI Harry Lawler. After a couple of minutes' delay, he got a reply.

"Hello Harry, how goes it? Is JP one of the dead?" DI Spearing asked almost callously.

DI Lawler replied: "Yeah he is one of them. Both him and his minder stabbed with what looks like an army knife. Over"

"OK Harry, let's take the opportunity before 'The Firms' lawyers ascend from hell. Take out any meaty looking files you can get your hands on; get them to one of your outlying stations where they can be lost for a few days and let us read through them before they can get an injunction. Get his safe opened and do the same with the contents." DI Spearing was now acting and sounding like the complete professional, the boozy voice had disappeared "I have already organized the removal of the files, but the safe is locked and needs a pro to open it!" DI Lawler replied.

"Good lad. Good. - Don't you know any local safecrackers?" DI Spearing asked.

"Steve Martin – you know Steve - one of the best in the business, lives in Guildford." DI Lawler replied.

"Get him quick Harry and get the stuff out of there, the money included. We can make this work for us if we move really quickly like." DI Spearing was now crisp and straight to the point. "I will organize the same at his offices. We might crack the 'The Firm' as well as the murder case in one move. See you in an hour or so Harry." DI Spearing hung up the telephone then re-dialled.

"Hello John, it is me – Andy! Need a very fast favour from you. I want you to get a warrant out on John Palmer's offices. This is a murder investigation. We want to grab any files or anything else incriminating."

"Who has been murdered?" DI John Sanderson asked.

John Palmer and his minder, his name escapes me. Could be anybody done it, Mafia, his own mob, Hammond's, – even our lot – just about anybody." DI Spearing answered

DI John Sanderson replied; "Bloody hell Andy this is getting serious. On top of Joseph Bolger disappearing, this could be the start of gang wars."

"Tell me about it John. Can you take care of it? Use the new girl Judith what is her name? Is it Clements? She is still wet enough behind the ears! Not too influenced just yet and will want to appear cooperative with us, although her bosses may not like it, but you know how it goes John." DI Spearing replied in a rather monotone voice, but knowing it may help to move the case.

"OK Andy, you will cover me on this though? It is evidence which may be attached to the murder case?" DI John Sanderson sounded concerned

"Yes of course John. You know me, better cover than Dulux paint. Oh, and make sure you take somebody who can get into his safe to take the contents and you will need a few heavy 'Wooden Tops' with you, in case his heavies turn up. If a lawyer turns up, just show him the warrant and emphasize this is a murder investigation and the files are evidence. Then ask him how he knew that there had been a murder? Put him on the wrong foot. You know the score. We need to move real fast on this John, I don't want to get frozen out by lawyers like I did with Joseph Bolger. I finished up with a pair of brass monkeys on that one. Thanks John" DI Spearing hung up quickly with a smile before DI Sanderson could ask any more questions.

"You did not hear any of that Devlin?" DI Spearing stared with just the right amount of menace towards me.

"What was that sir?" I replied with a smile.

"Good answer lad." DI Spearing replied with a broad grin. From all this I was beginning to see why he was rated as the best policeman in the squad.

"I thought signing in and out on the board was a safety thing to make sure in the event of fire and emergencies that this floor was evacuated?" I asked all innocent like.

"Aye it may well be laddie. Looks like I will have to go out on this job" He replied almost absent-mindedly. He lifted the phone and ordered a pool car and requested a driver asking for Sergeant Thomson.

"Here!" He said passing over the pile of folders from his in-tray. " You can read these while I am away bring yourself up to speed." He smiled as he said it.

"I don't think so sir. I am supposed to get on the job training with you and I won't get it sitting here reading in the office." I did my best to sound annoyed.

"This is not our job. It is only a possible link to one of my, sorry our, jobs and I have only been invited to sit in on this one." He replied with a harsh tone to his voice.

"All the more reason for me to tag along sir! Get experience of interfacing with other forces?" I stated quite firmly.

"There is no need for the two of us. I will only be looking over their shoulders seeing if there is any link to our job." He replied almost flippantly.

I decided to dig my toes in. "It did not sound like that to me on the phone sir. I think it is very important for me to go with you sir. I would only have to get a car and follow you."

"I thought you never heard any of that? Anyway, you need to get a DI to approve a car from the pool and I don't see any need for it." He replied with a sly grin.

"Oh, that is alright sir. I can always go upstairs to the chief and explain to him why I need it. I am sure he will understand and sign a chitty for me." I replied with a grin.

"Are you trying to threaten me laddie?" He asked angrily.

"Me? No! – Not at all sir. I am just trying to do my job." I replied smugly.

He then surprised me by replying "Well if it means that much to you come along then. We are leaving in five minutes."

I grabbed my jacket and put it on as I followed him to the exit without stopping to sign out.

We went into the Pool Car in the underground car park and there was a giant of a policeman leaning with his elbows on the roof of a brand new nineteen sixty-seven black
Jaguar S-Type Police Car. At the time a beautiful machine a real joy to drive and so cool!

"When did they start letting you loose with the classy stuff Tommy?" DI Spearing asked with a cheeky smile.

"They only give these to the best driver's sir!" Sergeant Thomson replied with a smile.

"That's what I mean Tommy! How come they let you loose with it?" DI Spearing gave him an evil grin.

"How come I knew you were going to say that sir? It must be the boredom!" Sergeant Thomson replied without a smile.

DI Spearing introduced me to Sergeant Thomson who was to be our driver for the day. A big man in every way, probably thirtyish, he was around six feet four, more with his London 'top hat' bobby helmet, carrying a bit of extra weight around his middle, but he looked every inch a rugby player which, it turned out in conversation, to be the case. He turned out every week for the Metropolitan Police Rugby Club playing against the best rugby teams in England; this was prior to the creation of the professional game for rugby union.

"Do you know how to get onto the fast way to Weybridge in Surrey Tommy?" DI Spearing asked.

"I should do sir. It is where I live, at least at the weekends!" Sergeant Thomson answered cheerily.

"They must be paying you sergeants too much these days if you can afford to live in Weybridge Surrey 'With the fringe on top.' The house prices down there are awesome." DI Spearing was sounding almost cheery.

"If only sir. No, it was the old man; he bought the place in forty-six when prices were rock bottom. I think it was a few thousand quid for a six-bedroom mansion. It is worth about a half a million now." Sergeant Thomson said and smiled.

DI Spearing did not reply and simply looked thoughtful.

We got into the back of the Jag, luxury leather seats, with the manly smell of new leather and Sergeant Thomson somehow wedged himself into the driver's seat and threw his helmet onto the front passenger's seat.

"How is your dad then Tommy?" Andy Spearing shouted across the front as the car started up and pulled out of the parking bay.

"Oh still pottering about in the garden all day and down to the 'Old Crown' in Weybridge every night for a few. He is still the same old mischievous character sir. He is seventy now and he is still always poking around in other people's business. I suppose that was his job for all those years in the squad. At least he is still managing to get around. Thanks sir." Sergeant Thomson replied with a ready smile.

Andy Spearing looked at me and explained; "Tommy senior was my DI when I joined the squad in nineteen forty-six. Taught me everything I know about being a detective, especially around the bars and joints in Soho." Andy laughed as he reminisced, but he had obviously decided to lighten the conversation and added; "A hell of a character, but he was a really good policeman. One of the best" Andy added.

"I am sure he would be delighted to hear you say that sir." Sergeant Thomson replied once again cheerfully.

"Maybe we could look him up for an hour when we get through out there?" DI Spearing was full of surprises today.

"That would be nice sir if we get the time. Where are we going anyway?" Sergeant Thomson asked.

"Oh, sorry Tommy, I forgot. We are going to John Palmer's mansion. Just outside Weybridge on the Kingston-Upon- Thames road. Do you know it?" DI Spearing asked.

"Oh, yes I know it sir. Now that is a mansion, swimming pool, acres of grounds, tennis courts,
horse paddocks, the lot. How can a turd like that get a place like that?" Sergeant Thomson asked with a disgusting tone.

"Well if you dealt with what he was dealing in, you could probably afford a lot of those mansions across the world. Still he will not need any of that where that turd has gone." Andy added with a smile.

"He copped it then sir?" Sergeant Thomson asked.

It appears so Tommy. It certainly appears so." Andy Spearing added thoughtfully.

"Who is handling it in Weybridge sir?" Sergeant Thomson asked.

"Harry Lawler, you remember old Harry from the squad? He left a couple of years ago." Andy replied.

"Oh, yeah I knew old Harry. He was another of the good ones who got away. Never did find out why he left though?" Sergeant Thomson left it like a trailing question.

"I think that was the problem. He was a damn good detective, but just could not take what was going on in the squad from the top to the bottom, so he got the hell out while he was still good enough to make it elsewhere and was sane enough after our lot." Andy had an edge to his voice, but also sounded weary.

"So, what were those bastards in the squad room saying about me young Devlin?" DI Spearing suddenly changed the direction of the conversation.

"Oh" I said giving myself time to think a reply. "They were actually saying you are the best DI in the squad sir." I managed to blurt out.

"But?" Andy raised an eyebrow as he posed the question.

"But they reckon you are going nowhere, because you are always taking on the men upstairs who don't want to know and who will get rid of you at the first opportunity." It was the best I could do without getting on about the drink problem in front of Sergeant Thomson.

"Yes, well they were spot on about them upstairs. A crowd of morons with their hands in the tills and deep pockets most of the time, except for the Chief, but as sure as eggs are eggs he will be beaten and eaten before too long, then I will follow." Andy Spearing was again sounding very melancholy.

"They were also right about you being the best DI in the squad sir. They could not afford to lose you." Sergeant Thomson piped in from the front.

"It is like this Tommy. Those bastards don't want the real criminals caught. They don't mind you catching the men who have murdered their wives or such like. Just try going after the real criminals, the gangs, and suddenly you are moved onto another case." Andy Spearing was amazingly frank and open, but again sounding very weary with it all.

I found it all a bit of an early, fascinating insight into the real world of 'The Met' at that time. It has probably not changed much over the years.

Unfortunately Andy Spearing started nodding off, the day after the boozy night before and the rest of the journey was quiet and there was little further conversation.

Book 1 in the DI Spearing and DS Devlin series

Chapter 07 - The first case scene

The two huge entrance gates to Palmer's Place mansion had been drawn closed and police 'no entry' blue and white tape had been stretched across each gate so that the gates could be opened and shut without the breaking the tape.

There were already around six newsmen and photographers at both sides of the gates. I looked at my watch and it was ten forty-five in the morning.

"It looks like Weybridge station is leaking the news already. The wolves are coming out in force." Andy Spearing said with more than a little sarcasm.

Sergeant Thomson stopped the Jag outside the gates and walked over to the two policemen who were on the inside. "DI Spearing from New Scotland Yard to see DI Harry Lawler" Sergeant Thomson said in a low tone.

"He is expecting you? " The bobby on the inside asked with a deep irked tone to his voice, obvious resentment to the London boys moving in.

"Yeah, just give him a bell please." Sergeant Thomson made it quietly clear he was not standing for any nonsense.

The bobby shook his head, but took the walkie-talkie from his belt and pressed a button. "DI Spearing from New Scotland Yard is at the gate to see DI Lawler." he announced loudly enough to be heard from inside the car and letting the news hounds know. "Oh – yes Sergeant." He hurriedly replied pressing the red button and re-hung the walkie-talkie on his belt and started opening one gate while the other bobby opened the other.

Sergeant Thomson got back to the car, wedged himself back in, and drove through. "You are to report to Sergeant Doyle at the main door." the first irked Bobby shouted as the Jag sped past.

"They don't like it when we move in on their scene." Andy Spearing had a little evil grin on his face as he nodded to the irked bobby. "By the way Tommy would you, as you usually do, get into a chat with Sergeant Doyle and the local Wooden Tops? See what you can find out while we dig through the murder scene." Andy Spearing smiled nicely as he asked.

"Yes sir. No problem." Sergeant Thomson sounded like he was eager to please.

The front door to the mansion opened as the Jag pulled up. Sergeant Doyle stood in the frame and in his hands, he had various pairs of plastic gloves and covers for over shoes.

As DI Spearing's party approached, Sergeant Doyle nodded to Sergeant Thomson. "Tommy!" He said in a curt manner with an Irish accent.

"Paddy!" Sergeant Thomson replied with a nod of the head.

Then Sergeant Doyle nodded to DI Spearing and simply said "Sir."

DI Spearing acknowledged with a nod of his head. It was obvious all three of them knew each other.

"Paddy this is my DS Kevin Devlin, new start yesterday and on his first murder case with me." DI Spearing added without much enthusiasm.

Sergeant Doyle went to shake hands then realized he had the plastic gloves and covers in his hands so he passed them out to each and then shook hands. "Kevin – 'Irish' are you with a name like that?" Paddy smiled

"No Scottish, but Irish blood in the ancestors," I replied with a smile and shook hands. I could feel he wanted to ask the usual question regarding which side I supported in Glasgow, but thankfully he suddenly felt it was not the time or place.

We all put on the gloves on hands and covers over feet. "Do you know the way to the study sir?" Sergeant Doyle asked.

"No, I have only been here once and I never got past the reception room." DI

Spearing replied and lied without thinking about it. Anyway, he thought, it was two weeks ago.

"OK I will take you all on through." Sergeant Doyle replied in an easy-going manner.

"Tommy, would you wait here for Paddy to come back. See if you can help with anything until we get finished at the scene." DI Spearing nodded as he spoke.

"Yes sir. I will see what I can do to help." Sergeant Thomson smiled and stopped to look around in the hallway.

"Right gentlemen, if you will follow me then." Sergeant Doyle moved off. Passing the two downstairs bedrooms Sergeant Doyle suddenly stopped and turned around to talk to DI Spearing. "Two of the so-called bodyguards apparently found themselves locked in their rooms this morning when they were woken by Mrs Palmer screaming having found the bodies. They both did a runner before we got here." Sergeant Doyle laughed and shook his head.

"Do you know who they were?" DI Spearing asked almost nonchalantly, but just a little anxious.

"Yes, it was Tommy Smith and Bobby Cosgrove. Know them sir?" Sergeant Doyle asked.

"Oh, yes I know them. A couple of real thick planks, but they can be nasty when they are two on one. They were Joseph Bolger's minders, so they must have switched to Palmer, when they lost Bolger. You can see how thick they were leaving their keys on the outside of their doors. Could you do me a favour and get Tommy to make a call for me when you get back to your post?" DI Spearing was again sounding very edgy as they started walking again towards the study and the crime scene.

"Yeah sure that is no problem sir. We have our own communications all set-up already and working in the reception room." Sergeant Doyle replied.

"Good. Tell Tommy to get on the phone straight away to the squad and get patched through to DI John Sanderson, he knows him. Tell him to tell DI Sanderson, that if Smith and Cosgrove show up at the offices, to arrest them immediately and charge them with fleeing the scene of a crime and to hint at suspicion of murder. Oh, and tell him to take them to Paddington and not Scotland Yard and wait for me to get back to quiz them." DI Spearing was again sounding very precise and professional, covering all the angles.

"Yes sir, no problem. Do you think they were the murderer's then sir?" Sergeant Doyle asked in a rather surprised tone.

"No, those two are lucky if they could make up their minds to go to the toilet before it is too late. We need to throw them onto the wrong foot though and then we might get some truth from them. Also, it is not a bad idea to let, whoever did this to think we have arrested those two, sort of put them off their guard - you know what I mean?" DI Spearing gave a little wink and nod.

I replied rather too enthusiastically "Sounds like good ideas sir." I did not mean it to come out sounding like ass licking, but that is how it sounded. DI Spearing gave me a quizzical look and turned away.

We came to the open study door and looked in. "I'll go and get Tommy to make the call for you sir." Sergeant Doyle said as he turned back towards the entrance hall.

"Yes, thanks Paddy." DI Spearing replied as he entered the study, then swung back round. "Oh, and Paddy, can you find out who leaked to the press and leak the arrest story to them, let them put it out and then pull them in."

"Yes sir" Paddy answered over his shoulder without stopping, or showing his angry face.

DI Harry Lawler came out to meet them. He was smallish for a policeman at that time, I would say about five feet ten, wiry thin, but looking fit. He was very smartly dressed in a three-piece dark grey suit, with starched brilliantly white shirt and dark grey silk tie. "Hello Andy, how the devil are you? Still hanging on in there fighting the good fight eh?" DI Lawler had a friendly smile and another with a northern Irish lilt to his voice. He held out his right hand to shake.

"Don't know about the good fight anymore Harry – more like another war again, just like fighting in the jungle again. How is it going with you out in the backwoods? Is it any easier for you than the Yard? DI Spearing laughed and took his handshake.

"Anything would be easier than that yard full of rats. I don't know how you can stomach it Andy." DI Lawler replied, looking over his shoulder at me.

"Oh Harry – yes sorry – this is my DS, Kevin Devlin, just started yesterday." DI Spearing turned around and pointed to me.

"Nice to meet you sir." I said and offered my handshake which he took with a very firm hand trying to unsuccessfully squeeze my knuckles; instead I caught his and made him squirm.

"Well you could not get a better DI in that place Sergeant! He will lead you well astray from the baddies in there." DI Lawler laughed at his own little joke and turned back to DI Spearing. "The forensic team has just finishing Andy and the coroner's lot is just about to remove the bodies. Want to have a look at the scene before we move things along?" DI Lawler asked quietly.

"Yes, if you don't mind Harry. We might put our view on it and see how it compares to yours if that is OK? DI Spearing was, for now, not pushing to be in charge.

"Yes sure, no problem Andy. Mind your feet, there is a lot of blood from the cut throat victim. He is not a pretty sight; the blood has all practically drained from his body into the carpet." DI Lawler led the way, side stepping the face down body of a six foot-three man with a gun stuck in his belt on his right side.

"Identified him yet?" DI Spearing asked matter of fact.

"Not formally, but Mrs Palmer tells us he is Tony Marks who was John Palmers main minder for years." DI Lawler replied.

DI Spearing knelt and gently pulled his face round revealing the slash from ear to ear across the jugular vein and wide open, piercing eyes. "Yeah it is Tony Marks all right. He has been with John Palmer a few years, not a nice way to go. By the way if forensics are finished why is the gun still in his belt?" DI Spearing sounded almost sympathetic and he gently closed Tony Marks eyes which appeared to have surprise and terror written into them.

DI Lawler replied "Shit!" He bent down, pulled out his handkerchief and carefully removed the gun before adding; "These people are supposed to be the experts!" He then went to the door and shouted; "Mason - come and bag this gun!" We heard Mason running and come in and apologetically say; "Sorry sir – an oversight!"

Harry Lawler was angry whe he replied; "More like bloody blind!" He handed over the gun, which Mason took and scuttled away. Harry Lawler turned back to DI Spearing and as a matter of fact said; "The coroner reckons Marks was dead before he hit the ground - about 3am." He nodded and went around the body and over to the desk where John Palmer's body lay with his head on the desk.

"This, as you know Andy, is John Palmer!" DI Lawler nodded towards the desk. "Forensics reckons it was the same knife as used on Marks. Threw it with a lot of force, probably from over there and with accuracy straight through the heart, again he died instantly. He managed to get a shot away but only into the desk as he pitched forward. Nobody heard anything, probably the silencer. It was just one hell of a throw of the knife!" DI Lawler shook his head as though in disbelief.

"Any prints do you think?" DI Spearing asked as a matter of fact.

"I doubt it. He probably had gloves on but you never know. A partial footprint on the window sill over there - must have gone out that way. A couple of size ten boot prints in the earth below the window, but they disappear on the lawn further down." DI Lawler shrugged his shoulders.

I went over to the window and asked. "Mind if I look out?"

DI Lawler looked across and replied. "No go ahead. We have already dusted the place so there is no problem."

I opened the old-style pulley window and looked down at the earth and sure enough there was what looked like size ten boots planted firmly in the soft earth under the window and going to the right, skirting the building towards the far end, then changing direction to go over the lawn in the direction of the plantation of trees and shrubs opposite. I closed the window and turned around to see both DI's staring at me.

"Well what do you think young Devlin?" DI Spearing asked tinged with a certain amount of humour.

"Well, what I don't think sir is this was a burglary gone wrong." I replied, slowly and deliberately.

"You don't say? DI Lawler was obviously amused, but I noticed DI Spearing did not say anything except "So?"

"So" I replied as thoughtfully as I could sound; "No professional burglar would take on a job like this. Look at it this way, three minders, a London east end gang leader, servants plus the wife and family all in the house. No way would a pro burglar even think about it, unless he had a team and for what? It not as if it was a club with lots of loot." I shook my head with some vigour.

"So?" What do you think went down here Devlin?" DI Spearing was obviously trying to encourage me to express an opinion.

"This was a professional assassination job that went wrong sir." I replied. "It looks to me as if these two were waiting for him. Otherwise, why were they here with guns ready at 3am in the morning?" I was beginning to get into the swing remembering how we were taught to analyse a crime scene in the criminology class at university and I had already used it at crime scenes in Glasgow.

An afterthought just occurred to me, looking from the minders body, trying to see him standing up. Then I realized he must have been blocking John Palmer's view, so I added; "Thinking about it from this position in front of the minders body; I think the minder Marks got over confident and made a mistake after putting his gun in his belt. He must have come across John Palmer's view and that was a fatal split second which gave our assassin the chance to somehow produce the knife, slash the throat, roll to the side and throw it straight through Palmer's heart." As I said the words, I acted the part of the killer, even pretending to throw the invisible knife from eye level with the desk.

"What is this lad then Andy – paranormal? That is one hell of a stretch of the imagination!" DI Lawler asked sounding astonished.

"He was educated in criminology at Cambridge don't you know?" DI Spearing smiled, but was rubbing his chin thoughtfully.

"You don't say? Yes, that would explain a lot." DI Lawler replied with a smile, but sounded full of sarcasm.

"I was also educated on the streets of Glasgow of which I am equally as proud. By the way, it looks like, from the tracks out there, he headed for that plantation from where he may have done a bit of observation." I replied, and added; "You know sir, sarcasm they say is lowest form of wit." I replied without thinking, but with a smile.

"My oh my - A Celt paranormal with a thin skin. That makes a change!" DI Lawler smiled nicely and DI Spearing laughed.

"Okay you two Celts. Let us settle down. – Harry, have you looked into the plantation?" DI Spearing bristled ever so slightly.

"Wooden Tops squad has been out there searching inch by inch for half an hour. If there is anything useful out there we will find it. We have not been sitting on our asses either Andy." DI Lawler was just beginning to lose his cool.

"No – No Harry- nobody was suggesting that at all. Just making sure we are covering all the angles before the weather changes and wipes any clues away. Have you any other thoughts young Devlin?" DI Spearing asked quizzically turning to me.

"I have just a couple of additional things sir!" I answered, ignoring DI Lawler. "First, this assassin, to be that good with a knife, he had to be highly trained. It is not really something you can teach yourself. So, I think he has to be ex-army. That is confirmed by the time he came in – just before dawn, a favourite time for army raids – and the fact that he was wearing what looks like rubber soled ex-army boots. Not many people, except ex-army, would wear boots on an exercise like this one. Judging from the size of the boots and the depth they sunk into the soil he is a big man probably over six feet and quite heavy, but almost certainly very fit and muscled."

Then I added; "Oh and one last thing sir, there are not many regiments who train their soldiers to kill with the knife like this, although you would know better than me sir. I can think of the Paratroopers and the SAS, but not anymore?" I finished with the question.

"I was in the Yorkshire Regiment young Devlin and because we were in the jungle in Asia, we had to be able to use the knife. I must admit though; I don't think any of us were this good with it." DI Spearing replied with a nod towards the dead bodies.

"So now we have deducted from this scant 'evidence' that we are looking for a guy over six feet, probably ex Paratrooper or SAS, heavy but fit and muscled. I don't know how you can put together that lot from this information, other than if you really are a Celtic paranormal." DI Lawler was now sounding exasperated.

"He is also a psychologist as well Harry – don't you know?" DI Spearing said with a a certain amount of sarcasim.

"Oh, yes that would explain a lot. I read recently, in one of the Sundays, these psychologists in America could make a good story out of anything you throw at them. I suppose you are one of the new 'Trained Brains' we have been hearing the squad is recruiting? I suppose you are also going to give us your theory on who he was working for?" DI Lawler turned away and signalled to the coroner's crew to start taking the bodies away. They started bagging the bodies and lifting them onto stretchers leaving chalk marks where they had lain.

"I was also called 'A Trained Bairn' this morning sir, but that didn't make me shit my nappy either." I replied with my most disarming smile. I noticed DI Spearing smiling quietly to himself. I added; "I cannot believe how quick this 'Trained Brain' thing has got around. Anyway, if I were a gambling man, which I am not, I think I would bet it is probably the start of a gang war. It is unusual for two bosses from the same gang to be wiped out together, especially with some of the gangs depending on them for their drugs distribution. But the word is 'The Mafia' is trying to break into the UK drugs market, so my guess it could be them. They are known to hire outside assassins to do their dirty work. Then again, it could be one of the others trying a takeover for whatever reason."

The Surrey coroner's people took the bodies out of the study and away towards the rear door where they had parked their white ambulance wagon out of sight of the watching press.

"DI Spearing was again thoughtfully rubbing his chin as he said;" Yeah okay, let us try going down the more conventional road Harry. Have you had words with Mrs Palmer yet?"

"Well not really, only briefly, she is in a hell of a state after finding them. She got her doctor to come and give her a sedative. Before she took the sedative, she asked if the kids could go down to their grandparents down Bournemouth way. We taxied them down there. She is upstairs under sedation." DI Lawler replied in a matter of fact tone.

"Any mileage down there do you think Harry?" DI Spearing asked without any expression.

"Naw I don't think so Andy, although I am no psychologist." He replied looking amusingly at me. "But I think she is grieving sincerely. She did seem to be rather cool and accepted he was dead. She said she did not know very much about Palmer's business affairs." DI Lawler replied with a slight smile and a nod towards me.

"Did you know Harry that Mrs Palmer's dad owned the accountancy firm and she was the head accountant after John Palmer and 'The Quiet Firm' bought it over as a front for their operations? That is how JP met her." DI Spearing asked, almost nonchalantly.

"Obviously not Andy. Now that puts a new light on her answers." DI Lawler replied, now it was his turn to rub his chin thoughtfully.

"You know what we are searching for in his files here and at his office Harry? Did you find anything?" DI Spearing asked.

"No nothing of significance. I guessed it was for anything incriminating within the files, plus the second set of books?" DI Lawler replied smoothly enough, but left the trailing question.

"Exactly Harry. The most likely place to have the second set of books was to have them hidden here. The office was too obvious. So, when did Mrs Palmer report the murders Harry?" DI Spearing asked.

DI Lawler took out his note pad and replied "07-45 by the look of it and we arrived here about 08-20."

"So, in theory, Mrs P. could have 'discovered' the bodies anytime between say 03-30 hours and telephoning the police at 07-45 hours and you arrived at 08-20. So, she would have had plenty time to get things organized with any files that had to disappear, including the second set of books. Do you agree?" DI Spearing was back on top of his game.

"Yes, in theory, at least if that what she was up to." DI Lawler reluctantly agreed.

"Well you did say she was quite cool and collected. Next question Harry. Did you see the kids leave in your police car and at what time?" DI Spearing asked.

"Yeah I did watch them going out to the car. It must have been around 09-00, because Mrs P had asked at about 08-40 like I said, not wanting the kids to see their dead Dad and going to their Granddads at Bournemouth" DI Lawler replied.

"Did they have any luggage with them?" DI Spearing looked inquisitively and spoke quietly.

"Yes, they did have a case each. You don't think?" DI Lawler left the trailing question.

"Did they look heavy? DI Spearing asked.

"Shit, they got two of the Wooden Tops to carry the cases out to the car. Shit I did not think Andy – sorry." DI Lawler sounded very guilty in his reply.

"It is only a retrospective thought Harry. It may not be right, but if it is the case, if it is any comfort, I don't think I would have caught it at that time. I am possibly only being wise after the event. Either way, it is too late now. Granddad will have the files buried in deepest Dorset by now." DI Spearing was back in his nonchalant mood.

"Did Mrs P tell you anything before she took the sedatives?" DI Spearing asked again sounding a bit edgy.

"Yes, a couple of things. First, her two minders did a runner practically before she had finished telling them about finding the two bodies." DI Lawler replied, with another smile.

"Ah yes Smith and Cosgrove. I have a call out on them, hoping we catch up with them this morning with any luck at Palmer's offices. I'll let you know how we get on there." DI Spearing replied quietly.

"Bloody hell Andy, you are certainly on the ball today." DI Lawler's replied.

"We need to be on top of these things Harry. In some ways, this is like any murder - we must make our own breaks as early as possible. Could you do me a favour Harry and get on that walkie-talkie thing? Contact Tommy, and find out how John Sanderson got on at Palmer's offices. See if he picked-up the two plonkers of minders. If he has caught them, tell him to put more pressure on them. See if Mrs P sent them there, rather than them doing a runner." DI Spearing appeared to be relaxed about the whole thing.

"There is a phone over there. You can use that." DI Lawler answered.

"No, I assume that is connected throughout the house and upstairs?" DI Spearing looked upwards as he replied.

"Oh, yes Andy. You do have a suspicious mind, but good point. That is if she is actually moving to take over." DI Lawler replied as he moved towards the walkie-talkie. He picked it up and spoke quietly requesting Tommy to do as DI Spearing had asked.

"Yeah don't forget Harry. Mrs P has quite a lifestyle here to maintain and I don't think she is the type to want to start over again with a couple of kids. Also, she may not be involved in the murder, but we must keep in mind, her dad, good old Granddad, is Joseph Bolger's cousin. He was in the family business; he owned the original accountancy which Palmer took over along with his daughter. If there was a dispute between Palmer and Bolger and our dead friend Palmer had anything to do with the Joseph Bolger disappearance, there could be a family feud here. The old boy still knows enough people to hire an assassin to do this kind of job, especially with his daughter's inside knowledge of the house. It is another bit of food for thought eh?" DI Spearing gave one of his little, knowing smiles as he finished his theory.

"How come you know so much about this lot Andy?" DI Lawler asked the question with a little puzzlement in his voice as he came off the walkie-talkie.

"I have had a wait and see watching brief on 'The Quiet Firm' for several years Harry. Not that my superiors would make a move on them without mountains of proof and you know the score with them upstairs. They have deep pockets. This is my chance Harry to get that proof and not allow anybody to take over their drugs racket." DI Spearing hoped he sounded convincing and sincere.

I asked; "Do you think that is how it is going down sir?"

"I don't know Sergeant!. But it is another possibility we cannot ignore. My gut feeling is she is only moving to keep the business and the lifestyle. But in doing that I think, whether she knows it or not, she is putting herself and her family into a very dangerous position." DI Spearing nodded as he spoke, like he was convincing himself.

Just as DI Lawler reached the walkie-talkie sprang to life with a voice saying; "DI Lawler please? Over."

DI Lawler picked it up and pressed a button as he lifted it to his ear and replied; "Yeah, what is it? Over" After listening he said;. "Oh, yes I see, hold on a minute." DI

Lawler hit another button before looking to Andy and saying; "It is MI5 wanting to talk to me. What do you want to do Andy?" DI Lawler suddenly sounded very unsure of himself.

"Ask who they are and their bosses name so we can check out their ID's. I want to find out who is pulling their strings at MI5 and how they found out so quickly about this murder. If they go on without giving any names just tell them 'The Met,' namely me, has taken over the investigation, because it is attached to a case I am currently on and I am too busy on the scene to be disturbed."

DI Lawler hit another button and spoke; "Okay put them through." as he shared the earpiece with DI Spearing.

"MI5 here" A youngish sounding voice said. "Am I speaking to DI Lawler?" The youngish voice added with a touch of arrogance.

"This is DI Lawler and to whom am I speaking?" DI Lawler sounded rather annoyed.

"As I said sir, this is MI5 here and we need to have a conversation about the murder at Palmers Place." The youngish voice was getting more arrogant, which only served to annoy DI Lawler.

"Like I said lad, I need to know who you are so as I can get you identified and cleared before I can speak to you. You could be the bloody press, or the murderer for all I know" DI Lawler had the beginning of a devilish grin. He was beginning to enjoy himself again.

"What do you mean sir?" The youngish voice was beginning to waiver.

"What part do you not understand about identifying yourself before I can speak to you boy?" DI Lawler was now obviously enjoying himself.

"We will identify ourselves when we come over sir." The youngish voice was now unsure of his ground.

"Look boy, unless you give me your names and your bosses name so I can check you all out, you will not be getting past the front gate. End of story" DI Lawler was now sounding very forceful.

"I don't think we are cleared to give our names over the phone sir. However, we have been authorized to take over the investigation. It is a matter of home security" The youngish voice was trying to regain his composure.

"Really - Is that so? Who authorized you to take over then?" DI Lawler was now getting annoyed, but still trying to get names.

"My boss got in contact with your boss at Guildford and he agreed." The youngish voice was again beginning to get arrogant.

"Well lad, tell me your bosses' name and my bosses' name, and then I can check it out." DI Lawler was now just beginning to lose his cool.

"As I said sir, I am not authorized to hand out names over the phone." The youngish voice was now sounding feverish.

"Look lad, you and your buddies go get your comfort blankets and go back to your cots. Let your boss man know that this is simply a police murder investigation, if it has home security implications or not remains to be seen. I am sure your bosses will explain how that works to you. Also, this investigation has already been taken over by 'The Met' with DI Spearing in charge, because it is part of an ongoing investigation by them. Good day to you." DI Lawler laughed as he hung up by pressing a button.

"Comfort blankets and cots indeed Harry - I ask you!" DI Spearing laughed and continued; "I think you are right though. Most of that MI5 lot would be lucky to hold down a junior office boys job. They get recruited from the local dole offices. It's that other lot from MI6 who are the real tough nuts. Mostly all ex-army and they know how to take anyone out of the picture permanent like, the trouble is, most of the bosses in MI5 got promoted from MI6 operatives, so they know the score and can be mean bastards."

"So, you are alright to take over the investigation Andy?" DI Lawler asked without a smile.

"Yes, no problem. The way I figure it is we are not likely to find the assassin unless we find out who hired him. By the way Harry, you said Mrs Palmer told you a couple of things. The first was about the two minders doing the runner. - What was the other?" DI Spearing asked in an off handed manner.

"Oh Yes! The other thing was she could not sleep and awoke about 03-00 hours, looked out the window and saw a local gypsy poacher, John Fitzgerald, coming up from their river with some fish in his hand. She said he did it regularly and Palmer was going to give him a fright one of these nights and fire a shotgun over his head. It could be he saw something on his way out." DI Lawler said as he shrugged his shoulders.

"Picking him up?" DI Spearing asked as a matter of routine.

"Yes - sent a squad of Wooden Tops up Turnpike Farm Lane an hour ago to bring him back here. There could be big trouble though. They are Irish travellers and they would fight with their own shadows if they thought they were not harming themselves!" DI Lawler again laughed at his little joke.

DI Spearing and I both still laughed at the thought. And DI quietly said; "A bit of a coincidence that Mrs P was looking out a window at exactly the same time as her husband was being murdered at three in the morning don't you think??"

Before anybody could reply the walkie-talkie sprang to life again and a voice said; "DI Lawler please? Over"

"Oh God – I hope it is not those MI5 kids again." DI Lawler said as he stretched over and answered. "Hello, Lawler here Over" After a short short pause he said; "Okay get them over here, but keep the bastards handcuffed. Over and out." DI Lawler sounded bemused and sat down.

"We got Fitzgerald out, but had to arrest him and three others for GBH. Three of our lads are down at the hospital in Church Street. I just told you Andy this would be big trouble." DI Lawler said shaking his head.

There are only three of yours in hospital. They must have come quietly then!" DI Spearing smiled as he said it.

"Yeah it is not very funny Andy. Two of them have broken jaws; one has a broken nose and two of them also have concussion. They are real hard men those Irish travellers. Good excuses for our lot to have a few months off work and a lot of compensation. I will be before an inquiry with the Chief Constable in the morning." DI Lawler was back to shaking his head again.

"You can always blame me for the decision to go in. After all I am running the murder enquiry!" DI Spearing just nodded.

"Good idea Andy. At least they can only swear at you, whereas he could have me back at a reception desk for the rest of my natural. Do you mind?" DI Lawler appeared to almost be begging.

"No, I do not mind at all Harry. I will just remind the CC that this Fitzgerald was a possible witness or the possible murderer and was seen fleeing the scene. So we had no alternative other than to go in after him. Yes?" DI Spearing flashed his evil grin again.

"Thanks Harry. I am due you one for that." DI Lawler sounded truly grateful.

There was a commotion in the hall and the four travellers appeared handcuffed hands in front, with four uniformed policemen looking a bit the worse for wear right behind them.

"Where do you want this lot Sir?" The tallest policeman with sergeant stripes and an upcoming black eye asked.

"DI Spearing is handling this case now Sergeant - Andy?" DI Lawler looked directly at DI Spearing.

"Which one of you is Fitzgerald?" DI Spearing stood close, too close, in front of the four Irishmen. No answer came. "Now look, unless you come forward you are looking at an accessory to murder charge." DI Spearing said loud and clear.

Suddenly one of them jumped forward and looped his handcuffs over DI Spearings head dropped them onto his neck and pulled him in.

I sunk two very rapid and powerful uppercuts into the guy's kidneys, quickly followed by a right-handed chop to his neck and his knees gave way. He just fell-down with his handcuffed hands around DI Spearings neck. I caught a glimpse of another guy making a move towards me and put an ultra-fast and powerful elbow and firm forearm straight across the bridge of his nose and his eyes. He collapsed like a sack of potatoes, blood spewing from his shattered nose. The others stopped dead and did not make another move.

"Bloody hell man I wish you had been with us today. I have never seen anything like that before." The police sergeant said and looked at me in awe.

DI Spearing lifted the handcuffed guy's arms over his head and let him fall face first to the ground with a crack of his forehead.

"Thanks Sergeant" DI Spearing said simply and quietly. "Now which one is Fitzgerald?" DI Spearing asked.

"That is him who had his arms around your neck sir." The police sergeant replied smiling and pointed at the guy face down on the floor.

DI Spearing looked down and said; "Great, just what we need. Give me a hand Sergeant. We will take him intoof the bedrooms for interview. You guys look after the others. Harry you want to join us?"

"No I will stay here Andy, get Tommy on the blower and help take care of this lot. Let me know if you need anything." DI Lawler replied with another of his smiles.

"Some food would be nice Harry. I am beginning to feel the pangs of lunch coming on. All this sight of blood, it must be the vampire in me." DI Spearing replied with a laugh. Police were the same the world over trying to hide their emotions behind a laugh when having to deal with some horrendous scenes of human carnage.

DI Spearing and I took an arm each and half carried and dragged Fitzgerald to the minders bedroom.

"I will get someone to go down to the local chippie for Fish and Chips – Okay?" DI Lawler shouted after us.

"Okay." DI Spearing shouted back over his shoulder as he huffed and puffed his way down the corridor and then added; "Oh and Harry, find out where your boys dropped off the kids in Bournemouth?"

"Sure Andy." DI Lawler shouted after us.

"Bloody hell sir you sound and look out of condition." I said, as I was beginning to do most of the lifting and dragging of Fitzgerald.

"Tell me about it. I will really need to start doing something about it. A few years ago, this guy would never have got anywhere near me with a lunge like that. Instead he almost strangled me." DI Spearing was back to that melancholy mood again. We finally made it into the room and shut the door.

DI Spearing disappeared into the en-suite and emerged with a pitcher of cold water and threw it over Fitzgerald's face, soaking the carpet at the same time. Fitzgerald slowly spluttered and quickly came to life.

"Okay get up and sit down on the seat." DI Spearing put a seat in front of him.

I took out my notebook and pen.

"Fuck off you limey." Fitzgerald almost spat the words out in a thick Irish accent and added; "Why the fuck should I?"

"I'll tell you why lad. Because if you don't I will do my best to lay an accessory to murder charge on you. I will also make sure you and your buddies out there go down for a minimum of five years. I don't think you, your wife and kids, or your buddies out there and their wives and kids will very much like you losing your freedom for five years. Do you? Especially when I make sure you are separated across the country and us limeys are beating the shit out of you, or pushing it up you. What do you think?" DI Spearing was sounding real hard and menacing.

"You have nothing on me limey and you know it." Fitzgerald was at the mumbling stage.

"No Fitzgerald? How about a witness saw you at the crime scene this morning at the exact time that two men in this very house were being murdered? No? Then of course we already have the lot of you fair and square with witnesses for GBH on four policemen. Those guys are in hospital and will be off work for months with serious injuries which have all been photographed for evidence. I think we have enough to put you away for a long time, probably life plus." DI Spearing was now in full flight.

"Don't talk hard, man. You know you cannot make any murders stick on me." Fitzgerald voice was beginning to quiver.

"You know 'man' – If I put my mind to it I can make anything stick, even to Teflon." DI Spearing smiled, but it was full of menace.

"Okay man. What is the deal?" Fitzgerald was now sounding very unsure and looking for away out.

"Well in return for the truth here, I can guarantee you; I will get you clear of the murder charges. However, I will have to speak to my colleagues out there, but maybe, just maybe, in return for a bit of revenge with no complaints and you and your families moving out of the south of England and never returning, I can persuade our boys to drop the charges."

"Otherwise?" Fitzgerald asked stupidly.

"I told you already. You are all alone spread in prisons across the country for a minimum of five years with limeys beating the shit out of you, or pushing it up you. It is up to you." DI Spearing turned away.

"Okay, okay, you got a deal. What do you want to know?" Fitzgerald was now subdued.

"Tell me what you were doing here this morning and what you saw? And the truth mind!" DI Spearing pointed at him like some sort of preacher screaming for the truth.

"Awe man I was only doing a bit of fish poaching down on Palmer's River, just to feed the family. I have done it for ages." Fitzgerald did sound a bit sorry for himself.

"Then what happened?" DI Spearing was not wasting any time.

"I was on my way back out when I came around the end of the mansion and there was this big guy climbing out of the window and turning away from me to skirt round the front of the house." Fitzgerald replied, with quick little bursts.

"What did he look like this man?" DI Spearing asked suddenly sounding excited.

"I did not get much of a look at him. I dived quickly back into the shadow." Fitzgerald replied, just too quickly to sound convincing.

"Come on Fitzgerald don't give me that crap. You are out at night every night.

You can probably see better than a rabbit in the dark. Come on, give or---" DI Spearing left the inference hanging there.

"Okay, okay. He was a big man well over six feet. He did not climb out of the window; he sort of stepped out of it." Fitzgerald was now getting into a talkative mood and I suddenly caught a whiff of his breath and realized he reeked of booze, even if it was only coming up on lunch time.

"Okay – we have established he is a big man, but what did he look like?" DI Spearing was beginning to show signs of impatience.

"He was built like a brick shithouse, thirteen to fourteen stones. A real heavy weight with no flab whatsoever, he was wearing one of those black turtle neck sweaters with black very tight black trousers. I would not like to run into him in a dark alley I can tell you. He had short, red hair and one of those goatee beards. He looked about fortyish I would say. Black face and hands, but I am sure it was a mud covering as I could see white eyelids. He was carrying a hefty tool sack like it weighed a couple of pounds and he had on those rubber ex-army boots. I would say an ex-soldier." Fitzgerald stopped.

"What makes you say an ex-soldier Fitzgerald?" I asked quietly

"Well he could be a current soldier, but definitely a soldier. I was one, the same as you governor, so I recognize a soldier. The way he ran using the building as cover, then cut across like a sprinter to the plantation of trees across the lawn looking calm and collected" Fitzgerald nodded towards DI Spearing who nodded.

DI Spearing and I nodded to each other.

"Right I am amazed how much you did see Fitzgerald, if, as you said earlier, you did not get much of a look at him, how come? DI Spearing asked.

"I caught him in the lights of the windows. Anyway, it was about three fifteen and starting to get light" Fitzgerald replied with a grin.

"So did you go into the room?"

"No I did not."

"You saw a window was open and you did not go in? That is what you expect me to believe?"

"I waited till the big guy was gone then I looked in and saw two guys lying there dead so I scarpered!"

"Okay Fitzgerald that is all. I think you are telling the truth. If I find out otherwise I will find you. Now come on and join the others" DI Spearing pointed the way out and I dropped behind Fitzgerald.

"What about our deal then?" Fitzgerald asked.

"I said maybe, but I don't think there is a hope in hell, I can swing it." DI Spearing just smiled that evil grin again.

"You are a filthy rotten bastard. I will deny everything. I will not identify the guy" Fitzgerald screamed as we led him out.

"Yeah, oh yeah! Look at it this way! I have dropped the murder charge. So let us face it Fitzgerald - you know and I know- when you came to court you were going to deny ever being here that is what you were going to do anyway, once you and your boys got off the assault charges. So, don't shoot me all that crap. You should not fight the police lad, you know that. As the good book says, let this be a lesson to you." DI Spearing just shook his head and laughed and walked out of the room and back to the study with Fitzgerald and I following.

"Get this fucking filth down the nick Harry and charge them with GBH. Make sure they are sent to different prisons around the country and get a minimum of five years each." DI Spearing turned around and grinned at Fitzgerald.

"You are a bastard. You will get payback for this. The brothers will find you." Fitzgerald spat out his words as he was led away.

"I am paid enough just to see you lot behind bars for five long years. You are a stupid cunt. Enjoy." DI Spearing laughed again. It was a side of DI Spearing I was to see again and again, ruthless and no sympathy for the criminal. As far as I was concerned, there nothing wrong with that, always assuming you were right.

The Wooden Tops led them off with truncheons drawn.

"You have lost your bet Harry. Young Devlin's description of our wanted man is almost spot-on." DI Spearing laughed.

"What bet was that Andy? I don't recall making any bet?" DI Lawler replied with a laugh.

"Not honouring your bets now eh Harry? On the slippery slope now" DI Spearing laughed again as he replied.

"What is going on here? Who are these men? Mrs Palmer had suddenly appeared as the travellers with Fitzgerald were led away and she sounded anxious, but not slurred as she would, or should, have been, if she had just come out of a sedative induced sleep.

She was still a stunningly beautiful dark haired woman with huge brown eyes, even if she was approaching middle age and having had two kids. Her figure was near perfect, flat washing board stomach, breasts a bit small but firm and pert; she obviously worked out most days. She was dressed in black, skirt just above the knees, displaying shapely pins, black silk blouse with a black cardigan and black high heeled shoes. Her eyes were puffed and reddish, but that could have been caused by rubbing them a lot.

"Oh, yes Mrs Palmer! That is Fitzgerald who you spotted this morning coming back from the river. The rest are a few of his travelling companions who have just been charged with GBH on the police." DI Lawler replied sounding slightly uncomfortable.

"GBH?" Mrs P asked with a puzzled expression on her face.

"Grievous bodily harm Mrs Palmer" DI Spearing interrupted to explain.

Mrs P was staring at DI Spearing and asked. "I know you from somewhere, don't I?"

"Yes Mam. I am sorry about your husband's death. I am DI Spearing from 'New Scotland Yard' I was here a couple of weeks ago investigating the disappearance of Joseph Bolger, who was Mr Palmers' boss. You remember?" DI Spearing sounded as smooth as silk, but there was just a slight edge to his voice.

"Oh yes, I remember. Did you find him?" Mrs P sounded vague but at the same time she was quite cool and collected.

"I think you know the answer to that one Mam?" DI Spearing gave Mrs Palmer a quizzical look before adding; "No, not yet Mam. We are associating his disappearance to your husband's death this morning. That is why I am taking over this investigation." DI Spearing spoke with all the assurance and sympathy needed in the circumstances. He had obviously done this scene many times in the past.

That statement from DI Spearing appeared to fluster the, up to then, ice cool Mrs P.

"Are those travellers involved in my husband's – murder?" Mrs P asked very quietly leaving the trailing 'murder' almost as part of the question.

A voice from the walkie-talkie "DI Lawler please? Over!

Harry Lawler picked it up. "DI Lawler. Over" After a pause he looked at Andy and said; "It is for you Andy. Tommy just returning the call we made earlier."

"Oh yes – excuse me Mrs Palmer. This may be important and may answer your question." DI Spearing moved over and accepted the walkie-talkie from DI Lawler: "Hello Tommy. Yes, how did John get on? Over." DI Spearing asked, making sure everyone could hear him. "Yes good. So, they arrested the two of them? Good! Oh yes? But DI Sanderson did get the files out? Good. No! - tell them don't worry about the solicitor. In fact, arrest him too. This is a murder investigation and we have the warrant etc. Yeah and don't forget those two minders did flee the scene of the crime down here, both with criminal records. Yeah let John know this, thanks Tommy – Over and out!" DI Spearing had a satisfied grin on his face as he hung up.

"I am so sorry about that Mrs Palmer. Had to take it though, it was very important." DI Spearing sounded almost apologetic and then paused before turning to me and added: "Can you take notes of this conversation Sergeant?"

"Yes sir" I replied while digging out my notepad and pen.

"In answer to your earlier question Mam; The answer is No! - We do not believe the travellers were involved in your husband's murder. They are only guilty of GBH on the police and of course poaching from your river, but Fitzgerald may have seen the murderer, or at least one of them, leaving your home." DI Spearing was back on the top of his game.

"Really? Has he described this man yet?" Mrs P was almost too quick in posing the question and in assuming it was not a 'she'.

"Yes, he has Mrs Palmer. It appears to be a good description and verifies our own assumptions looking at the murder scene." DI Spearing was obviously playing her along.

"Oh" Mrs Palmer could only manage before adding; "and what was that about the two minders being arrested?"

"Oh yes – As you know they were Smith and Cosgrove, your two minders. You reported they did a runner this morning straight after you discovered the bodies?" DI posed it as a question.

"Yes - well - they did go off like greyhounds after the hare." Mrs P was now sounding unsure.

"Well Mrs Palmer, they both claim you sent them off to your husband's offices with the keys. Why do you think that is Mam?" DI Spearing pretended puzzlement.

"Yes, well yes, that is right I suppose, now I come to think about it. I was so confused after finding the bodies I suppose." Mrs P replied, slightly flustered, but remarkably holding it together.

"Yes, quite naturally Mam, but why did you send them to the offices Mam?" DI Spearing asked with a natural tone to his voice.

"I wanted them to make sure it was secure, because of what happened here." Mrs P replied smoothly as if it was the obvious thing to do, just having found your husband lying murdered.

"Then why were they stacking and boxing files to take away when my police squad arrived?" DI Spearing asked ever so politely.

"I have no idea Mr Spearing, they were told to make sure the offices were secure, that is all." Mrs P replied with just a hint of anger.

"Well Mam, their story is that you ordered them to move the files out of the offices and take them to another address. Why do you think they would say that Mam?" DI Spearing asked obviously now toying with the lady.

"How the hell should I know? Those two plonkers probably thought they could make some money from the situation. They have not a brain between them." Mrs P was now sounding angry and losing her cool control of the situation.

"We are charging them with fleeing from a crime scene and possibly murder or accessory to murder Mam." DI Spearing was obviously in the process of getting her off balance.

"Those two bloody plonkers? They could not plan a monkey's tea party!" Mrs P was now sounding edgy.

"Don't be so sure Mam. After all it was those two who 'mysteriously lost' Joseph Bolger and he simply disappeared. It is so easy to pretend to be plonkers. Even the worst minders would not leave the keys to their bedroom doors on the outside, unless they wanted to look like plonkers. Also, Mam, if your husband was expecting someone last night, don't you think he would have had all his minders in there? So, what were they up to?" DI Spearing just hung the question playing mind games.

"Well don't forget Detective Spearing – Both their doors were locked from the outside. So how could they do that?" Mrs P asked with a triumphant tone in her voice.

"That could easily be arranged Mam with the help of an accomplice." DI Spearing replied wryly with a smile.

"What are you insinuating Detective Spearing?" Mrs P asked, now sounding defensive.

"I am not at this stage insinuating anything Mam. I am simply asking questions as I am supposed to do during a murder enquiry. You and I know Mam, when I was here last month, I did warn you and Mr Palmer, as far as I can remember that the Joseph Bolger disappearance and your business together could be connected. That meant your whole family could be in danger. Your husband was concerned enough to give you and the kids two minders to live in with the family here in the mansion. Do you recall that Mam?" DI Spearing was now putting leading questions.

"Yes – But." Mrs P replied with some hesitation, like she was expecting the trap to shut.

"Then why Mam did you send the two minders away knowing that a hired assassin had just murdered your husband and his minder and could still be around this place?" DI Spearing was now warming to the task.

"As I said - I was confused----" Mrs P was now getting rattled.

"Ah yes, confused Mam! Yes, but you were not that confused – you still had a very clear mind to be able to send your two minders off to clear out, possibly incriminating files, and to secure your office with your solicitor Mam?" DI Spearing was now putting the knife in.

"What incriminating evidence – what the hell do you mean?" Mrs P almost shouted her reply.

DI Spearing appeared to ignore the outburst and added; "Tell me Mam, at what time did you find the bodies in the morning?" DI Spearing turned and stared directly at Mrs P with an almost challenging look.

"I, I think it must have been around 7-15 or so, as I came downstairs at about 7-00 to start breakfasts and get the kids ready for school and I noticed the light on in the study. I cannot be exact. The confusion you know – Mrs P trailed off in her reply.

"Ah yes the confusion. Mam, assuming it was between 7-00 and 7-15 you found the bodies then you got the minders and sent them off to London and phoned your solicitors at what time was this Mam?" DI Spearing started pacing the room.

Mrs P was now getting quite agitated. "How the fuck do I know? I was not keeping a check on the fucking time was I?" Mrs P was now clearly losing it almost screaming her reply.

"Don't worry Mam – I dare say we can check your call records and find out when you phoned your solicitor. It is only detail." DI Spearing was now staring down Mrs P.

"Oh, Oh - I don't know. It was sometime just after seven." Mrs P almost murmured her reply.

"Oh, so you could have discovered the bodies even earlier than you said Mam?"

DI Spearing was straight in with the knife, twisting it as he went along.

"You are trying to confuse me again; I can tell what you are doing." Mrs P was now beginning to sound a little desperate.

"There it is again Mam. This confusion thing, but all we are only trying to do at this stage is to get to the facts. Now DI Lawler – at what time did Mrs Palmer contact the police station again?" DI Spearing made a big show with both of his hands and then again began started rubbing his chin.

DI Lawler made an equally big show of pulling out his notebook and looking it up, which he had checked just a few minutes before and replied in a clear precise voice; "It was 07-45 hours Andy."

"So between approximately 07-00 hours, when you say you discovered the bodies and 07-45 hours, when you phoned the police, you quite coolly, despite just discovering your husband's dead body, phoned your solicitors and ordered the minders, who were there to protect you and your family, to all go to your offices and make sure any incriminating files were removed. No confusion there then! Tell me is that correct Mam?" DI Spearing asked.

"You know I never ordered any removal of files. I already told you that." Mrs P was now back in a very defensive stance.

"Maybe, as you say Mam. However, on your own admission, those two minders were a pair of plonkers. Yet they were caught with your solicitor in your offices removing possible evidence less than two hours after they were here in this house and you discovered the dead body of your husband. They say you ordered them to do that Mam, so how do you explain that?" DI Spearing was now asking the questions with piercing penetration.

"I have had enough of this. You are just twisting everything. I know what you are doing." Mrs P replied and started to turn away.

"Mam, you can either answer my questions now, or we shall go down the local nick. It is up to you Mam. However, down there it will not be so nice for you with the press and all." DI Spearing was threatening, but still managed to somehow sound almost accommodating.

Mrs P stopped in her tracks and turned back to face DI Spearing. "What do you want from me Detective Spearing?" Mrs P asked again, almost despairingly.

"What I want Mam is the truth from you - plain and simple. Tell me Mam, why did you tell DI Lawler here that you did not know anything about your husband's business?" DI Spearing was back on track trying to knock Mrs P off balance.

"Because I do not know anything about his bloody business, that is bloody why!" Mrs P replied with a lot of irritation and rather too quickly, it was so obvious to all present.

"But Mam you were the chief accountant for the company for many years and it was only two weeks ago your husband said to me, in this very house, that you were still such a wonderful help running the company from home. Now you say you do not know anything about the company. How is that Mam?" DI Spearing appeared to be almost holding back a smile as he asked the question.

"Oh yes! I was the chief accountant, but that was before the kids were born and before I married John!" Mrs P was now scratching around for answers.

"Then can you explain Mam why your husband said to me - about your help in running the company from home Mam?" DI Spearing asked with another nonchalant look on his face.

"I don't know why he would have said such a thing. It is preposterous! I have not been involved with the company for years." Mrs P replied red faced and again sounding defensive.

"Then why Mam did you send your minders and your solicitors up to London to get rid of the files and any other incriminating evidence? Are you trying to take over the company again Mam?" DI Spearing asked with an inquisitive tone to his voice.

"I shall be honest with you Detective Spearing. I need to keep the company operating. It is now the only money I will have coming in to support me and the kids. Surely you can see that Detective Spearing?" Mrs P sounded as though she was once again getting to the desperate stages.

"Oh yes - I understand that Mam!" DI Spearing replied. "The only thing I hope you understand Mam is that you are putting yourself and your children in terrible danger – you do know that, don't you?" DI Spearing sounded sincere.

"What the hell do you mean?" Mrs P now sounded more than anxious.

"Well Mam – I think you know exactly what I mean! Like I said earlier! I told you two weeks ago – that the people who caused Joseph Bolger to disappear may be after taking over the company and I said then that you and your husband could be in danger. I think it is maybe the same people who made Mr Bolger disappear who have now arranged your husband to be murdered. There were also many more murders and disappearances before that. They are ruthless people Mam. If you think they are going to allow you to waltz in and take over the business then I think you are very much mistaken. They will use any means possible, including abducting your children, to keep you out, you understand?" DI Spearing stared at Mrs P without expression.

"What are you talking about many more being killed and who are these so called ruthless people?" Mrs P asked with a slight quiver in her voice.

"Mam, what we are dealing with here is a hired assassin who has been hiring his trade for many years to the highest bidder. Until now we have never even got a description of this man. The best we can hope for is to find out who hired him because they are the real murderers, they are ruthless people and they are probably in many cases different people who hire him." DI Spearing was now suddenly looking and sounding tired, perhaps the night before catching up on him.

"So that is what you were insinuating earlier. You think I am involved in this? I am one of these ruthless people is that what you think?" Mrs P was again sounding challenging.

"Mam I did not say that at all. As I said earlier I am only asking the questions that I should do. Because of the business your husband was in, there is a wide choice of ruthless people. However, because of your actions in attempting to remove possible evidence from the offices and, perhaps from this house, and ordering two minders to flee from the scene of the crime, then I am duty bound to consider you may be implicated Mam." DI Spearing again stared with a blank look on his face directly at Mrs P.

"Right that is it! I have had enough of this! If you want to talk to me again it will be with my solicitor present." Mrs P retorted and spun around this time walking away.

"That of course is your prerogative Mam. It will not look good to the outside world. Just remember Mam about the danger to you and your kids." DI Spearing shouted after her as she disappeared from the room and headed upstairs.

"You were a bit hard on her Andy." DI Lawler said in a matter of fact, low tone.

"Not half as hard as I should have been. I should take her into protective custody for her own good, but she would not come and I cannot force her." DI Spearing just shrugged his shoulders and at the same time wearily scratched his forehead.

"So, the two minders are talking sir?" I asked.

"Not a bloody word. They have taken what I believe the Yanks say as the 5th

amendment and the solicitor is squealing like a banshee." DI Spearing replied with a sly grin.

"You mean all that you just said about minders and the solicitor just now---"I started to reply but was interrupted.

"Look lad – you will learn that in this business, sometimes you have to throw these things up in the air and see what comes down. Now we do know she ordered the minders to flee the scene of a crime and sent them up to the offices. Akso we now know she got the solicitor over there. She also did not deny, you will have noticed that she removed files from the house after the crime. So now when we come to interviewing the minders, later today, we can let them think she has dropped them in it and they are left holding the baby. Also, don't forget we have left them to stew for a few hours and they think they are facing accessory to murder charges. Don't worry, they will be singing like a couple of larks within half an hour of us getting there." DI Spearing oozed self-confidence and again gave out his sly little smile.

"You don't think she is involved though do you sir?" I asked with a worried look on my face.

"To tell you the truth Sergeant, I don't know. I could say I don't think so, but she is a cool customer. Considering her husband has just been murdered. We will know better when we get the plonkers talking. In the meantime, she is holding out on us and she is probably obstructing the course of justice. It could be she is delaying us from catching up to the real culprits. So, in reply to you Harry, just more reasons for giving her a hard time." DI Spearing again sounded weary.

The walkie-talkie voice again; "DI Lawler please! Over."

DI Lawler answered with his back to us. "Yeah okay we will be there in a couple of minutes. Over and Out" He pressed the off- button and turned around to face us. "That is the fish and chips arrived in the kitchen." DI Lawler smiled as he said it.

"Oh, great I am bloody starving." DI Spearing replied and we all headed to the kitchen.

There were six 'Wooden Tops' around the kitchen table all already eating either fish or sausage and chips and we three all went over to the worktop and picked up ours. DI Lawler went and sat beside Sergeant Doyle and Sergeant Thomson, immediately started a conversation as he ate, but there were no more seats at the table. DI Spearing and I stood at the worktop eating out of the old newspapers covering the fish and chips.

"That was good work on the scene today Sergeant." DI Spearing said it so quietly I only just heard it and I was visibly taken aback.

"Thank you very much sir. I am a fast learner. It is amazing how much good stuff they stick into these 'trained brains.' I don't think DI Lawler thought much of it though." I replied with a slight smile.

"Ah don't worry about old Harry; he was only jealous because he did not see it. In fact, that was not only 'trained brains' you showed in there, you showed you have real intuition at a murder scene and not many have it. Harry would not know intuition if it hit him in the face." DI Spearing spoke quietly, but laughed a bit louder. The others turned around to see what the laugh was about.

"Harry, after this we are going over to see old TT, Sergeant Tommy's dad. He lives in Weybridge. Do you fancy coming over for an hour for a chat about old times?" DI Spearing had turned around eating a chip and was looking at DI Lawler.

"No, sorry Andy! I will need to finish up here, complete the search of the house, sort out keys and somebody, probably a woman PC, to stay here for a few days till the funerals. I will also have to get back and pacify my governor. Sorry Tommy, but tell your dad I will look him up soon. I promise." DI Lawler replied and nodded to Sergeant

Thomson.

"No problem sir. I am sure he would appreciate a visit anytime." Sergeant Thomson said with a friendly smile.

"Harry I don't think there is much more we can do here. Could you have a word with Mrs Palmer and try to make her see a bit of the old common sense instead of those money signs in front of her eyes?" DI Spearing asked with his mouth full of fish.

"Yeah, I guess you are right Andy, there is not much more to do here until we get finger prints or something back. Yeah, I'll try with her, but if you could not get through with your natural charm and wit, what chance have I got?" DI Lawler replied with a broad smile.

"Sure, be Jesus with your Irish blarney Harry and natural rugged well-worn looks, I am sure, you can do a better job than me to be sure and begorra" DI Spearing laughed and stuffed the last of his fish in his mouth.

Everybody laughed again another sign of the releasing of the policemen's pressure valve on gruesome murder scenes.

"To be sure Andy, after your performance this morning with her, that is not even a challenge for me to do better. Well at least, as you say, my looks are well worn." DI Lawler laughed and offered his handshake to DI Spearing. "Thanks Andy and I hope it goes well in the smoke with your parasites of bosses."

"I doubt if it will ever go well with the present lot up there." DI Spearing took the handshake.

Harry Lawler added; "And as for you Sergeant Devlin, thank you very much for your 'trained brain' lad. Yes, and Andy is probably right I would have trouble recognizing intuition if it did slap me on the face. Well done." DI Lawler smiled at me and winked as he offered his handshake.

"You see he is a white witch. He could hear a pound note drop in a crowded room with people shouting." DI Spearing laughed as he said it and patted DI Lawler on his shoulder in a friendly way. Again, there was laughter all round.

"Thank you very much sir." I replied with a smile as I took DI Lawler's handshake.

"Harry – do you think you could get onto Bournemouth police? Get them to get a search warrant on Mrs P's old man's place in Bournemouth. If we get there quickly enough we may catch them before they stuff the real dirty books out of reach." DI Spearing grinned and winked as he spoke.

"I will try Andy, but we will need more than a hunch to get a search warrant!" DI Lawler replied.

"Tell them we have independent witnesses to them removing evidence from a murder crime scene. Also, independent witnesses saw the evidence being delivered to the old man's address in Bournemouth. No need to mention it is policemen who are the witnesses – Know what I mean?" DI Spearing gave another evil grin with a nod and a wink.

"Bloody hell Andy! You are just as big a rogue as they are! I will see what I can do." DI Lawler shook his head in disbelief as he replied.

We all washed the grease off our hands in the kitchen sink and dried them with a common tea towel before DI Spearing, Sergeant Thomson and I said our farewells and headed back to the Jaguar.

I thought to myself as we drove out of the gates, it is amazing how one's opinion of people can change within a few hours of working with them.

Book 1 in the DI Spearing and DS Devlin series

Chapter 08 - Old Chums

Sergeant Thomson drove down the A317 Weybridge Road, but just before turning into the Weybridge High Street he hung right onto the B374 Heath Road. Then about half a mile down that road he hung left into Melrose Road which turned out to be a lovely tree lined road less than a one mile walk to Weybridge town centre.

About half way down Melrose Road, he pulled into the broad driveway of a lovely, large Edwardian black and white-detached property and stopped.

"Well here we are." Sergeant Thomson said with a hint of pride.

"Nice place." Andy said his only rather dry comment.

All three of us got out of the car and Tommy Thomson senior opened the front door and went straight over to Andy offering his handshake.

"TT how the devil are you keeping?" Andy walked over and took his handshake manly hugging each other as they did so.

"Ah ha - 'Sherlock Holmes' alias DI Spearing – Oh my good God! Fancy seeing you here! How long is it?" TT asked as they stood back and looked at each other.

"It must be ten years since you left the sinking ship TT!" Andy replied in an easy manner.

"Well that is one way of putting it I suppose." TT replied but with a melancholy tone to his voice. "And who is this?" TT asked, a smile reappearing on his face as he turned to me and offered his handshake.

"This is my new Sergeant Devlin and it may be that he is heading to be my new Watson." Andy replied with a light laugh.

"High praise indeed from Sherlock for you young Devlin." TT offered me his handshake which I accepted.

"Pleased to meet you sir." I replied politely accepting his handshake.

"TT is good enough for me young Devlin. That is how I have been known all my life. Only it is Big TT, because of 'Small' TT here! Now come in and have a beer on this lovely day." TT laughed as he pointed us into the house.

"Marrge has gone down the shops with the kids to pick up a few things young Tommy." TT said with a smile.

"You would think she could have left that to later when she knew we were coming." Sergeant Thomson alias 'Small' TT' replied, with more than a little irritation in his voice.

"Yes, well maybe son she did not want the kids running all over us when we were talking?" TT said with a smile.

"Sounds like you had a hand in it. That right Dad?" Tommy looked amused.

"Who me? - When did I ever have a say in what Marge and the kids did?" TT just shrugged his shoulders and smiled as he disappeared into the kitchen and shortly re-emerged with four bottles of cold lager which he passed round.

"Nice place you have here TT. Handy for the local, is it?" Andy asked with a smile.

"Aye Sherlock, about a ten-minute walk at an easy pace from my local, - just enough to build up a thirst!" TT replied with a smile and added; "Hey Tommy, how about you keeping young Devlin here company and I'll show Sherlock the house?"

"Sure, Dad you carry on into the Edwardian days." Tommy replied with a nod and a smile, obviously now having recovered his composure.

"Come Sherlock we will start with my study. I am now an out and out radio ham." TT laughed and pointed the way through to the study.

"I always knew you were one for hamming it up TT, but never put you down for a radio ham!" Andy laughed and followed TT into the study.

The room was packed full of amplifiers with microphones sticking out the front, speakers, radios, two walkie-talkies, two old Philips tape recorders, an old black and white television set with a jaunty bent aerial on top. A couple of antique looking radios, a couple of pairs of earphones, electrical wires strung all around and a two leather chairs completed the 'furnishings.' They both sat down on the chairs.

"I never would have imagined you would ever get into this technology thing TT. I always thought you were a few pints a night man and a piss up at the weekend. Whatever happened to the sociable man about town TT?" Andy asked with a smile.

"It is not the evenings that are the problem Sherlock. It is the days and sleeping times when you are retired - that is the problem. You cannot piss it up all the time, can you?" TT replied with a melancholy tone to his voice and added; "I now have friends all around the world from Australia to America, I talk to them day and night but that is not all." and then TT added with a soft smile; "and how about you Sherlock? – I don't suppose you have joined the twentieth century yet? I bet you still don't know how to work a walkie-talkie yet, never mind technology?"

"No, that is just not me TT! I have never taken a walkie-talkie out of stores to this day!" DI Spearing replied with a touch of triumph in his voice.

"You know the world is moving away from your type of policeman Sherlock? Technology is taking over and they will eventually throw you out with the baby's bath water. These new-fangled computer things will take us all over. You know that, don't you?" TT asked with that bemused look again.

Andy replied with a nonchalant shrug of his shoulders. "Don't think it will happen in my lifetime in the force TT. Although I must admit the Chief introduced our new computer 'trained brain' on Monday opening up a new department with something called IBM computers."

"There you go then Sherlock that is the start, but with you it is more than that, isn't it? I hear you have got 'Flash Harry' Tomlinson as your super these days. So, what chance have you got?" TT asked with a quizzical look on his face.

Andy replied with a wry smile; "Yeah there is that I suppose TT."

"Yeah you know him and his mob upstairs cannot afford to have straight coppers around - and with you getting so out of condition – you should not be giving them the excuse. Then what Sherlock? Do you know anything else except how to investigate? You will be lucky to get anything except a front desk security job unless you get some other skills along the way." TT was offering sincere advice.

Andy replied with a hurt tone, but still smiling; "Gee thanks for that vote of confidence TT. I really feel I am worth nothing at all now!"

"You know what I mean Sherlock. I would and you would hate to let them bastards push you out like me – you know? At least I was sixty and could retire on full pension, but you are only forty odds, although you may look sixty now." TT laughed as he said it.

"Hey what is this? Kick old Spearing day? I had enough of this from young Devlin already today!" Andy was taking it in good part.

"I am not surprised - by the sound of it young Devlin is a sensible lad." TT replied and just smiled.

Andy replied in a mocking tone "He has still got a lot to learn though!"

"That is for sure, but he already has a lot of skills you don't have." TT replied and paused before adding in a low tone key; "Now Sherlock back to more important things. Do you think this today is 'The Fox' again?"

"How did you know about it? Has young Tommy been opening his mouth?" Andy asked in a haughty sort of way.

"Look Sherlock – that is what I am trying to tell you! All this gear around me is not just 'radio ham' stuff as you call it. I could even tell you that you lot had fish and chips for lunch and that you had problems with the two minders and the Palmer's solicitor in London. How about that then Sherlock?" TT sounded smug and he had a sly little smile on his face.

"What are you up to TT?" Andy asked with another quizzical look on his face.

"Like I said earlier Sherlock! - This technology stuff! You don't have a clue, do you? I listened to all your communications, since the moment you arrived at the front gates, with that obnoxious young constable talking to Sergeant Doyle, until you left to come here." TT was now sounding even more smug and smiling broadly.

"You mean you have been listening in to police communications?" DI Spearing asked with an incredulous look on his face.

"I say Sherlock - I think you have lost all your powers of deduction along with your youth. I think it may be time to stop calling you Sherlock?" TT replied with a tone of sarcasm.

"I think it probably is." Andy sounded downcast then added; "So that is probably how our MI5 friends found out about the murders this morning?" Andy made the statement but phrased it as a question.

"It almost certainly is Sherlock. But they have a lot better gear than me and they have people listening in around the country. They are our bloody security lot, God help us." TT replied with that big smile again.

"Anyway, let us go onto better things. The good news is I also had a bug in the Palmers study for the past couple of weeks since Joseph Bolger disappeared." TT added with glee and a smile.

"What you mean a bug? How the hell did you do that? Wait a minute - You mean you listened into the ---?" Andy voice sounded more in hope than any conviction as it trailed off.

"Exactly my dear boy! I could only afford one bug so I had their maid plant the device under Palmer's desk. She happens to be a fellow customer at The Old Crown in town don't you know and I cultivated a friendship last year. Thought it might be useful. Unfortunately, being a bit lubricated and too tired to stand up last night, I had to go to bed at 02-30 hours, but I switched on my tape recorder and it lasted for an hour so we caught the sounds of the murder scene!" TT was now sounding positively gleeful.

"Oh, my good God TT! - You are a genius you know that?" Andy smile was as wide as the Grand Canyon and added: "Let's hear it then."

TT moved over to one of the Philips tape recorders and switched it on. It had been pre-set to begin as Sam Aldridge alias 'The Fox' came into the study.

"Drop the piece or you drop right there." Tony Marks voice was the first one to be heard as he spat the words with a deep menacing voice.

"Well now we would not want that, now would we?" A voice with an Irish accent, probably 'The Fox' answered.

Then the sound of metal hitting the floor, probably 'The Fox' gun, as ordered. This was followed by another clatter, like the sound of tools hitting the floor. Andy thought to himself, clever move, and both his hands clear and ready to do whatever he had to do.

"Well, welcome Mr Fox. We thought you would never get here. You army types are so predictable, waiting till the dead of night, which is always just before dawn with you lot." John Palmer's voice was sounding very confident.

"Presumably you were expecting me then?" 'The Fox' asked casually.

"You should check out your customers. They are more bent than a corkscrew. To

tell you the truth Mr Fox, we thought you would be a bigger challenge, given your reputation." John Palmers voice again still sounding very confident.

"You don't know much of my reputation Mr Palmer." The Fox replied.

"Don't be so sure Mr Fox, but right now your reputation appears to be in tatters. Search him Tony." John Palmer voice was arrogant.

"Tony, you bloody idiot -" John Palmer screamed, but then there was only a sound of a dull gurgling, which Andy thought was the sound of Tonys throat being cut. There followed a loud thud which DI Spearing assumed was Tony hitting the floor. A microsecond later there was another thump, which DI Spearing assumed was the knife hitting John Palmers chest.

This was followed by the sound of a pop which Andy again assumed was the sound of John Palmers gun, fitted with a silencer, going off into the desktop.

"My oh my Mr Palmer you did underestimate me. Not even a vest. Normal service resumed. I guess my reputation is fully restored don't you think?" The Fox was now speaking in a London East End accen.

This was followed by the sound of someone wiping something clean. Then silence.

"Is that it then TT?" Andy asked with his little sly smile.

"What more can you ask for Sherlock for free gratis?" TT replied and added; "Unfortunately the tape ran out, bloody thing, so we did not get Mrs P coming into the room."

"So, we can assume she came in any time after 03-30 when the tape ran out TT?"

"Your maths is still as good as ever Sherlock. So, what do you think? Is it 'The Fox' resurfacing?" TT asked.

"I have no doubt about that one. The good thing is, this time, for the first time in twenty years, we have a description and now, thanks to you, we have the sound of his real voice. Can you give me a copy of the tape?" Andy replied with a certain amount of confidence.

"Yes - You can have the original I don't have any need for it. A bit of a break this time then! What do you think the chances are of collaring him Sherlock?" TT asked with an inquisitive look on his face.

"One to five percent chance I reckon, unless his present employers have decided to foreclose on him this time around. That looks like a possibility. According to that tape, they were waiting for him and just like young Devlin analysed." Andy replied as a matter of fact.

"To be honest Sherlock, I don't care if he gets away with it. He is getting rid of the real criminals we cannot, or will not touch. That was an amazingly good analysis from young Devlin though." TT said with his usual big smile.

"Absolutely! It was amazing! – What can I say? I think he is going to be good!" Andy replied without rancour.

"Now then Sherlock, what do you think about Joseph?" TT asked quietly and confidentially.

"Yeah, well if he is not already dead, then now Palmer is gone I don't think he will last much longer. Unless of course our old friend Joseph, turns out to be the one behind this caper." Andy replied quietly.

"You don't think that do you really?" TT asked.

Andy replied with a shake of his head "The longer this is going on TT, the more I don't know what to think!" There was a pause and he then suddenly added; "I seem to be getting moved from pillar to post with this one."

"You don't think if he is alive he will shop us now do you Sherlock?" TT was sounding anxious and on edge.

Andy replied with more conviction than he felt; "I doubt it TT. He has had twenty-one years to shop us for that little caper TT and it has never been mentioned. Anyway, you are assuming he is with our lot and that is not worth worrying about TT."

"The thought must have crossed your mind too Sherlock. If it is the case this could turn very nasty for us lad." TT sounded worried again.

"Yes, it did cross my mind TT. Then I thought after twenty-one years I doubt if they could prove a thing. It would be Joseph's word against ours. I don't know about you TT, but I made sure that money was untraceable."

"The only thing I thought was that they might trace us with me buying this house and you buying yours in Harpenden. After all, on our low salaries in those days, they might look more closely where we got the money. It was such a hard time for us all, nearly starving to death in that bloody winter of '47."

"I told you about buying this house straight away TT. Did you eventually get the rest of the money into untraceable lots?"

"Yeah I managed to get it hidden as you suggested and I have it tucked into my bachelor uncle's will and I inherited it in nineteen-fifty." TT replied with his usual smile returning.

"Well there you go TT. If they ask anything about the house then you just say you got it from your uncle as an advance because you were going to inherit the money anyway. If it comes to it, then that is what I will be saying." DI Spearing was trying to sound confident.

"That is the main reason you came here to see me today isn't it Sherlock? To make sure I had the story, right?" You forget I know you too well. "TT smiled as he said it.

"I always said you read too much into things TT. I think we will have to go TT - got these interviews to do yet at Paddington." Andy replied with a mocking smile.

"Yeah right Sherlock. At least you got a bonus with the tapes." TT replied, handing the tapes to Andy.

Andy came back into front room and with a broad grin announced; "This genious TT has just given us a recording of the Palmer mansion killings. So we have a recording of the voice of 'The Fox' to go along with his description. Not bad after twenty years of hunting him!"

Book 1 in the DI Spearing and DS Devlin series

Chapter 09 - Helping Police

The journey back to London on that Tuesday late afternoon of July eighteenth was very quiet with Andy nodding off most of way, after all it had been a long day and the previous drunken night was apparently catching up with him.

At Paddington police station, we went to the reception desk and Andy appeared to be wide awake again as he spoke to the old looking Sergeant who was puffing on a woodbine plain cigarette without a filter.

"How are you Willie, still puffing those cancer sticks I see?" Andy said with one of his little smiles.

"Yes, Andy but they have not killed me yet and there are many of my friends who never smoked in their lives who are pushing up the daisies these days."

"Probably catching enough smoke from you Willie!"

"Could be when I come to think about it! I suppose you are here for the two plonkers and the banshee of a solicitor who John brought in?" Sergeant Willie just about smiled as he replied with a very rough as sandpaper voice.

"I hope they have been kept apart Willie?" Andy asked in the nicest possible way.

"They have been on separate floors all day moaning and waiting for you. What do you think this is – amateur night at the Victoria?" Sergeant Willie looked hard at Andy as he posed the question.

"I heard you sometimes put on a better show than the amateur night Willie." Andy laughed as he said it.

"Watch it big shot. You are not in 'The Yard' now, you are only a guest here you know." Sergeant Willie sounded angry, but it was obvious he was enjoying the banter.

Andy turned around to me and said; "Sergeant Willie used to be the desk sergeant at 'The Yard' before he decided to slum it with Paddington Green. - Sergeant Willie Thomas this is my DS Kevin Devlin, a Cambridge graduate don't you know?

"God what did you deserve to get he who thinks he is the best DI in the Yard?" Sergeant Willie asked with a grin.

"I won him in the raffle I think. – A lucky draw! – Anyway, it is nice to meet you Sergeant." I replied with my biggest cheeky grin.

"Never you mind that now Willie! Which room have you got for us?" Andy turned back to face Sergeant Willie as he asked the question.

"You being such a cheapskate – you could only afford the Second-Floor Room 2/1," Sergeant Willie replied with a sarcastic tone.

"My you do know how to spoil your guests don't you Willie? Can you send the thickest one of the plonkers up first, in five minutes?" Andy said matter of fact, but with a hint of a smile.

"I don't think there is much difference between them. Both are as thick as two short planks!" Sergeant Willie answered with a mischievous grin.

"In that case send the thinnest in first – I think that is Tommy Smith." Andy said as he flung his hand in the air.

"My, oh my, we are sharp tonight. You must have had a good day." Sergeant Willie nodded as he said it.

"As a matter of fact, I did Willie. I even went down and caught up with old TT." DI Spearing answered with a smile.

"Bloody hell he is still alive then?" Sergeant Willie replied with a look of astonishment on his face.

"Very much alive and kicking and learning all about these new-fangled things called computers. I forgot Willie, there will not be many older than you still alive, will there? Okay come along Sergeant; let us get up to our flash room." DI Spearing laughed as he waved so long to Sergeant Willie who just there shaking his head and mumbling.

The interview Room 2/1 was sparse to say the least. No windows, an old fashioned oak wooden table, with, on top, a mains plugged-in fifties style Philips tape recorder, an old black GPO telephone and a revolving noisy old forties style fan which pushed around stale hot air. Also, on top of the table, were a couple of ashtrays. There were three bare, very uncomfortable looking, wooden chairs one by itself and the other two facing on the other side. In the corner, there was a pile of labelled box files with what appeared to be ledgers piled on top.

"Welcome to the five- star interview room at the Paddington Station resort." DI Spearing said with a smile.

"I thought it was another cell for a minute sir!" I replied while looking around the room and added; "Looks like DI Sanderson has dropped off the Palmer office files and ledgers." I said, nodding to the corner.

"Andy will do while we are on our own lad. You only need to call me sir when any other policemen are around. Okay?" Andy said it with a nonchalant tone.

I was utterly astounded and taken aback. I could only mumble; "Yes sir – Eh Andy sorry."

"Yes, now we have that out of the way Kevin. We will drop the files off at the yard tonight and, first thing in the morning, you can deliver the ledgers, receipts and invoices up to that new boy in the fraud squad – what's his name – Whittington?" DI Spearing asked with a quizzical look on his face.

"Worthington is his name Andy. That Whittington guy is Dick with the cat." I replied with a smug smile and somehow knew I was feeding him a line- straight man for the comedian.

"Yeah that Dick- he sure is that. He thinks he is the cat's whiskers, doesn't he? By the way, I thought you handled him rather well yesterday morning and gently put him down with his sneering about being at Oxford and then you piped up with your honours from Cambridge and then said you felt the streets of the Glasgow Gorbals were just as important to you. I thought he looked like the cat had pinched the cream." Andy laughed at his own joke as he said it.

"Well he is a prat of the first order. I don't know if any of the others noticed." I replied slightly defensively.

"I noticed, but then I am a detective you know and I get paid to listen to that sort of thing." Andy replied with a faint smile.

"Do I have to drop them off to him?" I asked pleadingly and added; "I already had another row with the twit this morning!"

"Now there is a surprise. Two rounds already between the man from the Glasgow Gorbals and the English aristocrat's son. Who would ever have thought it?" Andy said sarcastically and shook his head before adding; "Don't worry - I will phone his boss man, Tony Raeburn, in the morning and you can just go in and dump the lot on his desk and walk away. Can you look through the correspondence for me? I doubt if there is anything between any of them, but they desperately wanted the stuff for some reason so it may be worth a shot. What do you think?"

"Yes sir – eh Andy – will do." I stuttered through my reply.

"Thanks Kevin -. Good God this has been a bloody long day already and it is not finished yet." Andy slapped his cheeks and rubbed his brow as he said it. He was beginning to sound positively comradely which was worrying. My preconceptions of him were fast disappearing after only a day.

"Now let me do the initial talking when each of these guys come in, especially the solicitor. I know him and he will turn nasty about being held all day, but I know how to handle him. Feel free to join in later if you have something important to say, you can be good cop to my bad cop. However, with the solicitor, be very careful with your choice of words with him. Okay?" Andy spoke quietly, but with conviction.

"Yes Andy. Yes, no problem with that! Shall I take notes?" I replied with what I hoped sounded like confident.

"Yes please but can you handle the tape recording? Use that for your notes unless you do shorthand?"

"Yes! - Sure thing Andy."

There was a knock on the door which was opened a foot, at the same time a youngish looking police constable stuck his head round and asked; "Are you ready for the first one sir?"

"Yeah bring him on in lad." Andy replied with a nod of his head.

A heavy-set man, in a grey suit, about six feet, fortyish, overweight with extra baggage hanging over his belt and with crew cut blondish hair stood in the doorway. He was handcuffed, with his hands out front, and the youngish looking policeman followed him in.

"Okay Constable, thank you very much. If you could close the door and wait outside, I would appreciate it." Andy asked in a surprisingly polite manner.

"Oh – oh yes sir!" The young constable stammered, obviously having expected to sit in, but then turned around and walked out.

"Sit down." Andy ordered using a brisk military style tone while he gestured to the chair opposite our two chairs and asked; "Your name?"

"I am saying nothing until I have my solicitors!" The man retorted with deep surly tones.

"Oh well, we will assume you are Bobby Cosgrove then." Andy replied matter of fact.

"I am not Cosgrove and you know it Spearing." The man replied with anger in his voice.

"Oh well you must be Tommy Smith. Now that was not so hard, now was it?" Andy said it with a smile.

"You knew that anyway - I am not saying nothing until my solicitor gets here." Tommy Smith replied like a little naughty schoolboy.

I swiched on the Tape Recorder and stated into the microphone; "This is an interview with Mr Thomas Smith at Paddington London Police Station Interview Room 2/1 on Tuesday July the eighteenth of 1967, at seventeen hundred hours. This interview is regarding an incident earlier today at the offices of Palmers Assocites situated in East Ham, London and the murder of Mr John Palmer in his home at Weybridge this morning Those present are; The aforementioned Thomas Smith who is being interviwed by DI Spearing and DS Devlin, both from New Scotland Yard.

"Ah, but you see the tape recorder did not know your name Tommy, but now it does. Now then Tommy, let us not play these childish games and face reality here. You are not under arrest, now Tommy! - You are helping the police with our inquires Now isn't that nice?" Andy said it with a touch of malice.

"What the hell do you mean 'helping the police with your inquires?' You will get us killed if you put out that story." Tommy Smith sounded genuinely scared.

"But that is what you are doing Tommy. But look, we don't have to put out any statement just if you two help us and we do not get involved with your solicitors. If you insist, then we must charge you. I don't really want to drop you two into it, but you know how these things go. Know what I mean Tommy?" Andy was sounding so convincing.

"Get stuffed Spearing – I know you too well! Anyway, if I am not under arrest then I am entitled to walk out of here right now. Aint that right Spearing?" Tommy Smith was sneering and sounded very cocky.

"Wrong - in fact you are very wrong - Smith! Of course, you can always try that old chestnut, but then I would be forced to charge you with a minimum of: one – fleeing the scene of crime, in fact the crime committed was murder. Two – Perverting the course of justice by removing evidence from Palmers Assosiates offices. Then there is number three – An accessory to at least two murders. Finally, number four - We may follow up with - after further investigation of course - charging you with the full capital offence of at least two murders. You know Smith with your record and you have to include GBH with a knife - it so happens that is the murder weapon in two of these murders – I think you would be behind bars for the rest of your lives." Andy was now in full flow again with his angry man voice.

"You – you don't have nothing on us Spearing and you know it." Tommy Smith was sneering again, but his voice did not sound so sure.

"No? You don't think so eh? Well now do you want to try these on for size Mr Thicko?" Andy was now sounding very irritated and he added; "One – How about an eye witnesses confirming that it was you two known villains who fled the scene of a crime of double murders? – Andy was just staring hard into Smiths face and about to add 'two' when he was interrupted.

"Who the hell said that?" Tommy Smith was almost screaming his question.

"The victim's wife - and she identified both of you very well by sight and name." AndyI replied in a matter of fact way.

"Mrs Palmer?" Tommy Smith asked with a puzzled look on his face then he suddenly obviously realized his mistake.

"Yes, exactly Mr Smith. Now then lad, tell me how exactly how did you know it was Mr Palmer who was murdered this morning?" DI Spearing asked with a confidential tone to his voice, a slight smile on his face and with both his eyebrows arched.

"Well I didn't – Well I guessed." Tommy Smith kind of stuttered his reply.

"I would say that is one hell of guess Smith. Wouldn't you Sergeant Devlin?" DI Spearing feigned surprise in his voice and gesture.

"Yes, that was one hell of a guess sir. I think the odds must be at least fifty million to one to get that right!" I replied with a smile and a shake of the head. - I was beginning to understand why Andy got the results. He was stretching facts and making it look desperate for the two bouncers.

"Now you see what I mean lad? And the thing is, Devlin here is a Celtic paranormal and even he could not have predicted that!" Andy could not hold down his laugh as he turned and winked at me. I could not help but laugh as well thinking back to the morning banter with DI Lawler.

"I – I must have heard it on television! That must have been it!" Tommy Smith replied, his voice sounding a little desperate.

"Ah yes, that must be it. You must also be paranormal as well as Devlin here! You have been at Palmers mansion, or his offices, or here in Paddington Green station all day. So, when did you watch television? Anyway, what is strange is that there has been no television news and we have not released any details to anyone yet! So, how do you explain that Smith?" DI Spearing asked with a sarcastic tone to his voice.

"You are just twisting things. You cannot prove a thing." Tommy Smith replied with an unsure shake of his head.

"Look Smith, I am only a simple detective and in five minutes I have already caught you lying about a murder scene. Now with a smart prosecution lawyer in an open court - you would not last even half that time. You know that lad, don't you?" DI Spearing was now trying the sympathetic approach.

"This would never get to court and you know it - don't you Spearing?" Tommy Smith replied with a challenging tone to his voice and his sneer returning.

"No? Well now lad, let us look at the facts again - At the risk of boring you by repeating myself." Andy looked thoughtful and rubbed his chin before adding; "One – like I said before lad - we have a reliable witness and she will testify that she identified you two known villains fleeing the scene of a murder – That alone is a chargeable, bookable offence for which two known criminals, on probation, and go back to prison without the need any of any other charge!" Andy paused to let that sink in! "Now then - Two – Your fingerprints are all over the murder scene and elsewhere in the house and yet you said you were not there. You really think that is defensible?" - Three – You, and your accomplice Cosgrove, have been caught red handed by police officers, perverting the course of justice by removing evidence connected to the murder case for which you are prime suspects. Four - You were both minders for Joseph Bolger who mysteriously disappeared in front of your very eyes in his club. We would then point out of course Joseph Bolger is, or was, the boss and John Palmer worked for him. Soon we may have to assume that Joseph Bolger is missing pressumed dead and you two are there right up to your armpits. Now how much more evidence do we need? What says you Sergeant Devlin?" Andy turned to me and winked with the eye that Smith could not see.

"I think sir, in the good old days that would be enough to have the two of them hanged." I replied with a smile.

"And nowadays Sergeant?" DI Spearing demanded an answer.

"I would say there is enough there to give them three consecutive life sentences sir." I replied louder than I intended.

"Look, we didn't flee from a murder scene." Tommy Smith was now visibly wilting with sweat running down his brow onto the bridge of his nose and hastily he added; "We were ordered to get up to the London offices and get those files and ledgers!"

"Ordered to? Who ordered you?" Andy sounded concerned and pretended astonishment.

"Mrs Palmer - that's who!" Tommy Smith replied, staring sullenly down at the table.

"Mrs Palmer? Now then you do surprise me lad" DI Spearing replied, still pretending astonishment.

"Mrs Palmer is the one with the trousers in that house. She is the real boss." Tommy Smith said quietly but firmly while nodding his head.

"Tell me Smith. Is she just being the boss now because her husband has just been murdered, or has she always been the boss?" I asked quietly as I felt I had to donate something to the interview.

"No! - She has always been the real boss as far as the money was concerned. She is the banker and handles the real accounts. She is a real bitch!" Tommy Smith replied with some venom.

"Tell me Smith, how did Joseph Bolger like that? I asked.

"He was okay with it. Her old man and Bolger are related, so he trusts her - more fool him," Tommy Smith replied with a shake of his head.

Andy and I exchanged knowing glances and nodded.

"Now that is very interesting Smith. Now then - what really happened this morning at Palmers Place? Andy asked.

"We don't have a clue. We got woke up with the bitch screaming and then we couldn't get out of our rooms, the doors were locked. I started climbing out of the window to go around the front, then the bitch opened the door and I rushed through --" Tommy Smith was about to add something when he was interrupted.

"What did these screams sound like Smith? Fake? Or did they sound like real screams? Andy asked.

"How the hell should I know? I was still asleep when I first heard the bitches first scream, at least what I thought was her first scream. I was still half asleep when she started screaming again and came to the door. I don't have a fucking clue if they were real or fake do I?" Tommy Smith was again losing his cool.

"Okay Smith, Okay, you stay cool. At what time was this at?" Andy asked.

"It was just gone six o'clock." Tommy Smith replied without hesitation.

"You sound very certain of that time?" DI Speared said more as a question.

"I am because I looked at my watch. Thought it was still the middle of the night and it was!" Tommy Smith replied with a slight smile.

"Yeah, I suppose for you two lads, six o'clock is the middle of the night." Andy returned his smile and then added a question; "Now tell me Smith – according to our information - Palmer was expecting his killers and was waiting for them. If we assume - for the moment - you two were not the killers, why did he not have you two in with him and Tony?"

"I am fucking telling you Spearing - we are not the killers." Tommy Smith was back with the irritation and then added; "We offered to sit in with them, much as we didn't want to, against that guy you need a small army. But Palmer said not to bother. He said they would have the drop on him!"

"So, you and he knew who he was up against then? How come?" DI Spearing asked.

Palmer said that it was 'The Fox.' Everybody in our business knows him as 'The Fox' and believe me Spearing anybody who has messed about with him, without an army, has woke up dead in the morning." Tommy Smith replied deadpan with what appeared to be genuine fear in his voice.

"So, you know this guy 'The Fox' do you?" Andy asked with a little smile on his face, thinking about dead men waking up in the morning.

"No I don't and I don't want to neither. He is bad news and works all sides of the fence, but it is always our side of the fence where the bodies turn up!" Tommy Smith replied grimly.

"Quite right too I would say. So, what did you do when Palmer said not to bother?" Andy was trying to throw Smith out of his comfort zone.

"We took off to bed about eleven." Tommy Smith replied.

"So, you really expect us to believe Smith, that you both went off to bed knowing that a killer was coming into the house and you both left your keys on the other side of the door. I don't think even you two would be that thick!" DI Spearing was acting astonished again.

"We all make mistakes Spearing, don't we?" Tommy Smith retorted with some innuendo.

"There are mistakes Smith, then there deliberate mistakes to make people think you are that thick. You just said you were about to climb out the window and come in round the front when Mrs P was screaming? What was to stop you doing that when it was time for you two to murder Palmer and Tony?" Andy asked the question with anger in his voice and stared straight at Smith looking for a reaction.

"We never murdered anybody. Can't you see? Why would we cut off the hand that feeds us?" Tommy Smith was now near tears as he spoke - he sounded almost desperate.

"Well if I was really cynical, which I am, I would say you found somebody with deeper pockets and bigger hands!" Andy replied with a smile.

"Listen Spearing - we have worked for Joseph's firm for a long time now. We are comfortable there and he took care of us when we got out the last time!" Tommy Smith had again that pleading tone to his voice when he was interrupted.

"As he should Smith – as he should. After all it was his business you two were doing when you got sent down for ten years and you covered for him, not a squeak from you two. I hope he also took care of your Mrs while you were inside?" DI Spearing did sound concerned.

"Yeah - like I say - Joseph always took care of everybody who worked for him. We all knew it so we knew not to open our mouths – You know what I mean Spearing?" Tommy Smith replied again with a touch of menace.

"Oh, yeah I know exactly what you mean and I know what Joseph would do. You open your mouths and you would be walking dead men within weeks. Know what I mean Smith?" Andy replied, appearing to counter the threat.

"Only saying - that's all!" Tommy Smith turned sullen again and stared down at the floor, apparently afraid to look anyone straight in the eye.

"Okay – I can swallow your story if it is backed up by Cosgrove!" Andy suddenly said, apparently wanting to get rid of Smith in a hurry.

Smith looked relieved and even managed a smile.

"Now then Smith - one more thing! What did the solicitor Aldrich say to you two?" Andy asked almost as an aside.

"He just kept on and on saying we have to get these files and things out of the offices before the police arrive." Tommy Smith replied.

"Those were his exact words? – 'get these files and things out before the police arrive'?" Andy asked while staring into his Smiths' face.

"Yeah definitely – He must have said it six or seven times." Tommy Smith replied.

"Did any go out before DI Sanderson arrived? Are they over there in the corner?" DI Spearing

"Yes, each of us had taken one lot down to the boot of Aldrich's car." Tommy Smith turned and looked at the files and things in the corner. "They were another six ledgers and they are not over there. Your lot arrived far earlier than we thought!" Tommy Smith replied as a matter of fact.

Andy immediately lifted the phone from the table. He asked for Scotland Yard and then asked to be patched through to DI John Sanderson.

"Hello John? It is me Andy Spearing! Listen John - when you pulled these files and ledgers today. Did you check out the boot of the Aldrich car for anything already out there?" Andy asked and listened and added; "No? Well look John - can you find out the Aldrich car registration number. Then get a warrant to search the car for evidence connected with the Palmer's murders. Could you then get some of the Wooden Tops over and find the car – it will probably still be around the Palmers office block. Take a photographer and 'independent' witnesses with you. Photograph the registration number, the independent witness, the time and demonstrate the boot is locked. Force the boot and find the ledgers. Photograph them as they are taken out one by one from the boot. Make sure they are identified as Palmer's ledgers. Okay John? Can you do it in the next hour? Great John - ring me at Paddington Green as soon as it is done. Thanks John I am due you one." Andy spoke with quiet authority.

"Right you are not of the hook yet Smith. I want signed statements from you two in the next hour, including what was said by Aldrich and the fact that he ordered these six ledgers to be taken to his car and these others were to follow. Sergeant Devlin will type them out for you and get someone to witness your 'freely given' signature." Andy said it and nodded to Smith as if to say on your way.

"I don't know about Cosgrove, but I am okay with that. What happens to us though?" Tommy Smith asked.

"I am sure Cosgrove will go along with it under the circumstances. We will sort it out as soon as you have both signed your statements. Sergeant could you give the PC a shout to take Smith here back and bring in Cosgrove?" Andy asked in a polite way, but he obviously wanted Smith out before he asked any other questions.

I quickly went to the door, opened it and spoke to the PC who came in and practically frog marched Smith out of the room.

Andy spoke into the microphone in the Tape Recorder stating; "End of Thomas Smith interview at seventeen thirty.

"Nice work Andy turning him over like that. I thought he was going to wet himself at one stage." I said as I sat back down.

"You know Sergeant; it is days like today that makes me love this job. I just love it! You saw the real police work today! You know those films and TV shows showing Scotland Yard police chasing people with flashing blue lights and jumping out of cars with guns and such like. Just bollocks, as you say in Scotland. If you did that once or twice in your working lifetime, then you are exceptional." Andy was speaking with such enthusiasm it was infectious.

"I think I saw the real you today as well Andy. I think I now know why everyone thinks you are such a good detective. You were thinking two moves ahead all day in your interviews." I said it in a matter of fact tone.

"Just remember this lad. It does not happen very often, if ever, but if you get a chance to get ahead of them and shake them up, then you have got to move real fast and throw up as much barrage as you can muster and be in position when it falls down to catch the pieces. Get in among them fast, because you will probably only get one good chance like this one. Joseph Bolger and his firm have been on my books for over twenty years and this is the first real 'in' I have had without our bosses being able to stop us, although in any case they will try that. It is also the first real break we have had with the assassin, we know as 'The Fox.' So, we have got to move hard and fast. Look I know I am not as good as I once was, but I still know enough to work it through." Andy was now juiced up and flowing.

"Why did you say earlier that we only have a one to five percent chance of catching the assassin?" I asked.

"Because lad, he is the one real professional in this lot. The one nobody really knows. The Scarlett Pimpernel if you like, nobody knows where he comes from, or where he goes afterwards. He is elite and covers his tracks." Andy betrayed a tone of admiration in his voice.

"But this time Andy we have a description, a rough age guesstimate, we know he is over six feet, his real voice sounds Londoner and probably ex-army, possibly Paratrooper, or more likely SAS. It is not a bad start." I sounded a little plaintive.

"Yeah well certainly it is a vast improvement on what we had. Forget about the description, it is probably a disguise, but everything else is good. Look Sergeant, this week, among other things, we have to shoot down avenues we have been down before - checking and double checking. You have a good feel for this assassin guy, so I want you with a fresh mind to start going through his old cases. Also, try getting into army SAS and then Paratrooper records. See what you can dig up. Nobody can be completely invisible; there has to be threads left somewhere along the road." Andy sounded convincing and thoughtful.

"Can I also stay on the murder case with you Andy? I need to learn real fast while you are still around." I now sounded as though I was pleading.

"Of course, you are. The assassin thing you will have to fit in between things. I need to bounce things off your fresh, young mind lad; my old head is getting pickled with the alcohol." Andy said it with a smile.

There was a knock on the door and the young PC stuck his head round the door.

"Cosgrove is here for his interview sir." The PC said with a nod.

"Okay lad - show him in." DI Spearing replied with a good-natured grin.

The Cosgrove interview went almost the same way as the Tommy Smith interview. It started with Cosgrove stating he was saying nothing and Andy, the cajoler, working him round with threats and disclosures until in almost the same time frame as Smith, Cosgrove too agreed to sign a statement.

I realized I was watching a master detective at work, digging out the truth and the facts ready for the next one to roll in.

"Okay Cosgrove. Like I said to Smith you are not of the hook yet. I want signed statements from you in the next hour, including what was said by Aldrich and the fact that he ordered these six ledgers to be taken to his car and these others were to follow. Sergeant Devlin will type them out for you and get someone to witness your 'freely given' signature." Andy said it and nodded to Cosgrove as to say on your way.

"I am signing nothing Spearing until I get a deal!" Cosgrove shouted at DI Spearing who shrugged and pointed to the tape and replied; "There will be no deal here as you well know!" Andy winked at Cosgrove and nodded at the tape recorder and continued in a monotone tired voice; "We already have a statement from Smith. So, unless you want to get left holding the baby Cosgrove I suggest you come along and tell the truth in your statement."

"Yeah, yeah - I see what you mean. Okay then I will." Cosgrove sounded so false it was almost laughable.

"Right Sergeant, get the PC to take Cosgrove back to his cell and tell him to bring Aldrich down will you?" DI Spearing was sounding all official again.

"Yes sir" I replied which came out sounding more mocking than I had intended.

Cosgrove went to say something, then he looked at the tape recorder changed his mind and turned away with me.

I quickly went to the door, opened it and spoke to the PC who equally quickly came in.

Andy stopped the tape recorder, recorded the closing of the Cosgrove interview and then asked; "Could you bring down Aldrich now constable?

"Yes sir, gladly. He is a banshee that one! Screaming and shouting all day doing all our heads in." The PC said it with a smile.

"Yes, well we will have to see if we can quiet him down for the night then eh constable? Andy replied with a smile.

"That would be good sir, although probably impossible." The PC answered and nodded to Cosgrove and, like Smith, practically frog marched him out of the room.

"Good work again Andy. I think you turned him even quicker than Smith." I said as I retook my seat.

"Yeah it is easier when you already know what the answers should be." Andy replied then added; "Aldrich! Now he is going to be the hard one though! Unlike those two thickos he is a solicitor – he knows all his rights. Still, because of our work with

Mrs P this morning and the two thickos statements, I think we are as close to nailing Aldrich as we will ever be." Andy was already preparing his mind for the interview.

"What about Smith and Cosgrove what happens to them now? I asked just to keep the conversation flowing.

"After they sign their statements we will charge them with perverting the course of justice and fleeing the murder scene. That, with their records, should get them five to ten." Andy replied with that matter of fact tone again.

"Really? I thought - you were giving them a deal? I replied without thinking.

"Those two thickos? Absolutely no chance! You know Kevin those two have beaten people to death and left others with permanent brain damage. Not to mention the stabbings. I have never been able to nail them in all these years except for one of the stabbings, because that time they were caught red handed. If we get real lucky and can possibly also nail them for accessory to these three murders - guilty or not - then I will." Andy sounded utterly full of revenge and nodded his head as if agreeing with himself.

"I suppose you are right, but everyone including them, deserves justice." I replied with a thoughtful tone, but did not expect the response.

"That's crap laddie. TT and I were just saying this afternoon we don't mind if the assassin gets away with it. He is doing a service getting rid of the scum. We cannot do it, even if we know they are guilty, and then, if there is a chance, most of our bosses stop us because they are in the scums back pocket!" Andy was angry, his face reddening.

"Vigilante police - surely you cannot mean that? Do you think that is what is going on here Andy?" I asked with a tone of disbelief.

"In answer to your first question - If all else fails then 'yes' - it may be the only answer. And 'yes' in answer to your second question too, at least it is not beyond the realms of possibility. According to the rumours I am hearing we may have some sort of vigilante group operating!" Andy replied in that matter of fact way of his.

I stood there in amazement for what I thought was minutes, but was probably just seconds, then came a knock at the door and the young PC stuck his head in and said; "Aldrich for his interview sir?"

"Yes, show him in constable." Andy replied quietly as though he was lost in thought again.

The constable frog marched Aldrich in. I was surprised to see that he too was handcuffed hands out front and he was looking very angry. He was a smallish middle aged man dressed in a dark grey 'Savile Row' suit, white shirt and dark grey silk tie with black shiny shoes. His jet-black hair was swept straight back and plastered down with Brylcreem. He looked every inch the solicitor although his face was now catching the five o'clock shadow. He had a dark complexion which only highlighted the shadow.

"Spearing! I might have known you were behind this. You have gone too far this time Spearing!" Aldrich was almost spitting out his words as he crossed the small room.

"Sit down Aldrich and shut it before you go too far and get me real angry!" Andy commanded and Aldrich silently did as he was told and sat down. DI Spearing added "Thank you constable..

"Thank you, sir." The PC replied with a smile and a nod at Aldrich as he left the room.

I swiched on the Tape Recorder and stated into the microphone; "This is an interview with Mr John Aldrich at Paddington London Police Station in interview room 2/1 on Tuesday July the eighteenth 1967, at seventeen-thirty hundred hours. This interview is regarding an incident earlier today at the offices of Palmers Assocites situated in East Ham, London and the murder of Mr John Palmer earlier this morning.

Those present are; The aforementioned John Aldrich who is being interviewed by DI Spearing and DS Devlin, both from New Scotland Yard.

"You can leave that thing off for a start Spearing. I am saying nothing until my advocate is here." Aldrich said, causally looking around the room and spotting the files in the corner before returning his gaze to stare straight at Andy.

"What makes you think you need an advocate Aldrich?" Andy asked and added: "You are only here helping the police with our inquiries"

"We all know you and helping with police inquiries Spearing. The next thing the innocent man is stitched up and facing a sentence." Aldrich blasted back, a small man who appeared to have a chip on his shoulder.

"Since when were you an 'innocent' man Aldrich? That must have been a long time ago when you were still a boy surely?" Andy asked with a sarcastic tone in his voice and a smile on his face.

"You may have appeared to be a 'smart ass' to those two thickos Spearing. That does not wash with me. You have got nothing on me." Aldrich replied with a touch of confidence.

"You know you are the third one who has said that to me today and they are all behind bars tonight. Still, let us see what we have got on you Aldrich shall we?" DI Spearing replied with a confident smile.

"It doesn't matter. I am saying nothing till I have an advocate here." Aldrich said, but this time there a slight quiver in his voice. Andy did not miss it.

"That's all right Aldrich. As you know I can question you until tomorrow afternoon on the twenty-four-hour rule. Then before your advocate gets here I promise you I will charge you and I can tell you since this is a double murder case I will be opposing bail. So, you look forward to at least the next few months in prison with the other slime balls while we slowly build up a case against you. It should be a horrible break that could go on for a long time. What do you think about that Aldrich?" Andy asked the question, again adding that sarcastic smile.

"I am a solicitor! I will not be threatened by you or anybody else. I have a business to run. I am due in court on Friday." Aldrich was not only angry, but he was also beginning to sound anxious.

"Not my problem Aldrich, but I think I can promise you this - you will not be there on Friday. – I wonder what the magistrate will think when he finds out you are in prison and you are applying to him for bail which is opposed?" Andy was smiling and obviously enjoying rubbing it in.

There was a delay with a long silence which did not appear to annoy Andy.

"I will be out before you know it Spearing. You cannot make anything stick." Aldrich finally retorted.

"See there you go again Aldrich making all these assumptions. Someone said that this morning and I said it then and I will say it again - if I have a mind to, I can make anything stick to anything, even to Teflon shoulders like yours." Andy smiled again and just shook his right hand in a dismissive gesture.

There was another silence for a couple of minutes.

"So, what do you think you have on me that you think will stick Spearing?" Aldrich asked, trying his best to sound nonchalant, but not quite succeeding.

"You are the solicitor Aldrich. I think after this morning's episode you can work that one out, don't you?" Andy was acting as smooth as silk.

"No, I don't think I can. If you are going to charge me you had better start telling me what you think I have done, don't you think?" Aldrich was trying to play a game of cat and mouse.

"I will ask the questions Aldrich, but if you refuse to answer, then I will charge you and that will be the end of it. You know as well as I do how juries interpret silence these days. Also, I shall oppose bail and you can rot in jail until your trial. Is that clearly understood Aldrich?" Andy spoke quietly, but clearly for the benefit of the tape recording.

"I hear the idle threats and it is understood." Aldrich replied coolly, with a touch of rancour in his voice.

"Right – First Mr Aldrich – You were caught by five policemen and a detective in the offices of Palmers Associates. You were acting with two known wanted criminals removing files and legers from from the premises at or around eleven o'clock this morning July 18th. Can you tell me what you were doing?" Andy asked the question while staring directly at Aldrich.

"I can tell you one thing, as I told your colleague DI Sanderson; I was not removing files or ledgers." Aldrich replied, with a sarcastic tone and a smile.

"Then what were you doing Mr Aldrich?" DI Spearing asked.

"I was getting the files and ledgers ready for my client to collect!" Aldrich replied in an easy-going manner.

"Oh, I see Mr Aldrich – you are one of the highest paid solicitors in London. So, with two known and wanted criminals, you were sorting out files and ledgers just like a lowly paid clerk would do. Who is your client Mr Aldrich? – He must be very well off to afford such pricey labourers?" Andy asked.

"I cannot disclose the name of my client." Aldrich replied in haste.

"No? Then am I to assume the three of you were stealing these items from Palmers Associates?" Andy asked the question and raised his eyebrows.

"Why do you assume we were stealing these items Spearing?" Aldrich asked the question with an incredulous look on his face.

"It is quite simple Mr Aldrich! These items are owned by Palmers Associates; therefore, if your client is not Palmers Associates then you three were stealing the items in question." DI Spearing was retaining his cool.

"I did not say I was removing the items. I said I was only getting them ready for my client!" Aldrich replied with an edgy tone.

"I say it again for the last time Mr Aldrich. – If your client is not Palmers Associates, then you were party to stealing these items. Is that so?" DI Spearing was now sounding more than a little irritated.

"I did not say Palmers Associates were not my clients!" Aldrich replied smugly.

"Really Mr Aldrich? You really do have to stop wasting police time, or I will have to add that to your charge sheet. Is Palmers Associates your clients or not?" Andy was suddenly forthright and obviously getting more and more irritated.

"Yes, Palmers Associates are my clients." Aldrich almost mumbled his response.

"I am afraid I do not understand Mr Aldrich. The sole director of the company Mr Palmer was, as you no doubt know, murdered last night. So, who is your client Mr Aldrich?" Andy asked with an expectant look on his face.

"Mrs Palmer is my client." Aldrich mumbled his reply and added; "As I am the family solicitor I also know that Mrs Palmer inherits the business under the terms of Mr Palmer's will!"

"Mr Aldrich – How many times have you represented a client involved with murder charges, or grievous bodily harm charges?" Andy asked the question completely ignoring the Aldrich reply.

"On several occasions, I guess." Aldrich replied with a defensive tone.

"So, Mr Aldrich you are aware that the removal of any possible evidence is an offence under 'perverting the course of justice' – are you not?" Andy asked with a brisk tone to his voice.

"Firstly, I told you already I was not removing any files, I was merely getting them ready for my client to review---" Aldrich replied, but was quickly interrupted before he could continue.

"Really Mr. Aldrich? – We have two signed statements, from your two co-conspirators, which clearly state that you repeatedly stated that you had to get the files and ledgers out of the office before the police arrived. What do you say to that Mr Aldrich?" Andy asked with a slight smile on his face.

"What? Aldrich asked and sounded astounded before adding; "They are not my co-conspirators and they must have misheard me or something."

"I don't think so Mr Aldrich. The two made and signed two separate statements during separate interviews. They both recorded word for word what you said to them regarding removing the files before the police arrived. So, what do you say to that Mr Aldrich?" Andy retorted with sarcastic undertones.

"They two are thugs who have never liked me. They are probably trying to frame me for their own petty reasons." Aldrich was now sounding edgy if not desperate.

"My, oh my, Mr Aldrich. Not a very original tale you tell. I would have thought, you being a solicitor, would have come up with something a little better than that lame, old excuse." Andy was now positively scathing.

"I don't really care what you think Spearing. You are in the same boat as them, so you are really out to get me for anything - just to get even for your past failures with me." Aldrich was trying his best to divert the interview.

"I really do recommend that you care about what I think Mr Aldrich. I don't really think you would like my thoughts about you now. Also, as to your little aside, regarding me, I would suggest to you this tape recording will prove beyond doubt that I have given you plenty of opportunities to explain your actions and have not heard anything remotely like a plausible reason." Andy replied, cool and composed.

"Oh, why don't you just go fuck yourself with that recorder of yours and see where that gets you?" Aldrich had now lost it.

"Mr Aldrich such language and you a solicitor too? You of all people should know better! I am afraid that you have ignored all our warnings and we will be adding additional charges of being abusive and obstructive to the police in their line of duty. It is all adding up to a lengthy charge sheet for you Mr Aldrich I am afraid." Andy replied quietly and firmly.

There was a moments silence when Aldrich just waved his right hand in a 'so what' attitude, then the phone on the desk suddenly rang loudly which startled everyone in the room. Andy leaned over and picked it up.

"DI Spearing here! Who is calling please?" Andy asked with a frown on his face and then added with a smile; "Oh John it is you! Yes? Good – oh that's good. Look John I am in an interview room now. I will suspend the interview for a few minutes. Give me a couple of minutes then phone back to the front desk and I can get the details then. Yes? Great, talk in a couple of minutes. Thanks again John – good work." Andy put the phone down with a comfortable sigh before adding; "This interview is suspended for ten minutes. - Sergeant - could you get the PC in here to stay with you as an independent witness and leave the recorder on – just in case Mr Aldrich has anything further to say while I am away." Andy Spearing asked with a slight smile and nodded his head a couple of times.

"Yes sir." I replied and rose, went over to the door and got the PC to come into the room.

Andy immediately rose and rushed out to the front desk to receive the call. The phone on the reception desk rang just as Andy reached it and Sergeant Willie picked it up and answered; "Good evening. - Paddington Police Station. How can I help?"

"DI John Sanderson here again Willie! Has Sherlock reached the desk yet?" DI Sanderson asked.

"Yes, only just! Puffing and panting like an old miner he is. - DI John Sanderson for you – Sherlock?" Sergeant Willie laughed as he passed the phone over to Andy

Andy took the phone and acted gruffly. "He is bad enough sitting here acting badly like old Jack Warner the policeman with his 'evening all,' without you giving him more ammunition John. "Well what is the story?" Andy asked, shooting a quick glance, with a mocking smile, at Sergeant Willie who just shook his head, but he too was smiling.

"Sounds like you and Sergeant Willie are still ribbing each other as much as ever." DI Sanderson said with a laugh and added: "Anyway just to clarify - we found the Aldrich car parked across the street from Palmer's office - a nice new shiny red Triumph Spitfire Mark 2 - believe it or not – it's on its way now to Charlton Police Compound. Those guys will have a bit of fun with it before it gets parked up!"

"Yes – that is good John! So, you found the ledgers in the boot?" DI Spearing asked with a rather anxious tone to his voice.

"Yeah – it was bingo time! Six of them all locked in the boot." DI Sanderson replied with a triumphant tone.

"Just brilliant John! – All done to the letter of the law?" DI Spearing asked.

Yes! – As each ledger was take out we photographed all entries in all ledgers as each ledger was taken out. We had independent witnesses watching us each step of the way and we had the search warrant for opening the boot and a warrant to remove the car to the compound. So, I think you can have him Andy." DI Sanderson sounded ecstatic.

"Great work John. We finally have something on the slimy bastard that will stick. Great! - I must get back to him now and charge him. Yippee! - I owe you one big one John." Andy replied and sounded equally as ecstatic as he went to put the phone down.

"No problem Andy. Depends on what you mean by one big one though." DI Sanderson replied and laughed then added; "Perhaps you can help me with a problem tomorrow morning – are you in? Oh, and I almost forgot - 'Flash Harry' your actual Detective Chief Inspector – if you ever knew you had a DCI – he wants to see you and young Devlin in his office as soon as you come in – He sounds loopy!"

"Well that sounds par for the course and a bit ominous. However, 'yes,' I am in tomorrow at least for the morning. So, 'yes' if I can help, give me a shout after I get away from 'Flash Harry' and his office – that is if I am not eaten before then. See you then, Oh John one last favour – could you drop the ledgers off at the yard - stick them under young Devlin's desk – not mine – could you do that John? – Thanks again John." Andy hung up the phone with a scowl on his face.

"You had better watch your back with that 'Flash Harry' geezer Andy. He is a man on a mission to fill his pockets with any money that is available." Sergeant Willie stated interrupting Andys thoughts.

"Yeah - tell me about it Willie. I hear tell he flashes so much, the 'Flash' toilet cleaning people are talking about hiring him for their toilet ads while he is down there among the shit." Andy replied with a smile back on his face.

"You have such a way with the words Andy." Sergeant Willie replied, laughing at the same time then added; "Are you going to be much longer up there?"

"No – just ten minutes or so! Just going to charge old Aldrich, then we must get statements signed. Have you got a spare typewriter anywhere?" Andy asked.

"Old Aldrich? You are going to charge him? I hope you lot at New Scotland Yard have plenty of money. He will sue the ass of you if you are not spot on." Sergeant Willie said and then added, almost as an afterthought; "Yeah we got one of those golf balls in room one behind me."

"Golf balls? What the hell do I want with a golf ball Willie? There isn't a fairway for miles around here!" Andy replied and Sergeant Willie took some time, and then thought that Andy was serious.

"You are so unbelievably out of touch Andy. The golf ball is one of those new-fangled typewriters that came out about six years ago. When did you last type out a statement Andy?" Sergeant Willie replied, thankful to get a little of his own back.

"Oh, one of 'those' golf balls? DI Spearing replied.

"Yeah one of 'those' Andy - that don't need no fairway. I bet you have never even used one, just like your walkie-talkie?" Sergeant Willie was enjoying having the upper hand.

"See that's the trouble with people using slang terms Willie. Now if you would have said the 'IBM Selectric Typewriter,' I might have known what you were talking about, you know that? Now - could you possibly reserve the 'IBM Selectric Typewriter' and Room 1 for me and Sergeant Devlin for half an hour or so Willie?" Andy asked with a quizzical, smarmy look on his face.

"That's the trouble with 'smart asses' Sherlock – They never know when to draw the line do they? Oh, I almost forgot, Sergeant Tommy is out the back having a chat to some of the lads while he waits for you" Sergeant Willie replied, again back on the defence, but still smiling.

"Thank you too Sergeant. I always know when to draw my lines." Andy replied, accompanied by another smarmy smile and a wave of the hand as he turned and made his way back to the interview room.

Andy re-entered the interview room and was met by silence. He spoke in a crisp business-like manner into the tape recorder; "DI Spearing re-entered the interview room after an absence of approximately ten minutes to continue discussions and enquires with solicitor Mister Aldrich."

Andy sat down on his chair, but surprisingly did not ask the PC to leave. There was silence for the next few minutes as Andy simply stared at Aldrich who began to move uncomfortably in his chair.

"Now then - Mr Aldrich. Earlier in our interview, you categorically denied removing any items from Palmers Associates offices and you denied telling your two co-conspirators that anything had to be removed from the offices before the police arrived. Is that correct?" Andy asked in a clear very precise tone in his voice.

The Aldrich face betrayed he recognised that a trapdoor was about to be opened below his feet, but after a minutes thought he opted to attack; "Damn right! Those two, and you, are just trying to shaft me." Aldrich replied with some venom, but there was a slight nervous or unsure undertone in his voice.

"Right Mr Aldrich! It is my duty to inform you that I will be arresting you tomorrow morning on several charges and you will be held in Paddington cells overnight. The first charge will be for attempting to pervert the course of justice. The second will be obstruction of the police in the course of their duty. The third will be for abusing police officers while carrying out their duties. We also reserve the right to charge you with a fourth offence of 'assessory to murder,' which will be held pending further enquires. I must warn you that anything you say from now on will be taken down and may be used in evidence against you, just as it would when you are formally arrested in the morning. Do you have anything to say Mr Aldrich?" DI Spearing asked staring straight at Aldrich with unblinking eyes.

Aldrich just sat there and stared in astonishment. The young PC just smiled and seemed to mouth the word 'Yes' but silently and punched in the air. I must admit I was taken aback myself, thinking 'bloody hell - -here we go.'

"What? – What? – What the hell do you mean?" Aldrich finally managed to blurt out a question.

"I thought it was quite clear Mr Aldrich. Which parts of these charges do you not understand? Or which parts do you need clarification on?" Andy replied with curtness and a smile.

"You – you cannot do this." Aldrich again blurted out, in a rather pathetic voice.

"I just have Mr Aldrich. Now, if you have nothing more to say Mr Aldrich I will wish you good evening. I still have a busy evening ahead to tie up loose ends on this case." Andy was again sounding very crisp and business like.

"You and I know it Spearing. I am not guilty on any of this – you know it!" Aldrich was now reaching the desperation stages.

"Afraid not Mr Aldrich! We now have proof you have been lying all along with this one. So, we have no alternative other than to charge you with these offences. So, I will say goodbye and will talk to you in the morning to hear how you feel then Mr Aldrich. Would you like to make, or do you wish to record a statement now? Andy was again smiling and sounding sarcastic.

"You can fuck off Spearing. You will pay for this – you know that?" Aldrich was back to losing his cool.

"I'll take that as a 'no' then shall I? Really Mr Aldrich, it is time you realized that it is time to stop this abusive behaviour! - PC Atkinson! - would you please return Mr Aldrich to his cell now?" DI Spearing was now in charge again and smiling.

"Yes sir. Most certainly sir!" The PC replied with a broad smile on his face.

"Wait a minute, now just wait a minute. Why am I not being charged tonight tell me that?" Aldrich had a pleading tone in his voice.

"Because you, Mr Aldrich, have been so uncooperative and abusive throughout today, we have still to make further enquires and it is getting on for six thirty o'clock so we will have to carry on in the morning. Enjoy your stay with us; we will move you to better accommodation in prison tomorrow where you will have some real close friends to share with. You will never have to be lonely up there!" Andy replied with that sarcastic tone and a smile before adding in a confidential tone; "Take my warning Mr Aldrich. The showers there are the most dangerous places to get caught. At least at night you know who is in the cell with you Mr Aldrich. You know what I mean? Now take him constable"

"Yes sir!" PC Atkinson replied, but could not hold back his laugh.

"Yes, make the most of it Spearing, but you will be the laughing-stock when I sue your ass." Aldrich practically spat out the words.

"Unfortunate choice of words there Mr Aldrich given where you are going. At least my ass will be my own for the next few years. Maybe after a few nights in the cells you will be more cooperative, what do you think Mr Aldrich? Shall we see in the morning how you feel?" Andy was barely hiding the mirth from his voice.

"Get stuffed Spearing!" Aldrich retorted angrily, but then heard all three of us laughing and realized what he had just said and added in frustration; "I have had enough of this, get me out of here now!" Aldrich turned away and walked to the door with PC Atkinson following, but still laughing. The PC closed the door behind him as he left.

Andy Spearing leaned over and before turning the tape recorder off said; "Interview with Mr Aldrich concluded at 18-30 hours on Tuesday the 18th July 1967."

I was still smiling and I asked; "I thought for a spell he was going to blow a fuse. Do you think we have enough on him Andy to make it stick?"

"Well John Sanderson found his car across the street from Palmers Associates and no guesses for what they found in the locked boot? Yep! The six ledgers from Palmers Associates, which we have him on tape, totally denying he had removed anything from the premises, and knowing that to do so was perverting the course of justice. We are watertight, within the law, on the opening of the car boot etc. We also have Smith and Cosgrove statements that he wanted the files out before the police arrived and we can prove the abuse charges. Mrs P also denies authorising him to remove the files which I held back in case we did not find the car! So, the answer is 'Yes we have enough to make it stick, as you say, but he has friends in high places, including 'The Yard,' so who knows? The slimy toad may slide out under the radar, but even if he does, in the meantime we will make it as painful as we can for him." Andy replied cynically with a smile.

"How can he possibly get away with it?" I asked and added; "He has practically put himself in jail and we have all the evidence we need. Surely? –"

"It is never as simple as that these days Sergeant. There are a lot of people out there with very large pockets and a lot more who owe quite a few favours to his firm. It is what makes his world go around!" Andy replied with a shrug of his shoulders and a sad look in his eyes.

"I think it looks like we are all in this seedy world." I replied. I sounded just as cynical.

"Yes - well - right Kevin. It is getting on and we still have a lot to do before we can go home. How is your typing with these new-fangled golf ball typewriters?" Andy asked with a smile returning.

"I can use them, but only with the two fingers." I replied with a nod of my head.

"Well that is two fingers better than mine!" Andy replied and added; "How long for you to type out two statements and a summary of the Aldrich interview if I give you use the recording?"

"About an hour, I suppose. Depending how long they are" I replied.

"That's not long?" DI Spearing said with an incredulous look on his face.

"Oh, we can use the Xerox Copier for the statements and just change the names over!" I explained.

"I am afraid it is not that easy Sergeant. The courts must see two signed originals without alteration. Anyway, we cannot have them exactly the same – it would look like too much of a 'put-up job' and we wouldn't want that, now would we?" Andy replied with a sly smile.

"Yeah I see what you mean. Not a good thing at all." I replied.

"Now first, before we draft their statements, I need to call Harry Lawler to see how he got on with Mrs Palmer! We don't want her appearing out of the blue." Andy said as he lifted the phone and dialled zero for the operator.

"Hello there. Can you get through to Guildford Surrey police station and then get me patched through to DI Harry Lawler please?" Andy asked and then added: "Yes I'll hold thank you." There was silence for a couple of minutes.

"Hello – DI Lawler here – who is calling? Over" DI Lawler appeared to be shouting over traffic noise at the other end.

"Hello Harry – it's Andy! Just to see how you got on with Mrs P?" Andy was also shouting as he was not sure if he could be heard.

"Bloody hell Andy – you almost burst my eardrum! It is only me who has to shout above the noise of traffic! Anyway, she would not listen to me regarding warnings about her health. She suddenly came downstairs about two o'clock and announced she was going up to the London offices. Nothing could stop her, she just went away in the car - said she was going to catch a train at Weybridge station." DI Lawler's voice suddenly disappeared from the line.

"Hello? Hello?" Andy shouted angrily and shook the phone, as if that would help, and added; "Bloody walkie-talkies, useless bloody things - always cutting out. These are the bloody things they want us to use."

"They lose the signal as you walk or drive around Andy. Sometimes the battery runs flat" I tried to explain.

"They should rename them walkies - 'no' talkies, then shouldn't they?" Andy retorted and slammed the phone down, then lifted it back up and redialled zero.

"Hello there." Andy replied coolly, before a pause, then replied; – "Yes we did get DI Lawler for a whole minute before he got cut off in his prime." Andy replied sarcastically, then added; "No – no point. I need to be put through to Palmers Associates of Bethnal Green please and ask to speak to Mrs Palmer." Another short pause while he listened, then Andy added; "Yes I will hold on thank you."

"Hello - to whom am I speaking?" Mrs P asked in a very cool manner.

"This is Detective Inspector Spearing Mam – I spoke to you this morning?" DI Spearing sounded calm.

"Yes, I remember Spearing. – How could I possibly forget? I also remember saying I would not speak to you again other than with my solicitor present." Mrs P retorted with a hard tone in her voice.

"As I said to you this morning Mam that is your prerogative. Now would you like to come with your solicitor to the station, or would you prefer that we come to your offices?" Andy sounded nonchalant.

"What do you mean? Why do you want me?" --- Mrs P sounded quite shocked.

"Well Mam I stupidly thought you may be interested in finding out how we were getting on with the hunt for your husband's killer. – You know the one that got murdered this morning?" Andy answered quietly and sarcastically before being interrupted.

"There is no need for that kind of talk Spearing, especially with Mrs Palmer's present state of mind. Now why do want to interview Mrs Palmer?" A man's voice came over - they were obviously talking into an intercom.

"Well now to whom am I speaking?" Andy stayed very calm and collected.

"My name is John Jacobs; I am acting as Mrs Palmer's solicitor in the absence of her own solicitor Mr Aldrich - the disappearance of whom I believe you know something?" Jacobs voice had a slightly foreign accent, but with excellent English.

"I see Mr Jacobs. Just to let you know, Mr Aldrich has not 'disappeared,' he and two of Mrs Palmer's minders – Cosgrove and Smith - are in fact helping the police with inquires into the murders of Mr Palmer and Mr Marks this morning. That is the reason why we need to interview Mrs Palmer again." Andy replied precisely.

There came a muffled cry of; "Oh" which sounded like Mrs P. Then silence, as though the line was dead.

"Hello DI Spearing – Where are these three persons that you mentioned being held?" Jacob asked.

"Actually, Mr Jacobs we cannot release that information now. They are in London Mr Jacobs and, as I say, all three are at present helping police with the murders enquiry within the twenty-four-hour period which is allowed under the law. We will be charging them tomorrow morning with several offences and will then be releasing information in the afternoon as to which prison they have been sent."

"Oh" Jacobs responded before adding; "I am afraid Mrs Palmer is unavailable and not well enough to be interviewed at present."

"I am afraid either Mrs Palmer agrees to answer my very urgent questions tonight, at New Scotland Yard, or at Palmers Associates offices, or like the other three she will be arrested and charged." Andy replied, with an edge to his voice.

"Charged with what Spearing?" Jacobs asked with a slight suggestion of astonishment in his voice.

"That will depend on her answers, or lack of answers, to my questions Mr Jacobs." Andy replied simply and to the point before adding; "In any case Mrs P was well enough to travel up to London this afternoon – was she not Mr Jacobs?"

"Can you hold on for a minute DI Spearing while I discuss this with my client?" Jacobs asked.

"Certainly, Mr Jacobs, but I must make you both aware that if we arrange it and we come over to Palmers Associates this evening and Mrs Palmer is not there, then we will put out a warrant for her arrest. Alternatively, if she decides to come in to New Scotland Yard and does not appear we will also put out a warrant for her arrest. Is that clearly understood Mr Jacobs?" Andy replied again, making the position very clear. Andy was building up the pressure.

"Yes, that it is now understood DI Spearing. Can you hold please?" Jacobs replied as his voice disappeared.

There was silence for a couple of minutes.

"Hello DI Spearing" Jacobs voice again, then he added; "We would prefer it if you come here. At what time shall we say?"

"Shall we say seven forty-five at the Palmers offices? Is that OK?" Andy replied.

"Why so late Spearing? Mrs Palmer would like to be off as early as possible as I am sure you will realize it has been a long, horrible day for her and her family." Jacobs replied with a sneer in his voice.

"I am sure you realize Mr Jacobs that we too have had a long day and are currently taking statements and have still to go back to the office to review the files and ledgers from today after interviewing Mrs Palmer." Andy replied with just a hint of a threat.

"Oh, very well Spearing. Just make sure you are here on time!" Jacobs replied as he hung up.

"Up yours too!" DI Spearing said before he hung-up.

"Why did you have to do that Andy?" I asked.

"We have to keep them all on the wrong foot Kevin, at least until we know they are not involved in the murders. Still I am going to try to charge them with anything I can catch them because – I will break up this firm right now if I can. – There will not be another chance for the next few years!" Andy was back on the ball.

Andy reversed the tape recorders back to Smiths interview and began to draft out Smiths statement with a pencil on a blank sheet of paper. This was quickly followed by Cosgrove's. They both included a signature box for both with a date and an independent witness signature box with PC Atkinson's name, job title and a date.

"Okay Kevin - if you can go through to Room 1, behind the reception desk, there is a golf ball typewriter in there. If you can get these two statements typed out and get the two plonkers to sign them off, by that time I will have a summary of the Aldrich responses to our questions. He will not sign it, so you can type it out in the morning in the office. We must not hand the tape over, only a copy of the signed statements and a copy of the summary on paper, so you take the tape and stash it with the typed originals in your flat. Make sure you get a copy of the signed statements and the Aldridge summary.".

"Okay Andy. Why so much caution?" I replied.

"Believe me Kevin. There are so many in the office who will be only too glad to get rid of any evidence. They are paid to get rid of things!" Andy replied, almost without thinking about it.

"Yeah okay Andy I will be off and get started." I replied and left the room and went direct to Room 1. Within forty minutes I had typed both pages and copied them and got both signed by Smith and Cosgrove and I had PC Atkinson witness the signatures and dated the statements.

A few minutes later Andy returned with a draft summary of the Aldrich interview summary and had a quick look at the signed statements. I had two copies of each.

"Well done lad – Now go find Sergeant Tommy through in the back room and then we can go catch Mrs Palmer and see what we can get from her, despite the solicitor. Then you can take the copies in tomorrow morning – we will deliver them to young Judith Clements to agree the charges." Andy said it all as a matter of fact.

"I can type the Aldrich statement at home tonight, so we can catch Judith Clements first thing - about eight in the morning? - Before we go to the DCI? - That way we will know where we stand before we go in? – That is if you can possibly make it in that early Andy?" I asked with a slight smile.

"Good thinking Robin." Andy replied with a passable imitation of Batman and added; "If you don't mind doing that. By the way – if I must get up at four, I can if I need to, so I do not need your little snide remarks Sergeant! I will phone Miss Clements tonight and set-up a meeting at eight fifteen – okay?" Andy said it with a smile.

I nodded and quickly walked through to the back rooms and duly found Sergeant Tommy chatting to another two sergeants.

"Sergeant Thomson - Looks like we are off to Bethnal Green. Handy Andy wants to talk to Mrs Palmer again!" I shouted across the room.

"Bloody hell - now?" It has been a long day already. I hope Andy is going to sign the overtime authorisation." Sergeant Tommy pretended annoyance and added; "Old Andy is like a bulldog with a bone. – He just won't let it go!" Sergeant Tommy shouted in reply, shook his head and laughed.

"Yeah and he is barking mad – ready to go" I replied with a laugh, and all the other three joined in. Sergeant Tommy and I came out while Andy was talking to Sergeant Willie.

"Willie just you remember! Make sure your 'wooden tops' understand! – We don't want anyone of the three making calls, or talking to each other, at any time tonight, or in the morning, or on the way to prison. I will make sure the prison keeps them separate as well." Andy said with a certain amount of threat in his voice and added; "At least I will make sure the prison keeps them separate, or preferably they go to separate prisons."

"This is not New Scotland Yard here Andy. I don't know for sure, but I don't think any of us are on the gang's payroll, but irrespective, I will personally make sure they will make no calls out of here tonight or tomorrow and they will all be brought to prison separately." Sergeant Willie replied earnestly.

"Thanks Willie – Tommy is just going over to pick up the car and then we will get the files and stuff out. Why don't you retire and get the hell out of this lot Willie?" Andy asked.

Sergeant Tommy disappeared out the door heading across the street to Sussex Gardens where he had left the Jaguar.

"Same as you Andy – It's in my blood I am still trying to catch the bastards!"

Sergeant Willie replied and added; "Futile task though."

"We managed to get some today Willie. So, don't give up just yet, despite your great age!" Andy replied with his sly little smile.

"Time, you lot went home and slept it off. You are still dreaming if you think you can put them to bed! Then again Andy, you always were a good dreamer!" Sergeant Willie dismissed us with a wave of the hand and a smile.

"It might not be much but we have caught some of them this time Willie. So, cheer up you miserable sod!" Andy gave him his big knowing grin.

"Well, just let us see how it turns out first Andy eh?" Sergeant Willie replied cynically with a smile.

Sergeant Tommy re-appeared a few minutes later and we loaded the Jaguar with the files and leftover ledgers and, seven fifteen, we set off for Bethnal Green and with the heavy rush hour traffic it took about thirty minutes until we rolled up outside Palmers Associate offices.

Andy and I went into the reception area and were greeted by two heavies, aged about thirty, dressed in open necked blue and pink T shirts both stretched very tight across their torsos to show off their muscles to best effect. They each had on the same tan coloured trousers, which were also stretched tight across their very big thighs and they wore dark brown leather shoes. They were both around six feet with the muscles protruding in their thick set necks and both had sandy brown hair swept back like the rockers.

As they walked towards us they looked like they could be twins, but weight lifters. It is that peculiar way all weight lifters strut as they sort of flex their muscles to impress while walking on the balls of their feet.

"What do you want?" Heavy number one asked in as gruff a voice as he could muster.

"I am Detective Inspector Spearing and this is Detective Sergeant Devlin. We are from New Scotland Yard and have an appointment with Mrs Palmer." Andy politely replied with a smile and went to his inside jacket pocket.

Heavy number one grabbed Andys arm with a vice like grip stopping him from getting to his pocket.

"Now lad, take your hand off me before I have to charge with assaulting the police and perverting the police in the course of their duty. That carries a hefty sentence even if you do not have any previous, which I doubt!" Andy said with a very cool and detached voice as they both stared at each other.

Finally, heavy number one let go and Andy went ahead produced his identity disc and I produced mine waving it at the two of them.

"We are going to have to search you before you can go up." Heavy number one again, with the same gruff voice, obviously, the spokesman.

"Afraid that is not going to happen lad! You have seen our identity discs and you know we are the police. So, get on your blower over there like a good lad and let your mistress know we have arrived." Andy said calmly.

"Afraid we cannot allow that sir. We have had two murders in this family already today and we aint going to allow another one during our watch!" Heavy number one replied again, this time a little more polite in voice and unsure.

"Lad, I am the Detective Inspector investigating those murders. I will only say this once more! – get on the blower over there and let your mistress know we are here. Otherwise, as I say, you two will be joining Mrs Palmer's other two minders in jail tonight on charges of perverting the course of justice, assault and obstructing the police. So, lad - what is it to be?" Andy just smiled as he spoke the direct challenge.

They both just stood there staring at us trying to convince us they were serious hard men.

"Okay Ralph – Get Mrs Palmer on the phone and ask her if she wants us to throw this pair out. They do not have a search warrant." Heavy number one replied with his gruff voice, while still swopping eyeballs with Andy who simply smiled, but did not avert his eyes.

"Rather fetching pink tops the lads are wearing today - don't you think Sergeant?" Andy laughed as he said it, but never averted his eye contact.

Heavy number one grimaced, his face showing anger and turning red.

"Yes sir. Rather nice, if you are into that sort of thing. Myself I like more manly colours!" I replied with a little laugh.

"Shut it Glasgow or I will shut it for you." Heavy number one was now getting visibly, and sounding, upset.

"I would not advise you to try that 'pinky'. Your blood will go all over your nice pink shirt and blot out the blue all together." I replied as I set myself expecting a head charge.

"She says for me to bring them up Bobby." Heavy number two shouted as he walked back to join us.

"Okay Ralph – you take them up" Heavy number one now known as Bobby replied and added; "I will take care of you later Glasgow." The tone of his voice suggested a bit of simpleton in there somewhere under the muscled body.

"I would not advise it my friend!" Andy said and added; "I just watched him taking two really hard Irish travellers out this afternoon and both were broken. You my friend would be in pieces. Besides you will find yourself in jail for a few years for attempting to assault a policeman!"

We went to the lift which was an open Victorian style and which just managed to accommodate the three of us to the top third floor with lots of jerks on the way up.

"Sorry about Bobby down there. Afraid he gets carried away with himself, he thinks his strength will carry him through, but that only happens if it is somebody who doesn't know what they are doing. He doesn't have the sense to know when to back off." Ralph the heavy number two apologized in the lift.

"You would think he would at least have the sense to back off when it is the police?" I replied quietly.

"No chance - he has had any sense beaten out of him by the pros he has run into - like a brick wall." Ralph replied with a faint smile.

I had to say; "You take care of him then?" I replied.

"Yeah usually, that is if I am around. I'll have to take you along to Mrs Pearson as she did not answer the phone. I just pretended she had answered to get you out of there before you flattened him and then arrested him!" Ralph said it with a shrug of his shoulders.

Andy broke into the conversation and said; "Good lad! Just you make sure he does not go looking for the Sergeant here. I meant it - you will be picking him up from the hospital and with a charge sheet attached to one of the pieces."

"I cannot guarantee anything with the state of his head. But I know the score, so I can only try." Ralph replied with a shake of his head.

We got off the bone shaker of a lift on the third floor and Ralph showed us to John Palmer's office. There was no reply to his knock on the door, so he turned away and walked further down the corridor.

"She is probably in the boardroom with that solicitor guy." Ralph simply stated.

Ralph showed us to the boardroom, knocked the door and we heard a male voice shout; "Come in." There was a huge antique oval oak table and twelve matching oak antique chairs. There was a Phillips tape recorder in the centre of the table and alongside an IBM Golf Ball Typewriter with single A4 sheets of paper lying by its side. On a small table in the corner was another smaller oak antique table with a coffee machine on top with china cups and saucers, and alongside it was a Flip Flop Chart mounted on an easel with pens on a ledge. On the opposite side of the table sat Mrs Palmer and a man whom we both assumed to be Mr Jacobs the 'new' solicitor.

"Come in Spearing - and this must be Sergeant Devlin I assume?" Jacobs asked in a much too friendly way, with a nod towards me, and signalled for us to sit opposite with our backs to the door which we did.

"Correct! - Mrs Palmer - Mam." Andy replied almost in a reverent manner with a nod, he ignored Jacobs. It was then I noticed the tape recorder was running.

"DI Spearing!" Mrs Palmer acknowledged with a humble note in her voice.

"Can we get straight to business Mam? Andy asked without hesitation.

"Well yes of course, as long as Mr Jacobs is present." Mrs Palmer replied with some hesitation.

Andy ignored the response and then handed me his notepad and asked me to take notes of the interview adding; "I assume you don't have any objection to Sergeant Devlin here taking notes of this interview?"

"No, not at all, as you see we have a tape recorder switched on." Jacobs replied with a show of confidence.

Andy then asked me for my notebook and read from it and stated; "Mam - this morning at your home, during our first interview, you said at first that your two minders - Smith and Cosgrove by name - had basically fled the murder scene at your home. Then, when we pointed out that both minders claimed you had sent them to these offices to remove the files etc. you stated, due to the awful circumstances, which I agreed is understandable, you had been confused and you confirmed you had indeed sent both to these offices. Is that correct Mam?" Andy looked directly at Mrs P.

"You don't have to answer that question if you don't want to Mrs Palmer." Jacobs placed his hand in a comforting way on Mrs Palmer's right forearm.

"Mr Jacobs – as I am sure you are aware. That was not a question. It was simply a request for confirmation of previously recorded statements, which Mrs Palmer has already made and any cooperative witness would be expected to confirm?" Andy sounded angry and looked directly at Jacobs.

"It may be DI Spearing that, as you say, due to confusion in these awful circumstances, Mrs Palmer may have by now remembered other relevant points." Jacobs replied rather too smugly.

"That may be so Mr Jacobs and I am sure you will ensure we cover those points. However, at this stage we are simply asking Mrs Palmer to confirm one of her statements we recorded this morning?" Andy spoke sharply.

"Oh, for goodness sake! Yes! I did make that statement. Now can we get on with it please?" Mrs P said with exasperation.

"Mrs Palmer you asked me to be here to advise and---" Jacobs angrily spat out, but immediately closed his mouth when Mrs P angrily waved her hand in an act of dismissal.

"Thank you, Mam. Now you also stated that you never ordered them, or your solicitor, to remove any files or ledgers from these offices. Is that correct Mam?" Andy was speaking patiently.

"Yes absolutely!" Mrs P replied instantly which drew a look of disapproval from Jacobs.

"Well Mam, can you explain why Smith and Cosgrove have both signed statements that they were ordered by your solicitor to remove the files and ledgers before the police arrived to seize them as possible evidence in the murder of your husband and the minder?" Andy S asked.

"Ah, but has Aldrich the solicitor signed a statement?" Mr Jacobs interrupted with a slight smile.

"Mr Jacobs please understand!" DI Spearing was now slightly irritated and added; "You should and do know the rules of solicitors being present. The police ask the person being interviewed questions and the person either answers the questions, or consults with their solicitor before answering the question. The solicitor does not answer the question with another question before the person answers, or consults with their solicitor on the question. Is that clearly understood?"

"I take that as a 'No' then shall I?" Jacobs replied with a smirk.

"Mr Jacobs, I will not repeat myself. You must understand I am trying to allow Mrs Palmer every chance to explain, or clarify, her actions this morning, before she faces possible charges." Andy said curtly.

"Charges? What possible charges?" Jacobs asked haughtily.

"Well - let us start with perverting the course of justice, shall we? Also, how about obstructing the police in the course of their duty? Other charges may follow if we do not obtain satisfactory replies to our questions. Is that clearly understood Mrs Palmer?"

"I wish to consult with my client privately please." Jacobs said it quietly.

"Certainly, Mr Jacobs. We will wait in the corridor. Just come out and let us know when you are ready to continue." Andy replied and rose from the chair while signalling to me to leave. We went out and I closed the door behind us.

After we got out of the boardroom I asked quietly; "How do you think it is going Andy?"

"Better than I expected!" Andy replied equally quietly and added; "Unless I can draw the statement that she did not order the solicitor to remove any files, then we will find it very hard to stick anything on her. But anyway, that will give us Aldrich on a plate!"

"What do you think about her now Andy – I mean for hiring 'The Fox?'"

"I don't think we have anything more on her. Like I said the last time Kevin, I just don't know! She is a very cool customer indeed. You know it is a fact that, in most family murders, either the husband or the wife turn out to be the murderer or behind it. The only difference with this case is the gangland thing, and the fact that she was on the premises when the murder was carried out, which would be a very stupid thing to do - and she is not stupid. However, she is guilty of perverting the course of justice and obstruction so I will try and nail her for that if I can." Andy replied very clearly and precisely.

The door to the boardroom opened and Jacobs appeared and said; "We are ready now." He turned away and went back into the room followed by us.

We all settled back into the same chairs around the oval antique table.

"DI Spearing, I have to advise you that Mrs Palmer has taken my advice and she is not prepared to answer any more questions at this stage. However, she is willing to make a prepared statement." Jacobs appeared to again be very smug.

"Sorry Mr Jacobs she can make a statement after we have finished our questions. to date Mrs P has not been charged with anything so there is no need to make a signed statement!"

"Okay Spearing – You ask your questions and Mrs Palmer and I will consult before answering!"

"We can see how it goes, but Mr Jacobs you cannot advise her on what to reply."

Mrs P suddenly exploded: "For goodness sake! Can we just get on with it! I am happy to answer your questions.

Mr Jacobs looked amazed and could only shake his head as he hesitated before lifting an A4 size paper and saying; "I will read out Mrs Palmers prepared statement and perhaps this will answer your questions. The statement is very short and to the point. He continued; "'Mrs Palmer totally denies ordering anyone to remove any files or ledgers from Palmers Associates offices. She only authorized her former solicitor Mr Aldrich and her two minders, Smith and Cosgrove, to get them out ready for her to review later today. She also denies any involvement in the murder of her husband earlier today. That is the end of Mrs Palmer statement. He passed the statement to Andy.

Andy read the statement and handed it to me and asked; "Could you type it out Sergeant and put a line for signing by Mrs Palmer and Mr Jacobs signing with dates? – Mr Jacobs could you give DS Devlin your business card for your company name and address?"

I replied; "Yes Sir" and collected the card from Jacobs and the statement from Andy and walked over to the typewriter.

Andy smiled and politely said; "I am afraid that leads us to a few more questions for Mrs Palmer! First, can you tell us why within a few hours of your husbands' death you felt the need to travel up to London to review these particular files?"

Mrs P thinly smiled and replied; "They were very important files for the future of this company!

"This was even though your children who had just lost their Dad needed you with them?"

"My children were safe with their Grandfather. Besides I had to ensure the staff was informed and the place was made secure"

"I see, but it is very strange under the circumstances you felt it necessary to come all that way when you could have called your manager to inform your staff and ensure the offices were secure?"

"I wanted to take care of it personally and I was still confused!"

"Not so confused Mrs Palmer that you did know the exact files to take out and you stated this morning that you had not been working for the company for years?"

"Those company account files do not change over the last twenty years Detective!"

"Okay! – You wanted to take care of it personally - so how come this morning you admitted that you sent your minders and Mr Aldrich to get the files ready for your review?"

"I was trying to save time when I got here so as I could get back to the kids!"

"The kids who you just said were safe with their grandfather? Anyway, can you know explain why Mr Aldrich - your solicitor - said you asked him to remove the files?"

"I cannot explain Mr Aldrich actions! All I can say is; I asked him to organise the files for me to review!"

Andy looked and sounded very serious as he said; "Mrs Palmer - I would like to record my warning to you this morning which you may recall was this" Andy paused for effect, staring intently at Mrs P for any response, got none, then continued; "Assuming you are not involved in any way with the double murders this morning and in the disappearance of Mr Joseph Bolger, then we must assume that, whoever hired this assassin are very dangerous and desperate people. As I advised you this morning, by taking over the company, you could be placing yourself, and your young family, in a very grave position. Just as long as you clearly understand what you are doing Mam." Andy finished with a nod of the head.

Mrs P simply nodded her head in response, but did look visibly shaken.

"Do you have your company stamp with you Mr Jacobs to sign as the witness?" I asked without looking up from the typewriter.

"Yes, I have Sergeant." Jacobs replied, leaning below the table he brought up a rather battered brown leather briefcase from which he produced a large red stamp and an ink pad. He pushed the stamp into the ink pad.

I finished the statement and passed it to Mrs P and said; "If you could please read it Mam and, if you agree with it, pass it onto Mr Jacobs to review and agree before both of you sign it."

Mrs P read the statement, nodded her head and passed it to Jacobs who read it nodded his head and passed it back to her.

"I would appreciate it if you could put in today's date and your full home address Mam and then pass it to Mr Jacobs." I said it as a matter of routine.

Mrs P did as she was told and passed it to Jacobs who stamped it, signed and dated it and passed it back to me. I ensured it had been signed correctly folded it and put it in my inside jacket pocket before returning to my original seat.

Andy had a slight smile on his face as he said; "Tell me Mam - where will you be for the next two days?"

"Why?" Mrs P asked, as though startled by the question.

"Well Mam, we are investigating your husband's murder and we may have a response on your company's books and files. Also, as I said earlier, we are concerned about your safety."

"When will I get the books and files back?" Mrs P asked ignoring Andys' question before adding; "I have a business to run here you know with people who are depending on the company for their livelihood."

"I do understand Mam, I really do, but these books and files have to be read and understood by the police investigating teams for any incriminating evidence connected with the two murders. They will also be required for the trials of Smith, Cosgrove and your solicitor Mr Aldrich!" Andy replied evenly and politely.

"You are charging John Aldrich?" Jacobs asked in astonishment.

"I cannot confirm that until tomorrow when we will be consulting our legal experts, but I would say, at this stage, it is highly likely to happen." Andy was as smooth as silk in his reply.

Mrs P and Jacobs exchanged confused, or was it fearful glances?

"Now Mam you must excuse us - we still have a few hours work to do before we get off home!"

Andy rose as he said it, but it was noticeable that both Mrs P and Jacobs looked stunned.

We left quickly and walked downstairs, rather than using the bone shaking lift, with a subdued Ralph for company, and quickly exited without talking to Bobby the number one heavy.

Andy suddenly said; "That is what I call a good result – still work to do tomorrow with Aldrich, but I think we have them all. If you like lad, Sergeant Tommy can drop you off at Paddington tube station and you can get off home. You still have that typing to do on the Aldrich interview - you have had a long day. Tommy and I will drop the ledgers and files under your desk for you to pass to 'Hooray' Nigel, as you like to call him, in the morning.

"Why yes, thank you Andy. I am rather tired and need to catch up." I replied quietly and thankfully.

"Again, that was good work today Sergeant. Oh by the way the next time you read my files, at least acknowledge my theories in your analysis. Perhaps you are not so much a genius as we all thought today – Eh?" Andy poked me in the ribs.

"Oh! Now I am already downgraded to just very good. Still I am not too bad for a 'Trained Bairn' – Eh Andy?" I responded with a laugh, but could feel my face going red for the first time in years.

"You have a quick silver tongue Kevin! I will say that for you." Andy replied with good humour in his voice.

So, ended my very first, full, long hard day at work with NSY.

As I made my way on the Metropolitan line to Kings Cross and swapped onto the overland line to Palmers Green I suddenly realized how weary I was. I also realized then that my whole preconception of DI Andy Spearing had been turned on its head. I had actually finished up liking and admiring the guy and was now looking forward to working with him.

Sometimes things have very strange beginnings and even stranger ends.

Book 1 in the DI Spearing and DS Devlin series

Chapter 10 - Judith Clements

Judith Clements arrived on Wednesday morning about seven fifteen, dressed in a black Marks and Sparks conservative woman's business suit which had a nice jacket tight-fitting at the waist which enhanced her tidy figure. She also wore a white T shirt showing underneath and shiny black high heel shoes. She still wore her hair in the same tight bun as on Monday.

She picked up a plastic cup of putrid coffee from the machine on the tenth floor of New Scotland Yard and walked diagonally across the open-plan office to her own office arriving at seven-twenty in the morning. Perhaps 'office' was an exaggeration as it was no more than the size of a large storage cupboard, about nine by nine feet, with three solid partition walls and a fourth solid partition containing a solid wooden door, the top half double glazed with clear glass. On the glass, someone had written in black ink with fancy lettering, 'Judith Clements' and under her name in plain bold capitals 'DPP REP.'

Inside, she had a metal desk with two deep drawers on both sides and a soft plastic imitation leather brown swivel chair with two arms. There was an old fashioned black BT telephone, an A4 lined pad with a biro pen and 'in and out' trays were the only items on top of the desk.

There was a metal, four-drawer, grey filing cabinet with a security bar latched on running the length of the cabinet. There was a combination padlock on top going through a metal loop on the top of the cabinet and through the metal bar which was also lodged into a socket at the bottom of the cabinet.

Opposite her chair were two hard, plastic, grey chairs for visitors.

The office 'furnishings' were completed by a small rotating fan situated on the top of the filing cabinet, which she had delivered by the office maintenance people yesterday when she had almost fainted from heat exhaustion. They had thoughtfully placed 'the black hole of Calcutta office' under an air conditioning outlet, but like most British offices, the AC did not really work. It simply circulated foul hot air and germs from around the floor. The fan did little more; unless you stood in front of it you could sometimes get a whiff of slightly cooler air. Today was forecast to be just as warm as yesterday, so Judith made up her mind to move into the main office, which was slightly more bearable, as soon as her only scheduled meeting with DI Spearing and DS Devlin was over.

Judith was in a reflective mood as she sat down in her chair and sipped the putrid stuff that was labelled as coffee.

Judith knew only too well that she had been moulded by her Mum and Dad to be a solicitor almost from the day she was born in nineteen forty-one. Both parents were solicitors and had a joint practice at Clements Solicitors in Bridge Street in the centre of the then market town of Northampton.

Her Dad carried out all the conveyancing work, which due to the house buying boom of the fifties and sixties in Britain, was very busy and highly profitable. Mum handled the divorces side and especially with more and more women wanting a taste of freedom in booming changing Britain of the fifties and sixties, her side of the business was also extraordinarily busy and profitable.

Judith could never remember being allowed to play child games, or do girly things. She was almost always with adults, even in her primary schooldays at Wooton Primary School in Northampton, it was straight back home and into books – always homework, or law books and then discussions with adults. Her parents lived in a large Edwardian house just around the corner from the The Yeoman of England pub in the village of Wooton in Northamptonshire.

In fact, she could always remember her Dad taking great pride in saying to people, when she was eight that she thought and acted like a twenty-year old. Then, when she was eighteen, he said she thought and acted like a thirty-five-year-old.

She had gone to a private girl's school from age ten out by Pitsford in the Northamptonshire countryside, but did not live in. She had been dropped off and picked up by Mum every day so the mould was very difficult to break.

She remembered it was when she went up to Cambridge University, to read Law, at age eighteen that she finally got the opportunity to break out of the mould. She only broke out to some extent, because she found it very hard having been so used to doing what was expected of her.

Her first act of defiance she remembered was selecting criminal law to study. Then her Mum and Dad finally accepted the idea, saying the firm could be expanded to include a criminal law section. There was always the assumption that she would come back to Northampton and join the family firm.

The Cambridge University Law Courses are quite notorious for the amount of reading involved. Of course, this came as second nature to Judith who had been reading and basically understanding Law books since she was seven years old and having discussions with her parents on the contents. It was no surprise when she sailed through the first year and was way out, head and shoulders, above the rest of the class.

Then at nineteen she met her first boyfriend, David Kencroft, a fellow nineteen-year-old student reading Engineering, Economics and Management and, with him, she had her first meaningful kiss. It brought on the sexual urges which she did not know anything about and so in character she began reading books on the subject including Sigmund Freud's 'Three essays on the theory of sexuality' and D. H. Lawrence's 'Lady Chatterley's Lover.' She read enough other snippets of information in the library to realize that she did not want to have unprotected sex, or children, which in the early sixties meant forcing the man to wear a condom, then commonly known as French Letters, or FL's for short. Men were expected to buy them in a chemist, but many found it too embarrassing to ask the young ladies serving in the chemist. The other source was usually the local gent's hairdressers who usually discreetly handed them over in packs of three with a nod and wink, but charged far more than the chemist.

Judith smiled to herself as she remembered her first attempts at sex with David Kencroft who was as equally naïve in sexual matters as she was, she remembered thinking at the time, at least she had read about it.

They finally fumbled their way through taking of each other's clothes started by sitting on the floral settee in her small Cambridge flat, in the dark, before they realized they would have to stand up and needed some light on the subject.

When she finally stood there naked in front of a man for the first time, in the light, she remembered how embarrassed she felt. She was not embarrassed with her body, because she knew she had a fine young teenage body with firm breasts and buttocks, all well- proportioned and a pretty good looking face, perhaps not a rare beauty, but nice on the eye. It was an embarrassment that she still had to this day, although she had only been seen naked by three men to date.

She then remembered the comedy of that first time with David and smiled again. She had insisted he had to buy and put on the FL, but he did not know enough to realize there were different sizes. When his penis was erected she remembered thinking he was quite large and then he fumbled to pull on the condom. The problem was they were too small and when he finally managed to stretch them across his penis they practically strangled the blood and it went bright red and very painful looking as it puffed up. He squealed in pain and tore at the thing to get it off. They both laughed nervously.

So, it became a heavy petting session, but Judith remembered refusing to let him touch her vagina, not minding him touching her breasts and kissing. She finally relented and masturbated him which was the first time she had ever touched a man. He came like a torrent within two minutes of starting, ejaculating all over her breasts. So, ended the first sexual experience, but it was another step in her new found freedom. They got dressed quickly and he almost ran out of the flat, seemingly embarrassed, leaving her feeling sore with frustration.

She did not see him again for couple of weeks and there was awkwardness between them when they finally met, but finally he apologized for his naivety on that first occasion, which she thought was very nice of him and they arranged another meeting at her flat.

This time they both had a better idea what was expected of them and there was not so much fumbling, and they were quickly stripped naked and he had the right size of FL's. The fumbling then started when he tried to enter her vagina to find it, as would be expected with a virgin, to be very tight especially with his fully erected rather large penis and he had no idea how to get it in. Finally, she grabbed his penis, opened her legs wider and gently put it in. He immediately plunged the full length in and started humping. She screamed in agony. He almost jumped out of his skin and did jump out of her landing on the floor in front of the settee.

"Jesus what is the matter?" David asked in astonishment.

"You almost ripped me apart David. I am a virgin you know you cannot just dive straight in. It has to be gentle?" Judith answered with the pain showing in her face.

"Oh, shit Judy – I didn't know – I am sorry! I will stop if you want me to." David's voice was emotional and he sounded genuinely scared.

"No David I want to do it tonight. But you have got to be gentle. You must go slowly and don't plunge everything in, just a little at a time. Do you understand?" Judith asked.

"Yeah – Yeah I understand – just let me know if it hurts and I will take it easier." David was obviously sympathetic and concerned.

"Okay David get it up then." Judith replied with a gentle smile. She had to again put it in for him, but before she could she noticed that it had gone soft so she played with it for a minute before it went hard again and she then put it in. This time he did put it in very slowly and gently and only a little at a time. She began moaning with delight and he stopped, saying; "Are you alright Judy?" Judith remembered saying in reply "Yes David, please oh please just keep on going." Suddenly she felt him coming with a loud exclamation of "Oh my God and a repeat of "Oh my God." Judith grabbed his buttocks and pulled him in saying: "Keep going David, oh please keep going."

David kept going until he heard a guttural sound coming from Judith and her body rose from the settee and she forced him in all the way with a cry of "Fuck me – Fuck me" as she climaxed for the very first time and she dug her nails into his buttocks until he let out a scream. They both collapsed, he on top of her and he shuddered as though he had come again. She had never forgotten the absolute bliss and the pain of that first climax.

Judith smiled as she recalled that night when she lost her virginity.

Suddenly she was brought out of her sexy thoughts by a knock on the door. A good-looking man in his mid-thirties with blondish hair and dressed in an expensive looking gray suit. He wore a brilliantly white shirt and gray tie which matched the colour of his suit.

"A penny for your thoughts!" He said with a nice smile and added "Are you available for a meeting?"

Judith's face coloured red before she answered "Afraid not – I have a meeting scheduled with DI Spearing and DS Devlin very shortly."

"Lucky old you – what did you do wrong to have that pleasure?" He asked still smiling.

"I dare say I will find out very shortly. I should be free at nine, if that is any good?" Judith replied with a smile.

"Nice one – that will do – see you then!" He replied.

"What is your name for my appointments calendar?" Judith asked flashing her best smile.

"Tony – Tony Booth!" He replied with another of his flashing smiles.

"Fine Tony – I will see you at nine." Judith replied giving him a smile back, the redness in her face now almost gone as Tony turned away with a friendly wave of the hand.

Judith returned to her sipping the awful coffee and her retrospective thoughts, again remembering with so much fondness that first climax with David Kencroft. She remembered finally feeling the complete woman, no longer the naïve girl, but a woman in control of her own sexual destiny. Unfortunately, that first night of climaxes was never repeated with David. After that it became the usual 'wham bam, thank you Mam' and their relationship soon petered out. She never felt any bitterness towards David, in fact, she still somehow felt grateful to him for getting her through that first awkward time.

She never felt she wanted to live with anyone; she was absolutely at peace with herself and her own company. She hated the thought of marriage and preferred the occasional night with a nice man, a good meal, a couple of glasses of wine and if she felt like it afterwards, a night of sex. She felt very much a sixties girl.

Then only a few weeks later came the sudden, life changing experience that Friday night in Cambridge – the night she went to the party in a student's rented house in Mill Road. The party was organised by Sally Thomson, her friend from her days at Northampton Pitsford school. Like everyone else at the party Judith had a few more wines than normal, and, feeling a bit drunk, she went for a lie down and fell asleep fully clothed in the spare room.

A few minutes later a totally pissed Robert Lindsay, a fellow law student on the same degree course, but three years ahead, staggered into the room swigging straight from a bottle of cheap red wine. He saw Judith on the bed sleeping and mumbled: "I have always fancied you darling Judith" and threw himself on top of her. He immediately pushed his hands up her skirt getting hold of her panties and tried to pull them down, only to find they were those, popular at the time, paper panties and they simply ripped off. Judith immediately awoke with a start and drunkenly shouted; "What the hell!" and then felt Lindsay press down on her pulling her legs apart and putting his penis in her. Judith tried to push him off but he was a big six-foot lad with solid muscle. He started humping her and she started to scream but he put his hand over her mouth stifling the noise. She then scraped at his face with her long nails.

"You bitch" Lindsay shouted and added; "I know you like it - David told me" and he continued humping.

Judith managed to move her mouth and managed to say quietly, with real hate; "Yes, but he was a real man with a decent size prick and he didn't have to rape me."

Lindsay suddenly stopped humping, his eyes glazed over and he started to come off her mumbling; "Rape? Oh, my God I am sorry Judith – I am drunk, I, didn't realize what I was doing!" There were tears in his pleading eyes and he added; "Please Judith! This will ruin me and I haven't even started out yet! Please Judith?" Lindsay was now crying as he zipped up his trousers.

"Get out of here you pathetic bastard!" Judith shouted at him through her own tears and pointed at the door. He jumped off the bed as Judith pulled down her dress. He turned away and staggered towards the bedroom door, but what Judith did not see was the little evil smile as he drunkenly staggered out.

Judith remembered Lindsay was a good-looking guy but a very cold person and even then was full of ambition and, as it turned out, he was now fulfilling that ambition nearby in London.

For several months afterwards she went to a shrink who, among other things, advised her to shop Lindsay, but as no harm had been done, except to her head, she decided to let it go.

Judith could not face another man throughout the rest of her university years. Then when she came to London she met Paul Casey, a thirty-year-old who thought of himself as a sophisticated man about town. He loved the sixties scene in 'swinging' London. In effect Paul turned out to be pretence, a hanger on, always trying to get in with one sixties 'in-crowd' or another, spending lots of money he didn't have and generally sponging of anyone he could, including Judith. It lasted as a friendship only on the occasional evening basis for about two years, but she had not seen him now for the past year and did not care if she never saw him again.

In fact, since then, Judith had been happy to go out with girlfriends for meals and the occasional London theatre show, pop concert or down the local pub. Then there was the odd weekend visiting her parents in Wooton Northampton, again spare time was spent with the family or girlfriends.

She never could get into the drugs scene, even during her university days. She liked a couple of glasses of wine with a meal, but that was as daring as she got except for that one night when the rape happened. She knew that getting caught and charged with drugs, or anything else for that matter, would put an end to any young lawyers promising career. She went to extremes to ensure nobody ever brought drugs into her flat in Red Lion Square. It was just around the corner from Grays Inn Gardens where she had worked in her Uncle Bill's offices of 'Clements and Beckhams' - well- known London barristers. Uncle Bill was her Dad's brother. She even went as far as to make some friends bury their drugs in the small, shared, front garden before allowing them into her flat.

Then her memory suddenly snapped into today and she remembered where she had met DS Devlin, that good looking guy from Monday, who had impressed her with his handling of the rude DI Spearing at Mondays' set-up meeting. She had not been listening to any of the introductions on Monday, instead concentrating on rehearsing her little introduction speech. Then just now, she suddenly remembered that she had seen him a few times at Cambridge University in the criminology lectures, which she had to attend once a week as part of her law degree course. It must be him – she seemed to remember he mentioned criminology and Cambridge during his introduction.

She remembered he was known as a bit of a loner in Cambridge, but had heard from a few of the girls on the university campus that he had a body that most guys would die for. He was ultra- cool, but a hard man if he needed to be and he really knew what it was all about between the sheets. He did not drink except for the occasional wine and detested drugs, so, for that alone, he had attracted her attention. The problem was he moved in completely different social circles, in fact he was seldom seen in any social circles. Funny old, small world she thought to herself as she gathered her thoughts.

In fact, it was those criminology classes at Cambridge that had persuaded her to move into criminal law and also persuaded her to move to London and join her Uncle Bill's firm of barristers rather than return to Northampton. That was shock number two for her Mum and Dad and they finally realized that she had now grown up and was an independent young, but mature woman going her own way. Uncle Bill had been very good about giving her a chance when she was twenty-two, but she had graduated in her law degree course with honours from Cambridge, so Uncle Bill knew that there was very little chance of hiring her.

The family mould was then completely broken and, although she still relied on Dad for support in the first few years, it did come willingly, if only after a bit of chastising about life in London. That was another laugh as they did not have a clue, or probably chose to ignore, about her life at university.

Then the problems soon emerged when she realized that life in Uncle Bills' barrister's offices was life in the slow lane at least until you had a lot of experience. A case could take a year to build up and Judith was a very small cog in the wheel, usually doing background research on the way the police had brought charges against clients and trying to find any way the police had broken rules and so get their client of scot free on a technicality. Often the clients were obviously guilty, but so many times the police had made mistakes bringing the cases to court, that the guilty parties walked away. Of course, the barrister's offices celebrated, but more and more Judith became disillusioned and came to realize she did not like the way her career was going.

So, she decided to apply to the DPP and when she was offered this unique opportunity as the representative at New Scotland Yard, she instantly accepted. It came as a shock to Uncle Bill and her family with comments like; 'one of theirs on the other side'.

She was so determined that she went ahead anyway, despite the protests and strong advice from the whole family. Already, by day three, she felt justified and had possibly two cases on her hands and was awaiting a possible few more with DI Spearing and DS Devlin – a bit of hunk to boot! – Both of whom were coming in shortly with a double murder case and a mob gangster leader disappearance which were somehow connected. Not bad for a new job and day three had not yet even started!

She thought about DI Spearing and his arrogance at the Monday morning meeting with Sir Mark Wright, the Commissioner of the Metropolitan Police. This had been followed by his obvious manipulation of evidence for DI John Sanderson to get her to draft out search warrants for the local magistrates to approve. This was to allow the search of John Aldrich's car. John Aldrich, a solicitor no less, was being held under the twenty-four-hour rules. It appeared there may be a connection to a double murder in Surrey yesterday morning.

Then there followed the phone call late yesterday evening from DI Spearing. He was ever so polite, as he arranged this meeting for eight fifteen this morning. It soon became obvious to Judith that he was again trying to manipulate her, hoping her inexperience in the job would allow him to squeeze through prosecutions. Well DI Spearing she thought to herself, this time you are in for a shock and you better have a lily-white case, or you are not taking this case nowhere, especially with a solicitor involved, seedy or otherwise.

She went into her filing cabinet and took out the only sheets of paper in the four drawers, which were all to support the search warrant for the magistrates for the search of John Aldrich's car. She had not heard about the results of the search, although her search warrant application had been granted by Judge Warner.

There was another knock on the door and she saw the good-looking DS Devlin standing there all smiles. He was dressed in a smart but inexpensive well cut dark brown suit, white shirt, plain dark brown tie and shiny brown shoes.

"Come in Sergeant please." Judith shouted at the same time waving her hand and smiling brightly.

"Good morning - Miss Clements" I said crisply, intending to try and find out if she was a 'Miss' with one of my big smiles, which usually got the girls drooling. I was immediately disappointed as it did not appear to work with the cool Judith Clements.

"Ah good morning Sergeant Devlin, you are rather early." Judith replied.

"Always sharp me! Do you know me?" I asked, still with a now rather inane grin on my face.

"Yes, you were at the Monday morning set-up meeting with the Chief!" Judith replied with her easy smile.

"Oh yes! You know I had almost forgotten that already! It seems like a week ago, how time flies as they say!" I replied still smiling.

"Yes, but I must admit though I knew you before – at least by reputation." Judith replied coyly.

"By reputation?" I replied rather too defensively.

"Yes – at Cambridge University – You were on the Criminology course which I had to attend once a week as part of my Law Degree course!" Judith replied with a slight smile.

"How could I have missed someone as beautiful as you?" I replied with my sexy voice and big smile.

"I gathered from a few of my girlfriends that you and your mate did not miss many in those days!" Judith said it with a knowing smile.

"A mate - me? I don't recall having any mates at Cambridge." I replied unknowingly walking straight into it.

"Yes! - I do seem to remember you being known as 'The Lone Ranger' and your mate – or should I say – your nearest challenger – being known as 'Tonto'?" Judith replied with a laugh.

"Ah yes that's right – I seem to remember - that was Prakash Patel – The wrong type of Indian though, but good looking and had a reputation as a lady's man!" I replied casually with my biggest sexy smile.

"According to what I heard from the girls he came a long way second to 'The Lone Ranger'?" Judith replied obviously enjoying the repartee.

"That was an unwarranted reputation!" I retorted acting hurt, and then added for good effect; "I still don't know how I missed you though!"

"According to what I heard you did not miss many on the campus!" Judith replied still smiling and added: "In any case I was a late developer!"

"No way – Nobody suddenly develops beauty like yours." I said without a second thought, but added my biggest smile.

"Yeah - that was the other part of your reputation. 'The Lone Ranger' with the silver tongue!" Judith said it with a laugh.

"No 'Silver' was a horse and he belonged to Roy Rogers!" I replied with a snigger.

"You cowboys are all the same - no matter which horse you ride!" Judith replied and we both laughed out loud.

There was a knock on the door at exactly eight fifteen and Andy Spearing came in dressed like a new pin with a new, dark navy lightweight summer suit, white shirt, navy tie, shiny black shoes, clean shaven with hair combed.

"Am I interrupting anything?" Andy asked with an inquisitive look.

"Not at all DI Spearing! Your Sergeant Devlin and I were just reminiscing!"

Judith replied while still giggling.

"You two know each other before then?" Andy asked with an inquisitive look.

"Only by reputation back at Cambridge sir!" I answered, trying hard not to get into hysterics.

"By reputation eh? I bet it was all bad?" Andy said it as a question.

"Not all bad – just some bits were a bit shady!" I replied without thinking too much.

"From what I heard it was mostly in the dark rather than shady!" Judith chimed in with a sarcastic but laughing tone.

"It must have been good times being a student?" Andy sounding envious.

"Yes sir! – They were good, but very hard times!" I replied, and this time both Judith and I couldn't help the hysterics.

Andy did not understand the joke and hastily moved on and said rather sourly; "Shall we get started as we have to get to DCI Tomlinson by nine?"

"Yes, well it is your meeting DI Spearing. – Do you want to show me what you have got?" Judith asked, but started laughing again and blushing before adding; "Sorry! – I didn't mean! I meant your cases – you know!"

This time Andy understood the humour and joined in by saying; "You don't have to explain Miss Clements. – I am not about to drop my trousers!"

This time all three of us laughed and finally we got down to business.

Andy opened the business with a very professional presentation of the facts as he summarized the findings to date; "As you are no doubt aware Miss Clements; we have only yesterday completed day one in a double murder investigation in Surrey. Because of our initial investigation, we have ascertained the following: 1) - The murders were carried out by a known professional assassin who has been operating for many years around the criminal fraternity. We do not actually know him only as 'The Fox,', but we certainly do know of him. 2) – As yet we do not know who hired him, although we are following several leads which we have received from an informant. 3) – During our investigations, we have found that two well known, but small time criminals – namely Smith and Cosgrove - who have incidentally previous GBH charges, had fled the scene in the early hours of this morning. We managed to catch up with them in the offices of one of the victims – John Palmer's offices in London Bethnal Green. They were caught by the police, with the families' solicitor - namely John Aldrich - in the process of removing possible evidence - which may be connected to the murders - from the offices. After initial denials, both have admitted in their signed statements, which DS Devlin has a copy of for your files, that they did in fact fled the murder scene, which is a punishable offence as they are both still on probation. They have also admitted in their signed statements, under orders from Aldrich, to start to remove the files and ledgers from the offices, which constitutes attempting to pervert the course of justice. Sergeant - if you would pass their two signed statements to Miss Clements please."

I passed the signed statements from Smith and Cosgrove to Judith without comment. She had a quick read of one.

"Are they both, more or less, the same?" Judith asked.

"Not the same as they were taken at different interviews, but in principal they both gave the same story, but separately!" I replied.

"What have we got from the solicitor?" Judith asked.

"Ah the solicitor was more difficult, as they always are of course!" Andy replied with his cynical smile.

"Yes, that is what they are paid for DI Spearing" Judith replied equally as cynical.

"Yes, indeed Miss Clements!" Andy replied with a smile and added: "Some are just a lot slimier than others!" However, we managed to get Mr Aldrich to admit on tape that he was acting on behalf of Mrs Palmer and he recorded that he had not removed any of the possible incriminating evidence from the offices, which, as you know, we can now disprove as a result of the car search yesterday - thank you again for arranging the search warrant - he in fact did remove six ledgers. Sergeant if you would give Miss Clements the records of the Aldrich interview." I handed over the paper record of the tape-recorded interview which she very quickly glanced through, speed reading I assumed.

"As you will see Miss Clements, this is a summary record of the interview we have tape recorded." DI Spearing said as a matter of fact.

"Tell me DI Spearing – Why do I not have the tapes of the interviews with Smith, Cosgrove and Aldrich? Judith asked quite abruptly.

"Because Miss Clements – of course before your time! – Evidence of this nature in this place has a history of suddenly being overwritten in a so called 'error', or simply disappearing. So, we are protecting it now along with the originals of the statements!" Andy replied almost nonchalantly.

"So, you are now saying you do not trust me or the police in New Scotland Yard. Is that what you are saying DI Spearing?" Judith asked coming direct to the point.

"As a matter of fact, I was recently told by a veteran retired NSY detective -this afternoon actually - that there are more bent coppers than corkscrews in London and I agreed and went along with that!" DI Spearing replied with his cynical smile.

"Yeah, but if you listen to the guys being screwed, there are also just as many detectives bending the rules to get the convictions. Are you one of those DI Spearing?" Judith was certainly not hanging back.

"Who me? – Now how could you possibly think such a thing?" Andy replied with that sarcastic tone and smiled again before adding: "Seriously Miss Clements - in here I think you will find several people coming in to talk to you about our case, including my chief, DCI Harry Tomlinson, and quite a few others, if they have not been in here already. I am assuming you will be treating our information confidentially until the ducks are all in a row and we have the charges in place?"

"DI Spearing please don't think of me as one of those naïve little barristers! In my previous life, I could act the dumb lawyer to the police and the DPP lawyers for as long as I wanted. Also, I can see you have managed to coerce these statements and if I can see that, if these people happen to get one barrister representing them all, which is not impossible, and then your case starts to fall apart. So, do not try it – I can smell bullshit a mile off." Judith certainly knew how to hit a home run as our friends the Yanks would say.

"Why Miss Clements I don't know what you mean. All I am going to do this morning is charge this lot and do my job" Andy replied his voice full of innocence.

"DI Spearing, since you do not know me, I will say this only once. I am on your side and believe me I want to catch the bastards just as much as you do! However, my job is to advise you on the law and if it is possible to obtain a conviction. I am telling you right now that you stand a chance with the two idiots, but the solicitor Aldrich - he won't sit back and be a fall guy. He will see that coming a mile off!" Judith replied in an easy manner.

"That is exactly what I am hoping for Miss Clements. You see we got a signed statement from Mrs Palmer last night, which is no way true, but I am hoping it forces Aldrich to realize he is going to be made the fall guy and come up this morning with the truth, the whole truth and nothing but the truth, when we charge him. Sergeant Devlin - can you give Miss Clements a copy of Mrs Palmer's signed and witnessed statement?"

Andy asked with that little sly smile returning.

I passed Judith the short signed and witnessed statement from Mrs Palmer. Judith had another very quick read.

"My oh my – you have been a busy pair yesterday, haven't you? Judith said and smiled before adding; "You know, don't you? - If they contradict each other you may finish up getting neither of them?" Judith said it plain and simple.

"I – we – would like to get them all if we can – They are all as guilty as each other in perverting the course of justice and obstructing the police. I think if we draw a statement from Aldrich this morning based on Mrs P's statement, - then we stand a chance. I am looking for your advice here Miss Clements?" DI Spearing sounded almost convincing.

"My - That is a smooth change from a minute ago DI Spearing!" Judith answered cheerfully with a smile and added; "Look it may come down to who is the worst of the pair? I believe if you go for Mrs Palmer you have a three on one there and it looks like she is trying to take over again as the boss of a drugs cartel. Whereas our 'friend' - Aldrich – Now he is still only a slimy solicitor. His reputation is well known in London! However, if he is worth his salt as a solicitor, he will probably slide out of it anyway. So, I would go for Mrs Palmer and the two minders." Judith replied.

"So, tell me - in your opinion – what are the chances we can get all four? – Assuming we can drag a statement from Aldrich this morning?" DI Spearing asked with a slight tone of desperation in his voice.

"At the very best I would say a fifty-fifty chance! In any case, with the children and so on, even if you get a guilty verdict, she would probably only get a suspended sentence." Judith thoughtfully explained slowly and clearly.

"Ah but it is not beyond the realms of possibility that Mrs Palmer is maybe guilty of arranging these murders. Also, the fact of the matter is that if we don't go for all four then Aldrich will simply say he was acting under orders, though we can then prove he stole the ledgers which he doesn't know we know about yet and we don't have to tell him until he has told us some more!" DI Spearing said it quickly.

"Oh, my what a tangled web we weave. – When first we practice to deceive?" Judith replied with her sly smile.

"I cannot tell how the truth may be; I say the tale as it was said to me. - Scott, I think?" I found myself saying it to Judith with a smile.

"You Scots have got an answer for everything. Still I like that reply - it is very apt - don't you think Miss Clements?" Andy replied with a nod of his head.

"No – it was Sir Walter Scott sir!" I replied, while just about stopping myself from giggling.

"Exactly Sergeant! He was a Scottish poet and novelist - eighteenth century I believe!" DI Spearing answered with a deadpan face and added with a smile; "You see, you university types always assume you are the only ones who read!"

Judith and I just sat there dumbstruck for a few seconds.

"Oh! Yes! Well Okay!" Judith finally managed to stammer and added; "I think that I will leave it to you DI Spearing to play it by ear. You are experienced enough to know how far you can push this." Judith said it with firmness.

"A girl after my own heart" Andy replied and added: "Afraid I don't know who said that one do you?"

"You did - I think just now." Judith replied without hesitation and we all laughed and then she added with a matter of fact tone to her voice: "Unfortunately, I am way past being a girl now DI Spearing. Just let me know immediately you decide and we can draw up the appropriate possible charges."

"Yes, I think we can work together Miss Clements. Strange I have already found two 'Trained Brains' I can work with!" Andy sounded pleased.

"Only if you two do stay within the rules of the law! Drop outside and you have me as an enemy and I don't think any of us will like that!" Judith replied sternly, but with a smile.

"We may have to bend the rules if we are to have any chance of catching the baddies Miss Clements!" DI Spearing said with bravado.

"Bending is good! Providing you have me on board and not running around like a headless chicken. Just remember that DI." Judith replied with confidence oozing out of her.

"How could I ever forget you Miss Clement?" DI Spearing replied devilishly and stood up offering his right hand to shake and added with a smile; "Do what you can, where you are, with what you have."

"Theodore Roosevelt I believe?" I said it with a broad smile.

"You know you two should take up a double act – you could rival Morecambe and Wise, or maybe more appropriate - Jekyll and Hyde?" Judith replied with a laugh as she shook hands.

"Yes, very good Miss Clements! We know where not to go for the one liners though!" I said, laughing as I shook hands and looking at her phone extension.

"Touché" Judith replied with her biggest, disarming smile as DI Spearing and I left her office.

As we walked towards the lifts to go up to the twelfth floor and our meeting with DCI Flash Harry, Andy suddenly smiled and turned around to me and said; "Nice girl eh Sergeant? You got designs there me thinks."

"You must be a really brilliant detective to work that one out Andy!" I replied sarcastically with a smile, but sounding kind of boyish.

"Ah Ha!" Andy replied and laughed before adding; "Anyway back to business. Did you get the ledgers up to 'hooray' Nigel this morning?"

"Yes, that bloody snob! – Wanted me to take them all the way back down until his boss Tony Raeburn told him to do the job. He was sitting there with his feet up picking his nose and scratching his ass as well!" I replied showing my anger.

"What did you do?" Andy asked smiling as though expecting the answer.

"Dropped them on his desk and accidently landed some on his feet, knocked them flying off his desk. He bloody swore at me until I gave him the stare, then he went quiet." I replied adding my own version of the devilish grin.

"Ah yes – the stare! It wouldn't surprise me if he pissed himself under that stare!" Andy laughed as we got on the lift.

"Come to think of it, he did put on a face like a little baby does when he is straining to drop one! Although that might just have been the pain from those heavy ledgers dropping on his feet! It got a laugh from the others around him though – He must be growing in unpopularity already." I said it with a poker face.

"You certainly have not lost time in making enemies and influencing people Kevin." Andy replied with a smile as he hit the twelve-floor button.

"By the way Andy - I did make a start on the Palmer's files. Mostly they are all full of invoices and correspondence. It is going to be long boring slog!" I said it with a bored expression.

"Exactly – That is why I left them to you!" Andy replied with a laugh.

"Yeah, thank you so much Andy. They all said you were good at leaving the rubbish for everyone else to sweep up!" I replied, trying to sound disgruntled but without success.

"That's what they also say about me Kevin - Heart of stone! – always willing to teach people how to sweep up the shit, saves you sliding on it on the way back down!" Andy laughed again at his little joke and added; "By the way, did you tell hooray Nigel to make sure they were secure every time he goes out?"

"Sure did! – Told him to book them into stores and to make sure they are kept under lock and key in the stores!" I replied curtly.

"Good!" Andy simply replied.

We arrived in the lift with a clunky click on the twelfth -floor and I followed Andy to the right. We came to an office door with the name 'DCI H. Tomlinson' stencilled in gold letters, obviously done by Flash Harry himself.

Andy knocked the door, "Come in!" A male voice with a strong London East End accent shouted and we went in.

Book 1 in the DI Spearing and DS Devlin series

Chapter 11 - Nigel and David

Nigel Worthington was the worst kind of snob. He was the arrogant son of a 'new money' arrogant snob.

Nigel had of course spent a privileged childhood in Surrey around the London stockbroker's belt and attended only private schools for boys. He had grown an unhealthy disregard for girls and then went up to Oxford. There, because of his 'old man's' money, he mixed with the sons and daughters of the aristocrats, the rich and the famous. In Oxford he followed up and took his liking for the so called 'good life' to new levels. The 'good life' was endless parties, smoking pot, drinking to excess and abusing girls or boys. He was at the end of the day bi-sexual, but with it, at times, abusive and loutish.

Following Oxford, where Nigel somehow managed to scrape a minimum degree, most of his so-called 'friends' moved up to London. Nigel managed to persuade the 'old man' to allow him to live in the four-bedroom penthouse suite, which he owned in the fashionable London area of Kensington. A perfect place to restart the Oxford wild parties' scene with his friends and they soon formed an 'in-crowd' of their own snobs who were fast becoming degenerates.

The 'old man' was James Worthington who had sexually abused Nigel from age seven to twelve until he lost interest. He was also an arrogant snob of a man, who had made his millions rather seedily in commodities during and after world war two. He had dodged national service with pretended colour blindness, deafness and with severe back problems, none of which ever showed after the medical in nineteen thirty-nine. Then, in the late fifties, he had got a chance through his commodities contacts to invest in the emerging UK supermarkets, which added to his millions.

In the early sixties, James Worthington began to believe his own publicity and the financial newspapers saying that he was a top international investor. He began pumping investment into mines throughout Africa, about which he knew very little. Soon he had lost the millions he had, although he still held majority shares in the worthless mines. He had to sell his shares in the supermarkets and this was quickly followed by the family home in Surrey. The 'old man' moved the family back to London and took back the penthouse in Kensington, which was by now the only property left that he owned.

This left Nigel Worthington very bitter. Very soon, with no money from the old man, he found most his so called 'wide circle of friends' quickly disappeared. The few who remained he had to avoid because he simply did not have the money to eat, never mind to party with, even on an occasional basis.

The one person who remained loyal was one of Nigel's longer term boyfriends David Long. David was Nigel's very own rent boy who lived in the Kensington penthouse for free in return for sex. David was a nice sensitive lad now aged seventeen with a very soft almost angelic face, wide brown eyes and his hair was shoulder length, a mass of black curls. He always seemed to be wearing very tight fitting jeans with a black silver studded belt. He had variety of tight fitting T Shirts and black or brown leather Chelsea boots which were so popular in the sixties. He was around five feet and eight inches tall and very slim. Although David had on many occasions been violently abused by Nigel when he was in his loutish moods, he had remained stubbornly loyal, bearing in mind in the beginning he badly needed a place to live. The alternative was living on the streets in cardboard city with the drunks, or druggies. That was not an appealing thought in those days.

David was like Nigel in that, as a boy up to fourteen years old, he had been sexually abused by his father, but there the similarity ended. In his schooldays, there had been very little money around his home and David was always poorly dressed. On top of this, David had become very girlish in everything he did, or tried including sports. Because of his poor appearance and his girlish ways he had suffered mercilessly at the hands of most school kids. The girls always seemed to offer sympathy and a few were his only friends. One of the girls, her name was Margaret Welsh; he always thought she could have been the one to pull him back to being straight. The problem was he was so shy and did not have a clue what to do with a girl and was scared shitless to become the laughing stock of his few friends, so he never even tried to ask her out.

It was no surprise that when David finished school at fifteen he ran away from his home in Walsall for the bright lights of London and to which he had no intention of ever returning home. It was also no surprise that his parents made no attempt to find him. They too had to take all the taunts and could see that their son was not 'normal.' His Dad had the audacity to comment on his disappearance that; "It was just as well, I don't know how a son of mine could turn out to be a queer."

David arrived in London with a couple of quid in his pocket and landed on the streets of London and soon fell in with a couple of 'rent boys' who quickly showed him the ropes and places to pick-up men with money to burn and wanted young boys. David had no real morals about using his body to make money to survive and he quickly became very popular in the seedy world in which he
lived because, at fifteen, he was underage and any man caught with him was heading for jail.

At the age of sixteen David, although he had accumulated some money and now rented a room in fashionable Chelsea, was sadly disillusioned with his lifestyle. At sixteen he was now nothing more than a male whore having to service gay men of every shape and size, many disgusting people who looked ridiculous nude, or otherwise and with equally disgusting habits. Many thought, because they were paying customers, they could do whatever they liked to him and sometimes he had to be strong to stop them, but with a few he was forced to submit, or be beaten to pulp - such a man was Nigel Worthington.

David first met Nigel at a mutual friend's party in Chelsea just over two years ago. At that point, Nigel was still riding the crest of the wave, his Dad was apparently still very rich and his downward spiral was just about to begin. That night, Nigel had been really all sweetness and light and asked David out for a meal the next night at the reasonably expensive, but excellent, Italian restaurant in Walton Street Chelsea. It turned out to be just around the corner not far from Nigels Knightsbridge penthouse.

After the meal, the red wine flowed freely and it did not take Nigel too long to suggest they go back to his penthouse for drinks at which point David suddenly became quite serious and said quite clearly, despite the drink; "Nigel I have to make it quite clear. I go out with men for a living." Nigel looked him up and down then replied leeringly: "So you are a whore David – Is that what you are saying?"

At that point, David should have known to cut out, but he was only sixteen and had very little experience of men like Nigel, He mumbled his reply along the lines: "It is the only way I can earn money Nigel!"

Nigel placed his hand on David's knee and gradually worked his hand up towards his groin on the outside of his trousers, but was too obviously aiming for David's fly zip. David put his hand on top of Nigels hand and said quietly; "Not here Nigel, not in public."

"Oh, a little prudish for a little whore are we David?" Nigel was leering again and was speaking too loudly. It should have been another warning for, the then rather naïve, David.

"Please Nigel – If you want to carry on any relationship then I am afraid if you don't stop right now then I am out of here." David said it and sounded like he meant it.

"Sorry David – I sound like a right prat, don't I? I promise I will not carry on like that anymore!" It turned out to be a very short term promise.

They were soon back in Nigel's Knightsbridge penthouse. Almost as soon as they were through the door they had very rough sex. David did not mind the rough stuff. He had previously had to endure a lot worse with guys who were older and horrible looking with their repulsive paunch bellies hanging so far down they could not even see their own penis.

They sat down afterwards with David in his pink satin Y fronts and Nigel still naked, but showing a well-developed midriff.

"I'll tell you what David!" Nigel started, faltering as he seemingly picked his words with some care before adding; "We seem to be getting it on. - If you fancy it – Why don't you move in here and live here rent free? In return we have sex a few times per month and the rest of the time you do whatever you want to do to live. Well - How about it?"

"No strings?" David asked almost ruefully.

"No strings! – As I say outside of our arrangement – we both do what we want to do – end of story!"

Nigel sounded very sincere.

David thought about it for no more than a minute, then with a little smile he replied; "That sounds okay – I think that's a deal." It was another major mistake that David would regret for the rest of his short life.

It was later, in that same week that David met up with another future benefactor in Jonathan Bridgewater, a middle-aged man, big at six feet three in his bare feet and very fit with a physique that most men half his age would have died for. Jonathan was the Chief Executive Officer for a company owning properties and a large estate agency in central London. They had paid sex in one of Jonathan's companies' empty, but furnished, apartments just off the fashionable Chelsea Road. He was big, but a gentle giant and very considerate in everything. Afterwards, he was obviously quite smitten by David and went on about how much he had enjoyed his session with David and he too suddenly made a proposal to David. He agreed to pay David a monthly cheque of two hundred pounds for his 'services' once a week on a Thursday. It was a nice tidy sum in nineteen sixty-seven for one day a week and David saw it as a way out of the whoring game and took up the offer. Well he thought to himself, it was still whoring, but at least it was with a nice enough bloke who liked straight, no kinky sex, with no attachments. Jonathan was a married man with a couple of kids, so everything was low key stuff. His wife and kids had no idea he liked boys and that was the way it had to stay.

How was David to know, at that point, just how smitten Jonathan would become over the next two years?

It was later that year that Nigel found out that his old man was in serious financial difficulties and money was very tight. Nigel's so called 'close circle of friends' were soon disappearing without trace and Nigel started taking out his frustrations by beating up David during very rough sex.

Truth be known, it had really started within a week of David moving into the penthouse when he discovered that Nigel was very much into the Marquis De Sade - sadism and sex with bondage. Later as Nigel's frustrations got worse so the beatings of David during sex became extreme. David often awoke with his upper body covered in black and blue whelps and his buttocks scratched sometimes raw and he had to have Nigel place Elastoplast's to take the sting out of sitting down and to stop the possibility of infections.

Finally, one morning David awoke after another night of bondage with beatings and found his anus red raw and swollen with rectal bleeding. The previous night Nigel had been shoving things up David's' anal passageway until the pain was excruciating that David cried out. Nigel had simply let loose with maniacal laughter and obviously found this sexually stimulating. He simply carried on taking pleasure from the pain he was inflicting.

David, bearing in mind he was still only sixteen at that time, was panic stricken with the sight of a pool of blood on his bed and, still naked, flew in a rage to Nigel's room with the blood running down his inner thighs. He burst through the bedroom doors and without stopping to look if Nigel was awake shouted; "Look what the fuck you have done to me. I am bleeding and red raw you - you bastard. That's it! -- finished! – I have had enough – No more you mother fucker - I am out of here!" David spun around and ran out of the room and into his own room and went straight into the shower and turned it up as hot as he could stand it.

Nigel had only come out of his sleep towards the end of David shouting and saw him turn to go back to his room. At first Nigel had a thin smile on his face and then he saw the blood around David's buttocks running down his legs. Nigel immediately panicked and jumped out of bed, taking time to put on a pair of his white Y fronts before running through to David's room. Hearing the shower running he barged straight through and opened the cubicle door.

"Get the fuck out of here – Jonathan was right you are a fucking pervert – Get out"

David was screaming and pushed Nigel with surprising strength away with the palm of his hand on Nigel's chest and with his other hand slammed the cubicle door.

Nigel staggered back and went through and sat on the bed until he noticed the pool of blood. He shot up and looking disgusted, said quietly to himself; "Oh my God." He strolled around the room until he finally heard the shower stopping and David came through to the room with a white towel, already with crimson patches, wrapped around his waist and his upper torso showing black and blue whelps.

"I told you to fuck off! Get out of here!" David had never shouted or even been angry with Nigel before.

"Look David, I am really sorry – I never knew" --- Nigel began for the first time to apologise to David.

"I cannot get it to stop bleeding Nigel – What am I going to do?" David sounded desperate like the young boy he still was.

"Look David – Water only makes it bleed more. Stick your towel up there and hold it tight in there for a while. It will stop. Then you had better go and see a doctor." Nigel did sound sympathetic.

"Oh yeah? And what do you want me to tell him Nigel? Doctor - I am sixteen years old and I have been letting this pervert stick these things up my arse all night and now I think I am bleeding to death?" David was as white as a sheet and now sounded harsh, but at the same time almost crying.

"To be honest David I don't care – Obviously, I would like you to lie to the doctor, but I don't care - just go and see him and get it fixed. If you go and see Doctor Johnston – he is in the A & E at the Chelsea and Westminster in Du Cane Rd, London W12. He is one of us, he will keep it quiet." Nigel did, for once in his life, sounded sincere.

"What will he want in return - a quick poke?" David was beginning to sound hysterical.

"Don't be ridiculous David. You look like a virgin bride on her marriage bed –

Who would want to poke that?" Nigel asked with just a little smile and just the right hint of humour trying to cool David down.

"Oh, for fucks sake Nigel. You just sink to the lowest depths to get a laugh!" David replied but he could not help but smile.

"Look David – I really mean this – it will not happen again – I really promise you that. – I am really just really sorry!" Nigel just shook his head and looked remorseful.

There was silence for a few minutes.

David did not miss the irony of the moment and deep down he knew Nigel would never live up to his promises. It was always the same the next morning after one of these battering sessions, although this one had been worse than ever. Today may be different, Nigel genuinely looked scared. Then again David still knew that Nigel was putting on a show, because he knew what could happen if David chose to report it. There was no doubt that for Nigel it would be jail and for several years. What was in it for David? He would have to endure going up in court and admit to the big wide world he was no more than a male whore, one of the infamous rent boys around the London scene. He would become a figure of ridicule and not only that, his clients would quickly drop him, not wanting to face the same fate as Nigel. Even Jonathan would be forced to drop him. Then what? He would have nowhere to live, no money and no way of making money?

The double irony was that during the last few months, Nigel fortunes had changed with his Dad losing his businesses and money becoming very tight. From being a millionaire's son to becoming a pauper had taken but a few months. David had understood Nigel's frustrations and the reasons for his bouts of depression and anger. David had been helping Nigel to stay afloat during the most difficult times until he could find a job. David gave him some of the money from what he earned with Jonathan. The deep-down truth was, David had come to quite like Nigel, at least when he was not in one of his loutish moods. He could never love him or anything like that; he was too scared of him, sometimes so scared he thought Nigel was going to kill him.

When David first gave him some money, Nigel had obviously been very moved and said some very nice things, including he would not forget, he would repay it all and things would change. Well, some things had not changed, but there were some very pleasant interludes between the bouts of anger and depression.

David felt the blood had stopped dripping from his anus, then suddenly made up his mind and said quite evenly; "I think it has stopped. I am going down the A and E at the hospital."

"Yes, that's good David. What are you going to say?" Nigels reply was almost pleading.

"I don't know yet. I will have to see what he asks!" David replied, seeing the anxiety, or was it anger? in Nigel's cold blue eyes. David quickly realized the possible danger and added; "I am sure I can come up with a good story – one of my clients did it – I don't have to say his real name or anything like that!"

"Yeah – yeah that sounds good. Well go, get ready and get it seen to." Nigel's voice was full of sheer relief.

"Nigel – this is the last time! I don't think my body can take it anymore." David was back to his more subdued self.

"Yeah – yeah you got it man – That is cool. I promise." Nigel's instant response did not sound genuine, but David decided to let it go.

At the hospital, David discovered Doctor Johnston was not on till the evening shift and in any case it turned out you could not book to see him in the A and E, only with a private appointment. Obviously, if Nigel had seen Doctor Johnston, it was when he had money and it was a private appointment. It was simple; one had to take who became free when it was your turn.

In any event, after a long two hour wait, during which he felt his anus was weeping blood again, he was invited through to a cubicle and it turned out to be, of all things, a lady doctor by the name of Alice Ward which was on a nameplate pinned to her white coat above her left breast. She was middle aged, but good looking and very fit. David panicked at first, but although he was obviously embarrassed when he explained what was wrong, the good doctor did not bat an eyelid. She simply handed him a hospital gown and told him to strip off and put on the gown and added to leave it open at the back. She then left the cubicle, drew the curtain closed and did not reappear for another thirty minutes.

She breezed in and told David to get up on the table, lie on his right side and put his feet up towards his chin. David did as he was told as the good doctor pulled on a pair of surgical gloves.

"My good God lad! - Who the hell has done this to you?" Doctor Ward asked, looking at David's buttocks and his red raw anus.

"It was a client Doctor! – Things got way out of hand." David replied quietly, hoping he could not be heard in the next cubicle.

"I would say things got a lot more than out of hand lad! Whoever did this to you is as near a psychopath as you can get! What did he put up your anus lad?" Doctor Ward was abrupt and straight to the point and no doubt could be heard, not only in the next cubicle, but also in the whole of A and E.

David felt his face go crimson and, before he could reply, let out a yell of pain as Doctor Ward stuck her gloved finger up his anus and felt around.

"Sorry lad – I will be a bit gentler, now I know what it is" Doctor Ward's voice was softer and gentle.

"I don't know what he stuck up me, but it was hard and cold, something like a round steel thing!" David finally blurted it out while trying to hold back the tears.

"You know lad – letting anybody do that - he or she – might not only damage your anus, but he could seriously damage your intestines and that is serious stuff!" Doctor Ward was now speaking quietly and was gently sympathetic.

"I did not let him do it. He sort of forced it and I was not able to stop it!" David's voice was rapidly becoming tearful and with the pain from the examination everything was closing in. Thankfully, Doctor Ward finally withdrew her finger and removed her gloves placing them in an insulator bin in the corner before washing and drying her hands and pulling on a new pair of surgical gloves.

"You know lad that is even more of a reason to report this man. – He is obviously way out of control. Now, turn on your back and pull down the gown from your chest." Doctor Ward's face was covered in a concerned frown.

Looking at the black and blue whelps around David's ribcage, Doctor Ward shook her head and her eyes betrayed her disbelief before she said; "Good God lad – this maniac has given you one hell of a working over. This is brutal assault lad, disguised as some sort of sadistic sex. I think it is time to call the police!"

David's eyes betrayed panic before he pleaded; "Please Doctor – No police – I will deny everything and do a runner."

"Don't you understand lad? You are in no condition to do a runner anywhere? For starters, you have a large anal fissure. In layman's terms, that is a large tear in the lining of your anal canal caused by whatever this guy was using, which is causing some of your rectal bleeding, not to mention the possibility of infections! Unless it is treated now, you will continue to lose blood until you conk out wherever and whenever that may happen, but certainly within the next twelve hours and any infections could be fatal. Then lad it is possible that he has damaged your intestines and, if he has, that could be extremely painful if not fatal. Now look at your ribcage lad - with luck they might only be bruised, but if some of your ribs are broken they could puncture your lungs and it is bingo! You understand lad?" Doctor Ward was speaking quietly, but firmly.

"Yes, I understand Doctor, but I cannot afford the police."

"You are on the game lad?" Doctor Ward asked with raised eyebrows.

"Yes Doctor." David replied simply with a little hunch of his shoulders.

"You do know you are far too young lad? It is illegal – The law only allows for consenting gay adults - even more so with an animal like this guy?"

"Look I don't know the guy Doctor. He just comes to London every few months. It is only me who would suffer. It is me who would finish up inside and you know what happens to people like me in there?"

"Yeah, so you say. But you know something David? I just don't believe you. I think you know this guy! But it is up to you my friend. It is your life, but just you remember, by not doing anything you could be causing other people to suffer and yes, maybe die, in the future. How would you feel about that David?"

"Look Doctor – I will think about it okay? Right now, I am just in pain okay?"

"Right, you are going to need an operation to rectify that tear. But first I am going to need X - Rays on your intestines, ribcage and that tear. You realize David you are going to have none of your type of sex for the next couple of months?

"That is nice way to put it Doctor! – My type of sex? I am gay and I am now a gay whore, hey-ho, but the way you put it sounds nicer."

"I am sorry David. – I did not mean it to come out sounding like that, but at least you have to take a holiday for a couple of months!"

"Yeah right Doctor – It sounds good to me!" David replied ruefully.

Nigel had meant it when he said he would not forget it and he found himself beginning to like David, rather than just using and abusing his body. Why he did the things he did to David he could not understand, but it was simply in his makeup. He made his mind up that in his present financial position to stop abusing David.

Later, in that same year, out of the blue Nigel's mum Maureen, still a very beautiful looking woman, blossoming in middle aged, decided to leave the old man and set-up home with a millionaire diamond dealer. To family and friends, it was never a surprise, because it was always obvious that Maureen had only married James Worthington for the money. Maureen was a former nineteen fifties top, and very beautiful model, standing at five feet eleven, with her long sleek legs, exquisite breasts, shiny black hair, dark brown pools of eyes and a body most women would die for, even though she was now into her mid forties.

The old man was certainly no catch for his looks, but at the time his money; well that was a different story.

Women like Maureen are the same the world over and follow the immortal code; 'No money – no honey.' That is their stock answer to the marriage vows about; 'for better or worse, for richer or poorer,' although at the marriage altar it is said with the most genuine feeling they can possibly drag up.

They got a quickie divorce and the old man changed his will and left what little there was to Nigel, which in effect was the Kensington penthouse and the rights to the worthless mines in Africa.

The old man could not stand the embarrassment of finishing up broke and, after the divorce, had no fight left in him to resurrect his fortunes. So, one fine winter's morning in January this year, it appeared he had topped himself in the garage behind their Kensington flat using the car exhaust.

Nigel now tried to remember the confrontation with his Mum at the old man's funeral, after the burial service, in Kensal Green cemetery on that bitterly cold afternoon in January with the rain and sleet swirling around the few mourners. They were mostly family – a couple of Uncles, Aunts, a few cousins and David Long – all dressed in black and standing around the grave. Nigel remembered thinking that was just like him, his old man's friends and workers had quickly disappeared into the woodwork with the money.

Nigel and David had a few drinks in a local Kensington pub before facing up to the funeral, so the memories were just a little hazy.

"How are you managing Nigel?" Maureen his mum asked with what sounded like more than a little false emotion, as they stood over the open grave looking down on the old man's coffin. Nobody knew if they were supposed to pray or what, then again nobody knew any prayers.

"Thank you for asking at last mum. How do you expect?" Nigel replied with a pained expression on his face.

"No need to be hypocritical Nigel. We both knew we used him and enjoyed his money!" Maureen answered very coldly and with a vacant stare from those big brown eyes of hers.

"Yeah, money gone and whoosh you are gone eh Mum?" Nigel almost spat the words and David leaned over and patted him on the shoulder in an act of consolation.

"Nigel I am sorry, but there was never any real love and we both knew it from the start. You of all people knew what he was like." She then almost blushed and hastily changed the subject adding, "Anyway how are you paying for his funeral and things?" Maureen asked as a matter of fact, as though dismissing her previous life with the old man.

"Don't know really. I suppose I will have to sell the penthouse and get myself a grubby flat somewhere! Did you actually know about him and what he did to me?" Nigel replied rather anxiously.

"You know you should try to hold onto that place. It will be worth a fortune in the next few years!" Maureen replied with a knowing smile on her face, trying to ignore the question.

"You did know, didn't you? - What he was doing to me when I was a kid? And you didn't do anything about it, did you?" Nigel looked directly into her eyes and saw that it was true before she hastily turned away.

"This is not the time or the place for that conversation Nigel. As I said, you ought to hold onto the penthouse!" She said it almost callously.

"And what shall I use for money eh Mum? I don't suppose you want to give up some of those diamonds he bought you in that 'loveless' marriage of yours?" Nigel was again sounding like the spiteful child, which in many ways he still was to say the least.

"Nigel! – Let me know how much for the funeral and the reception and I will sell the necessary diamonds. It is the least I can do! After all I am marrying a diamond expert!" Maureen replied almost smiling, but loud enough to let the family hear the offer.

Nigel just stared aghast and sounding unbelieving when he replied; "Yes mum, I am sure you mean that at this moment in front of all these people. I'll believe it when I see it."

"My, you are a doubting Thomas are you not Nigel? Then again you were always like that were you not?" Maureen replied crisply.

"Mum you never gave me any reason to believe in you. After all I saw more of the servants than I ever saw of you." Nigel replied with what possibly sounded suspiciously like his first ever heartfelt response.

"Perhaps you were just as responsible for that situation Nigel or have you conveniently forgotten your little confrontations nowadays?" Maureen replied, again coming over as very cold.

"Perhaps you forget mum that you and dad were away from Surrey most of the week. So, the confrontations were perhaps a kid crying out for help, but now I know you ignored that too, eh Mum?" Nigel now sounded very edgy.

"Why are you like this especially today of all days Nigel?" Maureen asked as she turned away towards the cars.

"Perhaps because we have never spoken to each other as adult's mum! What do you reckon?" Nigel shouted his reply above the wind noise.

Mum just kept walking away and out of his life. She never came to the reception in the local Kensington pub, but surprisingly she did sell some of her diamonds and paid for the funeral, the reception and it left several thousand pounds over for Nigel. However, he had no alternative other than, for the first time ever, to go out to work at twenty-seven years of age and it left him with a chip on his shoulder a mile high.

Nigel had intentionally misled those people at the commissioner Sir Mark Wrights introductory meeting on Monday into believing his old man's company had been able to withstand the loss of millions in the African mines fraud. Like his old man, he could not bring himself to admit failure, or that he was broke. Unlike his old man, he still had plenty of fight in him and intended using whatever means he could to get back into money and re-join his snobbish friends, whatever the cost. Why he needed to do that, he did not understand himself, but in his slightly warped mind he wanted that more than anything else.

Nigel smiled to himself at his own words at Sir Mark Wrights' introduction meeting on Monday and his portrayal of the rich man's son. He knew he could carry it off very easily and he believed that those at the meeting had all been taken in by his deceit.

He thought wrongly that, most of the people had been taken in, but of course a couple of the bosses knew the truth.

This job at New Scotland Yard, in the fraud squad, was his start to re-join the money brigade. It had nothing to do with morals about catching the fraudsters as he had suggested at the same meeting with Sir Mark.

Nigel was very much his old man's son. He had taken this silly job at New Scotland Yard in order that he could spot the companies who were into fraud and he could move in and take his share. He was also very like his old man in respect that he was not as clever as he thought himself to be, but he could spot the chance to jump in to money markets. He did not really care how he got in there, but he would jump in with both feet.

Nigel sat alone in the New Scotland Yard offices staring thoughtfully at the ledgers from Palmers Associates which the Glaswegian tough guy Devlin had earlier 'accidently' dropped on his feet. Nigel was still snobbish enough to think to himself it was unbelievable that a thug like Devlin had achieved an honours degree at Cambridge. He thought to himself; for God's sake, what is the world coming to?

Nigel began reading through the Palmers Associates ledgers, detailing the accounts for 'Joseph Bolger Associates,' an Import and Export Company operating from offices in Bethnal Green, London. He recognized the name of Joseph Bolger as the leader of a big London gang who had recently disappeared. He also recognized the name of John Palmer as one of the murder victims found yesterday in a Surrey mansion. He immediately began to get a warm feeling that there may be something in here that he could pick up on, more so when he noticed the accounts were counter signed by Mrs J. Palmer, Chief Accountant, who he knew from yesterday evening's television reports, had not been harmed.

After an hour or so on his first scan of the ledgers he began to spot the trends. Several years ago, a sudden huge increase in monthly orders to Japan for transistor radios, although on checking the UK sales they did not match anywhere near the size of the orders. Then he noticed the deliveries came via several Asian ports where some sales were recorded before eventually being reshipped to London.

In the same period, there was a sudden huge increase in monthly orders for pop records, fridges and freezers from America. Again, the UK sales did not match anywhere near the size of the orders. Then he noticed the deliveries came via South American ports to Antwerp where some sales were recorded before eventually they too were shipped to London.

Overall, there were considerable losses every year, yet the orders continued at the same levels. If these were the true ledgers then the company should have been nearly bankrupt and out of business. Nigel thought to himself; curious, indeed very curious and looking very promising. A plan started to form at the back of his mind. He had to get the ledgers out of here and hidden away in a left luggage locker at Victoria Station, before visiting Mrs Palmer. First, he had to show that he had booked the ledgers into the stores when he went out to lunch.

This lunchtime would be spent with a very quick visit to the supermarket getting two bags of groceries which he would bring back to the office. Nigel thought of Baden-Powell and said his phrase out loud; "Softly, Softly Catchee Monkey." He suddenly realized he had said it out loud, but nobody around appeared to have heard so he settled back down to more study of the ledgers and to wait impatiently for lunchtime.

Nigel then began to consider all aspects of the plan and suddenly realized that if the ledgers went missing now he would be the prime suspect and he would be watched very closely.

So, Plan B started to form, after all he thought to himself, there is no need to take the ledgers straight away! The police stores were as safe a place as any for the moment. Photographs as proof would suffice for now until the deal was struck.

Also, he had to show he was fully cooperating with DI Spearing and DS Devlin, the Glasgow thug, let them think he was open and frank with them, this way there was no need for them to get suspicious.

He got up, went downstairs to the stores and booked out a Kodak Instamatic 704 camera complete with a new spool. On his return to his desk, he immediately took photographs of all entries on all the ledgers pages, which used up most of the spool. He then removed the spool making sure it was not exposed to daylight which would have ruined most, if not all the photographs. He then placed the spool back in its little plastic canister and put it in his pocket.

He quickly went back down to the stores and booked back in both the camera and the ledgers. He made a lot of noise about the ledgers being held securely. He ordered that the ledgers had to be locked away and nobody but Nigel could book them out. The Sergeant then asked him for a signature on booking in so as, when being booked out, they would match the signature. He complied and quickly got back to his desk, all done in twenty minutes.

He then sat back and waited impatiently for lunchtime. Nigel thought to himself this could be extremely dodgy, but it is the beginning of a new life and he hoped he would be in a better place, at least for him, at the end.

Chapter 12 - DCI Flash Harry

We entered DCI H Tomlinson's, otherwise universally known as 'Flash Harrys' office, at nine sharp. The office was much bigger than Judith's and had windows looking out towards St. James Park. There was a nice, huge, oak wood desk, with a four-drawer oak wooden filing cabinet, but strangely the same three chairs, his being the imitation brown leather chair with the two armrests. The two opposite were the same cheap hard plastic chairs for guests. The only other furnishings were an empty 'in and out' black plastic tray on the left-hand corner of his desk, a lined notepad on which were several notes written, including the name DI Spearing underlined. On top of the pad were an expensive looking Parker fountain pen and a black cradle on which was the old, famous, black BT telephone would be mounted.

Flash Harry was dressed in an expensive looking dark grey suit, white shirt and dark grey pure silk tie with his feet planted on the desk obviously to show off he was wearing a pair of ultra-expensive Church's new black leather shoes and showing black cashmere socks. He had the old black BT telephone to his ear as we entered. Easy to see many of the reasons why he had been labelled 'Flash Harry.'

He signalled us, rather rudely I thought, to sit down, while still carrying on with his conversation on the 'phone.

"Tell you what Billy. Either get your ass in here tomorrow or forget you ever had a job." Flash Harry said it, not only rudely, but with a sneer as he threw the phone back on the black cradle on his desk.

"I assume you are Devlin?" Flash Harry asked and without waiting for answer added; "Now - where the hell have you two been Spearing?" Flash Harry asked as if he was speaking to a couple of dogs, which immediately got both our backs up.

"Nice to see you too - sir!" Andy replied and added a question; "Was that Billy Larkin you were speaking to 'sir'?"

"None of your dammed business Spearing! Now I asked you a question - Where have you two damn well been for the past twenty-fours Spearing?" Flash Harry was gradually getting beyond rude.

"I have been working on a double murder in Surrey – SIR!" Andy was obviously being sarcastic acting like a soldier in response to a commander, but he did stop short of saluting.

"Don't give me that shit Spearing." Flash Harry responded angrily and added; "Who gave you permission to go to Surrey? And you have disobeyed orders yet again. - You have not been carrying a walkie-talkie while out on patrol."

"Oh, yes that brick block that doesn't work mostly losing connection and it weighs you down if you have to chase someone. You could be dead and buried several times over before you get a connection. Is that the one - 'Sir'? Andy asked sarcastically.

"The last time you ran Spearing was from the Japs. So, don't act the 'wise-ass' with me Spearing. This is your last warning Spearing and Devlin it is your first!" Flash Harry was almost spitting his reply.

"Sorry sir!" I replied with a smile, "I am afraid the rules do not say anything about detectives carrying these 'walkie-talkies.' The 'good book' only states policemen, on patrol, shall always carry the walkie-talkies sir."

"Are you teaching him to be a smart ass too Spearing?" Flash Harry spun around to face Andy and then back to me and angrily said. "Well now - let me tell you 'smart ass' Devlin, if that is the case, then the 'good book' is out of date. 'We' have made it clear that we all have to carry walkie-talkies."

"Oh, very good sir, but 'we', who started on Monday, have not been told these additional rules. Do you wear one when you go out sir?" I asked sarcastically, anyway now he was beginning to annoy me.

"No of course not – I am a senior detective!" Flash Harry responded with a smirk.

"Oh, so there are separate rules for some Detectives as opposed to other Detectives is there?" I asked with a smile.

"Right now - stop right there!" Flash Harry responded, holding his hand up to me and turning to Andy added; "I have asked you Spearing - Who gave you permission to waltz off to Surrey to investigate a murder? Well?"

"Nobody sir – I did not need permission as the double murder in Surrey was directly connected to the disappearance of Joseph Bolger, which I was already in charge of and investigating, as directed by yourself sir. Also, I was requested to investigate by the Surrey police!" Andy replied quietly, but firmly, obviously angry.

"Well then Mr 'smart ass'. We have now been asked by MI5 to allow them to take over these murder investigations. "So ---" Flash Harry was about to conclude when Andy interrupted; "I do hope you told them where to go sir? These people have no experience whatsoever of investigating murders. It is more than likely they have committed the murders. It would be the most dangerous precedent ever to allow them to run a NSY murder case - don't you think SIR?" Andy asked the question with an absolute poker face.

"Well of course I have not said 'Yes' - yet. I understood there may be consequences, but I had to speak to you first and obviously, I could not contact you, so we have this mess." Flash Harry was on the defensive.

"Well at least that's good – Sir! - We don't have to escalate this upstairs now do we?" Andy asked with that devilish grin yet again.

"Are you threatening me again Spearing with your friends upstairs?" Flash Harry looked and sounded angry.

"No - not at all sir! - We don't want them getting all hot and bothered when there is no need - now do we sir?" Andy replied with a little sarcastic smile.

"You know Spearing – you will - before too much longer - you will lose your friends upstairs and then your defensive line will disappear. Then we will see to you." Flash Harrys' voice was full of venom as he spoke.

Andy appeared to ignore the threat and asked innocently; "Who was it in MI5 who asked that I be removed? – They apparently tried that yesterday."

"Oh, so you have been in contact with them then?" Flash Harry jumped right in as though he had caught Andy out.

"No sir – I did say apparently! - DI Lawler from Surrey police took the call, but naturally when they would not identify themselves he would not discuss it with them. - They could have been the press or anybody you know sir? So, the conversation went no further. Did they give you a name Sir?" Andy asked almost nonchalantly.

"Yes – yes of course they did." Flash Harry replied, but more than a little hesitantly before adding; "But of course they said it was a matter of our country's internal security, so I would have to get their permission before disclosing a name to you Spearing."

"It may be an internal security matter sir, but it is also a double murder - and it is a NSY' police enquiry and possibly a triple murder –that is if we assume Joseph Bolger is another victim! So, you see sir, we need to know what the MI5 involvement is in this entire scene?" Andy said it again straight faced and simply stared out Flash Harry who eventually turned away, took his feet off the desk and pretended to look out the window.

"Like I said Spearing, I will have to ask their permission before I can give you a name. Not that they will tell you anything anyway, they will hide behind the old national security gag – you know that, just as much as I know that." Flash Harrys' body language and his voice was showing and sounding edgy. It would have been no surprise to learn he did not have a name.

"That may be so sir, but if they do - then we will have to escalate it up to the Chief. As I say, this is a possible triple murder enquiry and you and I both know that the first forty-eight hours, in any murder enquiry, is the vital time." Andy replied with a slight smile.

"There you go again Spearing!" Flash Harry responded angrily and added: "Always threatening to go upstairs to your pals."

"It is not a case of threatening sir! It is a matter of procedure in these instances. You and I both know that sir - now don't we?" Andy replied sarcastically, with just a hint of a smile.

"There you go again Spearing. - All the big smart ass 'I am' attitude. It gets you nowhere and you know that, don't you? You are the nowhere man?" Flash Harry was now getting angrier spitefully pointing a finger at Andy.

Andy appeared to again completely ignore this new outburst and simply asked with an ice-cold tone to his voice; "Are you going to contact MI5 and get me that name, or not sir?"

"I already said I would – for all the good it will do you! Flash Harry limply responded.

"Can you please make it this morning sir? – As you know, speed is of the essence with this murder enquiry and we do have four very important interviews this morning with possible charges pending and we do not want to make a mistake if MI5 have their fingers in the pie - now do we sir?" Andy asked and was sounding precise as though he wanted the words recorded.

"Now don't you dare push me too far Spearing - I will contact them as soon as I possibly can. Like I say do not expect too much, they are national security for Christ's sake, how you think they are involved in murders is beyond me." Flash Harry was now beginning to lose the plot.

"I would appreciate it sir, if you would not use the Lords name in vain." I interrupted the conversation and was trying to look very sincere.

"What the fuck are you on about Devlin?" Flash Harry was getting red in the face and sounding irritated.

"I would appreciate it if you would cease talking to me in that manner sir! Swearing and using the name of God in vain like that! Otherwise I shall have to report you to the police authority." I replied holding his gaze.

I thought he was going to blow a gasket, his face was still red, but he slowly realized he was on a sticky wicket and he managed to regain his self-control.

Flash Harry broke the eye contact with me, turned back again to a smiling Andy and asked; "Who are these four people you have arrested Spearing?"

"I have not arrested anyone yet sir. I am conducting interviews and making contacts with Informant's this morning. I believe, depending on the information we receive, we may be able to charge several people today with offences connected with the murders." Andy said it with a monotone voice, like reading from a report.

"Have you run this past Miss Clements the DPP Rep yet?" Flash Harry asked quietly, but there was a devilish gleam in his eye.

"Why of course sir" Andy blandly replied.

Flash Harry had a look of disappointment on his face as he asked; "So you know who the murderer is then?"

"We know who the Assassin is, but have we don't know who hired him yet!" Andy answered crisply with his poker face showing nothing.

"So, it is 'The Fox' again? – the one YOU have been unable to catch for all these years?" Flash Harry was back to his arrogant mocking self.

"Not only 'me' sir, but it is the collective 'we'. However, this time we do have a description for the first time and a list of possible people who may have hired him. He was probably disguised, but at least we have a physical description." Andy was also back to his basic reporting voice.

"Yes, that's good. Let's get the description out there." Flash Harry replied, but was obviously very thoughtful, like he was thinking through some things.

"I don't think putting out the description now sir is a good idea. We would be warning him that we have a description and if it is a false beard and hair he will not wear it again," Andy replied with a matter of fact tone to his voice before adding; "Then again, we could get some copy-cat murders, or by nutters who want to get 'The Fox' blamed.

Flash Harry continued to look very thoughtful and then he suddenly made a decision and said rather too loudly; "Right then keep me posted on this Spearing – It could be an important breakthrough at last. Also, both of you remember - get your walkie-talkies from stores right now – If you are dealing with 'The Fox' you might need them. – They are very important to keep communication channels open."

"Yes, sir I can see they are very important." Andy replied with a sarcastic undertone and then asked; "Was that Billy Larkin you were speaking to earlier sir?"

"I also told you earlier that it was none of your dam business Spearing." Flash Harry replied angrily.

"You do know that Billy Larkin has been diagnosed with terminal cancer sir?" Andy asked with a cold as ice voice.

"Of course, I know – I am his boss aint I? Larkin has a long time to go and while he has been off he is still well enough to hit the bars every day and night getting pissed, so he could be at work - for which incidentally he is getting paid." Flash Harry replied without any feeling or concern in his voice.

Andy gave him an icy stare and said; "I think if you had just been told you had terminal cancer sir, you would be hitting a lot more than bars. You know sir, Billy Larkin is one of the best detectives you have got and has given his life to the force since before you were born. If that was him you were talking to earlier I will have your guts for garters." Andy looked cold as ice and made eye contact with Flash Harry.

"Did you hear that Sergeant? – This man just threatened me – did you hear it Sergeant?

Flash Harry sounded desperate.

"What was that sir? I am afraid I was not listening sir." I replied without smiling.

"I see." Flash Harry replied and added; "Well young man now let me tell you this - you may have just bounced your career into touch."

I moved over close to Flash Harrys face and gave him the special stare! Not a single word, the stare told him everything.

"Did you see that Spearing?" He – he was just threatening me!" Flash Harry was visibly shaken.

"No sir!" Andy replied and added: "What I saw sir was not a threat, but it was a promise. Knowing this young man sir - he will do what he says, even if he only stares."

"You two are thugs who do not deserve to be in the police. I will make sure you are both dismissed! Flash Harry responded with a little bravado, but he was obviously alarmed.

"I think you lost the right to be called a policeman a long time ago sir! If you are scared what your friends in the gangs will do to you if you let them down, then you had better think ten times more if you try anything with us." Andy just smiled, got up and walked out with me following behind.

"Get out of here before I have you both arrested." Flash Harry called after us from a safe distance.

The others working around Flash Harrys office looked up in astonishment as the shouted threat rang around the office. Andy just simply gave the loco sign pointing his finger to his brain and laughed. The others laughed nervously, without looking directly at Flash Harrys office.

Andy laughed and knocked me friendly like on the shoulder and quietly said; "Like I said earlier Kevin - You have this way of winning enemies and influencing people. Let's go and nail Aldrich and Co. By the way, I didn't know you were religious?"

"To tell you the absolute truth Andy, I am not in the least religious since I was a kid! I just had enough of him talking to us that way. Do you think he will try to do anything?" I asked smiling as we went towards the exit.

Andy laughed out loud shook his head and replied in a low tone; "You do have a way of stirring people up and wrong footing them Kevin. Put it this way - If I was him I would not even think about it after your visual threat. He will not do anything face to face because he now knows you would carry out that threat. No – he will come from behind your back, so make sure your back is covered. Speaking of which, I suppose we had better go to stores on the way out and requisition a couple of these useless walkie-talkie things. Do you know how to work them Sergeant?"

I replied; "Yeah I operated them in Glasgow. They are easy to operate I will demonstrate to you in five minutes when we get outside."

"Good!" Andy simply replied.

When we reached the stores an older Sergeant, Bob Thomas, issued the Walkie-talkies. As he wrote down the serial numbers he simply said with a little smile on his face; "Well I swear to God in heaven Andy – I never thought I would see this day."

"Well to tell you the truth Bob. On my way to Paddington I was hit by a great flash from the tenth floor and like old Saint Paul I am converted!" Andy said it without a smile.

"Yes, very good Andy! The only trouble is you don't want to get converted to a 'Flash Harry' policeman. That is the wrong side of the road Andy!" Sergeant Bob Thomas laughed out loud at his own joke.

"You had better believe it Bob and thanks." Andy replied as he signed out both walkie-talkies.

So, my career appeared to have ended before it started and I had the beginning of another very serious enemy.

It was nine forty-five as we left New Scotland Yard and headed for the Paddington Police Station.

Chapter 13 - Arrests

It was ten thirty when we arrived at Paddington Station and Sergeant Willie was again on the front desk and with a sly smile on his face said; "Welcome to 'Hotel Paddington' Andy. We have once again booked you both into our best suite – Room 2/1 again!"

"Why thank you so much Willie. You don't expect a tip, do you?" Andy replied with a smile on his face.

"The only tip I can expect from a tight fisted Yorkshireman and a Scotsman is to look for a tip hearing that you two are on the way out of here." Sergeant Willie replied with the same sly smile on his face.

"Well then let us make that sooner rather than later Willie. We cannot wait to get away from here can we Sergeant? Let us have Aldrich up first – How has he been?" Andy asked.

"Still sounding like the proverbial banshee. He is verbally abusing everybody who comes anywhere near him. Are you going to charge him Andy?" Sergeant Willie asked sounding hopeful.

"Sure, I am Willie." Andy replied with a wide smile on his face.

"Yes!" Sergeant Willie shouted out punching the air and added; "Yes, but can you make it stick to that slimeball this time?"

"I think so Willie. Caught him red handed perverting the course of justice. Obstructing the police in the course of their duties and, if you get the lads to make statements, we will throw in abusive behaviour!" Andy replied with a laugh.

"It will be my pleasure Andy!" Sergeant Willie replied with a smile.

Andy still smiling asked; "Willie - Can you make arrangements for the three to be transported strictly separately to three different prisons this morning? I think Aldrich to Wormwood Scrubs, Cosgrove to Kings Cross Prison and Smith to Wandsworth."

"I certainly will do Andy – I am going to love telling Aldrich he is off to the Scrubs." Sergeant Willie replied looking so happy as he lifted the telephone to start making the arrangements.

"Okay let's go Sergeant. Will you send Aldrich up first to room 2/1 then Willie?" Andy asked as he turned away, then added; "Oh and make sure the prisons know we are opposing bail."

"I most certainly will do Andy. It cannot get any better than this!" Sergeant Willie replied with a wide grin on his face.

"It seems to have made Willie's day." I said as we walked up the stairs to room one.

"More than his day – it is his best year for many a year! Yes - well that slimeball Aldrich has led us all a merry dance in the past. He has got more criminals off the hook than fishermen have fish on the hook." Andy replied with a smile across his face and added; "Well! let's not get into exaggerated fishermen tales today. Let's just get the bastards!"

"That sounds good to me!" I said with a wide smile.

It was ten thirty as we made our way back to Room 2/1 and Andy set-up the tape recorder while we waited for Aldrich. I asked, "How do you want to play it Andy?"

Andy replied, "Leave the main talking and set-up to me. Join in when you see an opening to put pressure on them."

There was a knock on the door and young PC Atkinson stuck his head in, his face all smiles, "Mr Aldrich for interview sir."

"Wheel him in Atkinson." Andy replied and added; "Oh and Atkinson - please stay as an additional independent witness and take notes, will you?"

"Yes sir – thanks!" PC Atkinson replied, but could not hide a smile.

I went over and I swiched on the Tape Recorder and stated into the microphone; "This is an interview with Mr John Aldrich at Paddington London Police Station on Wednesday July the nineteenth 1967, at 10-45. This interview is regarding an incident on Tuesday the eighteenth of July at the offices of Palmers Assocites situated in East Ham, London. Those present are; The aforementioned John Aldrich who is being interviwed by DI Spearing and DS Devlin, both from New Scotland Yard. PC Aitkinson based at Paddington Police Station is acting as an independent witness.

"You needn't bother with that recording thing Spearing. I have nothing to say until my advocate gets here" Aldrich shouted and waved his hand in a sign of dismissal.

"Oh, that's all right then Mr Aldrich! It will save us time all around. We will just record the charges and us reading your rights. Please sit down." Andy replied curtly and nodded towards the empty chair.

"What charges? What are cooking up Spearing?" Aldrich voice wavered slightly as he sat down.

"Oh, you cooked up your own stewpot yesterday Mr Aldrich."

"Oh yes, very funny Spearing. Now what are these charges?" Aldrich face was becoming quite red, probably high blood pressure, as he spoke.

Andy smiled and cooly replied;. "Now as I said just now and yesterday! - If you refuse to answer any more questions then I will read you the charges and your rights. Then you can see your advocate in prison this afternoon under the twenty-four -hours rule.

"What questions do you want to ask?" Aldrich was back on the defensive.

"Yesterday Mr Aldrich - You stated that Mrs Palmer was your client and she ordered you to get the files and registers ready for her arrival. Is that correct?"

"That is correct." Aldrich replied.

"Yesterday Mr Aldrich, you also stated that you had not removed any of the files or the ledgers from Palmers Associates offices. - Is that correct?"

"That is correct." Aldrichs' voice slightly wavered again for a micro second.

"Then how is it six ledgers were missing Mr Aldrich?

"What six ledgers missing? How the hell should I know?"

"Oh, you don't know? Then how come we found these same six ledgers in the boot of your car Mr Aldrich?"

"My car? You have my car? – This is a stitch-up Spearing!"

"Oh, you do keep right on using the same old chestnuts for excuses don't you Mr Aldrich? Just to let you know we had a search warrant for your car. Also, we had two completely independent witnesses who saw the car when we found the ledgers in the boot. By the way, the search was carried out in accordance with the terms of the search warrant. So, what do you say to that Mr Aldrich?"

"It must have been them two plonkers Cosgrove and Smith! They were working for Mrs Smith!"

"I am afraid that will not hang together Mr Aldrich! In the first place - how did they get your car keys? And second – You see they signed and dated their statements yesterday when you were still lying to us right through until now."

"All right! All right, I admit it! I was trying to protect my client! Mrs Palmer ordered that the ledgers be removed from the office." Aldrich replied, but was now sounding almost submissive.

"You see my problem Mr Aldrich? The fact is Mrs Palmer also made and signed a statement yesterday and she recorded in that statement that she never ordered you, or anyone to remove any files, or ledgers from Palmer Associates offices!"

"She stated what?"

"I think you heard what I said Mr Aldrich. You lied yesterday and you are still lying this morning - you are lying to us."

"I admit I lied to you before Spearing, but it is now the God honest truth! Mrs Palmer ordered me to remove the files and the ledgers."

"Too late now Mr Aldrich! While I will do my best and investigate your allegation, regarding Mrs Palmers orders. I am afraid three people made and signed similar statements yesterday and you have just admitted you lied yesterday and you have admitted you again lied this morning, so why should I believe you now Mr Aldrich?" Andy waved his right hand in dismissal and added; "Mr Aldrich – I am arresting you for the following offences:

- Perverting the course of justice by removing possible evidence connected with a crime of murder in the first degree.

- Obstructing the police in the course of their duty.

- Verbally abusing several police officers in the course of their duty and we reserve the right, pending further enquires, to charge you Mr Aldrich with accessory to murder in the first degree of one John Palmer and his associate Tony Marks. You do not have to say anything, but it may harm your defence, if you fail to mention now something which you may later rely on in court. Anything you do say may be given in evidence. Do you understand?"

"This is absolutely preposterous!"

"Is that all you wish to say Mr Aldrich?" Andy was saying it all strictly by the book.

"You know as well as I do Spearing I was acting under orders from my client."

"I do not know any such thing Mr Aldrich. What I do know is that I have two signed statements recording you ordered the files and ledgers to be removed. I also have a signed statement from Mrs Palmer, your alleged client, stating that she never ordered the files and ledgers to be removed." Andy replied with a smile.

"She is telling you lies Spearing and you know it."

"There you go again Mr Aldrich. The only person I know in this case who is lying is you Mr Aldrich! That was because you just admitted it – you lied yesterday and you lied today. Now you expect us to believe some other story because you have been found out? Okay if that is all you have to say Mr Aldrich, I have to advise you that you will now be taken to Wormwood Scrubs where you will be able to contact your advocate."

"You know Spearing; you are heading for serious trouble!" Aldrich voice was harsh, but at the same time anguished.

"Yeah, oh yeah! - Double, double, toil and trouble – Fire burn and cauldron bubble – Macbeth I think Mr Witch? Oh, I am so sorry fraudulent slip there Mr Aldrich" Andy replied with his little smile and PC Atkinson and I both smiled, but did not laugh out loud because of the tape.

"Yes, you may be acting the smart ass today Spearing, but just wait to see what tomorrow will bring."

"Don't worry about tomorrow, for tomorrow will worry about itself. Each day has enough trouble of its own! – Mathew Chapter 6:34 I think? Now PC Atkinson - handcuff Mr Aldrich and take him to Sergeant Willie and make sure he is taken immediately to Wormwood prison. Then bring in Tommy Smith first please. Thank you." Andy just nodded and waved his hand in dismissal.

"You will pay for this Spearing" Aldrich yelled as he was led away.

"I would not pay for you Aldrich even if you were free!" Andy replied coolly.

PC Atkinson closed the door as he left and Andy turned around and said into the tape recorder microphone; "Interview with Mr Aldrich concluded at 11-05 a.m. on the nineteenth of July 1967." He then switched off the tape recorder.

"Do you think the case on Aldrich is watertight Andy?" I asked.

"As tight as it can be with slimy toads like him. That is until his friends upstairs in the Yard find out, and then we will get the pressure!"

"You reckon somebody upstairs will try to get him off Andy?" I asked

"Afraid so – there are a few of those bastards in the back pockets of the gangs Aldrich represents. They will try with the DPP office to spring him!"

"Do you know who they are?"

"Yes, I know who they are, but knowing and proving are two very separate things. There is corruption from top to bottom in the yard Kevin! However, this time we have Aldrich red-handed. So, unless they tamper with the evidence, which we must make sure they cannot touch, then we have him!"

"How do we make sure they cannot tamper with evidence?"

"That is one of your jobs Kevin – This afternoon before the shit hits the fan, get all the evidence into a left luggage locker at Victoria Railway Station, including the stuff you took home with you last night. Also put the key someplace where they cannot find it and only you and I will know where!"

"That means going back to Palmers Green this afternoon Andy and then back to Victoria."

"Oh, so it does! Never mind you have your police pass for the travel. Anyway, I have to meet up with one of my snitches and you can attend to that business while I am away – Okay?"

"Yeah, I suppose so, still feeling a bit knackered after yesterday!" I grumbled.

"Yeah, aren't we all." Andy replied with a wry smile on his face.

There was a knock on the door and PC Atkinson stuck his smiling face around and said, "Tommy Smith for interview sir."

"Wheel him in Atkinson and stay again as an independent witness.." Andy replied, turned around and switched on the tape recorder and into the microphone said quietly, "Second interview with Mr Thomas Smith commenced at 11-10 a.m. on 19th July 1967. Those present; the aforementioned Mr Thomas Smith. Also DI Spearing and DS Devlin from New Scotland Yard and PC Atkinson from Paddington Police Station as an independent witness. He then turned back around and faced Tommy Smith.

"Ah Mr Thomas Smith please sit down." Andy said and pointed to the chair opposite.

"I have nothing further to add to my statement yesterday." Tommy Smith replied, nodding towards the tape recorder.

"That is not a problem and was expected Mr Smith. So, all there is to do today is to read your rights and the charges." Andy replied coolly and added, "Mr Thomas Smith I'm arresting you for the following offences:

- Fleeing the scene of a crime of murder.

- Perverting the course of justice by removing possible evidence connected with a crime of murder in the first degree.

- Obstructing the police in the course of their duty.

We reserve the right, pending further enquires, to charge you Mr Smith with accessory to murder in the first degree, of one John Palmer and his associate Tony Marks. You do not have to say anything, but it may harm your defence, if you fail to mention now something which you may later rely on in court. Anything you do say may be given in evidence. Do you understand?"

"Yeah, I understand Spearing - you bastard, I thought you were going to help us if we helped you?" Tommy Smith voice was full of emotion.

"All I said previously to you Mr Smith and to Mr Cosgrove was that I would inform the judge that you two have given the police full cooperation and would he or she consider that when sentencing you. Of course, if we found you were lying to us and you are later charged with accessory to murder then we would not have a word with the judge. Is that clear Mr Smith?" Andy asked, but with a slight grin on his face.

"Yeah it is clear Spearing you have stitched us up again, just like the last time." Tommy Smith just spat out his reply.

"Isn't it funny Sergeant Devlin when all these guys get caught red-handed with their hands in the till they all shout 'stitch-up' - don't you think so Sergeant Devlin?" Andy asked followed by a little giggle.

"If one was cynical sir, one would think they have all been rehearsed by their solicitors on what to say should they ever be caught red-handed. Then again, I am probably too cynical sir and they simply all say the first thing that comes into their head. Yet it is quite a coincidence - don't you think sir?" I replied with a smile on my face.

"I would think it is a little more than a coincidence Sergeant." Andy replied and turned around and spoke quietly into the tape recorders microphone, "Second interview with Mr Thomas Smith concluded at 11-17 a.m. on the nineteenth of July 1967.." He then switched off the machine.

"Can you PC Atkinson take Mr Smith directly to Sergeant Willie who knows to which prison he is to be taken? Then bring Mr Cosgrove for his second interview?" Andy said with a matter of fact tone to his voice.

"Yes, sir with pleasure!" PC Atkinson replied and took Smith's arm to lead him away.

Tommy Smith stared blankly at DI Spearing then turned away sullenly looking back.

The second interview with Bobby Cosgrove was almost a replica of the Tommy Smith second interview except Cosgrove got angrier.

When it finished Andy turned around around and spoke quietly into the tape recorders microphone; "Second interview with Mr Robert Cosgrove concluded at 11-57 a.m. on the nineteenth of July 1967." He then switched off the machine..

"God, I did not realize the time. I am supposed to be meeting my snitch at one o'clock. I will have to ring him and delay it for half an hour." Andy said as he lifted the phone.

"Do you want me to come with you Andy?"

"God no Kevin! These snitches would run a mile if I came with anyone. One- to-one deal all the time, no other way. I'll tell you what though, while I phone my snitch if you could use the telephone in the back office and give young Judith Clements a ring. You will enjoy that I suppose? Let her know who we have charged, what prisons they have gone to and make sure she makes the prisons know we are opposing bail. Oh, and you could give 'hooray' Nigel a ring - see how he has got on with the ledgers – I woud like to know how he got on before we go back to chat to Mrs Palmer this afternoon after my chat with the snitch. Oh, and take this tape with you as well for the locker at Victoria Station." Andy asked.

"Right sir – is that before or after I go out to Palmers Green?"

"The phone calls before you go to Palmers Green, but Mrs Palmer will be after. You will really have to learn how to manage your time Kevin!" Andy replied with a smile all over his face.

"Yes sir – three bags full sir!" I replied and headed out of Room 2/1.

I made the call first to Judith, but unfortunately, she was tied up in a meeting, so I quickly and rather blandly relayed the messages to her. She thanked me very politely without any banter. She sounded like she had someone in the room who she didn't want to know about my message, so I quickly hung up.

Then just before twelve I phoned through to Nigel Worthington.

Worthington lifted the receiver and simply said "Nigel Worthington here – How can I help?"

I responded; "Sergeant Devlin here Worthington. DI Spearing was just asking if you have had a chance to look at the Palmers Associates ledgers yet."

"As a matter of fact, I have Sergeant. I was just down stairs looking for DI Spearing, but he was not around. Studying these ledgers, I have found there has been a sudden vast increase over the last five years in the subject companies trading with Asia via Afghanistan and Holland and with the US of A, via South America. I don't think it takes a genius to work out what that trade may be? Secondly, these books are showing massive losses which most major companies would be unable to sustain. So, what I think we are looking at here Sergeant is that there is a second set of books somewhere which are the real books. Anyway, that is my own findings so far; although I am still working through them I have no doubt in my mind that is the case." Nigel thought the visit to DI Spearing's desk was a nice touch just in case anybody had seen him earlier.

"Well I am surprised Worthington." I replied, taken aback by his quick and almost certainly correct response. "Yes, well that is really good work Worthington. I will pass on the information to DI Spearing and thanks!" I responded hesitantly and hung up just as Andy stuck his face around the door.

"My snitch has already left for our meeting so I will have to scurry across to meet him. I will meet you back at the Yard later in the afternoon and we can then arrange a meeting with Mrs Palmer." Andy shouted and waved his hand in farewell.

"Yes sir." I shouted back in response. It was then, for some unknown reason, because of some gut reaction, I decided to follow Andy at a distance. I left it for a minute and went out looked both ways then caught him walking towards Paddington Underground station.

I stayed at what I considered a safe distance and watched as he made his way through the maze of underground tunnels heading in the direction of the Bakerloo Line. I followed and when we came to the platform I hung back in an archway at least two or three carriages length away from where he was standing. A tube train came almost instantly and I waited to the last moment before jumping on a carriage. I could see the nearest exit door to him, but could not see him and hopefully he could not see me. We carried on through five stations and finally he got up to the exit door at Piccadilly Station.

I watched him turning right, in the direction of the exit, before jumping off the tube train at the last moment and followed him, again at what I thought was a safe distance.

On exiting the station, he turned north-west and walked down Coventry Street in the general direction of London's Soho. He came to the junction with Wardour Street and turned left walking past the famous 'Marquee' club, once a jazz club, but now mainly a blues and rock venue with a recording studio in the back.

He continued down Wardour Street and came to 'The Ship' pub. Before going in, he opened the door and checked around, and then he entered. I idled nonchalantly towards the side doors which were open presumably because of the summer heat. I pretended to look at my watch as though I was meeting someone and took a quick glance inside the pub.

Andy was at the bar alone and ordered a pint of Speckled Hen best bitter.

Presumably his snitch had not yet appeared so he sat down at a small two chair table and gulped down half a pint, needed that I supposed. He looked at his watch twelve-thirty; he shook his head and gulped the remainder of the pint, got up and ordered another pint of bitter and while it was being poured he went over to the old black 'phone on the wall of the pub.

He dialled a number and stood waiting for someone to answer.

"Bethnal Green 3647999" A woman's voice with a London east end accent answered.

"Is Les Hall there please?" DI Spearing asked.

"Who is calling?" The woman replied with a slight waiver in her voice.

"A friend! - Les was supposed to be meeting me at one o'clock in town!" Andy replied.

"I am afraid Les will not be meeting anyone ever again in town. Mr - he was killed this morning trying to get on a tube train at Bethnal Green!" The woman sounded as though she was ready to break-down in tears.

"What? What do you mean killed?" Andy sounded agitated and had gone slightly white in the face.

"Well the police have been here and they said a big fella, about six feet something with reddish hair and a goatee beard was seen by a woman to push poor Les in front of the train as it pulled into the station. He took a direct hit and went under the wheels. It's going to be in the Evening Standard today with a description of the man"

"Oh, my God! I am so sorry Mrs – Are you Mrs Hall?"

"I am, but I am the mother of Les. His wife, the bitch, left him years ago and he has been taking care of me. Now I don't know what I will do. What is your name Mr?"

"Oh, I was just a business associate Mrs Hall." Andy replied and was just about to hang up when Mrs Hall added; "Yes I know what business Les was in Mr and I always told him he would come to a bad end."

"Well maybe you didn't know Mrs Hall. Les had been helping the police in recent years and had been trying to turn a new leaf." Andy replied hoping to make it a bit easier on her, but did not expect her instant response; "Is that why he was killed then Mr? – Was it because he was helping the police?"

"No! – At least not that I know of Mrs Hall Look I have to go – If I find out anything I will let
you know." Andy hung up and shook his head, while rubbing his chin. He went back to the bar and lifted his pint of bitter. By the time he sat down he had swallowed another half pint. As he supped his beer, he thought the description does sounds like 'The Fox' and perhaps Les Hall had found out who he was and that is what got him killed. Andy felt he was partly responsible for the low life Les Hall's death, but then quickly dismissed the thought, saying to himself that was how Hall had operated all his life, among villains and what happened today was inevitable, - just a wonder that it had not happened many years before. Still Andy thought, I owe Hall to at least try and find 'The Fox', perhaps tomorrow I will contact the Detective in charge and see what I can do.

As he finished the remainder of his 'Speckled Hen' beer he took out his nineteen sixty-seven W H Smiths daily diary and looked up today's date. He noticed he had to phone his solicitors Parker and Wynne today regarding his divorce. He went back to the bar and ordered another pint then returned to the pub phone.

He dialled the solicitor's number.

"Parker and Wynne Solicitors – How can I help?" A rather pleasant young girl's voice answered.

"Could I speak to Mr Wynne?"

"Who shall I say is calling sir?"

"Tell him it is Andy Spearing please. He is expecting my call!"

"Oh yes Mr Spearing. If you would please hold."

"Can't do much else dear – can I?"

"Yes well – Yes sir - please hold and I will see if I can locate him."

"Yes, do that dear and thank you."

There was a short delay and then a click on the line.

"Andy - Good to hear from you and on time! Just to let you know the decree absolute has come through. You are a free man at last!" John Wynne a friend, but a lousy solicitor, sounded jovial.

"Is that good news or bad news John?"

"Yes, well that is up to you Andy. It depends on what you make of it!"

"It also depends on what you charge me John."

"Always reasonable for a friend - you know that Andy!"

"Not so far John. It looks like I will have to sell off my family home to pay off you and her."

"Afraid it is the going rate these days Andy. Have to run it as a business even for friends."

"Yeah well if that is the charge for friends John. I would not like to see your charges for enemies. Mind you - you might have done a better job for your enemies." Andy replied, and hung up before John Wynne could reply. He shook his head and now looked even whiter than previously as he made his way back to the bar and picked up his third pint. He took another gulp, drinking a half pint in one go, and sat back down at his table looking utterly rejected.

I decided whatever news he had received it had driven him to spend the rest of the day drinking in the pub. I decided to head for home, pick up the tapes and the stuff from yesterday, get them to a locker in Victoria Station and drop back to The Yard. I need to check out with Judith in case anything was happening. I then intended to come back to 'The Ship' to pick up the pieces of Andy as it looked like he was in for a booze session.

Book 1 in the DI Spearing and DS Devlin series

Chapter 14 - The Sting

Nigel Worthington had been about to leave for the next stage of his Plan B when he received the call from DI Spearings Glasgow thug Devlin. He thought to himself that he had handled it rather well, but he decided to use his ploy of saying that he had been down to see them and to contact Mrs Palmer using DI Spearings phone.

He quickly bounded down the stairs and went to DI Spearings desk. The office was empty, it was just lunchtime and everyone had disappeared, probably off to the park for a bit of sun worshipping, or more likely, over to the pub for a quick pint.

Worthingtonl lifted DI Spearing's telephone and dialled Palmers Associates number which he had previously noted down from the ledgers.

A girl receptionist answered the call with the usual nice sounding voice and a middle of the road London accent; "Good morning – Palmers Associates – how can I help?"

Worthington shifted uneasily in the chair before replying in his posh BBC voice; "Can I speak to Mrs Palmer please?"

"Whom shall I say is calling sir?" The girl asked helpfully.

"Can you please tell Mrs Palmer it is a gentleman with knowledge on the whereabouts of certain ledgers, which are missing from your company. I am sure she will want to talk me." Nigel replied smoothly with an assured tone.

There was a click on the line and less than a minute later a mature woman's voice came on. "Mrs Palmer here - how can I help?"

"Mrs Palmer – I wish to meet up with you this morning. It is regarding the ledgers which went missing from your offices!"

"I believe the ledgers are in the hands of the police sir." Mrs Palmers was cool in her reply.

"That is correct Mrs Palmer. However, I happen to have a contact in the very police station where the ledgers are held and, for the right price, I can get them out to you before they can be used against you." Worthington was trying to sound very self-assured.

"What makes you think the ledgers can be used against me?" Mrs Palmer was sounding cool, calm and collected.

"Come on now Mrs Palmer. Shall I just pass on the message from my friend in the police station and talk about transistor radios from Japan, via Afghanistan, or how about the Freezers and Fridges from the good old US of A, via South America?" Worthington was back to his sneering and leering voice.

There was a long silence; "What price are we talking here?" Mrs P asked with an icy tone in her voice.

"Oh, shall we say £5,000 now and another £5,000 when we deliver?"

"Don't be so ridiculous!" Mrs P replied with exasperation.

"Well, let us make that £50 thousand now and £50 thousand when we deliver. Now is that so ridiculous Mrs Palmer? The companies you are representing are making millions from each shipment. So, what is one hundred thousand which will save you millions?" Worthington was back to his sneering voice.

"You go from £5,000 to £50,000 – I don't think this is serious!"

"Oh yes, believe me this is very serious. Look at it this way Mrs Palmer – do you want to save millions and not go jail?"

"I hand you over fifty thousand pounds and I do not even know if you have the ledgers. What do you think I am? – Some sort of an idiot?"

"No Mrs Palmer! You are certainly not an idiot. I know you are a very good business woman. You know a good deal when you hear one. I will bring photographs of all the ledger pages with entries. So, you can verify. Do we have a deal?" Worthington replied almost too casually.

"I will think about it!" Mrs P replied, but now with a nervous tone in her voice.

"I am afraid there is no time to think about it. You are either in now, or the chance is gone. It will be too late."

There was another long silence; "Okay – Okay! You have a deal. You will have to come to my offices." Mrs P replied with a little hesitation.

"Now do you think I am the idiot Mrs Palmer? The owner – the wife of a well - known villain who has just been murdered and you want me to come to your offices? I am afraid not Mrs Palmer. Shall we say Lyons Tea Rooms at Piccadilly at three pm?"

"How will I know you?"

"You won't Mrs Palmer. You come with a flower in your hair – just like the San Francisco song and I will know you. And you come alone! - If I see anyone around who looks remotely menacing towards me then I am out of there and there is no deal. Remember and bring the fifty thousand in cash. That is all Mrs Palmer." Worthington hung up the phone with a smile on his face and moved quickly towards the stairs and headed back to his own office.

Worthington left the office at just before 13-00 and took a taxi to Victoria Station. In the station a small shop advertised photo prints within an hour and Nigel paid an extra quid to get two copies of each within forty-five minutes. The assistant was only too pleased to do a deal for a quid in his pocket and placed the prints in separate envelopes while they dried.

Then he went straight onto the Victoria tube and switched at Green Park to the Piccadilly line and onwards to Piccadilly tube station. It was straight across the road from The Lyons Tea rooms on the corner. Worthingtonl managed to get a seat at the window on the first-floor restaurant area looking down Piccadilly. He would be able to see if anybody was following Mrs Palmer. He did a quick check, but could not see any suspects on any of the three floors. He ordered sandwiches and tea and settled down waiting and watching from behind the London Evening Standard newspaper.

She came into sight at about 14-20 approaching from the Piccadilly tube station. It was a large white flower she had in her hair and she carried a rather large carrier bag, her hand held the bag tightly to her right hip. No sign of anyone obviously following from Piccadilly, or approaching from the Leicester Square side. Well here we go Worthington thought to himself as Mrs P came to the doors. He decided to leave something on the table and went downstairs to meet her.

"Ah ha - Mrs Palmer I presume, how nice of you to come! Let us go upstairs where I have a table and have a chat!" Nigel felt the old smoothie again putting on his best posh accent. Mrs P nodded before following but did not reply. They sat down at the window table.

"All right, let me see proof that you can get hold of my ledgers then Mr?" Mrs P was certainly straight down to business.

"Ah ha, you're a woman after my own heart my dear. Right down to business"

"As far as you are concerned, I do not have a heart boy, so shall we get on with it?" Mrs P was cold and unresponsive.

Worthington produced one set of the photographs of one of the ledgers and handed them over to Mrs P without a word only a whimsical smile.

"Right these are copies of the ledger entries. Now – how do I trust you not to take the fifty thousand and scarper?" Mrs P asked, accompanied with a hard stare as she passed the brown carrier bag containing the money to Worthington.

"Because Mrs Palmer, there is another fifty thousand pounds for me when I bring the ledgers. It is that simple!"

"I will want these photographs and the negatives when you come back. When will that be?" Mrs P got up getting ready to leave.

"Oh, that will be early next week Mrs Palmer. By the way, please sit and wait here for five minutes before coming out. I don't intend to allow you to get someone to follow me." Worthington said it with another of his whimsical smiles.

He picked up the bag with the fifty thousand quid got up and hurriedly went downstairs and turned left as he exited walking towards Leicester Square. He looked both ways and across the road before quickly walking, as close to the shop windows as possible, to keep out of view of the Lyons Tea House windows.

He did not notice Mrs Palmers 'new' minder Ralph emerging from the Travel Agency opposite the Lyons Tea House and follow him to the Leicester Square tube station and all the way back to New Scotland Yard.

Worthington decided, on the spur of a moment, to celebrate and to finish mid-afternoon on the pretext of attending a meeting. He set off to the Sloane Square tube station and took the district and circle line to South Kensington. He still did not even notice Ralph following him back to his Kensington Penthouse.

Worthington rang the bell on the door of his penthouse and was met by David who he hit with a left uppercut to the solar plexus. David doubled up and hit the ground holding himself up on all fours while visibly panting in short quick breaths.

"That is it dog – where is your collar - dog?" Worthington was in one of his vicious, loutish moods shouting as he closed and locked the door.

"I don't know where it is – you said that you wouldn't do this anymore Nigel - please." David just stayed there on his fours and quivering, his eyes filling with tears.

Worthington swung a kick at David and caught him on the ass and shouted, "Get up you dirty dog and get your clothes off. I have your money to pay you back. I want to celebrate and have fun. If you play with me tonight I will pay you a bonus."

David yelped with the pain from the kick and quickly stood up and said; "Please Nigel – You know I don't like it this way."

"Shut up you dirty dog." Worthington shouted and swung a back handed fist which caught David just below his right eye and sent him spinning across the room and crashing into the coffee table.

"Now do as you are told and get your clothes off - NOW you dirty dog. I will find the collar to hold you in place." Worthington shouted louder and more viciously as he stormed off into the bedroom. He was now out of control and would exert the maximum pain to gratify his sexual desires.

David began to fumble and started taking off his clothes, quickly taking of his shirt and dropping his trousers and standing in his pink, silk, boxer, crying as he did so. He knew that beating was just the beginning and tonight was going to be a long hard night.

Worthington returned carrying a large dog collar and a lead shouting; "Get them boxers off dog and get down on your paws."

David pleaded; "Please Nigel don't hurt me anymore." But he obeyed, taking off his boxers and went down on the floor on his hands and knees with tears streaming down his face.

Worthington was suddenly back to his old vicious loutish self, which always happened when he had come into money and there was no telling how it would end. David only knew that tonight it would be very painful for him as the dogs' collar was put around his neck.

Chapter 15- Timely

I got back into Victoria Station at three thirty and rented a left luggage locker packing in the tapes and signed statements.

Since it was a beautiful summer's day I decided to walk down Buckingham Palace Road and got back to the New Scotland Yard offices at four o'clock.

I went straight to Judith Clément's office and found her alone, staring into space, with a frown on her face.

"Not a happy face then?" I asked putting on a false smile.

"No –I would say not at all!" Judith answered gloomily.

"What is the matter then?" I asked cheerily.

"I had a meeting with your boss 'Flash Harry' when you rang earlier!"

"Oh really? - I thought something was wrong. What did he want?"

"I think he wants to go to war with you and DI Spearing."

"Aye - I am not surprised after our meeting this morning. What was he on about?" I asked trying to sound as nonchalant as possible.

"He was actually trying to get me to lay off on the Aldrich arrest!"

"Well! Well does he know the evidence?" I asked.

"No – not at all! That didn't stop him though! He actually made a veiled threat as to my future."

"Don't worry about him. According to Andy he is all hot air and no substance." I replied trying to sound confident.

"Yeah – still - he seems to have a lot of friends upstairs."

"They cannot afford to do anything with us. The chief will not allow it." I replied, again with more confidence than I felt.

"Yeah well he seemed to be suggesting that the chief will not be around too much longer."

"Aye – He said something like that when we had a conversation earlier." I replied trying to sound cool.

"Yeah – then I got a call from his boss - a Detective Superintendent John Sunderland. He tried to get me to drop the case as 'not enough evidence'."

"Sounds like some heavy stuff. And did you?" I had to ask.

"What do you think?"

"I would be very surprised if you succumbed." I replied.

"I don't succumb that easy!"

"I am not surprised. You are not the type." I replied with the obvious innuendo and a little smile.

"You had better believe it!" Judith replied but she blushed ever so slightly.

"How about succumbing to a drink this evening?" I asked with one of my cheeky grins.

"Now that I don't mind succumbing to, but unfortunately I am not available tonight."

"Ah, just as I thought! A beautiful woman like you must have a full diary." I gave her my best devilish grin.

"Ah the silver tongue again. I suppose I should be honoured. The Lone Ranger has asked me out! Cannot wait to let my Cambridge pals know. Hi ho silver lining is alive and well." Judith put on her most brilliant smile.

"You are really funny. Another time perhaps?" I smiled but sounded a bit more desperate than I intended.

"Yes, definitely. Just can't miss the opportunity to brag about going out with the Lone Ranger. I'll look forward to it." She replied again with a most beautiful smile.

"Yeah right Kemosabe - Cool! – I'll see you then. Is everything else all right? – I mean with the arrests and things?"

"Yeah – I think so. Aldrich has John Ivory as an advocate. They are applying for bail tomorrow. I am using the possibility of accessory to murder to stop them getting bail, but I might not need that if their statements drop them in it. – Can you get the latest statements to me?"

"Oh shit! I forgot to type them out. I'll collect the tapes on the way home and type them out tonight. Meet you here in the morning about eight?" I asked.

"Yeah – okay! – The bail hearing is not till ten at Marlborough!"

"Thanks again Judith. See you in the morning." I flashed my best smile again and turned away.

I went down to my floor and sat down at my desk. Within a few minutes the phone rang on Andys. I leaned across and picked it up.

"DI Spearings desk! DS Devlin speaking" I answered.

"Is he there?" A man asked with an obviously false London east end accent, like a posh actor
trying to play the part of an east ender.

"I am afraid he is out of the office at present." I replied slowly.

"Can you take a message then?"

"Yes, I sure can." I replied at the same time lifting a pen and my notepad.

"Tell him that the man he is after - a 'Mr Fox' – will be appearing early in the morning on a job at The Centaurus Apartments, in Cadogan Gardens, Sloane Square - just around the corner from you at New Scotland Yard." The man's accent was still sounding very false.

"Oh aye? And how do you know that my friend?" I replied.

"Don't ask silly questions Sergeant Devlin and you will not be given silly answers. Just make sure he gets the message and make sure you don't go mob handed. This man is a pro and he can smell coppers at a hundred yards." The man hung up.

I sat there staring at the phone for a couple of minutes. How the hell did he know me? This didn't sound right at all. I quickly deduced that the only way he could have known me was that he had internal contacts, or in fact he was in these offices. No way of finding out, but maybe if it came through the switchboard. I dialled zero for the operator.

"This is the switchboard! – How can I help?" A woman with a pleasant voice answered.

"I just received a call on DI Spearings phone and got cut off. Can you tell me who it was so as I can ring him back?"

"No sir, there was not an external call through the switchboard to that number. It must have been an internal call and we cannot trace them." The switchboard woman curtly replied.

"Thanks anyway." I replied and hung up. Well, Andy had warned me about the ones upstairs on the gang's payrolls. Well it was one explanation anyway.

I decided to go back and pick up Andy, but go via Sloane Square and catch the layout of these Centaurus apartments.

The Centaurus apartments were housed in a huge London prestigious regency style building overlooking Cadogan Gardens. There was a huge reception area complete with four, brilliant white, concrete columns each four feet in circumference and with fluted shafts. There were wonderfully carved caps and plinths on each column which were about fifteen feet high to the white ceilings. The ceilings also had had wonderfully carved cornice all the way round.

Hidden behind the pillars, to the right of the entrance was a dark oak reception desk, behind which sat a fit looking porter probably late forties or maybe early fifties in full uniform, including cap, despite the warm day. He had copper or ex-copper written all over him.

I approached his desk and flashed my badge and said; "Detective Sergeant Devlin New Scotland Yard."

The porter just nodded then asked; "Yes sir, how can I help you?" He asked in a Geordie accent giving the impression he had a police officer visit every day of the week. He had a name tag above his left breast stating his name as Whitfield.

"Okay Mr Whitfield – We have information that a wanted and extremely dangerous man may be in this locality within the next twelve hours!" I replied.

"Is this the 'most wanted' man that 'The Evening Standard' is on about then?" Whitfield asked.

"Who is that then?" I asked and I guess I did sound dumfounded.

"It is in the late editions of 'The Evening Standard.' Is it still the right-hand not knowing what the left is doing in 'The Yard'? Here have a look." Whitfield replied smiling while passing the newspaper to me.

I snatched the paper and read the main headline story.

London Evening Standard
Scotland Yards Most Wanted Man? –
Hit man kills three in two days and then more!

A man fitting the description of 'The Fox,' an assassin wanted in connection with the double murders of accountant John Palmer and his associate Tony Marks, at Palmers Surrey mansion in the early hours of yesterday morning, has been matched to the same man who apparently pushed a known small time crook Les Hall off the East Ham tube stations central London bound platform.on the Hammersmith and City line.

Hall was hit and run over by the incoming train at eleven forty-five this morning.

The Hammersmith and City line London bound trains were stopped for several hours while Mr Hall's body was recovered.

A New Scotland Yard Detective, Chief Inspector Harry Tomlinson stated; "The man described by witnesses matches the description of the assassin known as 'The Fox' who is wanted for questioning in connection with the double murders of John Palmer and Tony Marks in Weybridge Surrey yesterday morning. He is also wanted for questioning in connection with many other murders and assassinations during the last few years. This man is armed and very dangerous and should not be approached by members of the public. If you see this man please phone 999 and inform the police of his whereabouts."

DCI Tomlinson went on and issued a description of the assassin as a six foot two or three and a very muscular man. He is thought to be around forty-five to fifty, almost certainly ex-army, possibly SAS or Paratrooper, with reddish hair and a goatee beard though this may be false.

Later today a man fitting the same description was seen in the vicinity of 'The Hoofers Club.' The owner, a Mr Joe Cole, was found dead and police are treating it as very suspicious.

There was a photo-fit of the assassin with a side view of his face.

I had read enough – Flash Harry was grabbing the limelight, acting the big 'I am' despite knowing that it could hinder our case. With a shake of my head I passed the newspaper back to Whitfield.

"You were a copper then?" I asked.

"How did you know?" Whitfield replied.

"Oh, just an educated guess. Where were you based?"

"At 'The Yard' – then at Paddington Green! You one of the new 'trained brains' then?"

"Jesus Christ! You know you London coppers must have a hell of an underground spy ring." I replied with a smile and added; "So you must have known Sergeant Willie Thomas?"

"Know him? He taught me all I know. One of the few straight ones left."

"Why did you pack it in then? - You are not that old" I asked.

Had enough of the corruption and fiddling. I joined the police to catch criminal's lad, not to be in their back pockets."

"This must be very tame compared to the police?"

"Yeah boring as well, but it is a job. I suppose it is the same as a security guard, but hey ho I am reading for an Open University course and this is ideal."

"Can I ask you about your security here?"

"Fire away especially if this guy is going to be knocking about here!"

"Yes, well it is a possibility. What do you think of the security at this place?"

"As far as this type of place goes it is damn good! We have these new CCTV cameras in the reception and on the front and back entrances and the emergency exits. We also have them on each floor looking down each corridor. I have the screens in front of me here on the desk."

"What happens if you have to go to the toilet or to one of the apartments?" I asked.

"Oh, I throw a switch which locks all the doors and the entrance doors to each floor. The tenants or owners then have to use their keys to get in and anybody else has to wait till I get back to the reception desk."

"Sounds good! How do the shifts work?"

Whitfield replied; "I do seven thirty in the morning for twelve hours and Tom Owen does the night shift from seven thirty for twelve hours - Monday to Friday"

"Tom Owen another ex-copper?"

"Oh yes – he was based at Lewisham before he retired ten years ago. Yes, Tom is a good old boy!"

"What about the weekends?" I asked.

"We have two coppers who are still working. They do moonlighters to make ends meet."

"That is fair enough. Do you reckon they are all straight?"

"Well the way I look at it is this – If they had been on the 'take' they would not be doing this dead-end job – Now would they?" Whitfield replied with more than a little anger in his voice.

"Aye I suppose there is that. Well I had better be getting along. Would you do me a favour? "Tell Tom about this guy - He may be around tonight and he ought to be extra careful and you too."

Whitfield replied; "Will do." And then he added a question; "Tell me - who is your DI Sergeant?"

"DI Spearing!" I replied.

"Oh well at least you have one of the decent ones left in 'The Yard' lad."

"Yes, so they tell me! He seems to be very good at his job despite the obstacles." I replied then suddenly had an afterthought and asked; "Tell me Mr Whitfield could you give me a list of all the tenants and the owners with their apartment numbers?"

"Well lad that is normally 'confidential' information. However, based on the circumstances I am sure no one will mind." Whitfield replied and went to the centre drawer in his desk and passed me a type written list.

These are the current occupants, it doesn't state who are owners or renters." Whitfield said with a coy smile.

"That does not matter." I replied and added; "Perhaps there is a connection?"

"Don't know I am afraid. Don't look too closely. These places are used to meet up with city girls, so it is best to keep out of it and my mouth shut. You know what I mean?"

"Sure." I replied, but is there anybody you recognize from the list?"

"Not really son. – They mostly use nom-de-plumes. I don't really pay too much attention. For the money I get, it aint worth getting too deep into this lot of charlatans! - That is what they are."

"How much does it cost to rent or buy a place here?" I asked being naturally inquisitive.

"Oh, to rent I think it is about one hundred pounds per week. To buy, they say three hundred thousand pounds."

"You are joking?" I asked in astonishment.

"Nope! - And what is more they reckon in another few years they will be worth millions to sell and thousands per week to rent. That's the new London for you lad." Whitfield replied with a wry smile.

"What are they into? They have got to be crooks to have that kind of money."

"They are business men mostly!" Whitfield replied again with the same wry smile.

"Aye well there you go, that is what I mean! You don't earn that kind of money and live in this style and be totally legal, do you?" I answered, my Glasgow working class background coming to the fore.

"Yeah you may be right there son, but there are crooks you can catch and then there are these ones."

"You take care now Mr Whitfield! This guy is a professional assassin and his employers, whoever they may be, are ruthless. Remember to let Tom know tonight. Keep your eyes on the screens tonight and not in your books." I said as I turned away.

"Will do and you take care too! The pros don't hesitate to kill to get away, even if you are a copper."

"Yeah – thanks for the reminder Mr Whitfield. See you later." I answered nonchalantly, but felt more than a little unsure.

I looked at my watch as I left. Time was moving quickly on. I decided I had to go back to Wardour Street and see if I could pick up Andy at 'The Ship' pub. He must be well plastered by now, but I had to give him the tip about 'The Fox' and see what he wanted to do.

I picked up a copy of the late edition of 'The Evening Standard' from a news stand outside Sloane Square tube station. It now had the photo of Joe Cole and the police appeared to be now linking his death to the assassin known as 'The Fox.'

I went into the tube station and decided the quickest route was to double back to South Kensington on the 'District and Circle' line and there pick up 'The Piccadilly' line to Piccadilly Circus. I exited at Piccadilly Circus station within fifteen minutes and walked back down Coventry Street and again turned left into Wardour Street.

I was amazingly back at 'The Ship' pub within twenty-five minutes of leaving 'The Centaurus' apartments. When the London Underground is working, there is no better way to get around London.

I stayed outside the pub doors and peered through a gap and sure enough Andy was still there supping another pint. I was just about to enter when he got up and walked towards the toilets. I then noticed a tall hippie guy with long reddish hair tied back in a ponytail looking around and follow Andy into the toilet.

I don't know why, but for some reason I did not like the look of that and I immediately went into the pub ignoring the barman asking; "Yes sir. What will you have?" as I quickly headed for the gent's toilet. I threw my copy of 'The Evening Standard' on Andys' table as I went past.

Andy was washing his hands when he heard someone come in the door behind him. The red-haired hippie sent a powerful right and left uppercut into Andys' kidneys and he let out a painful gasp and caught his breath as his pee went down the front of his trousers.

"Not so big now are you 'man'?" The hippie rasped.

As Andy tried to turn, the hippie threw another left uppercut into his solar-plexus. Andy threw up vomit and a lot of beer like a volcano and it cascaded onto the hippies' face.

"You dirty filthy bastard." The hippie exploded as he tried to wipe his eyes.

I tapped the hippie on the shoulder and as he turned around, still half blinded by the vomit, I gave him the Glasgow kiss across the bridge of his nose which splintered and spewed instant blood. I then caught him with a beautifully timed right knee to the groin which probably burst both of his balls and at the same time made him impotent for the rest of his life. As he pitched forward I drove my left knee into his cheek bone which I heard splintering with a sickening crack. He fell to the ground out cold.

"Are you all right Andy?" I asked as he was rather white, growing greyish.

"Could be better lad – then again I am sure glad you are on my side!" Andy answered with a grimace as he rubbed his kidneys and added; "Where have you been all day anyway since you left outside?"

"You saw me tailing you?" I asked feeling very embarrassed.

Andy was breathing in short gasps as he replied; "Laddie – A blind man would probably have seen you tailing me! Remind me tomorrow to teach you the basics for tailing someone and don't even bother to try and tail a pro!" Andy replied with a loud laugh.

"Do you know this guy?" I asked wiping Andys' spew from my brow with my handkerchief.

"Not really, but I recognize him from Monday. He kept interrupting when I was talking to my snitch in here." Andy replied.

"Really?" I said and added; "That a coincidence or what? Who the devil is he then?"

"Yeah, I don't like coincidences. Better see if he has any identity on him." Andy replied still grimacing with the pain in his kidneys.

I searched his pockets and found the old green driving licence in a battered brown leather wallet.

"Thomas Broadbent - he is from High Street Streatham." I announced.

"Take the license and get on that walkie-talkie thing if it works and run a check on him. Leave the wallet." Andy said in a matter of fact voice.

"While I am on, we had better get this guy arrested and get an ambulance. Assaulting a policeman in the line of his duty – that okay for starters?" I asked.

"I said already you are a quick learner lad. You get on that walkie-talkie thing and run the check – also tell them to check out where he works. Let them know a policeman is being attacked and ask for assistance and an ambulance."

I did as I was told, quoting my detective shield number and letting them know Andy had been attacked. I was assured there would be police and ambulance there within ten to fifteen minutes. I then asked them if they would run a check on the hippie guy and get back to me as soon as possible. I set the hippie up on his side so that he would not choke on his own blood or on his vomit when it came to.

"Okay let's go and have a beer." Andy said as he finished washing his face and gargling his mouth with the lousy London water.

"You alright for another beer Andy?" I asked.

"Yeah sure, that knockabout and spew sobered me up nicely. He aint going nowhere till the wooden tops arrive."

We walked through to the bar.

"Tommy – we had a problem with a guy in the toilet. He is out cold and the coppers plus an ambulance are on the way. Probably best to close the toilet till they arrive." Andy stated it as if it was a minor irritation.

"Yeah sure thing Andy." Tommy the landlord answered as though it was an everyday occurrence, then turned around to the barman and added;" Joey go and put a tape across the toilet door and tell any men needing the loo to use the ladies till it is sorted."

"Yeah sure Tommy." Joey the barman replied as he pulled some tape out of a drawer beneath the till and walked over to the gents' toilets.

"What are you having lad?" Andy asked.

"I will have a pint of Stella please Andy." I replied nodding at the Stella Artois pump.

"Head bangers stuff that. Most appropriate after that head job in the toilets." Andy laughed as he said it.

"The Glasgow kiss it is called." I replied.

"I guess that why the ladies don't like you Glaswegians kissing them?" Andy laughed heartily at his own little joke.

"Is that what it is? Here was me thinking all those years it was my bad breath" I laughed and Andy joined in, even Tommy the landlord laughed out loud.

"A pint of the head bangers stuff and a pint of 'Speckled Hen' Tommy and whatever you are having." Andy shouted still with a wide grin on his face.

"Thanks Andy. I will have a half of the head bangers stuff. It is lovely and cold on a warm day." Tommy replied as he started to pull the beers.

Andy was rubbing his kidneys and his solar plexus when he suddenly said; "You know lad, I will have to get myself back in shape. In the old days, I would have seen that guy off without trying too hard."

"Aye well that is second time in twenty-four hours it has happened. You had better start by cutting out the beer. What is that all about?" I asked a bit more forthright that I had intended.

"Well I had double bad news today, so I decided to drown my sorrows." Andy replied his face turning from laughing to a sorrowful look in a split second.

"That will be eight shillings and six pence Andy" Tommy the landlord interrupted as he handed over the beers. Andy paid with a scowl and replied; "We are going to have to get a mortgage shortly to pay for our beer every week."

"Yeah Andy, especially the amount you consume every week!" Tommy replied with a smile across his face.

"I mean - that is all I need today! - A smart ass landlord. Didn't they teach you at the booze school you are supposed to have a sympathetic ear for your customers?"

"Yeah, they sure did Andy, but only if it they don't have an effect on profits."

"You are a bit of a comedian Tommy, but don't give up the day job, will you?" Andy replied as we turned with our drinks and went to the table.

"Well who were you supposed to be meeting up with today?" I asked politely thinking I knew the answer.

"I told you he was my snitch, but it seems he went and got himself killed this morning!" Andy Spearing replied, but with a drunken slur in his voice.

"Les Hall, was it?" I asked.

"How the hell did you know that?" Andy asked with an amazed expression on his face.

"It is all over 'The Evening Standard' including a description of our assassin; 'The Fox.'. Our man 'Flash Harry' has been up to his tricks. Here - take a look." I said it as I passed the paper to him.

"Jesus Christ! We told him not to release that description. Oh my God and Joe Cole killed as well – He has, I should say had – The Hoofers Club – A real nice guy Joe – one of the few club owners who was not an out and out criminal, I can't see that being the work of 'The Fox' – that's not his style! He only kills real criminals."

"Why would he be in the area though Andy?"

"I don't know maybe he was visiting a friend or something! Andy suddenly had a flash, a gut feeling, but he couldn't get it out from the back of his mind. It will come eventually then he added; "Bloody hell we told him not to release that. Not much of a photo fit either. It will screw the case up a treat."

"Well he has gone and done it. The big 'I am' I reckon." I replied.

"The stupid shit bag." Andy sounded totally exasperated.

"Anyway, it was not Hall's death that upset you so much. He was just another toe rag! So, what else happened?"

"He still does not deserve that kind of death lad! Anyway, I got news of my decree absolute today. More than thirty years washed down the drain!" Andy replied sourly, still with a slur in his voice.

"I am so sorry Andy – I didn't know!" I replied sincerely.

"You were not to know lad. Now it's official, I have lost the family home in Harpenden and two thirds of everything. Bloody useless solicitor and he was supposed to be a friend!"

"What happened?" I asked, just hoping I was saying the right thing.

"She suddenly got up one morning and announced after thirty odd years she was going to have a divorce. She never even said why! "

"She must have said something. Was it money or drink problems?" I asked.

"Nope! - I can see the psychologist coming out of you now lad. No, hardly ever had a drink until she announced the divorce. Had the usual money problems – too much going out and not enough coming in, but we had two kids and starting up from scratch after the war, times were bloody hard. I think the main problem was being a policeman - my hours were diabolical as you know! I dragged her to one of those marriage guidance counsellors and she said the wife was only interested in the money!" Andy replied, sounding more than depressed.

"Right! So why did she say that?" I asked feeling my way.

"Just the way the questions and answers went, everything came down to money. Not least because she discovered, a week before she announced her intentions to divorce me, that the mortgage had been cleared for some time. Anyway, I knew for years the real reason was she never really loved me!" Andy was beginning to sound more slurred as he supped his beer.

"Why did you think that Andy?" I asked, not really knowing where this was leading.

"I had her followed several times over the years and had my house watched by a private detective. She had been having an affair for years."

"Anybody you knew?" I asked as a matter of course.

"Oh sure! – It was – a relative! – He was, and is, quite famous. – I suppose that was the attraction for her. It has been going on for years!"

"You mean to say it has been going on for years and you did nothing?" I asked.

"Yeah – I just could not face up to it! It would have split my family! Still cannot face up to it lad. Then during the divorce proceedings, which have been going on for two years, she told her and my family that I had been beating her – A pack of lies of course, but she let her mother die thinking that of me! And all the time she was carrying on with my relative. Jesus, it is a bloody mess. So, I took to drinking – I think maybe I am an alcoholic now and going down fast."

"God Andy – Have you been to see anybody to get some help?"

"I have never told a soul about it until today. Kept it all bottled up so to speak, no pun intended." Andy gave a little wry smile and added; "I am only talking now because of the booze. I didn't want to talk to the police psychology people – bloody waste of time they are – present company excluded of course – and anyway, with them it gets back and I get demoted. I could not take that. I am in a bloody mess, but somehow, I have to hold down this job. I have these problems, but I was and am hoping that by working like stink and hiding from the real world in the bottle I will get through them!" Andy answered.

"Look Andy, when you are working you have shown me - and a lot of people have told me - you are one of the best detectives in 'The Yard,' but I think you may need professional help to get through this and not the booze. It is a horrendous story and mentally it must be damaging you. The drink can only make it worse." I said it slowly and deliberately.

"Yeah well you are the psychologist so how can you help me eh lad?"

"I don't think that is a good idea. I mean of course I will help you in any way I can Andy, but you need a professional psychologist – I mean not one you work with day to day." I knew it had not come out the way I intended, but perhaps he grasped the meaning.

"Yeah, I can see that, but thanks for that anyway. I would appreciate it if you would keep this conversation to yourself lad?"

"Of course, Andy, but do think about it seriously. Longer term you could have some serious problems if you just let it all fester." I tried not to sound too dramatic.

"Yeah well that is enough of my problems for the day agony aunt! What else happened today?" Andy just shook his head as though he was dismissing everything and moving on.

"Well I went into the office this afternoon and answered your phone and picked up a tip for you."

"What was that? A winner for glorious Goodwood, was it?" Andy laughed as he said it.

"No, it was where we could find 'The Fox' in the morning." I replied with more than a little triumph in my voice.

"What? - What do you mean?"

"This guy phoned. He was like a posh guy trying to sound like an East Ender. He reckons 'The Fox' is going to turn up at some apartments on a job, near Sloane Square in the morning."

"You are joking?" Andy had an incredulous look on his face.

"No, and what is more, it was an internal call from within 'The Yard' - so it is, as you suspected, some sort of vigilante police group." I replied.

"Maybe and then again maybe not. How did you find out that it was an internal call?"

"I called the switchboard and pretended I had been cut off during the call and the switchboard girl said there had been no external call to your number. She said it could only have been an internal call!" I replied with a smile.

"My oh my, the plot thickens - more 'Double, double, toil and trouble' me thinks." Andy sounded apprehensive and seemed to be lost for a moment in his thoughts.

"I went to the apartments on my way over here. Expensive places and I spoke to the porter sort of cum security guard – an ex copper and he says he knows you. He was a Sergeant Whitfield?" I replied with a question.

"Steve Whitfield? It must be – Steve was a Sergeant at Paddington before Willie Thomas took over.

"Yeah anyway, I made him aware that our man may be around and to let the night man know – another ex-copper. They have a good CCTV System in the place so their security looks 'A' OK. I also
got a list of the owners or renters in there" I replied and handed over the list to Andy.

Andy appeared to ignore my report on the security rubbing his kidneys and his chin before suddenly stating; "By the sound of it and TT's tape, one of 'The Fox's 'employers are throwing him out with the bathwater. I also think, if Mrs Palmer was not his last employer, then she really is in danger. I think we will need to pay her another visit."

"What tonight?" I asked.

"Yeah --- well tomorrow may be too late for her!" Andy replied with a good deal of concern in his voice.

"What do you reckon with the tip?" I asked.

"Well if 'The Fox' has half a brain left there is no way he will go anywhere near that place - I suppose we will have to go around there in the middle of the night just in case, but knowing the way he operates I don't think he will be anywhere near." Andy shook his head as he replied.

"The middle of the night Andy? I live out in Palmers Green – I won't be able to get into town," I replied.

"You can grab a few hours' kip in my place – I have a flat in Buckingham Palace Road, just around the corner from Sloane Square. Then we can stroll over there about two in the morning and see if anything is going down – We should be back by five and you can catch up on your beauty sleep – Not that it seems to be working for you!" Andy laughed as he said it, but grimaced with pain trying to hold his kidneys.

"Yeah well I suppose so.!" I replied grudgingly, it was all I could think to say, but added; "Maybe you should go to the hospital.

There was a sound of sirens and outside two police cars each full of Wooden Tops screeched to a halt, followed seconds later by an ambulance with blaring horn.

Sergeant Tommy Thomson came bursting through the doors leading six wooden tops all of them with batons drawn. They stopped short in front of Andy.

"Sergeant Thomson! What the hell has got you out of New Scotland Yard Sergeant in such a hurry?" Andy said.

"Bloody hell sir – We were told you were being attacked?" Sergeant Thomson replied with an exasperated expression.

"And I was Sergeant and I have the black and blue kidneys and solar plexus to prove it, but you should see the other guy after Sergeant Devlin had finished with him!" Andy had a slight grin and nodded towards the gents' toilets.

"He is still here then? Sergeant Thomson asked.

"Yeah, well he aint going anywhere other than in an ambulance to hospital!" Andy replied.

"Let us have a look then!" Sergeant Thomson marched over to the toilets.

"Probably better leave him till the medics arrive!" Andy shouted after him.

The ambulance men came in looking very efficient and went straight over to where Sergeant Thomson was standing.

"Bloody hell sir! I see what you mean. It looks like he was the one assaulted!" Sergeant Thomson shouted from the toilet door while looking in.

"Yes, as you have seen before Tommy – Sergeant Devlin is very efficient in these matters wouldn't you say?"

"Bloody hell did this guy walk into a brick wall?" The younger of the ambulance men was heard to shout.

"No, he just got a great big Glasgow kiss from Sergeant Devlin here lad."

"A Glasgow kiss in the gent's toilet – Is he one of the limp wristed lot then? The younger ambulance man sounded disgusted, obviously not aware of the true meaning of the Glasgow kiss.

"I don't really know – Are you limp wristed Sergeant?" Andy was enjoying himself, smiling as he asked the question.

"Sir! ---" I could only stammer - my face going red.

"Well he is not denying it lad." Andy shouted across the pub.

"How long has he been out for?" The other older medic asked.

"About twenty minutes." I replied for the sake of moving the conversation.

"Where else did you hit him sir?" The older ambulance man asked.

"A knee in the balls –sorry testicles - and a knee to the jaw!" I replied, correcting myself just in time with the ladies' present. Most of the crowd in the pub, including the ladies, were smiling.

"Bloody hell – his balls– sorry testicles are swollen to the size of a football. His jaw and his nose looks like they are both broken. He paid a helluva price for that Glasgow kiss." The older ambulance man laughed as he said it, obviously, he knew what a Glasgow kiss was and playing up on the other one.

Thankfully, my Wallkie -Talkie rang and I quickly dived over to answer it in a brisk business type voice: "DS Kevin Devlin here – over" It was the guy I was speaking to earlier who had promised to ring me back with any information he could find on the hippie guy. He gave me the information which I could hardly believe. I had gone from red to white faced in seconds. When he said "Over" I could hardly reply but finally stammered: "I see – well thanks for the quick response over and out."

I must have looked shell shocked because Andy looked inquisitively at me and asked; "You all right lad?"

"Yes, sir but we need to talk privately." I replied.

"Can we use your back-room Tommy?" Andy asked.

"Yes, no problem, but keep your voices down - these walls have ears! – My missus in other words!" Tommy laughed and showed us through.

"I heard that Tommy!" A voice came from the snug bar.

"See what I mean?" Tommy said with a shrug of his shoulders and a smile.

We went into the spare room and closed the door before Andy asked; "What is the matter with you lad? You look as if you have just heard from a ghost."

"I wouldn't mind a ghost. You know who that guy, the hippie, works for? I asked a little too dramatically.

"Not a clue, but I am sure you are going to tell me." Andy replied with a smile.

"He is MI5 - Works at headquarters in Curzon Street!" I replied, brushing my fingers nervously through my hair.

Jesus Christ!" Andy simply replied and this time I was not caring about him using the Lord's name in vain.

"Exactly!" I replied it was all I could think of to say.

"Well, yet another of those coincidences that I don't like! Still it is not your problem lad! Don't forget he attacked me without warning nor did he identify himself." Andy was obviously working out a defence on his feet.

"Right lad let us get in there and organise Tommy and one of his wooden tops to go with him to hospital. When he comes round we will get Tommy to read him his rights and charge him with assault. Then we tell Tommy to keep him in there and not allow anybody to see him, or take him out until we get there. His office won't think anything is wrong for the next twenty-four hours at least."

"Will Tommy do that? I mean considering they are MI5 and all?" I asked, more in hope than anything else.

"Tommy will take great delight in throwing them out!" DI Spearing answered.

"If it was official, they might come mob handed – Tommy won't stand a chance." I tried to reason.

"I doubt it – otherwise they would have 'come' mob handed earlier – would they not?" Andy asked with a smile.

"Not being funny sir, but in your condition, I think he probably thought he could handle it himself?" I was never very good at diplomacy.

"Well thanks a bunch Sergeant!"

"Well he didn't know I had arrived back until I was in his face! Anyway, it was you who said you were out of condition sir"

"Yeah Okay – let's get organised Kevin before they all disappear."

"You sure about this sir?"

"No! – Not really, but what are the alternatives lad?"

"Tommy – you got a minute?" Andy stood at the door of the room and shouted and waved him across before adding; "You ambulance people stay put until we tell you to go – OK?"

"Yes sir, but make it snappy – This guy is not in a good way!" The older one replied.

"Tell me something I don't know lad!" Andy replied with a shake of his head.

Tommy came over into the room and closed the door behind him.

"Look Tommy we got a bit of a problem here. That hippie guy there – he turns out to be one of the MI5 operatives!" Andy paused for effect.

"Shit!" Sergeant Tommy replied, obviously aware of possible repercussions.

"Yeah exactly! However, it went down exactly how we told you. This guy attacked me from behind and gave me two very painful kidneys and followed up with one to the solar plexus. – Here!" Andy pulled his shirt out from his trousers and lifted it up over his ribcage revealing black and blue whelps around the kidney areas.

"You ought to go with this guy and get a check-up in the hospital Andy. That looks bad." Sergeant Tommy did sound sympathetic but added; "But I'll tell you what Andy – you two better get your stories straight, because those bastards may try and do you for unnecessary force."

"Listen Tommy I don't have the time to go to hospital right now – and - if you were in the elite MI5 or 6 force and you had got done like that by a twenty-six-year old,

I don't think they will want to go around seeking publicity – Do you? On top of that we think they have been up to something highly illegal - possibly murder!"

"Yeah? - Okay you got me Andy – I'll take him and book him into a private room and put a guard outside with strict orders not to let anyone in. Then I will move him to another room with a guard inside the room. I will hang around out of sight in reception and if I hear any inquiries I will drum up back-up. How does that sound Andy?"

"Perfect Tommy – Just what we need - I reckon we have twenty-four hours before they even start looking, but best play it safe."

"Are you going to authorise overtime for the lads Andy?"

"Certainly Tommy – arrange a swap after twelve hours though."

"The lads and I will appreciate it – Anybody else at 'The Yard' know what is going on Andy?"

"No Tommy! And keep it that way!"

"Say no more Andy!" Sergeant Tommy touched his nose to signify confidentially.

"I'll see you in the hospital tomorrow morning or maybe about lunchtime. Okay Tommy?"

"Sure thing Andy" Tommy marched quickly off and started ordering instructions to his six wooden tops and the ambulance people. Andy thought - one thing about Tommy Thomson, he knew exactly what he had to do and would not waiver.

"Thanks Tommy" Andy called after him and got a cheery wave.

"So, what are we up to now sir?" I asked.

"Back to the office – we will need to trace Mrs P and pick her up for her own good."

"Do you think you ought to go back to the office reeking of drink and looking like hell sir?" I asked politely.

"Oh, don't worry lad. - Flash Harry and co are all strictly nine till five merchants – It is getting on for six so they will be long gone even if there is an emergency. Let's go!"

It was looking like another long night and I really needed a visit to the gym. God I was feeling sore and in need of my regular exercise.

We walked back down Wardour Street and as we passed 'The Marquee' club I noticed a news board containing a poster advertising a forthcoming event and stopped, tapping DI Spearing on the shoulder. "Hang on a minute Andy I want to read this!" Andy turned and stood alongside me reading the poster;

Book 1 in the DI Spearing and DS Devlin series

Marquee

90 Wardour Street, W1   01 4376603
Open every night 7-11pm

*****One off special appearance*****

By the Scottish hit group who made their London debut in 'The Marquee'

'Black & White'
(Hits include; 'Looking Back,' 'Passing through the valley,' 'Ode to a working man' etc.)

With another Scottish group straight from their Savile appearance with Jimi Hendrix –

'1-2-3'

HERE! – Monday 24^h July - A sensational show not to be missed!

"Do you like this lot then?" Andy asked nodding at the poster.

"Yeah well when I was in Glasgow I used to go over to 'The Place' Club in Edinburgh and saw both. They are both very good live, so I might try and get to that gig. Do you like today's groups?" I asked, expecting the usual reply from the older generation, but was again surprised.

"Yeah well that lot 'Black & White' I have heard their records and they sound good. Not my type of music though! – They are really a white soul type harmony group. I am into 'The Blues' – I have been to see 'The Stones' in there, but my favourite UK group is 'Cream.' Did you know that Scottish guy Jack Bruce, the bass guitarist with Cream, writes most of the music? - A very talented guy. Although all the British R & B groups are really poor white showman imitations of the real Blues artistes from Memphis and New Orleans. My all-time favourite is Lead Belly – Now he is 'The Blues' – what is called the original country blues - and what a singer – what a musician! His twelve-string guitar is the epitaph of country blues! - Did you ever hear "House of the Rising Sun?" Andy was fully animated, obviously on one of his favourite subjects as we strolled back towards Leicester Square tube station.

I was astounded by the man's obvious passion for 'The Blues and could only meekly reply; "I have only heard 'The Animals' version of it!"

"Oh, come on – that was a massacre of it! – Lead Belly wrote that song and sang it how it was in New Orleans. Oh my God! –Now he was the real deal Bluesman - What an artiste!"

"I always thought 'The Animals' wrote it!" I replied.

"There you go! How about 'Black Girl,' or as it became better known; 'Where did you sleep last night?' Or maybe; 'Black Betty?' - Or what about; 'Cotton Fields?' - As in 'Cotton Fields Back Home'? Then 'Goodnight Irene' – That was just a few" Andy was now in full flow as we walked along Wardour Street.

"He wrote that lot?" I asked.

"Yeah and then some - and don't forget - they were written in the nineteen thirties and forties – Everybody who is anybody in pop today has recorded his songs from Elvis Presley to 'The Beach Boys,' to 'The Animals, ' to 'Credence Clearwater Revival' and 'Nirvana' – you name them, they have all done a Lead Belly number. You know, Lead Belly was a convicted murderer and served time on The Chain Gang?"

"Not heard of him until now. More your era" I replied, rather defensively. Suddenly I realised Andy Spearing had a lot more dimensions to his personality than I had ever imagined.

"Yeah it may have been my era, but his songs will live on forever. He never made any money during his life. Then, just as his career was taking off in Europe, he went and caught motor neurone disease. It was an absolute tragedy!"

"That was the good old days then eh?" I replied.

"Not so much of the good old day's lad! These black people in America had a hard life. Anyway, it is less than thirty years ago."

"Thirty years ago, it is taught as modern history in the schools Andy!"

"Watch it lad! I am not history –at least not yet!"

"Yeah well in thirty years they will be talking the same way about the music of the sixties – don't you think?" I replied again going on the defensive.

"Yeah, I daresay lad – I know there are a lot of good songs being written today, but the rock and rollers, rhythm and blues and folk rock guys ought to acknowledge the debt they owe the old bluesmen from Memphis and New Orleans – you know?"

"Yeah I know." I replied.

As we walked, my mind started wandering back to the 'Black and White' soul harmony duo from Edinburgh advertised in The Marquee for Monday night. Their names were Joe White and Adrian Black. The tune and words of their biggest hit came into my mind and seemed appropriate to me today:

Book 1 in the DI Spearing and DS Devlin series

Looking Back, from where I've come,

Looking back, when I was young

Looking back at the things I've done,

Looking back, it aint no fun.

Time I was moving on, I've been around too long.

I've seen all the places; I know all the faces,

I've been here a long time; I've lost all that was mine,

Time I was moving on, I've been around too long.

Looking back, from where I've come,

Looking back, when I was young.

Looking back at the things I've done,

Looking back, it aint no fun.

Time I was moving on, I've been around too long.

Book 1 in the DI Spearing and DS Devlin series

Chapter 16 - Out of control

Sam Aldridge, alias 'The Fox,' emerged from the toilets in Victoria Station on Wednesday afternoon. He had changed in one of the cubicles and was in what he called his old gentleman's 'home disguise.'

He was now wearing a very expensive grey wig and droopy grey moustache. He was dressed to match what he hoped was his perceived age. He wore a Savile Row fitted dark blue blazer, with blue striped open necked shirt, oxford grey flannel trousers and black polished brogue shoes.

To finish of the disguise, he had a telescopic highly polished stick and walked with a right foot limp and pronounced stoop hunching his shoulders.

To all, including his close neighbours, he could not be taken for anything but an old distinguished gentleman.

He went back down into the London Underground and took the circle line to South Kensington station where he switched to the Piccadilly Line to Knightsbridge station, which was just around the corner from his home. This home was in fact a top of the range luxury penthouse suite in a building containing only millionaires, many of whom only used their apartments for a few days year. A discreet place with tight security, he could not have found a better place.

Here he was known as a retired army officer Eric Liddell who had been badly wounded in the war. Sam told his neighbours he had made his fortune from 'Do It Yourself' stores and fast food outlets in the fifties and sixties which boomed as Londoners tried to rebuild their lives and homes. In fact, Eric Liddell had been his captain in the SAS and had been killed in action, somewhere in France, in nineteen forty-three and Sam had buried him while stealing his tags and planting them back in England between raids.

To the few in the building who knew him, including the security staff, he was known as good old Eric, the distinguished and very rich old gent in the penthouse. They all thought of him as a right old cad with a liking for very young ladies of the night, as London prostitutes had been known for hundreds of years. That was alright, because he was a rich old cad.

What none of them knew was that Sam owned the whole building through a holding company. It had been his first investment in the early fifties when property was cheap and Sam was earning huge money from his assassination business which had carried on into the sixties.

Sam knew that if Joe Cole had cracked he would have given his alias name and address. So, he was being extra cautious and went around the building several times looking for any strange vehicles or unusual people hanging about, but all seemed normal.

He then remembered that Joe Cole had said he had posted a letter to him yesterday so, when he finally let himself into the building, he went and picked up his mail from John the security man in reception and asked; "Anybody been asking after me today John?"

"No! - only the usual bunch of girls wondering when you will need an escort Mister Liddell!" John answered with his usual reply and a smile, so that appeared normal.

"If anybody – and I mean anybody - comes here enquiring about me John – make sure you hit that red button below your desk. And make sure Dracula Tony knows to do the same on nights. I will let you both know if I am expecting any girls and who they are. - Okay?"

"Sure thing Mr Liddell." John replied with his friendly smile, but he often wondered how old Liddell had managed to get the owners to put in a warning signal to his penthouse, but he never dared to ask.

Sam limped over to the lifts and went up to his penthouse. He went to his door, but did not go in. Instead, he stood there listening at the door and only after ten minutes, when he was satisfied no one was inside, he let himself in.

He closed and locked the door behind him and walked swiftly across the plush nineteen thirties art deco style sitting room still with his stick in hand. Sam had a taste for the high life and the decadence of the nineteen-thirties, hence the wonderful art deco throughout the place.

He then checked the three bedrooms, bathroom and kitchen, all done in the same plush nineteen thirties art deco real style. All clear, so he threw the stick and blazer onto the huge three corner settee.

He stripped off as he headed for the bathroom and ran a bath with Radox muscle relaxer in the seven-foot tub with the gold taps and fittings. Although nearly forty, his body was still packed with muscle, flat six pack mid-riff and stomach which all tended to betray his perceived age, which the young ladies of the night usually ignored, or did not notice, as the money was good. Sam always did show them his gym room where he worked out every day for three hours.

Anyway, they were the only ones who ever saw the body and Sam always did keep on his grey wig and moustache, plus kept the pretence of the limp. He did have his genuine scars from his war wounds so it always looked good enough to fool them.

As Sam settled into the luxury of the bathtub he reflected on the day. Today had been the first time since the war that Sam knew he had not been in complete control.

It had started as a normal Wednesday morning when Sam got up and dressed in his same 'home disguise' as he had just stripped off, complete with limp and stick in his right hand. He made his way limping along the High Street, Knightsbridge and got into the British Telecom red public phone box across the road from Harrods. He made his usual Wednesday morning call at nine-thirty to his old and probably – the truth be known – his only friend Joe Cole. It was of course the same Joe Cole who had given Sam his first job after the war and paid him an enormous sum to get rid of the protection gang from Joe's night club 'The Hoofers Club' in London's Soho district.

Since then they had remained friends and Joe took care of the post box bookings for Sam's business, although he had no knowledge what was going down and did not want to know. He almost certainly knew, but chose to ignore it. The way it worked was, the customers sent their bookings to one post box in the city under a false name, but it was automatically forwarded by the Royal Mail to a completely different post box in Stepney in the rough East End of London where it was picked up by Joe. So if anyone was looking at the original post box they never saw it picked up until it was too late. The forwarding mail box was changed every month.

Sam rang the number for 'The Hoofers Club' and it was almost immediately answered by a rather nervous sounding Joe Cole; "Hi we need to talk. I will give you a ring back. You on the usual number?"

"Yeah – The usual number – in fifteen minutes?" Sam asked.

"Will do" Joe Cole replied and hung up as he stood up and hurriedly walked out the office, locking up the club as he left. He walked down and cut through Wardour Street and got to the public phone boxes in Leicester Square within twelve minutes. The phone process was all part of the Sam Aldridge security system. It was a well-known fact that the police, other gangs and sometimes MI5 had bugged a lot of the club's telephones. Many of the clubs also had to employ specialists to regularly debug the clubs and so many high-tech tiny microphones with transmitters were found, for some it turned into a very profitable second business.

Sam Aldridge, alias Eric Liddell, simply stayed in the Knightsbridge phone box and ignored the queue of people waiting to use the phone. There were no mobile phones in those days. One either had a BT phone in your home, which Sam had of course, but he could not afford to have these important calls tracked back to his home hence using the red public phone boxes. He had his figure on the cradle and pretended to be talking.

Eventually there was a tap on the glass by a large man, dressed as a rocker with black leather jacket, trousers and boots with black greasy hair pulled back tight into a ponytail and tattoos covering his bare arms.

Sam turned around and opened the heavy door half way open and said; "Yes?"

"Right you old fucker! Out now! – we have been waiting for fifteen minutes – Now out!" The rocker went to grab Sam's shirt.

In a fraction of a second Sam brought up his walking stick in a vicious right uppercut to the rockers solar plexus and, as he doubled over Sam smacked the heavy phone booth door into his face. The rocker just simply tilted over and landed on his ass, eyes totally glazed and blood streaming from a broken nose.

The men and women in the queue looked in awe, first at Sam and then at the rocker most of them shaking their heads in disbelief.

"Now, I will only be another five minutes' ladies and gentlemen. So, unless any of you have objections, I will carry on." Sam said it with a smile and sounding like an old gentleman as he closed the door.

"Yeah - sure my friend. Whatever you say man - right on!" A painfully thin young hippie type with a Birmingham 'Brummie' accent answered. He had blonde shoulder length, flowery shirt and extraordinary tight faded blue jeans which showed everything he had and wore brown Chelsea boots on high heels. He added to anyone who was listening; "Have you ever seen anything like that man?"

"Yep! – Answered an old guy in the queue and added; "He is an ex-army man. They don't make them like that anymore. – A dollar to fifty he was in the war - I bet he was a trained combat officer!" A yank, overweight by four stones, mid to late twenties, in a loud 'Beach Boys' shirt and tan shorts with sandals, no socks.

"Guaranteed man!" The Brummie trying to react as he thought he should, trying to impress without success.

The phone finally rang and Sam answered; "Okay Joe what is happening?"

"There could be problems Sam. I just got the word that this little prick - Les Hall by name – has been asking around and seems to have turned up your name. Not from me, but somebody out there seems to have put it together. It seems Hall is a snout for somebody at 'The Yard' and he is aiming to pick-up the reward today. A loud mouth little turd by the sound of it! Not a pro, but it may be dangerous. Are you involved with the John Palmer thing and all that shit Sam?"

"Don't know a thing about that Joe!" Sam lied and added a question; "I think I remember that little turd. Where does he hang out now?"

"Bethnal Green! He lives in a flat in Clarkson Street, just around the corner from Bethnal tube station. But there is another, I think, more important problem." Joe was now sounding very nervous and Sam did not like the sound of it.

"What is that Joe?"

"It looks like somebody has somehow managed to by-pass the system and we have another post box letter this month!"

"How do you know Joe?" Sam asked.

"My best mate at Stepney Green Collection Centre sent it to me yesterday as usual. I posted it to you yesterday; you should get it in the post today. What do you think?"

"It could be just another job. Then again it could be a trap. I will have to look at it. I have decided I am going off to cool my heels for a few years down the coast so kill off the post boxes from now Joe." Sam stated it matter of fact like it was an everyday occurrence.

"Are things getting a bit hot down here in the old smoke Sam?"

"Not so hot Joe, more a few strange or not so cool things happening! You know what they say though - where there is smoke there is fire! By the way, since when did you stop picking up from the post box and who is this mate of yours?" Sam pointedly asked.

"John Tourney – he has been my mate since schooldays. He is one hundred percent okay Sam" Joe replied defensively and hastily added; "Even I don't like going back to Stepney these days Sam and it keeps me out of picking it up."

"Oh, for fucks sake Joe! Don't you know anything? They only had post box numbers. Now they have this John guy who can lead them straight back to you Joe." Sam sounded angry.

"John would not tell them anything Sam."

"Who are trying to kid Joe? The guy's I am dealing with don't mess around. They would have your name from Tourney in five minutes flat and my name from you in five minutes. Then they would just wipe you out. If you are real lucky it could be the coppers and you might live. Then again, some of them are bent as a corkscrew and would not be averse to saying good night to you both."

"Get to hell out of it Joe."

"You are kidding me aint you?"

"Would I kid about something like that?"

"No I guess not Sam – How long do you think before they move?" Joe's voice trailed away.

"Since they probably know about the post boxes – You can assume they are already on the job. So, I would close up now and disappear. You can always come back and pick up where you left off when things cool down, or flog the place if you are enjoying retirement!"

"I cannot just go and leave the staff in the lurch Sam."

"It is up to you Joe. It is either that, or face the music and that could be the death march." Sam replied not managing to hold back a laugh.

"Oh charming! So, you think it is that serious?"

"Well, it could be Joe and I personally would not take a chance. I cannot help this time because my ass is also on the line. I'll have to go Joe. Make sure you do it and do it now! See you Joe and take care."

"Yeah I'll see you Sam. You take care!" Joe replied and the line went dead.

Sam left the telephone box not forgetting to walk with his limp, a stoop and looked at the rocker who was still sitting there on his ass. With his left-foot he pushed the rocker over and he simply rolled over onto his right side with the glazed look still on his eyes.

"I think you guys can carry on – I don't think he will be able to use the phone for a while – Do you?" Sam alias Eric Liddell smiled at the queue.

As Sam limped away back towards his penthouse he suddenly spoke to himself; "I will have to sort this Hall guy out now. He has crossed the line." Sam then thought - but how did he get there – across the line?

He then thought about his friend Joe Cole and this guy John Tourney. I cannot take out Joe unless it is too late. No, he could never take Joe out. He was and still is his only real friend. So, it has to be Tourney. Sam regretted the decision. To some, he could see, he may have strange principals. He had always said he would only kill people who deserved to die, but like in any war, sometimes there had to be civilian casualties and it appeared Tourney may have to be one.

Sam went back to his penthouse and packed some clothes, including his red wig, reddish/greyish goatee beard and velvet hats into a brown canvas holdall.

He was still dressed in his 'home disguise' – Eric Liddell, the old rich gentleman complete with right leg limp, stick and stoop as he made his way on the District and Circle line to Notting Hill Gate tube station. There he went into the gents' toilets and changed into his red goatee beard and wig as worn last night at John Palmers, but this time he had on a lightweight tan suit with brown shoes.

He then joined the hordes on the Central Line and forty-five minutes later Sam stood in Clarkston Street in Bethnal Green near Les Hall's address. He decided he was too obvious in the street and quickly made his way to a café across the road from Bethnal Green tube station. He decided to wait it out and hoped Hall would take the Central Line into town which he thought was a fair gamble.

He sat there, having a cup of tea and a bacon roll, looking directly at Bethnal Green tube entrance. He was hoping he would still recognize Les Hall.

It was just gone twelve mid-day. It was now nearly two hours after Joe's call when the little turd Hall hurried across the road towards the Bethnal Green tube station.

Sam followed at a safe distance watching the turd join the crowd on the platform heading for London on the Central Line. He quickly followed him onto the packed platform and at the mid-point got directly behind him as the train hit the far end of the platform. It only needed a nudge as the train sped up the platform and Hall was spread-eagled in front of the incoming tube train. He was dead as Sam turned away and headed towards the exit as some of the other platform passengers screamed. Sam noticed a middle-aged woman cover her mouth, unfortunately a witness, but would probably only remember a minimum with the stress. She turned and ran battering through the crowd.

Sam headed for the exit from the station and found a quiet corner behind a pillar. There he tore off the goatee beard which was painful as it had been stuck on. He then removed the red wig and combed his natural blonde greying hair. He turned his jacket inside out and suddenly it was a black jacket, it had been specially made for just this type of quick change. He also emptied the holdall and turned it inside out and it became a black holdall, also specially made, and he refilled the bag with the clothes, wigs and stuff and placed a velvet black floppy hat on his head.

Within two minutes of pushing Les Hall from the platform, Sam had completely changed his appearance, fought his way through the masses entering or exiting the station and grabbed a London cab to Liverpool Street tube station. There he discovered the Central Line was closed because of an 'incident' at Bethnal Green, which made him smile, so he joined the Metropolitan Line to Kings Cross where he switched to the Piccadilly Line and in another fifteen minutes he was coming out of the Leicester Square tube station. He had decided to have a quick face to face word with Joe Cole at his Hoofers Bar before closing out John Tourney, although he had no intention of telling Joe what he was up to that afternoon. He made his way to Wardour Street and turned off into Berwick Street where the club was situated. As he turned into the street he saw the blue flashing lights of police vehicles and an ambulance outside 'The Hoofers Bar'. Television crews from BBC and London Weekend and reporters were swarming all over the place and the usual gawkers had gathered four or five deep across the road.

Sam decided to hang about the peripherals and try to pick up what was happening although his twisted gut feeling already gave him the answer. He edged up to a tall middle aged guy. "What is happening?" Sam asked, trying to sound all innocent.

"It sounds like someone has been shot in 'The Hoofers Club'. I was in there last night; it was a good night as well."

Sam looked across and happened to catch the eye of a man who was scanning the crowd. He looked like a policeman, but he could be one of a gang. Sam immediately moved out and hurriedly moved onto Wardour Street, heading down towards Leicester Square. He somehow knew the man was trying to get through the crowd and was in pursuit.

In a few minutes, he got to Leicester Square tube station and skipped down the steps. A quick glance over his shoulder confirmed the man was on the other side of the street trying to cross, but heavy traffic was preventing him.

Sam put on a sprint, but instead of going down to the trains he went straight past and headed for the exit at the northwest corner of Leicester Square which came out at the side of 'The Odeon' cinema. He ducked out of sight before the man appeared. He then watched as the man came into view and running, but the guy headed straight down towards the trains. Sam headed through the exit at 'The Odeon' and as he came out a black London cab came away from the cinema and he hailed it.

"Victoria Station" Sam shouted to the taxi driver as he jumped on board. They immediately pulled away and were gone from the square and going towards Shaftsbury Avenue - in a few seconds he was clear.

As he travelled, Sam thought, it had been a close call and if they had got a name or a description that would explain the man recognizing him. He thought to himself; 'damn you Joe why did you go and get someone else?' Tourney must have been taken out as well for them to get to Joe so fast.

Sam got the tube to Kensington after getting changed into his 'Eric Liddell' clothes he was back in his penthouse within twenty-five minutes of leaving Soho.

He picked up the A4 envelope forwarded by Joe Cole in yesterday's post. Inside was another unopened envelope addressed to a forwarding post code. Inside this was a foolscap page containing hand written instructions for the assassination of an associate of 'The Hammond's gang named as one Thomas Ricketts. Apparently, he had been a naughty boy with some bank robbery money and slit the throat of his accomplice. He was to be found in The Centaurus Apartments, in Cadogan Gardens, Sloane Square, where apparently, he would arrive in the early hours of Thursday morning. Payment of £50,000 would go direct to the Swiss Bank Account Number, but it did not have a name. This account belonged to Sam, but it was only an account number. The Swiss used to let you do that provided you had identification which matched the account when it came to withdrawals. Sam's account was in his original name of Peter Kirkham who had of course been pronounced dead – missing in action in nineteen forty-four.

Sam re-read the proposition for the assassination and instinctively he knew it was a trap. He could smell a rat, but he knew he had to check it out from a safe distance in the early hours of tomorrow morning without going into that lion's den.

He turned on the huge Philips television set, one of those with huge bulges of plastic at the back, packed solid with electronics. There were no such things as flat screen televisions in those days! He caught the ITV London Weekend news at six just starting. The lead piece was by a lady reporter who was reporting the murder of Joe Cole, the owner of 'The Hoofer Bar' in Berwick Street, London Soho. The TV pictures showed the frontage of the bar, a picture of Joe and then broke away to interview the Scotland Yard detective in charge – Detective Inspector John Sanderson.'

"Tell me DI Sanderson – Have you any clues about what happened here today?" The TV reporter lady asked.

"Well Joanne – What we do know is that victim, who cannot be named until relatives are notified, was shot in the right temple. At this time, we are treating this as a suspicious death. The angle of the bullet suggests it was not self-inflicted and there are other marks around his neck and arms. There is no suicide note which is unusual, so at this stage we are treating this as suspicious."

"Dammed right it is suspicious!" Sam shouted out loud at the television.

"Do you have any suspects at this time DI Sanderson?"

"Not yet, but it is early days. We are looking into several possibilities." DI Sanderson replied.

"I understand from newspaper reports that the wanted assassin, known as 'The Fox', was seen in the area of the club shortly after the death?"

"That is newspaper reports. However, the guy who ran away did not bear any resemblance other than his height. Really don't know how anybody could have recognised him against the photo fit" DI Sanderson replied curtly.

"So, it is possible that this may be tied into the recent murders of John Palmer and his minder and the murder this morning of the small-time gangster Les Hall?" Joanne asked.

"Well anything is possible I suppose as the photo fit of the person, who this morning pushed Les Hall in front of train on the central line at Bethnal Green, and the man who was seen leaving John Palmer's mansion in the early hours of Tuesday morning appear to be very similar. At this time, we cannot say if it is the same person, who was seen running away from 'The Hoofers Club' but anything is possible!"

Sam sat bolt upright on full alert. He had been seen at Palmers Mansions! Sam shouted out loud; "Jesus Christ!" He had not seen 'The Evening Standard.'

"I will now pass you to our reporter John Walters outside Bethnal Green tube station."

"John – what have you heard about this horrific murder that occurred just before lunch time today?"

"Yes, indeed Joanne, this was indeed a horrific murder, witnessed by a commuter, whom we now know, along with other commuters, have been traumatized by the horrific scenes here around noon. This murder closed the very busy Central Line into London for three hours. Earlier today I spoke to Detective Chief Inspector Harry Tomlinson from New Scotland Yard and this is what he had to say--."

The picture went to a press conference with lots of reporters, flashing cameras and microphones in front of a very expensively dressed man in his mid-thirties looking very serious, perhaps trying his best to look profound. A caption appeared at the bottom of the screen with the name DCI Harry Tomlinson and New Scotland Yard written underneath.

"The man we wish to speak to answers the description given by a woman witness pushing Les Hall from the Central Line tube platform. He also matches the description of a man wanted for questioning in connection with the double murders of John Palmer and Tony Marks in Weybridge Surrey in the early hours of yesterday morning. He is also wanted for questioning in connection with several other murders and assassinations during the last few years. He is known as 'The Fox.' This man is armed and very dangerous and should not be approached by members of the public. If you see this man please phone 999 and inform the police of his whereabouts."

DCI Tomlinson went on and issued a description of the assassin as "As six foot two or three, a very muscular man. He is thought to be around forty-five to fifty, almost certainly ex-army, possibly SAS or Paratrooper, with reddish hair and a red with grey streaks goatee beard, though it may be a wig and a false beard."

Then DCI held up a photo fit of the wanted man, but only with a side view of his face.

DCI Tomlinson then put up another photo fit and added; "This is what we think he may look like without the goatee beard and with black hair going grey! Again, I remind the public not to approach this man. He is armed and dangerous, so dial 999 if you see this man anywhere day or night. That is all the information I have at present." With that DCI Harry Tomlinson turned away ignoring all the shouted questions and walked briskly to a police car and was swiftly driven away by a police sergeant.

"So, there we have it from New Scotland Yard – this man!" John Walters pointed to the two photo fit pictures and added; "This man known as 'The Fox' is wanted for questioning in connection with the murder of Les Hall at Bethnal Green tube station and for two other murders in Surrey within the last twenty-four hours. Another of my police informants also told me this man is not thought to be a serial killer, but is an assassin; therefore, he is even more dangerous. There is no doubt he could also be linked to the victim at 'The Hoofers Club.'. So, there we have it and it is back to you Joanne in Soho outside The Hoofers Club."

Sam sat staring at the two photo fit pictures and quickly decided that neither looked remotely like him. He had to admit though that the verbal description of him was uncanny. Obviously, somehow, he had been spotted at Palmers Mansions this morning, probably just a bit of bad luck, the first time ever he had been spotted on the job. Then again, he remembered, didn't Palmer say he had been expecting him and even knew he was 'The Fox?' Still the police must have worked the scene well to connect dots to ex-military and so on.

Then he began to think more clearly. There were thousands, if not hundreds of thousands of ex-Paratroopers or SAS, most of them six foot plus and very muscular. So, with very little resemblance to the photo fit faces and no names to work on, it seemed to Sam he was clear from any problems. The only problem was Joe - Had he talked before they killed him? However, they would have been here waiting for him? Then again Joe Cole did not know his home address or his alias as Eric Liddell so they, whoever 'they' was, could not joint the dots. The only thing they could perhaps connect was the name Sam Aldridge and they may get a connection through Army records, but then the scent would die. Sam had never registered the name with any local authorities and not used the name, except with Joe, since nineteen forty-seven. He was just another statstic of the WW2.. However, 'they' may be a bit smarter than your average bear.

So 'The Fox' decided he more or less in the clear, he just needed to play safe and tie up loose ends, like getting rid and replacing murder weapons and his favourite knife. Burn the clothes, wig, beards and shoes, or boots he used in each operation. Then get out of the business for a few years. He started to collect the clothes, shoes, holdalls and boots used and bagged them before going up onto the roof garden of his penthouse. There he had installed one of those mini-furnaces which blasted everything with a minimum of smoke which could not be seen at night. He dumped all the stuff into the mini-furnace, but waited till dark to set it alight. Maybe it was not necessary, but it was simply a safety precaution.

As everything was burning up on the, he then took all the weapons and knives he had ever used on all of his assignments. He carefully wiped everything clean of fingerprints and wrapped them in old rags to stop them rattling about. He put aside a brand new Walther PPK with silencer and shoulder holster. Also, a brand-new knife and he tucked them under loose floorboards in the gym. He put the old guns and knives into an old suitcase, along with a holdall containing a new disguise.

He left a light on in the gym and a table lamp in the lounge.

Then, as an extra precaution, he drew all the curtains. Once again, dressed as the old cad Eric Liddell, he went down the lift and passed through the reception area.

"Hello Mr Liddell – going off on your hols?" John the security man at the reception asked..

"Not yet John – Just going down to the charity shop with some bits I am clearing out" Sam replied with a faint smile.

"Don't worry about that - put them behind here and I will take them down in the morning. The charity shops are all closed by now!" John was trying to be helpful, but this lot would not go down well in a charity shop.

"The one I am going to will be open all night!" 'Eric' replied with his old man voice and with a forefinger to the nose in the universal gesture. Sam always had the right answer ready, it was always the same, not because he was a genius, but he thought through most scenarios on what could go wrong, before he went out. Well, maybe earlier today was an exception, but he was back in control again.

John, the security man, shook his head and with a laugh and a wave of the hand which sent the old cad Mr Liddell on his way. He mumbled: "I don't know how he does it! All that money I suppose."

Eric Liddell was once again into his bit part playing. He looked around outside to make sure there was nobody around. He scanned the rooftops and the doorways in the gathering gloom. He did not see anything or anyone, but he knew that meant nothing. He went back through reception limping and using his stick, ignoring John's quizzical look he went down to the basement unlocking the rear door with his pass key. After a quick look around, he quickly exited, closed and locked the rear door. He kept up his limp and stick walk as he made for Chelsea Bridge and it was getting quite dark. Just before the bridge he saw a couple of young guys hanging around in the shadows. They both came slithering over with more than a little menace. Sam adjusted his hand on the suitcase so that he could have maximum leverage when he swung it into their faces. It was heavy with the weapons and ammunition so he knew there would be collateral damage.

"Can we help you with your case old man?" The first one asked with a cockney accent.

"Well now lad that depends if that is all you want?"

The first one gave a nervous giggle, which Sam took as a good sign – inexperience, probably your everyday London muggers.

"Well now we will probably have to take your wallet old man – You know as a tip for helping you out – you with a bad leg and all." The first one replied again with that same nervous giggle.

Sam dropped his stick and turned away at about at a ninety-degree angle as though looking for someone to help and replied; "Sorry you said that lad." Then suddenly he pirouetted with the case at shoulder height and it smashed into the first ones left cheekbone with a sickening smash. Sam then pirouetted in the opposite direction and with the case again at shoulder- height he smashed it into the second lad's right cheekbone with that same sickening smash. They both just dropped to the pavement, out cold for at least the next couple of hours.

"You should really know what you are dealing with when you try to mug old people in London lads." Sam said aloud as he picked up his stick and had a quick look around. Nobody about and he crossed the bridge. He slipped quietly down the other side by the river and went under the bridge on the embankment.

He had a quick look around up and down the embankments on both sides. Nobody around, so he quickly took out his holdall and emptied the rest of the suit contents into the river. With a splash, they quickly sank to the bottom. Luckily, the river was quite deep at this point under the bridge.

He sat for a minute again contemplating the day, which really could have been even more disastrous. At least now any evidence connecting either Eric Liddell, or Sam Aldridge, to 'The Fox' was effectively destroyed.

All of which brought him back to the thought which he spoke out loud; "How could they track packages through the Royal Mail post box system?" There was only one explanation for that! He had now worked it out and decided it had to be Flying Squad, or MI5. Nobody else had the power to interfere with the Royal Mail deliveries! Based on the policeman's – DI John Sanderson interview – it was not the police, so it had to be MI5? - Well maybe, but almost sure – but trying to find out who in that organisation was going to be very difficult.

Well, whoever it was, they were going to pay for Joe Cole. It was plain and simple for Sam. It would be his last act before getting out of the business for a well-earned break.

He got back up onto the bridge and hailed a passing taxi and booked the driver to take him back across the bridge and onward to Victoria Bus Station. They drove past the two muggers surrounded by a few night walkers. As they went past Sam said; "It looks like those two ran into a bit of trouble."

"Yeah, they look like a couple of muggers known in this area. You may have been lucky not coming across from that side of the bridge a few minutes earlier." The cab driver replied.

"Yeah well – you know what they say lad – You make your own luck in this life." Sam replied with a ruthful smile.

He decided not to take a chance and he dropped his case back at Victoria Bus Station in the lockers. He removed the holdall and went to the toilets to get changed into his 'new' disguise. He changed his disguise using a black wig, a black bushy beard and black Mexican style droopy moustache. He wore black slacks and a black top with black shoes, all good for night time surveillance. He stuffed his Eric Liddell disguise back in the holdall and, with the walking stick, dropped the lot back in the locker with the suitcase.

He then headed up, with no limp, to Sloane Square to get into a good position to observe the Centaurus apartments from a safe distance before anybody else got there. He would have to make sure he was not in a position that anybody else, like the police, were liable to use, or from where he could be spotted either on the street or from the Centaurus apartment. It was going to be a long and a difficult night.

Book 1 in the DI Spearing and DS Devlin series

Chapter 17 - Pieces falling into place

DI Spearing and DS Devlin sat in silence as they made their way on London Umderground back to New Scotland Yard from 'The Ship' pub. Andy Spearing was thinking about todays events.

Andy just loved it when the dots began to line-up, or as others put it, the pieces of the jigsaw all started falling into place. Maybe this time there was more than one jigsaw to piece together, but things were starting to happen. Some pieces were falling into place. He felt more than a little optimistic, why, he did not know, but he felt that this time they might get a few breaks.

Andy and I got back to New Scotland Yard at about six p.m. and went straight to our desks. Sure enough, the place was deserted, but DI John Sanderson was still there on the telephone and waved as we went past.

"Okay Kevin, let us try and trace Mrs P – You ring the hotel and the offices. I will try Weybridge and her Dad's place in Bournemouth. Let us see if we can reach her. Then we can go and have a kip before heading for Sloane Square around two? That sound okay?"

"Yeah I suppose so." I replied again, more grudgingly than I had attended.

"Don't sound so enthusiastic lad. – You know, this lady may be depending on us finding her pronto!" Andy replied with an edge to his voice.

"I doubt it Andy – It is more likely that lady is hoping that neither we, nor anyone else, will find her!"

"What do you mean lad?" DI Spearing asked with raised eyebrows.

"I don't have a clue Andy! I am just dog tired but I think it is time we had a brain storming session – Especially with DI Sanderson here and he is in charge of the Joe Cole thing!"

DI Sanderson looked across and smiled before getting up and joining us.

"Yeah Andy – I think it is time for one of those – What do you call them Sergeant?" DI Sanderson was looking at Andy and smiling.

"Brain storming session's sir!" I replied, knowing full well where this was going!

"Aye brain storming! These modern techniques are really something else aint they Andy?"

"Yeah you are right John - something else! But you and I have to have half a brain in the first place before we have a clue what is going on John!" Andy was laughing as he said it.

"I reckon, if we had half the brain of these 'Trained Brains,' I bet we could have solved most of our caseloads! What do you reckon Andy?" DI Sanderson was laughing as he said it.

"So, use the fucking trained brains and you might get there!" I was angrier than I should have been with their little light hearted jesting.

"Touché Sergeant – Let us go back to that later – First what do you think about the Joe Cole killing John?" Andy turned around and looked directly at DI Sanderson.

"Well, at the moment not a hundred per cent sure Andy! However, I think looking at the evidence it is a put- up job!"

"Yeah those are my thoughts from what you said on television John. Who found the body?" Andy asked it as almost a second thought.

"Well there is the rub Andy! It was MI5. Don't know who is in charge yet, but that in itself sounds ominous!" DI Sanderson replied with a little thin smile.

"Well there you go Sergeant – More coincidences! What does your 'trained brain' say to that Sergeant?" Andy asked a little sarcastically.

"Well sir – I was going to raise it in the Brain Storming later. Like you, I do not believe the Joe Cole killing was the work of 'The Fox.' Now by the sounds of it maybe – just maybe – it could have been MI5 just seeking to divert attention" I sort of trailed off at this point.

"What do you think John?" Andy asked.

"I think Andy – I think it could be MI5. How about trying this 'Brain Storming' thing?" DI Sanderson replied quietly, but with a smile.

"Yeah, well to me it sounds plausible, but probably not provable!" Andy replied and added; "Okay Sergeant let's get on with those calls to Mrs P."

"Just one thing before you go off Andy – remember our conversation the other day?" DI Sanderson sounded apprehensive.

"Yeah, you wanted advice?" Andy replied.

"Yeah, well I am starting to build up quite a case on 'The Hammond's,' although it will be another while before it is all ready to go. Still, somebody upstairs is pulling strings and making it almost impossible." DI Sanderson was obviously unsure.

"Tell you what John – Wait until it is watertight, then wait till the next bank holiday weekend – All them bastards upstairs usually take a week off on bank holidays – Get them charged during that bank holiday weekend before they come back." Andy answered quickly.

"Sounds like a plan Andy! I will do just that."

"Yeah John, but watch your back! Don't let anything out of the bag until you have arrested them; then I will let the rumour mongers loose saying they are 'singing' like and their so - called mates won't be long in knocking them back!"

"Yeah thanks Andy – I will keep it in mind." DI Sanderson went back to his desk.

"Okay Sergeant - let's make these calls for Mrs P, shall we?" I made the first call to 'The Dorchester' and they replied promptly with: "Good evening. The London Dorchester here – Can I help?! A posh lady's voice asked.

"Ah yes - I am Detective Sergeant Devlin from New Scotland Yard. Can I be put through to Mrs Palmer's room please?" I replied in my best Glaswegian accent.

There was silence for a few seconds then she replied; "Please hold sir while I put you through to the duty manager."

I cringed, but said nothing in reply.

"Good evening sir – John Westcott, the duty manager here. How can I help Sir?"

"I have just gone through that already Mr Westcott with your telephonist. However, I am Detective Sergeant Devlin from New Scotland Yard – I wish to be put through to Mrs Palmer's room?" I sounded nice and peaceful which was the opposite of the way I was now beginning to feel; the old class thing was beginning to boil.

"I am sorry sir, but I am afraid I do have to have a means of identifying you sir before we can give out any information on our clients." The office manager replied, sounded almost sneering, at least to my admittedly bias ears. I noticed it was clients these days and not customers.

"Tell me Mr Westcott; is this a one off, or are you just naturally obstructive to the police?" I asked, trying my best to sound irritated, but at the same time realizing I needed this man's' cooperation, which would now be hard to get.

Andy grinned across the desk and shook his head.

"Police or not sir I am afraid we cannot just hand out details of our clients to anybody who rings. After all Sir, you could be anybody?" Mr Westcott had that same sneering voice, but I suppose he had a point.

"Okay – okay! Just you ring New Scotland Yard in the next five minutes and ask to speak to Detective Sergeant Devlin. Is that good enough for you?" I asked bristling with anger.

"Yes sir, but I do not have the new number for 'New Scotland Yard.'"

"Well ring enquires! AND Mr Westcott, this is a murder enquiry. Mrs Palmer's life could be in danger, so make that call back to me within the next five minutes please."

"Oh, yes Sir, I will ring straight back!" Mr Westcott's replied, his voice suddenly full of urgency.

I threw the phone back on the cradle and it rattled.

"You have such a way with words Kevin. – Are you just naturally obstructive to the police? – A lesson on how to antagonise and not influence people!"

"My – My! - Talk about the pot calling the kettle black."

"Well at least I wait until the kettle has boiled Kevin!" Andy replied with a little sarcastic smile.

"Yeah there is that – I suppose I do have a short fuse, but usually it works!" I replied with a sly smile.

"Short fuse? Kevin! - you were almost blowing up before you have lit the fuse!" Andy said it with a laugh.

Luckily my phone rang before I could reply.

"Detective Sergeant Devlin! – Yes, Mr Westcott? - are you now satisfied? Yes? - Good! – Now can you put me through to Mrs Palmer? What the fuck? Are you joking? – You could have told me that ten minutes ago! Okay, yes okay Mr Westcott – Thank you for totally misleading this investigation. Client confidentially or not Mr Westcott – you are what our American cousins call a first-class asshole. Goodbye Mr Westcott." I answered with a snarl and furiously threw the phone with a hard crack, but it settled back into the cradle. Phones like everything else in those days were made to last for years!

"DS Devlin – you ought to at least try and control that Celtic temper of yours!" Andy was again laughing loudly as he said it.

"You know what that asshole just told me after all that Andy? Mrs Palmer checked out over the telephone this afternoon. What a fuckin waste of space he is!" I was now working up to a real lather!

"Listen – he was only doing his job." Andy replied still laughing.

"Yeah that's what the Nazis said in forty-six." I was getting into a right pickle.

"Cool down lad. I hardly think a hotel manager doing his job in nineteen sixty-seven warrants that kind of remark. – Even if he is an asshole. Now get onto her office and take it easy." Andy answered evenly, but obviously did not want to hear no more rants.

I felt the put-down, got a slightly red face, but instinctively knew Andy was right. I lifted the phone dialled zero and asked; "Please darling – Can you put me through to Palmers Associates in Bethnal Green?" There were no direct dials from your desk phones in those days; at least it was only starting to come in!

"Yes Kevin, if you like to hold it will take a minute." I recognised that sexy voice.

"Yes Sandra – no problem!" I replied and automatically put my hand over the mouthpiece which turned out to be a good move on my part.

"Oh, Sandra is it now Kevin? How did you know that so soon?" DI Spearing shouted laughing across the desks.

"Well I am supposed to be a detective sir and we 'young' detectives get our priorities right!" I replied sarcastically, emphasising the 'young' bit.

"Oh Cock-A-Doodle-Do" Andy replied making the sound of a rooster, followed by a real belly laugh and added; "You young chickens I don't know."

"Aint it better than being an old speckled hen?" I replied brightly with my little sarcastic smile.

"Touché again Kevin!" Andy replied with a wave of dismissal.

"A male voice I thought I recognised came on my line and said; "Good evening Palmers Associates."

"Good evening – Could I speak to Mrs Palmer please?" I asked in my best English accent, but it was still laced with my Glasgow dialect.

"Afraid Mrs Palmer left earlier this afternoon sir!" The voice replied with a little amount of uncertainty.

"Is that Ralph?" I asked with a little hesitation having recognised the voice of the 'good' minder we had spoken to earlier.

"Yes, it is! Is that DS Devlin?" Ralph replied.

"Yes Ralph! – The Glasgow accent gives me away every time. – "Tell me Ralph" (The buddy thing is always good when trying to extract information!) – "Tell me - did Mrs P say why she was going early, or where she was going?"

"Not really, but she was really upset when she got a call from her hotel and she seemed to panic. Told them to check her out and send the cases with the bill to her Weybridge home!" Ralph replied evenly enough, but did sound concerned.

I took out my notebook and pen and started to write down his answers.

"The hotel telephoned her and not the other way around?" I asked almost in disbelief.

"Yeah that's right sir! Right upset she was afterwards and hightailed it out of here within half an hour."

I was flabbergasted by this, but worse was to follow as I asked; "Tell me Ralph – Did she say what the message was from the hotel that sent her into a spin?"

"Not really – Only said 'Another of those leeches are after me and immediately afterwards she started packing up!"

"What did she mean by; 'another of those leeches'? – do you know Ralph?"

"I can only think it was another of you coppers Sergeant – sorry to say! Earlier in the afternoon she had paid a small fortune over to one of your coppers at the Lyons team rooms in Piccadilly."

"How did you know it was a copper?" I asked trying not to lead him too much.

"After she paid him off she had asked me to follow him for the afternoon!"

"How did you know who to follow if it had had gone down in Lyons tearooms?" I asked, thinking I knew the answer.

"I gave her a couple of minutes and then went into Lyons and spotted her with him in deep quiet conversation! Then I hightailed it out of there and went into a travel agency across the road, browsing the brochures until first she showed and then a couple of minutes later he came out. So, I followed him to New Scotland Yard and then half an hour later he came out and I followed him to his home. It was a very expensive penthouse in Knightsbridge. I think I saw him hit a young boy with an uppercut as he walked into the penthouse." Ralph sounded very pleased and almost boasting about his afternoons work.

"You got that close to him and he never spotted you?" I asked incredulous.

"Yeah that arrogant shitbag was so pleased with himself he was oblivious. If he is in the blackmail business he aint going to last five minutes, cop, or not."

"Yeah that's for sure. Tell me Ralph - what did Mrs P say when you told her?" I asked, trying to sound nonchalant as possible.

"She said only, 'thanks Ralph' and then said; "I will take care of it from here." – That's all she said and went to find a few files!"

"You sure Ralph - those were her exact words; "She would take care of it from here'?"

"Yeah – absolutely - for sure." Ralph was definite.

"A couple of final questions Ralph if you will – This thing - you think it is blackmail – What was it over?" I asked, but I thought I already knew and was not disappointed.

"It was something to do with company books!" Ralph answered again without hesitation and I felt a gut wrenching feeling deep down.

"So, Ralph – Do you have a description of this copper who was on the take?" I asked, but again I thought I knew and was not disappointed.

"Yeah, he is about twenty-six, around six feet and was dressed in a blue pin stripe suit with his black hair swept straight plastered down with Brylcreem. A bit old fashioned dressed and hair style for his age – Know what I mean? Ralph asked.

"Yeah I know exactly what you mean!" I replied rapidly feeling my gut in a knot. I thought to myself in a building rage; Nigel bloody Worthington, the fucker! I then noticed Andy waving over and signalling me to put my hand over the phone.

"Mrs P is not at home, or at her Dad's. I am going to get an all points issued on her, maybe too late. See if he has any clue where she might be?" Andy sounded a little desperate.

"Yeah sorry Ralph, well it's like this. We just got news that Mrs Palmer has gone missing. We are putting out an all points on her. Any ideas where she might be?" I asked out of hope but with little expectation.

"Not a clue, but like I say when she left here I got the impression she was going on the run and trying to get away fast." Ralph answered, matter of fact, as though his employers went missing every day. Then he suddenly added the question; "Do you think she has been taken?"

"Not a clue Ralph, but we have reason to believe some people may be after her. Anyway, thank you very much; you have been a great help this afternoon. Should she contact you please let us know, no matter what she says. Her life may be in danger!" I said it and sounded sincere, which I was.

As I hung up I heard Ralph say: "Yeah right!" I could not work out if he was pleased, or maybe disgruntled. I immediately lifted the phone again and spoke to the lovely Sandra, who brightened me up again; "Can you get me 'The Dorchester' Sandra and ask to be put through to a Mr Westcott? Give me a ring back?" I asked trying unsuccessfully to sound cheery.

"My 'The Dorchester' – you are moving in exalted circles these days." The lovely Sandra replied.

"If only my dear Sandra – If only." I left my rueful sounding voice trailing as I hung up.

"What's going on over there?" Andy asked from across the desks.

"Bring you up to speed in a minute when I get a reply to that call." I pointed at the phone as if that should mean something. Andy just nodded and got on with one of his telephone calls. I noticed DI Sanderson had disappeared.

My phone rang, irritatingly loud, and I quickly lifted the receiver and answered with a gruff voice; "DS Devlin here."

"Mr Westcott - the duty manager from 'The Dorchester' - here DS Devlin. How can I help?" Mr bloody Westcott voice sounded all sneering again.

"I'll tell you how you can help Mr Westcott – You can start by telling me how Mrs Palmer checked out of your hotel this afternoon?" I knew I sounded gruff and ready for a fight, but this guy was simply rubbing me up the wrong way.

"I told you earlier DS Devlin – it was by telephone." Mr Westcott sounded as smooth as silk.

"I know that Mr Westcott! But what you did not tell me was Mrs Palmer only checked out immediately after receiving a phone message from your hotel! Is that right? Why did you not tell me this earlier Mr Westcott?" I sounded, and was by now, extremely angry.

Mr Westcott did not reply for a couple of seconds before stammering his words in reply "I really did not think it was relevant and anyway you didn't ask!"

I immediately saw red and flew for his throat before catching myself at the last second and asked real cool; "Really? You did not think it was relevant that, immediately after a phone message from your hotel to Mrs Palmer, she has immediately checked-out of your hotel? You must have known her husband has just been murdered. Where is your brains man? Are they somewhere where you sit?"

"There is no need to be rude DS Devlin." Mr Westcott almost sounded irritated.

"I have not even begun to get rude Mr Westcott! Now what was this message you gave to Mrs Palmer and who was it from?

"I really don't think I should ---"Mr Westcott started to say.

"Stop right there Mr Westcott – Do not go down that path!" I shouted louder than I intended, but I was now past the point of caring, but added more quietly with a threat; "If you go down there Mr Westcott, I will come around in the next ten minutes and arrest you for obstructing the police from doing their duty during a murder enquiry. You can spend the next few nights in the cells – I promise you I will make sure that will happen!"

"Oh!" Mr Westcott replied very nervously before adding apologetically; "I am sorry, I did not realise it was so important."

"It is more than important - it is vital information Mr Westcott. Now – What was the message and who sent it?"

"Well, it came from a Mr Robert Lambert, who claimed he was from the Government Department of Information – He simply asked us to pass on a message saying; 'He would like to meet up with Mrs Palmer to discuss her husband's estate and he would drop by the hotel this evening' - that was it."

"There now Mr Westcott now that wasn't so bad was it?" I said it as sarcastically as I could muster before adding nicely: "Now are you sure that is everything you know Mr Westcott?"

"Absolutely." Mr Westcott replied now sounding full of cooperation,

"Right! Thank you for your help Mr Westcott. - I will be in touch if anything else turns up." I said and quickly hung up before he could reply.

"Who was that poor sod you just brow beat into submission? Andy asked quietly and with a smile.

"That 'poor sod' was that absolute asshole duty manager at 'The Dorchester' again who I should have arrested for wasting police time!" My 'Mr Angry' voice again.

"Your little red flag is waving above your head again you know!" Andy replied with that little smirk of a smile.

I had to smile, but chose to ignore it before replying with, some irritation; "Well - do you want to hear what I have found out or not?"

"Go right ahead Dr Watson." Andy replied again with that sarcastic grin.

Referring to my notes, I spent the next ten minutes without interruptions summarizing what I had learned from both Ralph and Mr Westcott. When I finished, I asked; "What do you think Andy?"

"I'll tell you what I think Sergeant. – First - that was some damn good work to dig out that information. Now to summarize my thoughts let us say:

    1.   First the name Robert Lambert rings a bell somewhere I think 'they' – whoever 'they' are – may have just made their first mistake by leaving that message for Mrs P. They probably thought it would never come out – So, again well done Kevin." I could not help but smile and purr a little – high praise indeed!

    2.   "Here is a 'wonder' point! Why I wonder did 'they' decide to warn Mrs P with this message? – Was it to get her on the run, or was it to get her out of her offices and away from her minders? Either way I don't think it is good news for Mrs P.

    3.   Then you're Hooray Henry – Mr Nigel Worthington – We need to pick him up. That can probably wait till the morning as he doesn't have a clue that we are onto him.

    4.   Finally - sorry Kevin! - but based on this information – I think before we go and catch some kip we ought to go to the hospital and interview this MI5 guy Broadbent? - What do you think?"

"Unfortunately, I agree Andy – one hundred per cent - with your entire summary! I think we ought to get there before they tumble to what has happened!" I could not think what else to say, I was getting so bloody tired!

"Okay – I will organise a car to take us to the Hammersmith Hospital and back to my place afterwards for a bit of kip before we head for those apartments at two in the morning. I have put out an 'all points' on Mrs P, so if she turns up I have given our walkie-talkie connections. OK?"

"Sounds good to me." I replied, not too enthusiastically, but matter of fact which is the way I now felt.

Five minutes later we were in the same Jaguar that we had travelled to the murder scene at Weybridge. This time driven by Sergeant 'Jocky' Weir, but there was little conversation as both Andy Spearing and I were nodding off most of the way. Twenty minutes later we arrived at the Hammersmith Hospital in the reception area. The cat nap appeared to have done us both good as we appeared bright and breezy. Sergeant Tommy Thomson appeared from the shadows in the far corner where he had obviously been observing.

"Andy – Sergeant Devlin." Sergeant Tommy was casual in his greeting.

"Tommy!" Andy acknowledged before adding the question; "Anything happening?"

"Not much! – They have been making inquires of course, but I booked him in under an assumed name and he is in a different room from the one registered at reception." Sergeant Tommy answered in a quiet clipped voice.

"Nice one Tommy - Which room is he in?" Andy asked equally as quietly before asking; "Is he conscious?"

"Oh, yes he is conscious Andy and screaming like a banshee about being assaulted by a member of the public! – Afraid I had to charge him with police assault before he would shut his big trap! I leave it up to you if you want to carry through the charge! - I will take you up to the room if you like"

"That's good Tommy. – Let us see if he is cooperative before we carry any charges. - Kevin you stay out! – it looks like he thinks you are Joe public, let us leave it like that until,
and if, we need to change his mind. OK?"

"No problem. I will be outside the room." I replied.

"Tommy, can you come in and take notes, when necessary, as an independent witness?" Andy asked. What he was saying was to only take notes when Andy was not threatening.

"Will do Andy!" Sergeant Tommy answered with a smile.

"Oh, it is you!" The MI5 Hippie greeted Andy with open dismay and hostility as he entered Room 303. Thomas the hippie was dressed in hospital issue pyjamas and had plasters across his broken nose, his right sided jaw was black and blue and he walked with a stoop like someone who has problems with their downstairs. His red hair was still in a pony-tail, but was matted and looked wet.

"Oh, you still recognise me then? You are certainly unrecognisable; looks like you have run into a brick wall!" Andy said it with his usual sly little smile. He had a pile of papers in his hand which he placed on the bed and he sat down next to them, before picking them up and pretending to read from them.

"Yeah, you would know all about that, wouldn't you? Now I am sure, by now, you know who I am and where I work, so let us stop the niceties and all the crap and let me get out of here." The hippie appeared to be talking though his teeth – it was obviously painful to talk.

"I don't think it is that easy now Thomas!" Andy replied with just enough threat in his voice.

"What do you mean?" Thomas the hippie angrily retorted, again hissing through his teeth.

"It is really very simple Thomas. This afternoon you carried out an unprovoked attack on a policeman, who you seriously assaulted. That my friend carries a five to ten stretch and, as you are part of the law establishment, you will probably get the top end towards the ten. If you have any brains, you'll know that is the basic truth and is inevitable!" Andy replied quietly, but again that threat was in his voice. It was noticeable that Sergeant Tommy had stopped taking notes in the middle of Andys' statement.

"Don't talk crap Spearing. You didn't identify yourself as a policeman! I am not one of your low-life criminals who you can threaten. I want to see the company solicitor." Thomas the hippie was trying to re-assert himself, but was beginning to sound a bit desperate. Sergeant Tommy had restarted taking his notes.

"That of course is your prerogative Thomas. However, if you choose to go down that path, let me make it clear, I have witnesses in the pub and in the toilets when you attacked me who will all swear that I identified myself as a policeman before and during your attack." Andy replied and waved his hand dismissively.

"You are a lying bastard Spearing and that will not hang together, especially when the company get to work!" Thomas the hippie was getting more agitated.

"I shall take that as a threat against my witnesses, shall I?" Andy asked, before quickly adding friendly like; "You know Thomas, you are assuming that your MI5 company will come rushing to your rescue. You know your boss better than I do, but, based on his record to date, I would reckon he will hang you out to dry! More especially when you have been caught red handed assaulting a policeman, even if he ordered it, which I assume he did! I reckon, either way, your career is over Thomas or knowing your bosses record to date, you will be lucky just to escape with a ten stretch!"

Thomas the hippie's eyes flickered and for the first-time betrayed real fear and probably recognition of his predicament. He suddenly responded sullenly; "OK Spearing what do you want?"

"It is not so much what I want Thomas, it is all about what you will give me Thomas!" Andy replied quietly and evenly, with a pause for effect, before continuing; "The first thing Thomas I want from you is your boss, or your bosses' names, the one behind this whole thing; The Joseph Bolger disappearance, what happened to him? Then, the John Palmer murder? And now today, the Joe Cole murder - what happened there?"

"I tell you that lot and my life aint worth a light!" Thomas the hippie sounded just as sullen.

Andy thought he was not the brightest bulb either, or he would not have attacked a policeman. Then he suddenly realised he knew his name as Spearing and rank as DI and he had not been introduced. So, this had not been a random attack!

Andy then looked straight into Thomas' eyes and stated; "Tell you what Thomas – If you don't tell me there will not be light at the end of your tunnel for the next ten years!"

"What do I get out of it Spearing?" Thomas the hippie said it slowly and carefully. He was getting ready to trade. Sergeant Tommy stopped taking notes and put his notepad back in his tunic pocket.

"I'll tell you what Thomas - if you give us bona fide information, I personally will take care of getting you a new identity tomorrow and getting you put into a protection programme where I will be your sole contact. You can start a new life away from London – perhaps in one of those hippie communes down Cornwall way? How does that sound?" Andy was trying his best to sound sincere.

"Right now, I don't see any other options appearing on the horizon" Thomas the hippie sullenly replied.

"Yeah, well, it is as good an offer as you are going to get from any of the sides in this mess. - But before we start - Do you have anybody you want to take with you?" Andy asked.

"Yeah, I do, but they will be watching her and they will be onto me like a wake of fucking vultures! So 'no' - best leave her for a while." Thomas the hippie replied in a matter of fact tone.

"Yeah, no love lost there then!" Andy looked directly at Thomas the hippie who did not respond, staring blankly into space, obviously ignoring the jibe.

"Okay Sergeant Thomson – If you would make notes and afterwards type up a statement, we can get it witnessed?"

"Sure thing sir!" Sergeant Tommy smiled and pulled his notebook and his biro pen back out from his breast pocket.

"I won't be signing any statement." Thomas the hippie said it quietly, but sounded determined.

"As I said before Thomas that is your prerogative. However, if there is no signed statement there is no deal and we revert to the GBH charge and throw you in jail for a ten stretch and that fucking wake of vultures will tear you to pieces in there – you do know what I mean?" Andy curtly replied and made a big show of tidying up his papers and notes.

The flicker of his eyes again betrayed the fear factor in Thomas the hippie before he said quietly; "I don't know that much anyway."

"Oh, that's all right Thomas – As I always say, every little helps to join up the dots! So, shall we begin?" Andy asked brightly. He only got a nod from Thomas the hippie in reply.

Andy continued; "Okay for the record, this interview and statements given by Mr Thomas Broadbent are given freely without any undue pressure at (Andy elaborately looked at his wrist watch) - at 19-15 on Wednesday the 19th July 1967. Present are; the aforesaid Thomas Broadbent, Sergeant Tommy Thomson and myself - DI Andrew Spearing both based at New Scotland Yard. Can I ask each of you to verbally confirm these stated facts?" Andy looked at both and they both replied "Yes."

Andy then continued; "Okay - duly recorded - let us get started. First Mr

Broadbent – How did you know my name and job title?

"I did not know you, but Segeant Thomson said you were coming!"

Andy thought to himself the simple explanation is always the best, but then asked; "So why did you beat me up?"

"I was upset because you had made me out to be a fool on the previous occasion we met!"

"I don't buy that Mr Broadbent. As I recall we only had a few words about you poking your nose into my conversation. So tell me the real reason, or we are going nowhere!"

There was a moment of hesitation before Thomas the hippie replied; "I just lost my cool man!"

Andy shook his head and replied; "I know you were there for an MI5 purpose Mr Broadment but I will leave it there for the moment. Now tell me what happened to Joseph Bolger who disappeared a few weeks ago?"

"I don't know squire! All I do know is that we were ordered to pick him up from an address in Brent Cross, which he dictated." Thomas the hippie replied.

"Who dictated?" Andy asked sharply.

"It was an assassin we all know as 'The Fox'!" Thomas the hippie replied smugly.

"So, let me see - what you are saying is 'The Fox' swiped him, but left him alive in Brent Cross for MI5 to deal with him! – but why?" Andy asked, but sounded as though he knew the answer.

"Because that was his contract, our boss wanted him alive to interrogate him like!"

Andy looked concerned then asked; "That brings us nicely to my earlier question - who is your boss?"

"Look I am -" Thomas the hippie began, but was immediately interrupted.

"Look Thomas –You know the score - Now stop fucking us about! Who is your boss?" Andy asked the anger bubbling up.

"Robert J Lambert, a right mean son of a bitch." Thomas the hippie replied spitefully.

"That's the second time that name has come up today! Now I know where I remembered it!" Andy appeared to speak his thoughts out loud, before shaking his head and continuing; "Right! – Where did you take Bolger?"

"It was to one of our safe houses – out Yiewsley way." Thomas the hippie replied.

"Where exactly in Yiewsley was it Thomas?" Andy asked with a threat in his voice.

"Falling Lane, a big barn of a house you cannot miss it – it takes up nearly half the lane!"

"Okay - so you left him there alive I assume? – Who else was there Thomas? Did your boss man take over?"

"Of course, he was alive when we handed him over." Thomas the hippie replied defensively and then added quietly; "How much longer I don't know when those two heavies were finished with him."

"What two heavies were they?" Andy asked before adding with an exasperated tone; "It is like pulling teeth with you Thomas!"

"Yeah! - Them two heavies do all that as well - extracting teeth without gas or injections. Jones and Wilkins – they are real nasty bastards – The in-terror-gaters – we call them." Thomas the hippie smiled at his own little in-joke ignoring the exasperated sigh from Andy.

"Yeah, they sound like you don't want to be mixing with them again." Andy replied, with just the right amount of menace in his voice, and added: "Do you think he is still there?"

"I doubt it - after Jones and Wilkins are finished with them they're usually carried out in a box so to speak. The boss is just as bad - lets them do whatever and it always ends the same way with the BIG E for the poor sods."

"So, was your boss there?" Andy asked almost nonchalantly.

"Not when I was there, but he would always be there towards the end. He likes to watch the end, but none of us plebs were ever allowed. No witnesses - his rules - other than Jones and Wilkins of course who were implicated anyway! And they took care of the body disposals as well" Thomas the hippie replied, he was now relaxed about handing out the information, but making sure he was making it clear he was only a peripheral player.

"What was the boss after from Bolger?" Andy asked quietly, but sounding a little tense.

"He wanted information on 'The Mafia' - who Bolger was negotiating with to take over his drugs operation, that sort of thing. After he got that, they would carry on with their torture until they thought they had every scrap of information in the guy's brain, and then they would finish him off. Unless of course the guy had already snuffed it before the end, which apparently often happened." Thomas the hippie said it matter of fact and without feeling.

"So, your boss has been using 'The Fox' – the assassin? How often did this happen? - Swiping guys, and then killing them for information?" Andy asked.

"Not a clue except for the ones where I was used and that was about four times in the past couple of years."

"Really – that much? And that was only the ones you were involved with? This boss of yours is running amok aint he?"

"Yeah! He is one of the top guys in Curzon Street. No bosses controlling him. Anyway, they don't appear to care, because he is getting rid of a lot of filth off the streets – know what I mean?" Thomas the hippie replied with a smile.

"Yeah, I know what you mean, but you know Thomas, even the filth deserves justice. Don't you think so?" Andy asked nicely, with a smile, then turned to Sergeant Tommy and asked; "Sergeant - Can you please give Thomas here a pen and paper so as he can write down the names of these four people, which I assume Thomas includes Joseph Bolger?"

"Yeah it does include Bolger." Thomas the hippie replied as he accepted the pen and the piece of paper from Sergeant Tommy and began writing down six names. When he finished, he handed the list to Andy with a nod of the head and gave the pen back to Sergeant Tommy who restarted taking his notes.

"Okay, I don't recognise them all, but the four I do recognise, all disappeared off the face of the earth. Did 'The Fox' swipe them all and passed them alive to your lot?" Andy asked with a little bit of anger creeping into his voice as he folded the piece of paper and put it into his inside jacket pocket.

"Yeah! - At least he did until recently." Thomas the hippie replied with a wary tone in his voice.

"So, what happened recently that changed things?" DI Spearing asked sounding a little weary.

"I don't really know except that the boss suddenly started searching for 'The Fox' and the word got about the office that he wanted 'The Fox' eliminated."

"Maybe it was because 'The Fox' knew all the victims had been handed over to your boss and he knew too much? What do you think Thomas?" Andy asked.

"Yeah, that wouldn't surprise me." Thomas the hippie replied.

"Would it not surprise you to find your boss had decided to eliminate all the witnesses, including you and your mates, so he would be clean and untouchable?" Andy asked sounding very concerned.

"I didn't think about that! – He wouldn't, would he?" Thomas the hippie replied, now sounding very nervous.

"Well you just said he was a vicious bastard! I think by the sounds of it he would not hesitate to have a clean-up and, if he did, he would have to make it a clean sweep - Don't you think?" Andy replied with a smile, he was now enjoying the wind-up.

"I don't know what to think anymore." Thomas the hippie replied again sullenly.

"Okay let's go onto John Palmer - what happened there?" Andy asked with a pretend knowing nod.

"Not got a clue! The only thing I do know is that the boss supported John Palmer because he did not want 'The Mafia' in this country. That is why he swiped Joseph Bolger out of the equation – Bolger was going to allow 'The Mafia' into the UK drugs racket. The boss thought that Palmer was the lesser of two evils until he had enough evidence to do Palmer. At least that was what the word was around the office." Thomas the hippie said it and it was noticeable he was beginning to sound a bit more confident.

Andy recognized a grain of truth in there somewhere as he remembered TT's taped conversation during the killing and John Palmer had been warned. "So, who was the office money on who had taken Palmer and associates out?" DI Spearing asked.

"No doubt it had to be 'The Mafia' – The UK gangs like 'The Hammond's and 'The Christie's had nothing to gain by ousting Palmer – In fact, if Palmer was eliminated, it was a loser for them!" Thomas the hippie replied still trying to regain his self-assurance.

"Yeah, but maybe they saw the chance to expand with the killing of John Palmer, then 'The Quiet Firm' were rudderless." Andy replied, but his voice trailed off as though he had just thought of something.

"Yeah could be, but with Palmer gone so were all the contacts across the world. That would do them no good at all, would it?" Thomas the hippie flung a good question.

"Not unless they had inside help Andy replied thoughtfully before asking: "Anyway what happened to Joe Cole?"

"Don't have a clue about that! I was in the pub with you all of this afternoon remember? That got me into this bloody hospital."

"You don't have a clue about a lot of things Thomas, do you? So, you have never heard of Joe Cole?" Andy was again sounding exasperated.

"I didn't say I had not heard of him now, did I?" Thomas the hippie replied with a smug tone in his voice and a smile, but seeing the anger in Andys' eyes he quickly added; "I was in the office yesterday afternoon and heard them talking about this other geezer – I cannot remember the geezer's name and Joe Cole's name came up – something about trying to find 'The Fox,' but that is about it I am afraid."

"Okay Thomas that is fine. Now the Sergeant here is going to type up your statement for you to sign and after you have signed it and it has been witnessed, I am going to arrange for one of our safe houses for you till we can get your new identity and get you moved to Cornwall or wherever. We will be back in half an hour or so – if you get ready to go I will pick-up some pain killers and fresh dressings from the doctors for you. Okay?" Andy was back with his Mister Efficiency voice.

"I suppose so." Thomas the hippie replied again sullenly as Andy and Sergeant

Tommy left the room.

Andy turned around to the young constable who was guarding the door and said; "Constable - Don't let anybody except nurses or doctors in there and, if any of them come along, go in with them. And lad! - Keep your baton in your hand and be ready to use it at all times. We will only be another half hour or so and then we will take him off your hands!"

"Yes sir, no problem." The young Constable replied as he took out his baton and I re-joined Andy and Sergeant Tommy in the corridor.

"How did it go sir?" I asked as we walked back towards the reception area.

"Oh, it went quite good Sergeant. We joined up another few dots." Andy replied cheerily, before adding; "We will fill you in as we go along Sergeant!"

Sergeant Tommy suddenly chimed in; "You realise Andy – Most of what he gave us is hearsay and wouldn't stand up in court. That is, if it even makes it there! Also I would suspect any decent lawyer would be screaming 'coerced' especially with the state of his health, which, don't forget those wounds were inflicted by the police and helped by the same DI Spearing, the interrogator at the interview."

"Tell me about it Tommy! - But at least we have joined up a lot of the dots and they have got to be worried about what he is talking about – He has a bit of inside information and they know that!"

"Yes, but this Robert J Lambert sounds like a right shitbag." Sergeant Tommy did sound concerned.

"Lambert – His name came up again?" I found myself asking with an incredulous tone to my voice.

"Yes Sergeant – one of the interesting things to come out of it! - It turns out our Mr Lambert is high up in our beloved MI5 wouldn't you know? That is where I had heard the name before, but I could not remember earlier. - And he appears to be running amok, dealing out life and death sentences without trial, to a lot of our low life." Andy replied evenly, but with a clipped tone.

"Shit – that puts Mrs Palmer in a very dangerous spot. That may explain why she did a runner." I looked directly at Andy as I said it, but saw little response.

"Yeah probably, but she may have done a runner straight into these MI5 vigilanties arms. As I said earlier, the phone message from the hotel may have been designed to scare her out of her offices and away from her minders."

"Yeah, according to Ralph her minder, she certainly panicked straight away after the phone message from the hotel. The only thing is - How would she have known he was MI5, the message only said Lambert was from the Government Information office?" I replied while trying to think about the conversation.

"She may have recognised the name! After all, she has been in the business for a long time - and probably still is. Alternatively, he may have threatened her! Well whatever! - We have an all points out on her and cannot do much more. I got a feeling that lady can take care of herself." Andy replied with a thoughtful tone.

"Not if she is up against MI5 vigilanties with no minders." I found myself replying as we reached the reception.

Andy went up to the receptionist cum telephonist. She was a middle aged, very large woman, who looked efficiency personified, dressed in very conservative clothes, her hair tied back in a bun, but she had a very pretty face with little makeup. She was half hidden behind the old type switchboard with all those plugged wires for incoming and outgoing calls. She had on a pair of headphones and a microphone on a stand was placed in front of her and the switchboard. She had a name badge above her left breast showing her name as 'Andrea Courtland.' Andy showed her his ID before he said; "DI

Spearing from New Scotland Yard – Mrs Courtland."

"It is Miss Courtland actually, but Andrea will do. How can I help you Inspector?" Andrea replied curtly and without a trace of a smile.

"I need my Sergeant here (nodding at Sergeant Tommy) to use your golf ball typewriter to type a statement. And I also need to get – What's his name?" (Looking at Sergeant Tommy) – who quickly picked up and hastily said – "Alan Thomson!" Andy immediately added; "Yes – of course – Alan Thomson - one of your patients – we need his doctor to prescribe him pain killers for the next few days and some fresh bandages and whatever else he may need to make his life comfortable. I am afraid we have to move him now because his life is in danger." Andy paused for effect and then added; "Oh and I need to use your telephone!"

"Yes sir – could I see all your identities again and badge numbers so I can record that you are removing the patient against the doctor's orders?" Andrea didn't only look efficient; she was efficient and taking care covering the hospitals back side.

"Certainly Andrea – Sergeants can you please both show the lady your badges with your numbers?" Andy replied and, with a flourish again, produced his badge and allowed Andrea to write down the details.

Sergeant Tommy and I followed suit.

Andrea immediately got on the switchboard phone to the doctor. While speaking, she signalled to Andy to the other telephone and Sergeant Tommy to the typewriter. I was beginning to feel a bit left out of all this.

As Andy went to go behind the desk to use the phone Sergeant Tommy called him aside and said quietly; "Andy – 'you know who' probably knows more about our safe houses in the London area than we do? – We even share a lot of them!"

"So, what are you suggesting Tommy?"

"I think we ought to get him out of the London area and to somewhere they will not be looking for him!" Sergeant Tommy kept his voice quiet.

"Yeah, I agree but where? That is the question?" Andy sounded a little tired and maybe desperate - trying to think.

Sergeant Tommy replied; "I thought we could drop him at my dad's - TT's place – out at Weybridge. They would never think of looking there!"

"Yeah that sounds good Tommy. Do you think TT would mind for the overnight?"

"Mind? He would be delighted – you know what he is like – he just loves to feel involved!"

"Yeah that is good Tommy. – You know, I need another giant favour from you! Sergeant Devlin and I have a late night and into the early morning surveillance! Do you think you could take over the car we have with us, drop us off at my place and you and one of your constables – could you then baby-sit Thomas the hippie for tonight at your dad's place? I will come down tomorrow afternoon with his new identity and take him on to his new abode."

"Yeah sure, no problem, if you sign off the overtime Andy we will do!" Sergeant Tommy replied with a smile.

Andy turned to me and, as though having read my earlier thoughts about feeling left out of things, asked with a smile and a wink; "Sergeant you are a good typist – do you think you can type if Tommy dictates? That way you can quickly get up to speed with the whole interview and we will not have to sit here all night while Tommy types a single sheet of paper!"

"Bleedin cheek! - I would only take half the night, and you Andy – you wouldn't even finish it after trying the whole night!" Sergeant Tommy replied with a laugh.

"Please Sergeant – mind your language – remember this is a hospital." Andrea quipped up from behind the switchboard.

"Yeah! – Sorry Andrea." Sergeant Tommy replied apologetically, before adding quietly, almost to himself; "I bet when some of the patients have a few more choice words when they are in pain!"

"That may be so Sergeant, but they have an excuse!" Andrea replied without a smile still with her headphones on.

"Obviously, nothing wrong with your hearing then Andrea?" Sergeant Tommy replied with a laugh.

"No Sergeant - thank God! I am in perfect health, but it is always good to be around a hospital if anything should happen!" Andrea replied, again without a trace of a smile, but everybody else just laughed.

Sergeant Tommy and I started work on the statement while I heard Andy on the 'phone to someone setting up a new identity for Thomas the hippie with Medical Cards, NHS Number and Insurance Cards, complete with work records and all the works, even a bank account with several thousand pounds.

I got up to scratch with the interview and finished typing the statement which was less than two pages, within thirty minutes. "What about witnesses?" I asked as I finished.

"Oh, I am sure Miss Andrea wouldn't mind being a witness if we bring Thomas out here to sign." Andy replied.

"It depends on what you want me to witness?" Andrea said it again without removing her headphones. We all smiled again.

"Oh, it is just to witness that Alan Thomson signed this statement without pressure, or duress and did it while in control of his faculties. That okay Andrea?" Andy was still smiling as he asked the question.

"I suppose so, - but he didn't look like he was in control of many of his faculties, the way he was holding his bits and pieces when he got admitted." Andrea replied, but this time there was a sly little smile on her face which helped her look so much nicer.

We all laughed again and then I asked; "What is your full name and home address Andrea? And do you have a home telephone number?"

"It is; 180 Burnthwaite Road, Apartment 1 Ground Floor. My telephone number is 01 8746 1818." Andrea replied curtly.

"Not far to come to work then?" Sergeant Tommy said it, obviously knowing the area.

"Yes – walking distance to the hospital – Walk it both ways every day or night for the exercise you know!" Andrea replied with her second smile of the evening.

I thought – yes you do need the exercise Andrea, but I did not dare say it! I finished typing the statement complete with a space for Thomas Broadbent's signature with his address at MI 5 Headquarters in Curzon Street, London and added a note under his signature that he was signing this freely without being coerced. Also, I was a witness with my address at New Scotland Yard and of course Andrea as the independent witness. As both Andy and Sergeant Tommy had held the interview, I felt they could not also act as witnesses to the signature. I handed the statement to Andy who appeared to read it slowly and thoroughly.

"Okay that is good Sergeant thanks – you included all the important points!" Andy said it with a little bit of innuendo, which I took to mean Sergeant Tommy had left out the bad nasty bits! Andy then added turning to me; "Sergeant - I like the bit about signing freely without being coerced – That is a nice touch."

"Well sir – I think as Sergeant Tommy said earlier, a lot of the stuff in there will not see the light of day in court, but if Thomas signs it like that, then he cannot cry wolf!" I simply stated the facts but Andy knew all that.

"Aye Sergeant – and it also helps to join up the dots – it shows MI5 are involved in killings, but proving who actually did the killings will be the difficult part." Andy replied, but appeared to be again in a different thinking world before he suddenly came out again and turned around to Sergeant Tommy and asked: "Tommy can you go get Thomas and your constable and we can get this signed and be on our way. I need some kip before I have to go on this surveillance in the early morning."

"Yes, sure Andy." Sergeant Tommy replied with a smile and marched off towards Thomas the hippie's room.

"We are slowly but surely getting there Kevin!" Andy suddenly proclaimed, but with a weary tone in his voice.

"My problem is Andy, I don't really know where we are going, - do you?" I asked it with a smile.

"Yeah, there is that I suppose!" Andy replied with a grin and then added; "But for a while there - we were going nowhere, now we are going somewhere!" Andy laughed as he said it and I had to join in, even Andrea grinned and shook her head.

A youngish doctor, aged about thirty plus, with shoulder length jet black hair and with oriental looks, probably Chinese, appeared with a pen and a prescription pad and without a word, signed a prescription and handed it to Andy before saying; "On your head be it Inspector. This man should not be moving anywhere, but if his life is really in danger, then good luck! You can get that from the Pharmacy on the way out - to the left of the exit!" With that the good doctor departed swiftly to the right towards the lifts.

Sergeant Tommy returned with Thomas the hippie in tow and his constable behind.

"Okay Thomas, sign this and we can get the witnesses to counter sign it and we will be on our way to a safe house!" Andy announced.

Thomas the hippie read the statement and then said; "My not coerced eh? I think you are stretching it a bit DI – don't you think?"

"That is up to you to sign Thomas, but I think what we are trying to point out is that we have not forced you in any way to sign this statement!" Andy replied quietly.

"Yeah – Okay, but you are stretching the point Inspector!" Thomas the hippie said, but he signed the statement and we – the witnesses – immediately countersigned.

"Okay! Let's get going before it is too late!" Andy replied and we all went out via the pharmacy where we picked up Thomas the hippies prescriptions. The five of us loaded into the Jaguar along with the driver, Sergeant 'Jocky' Weir.

Andy let 'Jocky' Weir know what was happening and asked him to transfer the Jaguar to Sergeant Tommy, which did not appear to be a problem. We arrived at New Scotland Yard and Sergeant Tommy took over the driving and dropped us off at Andys' place in Buckingham Palace Road, before going on to Weybridge with Thomas the hippie and the young Constable Badge Number 2693.

As we entered Andys' flat I decided to broach a subject that was bothering me and asked; "Andy - What if 'The Fox' shows up? – Are we really going in there with nothing but our fists against his gun and knives?"

"Well I have my old army revolver with six bullets." Andy replied, before adding; "The truth is that the revolver would probably be more dangerous to us than to him! I also still have my commando knife. I will look them out later, better than nothing I suppose!"

Andy and I went into his flat and I immediately dived down onto the bed settee fully clothed and within five to ten minutes I fell asleep.

Book 1 in the DI Spearing and DS Devlin series

Chapter 18 - Getting in place

Sam Aldridge, alias 'The Fox,' had intentionally arrived early, at around 19-00, in Sloane Square and was standing almost directly opposite 'The Centaurus' apartments building. He was there around eight hours ahead of schedule, not that he was going to do anything, only in position to observe what was going on. His principle was the early bird catches the worm.

Sam had noticed an apartment on the ground floor, almost directly opposite, but up slightly to the left by two blocks had a 'To Rent' Notice from a local estate agent. It also had a key pad for entry, but no security on the entrance. He thought; 'Ideal for hidden surveillance on 'The Centaurus' apartments, I only need the key pad number.'

He found the GPO red telephone box on the right-hand corner of Sloane Square and phoned the local estate agent. He asked the young sounding guy answering the telephone; "Is the apartment vacant?" and before he answered added; "I am only here for tonight before going back up north and returning next week to commence my new job. I would rather rent an apartment than live in a hotel - my company is paying of course, but I prefer an apartment to a hotel!"

"Of course, sir – Yes, let me see – yes the apartment became vacant only on Sunday, but they move so quickly in that area. It costs £100 per week (very expensive at that time!), but probably cheaper than a reasonable class hotel, you know what I mean sir? I can meet you there at 19-30 and let you view the property tonight if you wish?" The young guy's crawling certainly made it easier

Sam replied in the affirmative and added his name was Sam Wainwright and he would meet him there.

"Yes sir – no problem sir!" The young guy replied and hung up, obviously dreaming about the nice commission.

Sam made his way back to the apartment and made sure he had a good view of the entrance Keypad and settled down to await the arrival of the young sounding guy. He arrived about twenty minutes later driving a black Mini Cooper, dressed very smartly in a blue pin striped suit and dark blue tie with a spotless white shirt. He was about five feet ten inches and very fit looking. Smart, thought Sam, - An upper-class snob, or maybe a wannabe? The young estate agent introduced himself; "Frank Dobbins from Harley, Atkinson and Roberts the estate agents – Mr Wainwright?" Frank offered his handshake.

"Yes Frank – Nice to meet you" Sam shook Franks hand before adding; "Now let us have a look at the apartment as I have to catch the nine o'clock train at Euston station back up north tonight!" Sam lied easily and pushed the young lad into immediate action.

Frank hit the buttons numbered 1472 without thinking and making no attempt to hide the number. So much for security thought Sam and the entrance door opened with a little peep.

Frank walked across to the door immediately opposite the entrance and, in full view of Sam keyed in the number 1001, very original thought Sam, not hard to guess, into the keypad and the door clicked open and Frank entered first turning on the light. The curtains in the apartment were all drawn. As they entered there was a musty smell, which suggested it had been empty a lot longer than last Sunday, but then again, the furnishings looked nineteen fifties, maybe even pre-war and the wallpaper had certainly not been replaced since before the war. Frank noticed Sam smelling the place in disgust, as all estate agents apparently should, and hastily added; "Of course what you are paying for location Mr Wainwright is this exclusive address. – This is a very select area!"

"Yes, I am sure it is, but it is very dated don't you think Frank?" Sam replied before adding; "Like a pre-war movie set don't you think?"

"Yes, well all that adds a little charm Mr Wainwright don't you think? Anyway, the landlord has no restrictions on the tenants updating the property in whatever way they please!"

"Yes, I don't suppose he does - as long as I pay for it?" Sam asked with a disarming smile.

"But of course, sir! As I say it is the location you are paying for and the rent is cheaper to reflect the modernisation required!" Frank returned the disarming smile.

"Well Frank, if this is less expensive; I don't think I want to know the more expensive prices." Sam replied with a shake of the head.

"Well you would expect to pay at least two hundred pounds a month more! That is London for you" Frank said it with a little smirk.

"Unbelievable! Disgusting! Talk about taking advantage! Sam sounded angry. Little did Frank know that he was talking to the owner of two vast apartment buildings in the much more fashionable Chelsea and Knightsbridge area and was pulling in double and sometimes treble this rent from his six floor buildings, plus the penthouses, one of which Sam lived in as Eric Liddell.

"Well Frank - At the moment let me think about it – I think to modernise this place it would take several thousand pounds and at the moment I don't think I want to spend that kind of money on top of the extortionate rent you are asking!" Sam replied easily and without any real rancour.

"Up to you sir, but at the moment these properties are going like hotcakes!" Frank was trying his best to hide his disappointment as a possible big commission suddenly slid from his grasp.

"I am sure you are right Frank! But it really depends if you like hotcakes – don't you think Frank? And King Alfred managed to burn his – if you remember?" Sam smiled that disarming smile again and turned to walk away.

The response went straight over Franks head and he replied; "I suppose so!" as he put out the lights and followed Sam out through the entrance door. Frank didn't know it, but Sam now had all he needed to use the apartment for his surveillance tonight and in the morning. He turned away to the left, apparently to go around the back to the car park and shouted back; "Thanks anyway Frank – Sorry it did not work out this time."

"Yeah! – Yeah!" Franks reply sounded like he was well pissed off.

Sam just smiled, waved goodbye and waited at the side of the building until Frank drove off in his Mini Cooper. He immediately came around the front, removed the 'For Rent' signpost and brought it with him into the building using the keypad number 1472 and then took it into the apartment using the keypad number 1001. He left the lights off, but opened the windows.

He pulled up a chair to the window and prepared to nod off - another long night ahead!

At about ten p.m. darkness had just descended as Sam saw a large delivery truck draw up at the side entrance to 'The Centaurus' apartment buildings. Immediately he was on the alert. In London, deliveries just don't happen at that time of night! The drivers mate, a large burly man dressed in light blue overalls, with the logo 'Sofas Specials' emblazoned on the front and back in darker blue letters, emerged from the nearside and walked straight into the reception area. A couple of minutes later he emerged from the side door and signalled the driver up to the side door entrance.

The driver pulled up and emerged, another burly six-foot man, dressed like his mate. They both went around the back of the truck and pulled out a large wooden box with the same logo 'Sofa Specials' stencilled on the sides and between them they both struggled to carry the crate into the building. Sam thought to himself, it was a strange way to deliver sofas, all that extra weight of the crate on top of the weight of the sofa and those two were not professional furniture movers! In fact, Sam suddenly recognised both men.

They disappeared and within thirty to forty minutes they both reappeared. They had the 'Sofas Specials' box, which was now obviously empty as they carried it with ease and loaded it onto the truck. They then drove off in the general direction of Buckingham Palace Road. Very interesting thought Sam.

It was near two am when, almost nodding off to sleep, Sam heard the rather loud voices of two men in the alcove of the next block. It soon became apparent that they were police on surveillance and they could not have announced themselves more loudly. With the window's open Sam could hear the conversation in the quietness of the night.

"This is a complete waste of time! – You know 'The Fox' is too good even to show anywhere near this!" Andy said, but Sam did not know who it was.

"I dare say you are right!" A voice, with a Scottish accent replied, - DS Kevin Devlin, again a voice Sam did not recognise.

There was a quiet period and then Sam heard the Scottish voice say; "Do you have that list of tenants in the buildings I gave you Andy?"

"Yeah – here it is!" Andy replied and could see a torchlight to his right

"No! - This is the MI5 guy's statement – I gave you the list of tenants at 'The Centurions' apartments earlier?"

"Oh yes, sorry – Here it is!" Andy replied.

There was a delay for a couple of minutes then Scottish voice suddenly said; "Look here Andy – I did not spot it before, but there is a tenant here by the name of 'Lampers' – that is an anagram for 'Palmers' – What do you think?"

"What the fuck is an anagram Sergeant?" Andy asked.

"Well it is like a scrabble of letters that can be made up to another name, or meaning, they use them in crosswords – Know what I mean?" The Scotsman replied.

"Not a fucking clue lad!" Andy replied with a grunt before adding; "Are you saying this Lampers flat may be Palmers flat?

"Exactly Andy! – Well maybe!" The Scotsman replied.

"Well lad I think we had better get our arses into gear and go have a look!" Andy replied and Sam saw them both heading towards the entrance to 'The Centurions' building.

Sam could not help but smile at the conversation, but stayed in the shadows of the apartment and watched as they both disappeared into the reception area. What was interesting to Sam was the mention of a statement from an MI5 guy.

"Shit! - There is nobody on the desk!" Andy announced loudly.

I went around to the back of the reception desk and found who I assumed to be Tom Owen, the night security man. He looked very white, cum grey, and there was a pool of blood behind his head. I felt for a pulse and found a very weak beat. I found a towel and pressed it to his skull and raised his head on top of the towel to ensure his windpipe was clear.

"He is still alive, but needs urgent help. I will phone for an ambulance." I stated as I came around the table. I got on the walkie-talkie and called for an ambulance and police assistance.

"I am going up to Palmer's apartment." Andy shouted and moved fast towards the lifts.

"Hang on Andy – I think we ought to go in together - just in case." I shouted after him.

Andy took out his old army revolver and handed me his commando knife as we entered the lift.

Andy knocked the door to what we thought was Palmer's apartment, but the door just swung open. We entered led by Andy and his gun held with both hands and I followed with the commando knife held in an attack position.

"Police! - Do not move and put your hands up." Andy shouted as we entered the hallway.

We checked the rooms left and right - two bedrooms, then the kitchen and a smaller room which had been converted into an office. – All empty!

We then entered the lounge and there bound with rope to a chair was an elderly man dressed only in a pair of white Y fronts which were stained dark red with dried blood and the stench of excrement. There were red blotches and welts all over his skin and his face was a horror mask. He had obviously died in agony.

"Hello Joseph – so they got you as well?" Andy asked the question quietly and ruefully as though the man was still alive. He walked over and felt for a pulse, but he already knew it was a waste of time.

Is it Joseph Bolger?" I asked feeling the bile rising towards my throat.

"Indeed, it is, or what is left of him!" Andy replied, before adding with real feeling; "He was a gang leader, but nobody deserves to die like that!"

"What are these people? This is a bloody sadistic killing." I found myself shouting with real anger.

"These 'people' a you call them Kevin – animals more like – think they are above the law – and the worst thing is they probably are, but even they cannot get away with murder! Now let us be professional and coolly provide an analysis of the crime scene. What do you see Kevin? Andy asked.

"Don't you think we should wait for forensics Andy?" I asked as I took out my notebook and pencil.

"Oh, indeed Kevin – have to follow protocol. In fact, get on that Walkie - talkie thing and get forensics and photographers plus, you might as well get the coroner's people on standby to follow them." Andy was in his professional mode.

I got on to headquarters at New Scotland Yard and did as I was told adding that DI Spearing had assumed command. As I turned back to Andy he said; "Well lad, using that criminology trained brain of yours - what do you think happed here?" Andy asked with more than a hint of sarcasm.

I ignored the jibe and walked around the body looking at the burn marks and smelling the stench and something else which I could not quite grasp. I then noticed the jaws clenched showing several teeth missing and congealed blood around the gums. There were also several wood splinters in his bare back which led me to recognise the other smell.

"Well one thing is for sure Andy - this is not the crime scene!" I stated with confidence, before adding; "There has been a lot of blood lost during this sadistic torture and no sign of any blood except dried congealed stuff. I think by the look of it there - without taking off his underpants - they may have cut off parts of his manhood! Looking at the mouth it looks like they have extracted teeth without pain killers or gas which may suggest our hippie friend was right about this being sadistic work of those two or three guys from MI5." I replied tersely.

I then pointed at Joseph Bolger's back before adding; "I would say he has been moved here in some sort of rough wooden box. There are splinters in his back and the smell of a crate," I stated before adding; "And this is not the M.O. of 'The Fox' that's for sure!"

"What the fuck is M.O?" Andy asked with a sigh of exasperation.

"Modus Operandi!" I replied without thinking and added by way of explanation; "It is 'modern' police terminology!"

"I don't think you want to go down that 'modern police' road lad!" Andy replied with a faint smile and added; "Okay 'trained brain' – What the hell does that modus opus mean?" DI Spearing sounded angry.

"It means this crime does not follow the usual methods of 'The Fox!'" I replied.

"Why not say that in the first place? Keep it simple for me lad! Anyway, good work Kevin! I think you may be spot on!" Andy replied with a smile.

I did not get time to reply before there was the sound of sirens from the street outside.

"Best get downstairs and tend to that lot Kevin. Seal off the building and tell the wooden tops to stop anybody leaving and interview anybody entering, but stop them from getting out of reception," Andy instructed.

I got downstairs just as the ambulance people arrived quickly followed by four wooden tops coming from two pandas.

I showed my NSY badge to the ambulance people and said pointing; "Over there lads behind the reception desk our first victim."

"There are more?" The senior looking paramedic asked.

"The other is beyond your help. The coroner is on the way!" I replied as the four wooden tops came into the building.

I again flashed my NSY badge and told two of the wooden tops to take the back entrance and the other two to take the front door before adding Andys instructions on anyone leaving or arriving. I then again got onto the walkie-talkie and asked for more help to seal the building and a car to transport Andy and I back to New Scotland Yard.

I went around the reception desk and saw the ambulance men giving Tom Owen some oxygen and asked; "How is he?"

"Not good - very weak!" The senior ambulance man replied shaking his head before adding; "We need to get him to the Hammersmith Hospital a.s.a.p."

They man-handled Tom onto a stretcher making sure his skull was supported.

Tom Owen was six foot and overweight and the paramedics had difficulty lifting the stretcher, but they struggled manfully out to the waiting ambulance and they went off, sirens screaming in the night.

My walkie-talkie suddenly rang and I answered on the second ring; "DS Devlin here – over."

"Hello Sergeant sorry to bother you this late - it is Sergeant Tommy Thomson here ringing from Weybridge. He sounded agitated and he paused before adding; "I have been trying to urgently get Andy, but his walkie-talkie appears to be switched off. Any ideas how I can contact him? – Over"

I replied; "Yes Sergeant – We are on a crime scene at the moment – another murder and a GBH. Can I pass on a message? - Over"

"Anybody I know? – Over" Sergeant Tommy asked with some concern.

"Yes, the murder victim is Joseph Bolger and the security guy with GBH is an ex-copper Tom Owen. I think you knew him? – Over"

"Oh shit! - Poor Tom! Is he going to be OK? Over" Sergeant Thomson asked noticeably about the ex-copper and making no comment on the murder victim.

"It's not looking good for him Sergeant. Hard knock on the head. He has just been taken to the Hammersmith Hospital. Can I give Andy a message when I go back upstairs? Over"

"Yes, can do!" Sergeant Tommy replied with some concern in his voice and added; "Tell him his hippie friend has done a runner. Must have been between one and two ish – I got up for the toilet at two-thirty and checked his room, but he was gone! He seemed okay when I left him at one, so something has spooked him. Tell Andy to ring TT's number if he needs me. I will be around the phone for the next hour and tell him for fucks sake to switch on his walkie-talkie. Over"

"Will do Tommy. Talk to you later. Over and out."

I quickly went back upstairs and relayed Sergeant Tommy's message to Andy who responded with; "Oh shit – the fucking idiot – I thought he knew his life was in danger. What has he gone and done a runner for now?"

I could only reply with; "Like Sergeant Tommy said something must have spooked him! – Anyway, Tommy said to ring him at TT's house and to switch on your walkie-talkie in case Thomas the hippie tries to contact you. I need to get back down to meet the forensics."

"Yeah – Yeah! Alright." Andy replied sarcastically, but nevertheless walked over and switched on his walkie-talkie. The thing rang before I got to the door, but I carried on downstairs and left him to it.

"DI Spearing here! – Over"

"Spearing! What the fuck are you up to?" Thomas the hippie sounded angry.

"Is that you Thomas? Why the fuck did you do a runner? Over" Andy could not hide his irritation from his voice.

"I'll tell you why I did a runner Spearing! I went back down quietly to get a drink of water from the kitchen and overheard your old mate TT talking on the phone telling MI5 exactly where I was – Some safe house that! - so I hightailed it out of there before they had a chance to get there."

"Do you mean the old man or the son? Over" Andy was aghast. He then realised that is how MI5 got to Palmer's place in such good time. The listening gear in old TT's house was obviously MI5's stuff.

"Yeah – the old man who else? His son could be in it too for all I know. " Thomas the hippie was now sounding nervous.

"I don't think so Thomas! Young Tommy has just been on the phone to me saying you have done a runner and doesn't know why. - Where are you now Thomas? Over"

"I am not so silly to tell you that over the walkie–talkie. They – you know who – could be eavesdropping your walkie-talkie. Anyway, young Tommy would say that anyway, now wouldn't he?"

"Fair enough! - I'll tell you what Thomas – get your ass into the nearest police station. I think the nearest one is Epsom or Woking and I will arrange for a DI from Surrey to pick you up and get you back in protection. Over"

"How am I supposed to do that? I only have a few quid on me and stuck in the middle of nowhere in this very expensive hick town."

"Okay – Okay Thomas – I will tell you what I will do. Just you get yourself out of that phone box and into a nice dark corner out of sight. I will arrange for a DI from Surrey Headquarters in Guildford to come over and pick you up in about an hour and a half. Ring him in about an hour and a half on the following number – 01483571212 – He will be in Weybridge by then on the High Street - They will patch you through to him on a priority basis. He will pick you up within ten or fifteen minutes of your call and take you to a safe place until we can get you moved. How does that sound? Over"

"How do I know it will not be the same as the last so called 'safe house' and I am walking into another trap?"

"Tell you what Thomas – If you don't trust us right now – you are a walking dead man! They are on your tail, so you will have to stay out of sight and not on the road. Over"

There was a short pause then came Thomas' reluctant voice; "I suppose so – How will I know it is him and not them?"

"He will identify you as number twenty and he will identify himself as number seven. Got it? Over"

"Not very original – today's date!!"

"My you are on the ball Thomas. You have done this sort of thing before! - I can tell. Now get your ass out of that box and out of sight. Over"

"I'm off." Thomas the hippie responded and there was a click of the phone being slammed down onto a cradle.

"Thanks to you too!" Andy said it sarcastically into the dead walkie-talkie as he looked around the room for a phone and spotted one on a table. He took out his nineteen sixty-seven diary and looked up the personal phone number of DI Harry Lawler. He dialled the number.

"Hello who is calling?" A disgruntled sleepy voice, but there was no mistaking that Irish brogue belonging to Harry Lawler.

"Good morning Harry – sorry to disturb you at this unearthly hour – Andy Spearing here!"

"Andy? You know what time it is?"

"Yeah I know Harry. I am afraid we have got a bit of an emergency here!"

Harry Lawler was immediately awake and on the ball and asked; "Yeah? - What is happening Andy?"

"We have found Joseph Bolger! Dead of course! – Needless to say, murdered and tortured. We are at the scene now where they dumped him! Now our main witness has had to do a runner, he is in big danger and running scared. - He put two thugs, known torturers, namely; a Mr Jones and a Mr Wilkins together with Joseph Bolger just before he appears dead"

"What can I do Andy?"

"Two things Harry if you can – The first is I have located my witness and he is stuck in Weybridge absolutely petrified – the murderers know he is in Weybridge and are trying to find him as we speak." Andy was getting into full flow when he was interrupted.

"What is he doing in Weybridge Andy?" DI Lawler asked.

"Yeah well that is a long story. Suffice to say I thought I was getting him into a safe holding house in Weybridge, but it turned out to be anything but that! Anyway, I have arranged for you to rendezvous with him – he will be ring you on the walkie - talkie thing in about an hour and a half and let you know exactly where to pick him up. You will identify yourself as number seven and he will identify himself as number twenty."

"Wow it sounds like real cloak and dagger spy stuff Andy."

"Yes, in a way it is. Harry, but listen! - I want you to go in there with a bullet proof vest and tool up."

"Is this MI5 involved again Andy?"

"Afraid so Harry, but I think it is only one boss man and two of his henchmen involved. They are running amok - out of control. Problem is all three are maniacs, but with any luck they won't be around."

"And what if they are Andy? – You want me to go up against three, MI5 trained, maniacs?"

"No Harry – That is the second point. This witness has signed a statement detailing where they took Joseph Bolger and it is located around your patch. In fact, it is in Yiewsley in Falling Lane – apparently, a big barn of a house you cannot miss it. Do you know it?"

"Yeah I know it – supposed to be an MI5 safe house aint it?"

"That is the one Harry! – So, the second thing is I need you to get a local magistrate to sign an arrest warrant for Jones and Wilkins and a search warrant for the house in Falling Lane. Then I need you to set-up a stand-by, 'vests and weapons' squad, to raid the house and secure it for forensics to go over it with a fine-tooth comb. Remember, you have to pick-up number seven first then do the raid on the safe-house!"

"How do you expect me to do that Andy? – I don't have any proof to offer a magistrate!"

"Tell her New Scotland Yard will send proof in the morning. We must raid the place tonight, or should I say this morning, or they will escape and will be off scot free. Do you know any friendly local magistrate Harry?"

"You know I do – You just made a Freudian slip when you said 'her' Andy. – As you already know my sister-in-law has her magistrate's court in Aldershot so is local enough! You know we will both be out on a limb with this Andy, if you do not have sufficient proof and this thing goes tits up?"

"Yeah, I do know Harry, but we have statements, with independent witness signatures, so there will be no problem. Look Harry time's ticking on so you better get ready and go!"

"I am already Andy – I was dressing while we were speaking!"

"Good! - Remember Harry – Get Number seven out first to a safe place and then get your 'hit squad' over to Falling Lane. Don't let anybody know where they are going – either in the hit squad, or in forensics, until they are on the way in the van to Falling Lane. Okay?"

"Yeah right Andy! You owe me big time for this - and don't let me down in the morning." Harry sounded worried or disgruntled and he hung up.

Within fifteen minutes three very smart, but casually dressed young men all aged around twenty-five, were led into the building by a middle age man, probably around fortyish, with a scraggy sour face and a crumpled dark grey suit with a white shirt, but no tie. They were quickly followed by a guy carrying a camera, obviously the photographer, dressed in another crumpled brown suit, cream shirt and again no tie. He was the oldest, about sixtyish, with a well-worn face and smelling of tobacco and whisky. The sour face guy was obviously the lead man and identified them all as New Scotland Yard from the forensics department.

As I gave them directions to the Palmer's apartment, the extra wooden tops arrived and I directed them to secure the murder scene.

I followed the forensic people and the photographer back upstairs and found Andy introducing himself as the DI in charge.

Sour Face appeared to almost ignore DI Spearing and there was obviously a bit of an under-current of animosity between the two. Andy walked away and stared thoughtfully out of the lounge window towards the street, but with a lot of side glances in the direction of Sour Face. It was obvious that Andy was keeping a watchful eye on proceedings.

Sour Face directed two of the young men to try and find any fingerprints around the place and they wandered off in the direction of the bathroom and bedrooms carrying a box which contained the equipment for lifting finger prints.

Sour Face then directed the photographer to take photographs of the victim from every possible angle. Sour Face then put on a pair of rubber gloves and began a visual inspection of the victim and had the other remaining young man take notes of his statements on the injuries.

After twenty minutes or so inspecting the body and taking photographs of the abrasions, the mouth with the missing teeth and cigarette burn marks, I was astounded to see Sour Face produce a pair of scissors from a case and proceed to cut open Joseph Bolger's' underpants at the crutch. I shook my head and looked over to Andy who raised a quizzical eyebrow.

The underpants fell off to each side and revealed that indeed Bolger's torturers had cut off not only his penis, but also his testicles, all were missing. Sour Face suddenly stated; "I don't see anything else on the body which may have killed him, other than possible heart failure under torture. It is probable that they left him to slowly bleed to death, not a nice way to go. Judging by his colour, he has been dead for at least forty- eight hours and of course he has been sadistically tortured prior to his death. He was of course killed somewhere else. Not much more we can do until the coroner does his job."

"I understand it is possible to get fingerprints from the skin, the blood and clothing?" I asked anyone who was listening.

"Yes, it is possible!" Sour Face replied and added; "It is not so difficult from blood, but from the skin it is very difficult and has to be done under a controlled environment. Probably better to wait for that until we get him into the coroner's office. The problem with skin fingerprints is they mostly disappear or at best are smudged if the victim – like this one – has been man-handled and moved to other locations. However, we can try to get fingerprints from the blood and we will take samples of the blood to make sure it is all his. The trouble with that is, his bowels and bladder have emptied and probably contaminated the blood and any finger prints have probably been obliterated. Still we need to give it a go! Sour Face looked towards one of the fingerprint lads and said; "After we take a few blood samples Charlie - can you try and see if you can lift any fingerprints in the parts covered in blood?"

"It would be better for us to try before you take samples Phil! – Just in case!" Charlie replied with a slight nervous voice and smiled as he added; "Though with that amount of contamination I don't think there is much hope of getting anything!"

"Yeah of course Charlie - that is what I was just saying – that is fine go right ahead." Sour Face, whose name now appeared to be Phil, replied with a tired look on his face, like it was time to go.

Andy suddenly came out of his apparent deep thoughts and simply stated; "I would like Doctor John Harvey to now take charge of the forensics on this scene."

"Doctor Harvey appointed me to this case – Are you implying that I am incompetent DI Spearing?" Sour Face Phil asked with a hint of anger in his voice.

"I am in no position to judge your competency Phil." DI Spearing replied angrily, then paused before adding; "However, put it this way Phil – I have just seen you cut off the victims' underpants and you, as a forensic man, must realise that in order to cut-off his penis and his testicles the murderers must have had to pull down and pull back up his underpants. – There was a good chance there could be fingerprints on the underpants, but by cutting them open you may have sliced through the prints or smudged them. I may be one of the old- school policemen Phil and I am no forensic man, but even I know that is a no-no!"

Phil Sour Face replied defensively; "How was I to know his penis and testicles had been cut off?"

"Phil – my Sergeant here – without even looking stated that they had probably cut off his manhood. – Then again - my Sergeant has qualified in criminology at Cambridge." Andy replied with an ironic tone in his voice.

"Criminology?" Phil Sour Face could only ask and was obviously astounded.

"Yes Phil – it's the study of crime scenes and criminal minds!" I replied, rather sarcastically.

"Well there is a difference between studying and actually applying these things." Phil Sour Face responded.

"Exactly Phil – That is exactly why a man of your experience should not be making these mistakes!" Andy replied then paused again before adding; "Then again you had to be corrected by one of your juniors here about taking blood samples before you had tried to lift fingerprints. – Why was that?" Andy asked.

Phil Sour Face did not reply and just shook his head. The other younger men and the photographer appeared to be embarrassed by the interchanges.

"Then again Phil – Why did you send your fingerprint lads off around this apartment? Should you not have started with the victim and the chair where you are more likely to lift prints of the murderers? These guys are professionals – do you really think they would have hung around here in this apartment? After all you have just confirmed the body was brought here." Andys voice trailed off, then he suddenly added; "Now Phil, I want you to contact Doctor Harvey! – It has been stated by the Chief himself that Doctor Harvey would head up all NSY murder forensic investigations. I believe, for this case, I need the very best. So please get him here now!" Andy added with more than a hint of needle in his voice.

"It is nearly four in the morning!" Sour Face Phil replied beginning to sound both exasperated and defensive.

"So?" Andy fired his questions angrily and added; "My Sergeant and I have already been on the job for twenty hours and we are probably facing another twelve hours – So Phil - please get Doctor Harvey here – Tell him it is me and I am sure he will come running. As I say the Chief has already said, only on Monday, that Doctor Harvey will head up forensic investigations on New Scotland Yard murder scenes - so this will be no reflection on you."

Phil Sour Face just shook his head and retorted; "Doctor Harvey is still heading up this investigation!" He looked directly at Andy, but seeing his expression just walked off with his walkie-talkie and made the call.

Just over an hour later Doctor Harvey arrived. He was looking rather grumpy, nothing like the jovial character from the Monday meeting with the Chief.

He immediately acknowledged Andy with a nod and a quick word; "DI Spearing – Now what have we got here?"

"A murder victim – one Joseph Bolger – who appears to have been mercilessly tortured to death. He appears to have bled to death, although apparently, heart failure cannot be ruled out!" Andy replied in a matter-of-fact tone.

"I see" Doctor Harvey hesitatingly replied before asking and looking directly at Andy; "Who cut open his underpants before taking fingerprints?"

Andy looked directly at Phil Sour Face who blushed bright red and gave a blustered reply; "That was me sir!"

"I see!" Doctor Harvey replied raising a quizzical eyebrow and then asked; "And obviously, you have not tried to first lift any prints from the chair – judging by the lack of dust on the chair?"

"No sir! - I was just going to do that when DI Spearing intervened!" Phil Sour Face was almost snivelling.

"I am not surprised DI Spearing intervened Phil. These are just basics!" Doctor Harvey's clipped reply said all there was to say.

Phil Sour Face blushed again and mumbled something indistinguishable to himself.

"Right Doctor Harvey - thanks very much for coming out. – I will leave it in your safe hands. – Can I expect a report by the afternoon? – At least on fingerprints? Maybe a coroner's report in the next day or so?" Andy asked, again in that matter-of-fact voice.

"I will do my best DI Spearing. At least you will know by this afternoon if there are any fingerprints and if they match any known prints!"

Andy responded in a friendly tone; "Thanks again Doctor Harvey. I will look forward to it." And looking at me added: "Right Sergeant it is time for us to get going."

We exited the room and Andy said; "I think we had better go get some shuteye Sergeant – I don't know about you but I am cream crackered! - If you want to walk over to my place? We will have to be in The Yard for nine ish." Andy was looking at his watch, which told him it was almost five in the morning.

"I got us a car sir – thought we would need it. I really need to get back and get changed – I have been in these clothes for twenty-four hours! – If I go to sleep I will not surface till the afternoon! – So, I will just get back have a bath, change and come back – if that is alright Andy?" I asked my voice sounding tired.

"No problem Kevin - great idea getting the car – that shows your trained brain." Andy replied with a smile before adding; "But, by the sound of it, you won't last the day without a sleep."

"I'll catnap in the car both ways. Usually I can cope though I will not be too bright, but I'll be okay with that." I replied without humour as we reached the car with Sergeant 'Jocky' Weir behind the wheel.

Andy gave Sergeant Jocky instructions to drop him of first in Buckingham Palace Road at his flat then take me to Palmers Green and wait for me to get bathed and changed and then take me back to NSY. We were both nodding off even before we got to Andys' place which was only a couple of miles.

At Andys place as he went to open the car door he suddenly turned back and said; "Kevin I forgot to say. Thomas the hippie has done a runner. It appears TT sold him out to MI5, but Thomas overheard TT's call and hightailed it out of there."

"Bloody hell – TT with MI5? I sounded and was astonished, but could not hold back a yawn.

"Looks like it, but Broadbent has called in and I have got DI Lawler with a squad to go pick

him up!" Andy replied over his shoulder as he got wearily out of the car before adding; "See you for nine at the Yard Kevin."

"Yes Andy!" I answered with my eyes drooping and I gave a wave of the hand.

Andy trudged in to his small flat and immediately picked up his phone. He dialled TT's number.

"Hello – you know what time it is?" TT answered while trying unsuccessfully to stifle a yawn.

"Yes, I do TT it is around five in the morning. I just wanted to ask you WHY TT?"

"Why what? Andy?" TT replied suddenly awake.

"Why did you sell my witness to bloody MI5?"

"What are you talking about Andy?"

"You know damn well what I am talking about TT. You TT! – You of all people?" Andy sounded disgusted.

"Look Andy – I have been working with them for a few years. Our mob had no use for me and I just wanted to be useful. I was good at my job Andy and I did not fancy sitting in a reception desk acting as security man!" TT did sound contrite.

"Not like old Tom Owen eh?" "You know your man arranged a body to be dumped last night and old Tom was on the security desk. Got his head bashed in – he probably won't make it. So how does that fit with you TT?" Andy was almost spitting the words out with venom.

"I had no idea. How was I supposed to know?" TT replied sounding astonished.

"You know this guy is a psychopath TT? Did you not check him out?"

"He sounded okay to me when I started. It maybe he has changed, but he checked out in the beginning!" TT sounded defensive.

"Well TT I think you ought to find new contacts in Curzon Street. This guy has been running amok torturing and killing victims for the last few years and even the Opos know about it! The victims may have been criminals TT, but that does not entitle him to be judge and jury – now does it?"

"I had no idea Andy! Honest to God – You know me – I would never go along with anything like that!"

"Well TT – You knew it was me, a lifelong friend and your own son who wanted a safe home for him for the night. Yet you still snitched on us. How does that make you feel TT? Andy asked and then added: "Now you know so it is up to you TT? I just hope they don't grab my man because of your calls. I am off to bed. Over and out!" The line went dead.

TT stared at the dead walkie-talkie before he said with some real feeling; "I am sorry Andy! I am a bloody old fool!" He then thought to himself – 'Why could I not say that when he was on the phone?'

Book 1 in the DI Spearing and DS Devlin series

Chapter 19- The Hit Squad

DI Harry Lawler was wearing a police bullet proof vest with a Smith and Wesson Model 36 Revolver tucked in a holster under the left shoulder of his dark grey suit jacket. He was driving a Surrey police unmarked brand new nineteen sixty-seven black Jaguar 3.4 Mark 2 Sedan as he turned left into the High-Street Weybridge. There was three of his hit squad hidden on the floor in front of the back seat of the Jaguar. All were dressed in black with the same police issue bullet proof vests, and with the same revolvers as DI Lawler openly shown in shoulder holsters.

DI Lawler's walkie-talkie lay on the empty front passenger's seat as he turned left into the deserted High Street in Weybridge.

"Okay you guys." DI Lawler said firmly as he glanced over his shoulder before adding; "We have arrived on the High Street in Weybridge. I should be getting a call shortly to tell me where to pick-up this guy. You stay down and quiet until I pick him up unless you hear me in trouble. If I have to get out I will be leaving the windows open so that you can hear what is going on." DI Lawler thick Northern Ireland accent was pronounced and sounded full of stress as he mechanically wound down the driver's window.

He drove the car quietly and slowly along the full length of the empty High Street and stopped on a right-hand bend leading to Monument Hill. He was just short of a left turn into a road signposted Monument Green. He leaned over and wound down the front passenger's window. He left the engine ticking over; the finally tuned machine could not be heard above the barking of a dog and the baby like crying of a cat somewhere close at hand.

Five minutes passed before the walkie-talkie suddenly rang shattering the quiet spell.

"This is DI Lawler here! Over" DI Lawler answered as he quickly picked up the device.

"I am supposed to be given a number?" Thomas the hippie asked quietly.

"Oh, yes sorry!" DI Lawler hurriedly replied and added. "Number twenty and which number am I speaking to? Over"

"Don't you know anything?" Thomas the hippie sounded exasperated as he added; "Now anyone listening in knows who number twenty is, so at any time they can come looking for you and you can lead them to me! I am number seven!"

"Okay – okay – I am just not used to this cloak and dagger stuff! Over" DI Lawler replied with an angry tone.

"This is not cloak and dagger stuff DI - With these people it is life or death!"

"Okay – I have apologised number seven – now, where are you? Over" DI Lawler did sound contrite.

"I am at Walton-on-Thames Railway Station at the payphone boxes. – I will wait for you around the station. Do you know where it is?" Thomas the hippie was sounding more nervous as he looked around.

"Yes of course. I will be there in ten minutes – maximum! Over and out." DI Lawler replied with a tinge of arrogance and dialled another number.

"DI Lawler here. We are heading for Walton-on-Thames Railway Station - Follow me at a safe distance. Do not - repeat do not - show yourselves unless I call for additional help – Is that understood? Over"

"Yes sir – understood! Over and out." The driver of a black Ford Transit van responded. The van was parked fifty yards back along the High Street, Weybridge. The driver was dressed in black complete with bullet proof vest; gun and shoulder holster the same as the four in the back of the DI Lawler's Jaguar. In the back of the van sitting on the floor there were another five men all dressed the same as the driver.

Thomas the hippie went to move out of the red BT telephone box and for the first time saw the MI5 thug Jones standing with a Smith and Wesson Model 36 Revolver in his right hand pointing the sights straight between his eyes as he signalled with his left hand to come out. Thomas then noticed a black van with its bumpers almost up against the telephone box door, the other MI5 thug Wilkins behind the wheel with an evil grin on his face. There was only enough room between the telephone box door and the vans front bumpers to squeeze out.

Thomas knew instantly there was no escape, so it was either put up a fight and die right there and then, or go along with them and hope there would be a chance of getting out of this with the police already on the way. He chose the latter and eased himself out of the telephone box.

"Get in front of me now and don't make a sound, or you are a dead man walking." Jones rasped as he prodded Thomas with the Smith and Wesson Model 36 Revolver which had an ominous silencer fitted. Suddenly Jones swung his left arm in an arc and his hand held a syringe which had quite a long needle. It came down and jabbed into Thomas neck under his left ear.

"Oh shit!" Thomas automatically reacted and, too late, reached towards his neck. Whatever had been loaded in the syringe was already released and into Thomas the hippies blood stream. Within seconds Thomas' head began to feel woozy and his legs began to buckle. Jones grabbed him under his armpits and pushed him through the back door of the van, then swung Thomas' legs over and his whole body landed on the floor of the van. Jones slammed the rear door closed and leapt into the passenger door of the van.

"Sweet as a nut! Let's get out of here and have some fun with this guy" Jones said and nodded with a wink to Wilkins.

"Nice one Jonesy" Wilkins replied as he causally reversed the van and moved off without speeding.

Neither had noticed the tramp guy lying on the railway bench in the dark night shadows within the alcove to the station building. The tramp had witnessed the whole thing and had the foresight to mentally take down the registration number of the van.

Ten minutes later DI Harry Lawler rolled up in his jaguar with the three hit squad guys hidden in the back, driving straight towards the station and noticed the BT Telephone boxes. He slowed down and stopped at the BT Telephone red boxes. Nobody came out and so DI Lawler started to get out of his car and then seeing it deserted, dark and quiet he hesitated and quietly said without turning his head; "You guys get out the other side while I draw attention, work round and come in from the back of the station."

"OK boss." Someone answered from the back seat well.

DI Lawler hesitated again and then grabbed a torch from the glove compartment and noisily got out of his car, deliberately closing the door with a bang. He decided not to turn on the torch, too easy a target he thought if it is not who we are expecting.

"Number seven – are you around?" DI Lawler called out, but not too loud as he walked towards the station building. No reply.

"Look number seven - We got to get out of here sharpish – So let's move it." DI Lawler said it, sounding a little nervous. He noticed in the corner of his eye the three hit squad guys getting into position going around the back of the station.

"Are you looking for that guy who was in the telephone box ten minutes ago?" The tramp quietly asked - his voice coming from the shadows of the station alcove.

"Come out here man where I can see you." DI Lawler shouted as he took out his gun.

"Not bleedin likely mate! – I see that gun you are carrying! Those others had guns too and they stabbed your man in the neck with a bleedin needle." The tramp had an English, probably west-country accent.

"Okay I am coming over to you. Take it easy!" DI Lawler walked purposely towards the direction of the voice in the alcove.

Suddenly there was a crashing noise as a bench was turned over followed by a voice shouting loudly; "Police! - Don't even move a muscle man, or you are dead meat!"

"Okay! Okay! I can't move you great lummox! You got me jammed with this bench!" The tramp shouted out obviously sounding like he was in a bit of pain. Three guns were suddenly pointing at his head and as he tried to look up DI Lawler turned on his flashlight and lit up the scene.

"Jesus! What is this? – World war three? For fucks sake let me up!" The tramp tried to move, but was jammed with the three hefty hit squad members smiling, sitting on top of the upturned bench which acted as a kind of cage. He wore old baggy trousers with a crumpled old checked sports jacket, but almost new size ten Chelsea boots. An old British army coat was under him where it had fallen when the bench had been upended. His long, grey, dirty hair was all over his face and tangled in his bushy grey beard and moustache. He was in his late fifties, but looked in his seventies. He no doubt had suffered a hard life.

"Who are you Mr? What's your name?" DI Lawler asked.

"I am a nobody Mr! - Really,! I was just trying to get a bit of kip before going back on the road to nowhere in the morning! Then those blighters came along and carted your guy off" The tramp now sounded genuinely scared.

"What is your first name Mr Nobody?" DI Lawler asked with a thin amused smile on his face, the relief of the previous tension clearly now showing.

"Johnny sir! I am a man of the road sir. I don't get involved with any of these shenanigans. Honestly sir!" The tramp was getting upset and close to tears.

"Okay - Johnny Nobody! – Now tell me what you saw earlier when those guys took our man away! When was this?"

"It were about ten or fifteen minutes ago sir. - Like I said this van jams your man in the box – and then this other guy points a gun at your man's head - and then plunges this great bleedin needle on a syringe into your man's neck! Then they bundle him through the back door of their bleedin' van and take off." The tramp reply was staccato like and he was sounding desperate.

"You never mentioned a van before?" DI Lawler replied more a question than a statement.

"Your lot here didn't give me a bleedin chance to did they?" The tramp replied ruefully.

"Okay – now then Johnny – Did you notice what type of van it was? Or the colour? Or the number? DI Lawler was now sounding sympathetic.

"How much is it worth Mr?" The tramp was suddenly getting his courage back.

"Well now Johnny! I'll tell you what it is worth. Let's see – The maximum it is worth is this! We will not break your skull if you answer our questions! Nor will we break your knee caps! - Now do you think that is worth it?" DI Lawler retorted angrily.

"Okay – Okay – Keep your hair on! No need to get all nasty." The tramp replied with a smile.

"Don't you go smiling Johnny!" DI Lawler shouted angrily and added; "That was a policeman who was taken here and every second counts. So, give Johnny! – What type of van was it and what colour?

"It was dark coloured – one of those Bedford vans with no windows and sliding front doors." Johnny suddenly sounded frightened again as he cowered away from DI Lawler.

"A Bedford panel van?" DI Lawler asked again shouting down at Johnny.

"I suppose so – I don't know what a panel van is Mr Detective do I?" Johnny answered apparently getting some confidence back.

"Okay you slimy toad. Now! Did you take down the registration number?" DI Lawler was obviously trying to intimidate Johnny who was now having none of it.

"Do I look like I am the type who runs around with a pencil and pad in my pocket Mr?"

"No – that's true – more likely a bottle of beer and an opener!" DI Lawler replied with a rueful smile and then again shouted angrily; "So Johnny - did you see any of the registration number?"

"Of course, I saw the bleedin registration number. – It was in the light from the telephone box!"

"I think I am going to break your skull anyway just for a bit of fun Johnny." DI Lawler had now completely lost his patience and angrily added; "For the last time! – What parts of the number do you remember?"

"I remember all the number you great big." Johnny's' voice trailed off deciding, with a little wisdom, not to antagonise this guy any further and then added by way of an explanation; "When I am sober I have a photographic memory Mr – See it once and I remember every detail."

"Well, you having to be sober – that photographic memory won't happen very often now will it? Now Johnny - for fucks sake! What is the registration number?"

"RGT705E. It was nearly new!" Johnny replied without hesitation.

"Which direction did they go Johnny?" DI Lawler asked.

"Towards Kingston!" Johnny replied again without any hesitation.

DI Lawler wrote the registration number down in his notepad. Then took out his leather wallet removed a pound note and threw it at Johnny and said almost sympathetically; "Try and use it for food and not the drink Johnny." He turned and quickly walked back to the car at the same time signalling to his three men to lift the bench and said with a smile; "Let him out lads and come with me."

"Thanks Governor, but I think I need a drink after your lot pushing me about. Perhaps I will sue for GBH?" Johnny replied, while slowly getting to his feet and rubbing his back.

"Don't push it Johnny, or you might find yourself in the nick" DI Lawler laughed as he walked away before adding; "And you being a man of the road Johnny – I don't think you would like that one little bit!"

"I was a Japanese prisoner of war on the Burma Railway Governor. So, your poxy nicks do not bother me in the least!" Johnny retorted with a rueful smile.

DI Lawler turned back with a quizzical look on his face as though he was going to reply. He thought to himself – Can it be true? I would not be surprised, nothing surprises me anymore. After fighting through all that – he finishes up like this? Killing himself slowly but surely? DI Lawler shook his head in disbelief, but said nothing and turned back towards the car.

He stood outside the car and lifted his walkie-talkie from the front passenger's seat. He asked to be patched through to DI Spearing at New Scotland Yard.

"DI Spearing here! Over" Andy answered wearily, just about stifling a yawn. He sounded as though he had been using his walkie-talkie all his life.

"Andy, it is Harry! I had contact with Thomas the hippie but when I got to his location there was no sign of him. I have been waiting and looking around here for ten minutes, but no contact. Now I have an old tramp here who says he saw a man being forced at gunpoint out of the telephone box about fifteen minutes ago. Then they stuck a syringe in his neck and drove off towards Kingston! Over"

"I see Harry. Tell you what Harry – leave it another twenty minutes. Then take your hit squad and hit them hard at the address we discussed. Cover all entrances and exits. Make sure you all have vests and tools! Then get the forensics in. Give me a ring back and let me know how it went. There may be a chance our man may be there, but watch out for our two friends! – They can be nasty! Over"

"Will do Andy." We will get over there and be set up in twenty or thirty minutes. Over."

"Good man Harry – and thanks again! Over"

"No problem Andy – just make sure you cover my ass in the morning! Over"

"I don't think I like the thought of that Harry! I am not that way inclined! - No shirt-tail lifter me! But I'll see what I can do!" – Over and out for now!" Andy replied with a laugh and a silent smile.

Andy turned over in his single bed turned off the light and dropped straight back into a fitful sleep.

DI Lawler went around the car and got into the driver's seat as the other three guys arrived and got back into the rear seat well, all hidden from view. DI Lawler again got onto the walkie-talkie.

"Ged? -   It's Harry here! Okay we are going in to the lion's den. Get up close to me and we will go in on the quiet. No sirens! - Let's make it look like we are just another convoy with some more meat to deliver. When we get near the front door you peel off and come in from the back door. Try the door first for silent entry. If not use the battering ram, but get in there fast. Try not to use any guns unless you are fired upon. Understood? Over."

"Understood sir! Over and out." Ged replied with a little nervous laugh.

"You guys hear and understand all that?" DI Lawler turned around to the three guys in the rear seat well

"Yeah! Understood sir!" All three echoed.

DI Lawler saw Ged's van coming in his side mirror, he pulled out and headed towards Kingston-on-Thames. He turned towards West Drayton and soon after crossed over the, then 'new' M4 and came into Yiewsley. With little traffic, it only took only a further five minutes to go through Yiewsley and reach the target house in Falling Lane. It had been twenty minutes in all from Walton as they swept through the gates and up the driveway. As planned, DI Lawler took the car up as near as possible to the front door; there he noticed the dark green Bedford van with the registration number RGT705E. "Bullseye!" He exclaimed, as he alighted from the car carrying his walkie-talkie on his belt and a torch. He was quickly followed by the other three equipped with a battering ram.

They raced up to the front door, all four releasing their guns from their shoulder holsters as they ran. The first one there at the front door tried the handle and walked straight in.

"Assholes think they are immune!" DI Lawler mumbled quietly before adding; "Tony you stay out of sight at the front door and take out anybody who tries to get away. Bobby, you and Alex come with me. We are for the basement and take that battering ram with you. Tony, you tell Ged and Co to hit the upstairs bedrooms."

"Will do sir." Tony replied quietly.

DI Lawler led the way, as though he knew exactly where to go, and was quickly followed by Bobby and Alex. They reached a door, which was in effect a fully insulated and sound proofed fire door. They tried the handle first. No problem – opened not locked! - and they walked straight onto a stairway. From below, they could hear voices and someone screaming, obviously in pain. They quickly and quietly went down the stairway and turned around a left corner and came face to face with Jones and Wilkins on either side of Thomas the hippie who was still screaming, albeit he was in a semi-conscious state. He was bleeding from the mouth which looked like a cold teeth extraction. His arms were covered in cigarette burns, with several cuts around the quick of the finger nails. They had not wasted any time getting into the torture routine.

Wilkins and Jones looked aghast, both of their jaws dropping in disbelief before Jones went to move towards his jacket which had been hung on the back of a chair a few yards behind him.

"I would not advise that asshole! Not unless you like your body ventilated!" DI Lawler shouted the warning, sounded as though he meant it, and it stopped Jones in his tracks.

"What the fuck!" Wilkins announced and added; "Do you lot know who you are fucking dealing with here?"

"A couple of low grade punks from MI5 who did not even have the sense to maintain minimum security on the doors to their so called safe house! Am I right?" DI Lawler replied with a sarcastic tone as they all heard a door caving in somewhere upstairs.

"You are making a very big mistake here – asshole! You know who this house belongs to?" Wilkins again, but sounding slightly more nervous.

DI Lawler retorted; "Yeah – Do I look as though I am afraid asshole? – You see I had to get this warrant from a judge to search these premises for this man here who had been abducted by you two earlier tonight at gun point! Also, you see, we had evidence to suggest that this house has been used in the past to torture and murder other victims in which you two have been implicated. So yes! - In answer to your question! - I do know who this house belongs to asshole - and I am now charging you and Jones with abducting, at gun point, this man Thomas Broadbent and subjecting him to torture. We will also be charging you with other offences including abduction, torture and murder of at least one, or more, victims." DI Lawler paused for a deep breath, and then stated; "Jones and Wilkins - I am now charging you with the aforementioned offences and I must warn you that you do not have to say anything. However, it may harm your defence if you do not mention when questioned something which you later rely on in court. Anything you do say may be given in evidence. Do either of you have anything to say?" DI Lawler was now in full swing with a lot of venom in his voice.

"Fuck off asshole. Once the company finds out about this, your ass is in a sling!" Wilkins was obviously the talker.

DI Lawler replied with a sarcastic tone; "You really think that you two - Having been caught red handed abducting and torturing people and almost certainly murdering people – do you really believe that anybody in your 'company' is going to stick his or her heads above the parapets to defend you – Really?"

The doubt could be seen spreading over their faces, then they realised they had to believe.

DI Lawler turned to Alex and asked; "Have a look around the basement Alex – See what you can find!"

Alex replied; "Yes sir." And he wandered off looking first at shelves around three walls.

Wilkins finally found his voice and said; "You may think that, Mr DI, but you cannot prove a thing. As for this guy (he pointed at Thomas the hippie) - He is a threat to national security and as such MI5 has priority over the police - eight days a week as 'The Beatles' say! - So, you see you had better get our 'company' lawyer here pronto mate, or you will be paying the pied piper!"

"Oh, if it was all that simple me old chums. You see - not even MI5 can get away with torture and murder. That is police business. I am willing to bet some of the dried blood around here and the fingerprints, which you two idiots have not even bothered to try and clean up, will match at least one of our murder victims. I am not normally a betting man, but I hear that at the scene of a murder last night we lifted some fingerprints and I bet they will match one or both of you. On top of that, we have a witness putting you two with this same guy on the day he disappeared and then he turns up tortured to death. - He died in the same way as you were torturing this poor sod. Of course, we have caught you red-handed with this victim so there is no chance you can escape this one. So, there you have it, me old chums, as former members of security and law enforcement, I reckon the best both of you can look forward to is life. It couldn't happen to a nicer pair!" DI Lawler simply laughed and turned away from the pair. He had played a couple of long shots, which were far from the truth, but he was trying to intimidate both.

Jones was now white and looking scared. DI Lawler thought he is the one to work on, but now Wilkins was not looking, or sounding, as confident as he hesitated before replying with nothing more than bravado; "That's what you think DI, but you and I both know we are protected under homeland security!"

DI Lawler looked hard at Wilkins and bluntly said; "That's what I am telling you 'bonnie lad' – you are not protected and you are now charged with kidnapping, torture and causing actual grievous bodily harm. In the next few days, when we get the forensic reports from here and the other crime scene, we will also be charging you both with murder in the first degree. You can both think about that for the next forty-eight hours. DI Spearing from NSY will come over tomorrow for a chat and see how you both feel then. Bobby - can you get these two chumps fingerprinted and blood samples and then take them to Kings Cross Prison? Make sure they isolate them in separate wings - no phone calls, no visitors, no MI5, or lawyers for the next forty-eight hours. Only access will be for DI Spearing and his DS Devlin. Oh and no bail; we are extremely opposed to any bail. Got that?"

"Loud and clear sir!" Bobby replied with a smile as Ged and his team came into the room with four people.

Alex came back with a jar in his gloved hands. The jar appeared to be one of those large jars for pickling onions. Alex held it up to the light and with a disgusted expression on his face said; "You know what these bastards have been doing sir? They have been cutting of penises and testicles and pickling them!"

Everyone in the room turned around to Wilkins and Jones with a look of anger and disgust on their faces. Wilkins and Jones just stared at the floor.

"Okay Alex put that jar back and don't touch any of the rest till forensics get here. Bobby - could you and Alex handcuff them both separately and take them upstairs and wait in the lounge for Ged and his team. Make sure we keep it tight Bobby!"

"No problem sir" Bobby replied with a smile as DI Lawler turned to Ged and his team and asked; "Okay- What do have we here Ged?"

"These two guys claim to be Polish, but neither have passports or any identification. These other two (He pointed at two youngish looking guys probably both in their twenties, one with bright red hair and the other jet black) are 'supposed' to be their MI6 minders sir; they have given us their identification badges. However, we had to waken them up in the same bed to tell them we were here. We could have been anybody!" Ged replied with a smile. The two MI6 guys looked ashamed and their cheeks went red.

"Oh, that was very cosy lads. Feeling a bit cold tonight?" DI Lawler asked with a smile. Geds' and Bobbys' squad all had a laugh.

"Fuck off!" The red-haired guy shouted angrily.

DI Lawler just smiled and said; "Now, now, 'bonnie' lads! - Don't go getting your knickers in a twist and adding abusing the police to your charges! – There has already been enough abuse here tonight." More laughter followed from the squad as Bobby led Jones and Wilkins, followed by Alex, up the stairs

"Okay!" DI Lawler said it breezily and asked the two who appeared to be Polish: "Do either of you speak English?"

"Yes, sir we both do!" The older one with the greyish hair swept straight back from the brow replied with not a hint of an accent. He was obviously well schooled in English and that just did not happen in Poland. He wore black suit trousers, a white button down collar long sleeved shirt. The other younger Polish guy aged about thirty had a more modern almost, but not quite, Beatles hairstyle and a bushy beard with full untrimmed moustache. He was dressed in ill fitting, rather tight black trousers and a nylon black turtle necked sweater. Both had only socks on their feet.

The two MI6 guys still looked sheepish. The one with the bright red mop of hair had short back and sides and the other jet black hair, also with short back and sides. They were dressed in the standard MI6 'uniform' of charcoal grey suit trousers, white open necked shirts, no ties and only grey socks on their feet. The charcoal grey suit jackets and matching plain grey ties were almost certainly left upstairs.

"Okay, suppose you tell me what you are doing in Britain without a passport, or a visa?" DI Lawler asked staring intently at the older of the two Poles.

"We are guests of your government!" The older Pole replied without hesitation.

"That is all you need to know Inspector." The red mop hair interjected.

"No bonnie lad!" DI Lawler retorted as he turned around to face the red head and added; "As I had to explain to those other two MI5 wankers earlier. This is a New Scotland Yard abduction and murder enquiry. We have just found an officer who was abducted earlier this evening in Walton and we find him here in this house drugged and being tortured by two men who have been identified as two who were the last seen with another man who was found tortured and very dead this morning! We have reason to believe that this man was murdered along with others in this very house. Now we find you two and another two, as yet unidentified aliens, in this same house where an abducted man is being held and tortured and others have been murdered. So, no bonnie lad, I am afraid that is not all we need to know – not by a long way!"

The red head responded angrily; "Okay, okay! - We are only guests in this MI5 safe house for tonight. These two were flown into Stanmore Military airfield late last night and we are moving them on in the morning down south. We have no part in what MI5 are up to in here, nor do we want to get involved."

"Could only afford a double bed then? Not much of a 'safe' house this, is it?" DI Lawler asked with a smile and a sarcastic tone in his voice. However, he thought to himself, while we may be able to take out the MI5 guys, the MI6 guys were a totally different proposition.

"We have to make this very clear Inspector. This is a top-secret operation and you are obstructing a government agency in the course of its duty." The red head again, he was still blushing, but getting his point across.

DI Lawler turned around and spoke to Ged; "Tell me Ged, have you taken their details for MI6?"

"Yes sir! Both are in my notebook. The flaming red head over there is one John Brooks and the other sultry dark one is John Birch – Two Johns!" Ged replied, still smiling, obviously enjoying the MI6 men's discomfort.

DI Lawler turned to the two MI6 guys and said; "Okay Mrs Birch and Mr Brooks – or is it the other way around?. Here is what we are going to do! We are going to leave you to get on with your business in the morning. We will say nothing about what has gone on here tonight, provided you two say absolutely nothing to your bosses. You see if you do say anything at all – anything to anybody - then we will be compelled to let your bosses know exactly your cock up." DI Lawler paused for a second smiled and added; "Excuse the unintended pun - right up to the fact that you were in bed together! Is that understood and agreed?" There was more laughter from Geds' squad.

"Yeah – we agree!" The red head answered for the two, again blushing and sounding relieved.

"Now you can all go back to your cosy beds and let us get on." DI Lawler smiled as he said it and as an afterthought added; "Oh, by the way, our forensic men will want your fingerprints later to exclude you from any further investigations. - Understood?"

"Yeah - sure!" The red replied as they both rushed to get up the stairs.

"Also, you had better make sure your Russian friends here are kept under lock and key!" DI Lawler said it with a smile and a wink to both the MI6 guys.

"They are not Russian – They are Polish! John Brookes replied a little too hastily.

"Yeah! – Whatever!" DI Lawler responded and waved his hand in dismissal before adding; "Follow them up Ged and make sure they go straight to bed! No calls!" DI Lawler said it with a smile.

"Yes sir – as long as you don't expect me to follow them to bed!" Ged replied with a broad grin and the others laughed.

"Up to you Ged – if you are into that sort of thing." DI Lawler replied smiling but with a quizzical look. Again, the whole squad laughed, but Brooks and Birch looked angry.

DI Lawler suddenly remembered and said: "When you have finished in the bedroom Ged, could you go out and check the van? Then tie in with Bobby and talk through our plans for the MI5 guys. I want two guys left here on the front and back doors for anybody coming or going. Then I want you and one of the others to accompany me with Thomas here to a safe house. The two of you will have to stay with him until we can safely move him to wherever he is going! The rest of the squad to go with Bobby. Understood?"

"Yep – no problem sir." Ged replied as he and the rest went upstairs leaving DI Lawler with Thomas the hippie who was still quietly moaning and under the influence of whatever drug they had given him. DI Lawler started writing into his notes.

After ten minutes Ged came back in and said; "Been out to the van and there is a big box in there from some sofa company. There is what looks like blood marks inside the box with hair and cloth fibres."

DI Lawler replied angrily; "Jesus those arrogant shitbags! Okay – Ged make sure we have forensics quarantine the van and go over it and the box with a fine-tooth comb."

"Well Thomas can you hear me?" DI Lawler asked loudly trying to get Thomas out of his stupor, but there was no response.

DI Lawler picked up his walkie-talkie and got through to his Surrey headquarters. He first asked for an emergency ambulance to be sent to the house in Falling Lane Yiewsley and then asked to be put through to Forensics. He told the Forensics team he had set-up on standby and to get out to the house and meet him as quickly as possible.

He then had a call patched through to Andy Spearing.

"DI Spearing! Over" He answered it with a thick tired tone in his voice.

"Harry here Andy! – We just caught the two-bastard's red handed with your hippie friend – torturing him. I've got forensics coming on the job – plenty of old blood marks, fingerprints and everything! – It looks like they never wiped the place clean – arrogant shitbags, thought they would never be caught in this place. Over." DI Lawler was almost shouting and sounded very excited.

Andy was quickly fully awake and replied; "Brilliant work Harry - How is Thomas – the hippie? Over"

"I think he was drugged but other than ciggy burns on his arms, a few razor blade cuts and a missing tooth, I think he will be alright! I am just waiting on the ambulance coming! Over." DI Lawler replied.

"Don't let them take him to no hospital Harry. Get them to give you pain killers and bandages and whatever else is necessary. Was there anybody else in the house? Over" Andy asked with a hopeful sound in his voice.

"There was couple of foreigners – maybe Russian! They appear very irritated and they had a couple of English minders with them – MI6 guys they claim and they are screaming blue murder Andy! We caught the minders in bed together! Gave me some leverage! We just walked in the front door! Over" DI Lawler sounded amused.

"Okay Harry – You have got to work fast now. "First, get Thomas to a safe place where they will not be looking. – NOT in Weybridge! – Oh, and get him a doctor to attend to his wounds. Use your most two trustworthy guys and keep them armed and stay with him until we can get this mess sorted Harry. Second, don't arrest Jones and Wilkins just yet, tell them you will be charging them initially with torture and kidnap and pending murder charges! – Try and get them talking before you charge them. Take them to your headquarters and hold them under armed guard and under no circumstances allow anyone to take them. Third, take the two minders and the foreigners to another of your holding cells and hold them under armed protection. Tell them you are holding them pending investigations into the two foreigners who we believe are illegals and they will be charged with aiding and abetting illegals to get into the country. See if they will talk. Also, Harry - make sure they are all kept away from 'phones for the statutory forty-eight hours. – Is that all clear Harry? Over"

"All clear Andy, BUT I am afraid I have already taken most of the steps, but some you may not like! Over"

"Okay tell me the worst Harry? Over"

DI Lawler relayed the actions he had taken to date and made it clear that they were now not reversible He added details about finding the sofa box in the van and gruesome pickled penises and testicles. He also let him know his thoughts on Jones looking the most likely to break.

Andy replied; "They are bloody animals, - Okay Harry – Great work! That sofa box is vital evidence in the Joseph Bolger case so after forensics are finished with it quarantine the van with the box. It was a pity about charging them, but as you say we can hold them for twenty-four hours. Thanks for arranging Kings Cross Prison! It is so much easier for me – I have so many things going on at the moment! Getting cream crackered too, but I think we may have an outside chance of nailing some of them this time around. Talk to you later – I need some kip! Over"

"Yeah – you and me both Andy. Over" DI Lawler replied.

"Good man Harry – and thanks again! Over"

"No problem Andy – just make sure you cover my ass in the morning! Over"

"I don't think I like the thought of that Harry! I told you already - I am not that way inclined - no shirt - tail lifter me! But I'll see what I can do!" – Over!" DI Spearing replied with a laugh and a smile.

"Yeah Andy – Make sure it is with me in the morning. Over and out!" DI Lawler replied with a rueful smile.

Chapter 20 - Breaking Up is so hard to do

David Long awoke that fateful Friday morning just before seven a.m. He was completely naked without covers and lay in a baby's fetal position on the top of the double bed in Nigel Worthington's room. David was aching all over and shaking as though it was cold, but it was a reasonably warm mid-July morning in London's Kensington area. Pain racked his whole body and his anus felt red raw.

Nigel lay next to him, also naked, but under the bed quilt covers.

A minute or two later the alarm suddenly went off with a loud shrill.

Nigel started to awake, turned over and suddenly shouted: "Turn that fucking thing off."

David reached over and without moving position stretched over and turned off the alarm before stating; "I thought you were going to work?"

"I aint going this morning – no way. I'll go in this afternoon about two ish!" Nigel replied wearily.

"They won't like that, will they?" David replied quietly and tentatively.

"Who cares a fuck what 'they' like?" Nigel replied his voice full of aggression.

"Just saying!" David replied.

"Well don't bother 'saying '- asshole!" Nigel replied and David knew to clamp up.

Nigel then suddenly added; "This is Thursday – aint you going to meet your friend Jonathan –What's his name?"

"Jonathan Bridgewater" David replied without thinking.

"Yeah well why don't you toddle along and service your friend Jonathan? I tell you what David – don't bother coming back."

"What do you mean Nigel? I thought you said you loved me?"

"Don't be ridiculous David! – Do you really think I could ever love a little whore?" Nigel said it spitefully and added; "After all, that is what you are! Living here as a rent boy and then whoring with your friend Jonathan."

"You were all right taking the money from me when you were skint though?"

"I'll tell you what David – Go into the top drawer in the cabinet over there. You will find five thousand quid in there. It is more than double than what I borrowed from you in the last couple of years. Take it and fuck off NOW!"

"Nigel please! - You know I don't want this!" David's voice was quivering.

"Who the fuck cares what you want? - Whore! This is your last chance 'Whore' to get out of here in one piece– Now for the last time - fuck off out of here! - I have had enough of your whining!" Nigel turned away.

David jumped up out of the bed sobbing and pulled on his red satin underpants, his jeans and blue T Shirt with blue socks and trainers. He quickly went over to the cabinet and collected the five thousand quid and stuffed it into his jeans. He found the key to Jonathan's apartment and stuffed that in his pocket. He spotted a case on top of the wardrobe, turned back to Nigel and asked; "Can I borrow that case?"

"Take what you like 'Whore' – that was my old man's case!"

David pulled the case down and started throwing in his underwear, socks, trousers, shirts, jackets, trainers and sandals. He went through to the bathroom and collected his toiletries. He saw some pain killers which he had been given by the hospital the last time he had been badly abused by Nigel and he grabbed them. As he took them he saw the cream he had used on his anus and stuffed that into jeans pocket with some rubber gloves. He took all the stuff through and tossed them into the case which he then closed.

He went to walk away without saying a word.

"What about the rest of your stuff?" Nigel asked.

"Stuff it up your ass like you did to me!" David replied with a quivering voice and walked out of the apartment slamming the door on his previous life, but the pain was written all over his face.

Nigel felt awful, but deep down he knew that if David had stayed he - Nigel! - maybe in one of many dark moods would have at the least seriously injured the boy.

David walked out onto the street to be met by a beautiful, summer, July morning.

He decided to hail a taxi - with five thousand quid in his pockets - he could afford it and he did not fancy having to haul this case. By luck a free taxi came past and he hailed it to stop.

Fifteen minutes later he reached the building in the fashionable Kings Road Chelsea where he usually met Jonathan every Thursday morning around nine. He was early. He made his way to the third-floor luxury apartment which had been advertised for rent for the last few months at a rate of £200 per month by his friend Jonathan's 'Bridgewater Estate Agency.' - He got out the key and let himself into the apartment.

David lay down on the bed fully clothed to rest, but at nine o'clock, although half asleep, he heard a key being put in the door and Jonathan entered.

Jonathan was a forty-nine-year old six foot and two inches. A good-looking guy, in a rugged kind of way, and still a very fit man thanks to his daily gym workouts. In World War Two he had been a Royal Navy man with Special Projects, forerunners of the Royal Marines in the South-East Asia theatre of war. He had been trained to kill quietly and quickly. He had also been trained to survive torture and interrogation. Like many who had survived, he resolutely refused to talk about the war. Although the horrors of war did that to many people, it was also during the war that he had become bi-sexual. It may have been simply down to the absence of women in the Special Projects, but Jonathan found that he enjoyed sexual relations with boys just as much as he did with women. The problem was, at that time, it was illegal to have any type of gay sex with boys under twenty-one, hence the reason for secrecy.

"David – How are you?" Jonathan asked as he entered the apartment.

"Not good! He has chucked me out Jonathan!" David replied now feeling a bit sorry for himself and sobbing.

"What's the matter love?" Jonathan asked as he crossed the room before adding the question; "He has not been acting the yob again has he?"

"Worse than ever Jonathan – He has also chucked me out!" David replied with a soulful expression, tears running down his cheeks.

"Don't worry about that love. You can stay here until we can sort it out!"

"Thanks Jonathan – I don't know what to do."

"Let me see what he has done to you this time" Jonathan said with a painful expression. He pulled down David's shirt collar and revealed the painful looking welts around David's neck caused by the dog collar.

"Oh, my God – What has he done to you David?" Jonathan asked as he caressed David's neck and started to undo the buttons on David's shirt which, when removed, revealed the bruises around David's rib cage.

David saw the bulge in Jonathan's trousers around the crutch as he removed his shirt.

"Please Jonathan – I am in real pain especially down there!" David pleaded, tears beginning to roll down his cheeks.

"David – you know this is my only day off this week. I will be very gentle - Not like that brute" Jonathan replied as he undid the button at the top of David's jeans and pulled down the zip. The jeans dropped to the floor, leaving David standing in his red silk boxer shorts and socks. Jonathan sighed and then pulled down the boxer shorts leaving David naked, bar his socks.

Jonathan turned David round and looked at his buttocks, red and sore looking and asked; "God he has been shoving stuff up you again! And look at your buttocks!"

"Jonathan please! - If you have to - Please I need to put on some cream – Please!" David pleaded.

"Of course, David – I will put it on for you – Where is it?" Jonathan was as ever most considerate.

David bent down and took the cream and rubber gloves from the pocket and felt Jonathans hands touching his buttocks. David stood up and handed Jonathan the gloves and cream and noticed Jonathan's trousers and underpants down at his ankles and his huge penis fully erect. He was bigger and therefore, at the moment, more painful than Nigel. Jonathan stepped out of his trousers as he pulled on the rubber gloves and quickly put on the durex condom.

"Lie down on the bed David and I will put the cream on!" Jonathan said it very gently and slowly.

David did as he was told and felt Jonathans finger apply lots of the cream around and in his anus.

Jonathan then suddenly started bonking David for the next thirty minutes. David murmured, obviously in pain each time Jonathan thrust deeper. Jonathan carried on regardless until he climaxed.

"You okay?" Jonathan asked as an afterthought. David simply nodded. "I thought Nigel was working now?"

"Yeah, he is, but he is not going in until this afternoon for two." David replied, tears again welling up.

Jonathan continued in a low quiet voice; "I'll have to go into the office this morning. I'll be back at lunch. But as I said, you can stay here until we rent this place, then we will find someplace else – Okay? No need to go back to that bastard!"

"Yeah - right!" David replied drily as he moved stiffly and pulled on his red silk boxer shorts.

"Right – I'll see you later." Jonathan replied hesitatingly as he got up and dressed. He felt so guilty at having to force himself on a very sore David who was racked with pain, but quickly dismissed it as not his fault. It was that bastard Nigel's fault, it was he who had beaten him and physically abused him. Jonathan hurriedly left the apartment without another word, but heard David sobbing as he left.

David's pains seemed to be shooting all over his body. He got up on wobbly legs and went to Nigel's case and found the pain killers. He then staggered to the bathroom and took a tall glass full of cold water. He went into the sitting room and found a piece of A4 paper and a pen. He returned to the bedroom and lay back down on the bed but on top of the covers.

He wrote on the paper; 'I have had enough abuse. Fuck you all! Goodbye!' He signed it 'David Long.' He then took a handful of the pain killers and swallowed them one by one with a sip of water following each one down.

Probably, for the first time ever, David thought about his miserable life. He thought; what had he achieved? What had he contributed to life's rich tapestry that people would remember about him? Not a bloody lot! Since a young child, he had been abused physically and mentally first, by both his parents, then a list of men. There had been a few kinder ones, like Jonathan, but at the end of the day all they wanted was a quick bang thank you man, although some did recognise he was only a boy. Even then, all they wanted was to get his pants off.

The girls had been attracted to him - with his angelic face and big wide brown eyes he could easily have had his pick. The truth was he was scared shitless of girls ever since sweet little Marie Toner, when he was fifteen years old and had stripped of at the riverside. She had laughed out loud at his small penis which was not even hard. So, it could never be again with a girl.

David began to feel drowsy. He emptied his head and lay back to await his end.

Book 1 in the DI Spearing and DS Devlin series

Chapter 21 - Day of reckoning

I got back to my digs in Palmers Green about 6 a.m.I decided to break the lanlords rules and took a bath, washed my hair, shaved and changed from the skin outwards. I splashed plenty of deodorant and after-shave before putting on a crisp new white shirt, a dark plain navy blue tie, which matched the freshly dry cleaned navy suit. Somehow, I had a gut feeling that this was going to be another big day.

About an hour or so later, I was back out, and in the front passenger's seat beside the driver Sergeant Jocky Weir who also looked exhausted. Of course, it was the London morning rush hour as we slowly went through Palmers Green and within minutes we were down the hill towards Wood Green, passing the infamous Cock Pub on the left. Within another minute, I was napping.

I awoke in the police car park at New Scotland Yard and if had not been for Jocky Weir pulling my sleeve and shouting I would probably have spent the day in there. I looked wearily at my watch, it was 8 a.m. and I looked at Jocky and could only say; "Thanks Jocky!"

I staggered out of the car and went around to the reception and signed in as DS Kevin Devlin at 08.05. I looked down the signatures, but noted no Nigel Worthington or Andy Spearings signatures, although the latter was not a surprise. Somehow, I doubted if Andy would even bother to sign in. It was a police constable behind the desk this morning, no sign of lovely Sandra the receptionist.

I took the steps up to the third floor, an attempt at some exercise. I went up to my desk and quickly walked over to the coffee machine. I needed a quick injection of caffeine.

It seemed a permanent scene beside the coffee machine. There stood Tony Booth, he with the blond hair and expensive flashy clothes. Next to him stood Bill Brown the Edinburgh Scotsman, he with the high blood pressure face and expensive flashy clothes.

"Well if it aint the number one 'trained brain' himself – the infinite DI Spearing's lap dog!" Tony Booth the ever-effervescent blonde said sarcastically.

I just could not stop myself and replied; "Well if it is not Tweedledum and Tweedledee - the New Scotland Yard coffee drinkers!" That put an end to any polite conversation as I pushed up to the coffee machine put in my six pence and got a cup of the foul stuff.

"You know it doesn't pay to be a smart ass around here boy!" Bill Brown murmured.

"Yeah I can see that!" I replied breezily and looked hard at both and walked off with my plastic cup full of the foul coffee.

Tweedledum and Tweedledee could only stare, but were so taken aback by my attack, they apparently could say nothing. I smiled nicely to them and sat down at my desk. There was a message on my desk which read; 'DCI Tomlinson wants you and DI Spearing in his office as soon as both of you arrive.' I looked at Andy's desk and saw the same note. It was now eight fifteen. My desk was clear except for the brand-new IBM golf ball electric typewriter loaded with bright white paper.

I decided to start to write the report on this morning's Joseph Bolger murder scene and took out my notebook. Time sped by and about nine o'clock I was halfway through and looked up and saw Andy staring down at me. He looked exhausted, but dressed smartly in a clean grey suit, shirt and plain grey silk tie. Obviously, he too was prepared for another big day.

"Busy?" Andy asked nonchalantly.

"I am just writing the report on the Joseph Bolger murder scene from this morning sir." I replied with ease.

"Good lad! Let me read it when you're finished. Keep out the obvious bits beforehand" Andy replied with a tight little smile.

"Understood sir – Don't want to give the wrong impression, do we?"

"Exactly! Andy replied, paused and then added; "Seen this note?" He waved the sheet of paper.

"Yeah – I suppose we had better go up?" I replied with my own inane grin.

Andy replied; "Yeah I suppose so. – I have just been talking to John Sanderson on the way in. He tells me Flash Harry has a Mr Robert Lambert waiting in his office to chat to us!"

I replied; "Oh shit!" The only thing I could think to say, not for the first time in the last few days.

Andy replied with a smile; "Exactly! It could be it is about to hit the fan! The good news is that, a couple of hours ago, Harry Lawler rescued our Thomas and caught Mr Robert Lambert's two Opos - Jones and Wilkins - red handed torturing our Thomas. They are both arrested and in Kings Cross Prison! So, we are in pole position."

"You beauty!" I cried punching the air with my right fist, before standing up.

Andy just smiled and said; "Yep! – The Gods sometimes smile on us. Let's get on up there and see what he has to say for himself. Like I say, leave the talking to me unless you spot me making a mistake."

As we passed the stairway I stopped and said; "Let's take the stairs up." I turned left towards the stairwell.

"What to the tenth floor?" Andy asked with an incredulous look on his face.

"Well you said you had to start to get fit!" I replied laughing.

"I said I had to get exercise, not kill myself. Oh, well might as well - I have made my will out." Andy turned and joined me going to the stairs.

Half way up I realised it may have been a mistake. Not only was Andy struggling to breathe, but I also realised that in the last week my fitness condition had quickly deteriorated. We both struggled up the final three floors and on reaching the tenth floor we silently agreed we could not go into the meeting without a breather. Eventually, we went through the stairway doors and walked down the corridor to Flash Harrys office. Andy was still breathing heavily as we knocked on the door.

"Come in!" Flash Hurry's voice resounded around the half empty office. Andy led the way and I followed. We were faced by Flash Harry behind his desk, dressed in yet another expensive looking dark brown suit, immaculate white shirt and dark brown tie. Alongside him seated was a man in his thirties, bright blue eyes, expensive Italian cut dark grey suit and matching plain silk tie.

"Where have you been DI?" Flash Harry asked with a lot of irritation in his voice.

Andy replied rather sarcastically, while still apparently struggling for breath; "As you should know (Looking from Flash Harry to the other man) - I was on a murder scene until five ish this morning. We managed to get a bit of shut-eye about six!"

"Oh, I see!" Flash Harry hesitantly replied before turning towards the other man. "This is Robert Lambert from MI5 – He wants to have a word with you."

Robert Lambert stood up and offered his handshake, but Andy ignored it, so I ignored it as well and we both sat down on the two spare chairs.

"I see." Was all that Robert Lambert could say, but he grinned and there was silence.

"What is this word you want? I have a busy morning scheduled." Andy said curtly while looking at Flash Harry and ignoring Lambert who looked perturbed.

Lambert replied; "Well DI Spearing - I have had a complaint from one of my men stating that you and your DS here had a confrontation with him. Your DS here beat him up and you falsely arrested him! I am here to make a formal complaint to your commanding officer!"

"Oh really? What is this man's name?" Andy asked coolly and without rancour.

"As you well know, DI Spearing – His name is Thomas Broadbent." Lambert grinned as he replied.

"Oh really? When was it he reported these preposterous allegations to you?" Andy asked, still not looking directly at Lambert. Andy now realised Lambert was not up to date with the current situation and was quickly trying to make the best use of the information.

"Yesterday in The Ship – a pub in Wardour Street!" Lambert replied, but he was beginning to feel and look uncomfortable.

Andy turned his head and looked directly into Lambert's eyes and asked; "I see! So, Mr Lambert where is Mr Broadbent now?"

"He escaped from your custody and is now under our protection. He told us the story!"

"So, what you are telling me is you are hiding a fugitive from the law? Is that right Mr Lambert?"

"Don't play your silly little games with me Spearing. This is not one of your petty little criminals you are dealing with here. Remember, if you play with fire Spearing you are going to get burnt and I have the information to burn you!"

"My Mr Lambert - Is that a threat?" Andy smiled, but he now knew from that threat Joe Bolger had been broken.

"You take it whatever way you want Spearing."

"Whoa right there Mr Lambert." Flash Harry suddenly interrupted with a touch of anger in his voice and added; "MI5 or not - You cannot threaten one of my officers who is simply doing his duty. Let's remember - you have also just admitted to harbouring a fugitive!"

Andy and I looked at each other with astonishment written all over our faces – Flash Harry had just defended us against MI5 – whatever next?

Lambert took a short pause to gather his thoughts before replying; "I did not admit we were harbouring a fugitive. What I did say was - We had taken Mr Broadbent into MI5 protective custody! – He has been involved in some internal security matters which take precedence!"

Andy replied; "I am afraid that is not the case Mr Lambert, but let us leave that aside for a minute. What if I told you that we have an eye witness who has testified that he saw two of your MI5 operatives taking Mr Broadbent at gunpoint from a telephone box in Weybridge? This person then saw your men inject Mr Broadbent in the neck with a syringe - at this stage an unknown substance, before then bundling him into a Bedford panel van?"

Lambert looked visibly shocked and turning red around the gills before responding with; "Utter nonsense! Who could have identified two MI5 operatives?"

Andy again looked Lambert straight in the eye before replying coolly; "Oh that was the Surrey police Mr Lambert. That is when they caught up with their van in Falling Lane - that street is in Yiewsley! I do believe you will know the house we found them in - it as one of the MI5 'safe' houses?"

Lambert was again visibly shaken, the smirk and confidence draining from his face which was now turning white. He suddenly realised that the cards he thought he held were now stacked against him. There was a pause before he replied with a little shaking in his voice; "I don't know what you are talking about Spearing. If two of my MI5 operatives were acting illegally – I didn't know about it!"

"I was wondering when you would get around to 'hanging-them-out-to-dry.' Still, I thought you just said that Mr Broadbent was in your 'protective' custody and that he had 'told you a story' as Mr Max Bygraves usually says? How come? – If, as you now allege, your two operatives were acting illegally?"

"I don't have to take this!" Lambert said as he got up apparently to leave.

Andy put a hand on Lambert's shoulder and said; "I am afraid you might have to put up with a lot more than this! You see Mr Lambert your information is out of date by a few hours! You really must get your lines of communication sorted out! You see, your Mr Broadbent is back in police custody and your two operatives - Jones and Wilkins - are both also in police custody charged with abduction and torture of Mr Broadbent causing him actual grievous bodily harm. Both have also been notified of possible pending murder charges. We have picked up a lot of forensic evidence in your Falling Lane so called 'safe house.' – So, you see 'Mr' Lambert - I am certain Messrs Jones and Wilkins will not take too kindly to being as I say left 'hanging-out-to-dry.' I am sure when we have our little chat later, in Surrey; they will be more 'amenable' as they say."

"Those two operatives will say nothing Spearing. So, you will have nothing!" Lambert almost spat out his reply.

Andy replied with a smile; "Oh that is where you are wrong Lambert. We have caught those two-red-handed abducting and torturing Mr Broadbent. Also, we have a witness and forensic evidence linking them to our torture and murder victim – one Joseph Bolger- in Sloane Square last night. They are going down for a very long time and I think they will want a deal. They will start talking don't you think?"

Lambert was now very white and flustered, but when he replied, he smirked; "You hope! - You know it won't even reach court. It is not in the national security interests."

"That will be interesting to see – How do the national security interests cover MI5 getting involved with the torture and murder of our citizens?" Andy replied with a crisp even tone in his voice.

"Won't it just?" Lambert replied again with a smirk as he again rose to leave the room.

Andy suddenly asked; "Mr Lambert I am afraid you are also personally going to have to answer my questions in connection with the disappearance of Mrs Palmer?"

"How should I know what happened to a Mrs Palmer?" Lambert replied trying to sound cool, but obviously still flustered.

"Well Mr Lambert it was shortly after you spoke to her that she disappeared!" Andy replied and looked quizzically at Lambert.

"How the hell did you?" Lambert started to reply and cut off, before adding; "You don't know what you are talking about Spearing! I am out of here - Now!" Lambert moved away towards the door.

Andy replied with a smile; "Well Mr Lambert as they say in the old westerns – Don't leave town – I will want to at least talk to you again."

No response from Lambert except the slamming of the door behind him.

Flash Harry leaned across his desk and spoke quietly to Andy; "You absolutely sure about all these facts Spearing?

"Most - but not all – YET!" DI Spearing replied with a cheeky grin.

Flash Harry sounded agitated when he asked; "When did all this happen? Why was I not informed?"

"It all started happening late yesterday afternoon after you had left work. It then evolved in the early hours of this morning. There was no way to contact you sir as you were not on your walkie-talkie!" Andy replied with another cheeky grin.

"You could have called me at home Spearing!" Flash Harry said it, but sounded unsure.

Andy decided to take a chance and replied; "We did sir, late yesterday afternoon, but there was no reply! Then, by the time the murder was discovered, it was three in the morning and I figured there was no point in waking you from your sweet dreams! So, I reported it to the Yard during the night and thought I would tell you face-to-face this morning."

"You know Spearing one of these times you are going to push it too far!" Flash Harry replied when the phone on his desk rang. He picked it up and said; "DCI Harry Tomlinson."

A familiar voice replied; "DI John Sanderson here sir! I am still with The Randalll family sir. I am afraid the girl Mary is badly stressed. I am not qualified to deal with the girl sir. – Then her parents are interjecting all the time and making her worse. I was wondering if you could get young DS Devlin to take over. I believe he is a qualified psychologist and a criminologist so he would be better for this one?"

Flash Harry replied; "Good idea John. DS Devlin is with me now. I will send him straight down!"

"Yes I understood he was sir. I am in Interview Room 1 on the second floor – and thanks sir!"

"No problem John." Flash Harry sounded friendly and that should have been a warning to DI Sanderson as he hung up the phone.

"DS Devlin – I have a case for you to take on. We have a Mary Randalll and her Mum and Dad downstairs on the first Floor in interview room one with DI Sanderson. It seems the daughter Mary, who is a teenager, is in a stressed state and crying about a gang bang rape a few days ago. As you are a fully qualified psychologist can you go down and take over from DI Sanderson who seems a bit out of his depth!"

I replied slowly and looked at Andy as I said; "Yes sir, but we have two current murder charges, several other aiding and abetting cases and an abduction and torture case all going on?"

Flash Harry replied unsympathetically before Andy could say anything; "Oh no need to worry about this one Sergeant. Just listen to her moaning, apparently, she is incoherent anyway. Just sound sympathetic and then refer her to a private psychologist. It will only take an hour at most. Her parents are apparently being a pain interjecting all the time! Anyway, there is nothing much we can do after three days and an incoherent teenager – You know what I mean?"

I looked at Andy who just nodded without saying anything.

I replied; "Yes okay sir – I will see what I can do." And I rose to leave and was joined by Andy..

"Good! Well done Sergeant!" Flash Harry shouted after us as we left the room.

Andy and I walked down the corridor and when out of earshot Andy quietly said: "Be very careful with this one Sergeant. I have a gut feeling Flash Harry is up to something – way too friendly by half!"

"Funny – that is exactly what I thought Andy. I think I will try and talk Judith Clements into coming in with me. She is a lawyer so will cover that side for me and as a woman, maybe the girl will open up more to her and calm down!"

Andy simply smiled and said; "Good idea! Always better to get to the pretty ones through work – Eh?"

I replied with a wicked smile; "The thought never entered my head Andy!"

Andy replied; "Yeah sure I believe you – not many would though! I will see you later alligator!"

"Yeah! - In a while crocodile!" I replied without thinking, but we both laughed.

"Oh, and when you're with her Sergeant. - ask her if she could get one of her friendly judges to put an injunction on anyone and I do mean anyone - except you or I - from removing Jones and Wilkins from prison. And to have a recorded no bail on the grounds they were MI5 officers who have been caught red handed abducting and torturing our citizens and they will almost certainly be charged shortly with murder. Most decent judges just love – like us - to put one over on MI5. Oh, and do not disclose which prison they are in – If asked, tell her to say - obviously in the circumstances, she believes it is a top security prison!"

"Right sir." I replied saying 'sir' because a young constable was passing.

I went directly to Judith Clements' office and knocked on the door, waited for the "Come In" from Judith's sweet voice and stuck my head round the door.

"Got a minute?" I asked with my best, big, friendly fox like smile.

"Come in my Lone Ranger!" Judith said again, so I slunk in and sat down on the chair opposite her. She had three or four files and a notepad and pen spread across her desk. Today she was dressed in a navy blouse, navy skirt – almost a mini - and had make-up on. I thought very attractive.

"I have revealed my face to a pretty lady! Now I have to ask a favour! I replied with my best American Lone Ranger imitation.

"Just as long as you do not want me to reveal anything to you Lone Ranger." Judith laughed as she replied.

"Would I dare to ask Kemosabe?" I replied and added; "Are you available for an hour or so?"

"That long? Are you bragging again my Lone Ranger?" Judith laughed again, though her face went red.

"Never brag Mam. I am always as good as my word!" I replied again in my best American Lone Ranger imitation and added in my own Scottish voice; "No really! – I have been given a case downstairs in my police psychologist role. It is a young teenager who claims to have been gang raped, but by the sound of it she is stressed out. I need a good woman to hold her hand and soothe her, while I get the parents out of the room. They are making things worse. Then I will come back in and do my psychologists' bit! Are you okay with that?"

"I don't know if I am up to that Kevin!" Judith said it with a good deal of hesitation.

I replied "You don't have to be qualified or anything! I only need you both as a witness to what is said and to hold her hand!"

"I didn't say I wasn't qualified. At least I am qualified by experience!" Judith replied and I noticed a tear rolling down her cheek."

I could only say; "Oh! I see – no problem! - I'll fly by the seat of pants." I got up and turned away.

"Kevin – wait – If I can't help her then I don't know who else in this place is any better positioned to do so! Okay just give me a sec to go to the loo and I will be right with you."

"You sure about it?" I found myself asking.

"No!" Judith replied and added; "But the poor girl needs somebody if her parents are not helping!" Judith got up, picked up her handbag and walked past me towards the ladies' toilets.

I walked behind and waited outside. When Judith came out she had dried her eyes and obviously tidied her make-up.

"What's the girl's name?" Judith asked as we got into the lift.

I replied; "Mary – Mary Randalll."

We headed for the lift and took it down to the first floor.

Judith and I got to interview room one on the second floor. I stopped and said; "I will get DI Sanderson out first and find out the score before we go in. – Okay?"

"Sounds like a good idea." Judith replied, she sounded rather nervous.

I rapped the door loudly and I stuck my head round the door and saw DI Sanderson and said; "Could I have a word in private sir?"

DI Sanderson replied; "Yes certainly Sergeant. Excuse me folks - this will only take a minute."

DI Sanderson came out and closed the door behind him.

I simply said; "I understand you have requested I take over this case sir?"

DI Sanderson replied; "Yes Sergeant – the girl badly needs a psychologist and the Dad is an overbearing arsehole, but who can blame him? Good luck Sergeant. I will introduce you and then let you get on with it."

"Thanks sir." I said it, but at the time I was not sure if I meant it and I then added; "Oh and this is Miss Clements who you may have already met. She will be coming in with me to help soothe the girl."

"Hello Judith." DI Sanderson greeted her with a smile and then added: "Yes, that is a good idea Sergeant – I think Mary needs more than a soothing touch though." DI Sanderson replied without rancour.

"I appreciate that sir, but we need to get the parents out of there before we can maybe get some sense out of her?"

"Agreed Sergeant – I will keep them out of your way! - Let's get to it." DI Sanderson replied and went back and strode purposely into the room followed by Judith and I.DI Sanderson stood in the middle of the room facing the two parents and said; "Right folks let me introduce Detective Sergeant Kevin Devlin who is a police psychologist. He will be taking over this case from me – DS Devlin." DI Sanderson pointed to me as a form of introduction and turned to go back out of the door.

"What the hell is this?" Dad Randalll shouted. He was a middle-aged man with a middle-aged spread and dressed in early fifties style. He then added; "He is no more than a kid - not much older than my daughter. Who says my daughter needs a shrink?"

Mary let out a sob. She was a natural looking blonde, a beautiful looking teenager dressed rather sedately in a long summer printed frock cut noticeably below the knee and she sat staring into space alone on a chair in the corner.

I quickly moved forward and said firmly, but coolly; "Mr Randalll sir – If you and Mrs Randalll will step next door we can discuss this without further upsetting your daughter?"

Dad Randalll looked at his daughter who appeared to be in a trance, but she was sobbing uncontrollably. Dad shook his head and said; "Right let us get this over with!" He turned to his wife and gruffly said "Rosemary." And he pointed out the door.

"Miss Clements here will stay with Mary to make sure she is alright." I said and Judith immediately moved over taking a chair with her and sat down opposite Mary. She held her hand, rubbing it gently and said; "Hello Mary I am Judith, I am sure it is going to be alright." Mary suddenly turned to Judith and hugged her and said; "It will never be alright again Judith. It has never been alright!" At least she understood what was being said.

Dad Randalll had turned at the door and had witnessed the scene and simply said; "Yes of course." He then followed his wife out the door and I came next.

DI Sanderson led the four of us into the interview room two leaving Judith with Mary in interview room one. I, being the last one in, closed the door.

I knew I had to keep this conversation low key and play it very cool and I opened the conversation; "I do appreciate Mr and Mrs Randalll the hurt and anxiety you feel for your girl!"

Mr Randalll immediately intercepted and said almost venomously; "You – You have no idea. How could you possibly know anything about how we feel?"

"John – please let the man finish!" Mrs Randalll pleaded.

"You – you shut that big gob of yours! If it was not for you she would never have been here in the first place." Mr Randalll was vicious with it.

"You know that is just not true John. It was you who drove her away." Mrs Randalll started to retort, but was immediately interrupted.

"You had better shut it now lady." Mr Randalll said it and looked ready to be moving to hit Mrs Randalll. I got in between the pair and gave Mr Randalll the cold hard stare.

I said it coldly; "Now look, this is not helping your daughter in any way. In fact, it is probably what is causing a part of her problem. I don't have to tell you squat Mr Randalll, nor do I have to defend myself. Now let me tell you as far as I am concerned - I was brought up on the streets in the Glasgow Gorbals. I have seen rapes, murders, razor slashings, the lot! I have honours degrees from Cambridge University in criminology and psychology from Keele University. I have also policed in the same Glasgow streets. This week alone in London, I have been involved with three murder scenes, or assassination cases, abduction and several aiding and abetting cases. Now it is your daughter's gang rape. So, don't you dare tell me what I know or don't know Mr Randalll, or I may be questioning you a lot more closely"

"So, what is wrong with my daughter Mr know all?" Mr Randalll bounced straight back.

"Oh John - for goodness sake– just listen for once in your life!" Mrs Randalll said it and then shrunk back. Mr Randalll spun around towards Mrs Randalll, but I was too quick for him and got between them again.

I again looked him straight in the eye and said coldly; "I'll tell you what I think is wrong with her after watching her for only a few minutes. I think your daughter may be suffering from Gross Stress Disorder. It is a form of shell shock which soldiers in the First World War suffered from, but it was all stress related. And let me tell you this Mr Randalll, your shouting and attitude is not helping her one little bit. In fact, it is probably making her worse. And that young lady who just went in there and hugged your daughter Mr Randalll? She knows all about rape. I am now going in there and hope somehow, between Miss Clements and I, to get some sense from your daughter. However, let me warn you, that it is often weeks, or months, before we can get any sense from people suffering with stress disorders. Shouting will not help in any way. Now I am leaving you with DI Sanderson here. I will go, and with Miss Clements' help, try to talk to your daughter and find out what has happened."

"You cannot do that. The parents have to be there!" Mr Randalll was now sounding anxious.

I retorted, now getting angrier; "I can and I will Mr Randalll. Your daughter is eighteen and is therefore an adult and she is a victim, not a suspect being questioned. Let me now say this Mr Randalll - if I as much as hear you through these walls, or you knock on the door I will put you under arrest and charge you with obstructing the police in their investigation and you can spend the night in jail thinking about it!"

Mr Randalll came straight back again and said; "You wouldn't dare!"

"Just you try me!" I replied as I walked out of the room and, on closing the door behind me I noticed both DI Sanderson and Mrs Randalll smiling, while Randalll looked aghast, but said nothing.

I knocked gently on the door to Interview One room and went in. I saw Judith still sitting holding and stroking Mary's hand and caught the last bit of the conversation as I slowly walked across the room Judith was saying; "It is alright Mary. DS Devlin is the right one to help you. Try to remember Mary."

I felt good and I must admit a bit proud at catching that bit. I knew this was my first big test in the big real world for me being, or becoming, a fully-fledged psychologist. My gut feeling was that it would take more than a chat to unlock this girls mind and relieve her stress.

I opened with my gentle re-assuring voice and said; "Hello Mary – My name is Kevin Devlin. Judith and I are hoping to help you recover from your ordeal. Can you remember anything that went on Mary?" She just sobbed and sobbed, nodded her head as though saying yes, swaying back and forth, but her bright eyes were unblinking and she just stared vacantly into space somewhere around the wall behind me.

Judith again interjected as she continued gently rubbing Marys hand and said; "Try to remember Mary."

I looked at Judith and said; "Would you rather tell Judith what happened Mary?"

She again nodded her head as though saying yes, but continuing to sway back and forth, but this time her eyes filled with tears.

"Nobody can help me!" Mary replied and added; "Not now - not now he is back!"

"Who is back Mary?" I asked quietly trying not to frighten her again.

"Him who was here just now!" She whispered like a demented soul.

"Who - Your Dad Mary?" I asked trying to probe an answer.

"Yeah that – that slime pot! It was him who caused it!" Mary replied from somewhere in her subconscious.

"What did he cause Mary?" I asked gently.

"Me to run away and be here in London – you know that, don't you? The slime pot!" Mary began rocking back and forth again shaking her head.

"Why did you have to runaway Mary?" I asked slowly and quietly.

"Because – you know – don't you?" Mary replied, but she was becoming more and more agitated. I recognised I might lose her, so I decided to change the subject and try to go back to the Dad later.

"What happened to you last week Mary here in London?" I was gentle and slow, but Mary did not respond.

"Try to remember Mary." Judith again interjected with the same words and she was still gently rubbing Mary's hand.

Mary suddenly screwed up her pretty face and said; "It was that bastard Johnny Eden and his mob of mates!"

"Johnny Eden? – The big-time disc jockey Mary?" I asked, and I knew I was sounded a bit surprised.

"Yes, Johnny fucking Eden – the bastard!" She replied with some venom.

"What happened then Mary?" I asked quickly.

She began to sway back and forth again. Her tears were rolling down her cheeks. She began to shake and cry!

"I cannot remember. – I can't remember. The bastard stuck a needle in my arm. I can't remember - the bastard." She said it between great sobs.

"Try to remember Mary." Judith again interjected the same phrase and still gently rubbing Mary's hand.

I suddenly realised Judith had somehow managed to hypnotise Mary. I looked quizzically at Judith, but she pointedly did not look at me and concentrated instead on

Mary. With my experience, I realised it could be extremely dangerous to hypnotise a person with a recent stress disorder.

"Was it bad things Mary?" I tried to keep up the pressure - trying to probe her into remembering without disturbing her too much.

"What do you mean was it bad?" Mary screamed at me and then shouted; "It was excruciating you fucking idiot! They were a crowd of fucking morons!"

"Who were 'they'" I asked gently, again hoping not to get her worked up and get out of control.

This time she shook her head violently from side to side, her mind obviously in turmoil.

"Try to remember Mary." Judith again interjecting repeating the same phrase.

"It was that fucking Johnny Eden and his four mates. Bastards!" Mary replied and her sobs restarted, only louder.

"We know about that bastard, but who were the four others?" I asked quietly.

"I didn't know all the fuckers. – That politician guy Philip Hawkins – yeah him! And that pop star fucker who thinks he can sing - Tony Walters." Mary replied without any hesitation.

I wrote down the three names in my notebook and asked; "What exactly happened Mary?" I asked ever so gently.

Mary again started violently shaking, crying with heart wrenching sobs.

I looked at Judith and said; "I think you are going to have to waken her. This is getting to dangerous levels!"

Judith looked at me with a cold stare and replied quietly, but sarcastically, to me;

"Give her a minute professor." And turning back to Mary she said smoothly; "Try to remember Mary" and she again started rubbing her hand.

Mary continued shaking and violently moving her head from side to side. I was about to call a halt when Mary quite suddenly was very cool and collected, quietly said; "They took me to a mansion near Henley- on- Thames. They took me into a big room the four of them!"

"Were you not worried about four of them and you being the only girl? I asked, to make it clear if she had agreed to or not.

"No, there were other women and people in the house. That bastard Eden asked me through to another room to see his record collection. When I went into the room, there were three others in the room and I heard Eden locking the door behind him and taking the key out. Then I knew there was something wrong!"

"What happened then Mary? I asked trying to keep her mind on the subject.

"The next thing I knew that bastard Johnny Eden stabbed me with a needle in the hand. He said it was a pin in his gold bracelet, but I saw a needle in his palm. Then my head started getting fuzzy and the four of them got around me. Their hands were all over me. I screamed – 'No I don't want this,' but they pulled of my clothes, they were all laughing and lifted me." Mary paused, as though that was it, but suddenly added; "They threw me over the back of a Chesterfield settee opened my legs and that bastard Johnny Eden jumped in and shouted he was first and just fucked me from behind. Then the other three followed. One of them put it up my arsehole and was spanking me hard, it was so, so humiliating. I couldn't do anything except scream for them to STOP – STOP – STOP, but they just carried on laughing and thumping it into me. I am scared – I don't even know if they used condoms! Oh, my God, I might be pregnant!"

She started sobbing again, uncontrollably, but I decided I had to get as much information as possible before she awoke from the trance.

"Can you remember what happened after that Mary?" I was moving towards the final questions I needed answered.

"Oh, yes I can remember. That fucking bastard Eden gave me my clothes and said; 'Thanks Babe for agreeing to accommodate my friends and I this afternoon. I'll get my chauffeur to run you home.' They all just stood there and laughed as they pulled up their trousers and zipped up. – Those fucking Bastards!" Mary answered and started sobbing quite violently yet again.

I thought there it was - covering their ass in case there was any comeback – and then I asked; "What did you do then Mary?"

Mary answered quickly; "I went home and scrubbed myself everywhere for two days and threw out every bit of the clothes from that day!"

"I understand!" I heard myself say, but thought there goes any real evidence.

I then asked what I thought was my final question; "Where did you meet this Eden character Mary?"

There was a short pause and then Mary replied still sobbing; "At that BBC TV show 'Meet the Stars' – I was one of the audience chosen to meet the stars!"

I suddenly thought of another 'final' question and asked; "Was one of the stars Tony Walters?"

Mary replied, almost instantly, though still crying; "Yes he was the ass fucker!"

I turned to Judith and said; "I think it is time to waken her up Judith."

Judith nodded and turned around to face Mary and spoke quietly into her ear; "Mary when I say the words - I want you to waken - when I say the words you will feel great about yourself." There was a pause then Judith said; "Snap out of it Mary and you are now feeling great!"

Mary blinked and looked at Judith then threw her arms around Judith, gave her a kiss on the cheek and said; "Oh Judith – thank you."

I was surprised and if I was honest a little taken aback by the hugging and kissing. I tried to find my voice and could only find a mumble; "Okay – Mary we have enough details from you to start the enquiry. With the evidence we have got, we cannot promise anything, but we will do our best."

"That is all I can expect!" Mary replied with her first smile and I noticed she had a beautiful smile.

I went on and said; "Now Mary - you said in the interview you were worried in case you were pregnant. Do you want to see a police doctor Mary? I don't think we can find any evidence as such, but now that you have reported rape it would make it easier to get an abortion – If that is what you want? The sooner the better."

I knew it may have been the wrong thing to say almost as soon as I said it. There was a pained expression on both Mary's and Judith's faces.

Mary replied; "I don't know if I can cope with that right now, - maybe in a week or two?"

I nodded and said; "Just let me know." I paused and asked; "Do you want me to get your parents and get you off home?"

"No fucking way – I am going home on my own and he aint coming with me." Mary answered clearly and showing there would be no discussion on the point.

I suddenly remembered and asked; "I am sorry Mary, but during the interview I meant to ask – Did your Dad abuse you as well? Is that why you do not want him near you?"

"My Dad?" Mary started to reply, but paused to consider her words carefully before adding; "No, my Dad did not abuse me. - At least not in a sexual way! My Dad is one of the most bombastic men I have ever met. You just heard him and he is usually a lot worse. He is a control freak, but the worst he has done is slapped Mum and me about a bit, more so Mum. He has done it to me for the last time. That is why I went off to London, which is why I am here today. So, no way am I having him around me!" Mary finished with a shake of the head.

Judith suddenly intercepted and said; "Mary they came all the way here to London to see you and take care of you. That is surely worth an explanation why you don't want them around?"

Mary responded; "Bollocks! – He only came down because he thought he would get control of me again! No fucking way! But I don't have a problem telling him! – Where is he?"

I replied; "Next door, but take it easy. Remember your Mum has still to live with him."

Mary just looked blankly and replied angrily; "Yeah right – Let's get in there." The change in Mary was quite remarkable, whatever suggestions Judith had implanted in her mind were certainly working.

The three of us went in next door and DI Sanderson was still with Mr and Mrs Randalll.

Mary walked right up to her Dad and said without any hesitation; "Dad you are the most bombastic man I ever had the displeasure to meet in my life. Furthermore, you are a control freak and you have slapped me for the last time. And if I ever hear that you have hit my Mum again I will make it my business to get you arrested. Now don't ever come near me again." Mary turned on her heel and went to walk away, but Mr Randalll put his hand on her shoulder.

Mary spun around and angrily said; "Take your hand off me you slime pot!"

Mr Randalll was startled, hastily withdrew his hand, and looked contrite when he said: "Mary I am so sorry."

"You should have said that fifteen years ago Dad when you spanked me as a three-year-old for wetting my nappy during the night. And you should have said it hundreds of times since then. Now it is too late!"

"Mary - Please?" Mr Randalll appeared to plead before being interrupted.

"Fuck off Dad - I should have done this years ago!" Mary replied and walked out of the room, quickly followed by Judith and I. DI Sanderson blocked and closed the door and did not allow Mr or Mrs Randalll to follow us.

I called after her; "Mary – Hang on I will get you a car to take you home. You are a victim and a witness!" Mary stopped and went back into Interview Room One followed by Judy and I and I again closed the door.

I went over and lifted the phone and said; "DS Kevin Devlin here" I then asked; "Can we have a Panda car out front in ten minutes to take our witness a Miss Mary Randalll to her home address?"

"Yes Kevin." Sergeant Thomson replied and I hung up.

I turned back to Mary and asked; "Mary – Can you - for my report - write down your address and telephone number in my notebook?" I passed her my notebook and a pen and she started to write it down.

Judith went into her bag and produced a card and said; "If you ever need Sergeant Devlin or myself you can ring me on this number. For Sergeant Devlin ring New Scotland Yard and they will patch you through. Okay?"

Mary took the card and once again threw her arms around Judith, hugging her tight and kissing her cheek, before saying; "Judith thanks for everything and I will be in touch."

I noticed Judith's cheeks go red as she looked at me over Mary's shoulder. I thought there must have been some bonding going on with those two today.

I felt a bit awkward at breaking up the scene and sort of mumbled; "Judith could you do me a favour?" Judith did not reply, but looked at me with another pained expression, so I continued; "Could you take Mary down to the reception entrance and make sure she gets into the panda booked for her?"

Judith suddenly smiled and replied; "Yeah sure no problem Sergeant!"

I then remembered and again asked; "Oh and Judith – Could you come back here afterwards? I must draft a report on this? Also, I have a message for you from DI Spearing which needs your urgent action."

"Yeah sure thing Sergeant!" Judith replied with a grin. Mary and Judith went out and left the door ajar leaving me drafting my report ready to type later. A few minutes later I heard next door being closed with a bang.

"What have you done to my girl?" Mr Randalll was in the doorway looking angry, with Mrs Randalll and DI Sanderson in the background.

I replied coolly without emotion; "I have done nothing to your daughter Mr Randalll. She has gone home and I think she has made it plain, for the moment, she wants nothing more to do with you."

"My girl would never have talked to me like that! You must have hypnotised her! You psychologists are all the same!" Mr Randalll was building up another head of steam.

I replied truthfully, if just a little evasively; "Mr Randalll I suggest you watch your tongue or one of these days you may find it attached your teeth! For your information Mr Randalll, I did not hypnotise your daughter. Your daughter is - as I suspected earlier and advised you – she is suffering from Gross Stress Disorder. During this time, she will have short lucid moments, like ten minutes ago. Then she will retract under any pressure. We have managed somehow to get her side of the story and I am now proceeding to investigate her allegations."

"Allegations? You call them allegations? She has been gang raped and you talk about allegations?" Mr Randalll was shouting again.

I replied very coolly again; "Mr Randalll – I suggest you go and cool down. At this stage that is all we have – 'ALLEGATIONS!' - I can advise you this Mr Randalll - Because of the delay in reporting these 'allegations' of rape and the fact that Mary has understandably destroyed most of the evidence, we will find it very hard to prove any of it, especially if the perpetrators deny the allegations. Even Mary in her present state understands that much!"

Mr Randalll again exploded with rage; "You see! Covering up already because these are public figures! - I want to talk to my daughter. I am going there right now!"

I replied with a steely tone in my voice; "Mr Randalll - you really do not understand, do you? If you carry on bawling and shouting at your daughter then she is going to recede into her shell and she may never come out of it! I can assure you there will be no cover up – if we can prove it we will."

Mr Randalll replied loudly; "Bullshit – you are all the same! - Covering for each other."

I rose and displayed my anger in my reply; "I think you had better go home Mr Randalll, before you say something you may regret for the rest of your life."

"Are you threatening me Sergeant?" Mr Randalll now sounded a little nervous.

I was beginning to lose it when I replied; "No I am not threatening you Mr Randalll. I am promising you, if you make one more such allegation, I will arrest and charge you."

At that, Mr Randalll began to bluster and did not respond. Finally, Mrs Randalll took his arm and said: "Come on Dad – let's go home."

Mr Randalll again retorted angrily; "Take your paws of me woman" and he violently pushed her hand away and walked off.

I shouted to DI Sanderson as he followed Mr Randalll out; "DI Sanderson please explain to Mr Randalll that he must not contact his daughter Mary - unless she invites him! - otherwise he will be arrested." DI Sanderson nodded his head and followed Mr and Mrs Randalll towards the stairs exit.

Five minutes later DI Sanderson returned to the interview room, smiled and said; "That was good work Sergeant. You handled it all perfectly, although at one point I thought you were going to break his jaw!"

I replied with a smile; "At one point I was severely tempted DI! – What an absolute arsehole he is!"

DI Sanderson replied; "Tell me about it Sergeant! Is there anything else I can do?"

"Well if you could counter sign the report at the bits you witnessed?"

"Certainly, Sergeant no problem! What do you think?"

"Like I said I doubt if we can make any of the charges stick – especially if they deny the allegations, which I have no doubt they will!"

"Talk to Andy! – With these things, he can usually come up with a cunning plan!"

I replied; "Yeah I know what you mean. I'll try to catch him before lunch."

"Are you not coming up now?" DI Sanderson asked.

"No I am waiting for Judith to come back here, she has been gone a while. Then I think I will go through everything and draft my report. Could you let DI Spearing know that I am here if he needs me?" I asked.

"Will do Sergeant. - That girl Judith did really well to calm Mary down like that, especially her being a lawyer don't you think?" DI Sanderson said it with a knowing smile.

I decided not to bite and simply replied "Yes she did sir – There is more to that girl than meets the eye!"

"You are telling me Sergeant!" DI Sanderson replied with a huge grin and left the room.

Andy got back to his desk and sat-down to collect his thoughts. He suddenly remembered he had to send Harry Lawler the back-up information - a copy of Thomas Broadbent's signed statement on the MI5 pair Jones and Wilkins involvement with the torture and possible murder of Joseph Bolger. He rang reception and got the fax number for DI Harry Lawler at Surrey Police Headquarters. He wrote a quick covering note stating: 'FAO of DI Harry Lawler – "Harry – herewith to cover your A_ _ - Please keep it covered! He signed it - DI Andy Spearing NSY.' He walked over to the Fax machines, which were the Emails of those days. He dialled the number and pressed send. Off it went and a couple of minutes later up popped a confirmation that it had been sent successfully.

He pocketed the confirmation and walked back to his desk just as his phone rang. He ran the last few yards and picked up the 'phone and breathlessly said; "DI Spearing here!"

"My oh my DI Spearing!" A man with a heavily disguised voice spoke and it sounded like it was through a handkerchief. The voice then added; "It does sound like you will have to get a lot fitter before you can ever catch 'The Fox!" The voice laughed.

"What the hell! - Is that you Mr Fox?" Andy asked incredulously.

"None other DI Spearing! – Now listen very carefully I will not be giving you time to trace this call. – I just want you to know you were wrong last night when you said – "you know 'The Fox' is too good even to show anywhere near this!"

"You were there?" Andy sounded and was astounded. He looked around the office trying to get attention, but nobody was looking up from their desks.

"Of course I was, nearby in my little lair!" But you were right in that I would never go into that trap!" The Fox replied evenly, but speaking through the handkerchief it sounded like he had a heavy cold and a German accent trying to hide the London east end.

"Okay – What do you want Mr Fox?" Andy asked while still throwing his arm up in a wide circle. Finally, Bill Brown noticed and Andy pointed to the earpiece. Bill Brown immediately understood and lifted his phone and mouthed in some instructions.

'The Fox' finally replied; "I just want you to know that I had nothing to do with that thing this morning, or with the Joe Cole murder yesterday! However, I did witness yesterday evening two guys taking a big crate into that Centurion Building!"

"Oh really? Was it the two MI5 thugs?"

"My oh my DI Spearing you are beginning to sound like a real detective!" The Fox replied.

"You had better believe it! And my packs of hounds are now on your tail Mr Fox!" Andy retorted, but with a smile.

"Yeah but they may have the wrong scent DI Spearing." The Fox answered and there followed a short nervous laugh.

Andy decided to throw in a wild card and asked; "So what happened to your friend Joe Cole?"

There was a short delay, which told Andy everything he needed to know, - Joe Cole was a friend - then The Fox replied; "Afraid I have to go DI, but I had nothing to do with Joe Cole - end of story, or the body at The Centurions!" The Fox hung up.

Andy looked across at Bill Brown who signalled with a cut across his throat, but shouted across; "They recorded a bit!"

"Right – Thanks" DI Spearing shouted back, but looked and felt disappointed.

Andy sat back to think again. He needed to go back to Joe Cole; there is a connection there somewhere! The phone rang again he lifted it and said; "DI Spearing here."

"How would you like to do a trade DI Spearing?" Mr Fox again, back to his smoothie self.

"What sort of trade Mr Fox?" Andy asked quietly.

"I want the name of the guy behind the two MI5 thugs!"

"Ah - wouldn't you like to know?" DI Spearing asked and suddenly added; "You know I cannot tell you that. Maybe some other trade?"

"We both know you haven't got a snowball's chance in hell of nailing this guy DI Spearing. I can do that at absolutely no cost to the taxpayer."

"I believe that is true Mr Fox. But if you can give us a few pointers we will get him legally. I want him more than you. Contact me at this same number Friday around the same time." Andy replied and hung up with his fingers on the phone cradle. He waited, and sure enough there was a second click on the line. Someone had been listening or recording the conversation.

No matter what - Andy now knew there was an outside chance of catching two birds with one stone. He dialled reception who answered immediately.

"DI Spearing here. Did you just record a call on my line?"

"Yes sir – It was authorised by DS Brown apparently on your orders, but we could not get a trace in the timescales."

"Good – very good! Can you get all of the recordings up to me and then cease any other recordings? Do you understand?"

"Yes sir. I will get security to deliver it in the next few minutes."

"Thank you." Andy replied. He knew he had to report the proposition because somebody had recorded it, but he decided to wait until DS Devlin returned to act as a witness. He checked his watch. It was nine thirty, so nine twenty-five tomorrow morning not long to wait after all this time.

Andy made another check to make sure his line was clear. He dialled the direct number for Harry Lawler knowing full well that he would not be in as he must have got to bed after seven this morning. Sure enough there was no answer. After three rings he hung up, putting his fingers on the phone cradle. Again a few seconds later there was a click as whoever was the listener hung up.

Andy then got up and went directly to the car pool where he found Sergeant Jock Wilson and asked; "Jocky I need a run, ten minutes down the road, to drop me off at Victoria Railway Station main entrance and then for you to pick me up at the Buckingham Palace Road side entrance and take me back here. Okay?"

"Why the cloak and dagger stuff Andy?" Jocky asked with a smile.

"Same old - Same old Jocky!" Andy replied and added; "I think somebody may be trailing me so we have to keep sharp eyes."

"Why would anybody want to be so stupid as to follow you Andy?"

"Well it is certainly not for my pretty ass Jocky!" Andy laughed as he replied and waved towards the car pool.

Jocky laughed and replied: "Aye that's for sure!" as he went over and again got into the brand new black Jaguar S-Type 3.8 Police Car.

"Hoy you! Just watch it!" Andy shouted back laughing as he got into the rear seat and asked; "Not the Panda Jocky?"

"Not if I can help it Andy – It's like driving a tin can!" Jocky replied.

"Yeah so I hear, but a bit more economical." Andy replied with a laugh.

"A night shift in a tin can is no joke Andy! – The youngsters are so big these days they come out like a squashed sardine!" Jocky responded with his usual quick Glaswegian humour.

"Anyway - keep an eye out in the mirrors Jocky for anybody following us." Andy asked as he fitted a little hook with a mirror attached around his right forefinger. A little contraption he had used for years to catch anybody following him, like DS Devlin yesterday afternoon, without them knowing they had been spotted. The only time he could not use it was when the sun was in his back then the glint from the mirror gave him away.

They went down Buckingham Palace Road past the exit to Sloane Square and carried on straight down and swung a right into the Victoria Railway Station main entrance opposite the Victoria Palace Theatre.

"Notice anybody following Jocky?" Andy asked without turning around.

"One or maybe two possibilities Andy, but it is hard to tell! It maybe they are just stuck in the traffic!" Jocky replied with one eye on the mirrors and the other on the road ahead.

"Keep an eye out when we pull into the station forecourt. See if anyone follows me in and then tries to follow me. Okay?" Andy was cool, calm and collected.

"Will do Andy. I'll do a 'u' turn and meet you at the Buckingham Palace Road exit in five. Okay?"

"Nice one Jocky. See you shortly." Andy quickly got out of the car and strode towards the station's main entrance. As he reached the main entrance he had a quick sideways glance without moving his head and he noticed one of the two cars, a silver Bentley that had followed them down Buckingham Palace Road, had pulled in behind Jocky. A tall guy with a tan trilby hat and dark brown suit started to emerge as Andy disappeared into the main entrance. It could of course be a coincidence, but Andy was not a great believer in coincidences. He quickly made his way to the public telephones which were hidden behind an advertising hoarding. He noticed something advertised about Jimi Hendrix at The Savile Theatre with Denny Lane and his String Orchestra plus 1-2-3 the Scottish group Devlin had mentioned, on 4th June 1967 – an old poster. His passing thought was he must try and get a ticket to see Hendrix one day. Hendrix had a growing reputation as a guitarist some said better than Eric Clapton, but that he doubted, may be a better showman.

He went to the far end telephone booth checked that it and the next one were both working and quickly noted down the telephone numbers. It was amazing most people coming in would not take the first booth and usually took the near middle booths and ignored the far end booths. Without breaking stride, he walked across the concourse towards the right where the Buckingham Palace Road exit was. He again glanced right and left without moving his head. He noticed the guy with the tan trilby scanning the crowd as he ducked into the alleyway leading out to Buckingham Palace Road.

As he walked out Jocky Wilson rolled up with the Jaguar and he dived into the backseat.

"Back to the yard Jocky. Did you see the guy with the trilby following me?" DI Spearing asked with a smile on his face.

"I saw him go in a minute behind you and he was in a hurry. Couldn't tell if he was following you, or in a rush to catch a train." Jocky replied.

"Yeah – he was scanning the crowd looking for somebody as I went across the concourse. I think he saw me as I went into the exit, so they will be following."

"Any idea who?" Jocky asked.

"MI5 I think – only they could be so incompetent, or maybe one of ours!" Andy replied with a laugh and asked; "Any sign of the silver Bentley in your mirrors Jocky?"

"Aye!" Jocky replied and added with a laugh; "Three cars back, hot on our tail!"

"Wonder what they think they are doing?" Andy replied. He decided it was time to have a meeting, or to use the new modern terminology a 'drains brain' this morning with DS Devlin and try to pull all the threads together.

About ten minutes later Judith came back quietly into the first-floor interview room one, looking thoughtful and maybe a little pensive.

I looked up and asked; "Everything okay? Did Mary get away okay?"

Judith replied; "Yeah no problem!"

I looked directly at her again getting eye contact and asked; "Where did you learn hypnosis?"

"I didn't." She replied and added: "I learned self-hypnosis and I just adapted that!"

I thought I knew the answer, but I thought I should ask the question anyway; "When was that?"

"After 'IT' happened to me!" Judith replied causally, but at the same time she was tense.

"From what you said earlier, I gathered you have been raped? Where did that happen?" I asked the question slowly and very deliberately.

Judith replied coldly; "At Cambridge! - One of those drunken student nights with friends. I awoke to find a drunken guy on top of me, not having been invited – needless to say."

I automatically replied; "Oh God I am so sorry for you! Did you report it?"

Judith looked away and whimsically replied; "No – he was a guy I knew – and if I reported it, his career was finished before it had started. So, I let it slide."

I replied quickly, without too much thought; "Really? You know the statistics are that if they get away with it once they are likely to do it again?"

"Yeah, I know, but if I did report it - it would have destroyed his whole life. Anyway, I don't think he would ever do it again. He is a top barrister already and he is being tipped to be the youngest judge ever in England. If I had reported it his whole legal life was destroyed before it started"

"What about your life Judith? Has it changed your life?"

"Yeah I guess it has! But I have learned to live with that!"

"Why should you Judith?" I knew I was scratching at old sores lifting off the scabs.

"Because I liked him and did not want to destroy him! Is that good enough?" Judith snappily replied, but I could see the tears coming to the eyes.

"Well I hope he was suitably grateful?" I said it a little harder than I had intended.

"He offered to marry me, but I refused!" Judith defensively replied and tears ran down her cheek.

I suddenly wakened to what she was struggling to tell me, but I could see that this was not the time or the place. I went over to her and put my arms around her and said quietly; "No need to talk about this now we can do it another time."

"Yes please!" Judith replied and added; "It was such a difficult time you know."

She wiped away her tears with the back of her hand.

I withdrew my arms and tried to lighten up and said; "You did brilliant with Mary. Don't know what I would have done without you."

Judith smiled that dazzling smile and replied; "You know Kevin, although I didn't think I could do it, I actually felt fulfilled after I had done it. I went to the canteen for a cup of tea after I sent Mary off - she is a lovely girl. Anyway, I think I could get the kind of fulfilment out of psychology that I don't get from my own job. I think I would like to go for it and change careers. What do you think?"

I paused for a moment trying to formulate the right words then I replied; "You know Judith, my tutors and my job experience as a psychologist during the summer breaks from university, they all warned me not to expect too much job satisfaction from psychology. They all said that the majority of the real psychology work is long term and can take years to break through a sick mind, if ever. The stuff with movie stars and pop stars is mostly to put money in the bank." I finished and noticed the look of disappointment on Judiths' face.

I then decided to hastily add; "You know Judith, what I would suggest is you could take a psychology course in your own time working from home with the new open university at Milton Keynes? That way you can carry on working with the police and get yourself ready at your own pace!"

Judith smiled at that and asked; "How long does that take?"

"I think it is a minimum of three years!" Again, I saw that look of disappointment in Judiths' face, so I again hastily added; "You know, I think the Chief is a modern policeman and is open to new ideas. He has proved that by hiring us; 'trained brains' as we are now known. I really believe with rape cases we should have available a specialist team with a woman who knows what it is the victim – man or woman - is going through as well as a psychologist. I bet if we offered our services we would be snapped up. That way, you and I have the best of both worlds! - What do you think?"

"I think you are a genius Sergeant Devlin." Judith replied with a beaming smile and gave me a peck on the cheek.

"Some say that Kemosabe, but then some talk with forked tongue!" I replied with my Lone Ranger imitation and a smile.

"You know, you are an idiot at times!" Judith replied, playfully hitting me on the shoulder.

"Now you tell the truth Kemosabe!" I replied feigning being hurt and I then added; "How about that drink tonight?"

Judiths' face clouded again and she hurriedly replied; "Yeah sure Kevin, but I just want to be clear on one thing! I would like to get know you as a friend, but I cannot get into a relationship right now you understand?"

I paused tried to look hurt, but could not hold it and with a smile replied; "You know Kemosabe means 'Faithful Friend'?"

"It never does?" Judith replied waving her finger in a gesture of 'no'

"It does too." I replied and added; "Anyway I need a friend – too many acquaintances and not enough friends!"

"You are a bloody fool my Lone Ranger!" Judith replied and gave me another peck on the cheek.

Just then there was a knock on the door and in bustled Andy carrying an easel and Flip Chart with coloured pen's. He caught Judith in mid peck, on my cheek, and looking quizzically at us smiled and asked; "Not party pooping, am I?"

"No party here sir – just friends!" I replied rather shyly. Judith also shyly smiled.

"Yes, I see Andy replied still smiling and added; "Thought I would have one of those 'Drain Brains' to pull all our investigation threads together. You can stay and contribute Judith – I need to talk to you anyway!"

"Oh yes – Lone - Sergeant Devlin mentioned it!" Judith replied sounding rather flustered.

"It is 'Brain Storming' sir! Not drains brains" I heard myself saying.

"Oh yeah – whatever!" Andy said it nonchalantly and went on; "Since you know all about these things Sergeant and you are one of the 'trained brains' - you can take the chair." He handed me the Flip Chart, the easel and the coloured pens and promptly sat down.

"I walked into that one, didn't I?" I replied with a smile and set up the easel with the Flip Chart and folded back the cover, leaving a white blank sheet. I picked up the black ink pen and left the rest on the little shelf on the easel below the chart.

I paused for a moment trying to gather my thoughts and then started to draw a box at the top of the sheet on the Flip Chart and said; "I suppose we start with the murder on the morning of Tuesday 18th July in Tunbridge Wells of one John Palmer. He was the owner of Palmers Associates, who were the accountants for one Joseph Bolger. We shall talk about him later as he has also turned up as a victim! – Suffice, for the moment to say, Bolger was the head of a gang known as 'The Quiet Firm' Importers of Drugs and other fancy goods into the UK. They were sellers to organised crime gangs. I paused and pointed at the box and the information.

Book 1 in the DI Spearing and DS Devlin series

> John Palmer:
> Murdered at home in
> Tunbridge Wells
> Tuesday 18th July 67

I continued by talking and adding threads of information to the right side of the box;

"The first thread is the question 'WHO DID IT?' – We believe we know the answer to that question i.e. an assassin known as 'The Fox'. I drew a thread and a box into which I inserted 'The Fox.'

I continued; "The second question is; as 'The Fox' is a known assassin - Who Hired Him?" – I drew a thread with a box and entered WHO HIRED HIM?

I then continued; "We have a few suspects, for example;

1) I drew a thread with a box and entered 'The USA Mafia.' – I then just spoke without writing; "They are trying to move into the huge UK drugs market through Joe Bolger and John Palmer is known to have tried to stop them! We may also have MI5 involved trying to stop them through making Joe Bolger disappear and turning up dead - So we put down MI5 as possible suspects.

2) I drew a thread with a box and entered 'MI5.' – I then spoke without writing;

3) "They have been linked by a witness – a Thomas Broadbent" (I drew a thread and drew a box and entered 'Thomas Broadbent' and added; – "More about him later - He is now under police protection. He witnessed two MI5 Operatives taking Joseph Bolger, who we will come back to later, into their custody. Now of course Joe Bolger has turned up badly tortured and murdered!"

Andy interrupted with a quip; "I love your Scottish pronunciation of 'murdered' Sergeant."

I replied quite quickly with a pained smile and a pronounced Scottish accent; "Aye weel it disnae maiter the pronunciations of 'murder' sir – It still means he is very deed."

Andy laughed and replied with a ridiculous attempt at a Scottish accent; "Aye very good laddie – Carry oan noo son!"

I replied in a very English aristocratic accent; "I say sir – that was jolly funny – What?"

Andy laughed and replied; "Yeah touché again Sergeant – carry on."

Judith was having hysterics, but keeping the laugh in. It was good to see her getting back to almost normal.

I then got back into my routine and continued; "Early this morning we arrested and charged two MI5 operatives - a Mr Jones and a Mr Wilkins who were caught red handed torturing Mr Broadbent our witness. We also have a witness who saw them abducting Mr Broadbent at gunpoint!" I paused, drew a thread wrote the names 'Jones and Wilkins' alongside MI5. I thencontinued; "I believe we have the evidence to link the MI5 pair, to other tortures and murders including Joseph Bolger. And of course, we have one of the MI5 Chiefs – A Mr Lambert!" I paused again, drew a thread and wrote his name with a question mark alongside the other two and continued; "Lambert has been directly linked to these two operatives, but is now naturally denying authorising any abductions, tortures or murders. He is hanging the other two 'out-to-dry', but we are hoping, when we question them later the worms will turn."

I then continued; "The bottom line, as far as the murder of John Palmer is concerned, is - we do not think MI5 are involved, the reason being, at this stage, we do not believe it would be in their interests to have him eliminated. But there is an outside chance they may be covering their tracks."

4) "Other UK Gangs? For example; 'The Hammond's or The Christie's I paused and drew a thread with a box and entered 'UK Gangs' and continued; "Well, we came to the conclusion that the only reason they would have was if they saw a chance to expand their organisations. Then we thought – how could they do it without the help of John Palmer or, as it turned out, Mrs Palmer? – They both had all the contacts for the drugs! – We will now talk about Mrs Palmer. I paused and wrote on the chart;

5) I drew another thread with a box and entered 'Mrs Palmer?' I then continued; "Mrs Palmer?" I paused again and added; "Well, as in all good 'who-done-it's,' it is usually the wife or the husband who are the prime suspects. Certainly, she appeared to be very cool, calm and collected BUT she has now disappeared and our Mr Lambert of MI5 fame was the last known contact before she done a runner!" I drew a curved line back to Lambert in MI5.

I said and wrote two more names; "Tommy Smith and Bobby Cosgrove?" I then said; "Two bodyguards - known convicts - who have been charged with fleeing the murder scene and then removing evidence from the premises of Palmer Associates. In this respect, they have been charged with a Mr Aldridge" – I paused and wrote the name down – "Aldridge is the company solicitor and besides being charged with removing evidence, he has also been charged with obstructing the police etc. – All three are still in custody as far as I know?" I looked at Judith who nodded.

6) "Finally, there is our very own - Nigel Worthington?" I wrote the name down on the chart and added; "Nigel Worthington is not a suspect in the murder, but we have a witness who tells us Worthington may be involved in a blackmail scam on Mrs Palmer." I paused for effect and added; "Incidentally sir – Worthington has not turned up at work this morning!"

"Jesus! Where are we going with this?" Judith asked sounding astonished and added;

"This is escalating all over the place. This case is like a giant octopus there are tentacles everywhere! When did this happen?" Judith looked anxiously at both of us and added; "This could reverberate through this whole place! How the hell did he ever get involved?"

Andy just smiled and replied; "We likened it to a spider's web with all those threads going everywhere! We were informed about young Worthington late yesterday afternoon. We chose to leave it till today and question him when he came in! – It may have been a mistake leaving it till today."

I looked at Andy who nodded and I replied; "He was given the books from Palmers Associates and he obviously found something incriminating and immediately set about blackmailing Mrs Palmer."

Judith asked; "So where do we go from here?"

I replied; "That's why we are here doing this Brain Storming!" I pointed to the chart and added; "so there we have it! – These are all the threads we have to the first murder this week. I suggest we have a 'Brain Storming' on this one (I pointed at the chart) and added; "Before moving onto the other cases! What do you think sir?"

Book 1 in the DI Spearing and DS Devlin series

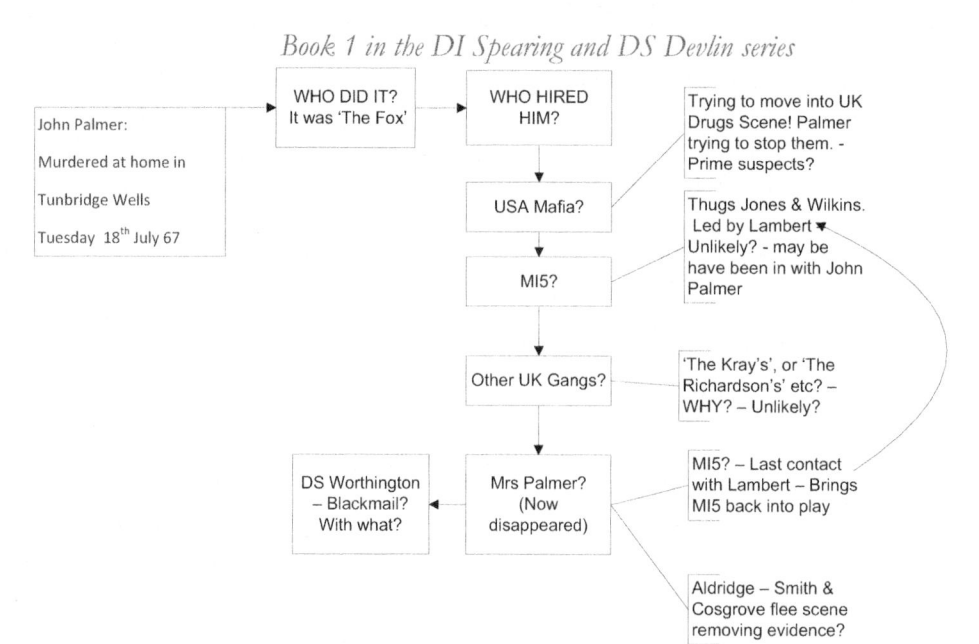

```
John Palmer:          ┌──────────────┐    ┌──────────────┐   Trying to move into UK
Murdered at home in   │ WHO DID IT?  │───▶│ WHO HIRED    │   Drugs Scene! Palmer
Tunbridge Wells       │ It was 'The Fox'│ │ HIM?         │   trying to stop them. -
Tuesday 18th July 67  └──────────────┘    └──────────────┘   Prime suspects?
                                                 │
                                                 ▼
                                          ┌──────────────┐   Thugs Jones & Wilkins.
                                          │ USA Mafia?   │   Led by Lambert
                                          └──────────────┘   Unlikely? - may be
                                                 │           have been in with John
                                                 ▼           Palmer
                                          ┌──────────────┐
                                          │ MI5?         │
                                          └──────────────┘
                                                 │           'The Kray's', or 'The
                                                 ▼           Richardson's' etc? –
                                          ┌──────────────┐   WHY? – Unlikely?
                                          │ Other UK Gangs?│
                                          └──────────────┘
                                                 │
        ┌──────────────┐                         ▼           MI5? – Last contact
        │ DS Worthington│    ┌──────────────┐                with Lambert – Brings
        │ – Blackmail? │◀───│ Mrs Palmer?  │                MI5 back into play
        │ With what?   │    │ (Now         │
        └──────────────┘    │ disappeared) │
                            └──────────────┘                Aldridge – Smith &
                                                            Cosgrove flee scene
                                                            removing evidence?
```

Andy responded; "Yeah – Good idea Sergeant! – I like this 'Brain Storming' thing. It gets us thinking! These threads - they clear the mind - it gets us concentrating on the important points."

I was surprised by his enthusiasm and responded; "Yes that is the point of it sir!"

Andy then stood up and began walking around the room and asked; "Just thinking out loud. I was always taught by my old commander that old cliché, that when you are stuck, you have got to go back and follow the money. - Who had the most to gain by Palmer's death?"

"I would say 'The Mafia' sir – There are now hundreds of millions of pounds in the UK drugs market!" I replied without too much thought.

"Exactly Sergeant! Then who had the most to lose do you think?"

I thought for a moment and replied; "Possibly the UK Gangs! - The Mafia could run the whole operation themselves."

Andy retorted; "Yes, but so – The UK Gangs would not want John Palmer dead, now mmn would they?"

I paused and thought again before replying; "Only if they saw an opportunity to expand by taking over the lot and therefore making sure 'The Mafia' could not get in?"

Andy immediately replied; "Yes maybe, but why now? I mean they have been working with John Palmer for a long time now and they were all making big money! So why upset the applecart now?"

I replied without thinking too much; "Yeah I can see that! So, we can cross the UK Gangs out?"

Andy replied; "Well let's do that for the moment, unless we think of something else later to put them back in the equation!" - Andy paused, then again started walking around in a small circle, before adding; "So what about MI5? As you said Sergeant - they are definitely involved in all this – we know they were involved in the Joe Bolger abduction and his murder and in the Thomas Broadbent abduction and torture."

"We only know for sure they were in on Thomas Broadbent, and think but are not certain about Joe Bolger are we sir?"

Andy shook his head and replied; that is one of the things I wanted to talk to you and Judith about later. - I have just had an informant who says he is a witness to our two MI5 lads - Jones and Wilkins - delivering a wooden crate to 'The Centaurus' apartments last night!"

"What, somebody witnessed it and actually recognised two MI5 operatives?" I asked incredulously, before realising it could only be one person and added; "But that could only be?"

Andy interrupted; "Exactly Sergeant – our 'Mr Fox' has finally come out of his lair and spoken after twenty odd years. Not that he will come out and be a witness, but at least we now have confirmation it was those two and our Mr Lambert is involved."

"What did he want in return for the information?" I heard myself asking the question, but seeing the pained expression on Andys' face I realised it was the wrong question.

Andy replied; "Nothing other than making it clear he was not involved in either Joseph Bolger's or the Joe Cole murders. – I got the impression that at some point he and Joe Cole were friends! Something to consider don't you think?"

I didn't know quite how to react and mumbled my reply; "Yeah interesting!" and after a little thought added; "Okay! - We will be going onto the Joseph Bolger and Joe Cole murders later – let's get the John Palmer murder over with first and then move on! So, we don't think the UK Gangs are in the frame for hiring 'The Fox'? So going back – do we agree it is unlikely MI5 were involved in JP's murder?"

Andy quickly replied, quietly and thoughtfully; "I would have said 'Yes' until they got involved with the disappearance of Mrs Palmer. For some reason, they may also have got involved in Joe Cole's murder it was certainly not 'The Fox' as they tried to get us to believe! For now, I think we should leave them in the frame for John Palmer and they are as sure as hell, up to their necks with Joseph Bolger and Joe Cole! I believe they are running out of any control."

I nodded my agreement and then added; "OK - Let's leave them in the frame – What about Mrs Palmer? If she takes over the business she sure as hell benefits! Don't forget she also lied to us about her present involvement with the company!"

"That's true, but why would she do that now? She virtually has the money anyway! Also, she has either disappeared of her own accord and is running scared! Or whoever has abducted her. – The Mafia? MI5? Hard to see any other others involved. Then there is the Worthington angle, but that may only be blackmail, although he has not appeared at work today which could be ominous!" Andy was suddenly sounding a little anxious.

"Right so do we want to leave Mrs Palmer in the frame?" I asked, thinking I knew the answer, but got a surprise.

Andy shrugged his shoulders and again rubbed his chin before slowly and deliberately replying: "I think for now we leave her in there, until we can say for definite. For my liking, she was just a little too cool about her husband's murder, so for now we have got to keep her in the mix." Andy looked at his watch before adding; "Okay – look it is getting towards lunch and we have a lot to do this afternoon. Let's leave Joseph Bolger and Joe Cole till later – I think we agree they are the work of MI5 so we can hit Jones and Wilkins with it when we see them at Kings Cross Prison later. Is there anything else?"

I quickly replied; "One thing sir! That gang rape case of the teenager I got this morning. It involves a top disc jockey, a pop star and a member of parliament. She has identified three of the four. She had been doped by the disc jockey. Problem is she has scrubbed herself clean and threw the clothes out and the case is now over three days old. How do you think we should handle it?"

"How is the girl?" Andy surprised me again by his first question.

"I think at the moment she is suffering from GSD – sorry sir - Gross Stress Disorder."

"Isn't that something the troops suffered from in the war?" Andy again surprised me with his general knowledge.

"Yes, it is a form of shell shock which soldiers in the First World War suffered from, but it was all stress related, although not recognised until too late in the war."

"So, would she be any good in the witness stand?" Andy asked as usual coming straight to the point.

"At this moment I don't think so, but maybe by the time it came to the trial she may be okay?"

"With this type of case with the mass media putting it under the spotlights and our gutter press hounding for every dirty detail – you will need a lot more than maybe Kevin. Between their top barristers and the mass media against a little unstable girl, it would be a massacre. She might never recover and she would probably recede into a shell. Especially when they make it appear she was on drugs - and they will"

"So, we just let them away with it sir?"

"I didn't say that Sergeant! I am just trying to let us all be aware that it would be very difficult both for the girl and in law, as I am sure Judith here would advise?"

Judith's face flushed and she took a short time before replying; "I agree it would be difficult sir, but surely we are duty bound to at least try for the girl and not let these bastards get away with it?"

"I agree with your sentiments Judith, but we have little time, or room to manoeuvre. I suggest we have three separate teams to bring them all in here for questioning only, hopefully, without their barristers and let them sweat. Then try to break their stories, because they will have one in place. Have any of them been involved or been questioned about anything like this before Sergeant?"

"I have not had a chance to check yet sir!"

"Well you do that, but don't let anyone know what you are up to. Otherwise the top brass will jump in for the career publicity, or to crush it on insufficient evidence before it starts. I will get two other trustworthy teams to pick-up the MP and the pop star. Write down their names for me Sergeant. You and I will pick up the DJ. If he is a BBC DJ he is probably based in Portland Place so we can pick him up easily and drop him back here and let him sweat while we go over to Kings Cross Prison to question Jones and Wilkins. How does that sound?"

"Like another day blasted out of the water sir! But it sounds good to me; at least we are giving it a shot!" I replied as I wrote the two names down on a piece of paper and passed it to Andy.

"Yeah, but I don't know how successful it will be Sergeant. - Judith - Could you stand - by in case their barristers turn up?"

"Certainly sir – it would be my pleasure!" Judith replied with a Cheshire cat grin all over her face.

"I hope we can all smile at the end of this Judith. It could be at best broken nose time, or broken careers, so everybody let's watch each of our backs." Andy sounded as cautious as I had ever heard him, so we somehow knew we were about to go into swamp land.

I decided to gamble and went off down to the basement and went into the computer room. There were stacks of IBM 360 mainframe computers wall to wall. It was all very impressive and high tech for the time, but noisy as they churned out reams of paper prints at frightening speed from massive printers in the middle of the room. There were stacks of other machines against the walls containing massive magnetic tapes whirring around behind glass doors.

I obviously felt and looked bewildered and then I noticed someone I recognised coming out of an office at the far end of the room. It was the geek Charlie Wynne who I had met at the Chief's inaugural meeting with the 'trained brains.'

I shouted across the room trying to be heard above the noise; "Hello – Charlie, isn't it?"

Charlie heard me and walked across with that awkward shy grin on his face and he surprisingly offered me a handshake as he replied; "Kevin – Yes? It's nice to see you again. - DI Spearing's not venturing into the modern technical world already?"

"No chance of that Charlie – at least not yet!" I replied with a grin and added; "I thought you said these things were getting smaller and the noise is bloody awful. – How can you hear yourself think?"

Charlie just smiled and replied; "I didn't know you had to hear to think? I hear even deaf people can think? – Anyway, the smaller computers are just coming on the market in the USA, although the space programme helped them!" Charlie laughed at his little joke then added; "Anyway, how can I help?"

Suitably admonished, I realised there might be something personal behind his retort and rather sheepishly replied; "Sorry I didn't mean any offence! - I was hoping you might have the criminal
records on computer - save me searching the old hand written stuff?"

Charlie replied with a very straight face; "No offence taken." What names do you have?" Charlie asked.

I wrote down the names on a piece of paper with minimal information; Johnny Eden a DJ, Philip Hawkins an MP and Tony Walters Pop Star. I handed them to Charlie and then said quietly; "This is strictly confidential at the moment Charlie – It must not get out of these four walls!"

Charlie replied again with his sly grin; "No worries about that Kevin. After they are in these IBM monsters only people with warped minds like mine will ever recover it. This is called job protection these days!" Charlie gave me another wicked grin and winked before reading the names and adding; "It looks like you are in luck - at least with two of the criminal records. We are doing them alphabetically and we are down to the L's for the last forty years. However, we have previously completed all the formal recorded interviews with anyone in the greater London area and if they have been questioned or any information has been collected by any law enforcement agency it will there!"

"That's great Charlie. How on earth are you getting that lot on the computers so fast?"

"We have teams of Data Inputter's working 24x7 on the consoles to upload the lot. They are in the back office over there!" Charlie pointed towards the door he had just come through and added; "They have the best typing speeds available so it is just a massive churn! It's been in place for the past few months - apparently before the building opened. Look, I will start with the other two and get out any criminal records, plus for all three, I will find any interviews or information. – In the meantime, you can look up any criminal records on Tony Walters. How does that sound?"

"That's cool Charlie. Which floor is Criminal Records on?"

Charlie smiled and replied; "That's the good thing! They are all in the back office ready to be put into the big melting pot machine! Follow me!" Charlie turned and surprisingly quickly walked to the back office. In there were racks stacked floor to ceiling with box files on both side walls. On the other two walls, again stacked floor to ceiling, were card index boxes, there must have been millions of records. There were twenty-four consoles running through the centre of the room some with men but mostly woman working the keyboards at alarming speeds, leaving my two finger keyboard skills looking like a drunk man running against supremely fit, track athletes.

I looked in amazement, but Charlie just said; "The box files are the criminal records and they are in alphabetical order. The card index boxes are also in alphabetical order, but contain interviews or information on individuals after they have been questioned. I will get on with these and let you search the box files for any Tony Walters criminal records.

I went off and eventually found the W file boxes. Then I found the files for people with the name of Tony Walters. After twenty-minutes I ran out of Tony Walter files and had found nothing that resembled Tony Walters our Pop Star, so I made my way out and found Charlie looking over some computer print-out sheets.

Charlie smiled and handed me the print-outs before adding; "Looks like one has a criminal record and all three have been interviewed at some point, but it may not be what you are looking for?"

"Really? – You found them that quick?"

"They have been ready for ten minutes! Just picked them up to make sure they are legible!"

"These things really work then?"

"One day they will run the world Kevin – mark my words! – You should start getting involved for your future."

"Charlie - at the moment I don't have enough time to run my own life, never mind try to learn computers!"

Charlie just shrugged his shoulders and replied; "Believe me, one day you will not be able to do your job without these things sitting on your desktop then you will have to learn but it may be too late! – You can use that desk over there, afraid you cannot take them away."

"That's fine Charlie and thanks for your help." I replied and went over to sit and read.

The first surprise was who had the criminal record? – The name was Phil Hawkins - the Member of Parliament no less! I thought MP's could not be elected if they had a criminal record, then I read why he had been able to get in. It appeared as a nineteen-year old in his home town of Hemel Hempstead he had punched a Chinese waiter following a row in a restaurant. The waiter fell backwards and cracked his skull on an old iron radiator, one of those types with the very sharp protruding edges. The Chinese was dead before he hit the ground. Hawkins was charged with manslaughter, but claimed self-defence as the waiter had inexplicably attacked him with a vicious assault. He claimed that a woman sitting at the next table was a witness to the assault, but she had disappeared in the confusion before the police arrived. Hawkins was found guilty of manslaughter and sentenced to ten years in prison.

Anyway, it turns out, after Hawkins had spent a month in prison, the mystery woman witness came forward and substantiated Hawkins' story that Hawkins had indeed been viciously attacked by the Chinese waiter. It turned out she was a married woman and had been out having an affair with another man. On top of all that, it was discovered that the Chinese waiter was a registered Chinese boxer and a black belt in Karate, therefore could kill with his hands. The police had not revealed this at the trial.

On appeal the sentence was quashed and the criminal record was ordered to be removed. Obviously that had not happened; it seldom does in these cases.

"What do you think you are doing?" Kay Turner, the sexy lady from the Chief Constable's introductory meeting last Monday, stood looking down on me with her hands on her hips, a dominant expression on her face. She was dressed in the same way as last Monday, right down to the sexy black stockings.

"Mam - I am looking up criminal records and any information on three suspects in a rape case I am involved in at the moment!" I tried to sound cool, calm and collected.

"Don't 'Mam' me Sergeant – My name is Kay Turner – Miss Turner to you – Now - where is your authority to look up these records man?" She was getting louder and attracting everybody's attention in the office.

"Miss Turner – I am a Detective Sergeant based here in New Scotland Yard. I believe I do not require any authority to look up criminal records!" I realised I did sound rather tetchy.

"The rules here DS Devlin is you do require your supervisor's approval to look at these records. Where is that approval?"

"Mam – Sorry Miss Turner! – Can you tell where this rule is written down?"

"Don't be a wise ass with me Sergeant! – I told you all on Monday this was the rule and a memo has been circulated and authorised verbally by the Chief to this effect!"

"So, what are you saying - Miss Turner! – Is there or isn't there a rule written down regarding this approval?"

"I see we have another Scottish union upstart, here have we?"

"Mam – I am afraid all you have got is a Scottish DS just trying to do my job! I take it that is a 'no'? Not in the rule book?" I knew that it sounded, as it was, – raw sarcasm - not the best way to win friends and influence people, especially in front of her minions!

"Have you or have you not got DI Spearing's approval?"

"Of course Mam – I have DI Spearing's verbal approval – if you care to ring him? We have got to move very quickly with this rape enquiry!"

"Get on with it lad and make sure you leave those print-outs with Charlie." Kay Turner turned away and walked off into the main office without another word.

I was beginning to get annoyed, even if she was a sexy lady and I rudely replied; "I am not a lad Mam. I am DS Kevin Devlin!"

"Yes, and I am not a 'Mam' Sergeant – Miss Turner or just Turner will do?"

"Kay all right?" I asked with my best cheeky grin.

"Whatever!" Kay replied and stormed off. Charlie just grinned.

"What is up with her Charlie?" I asked.

"Typical Yankee lady these days I am afraid Kevin. A little power goes straight to their head!"

"How is it with a woman for a boss Charlie? - More especially one like that?"

"To tell you the truth she is good Kevin - if she sticks to her own job!"

"No problem with that, but she has got to be helpful not obstructive!"

"I doubt if she sees it like that Kevin." Charlie replied with a grin.

I decided to concentrate on the information print-outs and first up was Tony Walters, the Pop Singer. It appears he had been interviewed by my Tweedledee and Tweedledum pairing – Tony Booth and Bill Brown. I decided to take notes as I went along.

It had been reported by a nosey neighbour in Surrey that in nineteen sixty-three Tony Walters, who was then at the height of his stardom, had been seen by the neighbour bringing young boys into his mansion. There were innuendos that there may be some queer sex ('Gays' were then known as 'Queers'!) going on which was still illegal back then with under twenty one year olds..

The two dickheads had carefully recorded that DCI (Now Detective Superintendent) John Sunderland had ordered them to go up to the Walters' mansion and ask him (Walters) straight out if he was having unlawful sex with boys. As expected, Walters vehemently denied the allegations. I read between the lines that this was the police practice in those days. Fire a warning shot across to make sure that if it was going on they should be more discreet in the future. In other words, the police were turning a blind eye to it, not wishing to get caught in the then controversial homosexual law tangles.

Just to sweep the whole thing under the carpet, the two dickheads had recorded going back to interview the nosey neighbour – a John Thomas – and concluded that the man may be a homophobic. They must have looked that one up in the Oxford dictionary, or someone, like their boss Sunderland, had told them what to write. Anyway, the case was closed.

Next up was the MP Phillip Hawkins. He was then, and was still, the Conservative MP for an area in St Albans, Hertfordshire, not far from his home in Hemel Hempstead. He was interviewed in January of nineteen sixty-four in connection with some of his controversial hard right wing, or as the Americans say 'rednecks,' statements on immigrants. Another innuendo came out that he was a Neo-Nazi sympathiser. Nazis were far from popular in England at that time, but the immigrant problem was coming to the fore and right wing views were getting a lot of support.

Once again, our Superintendent Sunderland had been put in charge; I thought he appeared to be ensuring he got on to the high-profile cases.

It appeared that the MP had used the old chestnut that he had been misquoted by a press reporter who had sneaked in unauthorised to a private meeting. No way of proving anything as the people attending the meeting were all right-wing Conservatives and were not about to admit to any misdemeanours. Then I noticed one of them was the then Home Secretary the 'Honourable' William Turnbull, who was also boss of New Scotland Yard. The Conservatives version of events was quickly accepted by DCI Sunderland without too many questions, although the press guy had stood by his story. Coincidence or what? - Later that same year, in July, DCI Sunderland found himself promoted to Detective Chief Superintendent and kicked upstairs.

Then it was time to consider the DJ Johnny Eden's interview notes. Ah - this in a way is related to our case. It was in June this year - only a few weeks ago - that our DJ was interviewed following an alleged groping of a seventeen years old girl in his dressing room at the BBC Television Studios in Lime Grove, Shepherds Bush, W12. Once again, our DCI Sunderland put himself in charge. Yet again there was another coincidence? – His number two was our present DCI 'Flash' Harry Tomlinson.

It appears that the DJ denied the charge, stating that nobody was allowed into dressing room which was confirmed by the BBC Producer. Apparently, there were no witnesses and so DCI Sunderland had quickly closed the case with no further action. For me it was all a bit too neat and tidy, but there again I may have been looking for too much.

Anyway, it was time to get back to Andy, so I completed my notes, thanked Charlie for his help who responded with his sly smile a wink and said; "Just doing my job Kevin!" I headed back to the office.

Andy was just coming off the phone as I arrived back in the office and immediately aasked; "Find anything in records?"

"Sure did" I replied and conveyed what I had found, highlighting DCS Sunderland's involvement.

"So, what are you thinking regarding Sunderland?" Andy asked with a quizzical look on his face.

"Well, on the surface, it appears like there is no proof on any of the cases, but if it was me looking - I would have looked at the fact that Walters is heading towards thirty, a pop star and not one single steady girlfriend? Nothing reported that he ever spent time with any of the thousands of his adoring girl fans? Well that does ring true. Then Sunderland sends Tweedledee - err sorry - Tony Booth and Bill Brown marching up to Walters' front door to ask him about these young boys going into his house at night and practically asked if there was anything going on? Sunderland might as well have sent him a written warning to watch out, if he was doing anything, there were nosey neighbours about."

I continued; "Then came Hawkins there was no look at, or at least no mention, that he had been charged and found guilty of manslaughter of a Chinese immigrant. – Even if it was quashed on appeal it ought to have been looked at because of the Neo Nazi attributions. It probably was, but with, at the time, the Home Secretary involved the whole thing was swept under the carpet quicker than a Hoover. Then within a couple of months Sunderland is promoted to DS."

"Finally, there was an allegation against Eden only a few weeks ago that he had groped a seventeen-year-old in his dressing room at the BBC Shepherds Bush studios. Again, there were no witnesses and it would have been difficult to prove, but at least the DCS should have contacted Manchester police where Eden hails from to enquire if had any previous in sexual assaults". There is nothing in our records! Again, it looks like a Sunderland warning to watch it!"

Andy raised a quizzical eyebrow and asked; "Have you contacted Manchester then?"

I replied with a smile; "Not yet, but now I know this I will ring them before we go!"

"Better be quick! I have arranged for two teams to pick up the other two at twelve fifteen and we need to pick Eden up at the same time. Get them all back here for questioning in separate interview rooms without phones and let them sweat until we get back from Kings Cross Prison this afternoon. How does that sound?"

"Sounds good to me I'll ring them now!" I replied lifting my phone and asked for Manchester Police HQ in Chester House. Eventually I was put through and I managed to persuade a desk sergeant to urgently fax me, by early afternoon any interviews with, or any charges against, the DJ Johnny Eden. I hung up and got my things ready including handcuffs.

I joined Andy at the lifts and again persuaded him to take the stairs. Although it was downstairs I soon realised how unfit I was getting with just a few days away from the gym. Then I looked at Andy and he was really struggling and he said through his heavy breathing; "Aye laddie, next time it is the lifts before I have a heart attack!"

I replied; "Well Andy – you have to start somewhere and this is the easy bit!"

Back came the quick reply; "If this is the easy bit lad, then it is going to be several strokes and a heart attack on the hard bit."

We got out to the basement car pool and while waiting for a car I explained my proposal for a specialist team consisting of Judith and I on rape cases.

Andy responded positively by replying; "I think that is a brilliant idea Kevin. Our lot of big macho-men with their size ten boots do not have a clue how to deal with these things. I will talk to the Chief when I get back, but don't forget we don't get many rape cases handed in to NYS – Usually the locals take care of those cases!"

He must have seen the disappointed look on my face, because he quickly added; "Of course we could suggest we place you both out as consultants to train people on the first cases in the home-counties, but that might interfere with your day jobs. Still, I think it is a very good suggestion Kevin. It falls into line with the Chief's current forward thinking policies! I think he will go for it! Mind – in the London area you might have to deal with as much male rape as female rape if you can handle that?"

"I think we could handle both – it is a matter of violation of peoples' bodies."

"Yeah, but it will be different. I know if I was a bloke, I would not want people to know that I had been raped!"

"Yeah Andy I can see that, but there are also boys who are just prostitutes, so called 'rent boys' but they deserve protection as well – don't you think?"

"Yeah, I suppose so, but not any more than women prostitutes and they don't get much protection from us. Usually a customary look and; 'okay we will see what we can do' before placing it in the unsolved bin. Anyway, I will have a word when we get back and see what the Chief thinks."

"Thanks Andy" I replied, there was not much more I could say.

Sergeant Thomson again picked us up in the Jag and we headed out to Portland Place to pick up DJ Johnny Eden for questioning.

Sergeant Thomson looked very serious and disturbed before he said without looking back; "Look Andy – I am really sorry about last night with Dad. I could not believe it!"

"Me neither lad. Me neither! I suppose I understand though, it must be hard dropping out after a life time chasing shit bags to counting how many shits you have in a day."

Sergeant Thomson and I both laughed and then Sergeant Thomson added; "Yeah but there is no excuse for it!"

Andy shook his head and replied; "Don't worry about it lad. I was thinking - TT only thought he was working for the good guys – how was he to know he was working for an MI5 guys who were bent as a corkscrew? We both laughed again and Sergeant Thomson replied; "I hope you don't mind Andy if I tell him what you said?"

"Yeah you do that lad. – I treated him with a bit of roughcast this morning, but I could not apologise to the silly old sod – You know what I mean?"

"Yeah I know Andy and thanks – I will let him know you send your apologises in your own inimitable way! He is really down!"

Andy just smiled and retorted with; "Yeah – you do that lad - before the day is out."

I could see this was leading up to be another long day and possibly go on late into the night and I was already feeling weary.

Book 1 in the DI Spearing and DS Devlin series

Chapter 22 - Heartbreak

Jonathan Bridgewater came back to the Chelsea Road apartment just after twelve noon. He had an awful feeling that something was wrong as soon as he walked through the entrance door and saw the place was still in darkness with all the curtains still drawn.

He called out in an almost fearful tone; "David – are you in?" No reply and the hairs on the back of Jonathan's neck began to bristle. He closed and locked the door and walked slowly up to the main bedroom. For some reason, he decided to knock the door before entering and asked, louder than he intended; "David are you in? Are you alright?" Some sixth sense was telling Jonathan it was not alright. As he entered the room he saw David Long lying on top of the bed covers dressed only in his red silk boxer shorts. His arms were crossed across his chest like an Egyptian mummy, his face a grey mask with no movement.

Jonathan rushed across the room and put it his hand on David's brow. He drew it back as if he had been burned, his facial expression aghast. David's brow was ice cold. Jonathan realised he did not know how to take a pulse, so he placed his hand on David's heart, but did not feel any beat. He then ran to the toilet and grabbed the shaving mirror. He had read somewhere that if you placed a mirror in front of the mouth and nose and, if there is any breath, the mirror will cloud over. Nothing! Jonathan threw the mirror on the floor and then saw the letter and read it.

Jonathan's left hand went up to his mouth and could only tearfully say; "Oh David what have you done?" It seemed so inadequate. He pulled David up into his arms and gave the lifeless body a bear hug. "Oh, you silly - you are a silly boy David." Then suddenly thinking of Nigel Worthington he suddenly added; "That bastard!" It did not enter Jonathan's head that in any way he was responsible.

Jonathan then began to realise his own predicament. He lay David down and in a panic suddenly thought - It would come out he was a queer! It would kill his wife and the kids would be open to all sorts of abuse at school. What could he do? He then rushed through to the toilet and picked up some cotton wool balls as he began to think - how could he escape? He came back and turned David over on his stomach pulled down his boxer shorts and began, using the cotton wool balls, the disgusting job of cleaning David's anus. He thought at least he had worn a condom so there would be no trace of him in there except possibly his pubic hair traces. He carefully tried to make sure all were removed onto the cotton wool balls, even if some were bloody Nigel's. Slowly a story began to formulate in his brain. It was going to be dodgy, but no matter what he dreamed up, it was going to take sheer concentration to pull it off.

He then found the condom he had used and made sure he wiped around the area on the floor where it lay. He wrapped the condom in several sheets of toilet paper and sealed it with an elastic band. He had heard of used condoms blocking toilets and coming back up the away drain so he flushed the toilet several times to make sure and threw in the used cotton wool balls on the third flush and made a few more flushes to make sure everything was gone. He wiped clean all the stuff that belonged to David, but, when finished, put a few of David's fingerprints back on making sure he pressed them in using David right hand in approximately the right position. He then turned David onto his back pulled up his boxers, making sure he wiped them clean, again making sure only David's prints were on them and refolded his arms across his chest. Then he found the rubber gloves he had used to put the cream on David's anus. He carefully put some of the cream onto David's fingers and using the rubber glove, rubbed it in. Then what to do with the glove? He came up with an idea cleaned and dried the gloves then smeared the finger with cream and dropped it carefully back on the floor where it had been.

So, the altered death scene was in place. He then sat down and took several very deep breaths before lifting the telephone and dialling 999. A woman telephonist's voice replied;

"Emergency services – which one would you like please?"

Jonathan replied as shakily as he could muster; "Police – I think. Oh, and an ambulance, but I think the poor boy is dead!"

"What is your name sir and where are you calling from sir?" The telephonist asked as if it was an everyday response.

Jonathan tried to sound stunned and bewildered; "I am Jonathan Bridgewater. Oh, I just came back to one of the Chelsea Kings Road apartments my company are trying to rent and I found this boy there dead!"

"Yes sir – I understand sir!" The telephonist answered patiently and again asked; "Where in Chelsea Road sir?"

"The Kensington Apartments in Chelsea Road – the penthouse suite!"

"Right sir –The Kensington Apartments in Chelsea Road – got your location sir. Are you quite sure he is dead sir?"

"Well madam – I am no expert, but he is not breathing so I am assuming he is bloody dead!" Jonathan was beginning to try and sound a bit hysterical.

"Take it easy sir – We will have the police there in a few minutes. Probably be New Scotland Yard and they will identify themselves before entering the premises. She then added; "Thank you sir!" The telephonist quickly hung up.

Jonathan had not been expecting New Scotland Yard then realised they were only a few minutes' drive away. Panic again set in. – How could he explain how David got into the apartment? He rushed through to the kitchen found a tyre lever which had been left by a previous tenant and came back through. He remembered, found the spare keys in David's pocket and put them into his own pocket. He went out and locked the door from the outside. He then, with all his strength, tried to jemmy the door, but only managed to splinter some wood. Then, with the strength of a desperate man, dug the tyre lever alongside the locking mechanism and with an almighty heave and a loud crack the door burst open. He thanked his lucky stars the other apartment owners were usually all out working. He quickly lifted the splinters and stepped inside closing the door behind him. He moved the heavy Victorian hat and umbrella stand and laid it on the floor behind the closed door to make it appear it had been pushed aside as he opened the door. He then wiped the fingerprints from the tyre lever and pressed David's fingerprints before laying the lever beside the bed.

There was a faint sound of police sirens and David rushed over and scanned the streets below his panoramic view from the penthouse was awesome. He saw the police car, sirens wailing, entering the Kings Road from the New Scotland Yard area. He took another few deep breaths trying to control his tingling nerves.

The police car screeched to a halt outside the apartment buildings. Two plainclothes detectives rushed out and rang the bell. The intercom bell buzzed in the corner by the door. Jonathan rushed over and buzzed them through the entrance door. He heard the lift whirring and clunk click as it stopped on the penthouse floor. He waited until they rang the doorbell and swiftly opened the door.

The older of the two detectives who had on a smart dark blue, almost black, suit bright white shirt and dark blue tie in a Windsor knot, with a trilby hat and highly polished black shoes. He stood in front with a detective police badge held up in front.

DI Sanderson noticed the door looked like it had been recently jemmied but not by an expert burglar.

Book 1 in the DI Spearing and DS Devlin series

"Hello – Mister Bridgewater? I am DI John Sanderson from New Scotland Yard and this (pointing over his shoulder) is Detective Sergeant Tony Booth. DI Sanderson noticed that Jonathan Bridgewater was a big man; around six feet three inches with a muscular build and size ten highly polished black shoes. He was dressed in an expensive dark blue, almost certainly 'Savile Row' suit, white shirt and dark blue silk tie.

Tony Booth was also holding up his detective badge. He was a younger man, but flashily dressed in what looked like another expensive tight fitting grey silky suit, white silk shirt and grey silk tie with highly polished black Chelsea boots which were all the fashion in nineteen sixty-seven.

DS Booth just nodded.

"You are Mister Bridgewater who reported the body in the apartment?" DI Sanderson asked curtly.

"Yes – Yes I am!" Jonathan sounded a little more nervous than he intended.

"Right then! - Can you show us the body please Mister Bridgewater?" DI Sanderson was all business.

"Yes – Yes - I found him in the bedroom through here." Jonathan replied still sounding very nervous, he led the way quickly to the bedroom scene.

DI Sanderson noticed the empty bottle of pain killers beside a near empty glass of water on the bedside table. There was also an A4 sheet of paper lying there; he thought probably a suicide note. He picked it up with his finger nails and quickly read the short contents. He put the note down on the bedside table.

DI Sanderson leaned across and felt for a pulse first around the wrist and then the neck. He lifted David's arm which was already going stiff with rigor mortis beginning to set in. He noticed the serious black and blue bruising with whelps on the body and the abrasions around the neck.

"Yeah he is dead right enough – a young boy – what a waste! I would say he has been dead a few hours."

He then looked at the clothes – Good quality stuff he thought to himself and checked the pockets and turned out a wallet with a couple of quid and a ten-shilling note, but nothing else except a St. Christopher medal. He then pulled out an envelope and when he saw the contents he quickly shifted his body position to hide it from the other two. He had noticed the bundles of fifty pound notes in the envelope; it looked like several thousand pounds. He palmed it into his inside breast pocket. He hoped that nobody had noticed.

He then noticed a rubber glove on the floor, picked it up and popped it into clear plastic evidence bag which he pocketed.

"Any idea who he is Mister Bridgewater?" DI Sanderson turned quickly to look Jonathan straight in the eye. Jonathan looked flustered and turned away to avert his eyes, a little sweat trickling from his brow.

"No - afraid not Inspector, but the name on the suicide note says David Long!" Jonathan replied.

"You read the note? Did you touch anything else?"

"Yes, I read the note – I – I thought it might tell me who he was! I did not know how to take a pulse, so I felt his heart and then held a mirror to his mouth and held his head up to see if there was any breath! That is the mirror I used on the bed beside him. He must have been a dosser!" Jonathan replied very emotionally.

DI Sanderson looked quizzically at Jonathan and quietly asked; "What makes you think he was a dosser Mister Bridgewater?"

"Well he broke in - didn't he? That tyre lever over there plus the broken door. - And he does not own or rent this place - does he? We get a few break-ins like this around our properties in Chelsea."

"That doesn't make him a dosser does it Mister Bridgewater? Look – He was wearing expensive silk boxer underpants and the suit is Savile Row quality and very expensive! – He also had a large sum of money with him – Probably enough to rent this place for a year. I don't think a dosser would be wearing that kind of gear and have that amount of money. – Do you Mister Bridgewater?"

"No I don't suppose so!" Jonathan was back to being unsure and he shook his head.

"He is almost certainly a squatter!" Tony Booth began the sentence and hastily stopped, when he got an angry glance from DI Sanderson, but he still added; "Yeah! – They are up to their armpits in squatters in Centre Point at Camden and all over Kings Road and Kensington."

Jonathan Bridgewater appeared relieved to divert attention.

"Would you mind Mister Bridgewater? - If DS Booth and I look at the other rooms - before we concentrate on the main bedroom? Also, could you move through to the lounge? – We need to keep the scene clear!" DI Sanderson asked with a nice manner.

"No, not at all!" Jonathan replied apparently very glad to get away from the main line of questioning.

DI Sanderson pointed DS Booth towards the other bedroom and they both walked that way. DI Sanderson shut the other bedroom door behind him.

"Okay Booth – What are you trying to pull?" DI Sanderson was sounding very hard and fast.

"I don't know what you mean sir – I only said-----"

"I know what you said Booth. If you look at this crime scene ---"

Booth interrupted with; "I thought suicide was no longer a crime since 'sixty-one' – Sir?"

DI Sanderson shook his head in disbelief; "Even if the final act turns out to be suicide – How the hell do you think the lad got all those bruises and welts which will undoubtedly be all over his back as well? Not only that, didn't you notice the marks around his neck? I don't think those were self-inflicted, do you? It looks like somebody was trying to strangle him at some point!"

"Oh, it is probably, from what I hear, another of those sex games that these queers are into!"

DI Sanderson shook his head and replied; "Look - do you really not see the big picture at all Booth - do you? – Do you not see how nervous Bridgewater is around the scene? Shit Booth – How long have you been a DS?"

"Six years' sir!"

"Yeah, well that explains it all! – Can't you even feel there is something not quite right here Booth? He - Bridgewater - is so nervous he could shit his pants at any time! There is a guy there full of awful bruises and quite dead and the same guy who happens to own the place is trying to convince us this lad, David Long, is a passing dosser who is dressed in very expensive gear and expensive underwear. Also, there is a vast sum of money in his pockets and you are backing Bridgewater up saying he is a squatter! Come on Booth who taught you to be a detective?"

"Sorry sir – I thought it was an out and out suicide – So what is your point – sir?" Booths sarcastic tone certainly cut through the ice.

"I will tell you the point Sergeant – and only once for your education – For a real detective – this suicide may be OK, but the rest stinks to the high heavens Sergeant!"

"There is no need to be abusive sir!"

"I'll tell you what Sergeant – from now on keep your mouth shut. Let me do the talking!"

"I am happy with that sir! I think you are way out of line here both to me and Bridgewater!" Booth sounded rather challenging.

Yeah? – You may be right Sergeant!" DI Sanderson replied, but then sarcastically added; "Then again maybe that is why I am a clean DI and you are the DS despite all your crawling."

"I object to your inference sir!" Booth replied raising his voice.

"Right! – It is noted Sergeant! Now let us try and do a decent investigation and respect that young boy in there. At least give him a little bit of justice. You see Booth - the devil is in the minor points, but if you don't investigate the minor points you let the whole thing slip away! –That is what being a detective is really all about! - Do you understand Sergeant?"

"If you say so sir. You are beginning to sound more like DI Spearing everyday" Booth's reply was very dry, but was not meant to be funny.

DI Sanderson just smiled and replied; "I take that as a real compliment Sergeant. - DI Spearing is probably the only fully fledged complete detective in the Yard. Now let us get on with this investigation. You have a look around here and the other rooms – see what those big detective eyes of yours can see! Oh, and give the Yard a ring on your walkie-talkie thing and get the forensics and coroner's people, with a doctor, out here pronto and a couple of wooden tops to keep anybody out. Is that clear enough Sergeant?"

"It is very loud and clear – SIR!" Booths' reply was equally loud and sarcastic.

DI Sanderson went to go out and turned back before saying; "And remember Sergeant don't touch anything without rubber gloves on." Booth just waved his hand and silently mouthed "Fuck off!"

DI Spearing then returned to the lounge to find Jonathan sitting on a chair staring blankly into space.

"You sure you don't know this lad Mister Bridgewater?" DI Sanderson looked quizzically at Jonathan.

"No – of course not. I have already said, so haven't I?" Jonathan replied, trying to sound irritated.

DI Sanderson took out his notepad plus pen and curtly asked; "Right then Mister Bridgewater – Where were you yesterday afternoon and last night?

Jonathan looked bewildered and then nervously asked; "Why do you want to know where I was last night?"

"I will ask the questions Mister Bridgewater! It is really very simple – Where were you yesterday afternoon and last night"

"I was in the office all afternoon till five. Then I set off for home about five-fifteen and reached home about seven."

"Home is where Mister Bridgewater?" DI Sanderson asked as a matter of fact.

"Lightwater in Surrey!" Jonathan replied, again sounding nervous.

"That's a long time to get to there from Kensington?"

"It was the usual rush hour traffic and I don't have a police siren to get me there any quicker!"

DI Sanderson smiled while writing down the reply, but realising he had to keep the man on the wrong foot, he quickly asked; "Is there anyone who can confirm you were at the office and at home during those times?"

"Look, what is this - An inquisition? I have just discovered a body in one of the many apartments my company lets or owns and which, incidentally, has been broken into and I am being questioned like a common criminal!" Jonathan was again sounding nervous, but trying his best to sound indignant.

DI Sanderson just stared and repeated the question; "We will come to all that in a minute Mister Bridgewater – Now I repeat – Is there anyone who can confirm you were in the office and at home during these times?"

Jonathan suddenly seemed to flag and flopped down on one of chairs before replying with a disgruntled tone to his voice; "Of course there is – my office staff stay late - till seven. My wife and kids can confirm I got home around seven!"

"Anyone else - other than your wife and kids can confirm?"

"No – why should I have to? That was last night and has nothing to do with finding this body today?" Jonathan replied, but then suddenly apparently thought and smiled before adding; "Yes of course - I forgot! My next-door neighbour Bob Parker and I - we went down to our local 'The Old Wheatsheaf' about nine. We stayed there till closing about ten thirty, well ten forty-five after drinking up time. Came back to our house and we had a couple with our wives to finish off the evening. Sort of our mid-week ritual! My wife and I finished up just a bit later getting to bed about midnight – paid for it this morning!"

DI Sanderson wrote down the details before replying; "Okay – now since you mention it - what about this morning? What time did you leave home this morning?"

Jonathan paused apparently thinking; "Yeah as said, I had a late night last night. I overslept this morning for a bit. My wife set off on the school run about eightish, but I did not get away till about eight thirty!"

DI Sanderson wrote down the details and asked; "Did you go direct to the office Mister Bridgewater and didn't stop here?

"Why yes of course – I was running late I went straight to the office!"

"So, what time did you arrive at your office?"

"Let's see – It must have been the back of ten, maybe ten-thirty ish!"

"Again, that is an awful long time to get there from Lightwater – is it not Mister Bridgewater?"

"Yeah it was, but with me running late I caught the full blast of the rush hour. It was horrendous at Chiswick and then Hammersmith was just choc-a-block. I have never seen anything like it!" Jonathan replied using the information he had got from Jake the senior estate agent in the office who had arrived late, but before Jonathan.

DI Sanderson just stared at Jonathan and did not say a word for a minute. Jonathan moved in his chair, looking and feeling uneasy.

DI Sanderson suddenly decided to change tack with his questions and started by simply saying; "Yes well we can check-out these things." Then asked, in another attempt to throw Jonathan onto the back foot; "Are you a rich man Mister Bridgewater?"

Jonathan immediately became defensive, realising where this was going and replied evenly; "No – not rich. I suppose I am comfortable!"

"Well your company own some very large properties like this in central London and you appear to be renting high value places." DI Sanderson waved his arm around the room and then added; "You also own a home in Surrey – the stockbrokers' belt. So, I think you are more than just 'comfortable' Mister Bridgewater?"

"We do not own this house. We rent it for some foreign clients. Also, my home has a small mortgage!" Jonathan again sounded defensive.

"Yeah I bet it is only a mortgage for tax reasons eh Mister Bridgewater?"

"There is no law against that – is there DI Sanderson?"

"No, there certainly is not Mister Bridgewater, but it should not be offered as an excuse that you are only comfortable - now should it Mister Bridgewater?"

Unbeknown to them both Tony Booth had quietly re-entered the room and gave a small cough to indicate he wanted to interrupt.

"Yes DS – What is it?" DI Sanderson sounded and looked angry at the interruption.

"Just to let you know sir! - Forensics will be here in ten and the Coroner's people will be here shortly after."

"Yeah thank you Sergeant – have you finished looking through the rooms?"

"Well yes sir, but my big beady eyes could not see anything unusual!"

"Now there is a surprise Sergeant!" DI Sanderson was being sarcastic and suddenly turned back to Jonathan and asked; "Have you seen anything which should not be here Mister Bridgewater?"

Jonathan looked agitated and stammered a little in reply; "No – not that I have seen." Then he suddenly realised that it would not look good because it would be found soon enough, he added; "Sorry – Yes! - there is a suitcase lying open in the bathroom over there!" He pointed at the en-suite door.

"Go have a look Sergeant and use your gloves or a handkerchief – don't touch it with your bare hands!

"Yes Sir!" DS Booth was being sarcastic this time as he headed for the en-suite.

"Did you touch it Mister Bridgewater?" DI Sanderson asked rather grumpily.

"Yes, I suppose I did! – Just to look and see what was in it!"

DI Sanderson could not get away from the feeling Bridgewater was always covering up and then asked; "And what is in it?"

"Oh, just some clothes and stuff – I don't know exactly."

"Very strange you know - young David just comes in and makes himself at home here as though he had been expected – don't you think that's strange Mister Bridgewater?"

"I'll tell you what I think DI Sanderson! You are putting two and two and trying to make it five while it only makes four, but you will not listen!" Jonathan was now tetchy, allowing DI Sanderson to get under his skin, which was exactly what he wanted to do.

DI Sanderson just smiled and quickly decided to again throw Jonathan onto the wrong foot when he replied; "Afraid we are not dealing with mathematical problems here Mister Bridgewater! - We are simply trying to establish facts. Now to get back to my question about your wealth – Which is it - 'comfortable' or just plain 'wealthy'?"

Jonathan was again knocked out of his stride and back on the defensive when he sullenly replied; "As I said I am comfortable."

DI Sanderson just smiled and replied evenly; "That's no problem - We can always check your Companies accounts with Companies House. The value of your house is on the market. So, we will need your private and company bank account details plus your home addresses – if you have more than one, including any holiday homes here or anywhere in the world? – If you could just please write them down here." DI Sanderson handed Jonathan his notebook, opened at a new page and passed him his pen

"You have no right!" Jonathan began, his voice wavering with nerves clearly showing, but still trying to hold it together and added; "You are really treating me like some sort of criminal Inspector. All I did was find a squatter in my empty apartment."

DI Sanderson immediately flared up in pretence of anger as he shouted; "Actually a 'dead' squatter Mister Bridgewater, there is a big difference. I'll tell you exactly what I have the right to do Mister Bridgewater! – I have the right to establish the facts on what has gone on here – Why a young lad is found lying dead in your apartment having been badly beaten up before – 'maybe' – and I do emphasise 'maybe' - having committed suicide. I also have the right Mister Bridgewater - if I find you are lying about any of this - to charge you with at least obstructing the police and anything else I can throw at you! – Do you understand that Mister Bridgewater?"

Jonathan just nodded and took out his chequebooks and shakily wrote his banks and homes details.

DS Booth had again quietly come back into the room and had witnessed most of the confrontation. Seeing there was a break in the questioning he suddenly stated; "I have looked through the case sir! – Just clothes, underwear, socks, T shirts - the usual stuff. Though there is a name and address on a label in the inside of the lid!"

Jonathan looked up from his writing in alarm, which was noticed by DI Sanderson.

"Well don't build up the suspense Sergeant – what is on the label?"

DS Booth took out his notebook and replied; "It is a Mister James Worthington and the address is; 'The Penthouse Suite', Grosvenor House, Kensington High Street, London W14."

DI Sanderson gave a sigh and replied; "Yet another man in a very wealthy location! My, my, - this gets more of a mystery this one! - Do you know this James Worthington – Mister Bridgewater?" He was again trying to wrong foot Jonathan.

"No of course I don't!" Jonathan replied too quickly.

"Oh well you don't seem to know anyone in your flat do you Mister Bridgewater?"

Jonathan appeared to ignore this question and asked; "I thought you would be looking at the body?" Jonathan's voice was croaked.

"The Forensic people must go in first, then us, then the Coroner's office. As you just heard, they are all are on the way!" DI Sanderson replied.

"The forensic people are coming? – I mean I thought it was a suicide?"

"It may look like a suicide Mister Bridgewater, but according to the apparent suicide note there is more than one person involved! - What it looks like and what it is can be two very different things! – Just like the magicians 'sleight-of-hand' – You know what I mean?"

Jonathan again chose to ignore the jibe and replied; "Look how long is this going to take? – I have a business to run!"

DI Sanderson looked very stern and replied; "Yes – well we have a really dirty business to sort out here Mister Bridgewater. The apartment, as it is a possible crime scene, - it will be closed for a few days until the forensic people are finished and we have satisfied ourselves there is nothing else to find!"

"And what am I supposed to do?" Jonathan retorted indignantly.

"You do whatever you have to do Mister Bridgewater. – But I am afraid you will have to stay here at least until the forensics are finished after that we may have some more questions for you. We will be checking your statements in the next couple of days and we will want to talk to you again." DI Sanderson turned away and then suddenly turned back, again trying to put Jonathan on the wrong foot, and asked; "Why did you turn up here today Mister Bridgewater?"

Jonathan was apparently taken aback and stammered his reply, another sign of possible lying; "I – I – always check out our empty places at least once a week!"

"So – young David could have been here for six days?"

Jonathan shook his head as though to say 'no', but took another thirty seconds before he quietly replied with; "We have a cleaner comes in every week and she was in here yesterday. She would have reported it if he had been here yesterday!"

DI Sanderson smiled and replied; "Unless of course she had been paid to keep her mouth shut! – Mister Bridgewater please write down her name and telephone number, along with your own office and home numbers."

Jonathan replied with a weary expression on his face; "Sorry I don't have her address and I doubt if she has a telephone – Her address is on my Rotadex card system on my desk in the office."

DI Sanderson took a business card from his breast shirt pocket, handed it to Jonathan and replied; "That's all right – Just give me a ring with her number – leave a message if I am not around. Write down your own and company address and telephone numbers please." DI Sanderson then went into the bedroom where David lay.

Jonathan started to write his address and telephone numbers down just as there was a knock on the entrance door to the apartment.

DS Booth went to answer and opened the door to find David Arkwright holding up his identification badge at eye level, with two youngish police constables behind him and a man with a Nikkormat FTN Camera which hung on the end of a strap around his neck.

David Arkwright smiled and said; "Good afternoon – David Arkwright from Forensics – These two constables arrived at the same time! And this is our camera man Joe Lacey" David picked up what appeared to be a large tool box, walked in and left the two constables with DS Booth before asking: "Where is the body?"

"He is along the corridor to the right - in the main bedroom!" DS Booth replied before turning to the two constables and quickly stating; "Rig up the no access crime scene tape and one of you stay outside the door and the other come inside the door. You know the procedure?"

"Yes Sergeant." The older constable replied while pulling out tape from a bag he was carrying. DS Booth left them to it and walked quickly after David Arkwright and Joe Lacey.

David rapped the door before entering the bedroom and saw DI Sanderson looking over David's body.

"Good afternoon sir – David Arkwright from forensics - DI Sanderson?" David asked perkily as he offered his handshake before adding; "Oh and this is Joe Lacey our photographer!"

DI Sanderson shook his hand and replied; "Yes, nice to meet you – I was expecting Doctor Harvey!" and added; "Joe" DI Sanderson acknowledged Joe with a nod of the head.

"Afraid it was reported as a suicide sir, so you only get the lackey!" David replied with a little nervous laugh.

DI Sanderson shot an angry look at DS Booth as he entered the room, but he just non-chantly shrugged his shoulders.

DI Sanderson replied rather tersely; "Well - we will leave that to the coroner to decide, but as you will see from the body the boy has been beaten up quite badly at some recent point."

David quickly replied; "Yes I can see that – poor sod – not had a good day, has he? – Anybody touched the body or anything yet?"

"I am afraid so David! – Our Mister Bridgewater – he is in the lounge! He 'discovered' the body when he came to check his empty apartment" DI Sanderson replied with a certain amount of sarcasm and pointed towards the lounge and continued; "He lifted and read the apparent suicide letter and felt David's – that is the victim's - heart and tried to see if he was breathing using that mirror. – When I arrived, I checked for his pulse on his wrist and neck! No signs of life!"

Jonathan Bridgewater had suddenly appeared in the bedroom doorway; he looked like he was in a trance and replied almost hysterically; "I don't know what you lot expected of me! If I had not checked David – and he had been alive – what would you have said then eh?"

DI Sanderson noticed the almost fraudulent slip of using David by name, but let it go for now when he replied; "Look Mister Bridgewater – Nobody is blaming you here – We are just establishing facts – Can I ask you to give your fingerprints to Mister Arkwright here – then wait for me in the lounge?"

"My fingerprints? Why?"

David Arkwright quickly replied; "Well Mister Bridgewater - We are hoping to find any other fingerprints that should not be here and so we can quickly dismiss yours as obviously, we would expect yours to be here."

DI Sanderson had to admire David Arkwrights' quick reply as technically, at that time, the police required anybody to give permission to take their fingerprints, other than if they were prime suspects in a crime.

"Well OK." Jonathan Bridgewater mumbled in reply.

David Arkwright quickly set-up and took Jonathan's fingerprints. He suddenly said to Jonathan – "Oh sorry we will also need your blood type – Do you happen to know it?"

"Of course, I do – I was in the Royal Navy in the war – It is Type AB+"

David replied; "Oh that is fairly rare so we will have little bother identifying if your blood is around the scene!"

"Nice to make your life easier!" Jonathan replied rather sarcastically.

When forensics had completed taking Jonathan's fingerprints, he took a lingering look at David on the bed, turned and walked away back to the lounge.

"Bridgewater appears to be a bit more upset than you would expect if the boy was a stranger!" David Arkwright said it casually to nobody in particular.

DI Sanderson raised an eyebrow and looked directly at DS Booth. He did not have to say anything; the message was in the body language – 'See even a forensic man could see it.'

"You're telling me David!" DI Sanderson retorted with another look at DS Booth and then walked over beside David Arkwright who was dusting the suicide note for prints.

"Only two prints here – probably the deceased's and Bridgewater's since he touched the note!" David Arkwright said it matter of fact and then added a question; "Joe can you take a few photos before we move him?"

Joe Lacey moved into position and took some long shots followed by a few close-ups.

David then proceeded to take young David's fingerprints.

"Can you get anything from the underwear or his skin?" DI Sanderson asked more in hope than any knowledge.

"Highly unlikely and certainly not here with the minimal equipment I am given. Need to take the underwear back to the lab and the skin would need to be looked at before the coroner's lot get a hold of the body and it would have to be in the lab. Could you two ease the body up so as I can take the underwear off without touching the boxers too much?"

DI Sanderson quickly replied; "Yeah OK! - Sergeant - could you take the other side and ease the body up to let David take off the underwear?"

"I suppose so." DS Booth sounded reluctant and nervous as he walked over to the other side of the body.

"Don't worry Sergeant he is not going to jump at you" DI Sanderson smiled and then suddenly shouted; "Boo!" DS Booth jumped back with fright, obviously startled, then settled, replied; "Yeah very funny sir."

"Now if you could both put your rubber gloves on and try to ease his buttocks up using his back so as I can ease off his underwear without smudging anything. OK lift on the count of three; One, Two, Three." David Arkwright gripped the boxers at the waist band and as the body was raised slipped them down over the buttocks onto the legs.

"That's very interesting DI! – The waistband is elasticated and is very tight. Look at his skin around the waist there!" DI pointed at the two waistband marks around the waist and added; "It looks like they have been pulled down and then put back on, but in a different place. Joe, can you take a couple of photos of his waistline detailing those two waistband marks?"

"Yeah sure David." Joe Lacey replied and took a couple of close-ups.

David then continued; "Now if you can both lift him by his buttocks and ankles I will just slip them down. Again, lift on the count of three; One, Two, Three."

The legs were raised and David slipped the boxers down to the ankles and then said; "Okay drop him down! – I will get them over the ankles." David did this one leg at a time without touching the skin. He placed the underwear into a clear plastic evidence bag.

Looking down at the body DI Sanderson shook his head and said; "You know, even when they are dead they don't have any dignity."

"He doesn't have much dignity to protect!" DS Booth replied with a smirk.

"You know Booth I told you already - Shut that big gob of yours!"

David Arkwright and Joe Lacey just nodded. DS Booth look startled.

"Oh well I might as well not be here!" DS Booth replied and went to walk off.

"Just stay where you are Sergeant – You are still needed again to move the body!"

DS Booth just mumbled and stood there.

David Arkwright broke the awkward silence and said; "Okay – Let's move him onto his right side, don't turn him onto his stomach. - DI Sanderson – If you can take his shoulders and Sergeant take his two legs together and gently turn him onto his right side. – Again please - On the count of three; One, Two, Three." It was achieved with ease.

"As you said sir, this young man has taken quite a beating in the name of sex Look at the welts across his back and his buttocks. I must say sir they look as if they may be twelve or so hours old judging by the congealed blood, they are certainly not a few hours old. There would be a lot of blood on the bed if they were recent! – There are only spots of blood, probably caused by the wounds weeping. The coroner will give you a better idea, but I think he has only been dead for a few hours!"

"Good – Thanks David - that gives me a good idea of timescales and since there is not much blood around I think the beating may have happened somewhere else. What do you think David?"

"Almost certainly sir. I will have to look at the anus to see if there any signs of anything there. Joe, before I move his leg – could you take close-ups of his back and buttocks?"

"Yeah – no problem David." Joe Lacey replied and moved his camera in to position adjusting the zoom lens his camera flashing quickly.

"Okay sir – If you could raise his left leg quite high I will look at his anus." David said it as he produced a small torchlight from his pocket with a magnifying glass.

DI Sanderson raised the leg and David pushed the left buttock aside with his thumb and at the same time flicked the torch on and went in close to the anus with the magnifying glass in his right hand.

"I see" David commented and then asked; "Could you pass me the small tweezers from my box over there Sergeant?"

DS Booth stooped down and passed the tweezers.

"Sergeant - Could you come around and hold this torch for me and shine it into the anus?"

DS Booth came around and apparently reluctantly did as he was told.

David picked up a few cotton wool ball threads with the tweezers and placed them in a small plastic bag he produced from his pocket.

"What is it?" DI Sanderson asked because he could barely see what was going into the bag.

"Cotton ball threads! I think young David here has been cleaned or cleaned himself using cotton balls. There is also cream, it smells like antiseptic cream in there and there are signs of recent sexual activity."

"Are you sure?" DI Sanderson asked.

"Positive about the cotton balls and cleaning. The coroner would probably be the best to confirm the recent sexual activity, but there is recent red soreness around there and the smell of sex is there, but probably condoms were used. David has probably had an ejaculation over himself which is where the smell of sex comes from, but he has not been cleaned in his front!" David Arkwright replied matter of fact.

David then had another look more closely this time again using the magnifying glass.

"Ah ha, what have we here?" He again used his tweezers and came out with a very small thread of pubic hair which he placed in another clear plastic evidence bag. "Could you label that sir as 'foreign pubic hair from David?" David handed the bag to DI Sanderson.

"Yes sure" DI Sanderson replied marking it with a felt tip pen he took out of David's tool box.

David then produced another thread of hair and placed it in another evidence bag and turned to DI Sanderson and asked; "Could you label this one sir as hair sample from the victims' anus area?"

David then went around to the front of David and with a pair of scissors cut a sample of young David's pubic hair and put it in another evidence bag handing it over to DI Sanderson and asked; "Could you label this one sir as David's pubic hair?"

DI Sanderson marked the bag and was impressed with the professionalism of David Arkwright.

"I saw some cotton wool balls in a glass in the bathroom!" DS Booth said excitedly and went to move towards the bathroom.

"Hang on Sergeant – Let me see if there are any prints to be lifted before you touch it!" David Arkwright shouted and then asked; "Joe – if I hold the left buttock open could you get a few close-ups of the anus – as best you can!"

"I'll try David, but it might be better to have the legs splayed." Joe replied.

"That will have to be at the post mortem Joe. Try and get something now while it is still fresh." David said it and added the question; "What has happened to the coroner?"

Joe moved in and again adjusting the zoom lens he set his camera flashing quickly.

"Don't know - They said they would be here in about half-an-hour!" DS Booth piped up.

David Arkwright got up and said; "Well that's as much as we can do on the body for now sir."

DI Sanderson responded; "Well thanks David – excellent work! – You have given me a lot to talk to Mister Bridgewater about me thinks. Sergeant you come with me and take notes at this part of the interviews"

David suddenly added; ""I'll get around and see if there are any other prints around and take a sample of the cotton wool balls. You know the cotton wool balls prove nothing sir? – There are billions of identical ones around - It only proves there were similar ones in the apartment for whomever to use!"

DI Sanderson replied; "Yeah – that's my problem David – I can prove very little unless I can get Mister Bridgewater talking! Oh David - Go over that tyre lever for prints or anything! Oh, yes and have a look at this rubber glove." And he handed it over in the clear plastic evidence bag.

"Will do sir – don't worry I will go over the place with a fine-tooth comb!" David shouted cheerily and then looking at the rubber glove he added; "By the way sir, there only seems to be cream on this glove you gave me. If it was used to clean the anus then you would expect either streaks of excrement or some blood!" David replied with a grin.

"Yeah right David – spare us the details for now!" DI Sanderson replied and laughed.

DI Sanderson and DS Booth went towards the lounge - as they walked down the hallway DS Booth suddenly asked; "How do you want to play this sir – Good cop and bad cop?"

"Yeah but wait for my signal before coming in with your bad cop! If we can get him to talk without threats it will be much better – OK?"

"Yeah sure – Your case sir!" DS Booth replied with a smirk as they entered the lounge to find Jonathan Bridgewater sitting on the settee, once again staring vacantly into space.

DI Sanderson just stood without saying a word, shaking his head, rubbing his chin and staring at Jonathan Bridgewater. It took a couple of minutes and Jonathan began to shift uncomfortably.

"Do you still have a problem Inspector?" Jonathan asked again sounding nervous, but slightly more settled, which was a bad sign as far as DI Sanderson was concerned.

"Yes, I do as a matter of fact Mister Bridgewater. In fact, since the initial forensic examination I have several problems."

"Oh" was all Jonathan could manage to say.

"Perhaps you can help me Mister Bridgewater?"

"If I can." Jonathan replied.

"Well you see Mister Bridgewater - as I said earlier – It appears to me to be inconceivable that a young man who wants to commit suicide would go to the trouble of breaking into a complete stranger's apartment to do his final deed. More especially when he has enough in his money in his pocket to go out in style at 'The Hilton,' or 'The Dorchester' or somewhere exotic! Don't you think Mister Bridgewater?"

"Who knows what a suicidal person is thinking Inspector?"

"Good answer Mister Bridgewater, but you know the statistics say that people, who have money, but have no one, choose to go out in style."

"Maybe young David was the exception to the rule Inspector?"

"Yes, may be so Mister Bridgewater, but would you say that David was also another exception in the way he was cleaned around his anus and testicles with cotton wool balls after he died?" DI Sanderson looked quizzically at Jonathan. For an instant, there was a flicker of fear in Jonathan's eyes, before they again glazed over. DI

Sanderson had taken a chance saying David had been cleaned after he died and by the reaction he now knew to be true.

"What the hell are you on about now Inspector?" Jonathan had dug deep and managed to control himself.

"Oh, our forensics people have just discovered that someone has cleaned David around his anus and his testicles using cotton wool balls with antiseptic cream."

Jonathans eyes flickered in that now familiar nervous way before he replied; "Yeah well he could have cleaned himself before he committed suicide!"

"Yeah – again a good answer! But do you think anyone who was about to commit suicide would bother to clean himself?"

"Again, Inspector, who knows what goes through a suicidal persons' mind?"

"Well you see Mister Bridgewater that is another problem. If David did clean himself where did all the cotton wool balls go?"

"Well maybe he cleaned himself before he took the pills?"

"Well it is possible I suppose, but I cannot see a young boy bothering too much about a mess left behind when he is gone - do you Mister Bridgewater? Oh, and that's the other mystery – The forensic people reckon there are signs of recent sexual activity around the anus and on David's body, that is certainly mysterious!"

"Well I didn't get here as I said till around twelve and I immediately reported the finding of the body. Perhaps he had someone else in here with him this morning?"

"Yes, another good answer Mister Bridgewater." DI Sanderson replied with more than a little sarcasm before adding; "You know Mister Bridgewater you do come up with plausible answers and so quickly as though you have been thinking about it for a long time."

"I am only responding off the top of my head to your questions Inspector and trying to help!" Jonathan responded with a thin smile.

DI Sanderson knew he had to change tack and try to throw Jonathan onto the wrong foot again he was getting too comfortable and suddenly he recalled the conversation about the blood type and asked; "You mentioned you were in the Royal Navy during the war - which ship were you on?"

"I was not on a ship I was in Special Projects."

DI Sanderson suddenly had a bit of inspiration and asked; "Oh yes they were the forerunners of the famous Royal Marines were they not?"

"Yes, they were" Jonathan replied somehow knowing what was coming next.

"Which theatre were you in Mister Bridgewater?"

"Mostly South East Asia, but had a short spell in the European theatre."

"Ah yes the Japanese in Asia, very tough times! You must have been trained in Resistance to Interrogation or RTI as you lads called it?"

Jonathan had a thin smile on his face as he replied; "Yes indeed Inspector."

DI Sanderson knew then he was up against a professional, all the nervous actions could be no more than an act. He knew it was highly unlikely he would break him down with this line of questioning. He knew the man or woman breaking down under questioning only happened in Detective films or in television shows like Perry Mason. It didn't happen in the real world, so he just said; "I reckon this interrogation must be a piece of piss to you with your RTI training Mister Bridgewater."

"Inspector I am now twenty-two years older and I am afraid nothing is a piece of piss anymore, except my prostrate problem. Today has been traumatic for me." Jonathan replied, but again that thin smug smile on his face.

"The thing is Mister Bridgewater I think you should know this; we don't really care a monkeys if you have been having it off with young David, although we cannot ignore it as it is illegal with a boy of his age. We want to collar the other guy who did this to David. I don't believe you gave him that beating and we must catch this guy before he kills the next one. Do you know who he is Mister Bridgewater?"

"How could I possibly know that when I do not even know the lad Inspector?"

DI Sanderson shrugged his shoulders making it look obvious he did not believe Jonathan and then decided it was time to bring in the bad cop routine and gave a nod to DS Booth. He regretted it almost instantly.

"You know what they say about you Royal Navy boys don't you Mister Bridgewater?"DS Booth asked with a smirk.

"I am afraid you are going to have to do better than that lad." Jonathan just smiled and turned away.

DI Sanderson stepped in with an angry glance at DS Booth and quietly said; "Look Mister Bridgewater – I will put it this way – We can put out a media release saying a boy prostitute was found by yourself in your company's apartment and he had been beaten and sexually assaulted before committing suicide – assuming it is a suicide. We then leave it to the public, your friends and your family to make up their own minds about you and your involvement"

"If you infer or even make an innuendo that I am a homosexual I will have my solicitors sue the arse of your trousers." Jonathan was angry, but DI Sanderson saw fear in his eyes for the first time. It had obviously struck a raw nerve.

"A most unfortunate turn of phrase Mister Bridgewater don't you think?" DI Sanderson said it quietly with a smile which also brought smiles to Jonathans and DS Booths faces.

DI Sanderson added; "Look Mister Bridgewater as I say, we are not interested in what you are up to, other than this boy is underage! – It is the other guy we want. We can just as easily make a statement saying a squatter has committed suicide in an apartment in Kensington - end of story" – it will probably not even make any of the newspapers and certainly not the television. We need your cooperation Mister Bridgewater that is all!"

DI Sanderson noticed the change in body language and in attitude, Bridgewater was thinking about it. Perhaps for the first time ever he was going to get a witness breaking down under questioning.

"I really have to think about it – nothing in writing of course." Jonathan was moving.

"Like bloody hell you will – you bloody shit pusher." DS Booth was still playing bad cop and totally misread the situation.

DI Sanderson and Jonathan just looked agape at DS Booth and it was Jonathan who recovered his voice first and responded; "There you have it Inspector – A bloody homophobic in all its glory."

"Hey who are you calling a homo whatever?" DS Booth replied with spittle coming from his mouth and rising moving towards Jonathan who just smiled.

"Sergeant please sit down right now - before you get hurt"" DI Sanderson spoke with some authority and then turned towards Jonathan and said; "Sorry about that Mister Bridgewater I understand where you are at."

"You are apologising to him? - Why? – It should be him apologising to me!"

"Sergeant sit down and just shut that big gob of yours."

Jonathan just smiled and said; "Well if there is nothing else Inspector I will be off." and he rose and started to walk confidently towards the door.

"I am sorry Mister Bridgewater, but I'm afraid you will need to wait till the coroner and the doctor gets here. We need to take blood samples and stuff from you when they arrive!"

"Bloody hell – When will they be here Inspector?" Jonathan asked obviously getting very hot and bothered.

"They should be here any minute and we will get them to take care of you first Mister Bridgewater." DI Sanderson said it very coolly.

Almost on cue there was a knock on the door and one of the wooden tops popped his head in and shouted; "The people from the coroner's office are here sir!"

DI Sanderson said to Jonathan; "Talk about the devil." And then looking round asked DS Booth; "Could you bring them into the lounge Sergeant?"

"Yes SIR." DS Booth replied sarcastically and went down the hallway and signalled to the incoming party; "This way gentlemen." There were four people in all, two paramedics with a medical box and carrying a stretcher and two others, one a doctor since he was carrying a doctor's bag.

At that point, David Arkwright and Joe Lacey emerged from the bedroom and they also headed into the lounge.

As they entered the lounge the youngish looking guy with the black rimmed spectacles on a hooked nose and dark brown almost black eyes was leading. He had jet black haircut short back and sides and he wore a charcoal grey suit and highly polished black brogue shoes. He smiled and looking at DI Sanderson said; "Hi DI Sanderson – Deputy Coroner Hugh Jenkins – I believe we have met before on another case?" Jenkins offered his handshake.

"Yes, indeed Mister Jenkins" DI Sanderson accepted his handshake and added; I think it was the Robinson case, wasn't it?"

"Yes, indeed sir – Nothing wrong with your memory! – A couple of years back I recall it was a successful conclusion! Anyway, this is Doctor John Henry – John - DI Sanderson!"

DI Sanderson and Doctor Henry shook hands and exchanged greetings. Doctor Henry was a middle aged man who looked very tired, dressed in a crumpled light grey open necked shirt no tie and brown cuffed hush puppy shoes. He was the one carrying a brown leather doctor's medical bag.

"I wonder if I could ask a favour Doctor?" DI Sanderson smiled nicely and then added;

"Before you go through to the body could you take a blood sample from Mister Bridgewater here" DI Sanderson pointed and paused looking intensely at Jonathan then said; "And could you supervise our forensic expert David Arkwright who has to take pubic hair and other samples from Mister Bridgewater?"

Jonathan just shook his head in disbelief went to say something then changed his mind.

"Certainly DI – Can we go somewhere private?" Doctor Henry replied with an equally tired sounding voice.

"There is a spare bedroom down the hall!" DI Sanderson replied

Doctor Henry still carrying his doctor's bag, David Arkwright carrying his tool box and Jonathan Bridgewater entered the spare bedroom.

"Which arm would you prefer the blood sample to be taken?"

"The left please" Jonathan replied rolling his shirt sleeve up.

"Would you please put your hand into a fist." Doctor Henry quickly inserted the needle and thirty seconds later the sample was taken and he asked; "That's fine Mister Bridgewater – What blood type are you?" Doctor Henry quickly labelled the blood sample and marked it 'Mr Bridgewater'.

"AB+ Doctor." Jonathan replied.

"That's quite rare." Doctor Henry replied marking the sample and then added; "Now Mister Bridgewater – Take off your trousers and your underwear and go over and lie on your back on top of the bed. David here is from forensics and must take samples from your pubic hair and things! I am here to see that it follows due medical process. OK?"

"Is this strictly necessary?" Jonathan asked as he moved over to the bed and started to take of his things as ordered.

David Arkwright replied; "Afraid so Mister Bridgewater. We have found pubic hairs in the deceased anus and we have to see if your hair matches - among other things!" David picked up a pair of small scissors, a pair of tweezers, some clear plastic evidence bags with a marker pen and his magnifying glass. He then took a brand new very fine white bone comb from his box and removed the cellophane packaging which he ensured Doctor Henry had observed.

Both David and Doctor Henry looked down on Jonathan on the bed.

"I am afraid I have to first inspect your penis under microscope not because of the size!" David grinned and added; "Only because we have to see if there is any foreign hair, or particles on it which matches what we found on the deceased. Is that OK Mister Bridgewater?"

"Fuck, it is already embarrassing enough! Just get on with it!" Jonathan replied his cheeks going red and turning his head sideways.

David first pulled the foreskin back on the penis and observed the head under microscope, but he could see nothing unusual. He then run his finger round the head and put his finger to his nose and asked: "You have had sex in the last few hours Mister Bridgewater?"

"How the fuck do you know that?" Jonathan asked angrily and sounding alarmed.

"I can smell the stale sperm on the head of your penis. It has obviously been in a condom!"

It was nearly thirty-seconds delay before Jonathan finally replied quietly; "Yes I have had – with my wife this morning – if it is any of your business!"

"I am afraid it is my business Mister Bridgewater. You see the deceased had someone up his anus and he - David- ejaculated as well. Did you not have a shower before you left home this morning Mister Bridgewater?"

"What?" Jonathan was speechless for the moment his mind in a whirl trying to find an answer.

"It is a fairly simple question Mister Bridgewater. Did you have a shower before you left home?"

"No – No - I already told your Inspector that I overslept this morning I had to rush out!" It was the best answer Jonathan could think of under pressure.

David gave a small thin smile and then said; "No that's good! Right Mister Bridgewater. I now must comb through your pubic hair to see if there are any foreign hairs caught in there. OK?"

Jonathan turned his head away and angrily said; "Just get on with it, will you?"

David slowly pulled the comb through the hair and when it came clear he held the comb up to the magnifying glass and saw a small curly hair which was a different colour and texture from Jonathan's pubic hair. He removed it from the comb with his tweezers and placed it in one of the clear plastic evidence bag. He then used a marker pen and wrote on the bag 'Foreign hair taken from J Bridgewaters pubic hair 20/07/67.'

David then said quietly to Doctor Henry; "You are a witness to the removal of this hair from Mister Bridgewaters pubic hair?"

"Yes I am." Doctor Henry confirmed.

Jonathan shifted uneasily on the bed but said nothing.

David just smiled and politely said; "Finally Mister Bridgewater, I am taking a small sample of your own pubic hair. This is to compare it against a foreign sample of hair we found in the deceased around his inner buttocks. OK Mister Bridgewater?"

"For fuck sake – Just get it done will you" Jonathans voice had a resigned tone to it.

David took the pubic hair sample bagged and labelled it as per the other sample and said; "Again Doctor – you are a witness?"

"Yes, I am" Doctor Henry again confirmed.

David then said; "Right Mister Bridgewater you can get up and get dressed now!"

David and Doctor Henry turned away as Jonathan got up and dressed and they all went back to the lounge.

David immediately caught DI Sandersons eye and they walked over together to the far corner of the room.

David very quietly said: "Sir - Under the magnifying glass, which is not as good as the microscope, the indications are unfortunately that the foreign pubic hair found in David's buttocks does not match Mister Bridgewaters pubic hair. However, the good news is that a foreign hair I found in Mister Bridgewater's pubic hair may match the hair sample I took from around David's anus. Also, he has had sex in the last few hours although he says it was with his wife. OK?"

DI Sanderson replied quietly; "Brilliant David! – Contamination?"

"No chance! I used a brand-new comb and made sure Doctor Henry witnessed it being unpacked!" David replied with a smile.

DI Sanderson also smiled and replied; "Great David – really well done! Make sure the Doc confirms that in writing in your report as soon as possible! It could be a while to the trial!"

"Yes sir." David replied feeling good.

They both joined the rest of the crowd in the lounge and DI Sanderson went straight over to Jonathan and looked him straight in the eye and stated loudly for all to hear; "Jonathan Bridgewater – I am arresting you for having unlawful homosexual sex with a minor. You do not have to say anything, but it may harm your defence if you do not mention when questioned something which you later rely on in court. Anything you do say may be given in evidence. Do you understand?"

Jonathans face was suddenly a contorted mess, he squeezed his eyes tightly shut, tears came in the corner of his eyes and he blinked. His shoulders crumpled, the raw emotion was almost touchable.

"I repeat - Do you understand Mister Bridgewater?" DI Sandersons own voice sounded emotional and sympathetic.

"Yes, I understand." Jonathan replied, looking away trying to hide his tears while wiping them away with the back of his hand.

"Mister Bridgewater, I also have to inform you that we reserve the right to charge you with further offences should the coroner's office or the Pathologist find any irregularities in the post mortem, other than suicide which is being assumed at this stage in the proceedings. It may be that the beatings that the victim has suffered may have contributed to his death in which case we may have to question you again. Do you understand this Mister Bridgewater?"

"Yes – Yes, I understand, but I never beat him up!" Jonathan replied his face now chalk white, looking likely to break down at any moment.

"Why did you have to sexually assault him in that condition Mister Bridgewater?" DI Sanderson voice was now emotional and then he added; "You know

Mister Bridgewater, when this (DI Sanderson pointed to his groin) rules this (DI Sanderson pointed to his brain) you are always likely to be heading for a downfall like this."

Jonathan just stared at DI Sanderson for a few seconds and suddenly pulled himself together, visibly trying to control himself and replied sounding really bitter; "I repeat it was not me who beat him up Inspector. Perhaps it is worth me pointing out, I read it somewhere - If you always allow your brain to rule your heart - then you can become an inhuman animal and an embittered lonely man, or woman." Jonathan wiped another tear away with the back of his hand and then asked; "Can I go now?"

DI Sanderson gave a thin smile and replied; "Mr Bridgewater, I cannot see anything but inhuman action here, having sex with a young boy in that condition" DI Sanderson angrily waved Bridgewater away and added; "Yes Mister Bridgewater you can go now. The Public Prosecutors office will be in contact, it could be a while before it comes to court. Mister Bridgewater (Jonathan turned back) we will do our best to keep this out of the media until the trial – OK?"

"Thank you, Inspector." Jonathan retorted and walked, rather slouching down the hall, shoulders slumped.

DI Sanderson looked sad as Jonathan disappeared down the hall and simply said; "There goes a broken man."

DS Booth suddenly said; "We have him by the short and curlies sir (Everyone laughed at the unintended pun) – Why didn't you throw him in jail and he could have got a taste of his own medicine in there?"

DI Sanderson just shook his head and replied sarcastically; "Tell me Sergeant - Why don't you pursue your mates - the real criminals - with the same vigour?"

DS Booth responded indignantly; "You all heard that – He just slandered me – You heard, that right?"

David Arkwright was the only one to respond; "What was that Sergeant? I am afraid I was not listening." Everyone else just shook their heads.

"I see." DS Booth said.

DI Sanderson just smiled and said; "Sergeant you will never get it, will you? As I said earlier - You know you are probably the original PC Plod walking over everything and listening to nobody – Now let us get around to tying this case down."

DI Sanderson looked around and said loudly; "Gentlemen – I would appreciate it if we could keep this very low key for the moment. If the press do get a hold of it, we just say we have found a squatter in this suite - He has apparently committed suicide and left a note. We are currently trying to identify him in order to let his parents know before we can release any more details." Is that clearly understood?" DI Sanderson looked directly at DS Booth and added; "In fact that is the absolute truth at this moment in time. - OK?"

Everyone, including DS Booth, nodded. He then added; "We don't want any media speculation, before we know where we are going ourselves with this case. We have the minimal proof at the moment and we don't have a clue yet who beat this boy up" He then paused before going on; "Oh Joe - how soon can you get those photos of David's face to us so as we can go around the apartments to see if he has been around here before?"

"These ones won't be ready until tonight sir, but I can do better than that! I have one of the new Polaroid Instant Cameras Series 210 out in the car – They give you instant photos – not brilliant, but they are good enough for a passport or identification photos etc."

"Brilliant! Go get it from the car and do your stuff." DI Sanderson replied and added: "Hugh – Can you hold off with your coroner's stuff and Doctor Henry for another few minutes? Tie up with David in the meantime into what forensics have found so far."

"Yeah sure sir – no problem – we will be here for a little while anyway!" Hugh Jenkins replied with a dismissive wave of the hand.

"Good – Oh and Hugh – Could you tie up with the Wooden Tops when you are leaving with the body and make sure this place is left secured? Thanks"

"Yes sir – Will do!"

DI Sanderson then looked at David Arkwright; "David – What about you?"

"I've covered the bedroom and the en-suite sir, I will have a quick look around the rest, but to tell the truth I don't expect to find much else."

"Up to you - Your judgement David" DI Sanderson just smiled as he said it.

Joe Lacey came back in with the Polaroid Instant in his hands and went straight through to the bedroom.

DI Sanderson looked directly at DS Booth and said; "Okay Sergeant – When Joe gets us those Polaroid photos – you and I will have to take them through the building, starting with the caretaker in the basement where we can get a list of the tenants, or owners. Then we need to go back to the Yard to write and file our report and the arrest record with the new girl Judith what's-her-name? I think we then must go check out the name and address on the suitcase. OK?"

"I was hoping to get away sharpish tonight sir. - Got to get a few things sorted out back home." DS Booth answered sounding less than enthusiastic.

"Well it is only one thirty in the afternoon Sergeant – If we get our arses into gear we should not be late. Assuming we are not called out to anything else." DI Sanderson replied with a faint smile.

"Yeah right I will believe that when I see it!" DS Booth retorted ruefully.

"You are so enthusiastic Sergeant." DI Sanderson replied sarcastically.

Joe Lacey emerged from the bedroom with a roll of film containing the photographs of young David and handed them across and said; "There you go sir. Not bad, are they?"

DI Sanderson looked at them and replied; "Bloody good Joe, thanks. Amazing how good they are in such a short time – the wonders of modern technology – eh?" He then turned and shouted across the room; "David – Thanks again for the good work today. – I will make do with the lackey any day!" Turning back to DS Booth he said; "Let's go Sergeant."

David Arkwright grinned and shouted back; "Cheers sir."

DI Sanderson and DS Booth made their way to the basement and found their way to the caretaker's apartment. There was a paper notice stuck to the door stating; 'Mister Felts – Caretaker'.

DI Sanderson rang the bell and it was almost immediately answered by an elderly, six foot man with thinning grey hair, a painfully thin man all bones showing beneath a - used to be white - T Shirt, dressed in dungarees with the bib hanging down to his knees and looking very tired, a cigarette dangling from his lips. He looked dirty and had at least two day's stubble on his painfully thin face with protruding cheekbones.

DI Sanderson flashed his badge and introduced himself; "Mister Felts – I am Detective Inspector Sanderson and this is Detective Sergeant Booth. We are from Scotland Yard. Can we have a word with you?"

"Scotland Yard eh? It must be serious then? I was wondering when you lot would get around to letting me know what was happening with a body in the penthouse." Mr Felts replied gruffly.

"Can we come in Mister Felts? Better not to talk out here!" DI Sanderson asked pleasantly with a smile.

"Aye I suppose so." Mr Felts replied and just turned around and walked in. DI Sanderson and DS Booth just smiled at each other until they got inside and caught the gut wrenching smell of the place. It was a mixture of cat's piss from at least five cats lying about in the lounge, body odour, sheer filth, stale tobacco, empty beer cans or bottles laying around and rotting food lying all over the place with flies buzzing around. Their noses turned up and their hands went to cover their noses and mouth. There was no air in the room.

"Sorry about the mess I haven't had a chance to clean up for a couple of days!"

DS Booth whispered to DI Sanderson; "More like a couple of years!"

Mr Felts turned around sharply with a sarcastic smile; "You asked to come in laddie, so you get us how you find us."

DI Sanderson replied through his hand; "Look Mister Felts you could be making yourself very ill living in this filth. Please at least open a window."

"My, we are sensitive souls, aren't we?" Mr Felts said it with a laugh, but he went over and opened a window.

"I think our souls don't mind Mister Felts. It is our stomachs that are complaining!" DS Booth replied with a smile.

"Ah yes – very good laddie – I like that." Mr Felts retorted, not feeling in the least sensitive.

DI Sanderson took out the photos of David and handed them to Mr Felts and asked; "Have you seen this lad around here before Mister Felts?"

Mr Felts took a cursory glance at the photos and rather too quickly replied; "Nope! – Can't say that I have Inspector." He handed them back.

DI Sanderson handed them back to him and asked; "Please take another look Mister Felts – Just to be sure."

Mr Felts took another cursory look and again handed the photos back too quickly before stating; "Nope Inspector, I cannot say I have ever seen this face around here. Then again, I am not the security guard nor am I paid to watch who comes in or goes out, so I don't pay much attention on the comings and goings.

DI Sanderson interjected; "Talking about security – What is the security around here?"

Mr Felts rubbed his chin before replying; "Aye well that's another long story Inspector. We had that there CCTV stuff put in brand new two years ago when Mister Bridgewaters Company bought the block!"

"Mr Bridgewaters Company owns the block?" DI Sanderson asked sounding astonished. He realized Mister Bridgewater had been economical with the truth earlier.

"Yes – Well at least he did until he had finished the upgrades. Then he sold three of the five apartments and from what I heard he nearly doubled his original investment of £400,000 with the first sale. So, in all, with the three sales, he damn near trebled his money and he still rents out the other two for phenomenal money. A very smart man is our Mister Bridgewater'"

"Yeah he must be. But the penthouse it seems to be empty now?"

"Yeah that's a strange one. He never had trouble renting it, but now it has been empty since the middle of June! Anyway, regarding the security – it all happened in June! – The CCTV suddenly broke down and the front door buzzer thing to allow people in suddenly stopped working in three of the apartments so we had to disconnect the lot."

"What's the matter - couldn't you fix them?"

"Me? Well I suppose I could have had a go, but Mr Bridgewater he said he would get the company back in as it was under guarantee."

"And it is still not fixed?" DI Sanderson asked quietly.

"No! That's the trouble in London – trying to get people to do their jobs you know?"

"Yeah I can see that Mister Felts!" DI Sanderson replied with a grim smile and Mr Felts didn't know if he was being sarcastic or not.

"Anyway, the bottom line is, other than when I got paid a bit extra to watch the security monitor, when I had the time, which was practically never, I have absolutely nothing do with security. It is not up to me to watch or challenge anybody going in or out so basically I don't."

DI Sanderson decided to change tack and quickly asked; "So there are five apartments in the block is there Mr Felts?"

"Five in all sir, excluding mine which of course is termed as a live in flat!"

"Do you have a list of the owners or tenants Mr Felts?"

"Yes, I have sir. Three of the apartments as I said earlier are owned – one by an American, the other two by 'foreign' gentlemen. They are all here usually in June for Wimbledon, the Derby and Royal Ascot. The American is a businessman and he probably comes another couple of times in the year!"

"Any of the three here at the moment Mister Felts?"

"Afraid not Inspector."

"What about the other two apartments?"

"One is currently rented to a nice young couple – Mr and Mrs Bootle. They own a couple of boutiques in Chelsea – Hard workers the pair of them – out from 8 ish till about the same time at night. I think they go out for a meal on the way back. The other one is the penthouse of course."

"So basically, there is no one around at the moment, or since eight this morning other than Mister Bridgewater? Did you see what time Mister Bridgewater arrived?"

"Nope – Can't say I did Inspector. As I say it is nothing to do with me so I just don't watch."

"Yet you seem to see Mr and Mrs Bootles' movements alright?"

There was a moment of hesitation before Mr Felts hesitantly answered; "What? Oh yes of course that was when I was watching the CCTV monitor."

DI Sanderson immediately retorted with a smile; "Yeah, when you had the time which was practically never - eh Mister Felts?" DI Sanderson decided to keep him on the wrong foot and asked; "How did you find out there was a body in the penthouse Mister Felts?"

Mr Felts moved uneasily; "I just assumed what with seeing the ambulance maen and the doctors, the police and all!"

"So, Mister Bridgewater did not drop off on the way out to let you know and that I was coming down to see you like I asked him to?" DI Sanderson lied just to get the reaction.

Mister Felts face went red, again he moved uneasily and after a few seconds delay finally mumbled; "Yes of course he did, but he never said anything as to what was going on Inspector."

"Is Mister Bridgewater your boss Mister Felts? What I mean is - do you depend on his good will for you to keep your job and this place?"

"Yes of course he owns and manages the place! So, what do you expect Inspector?"

"Just the truth! - That would do me Mister Felts. If he has told you what to say and not to tell the truth now that is a different matter. If this thing came to court, it would be a barrister asking these questions and if he found out you were telling lies you would get done for perjury and that is a few years in jail Mister Felts? So, what is it to be Mister Felts?"

"I am just an old soldier trying to make a living Inspector and have a place to put my head down at night that's all I want!" Mister Felts was putting on the old soldier act, almost crying, but then he suddenly added; "Mister Bridgewater really does only come once a week on Thursday mornings and afternoon, unless of course there is anything wrong."

DI Sanderson immediately asked; "So he comes morning and afternoons every Thursday? Was that the case today Mister Felts?"

Mister Felts looked and sounded very nervous when he replied quietly; "Yes he came at about nine then came back at about twelve – Will I lose my job and the flat Inspector?"

"Is that what Mr Bridgewater said Mister Felts?"

"Well not in as many words, but that is what he meant all right, if I told you anything."

DI Sanderson first looked at DS Booth and then at Mister Felts and said; "Well, if he tries that, let me know and I will have him for intimidating a witness to commit perjury. But you know Mister Felts with the state of this place he could easily get you chucked out for trashing it and not doing your job – you know?"

"Yeah I know – just getting a bit lackadaisical in my old age!"

"More like you have just stopped cleaning all together." DS Booth interjected with a surprisingly soft tone and a smile.

"Yeah! I suppose you are right there young fella." Mister Felts replied with a mischievous grin.

DI Sanderson smiled along with him and said; "Listen Mister Felts you are an old soldier, but not that old. It is in your blood - You know how to make a place spick and span. If you want to keep this place then you have got to get it done. You really need to fix it up, clean, paint and decorate – and let those cats outside in the air and teach them to do their stuff in their own litter trays outside, or get rid of them."

"Oh, I couldn't get rid of my cats – they are my only friends they would go off if I let them outside."

"Maybe it is the smell in this place and the pong from you that is the reason the cats are your only friends Mister Felts? If you sorted that out and started going down your local for a few then you might make a few friends." DS Booth retorted, but again surprisingly with a soft sympathetic tone and a smile.

"Used to do that young fella, but got out of the habit."

DI Sanderson suddenly got serious again and asked; "So what about this young boy Mister Felts? Still not recognise him?" DI Sanderson tried to hand over the photos, but Mister Felts shook his head.

"I could not swear it was him Inspector because he always sneaked in hiding his face. But there was a young boy came in every Thursday for the past month or so. Always just before nine and left just after Mister Bridgewater in the afternoon. None of my business what he gets up to, but him with a wife and a young family you know? It's just not right!"

"Yeah that's for sure Mister Felts. No way of telling with his type these days. Anyway, DS Booth here will get back to you today or in the morning with a statement for you to sign. I assure you we will not need to use it unless Mister Bridgewater pleads not guilty, which I doubt, as we do have some hard evidence."

Mister Felts suddenly looked alarmed and asked; "What is he getting charged with? Is it murder?"

DI Sanderson smiled and replied; "No nothing like that, but we have to wait until we formally identify the boy and contact his relations. So, we must keep it quiet until that is done. Anyway, we better get on and leave you to start your clean up if you want to hold onto this place?"

"Aye I am going to start right after lunch." Mister Felts replied sounding a little enthusiastic.

"Well make sure it is not a wet one!" DS Booth replied and Mister Felts laughed.

DI Sanderson and DS Booth were glad to get into the fresh air. DI Sanderson turned to DS Booth and said; "You know, you were very good with him in there."

DS Booth smiled and somewhat ruefully replied; "Yeah well I had two uncles who came back from the war the same way, so I could relate to him."

DI Sanderson replied, sounding melancholy, and added; "There but for the grace of God go I. Okay! let's go do our reports and statements and then we can, go over and check out this suitcase address later in the afternoon."

Book 1 in the DI Spearing and DS Devlin series

Chapter 23 - The Rape Case

Andy and I entered the beautiful nineteen thirties art deco reception area at the BBC Broadcasting House in Portland Place London. The reception area was practically covered in shining marble, it was clinically clean. They walked up to the receptionist, a young pretty blond wearing a skimpy pink mini dress and with a Mary Quant hairstyle. There was a six foot plus security guard to her right holding a walkie-talkie.

We produced our NSY Identity Badges to the receptionist and Andy asked; "Can you tell me which studio Johnny Eden is in?"

"Afraid I don't know sir! – I think he is in a rehearsal studio for the 'Meet the Stars' television show. The receptionist replied with a nice smile.

"Well can you find out where he is Miss please?" Andy asked nicely with a smile.

"I can get his producer John Richards to let him know." The receptionist replied helpfully.

"No, please – We have to pick him up - We don't want anybody informing him we are here thanks."

"Oh!" The receptionist replied and added; "Okay I will just ask Mr Richards which studio he is in."

Andy replied; "That would be good Miss."

The receptionist dialled an internal number which was answered on the third ring; "John Richards here can I help?"

"Oh, hello Mister Richards - Reception here. I have two gentlemen here who insist on talking immediately to Johnny Eden. Can you tell me which studio he is rehearing in?"

"Who are these gentlemen?" John Richards replied annoyed.

"They are detectives from New Scotland Yard Mister Richards." The receptionist replied and then noticed Andy signalling to speak. She passed the phone over.

Andy simply stated; "Mister Richards we have to speak directly to Mister Eden. We do not wish to forewarn him we are here. Can you please advise me which studio he is in?"

"I will be right down." John Richards replied.

Andy responded angrily; "No sir – I do not wish to speak to you – I have to speak directly to Mister Eden now on an important police investigation. So please Mr Richards, just give me the damn studio and floor numbers."

John Richards replied defensively "Oh I see. He is in rehearsals in Studio 3B that's the third- floor Studio B."

Andy replied very firmly; "Please ensure you do not phone or forewarn him we are coming – Thank you Mister Richards." He then passed the phone back to the receptionist.

"Are there lifts here?"

"Over to your right Inspector. But it is quicker to take the stairs, which are next door to the lifts." The blond receptionist replied with that friendly smile again.

"Thank you, Miss, – Miss?" I asked giving her my best shot.

"Rita Gallagher." She replied a little shyly, but sounded interested.

"See you later Rita." I replied, again giving my best white, flashy teeth smile and a friendly wave before joining Andy marching towards the lifts or the stairs.

"Do you ever stop trying with the girls Romeo?" Andy asked with a smile.

"Not with such a pretty one as Miss Rita. I never tire of trying." I replied.

"Yeah that's for sure. Shall we chance the stairs again?" Andy asked as he turned into the door labelled 'Stairs.'

"Do you think it is worth the risk of a heart attack?" I asked with a laugh.

"I seem to remember you were struggling just as much as me when we got to Flash Harrys' office!"

"I don't think so – a bit of selective memory there me thinks Andy. But I must admit it is amazing how quickly you get unfit when you stop the gym. All this work and no play is no good for the body."

"Tell me about it. I have no gym, no fitness and plenty of drink – A recipe for disaster!" Andy replied, breathlessly, as we reached the third floor and saw Studio B almost directly opposite us.

"Give me a minute." Andy said while gasping for breath and added; "Must start and get myself fit again." He bent over, hands on his knees, as he tried to recover. It took a couple of minutes before he could proceed. He walked up to the Studio B door rapped it loudly and marched straight in followed by me.

Johnny Eden was sitting alone reading aloud from a script which was titled 'Meet the Stars.' He was dressed in a bright red shirt with open neck and a gold medallion hanging round his neck on a gold necklace. He had on ridiculously tight striped trousers which practically showed everything he had around the crutch area.

"Mister Eden I presume?" Andy asked while flashing his NSY badge.

"Yep you've got me! - What is this about?" Johnny Eden sounded relaxed.

"I am Detective Inspector Spearing and this is Detective Sergeant Devlin. We have been ordered to bring you into New Scotland Yard for questioning regarding an incident in which you are alleged to be involved. Would you please now accompany us to New Scotland Yard sir?" Andy just said it outright. I must have shown amazement on my face but I pretended to shiver in the air-conditioned studio.

Johnny Eden just smiled confidently and put his two hands out; "Do you want me in handcuffs Inspector?"

"I don't think that will be necessary sir as you will I hope only be helping the police with our inquiries."

"Do I need my lawyer Inspector?" Johnny Eden sounded as if he was goading us.

"We are not arresting you sir. We are only bringing you in for questioning which we are entitled to do without a lawyer. Now if we were charging you with anything then you would need a lawyer." Andy replied patiently.

"Look I am in the middle of rehearsal for a television show tomorrow," Johnny Eden did not appear too bothered.

"Yes, Mister Eden and we are in the middle of three murder cases and we have been pulled in to this just to get you up to New Scotland Yard. We have a car outside - I am sure we can have you back to your rehearsal in no time." Andy lied again.

"Oh, very well I suppose if I have to." Johnny Eden appeared to be pretending and certainly did not appear upset.

We left and walked down the three flights of stairs, straight out through reception and back to the waiting Jaguar car with Sergeant Thomson leaning on the hood.

We sat with Johnny Eden between Andy and I in the back seat.

Johnny Eden suddenly turned to Any and with a thin smile asked; "Nice car. - Is Detective Superintendent Sunderland still with The Yard?"

"Yes he is Mister Eden, but I am afraid this case is too small for him to be involved." Andy responded as a matter of fact.

"Perhaps when he finds out I am involved, in whatever way, he may want to get involved?" Johnny Eden was sounding too smug for my liking.

"I am sure he will – He usually does get involved with high profile cases. I will be sure to let him know that you are helping the police with their inquiries." Andy sounded smooth and reassuring.

"Yes, you do that Inspector. So, I am a high profile case? What is this all about Inspector?" Johnny Eden was relaxed.

"Afraid that will have just have to wait Mister Eden. All we know is we had to bring you in for questioning. We may or may not be the ones to question you – it depends on what is happening with the others!" Andy lied again. I could only smile.

"Yeah right Inspector." Johnny Eden replied ruefully now apparently knowing the score.

On the way, Andy suddenly asked Sergeant Thomson; "Sergeant could you stop at that telephone box." He was pointing at the bright red box on the corner as we were about to turn left to head up to up to Oxford Circus.

"Yes, sure sir, but you can use the car radio?" Sergeant Thomson replied.

"No thanks Sergeant! – This is a private call and I don't want half of London and the whole of New Scotland Yard knowing my business!"

Sergeant Thomson laughed and pulled over. Andy jumped out and got straight into the box. I saw him putting in several pennies, dialling a number, pressing the connect button with his thumb and speaking for probably ten minutes.

Andy came back into the car and said; "Thanks Sergeant. Let's get to The Yard and get his thing sorted."

There was heavy traffic around Oxford Circus and all the way down Buckingham Palace Road, so it was almost thirty minutes until we got back to The Yard and parked.

We went straight up to the fourth floor where we parked Johnny Eden in a small interview room 4/3 with no phones and only a tape recorder.

I asked; "Would you like a coffee or something Mister Eden while you wait?"

"A coffee would be lovely Sergeant - White, with two sugars please." Johnny Eden replied still sounding very confident.

As we came out we locked the door and asked one of the PC lads to fetch the coffee. Andy also asked him to make sure that the door remained locked and not to allow any phone calls.

Andy turned around to me and said; "Let's go down to the third and second floors and meet the other two teams to see how they got on."

We again walked down the stairs to the third floor and on the way down I said to Andy; "You know Andy, I have a bad feeling about this one! Johnny Eden is far too comfortable and smug!"

Andy smiled and replied; "You know Sergeant that 'trained brain' of yours is almost as good as my rotten gut feeling! The call I made from that box was to hedge our bets and make sure he is going to be very uncomfortable, no matter what happens."

I replied with a smile, although I did not understand a word of it; "OK Andy – Let's make him a bit hot and bothered!"

We arrived outside of Interview Room 3/1 where we met DI John Barker who had DS Jack Thomson in tow. I had met Jack on Tuesday morning and he appeared to be a nice guy.

"How did the interview go John?" Andy asked curtly without introductions, although Jack and I nodded to each other in recognition.

"Well Andy – I have checked with DI John Robertson downstairs and we have both been hit with the same thing! They are both giving the same answers. It's like 'The Everly Brothers' in harmony - so well-rehearsed are they!"

"Why am I not surprised John?" Andy replied smiling and added; "Okay give us half an hour John. – I am not expecting any success with Eden. We will have a go, but it looks like an impasse."

Andy turned to me and said quite curtly; "Okay Sergeant I think we should get this over sooner rather than later. Since it is your case I will leave you to do the questioning!"

"Yeah – thank you very much sir!" I said it rather sarcastically, but with a smile.

Andy turned back to DI Barker and said quietly; "Keep them in there for a few hours - let them sweat! Tell them we are holding them pending further enquires – Let them all go about five o'clock."

We went back upstairs to room 4/3 and entered to find Johnny Eden sitting causally sipping his coffee.

Andy went over to the tape recorder and switched it on and spoke; "This is DI Andy Spearing and DS Kevin Devlin we are interviewing an entertainer with the professional name of Johnny Eden on Thursday 20th July 1967 commencing 15-00 hours. DS Kevin Devlin will be leading this interview as he is has been allocated the Lead Investigator in this enquiry. - Detective Sergeant Kevin Devlin.

"Thank you, sir." I found myself feeling a little uncomfortable with the formality, but recognised the necessity for the introductions.

"First, for the sake of the tape Mister Eden, would you please identify yourself as Mister Johnny Eden a professional entertainer and disc jockey?" I kept it to the basics.

"Whatever." Johnny Eden waved a dismissive right hand and turned away from me.

"Mister Eden - Would you please turn around and face the microphone and answer my question; 'Yes' or 'No.'" I knew there was an angry edge to my voice, but I spoke clearly and slowly.

"I suppose 'Yes' is the answer." Johnny Eden replied nonchalantly.

"The answer cannot be a supposition Mister Eden. – It must be a straight 'Yes' or 'No'? Are you Mister Johnny Eden a professional entertainer? 'Yes' or 'No.'" I replied having decided the minimum I could do with this interview was to establish that I was in control.

"Yes." Johnny Eden replied sullenly. First point to me! Andy just smiled.

"Okay Mister Eden this investigation is regarding an alleged rape in which you and three others, two of whom have been identified, are alleged to have been involved. I would like to ask you several questions in relation to these allegations Mister Eden!" I looked directly at him, but he just smiled.

"I knew it – that lunatic Randalll came storming into the studios this morning and started yelling about a gang rape of his daughter. What a fuckin idiot!"

I looked to Andy who shrugged and signalled for me to carry on.

"That lunatic as you call him Mister Eden is the very concerned father of an eighteen-year- old girl who is suffering from Gross Stress Disorder because of this assault!" I felt myself getting very prickly and knew I had to stay calm.

"I thought that was a world war one syndrome. Anyway, that does not excuse him from making these wild allegations." Johnny Eden was certainly staying cool calm and collected.

"It is not the dad who is making these allegations it is the eighteen-year-old girl who suffered from this horrific assault Mister Eden!" I was very close to the edge of losing it with this guy, the confident smug was now beginning to irritate me.

"Look Sergeant – There never was an assault – This girl was as high as a kite, but she was a very willing partner - as we will all testify." Johnny Eden just shrugged and acted unconcerned.

"You got that all organised Mister Eden?" I challenged him and then added trying to wrong foot him; "So you all took advantage of an eighteen-yea-old girl who was high on drink or drugs? Is that right Mister Eden?"

"Not the way we remember it Sergeant! She came out to my place all on her own – nobody forced her to come out to Henley-on-Thames and nobody forced her to have sex Sergeant."

"Not the way she tells it Mister Eden."

"No – I don't expect it is Sergeant. You know these young girls nowadays Sergeant – You are a good-looking guy I am sure you have had plenty. The next day they realise what they have done and instead of thinking of themselves as sluts - especially in front of their old man - they start shouting 'rape' – Well I am afraid it happens all too often." Johnny Eden could not hide the smirk on his face.

"Yeah, well maybe if you take advantage of a girl Mister Eden. Or inject her with something eh?" I found the anger beginning to boil.

"What the fuck are you talking about Sergeant? I can have my choice of half a dozen girls every night of the week by just snapping my fingers Sergeant. Why would I have to drug some weirdo just to have sex?" Johnny Eden was beginning to lose his cool at last.

"This was not sex Mister Eden. This was a gang bang on a girl who pleaded for you lot to stop."

"Not how we remember it Sergeant! She went along with it and loved it despite her morning after conscience. I bet she does not have a single bruise, or anything to suggest she was assaulted – Does she Sergeant?"

I reached across and turned off the recorder before I said; "You know Mister Eden you are a right nasty little piece of shit who thinks he can get away with it because you are a so called 'television personality.' But you know, we are going to get you and your shitbag mates."

"Is that all Sergeant? I think it is about time I was on my way." Johnny Eden stood up like he was about to leave.

"Just you sit down right there Mister Eden." I shouted angrily and added; "I am checking on reports about you from up North. You are going nowhere until I get clearance from them." I got up and went to leave.

"Oh, really Inspector – this is too much. I really need to talk to your superiors." Johnny Eden was smirking again.

Andy just stared him out and replied; "Like the Sergeant says Mister Eden – You just stay put until we get clearance." Andy then switched the tape recorder back on and simply said; "Interview suspended pending further enquires with Manchester Police station." He then switched the tape recorder off.

Johnny Eden just smiled, not looking so confident now and waved his hand dismissively.

Andy took the tape. He and I left the room together and locked the door behind us.

Andy looked sympathetic and simply said; "Well Sergeant – As we expected, we have lost the battle, but maybe not the war. Let's go find our Mr Randall at his bloody hotel and let him know he has blown any chance of us getting these bastards to court."

"What about Eden and Co?" I asked.

"Let's leave all the bastards to rot for a while. Let them fuckin' stew."

"Good idea Andy!" I replied, but could not hold back a laugh.

We walked out the main entrance to NSY and met a man with a Press Badge hung around his neck with a photographer in tow. There were also another two men, one holding a mobile London Weekend Television camera and the other a microphone. They all converged on Andy

The reporter spoke first; "DI Spearing - as you know - I am John Fisher from The

Book 1 in the DI Spearing and DS Devlin series

London Evening News and this is Bob Ashcroft from London Weekend television evening news programme. – I understand Johnny Eden – the well-known television personality, the pop star Tony Walters and the MP Philip Hawkins are all in New Scotland Yard at the moment being questioned. Can you tell me what it is in connection with?"

Andy looked surprised and replied; "Yes John – I don't know where you got your information from, but the three men have been helping police with our inquiries into an alleged gang rape of an eighteen-year-old girl at Mister Eden's Henley-on-Thames mansion. That is all I can say at the moment as our inquires are continuing."

Andy and I walked directly to the Jaguar with Sergeant Thomson behind the wheel. Andy spoke first; "Sergeant takes us to 'The Maddison' hotel in Sussex Gardens, then we will need to go to Kings Cross Prison to interview our MI5 chums.

"No problem Andy!" Sergeant Thomson smiled as he drew ought into the traffic.

"You had nothing to do with the media turning up there Andy?" I asked quietly with a thin knowing smile.

"Me? - Would I dare do such a thing?" Andy replied with a mischievous smile on his face.

"Well!" I replied, but just laughed and then added; "You know Andy; – I reckon it is you who should be known as 'The Fox.' I reckon the assassin is number two!"

"One thing Sergeant - they may have won round one, but we got in a few nice body blows right there. They are going to have to answer a lot of awkward questions from their friends and management. It will start a media frenzy – who knows where it will end?" Andy just smiled and shook his head and added; "At least it will take that smirk off Eden's face!"

"I only wish I could be there to see it!" I replied ruefully.

"Oh, you'll see it alright. Bob Ashcroft will interview them when he comes out and it will be all over the evening news!"

It took us twenty minutes to cut across central London towards Bayswater and on to Sussex Gardens and 'The Maddison' hotel. We both went in to the small reception area.

Andy flashed his badge and asked to speak to Mr. and Mrs. Randall. After fifteen minutes, they eventually appeared.

Andy stared very hard and long at Mr. Randall before he said; "Mister Randall, I am
Detective Inspector Spearing and I believe you know Detective Sergeant Devlin?"

Mr. Randall just mumbled to himself, but Mrs. Randall smiled and said; "Hello Sergeant – Do you have any news for us?"

"Well 'Yes' and 'No' I started to reply, but was interrupted by Andy..

"Well actually Mrs Randall we have come to thank your husband here for successfully blowing any small chance we had of bringing your daughter's alleged rapists to face justice." Andy and I just stood and stared angrily at Mr. Randall.

Mrs. Randall looked pleadingly at her husband and asked; "For God's sake what have you done now John?"

"I have done nothing woman! – I only went and gave that bastard Eden a piece of my mind. No more than he deserved!"

"What you have done Mr. Randall is forewarned the bastards that we were coming for them and, therefore, they had plenty of time to get their stories tighter than a ducks' arse. – Excuse the language Mrs. Randall – So now we have missed the chance to divide and conquer!" Andy was red in the face and almost spitting with the words.

Mr. Randall responded; "Well your man Devlin here said there was no chance of getting them to court and it sounded like it was going to be covered up – So what's the difference?"

"I beg your pardon Mr. Randall, but what I believe I said in front of witnesses was; 'We would do our best, but as Mary had thrown out the clothes she wore and had, understandably, constantly showered for two days before it was reported. In these circumstances, it would be extremely difficult to prove.' I believe you were the only one who was ranting about a cover-up and obviously not listening to anybody!" I found myself slightly on the defensive, but I decided to hell with that.

"That is just not true – Is it my dear?" Mr. Randall turned to his wife.

"Of course, it is true John - as usual you just never ever listen." Mrs. Randall said it with a faraway look in her eyes.

"Why you!" Mr. Randall shouted angrily and raised a balled fist. I hit him with a swift hard blow to the kidneys. In truth, a little harder than I had intended and he went down on his hands and knees, his face grey going chalk white.

"Now look what you have gone and done John." Mrs. Randall said it like an Abbot and Costello sketch; in fact, I am sure she was smiling, almost laughing.

"Me? Look, what I have done? You, stupid bitch it was him! I will sue the bastard." Mr Randall's voice came out like staccato as he searched for a breath of air.

"Mr. Randall I simply stopped you from assaulting your wife with a balled fist. As these witnesses will testify I am sure. A word of warning Mr Randall, if you as much as touch your wife I will personally come up and arrest you myself. Do we understand each other Mr. Randall?" I shouted the question into his ear.

"Yeah – Yeah" Mr Randall replied, still trying to catch his breath.

Andy interjected; "I suggest you listen to the Sergeant. He does not make idle threats Mr. Randall."

I turned to Mrs. Randall and said; "Mrs. Randall - if he assaults you again just make a call to 'The Yard. I will be right up and arrest him."

"Oh, yes I will Sergeant Devlin - thanks" Mrs. Randall smiled serenely.

Andy pulled Mrs.Randall aside and quietly asked; "Perhaps you can explain to your daughter Mrs. Randall why we could not prosecute her rapists?"

"I most certainly will do Inspector – make no mistake about that!" Mrs Randall sounded adamant.

Andy replied; "Good we will see you Mrs. Randall. Sergeant - we better be off to Kings Cross Prison and see the two MI5 clown's. It is getting late."

"Yes sir." I replied before turning back to Mrs. Randall. "I meant what I said Mrs. Randall – day, or night, just call me."

"Yes – and thanks Sergeant." Mrs. Randall replied, although quietly - she was once again sounding adamant.

We went outside and jumped back into the Jag.

"Tell you what Tommy, I am starving - Go to Kings Cross Prison via Kings Cross and we can pick up a sandwich for lunch at 'The Sandwich Bar' opposite St Pancras Station. Know it?"

"They have the best fresh sandwiches in town Andy!"

"That's for sure Tommy!" Andy replied.

Within twenty minutes we drew up outside 'The Sandwich Bar.' Tommy left the blue light flashing.

"Okay what do you want Tommy?" Andy shouted over the noise of the passing traffic.

"I think I'll stick to a cheese and pickle on their white bread Andy." Tommy shouted back.

"What about you Kevin?"

"I think I'll have a spicy chicken with salad." I replied.

"I think I'll have the same as Tommy – Their cheese and pickle on white bread you could die for! Okay Kevin here is two quid - make sure you get a receipt for expenses – Can you please?" Andy looked at me with a disarming smile.

I had to laugh before I said; "Well, I walked right into that one didn't I sir?"

I got out and walked into two wooden tops – A Sergeant and a Police Constable.

"Can we help Sergeant?" The Sergeant asked.

"How did you know I was a Sergeant – Sergeant?" I asked with a smile.

The forty plus year old Sergeant answered with a smile. "Not hard Sergeant! The one in the front – the driver is one of us – so the DI must send out the Sergeant. Simple!"

"You know I think you should be a Detective - Sergeant." I replied with a laugh.

"Been there – done that Sergeant! – Even got the T Shirt, but you know they chucked me out – Reckoned I was too clever for my own good! The Sergeant laughed heartily.

"Yeah – I can see their point!" I answered also with a laugh and added; "Any influence with 'The Sandwich Bar' staff?" I asked quietly.

"Well if the local Sergeant hasn't any influence then who has? - Probably only the local Kings Cross prostitutes and there are a lot of them!" The Sergeant winked and laughed and asked; "What do you want?"

I gave him our order and I gave him the two quid and asked him to get three coffees as well and a receipt. Off he marched to the front of the queue and ten minutes later came back out with the complete order.

"What can I say Sergeant?"

"Thanks, will do Sergeant!" Just remember me when you are up the food chain" The Sergeant replied. I really liked this guy's sense of humour.

"Then thanks Sergeant. I will more than likely see you on the way back down the food chain."

"Not what I hear about you 'trained brains.'"

There it was again. The amazing rumour control within 'The Met.' – I just waved and got back in the car. I could not help but grin.

We ate our sandwich lunches and drunk our coffees as we headed down Caledonian Road for Kings Cross Prison.

Chapter 24 – Closure

Pete Baker was only a private courier van driver around the London area. He was a van driver with ambition to better himself.

He was trying to get entrance into the London police. He had studied, through books, the observation techniques needed to be a detective. He was also studying psychology through the new Open University courses and had taken an interest in body language.

He took great pride in keeping up to date with everything that was happening in London by reading cover to back page of the London Evening Standard and with the national news through doing the same with the Daily Express.

He came into the very affluent Kensington Apartments just before two in the afternoon carrying a parcel for Apartment 3A, which was on the third floor. He took the stairs rather than the lift as he always did in these types of buildings, his form of exercise for the day. He was surprised to see a rather tall, well-built man about two floors above him taking the stairs two at a time, Pete thought to himself he is obviously very fit, but he was surprised to see anyone at this time of day in these apartments, especially taking the stairs. The fit guy was already on the fifth floor and still going up, probably to the penthouse, when Pete reached the third floor and went through to third floor apartments.

Pete rang the bell to Apartment 3A and had to wait a full two minutes before the door was opened. Old Mister Wells, an eighty-year-old and a regular customer, answered with his usual smile and the same greeting he had been using for the past two years that Pete had been doing this job; "Ah there you are, I thought it would be you!" Mister Wells said it as he accepted the parcel and dithered for another minute as he signed the receipt and adding; "Thank you so much – See you again in two weeks, I hope." Again, the same words he always used before closing and locking the door to his apartment.

Pete looked through his list of next deliveries for a few minutes then went back to the stairwell. As he took the stairs, he heard someone coming down quite fast above him. Pete looked up and caught a glimpse of the big guy from a few minutes ago, but this time caught a glimpse of his face before he quickly turned off the stairs into the fourth-floor apartment's level.

Pete quickly averted his eyes and his face which showed alarm and a little fear. Pete had instantly thought he recognised the man from yesterday's papers as 'The Fox' right down to his red hair and his red goatee beard. Pete did not want to show he had recognised the man so he just ambled along at the same pace down the stairs. As soon as he hit the ground floor he headed for the caretakers flat. On previous occasions, he had to leave parcels with the caretaker so he knew exactly where to find the flat and he hurried across and rang the bell keeping his finger on the button.

"Okay – Okay keep your shirt on." The Caretaker shouted as he unlocked his door and opened it before seeing Pete and adding rather angrily; "Oh it's you, what's all the noise about?"

"Can I come in?" Pete asked and before a reply he brushed past and pushed the door closed and locked it.

"Hey what the fuck do you think you are doing?" The Caretaker bristled with indignation.

Pete ignored him and looking around the flat he could not see a phone so he turned back showing fear on his face asked; "Have you got a phone?"

The Caretaker slowly began to realise there was something wrong and quickly replied; "Yes it's on the wall in the kitchen through there." He pointed to a door to the right of the lounge.

Pete practically ran over and found the telephone and dialled 999.

"Emergency! – Which services please?" Someone replied with a foreign accent.

"Police please – Urgent!" Pete replied quickly and quietly. There was few seconds' delay during which Pete became agitated saying to no one in particular; "Come on for fucks sake."

"Police" A voice came on and added; "How can I help you?"

Pete tried to now act cool, calm and collected and report the facts, but his voice came out rapid staccato style and he said; "I have just been delivering a parcel and going up the stairs I saw that guy you are after, 'The Fox.' He was going up to the penthouse."

"Oh, my God!" The Caretaker muttered, but the guy at the other end of the 'phone obviously heard.

"Okay, just take it easy for a minute mister? What is your name sir?" The voice asked.

"Pete – Pete Baker – I am a courier delivery manager. I was delivering a parcel here." Pete replied, trying to remain cool.

"And where is here?" The voice asked, sounding calm.

Pete shook his head trying to think clearly before replying; "The Knightsbridge Apartments in Egerton Street, Knightsbridge!"

"And the telephone number you are calling from sir?"

Pete looked at the number on the wall and replied; "012358907."

"And who owns The Penthouse Mister Baker?"

"That is Mr. Nigel Worthington's Penthouse" The Caretaker shouted.

"Who is that?" The voice asked.

"That is the Caretaker sir!"

"Okay Mr. Baker, – Are you quite certain that this man is 'The Fox'?" The voice asked.

"I am certain, it was the man described in yesterday's Standard. But to tell you the truth I didn't hang about there to find out!"

"Yes, well that's understandable sir! As you have read, this man could be armed and dangerous. Is he still in The Penthouse?" The voice was still calm and taking things slowly.

"No, he came out, but when I saw him on the stairwell, he dived off and went into the fourth floor!"

"Okay Mr. Baker – You have done a good job, but stay out of sight and lock the Caretaker's door. Wait there and we send an armed response team to the Caretakers within the next twenty minutes and we will take it from there. Is that quite clear Mister Baker?"

"Understood." Pete Baker replied, and was pleased with the comment about doing a good job, and hung up the phone.

"God this sounds all too bloody dangerous!" The Caretaker said anxiously.

Pete tried to act casual, although not really feeling it and replied; "We will be okay in here and with any luck he will have scarpered by the time the armed squad gets here!"

"Let's hope so." The Caretaker replied looking nervously all around the flat.

It was nearer thirty minutes when there was a loud knock on the door. The Caretaker went to answer it, but first looked through the peephole in the door and identified policemen standing there with guns drawn, hard hats, Kevlar vests and carrying walkie-talkies. He opened the door.

"Mr. Baker?" The Lead Policeman asked.

"That's me!" Pete replied and came forward.

"I am DI Turner the lead for the Mets Armed Response Squad based at Paddington!" DI Turner flashed his ID card and continued; "So where and when did you last see this guy?"

"It was about thirty minutes ago on the fourth floor, but he had been up at 'The Penthouse' before that and he just took off on the fourth floor, coming down when we saw each other!" Pete replied, feeling more relaxed.

"He didn't try to shoot you or anything?"

"No – but I took off from there - not letting him know I had recognised him."

DI Turner grinned and turned to the other six officers and said; "Right lads we will split up. You four," - He pointed at four of the officers and continued – will sweep through the fourth floor and then go up to The Penthouse – Which floor is that?"

"The sixth floor actually!" The Caretaker replied.

DI Turner continued; "How many exits do we have?

"There are three – Front and Back on this ground floor and one by the lifts in the basement!" The Caretaker replied.

"Okay Jones you take the basement. Andrews, you take the back door and I will take the front door and coordinate the operation from there. Everybody! - Stop anybody coming in or trying to leave. Shoot, only after you have given him or her warning, or if they shoot first. Understood?"

The officers all nodded 'Yes' and DI Turner added; "Okay lads – lets go and let's be thorough. Don't forget this guy is armed and dangerous."

They moved away so quickly, like a dust storm they were gone and The Caretaker quickly shut and locked the door and said; "No point in taking any chances. We might as well wait here until they give us the all clear."

"Yeah – Good idea – Thanks." Pete Baker replied and gave a slight shiver.

There was total silence for ten long minutes. The walkie-talkie crackled and a voice came through; "Keene here for squad leader. Over."

The squad leader at the front entrance took the call. "Turner here Keene – What have you got for me? Over."

"We have been through both of the apartments on the fourth-floor sir.

None occupied and no sign of any disturbance. So, we are going up to 'The Penthouse' now. Over."

"Okay Keene. Be careful up there. That is where he was seen to come out of. Over."

There was a five-minute silence. The walkie-talkie crackled again and Keene came over again; "Keene here outside 'The Penthouse' - We have a fatality up here Squad Leader – throat slashed, ear to ear, and blood coming from his back I think! - Not been dead long - still warm. Over."

"Any identification on him Keene? Over."

"Just looking Sir!" Keene replied and after a pause added; "This guy has a New Scotland Yard badge on him. His name is Nigel Worthington. Over."

"Could you repeat that Keene? You said he has a New Scotland Yard badge and his name is Worthington? Over."

"That is affirmative Sir. Over."

"Okay he has been confirmed as the owner of the penthouse Keene. Check his pockets for keys and then go on hold, on alert, outside the apartment. Do not enter the premises yet. – We are now dealing with a crime scene. I will get onto 'The Yard' and get Forensics plus the Coroner's office on the ball. Over and out."

DI Turner got onto the desk Sergeant at New Scotland Yard and explained the situation. At the end, he suggested that the desk Sergeant contacted the Detective in charge of ''The Fox' investigations and explained the witness positive identification of 'The Fox.' He also requested some Wooden Tops to secure the building and the crime scene.

Book 1 in the DI Spearing and DS Devlin series

Chapter 25 - MI5 Conspiracy?

Less than ten minutes after leaving 'The Sandwich Bar' opposite St Pancras station we arrived at Kings Cross Prison in Caledonian Road.

The huge Victorian prison at that time was depressive to me. I suppose as a young man in nineteen sixty-seven there was little appreciation of the wonderful Victorian architecture.

We entered through the main entrance, via two security checks, showing our IDs and eventually Andy and I walked through a gate, followed by a further door, and found ourselves in a reception area. There were prison guards on each of the doors leading into and out of the reception area.

The governor, James Mitchell emerged from one of the doors labelled 'Offices.' He was a distinguished looking guy about fifty, with ruggedly handsome face and black wavy hair going grey at the temples. He wore a classic Savile Row light grey summer suit, white shirt and matching grey tie with highly polished, black, Oxford brogues shoes. He was not tall, a little on the thin side, but he walked straight over and offered his handshake and said; "DI Spearing?"

Andy shook his hand and replied; "Yes Governor." And turning to me added; "And this is DS Devlin." We shook hands and simply nodded to each other.

Governor Mitchell said; "We have arranged for Wilkins and Jones to be brought down separately to the lawyers meeting rooms. As you know, they have been kept separate in solitary, but we have had their MI5 bosses on enquiring if they were here."

Andy looked anxious and asked; "What were they told Governor?"

Governor just smiled and replied; "We had no new admissions last night! That was basically the truth as they were not admitted till this morning."

Andy smiled and replied; "Nice one Governor, Thank you."

"No problem Inspector. - Officer Kavanagh over there will show you through to the lawyers meeting room and I think Wilkins will be brought down first. One thing to bear in mind Inspector! - We are not a high security prison here! Although we can cope with a few nights of solitary confinement we have too many vagrants in here. They get let out one day and after twenty-fours on the piss they intentionally get re-arrested. Treat this place like their private hotel for a few months."

Officer Kavanagh was a giant of a man, dressed in prison uniform without the jacket, wearing a thin brilliantly white shirt and you could see the muscles through the shirt. He came over, and without a word, signalled us to follow him.

The Governor spoke to Kavanagh; "Bring the Inspector and Sergeant back to my office when they have finished Officer - Thanks."

Officer Kavanagh replied; "Yes Governor." He led us off down a maze of corridors to a door labelled 'Lawyers Meeting Room 1 and we entered. There were four wooden chairs around a bare wooden table with a Phillips tape recorder on top and that was the total furnishings. It had the feel of a converted cell.

Officer Kavanagh hesitated and asked; "Do you want guards inside with you Inspector?"

Andy replied; "No, that's all right Officer. DS Devlin here can handle any problems inside. If you position yourselves outside the door we will shout when we are finished with each one.

"Okay, no problem – Just that Wilkins has been giving us some problems and has had to be restrained a couple of times so he will have the handcuffs on."

"Has he been hurt?" Andy asked as a matter of fact as we took the seats facing the entrance door.

"No – well - not that you would see anyway!" Officer Kavanagh smiled and there was a knock on the door. Another two officers came in and stood there with Wilkins between them and the second one prodded Wilkins forwarded and said; ""Wilkins here sir!"

Officer Kavanagh pointed Wilkins to one of the two remaining chairs. Officer Kavanagh then left the room.

Wilkins strolled over and sat down casually, flicking imaginary dust from his clothes with his two handcuffed hands. Wilkins was a surly looking thirty-three-year old with black thinning hair rapidly receding at the temples. He was around five feet ten inches tall with a stocky, strong looking body. He was dressed in the standard grey prisoner's uniform, unshaven, but looking clean.

I took out my notebook and pen and switched on the tape recorder before stating; "This is the recording of an interview with Mr Robert Wilkins in Kings Cross Prison on Friday the twenty-first of July 1967 at one p.m. Present are the aforementioned Robert Wilkins and Detective Inspector Andrew Spearing and Detective Sergeant Kevin Devlin, both from New Scotland Yard." I nodded to Andy.

Andy opened the interview; "I am DI Spearing and this is DS Devlin – I am the officer in charge of this investigation. As you know Mr Wilkins - you have already been charged with kidnapping, GBH and we are investigating your involvement with several murders. We have already
read you your rights. Have you anything to say?"

"Just you get the company solicitor."

"For the record, Mr Wilkins – Which company is that?"

"You damn well know which company Inspector!"

"I think I do know the company, but for the record Mr Wilkins please?"

"I work for MI5 and I want the company lawyer."

"Right that will be arranged after the twenty-four- hour period. However, I would strongly recommend Mr Wilkins that you do not contact them until you are transferred to a high security prison, which we will be arranging for shortly."

"What the hell are you on about now Inspector?" Wilkins asked, sounding irritated, but unsure.

"Well, it is like this Mr Wilkins. We have spoken to your boss, a Mr Robert Lambert, this morning and he now denies that you two were acting with his authority. In other words, he is hanging you two out to dry. Now you two must be extremely dangerous to him with all you know about him. So, he will take swift action as soon as he knows which prison you are in. You, of all of his people, know what that means don't you?"

Wilkins looked alarmed and retorted; "It is not only him involved!" He stopped himself abruptly.

Andy replied; "So there are more bosses involved?"

"I never said that." Wilkins replied appearing to clam up again.

Andy just smiled and said matter of factly; "Okay, look at it this way Mr Wilkins. You and your mate abducted Mr Broadbent from police custody; – we have a witness who saw you two at a telephone box - you took Mr Broadbent at gunpoint and injected him with some type of substance."

Wilkins interjected with; "We didn't know this man was in police custody. MI5 had been hunting for him for two days. He was wanted on a criminal charge for conspiracy involving the government and we found him in a telephone box, no police were involved."

"I can understand that, but I have a couple of problems. You see, MI5 deny you were working for them on this, so they are effectively saying 'conspiracy?' – What conspiracy?" Andy paused for effect before adding; "Then we caught you two red handed torturing our man and not taking him into custody. Now that does not add up, does it?"

Wilkins shifted uneasily in his chair, but said nothing.

Andy continued; "Now my other problem is, we also have a witness to you and Jones delivering a sofa in a huge box to an address in Kensington where we later found a body and a security guard with severe head injuries." Andy paused, watched Wilkins' eyes for reaction and there was a flicker of fear and certainly panic.

Wilkins finally responded with; "I don't know anything about that. You are trying to stitch us up."

Andy just laughed and added; "That old chestnut comes out every time you criminals get into a corner. Is it a stich-up that we found the same van that delivered the sofa with that same box at the address we picked you up?"

Again, Andy paused for effect and he saw the flicker of fear in Wilkins eyes before he added; "And is it a stich up that we found fabrics of clothing and blood in the box which will almost certainly belong to Joseph Bolger, the body we found in Kensington apartments? And is it a stich up that a metal bar containing blood which will, almost certainly, match the security man's blood and head wounds?" Also, is it a stitch up – when we have a witness with you and your mate bundling Mr. Broadbent into the back of that same van in Weybridge?"

Andy stared hard at Wilkins with a look of utter disgust and angrily said; "Do you know the most gruesome thing we found Mr Wilkins? – We found several jars in the room where we picked you up with pickled penises and testicles! – I am betting one of these belongs and will be matched to Joseph Bolger's body. So, Mr Wilkins in addition to the previous charges, regarding Thomas Broadbent, I am now charging you with first degree murder of Joseph Bolger and with assault and battery causing the grievous bodily of a Security Guard at the Kensington Apartments. I must warn you, that you do not have to say anything. However, it may harm your defence if you do not mention when questioned something which you later rely on in court. Anything you do say may be given in evidence. Do you understand? Do you have anything to say?"

The panic in Wilkins eyes was obvious. He now knew he was in a very tight corner with no way out. He then responded with a piece of bravado; "Its bollocks and you know it - the company will never allow it to happen."

"That's what I have trying to get you to understand lad! They cannot afford to allow you to live man! You are in for life or more and they cannot afford for you to talk, so they will get to you as soon as they know where you are. You know Robert Lambert better than us – Do you really think he will allow you to live?"

"Okay! Okay! – I will wait until tomorrow to get into the top security prison then I will contact the company lawyer. Which prison will it be?" Wilkins sounded afraid.

"It will probably be Parkhurst." Andy replied curtly.

"Parkhurst on the Isle of Wight? My wife and kids will not be able to visit me?"

"You have a wife and kids?" Andy asked sounding concerned.

"Yeah! Of course I have. Why?"

"I didn't think you would need an explanation. Your wife and kids are in danger. You know how Lambert operates – get to you through them! What is your home number and address? We will run a check."

"012228530. the address is 516 Eynsham Drive, Abbey Wood" Wilkins replied without hesitation but with some alarm.

Andy turned to me and asked; "Sergeant! - Can you see Kavanagh and make a call - and enquire if they are alright?"

"Yes sir!" I replied turning away and then turned back and asked; "Sir - Do you want me to send in the guard?"

"No, that's alright Sergeant. I don't think even Mr Wilkins is that stupid to try to escape from here?" Andy replied with a smile and Wilkins simply scowled.

I found Kavanagh who led me to an office phone with an outside line.

I dialled Wilkins' number and got an answer from a male with very low guttural voice, an obvious attempt to disguise his true voice; "Who is calling?"

"I wish to talk to Mrs Wilkins." I replied quietly, trying to catch any background noise or chatter.

"I asked who is calling, not who do you want to speak to!" The guttural voice angrily replied.

"I am calling on behalf of Mr Wilkins to see that his wife and children are okay?" I replied coolly.

"Just tell him 'we' have them. He will know." The guttural voice replied with a threatening tone.

"Who are 'we'?" I asked trying to stay cool, but the guttural voice just hung up the 'phone..

I dialled straight back to the same number and on the third ring the guttural voice again replied; "What do you want now?"

I swiftly and angrily replied; "I have to know that they are alive- Let me speak to them."

"Fuck off – just tell Wilkins we have them!" The guttural voice replied and again hung up.

I immediately dialled NSY and, having identified myself, got the duty sergeant to send armed police in a squad car round to 516 Eynsham Drive to check out a possible kidnapping, or holding Mrs Wilkins and the children against their will. I asked the Sergeant to ring me back on my walkie-talkie. I then headed back to the interview room.

I knocked on the door and put my head inside and asked; "Can I have a word out here Sir?"

"You certainly can Sergeant." Andy replied, rising, quickly coming out the door, and closing it behind him.

"What's up Doc?" Andy asked with a smile mimicking Walt Disney's Bugs Bunny.

I smiled and quietly answered; "MI5 have got the wife and kids. They told me just to tell him and then hung up. I have got armed police in a squad car on the way to his home address, but I doubt if they will be there. Shall we tell him?"

"No alternative I am afraid Sergeant. He will either open up to us or clamp up. Anyway, we are getting nowhere as it stands, so we have nothing to lose. Let's get on with it" Andy replied and quickly re-entered the interview room.

Wilkins immediately looked up with fear in his eyes and asked; "What is happening?"

Andy replied curtly; "It appears that your colleagues have swiped your wife and kids and told us to tell you they have them. We have a squad car on the way to your home."

Wilkins put his handcuffed hands to his face and mumbled; "I knew it!" and suddenly added; "They won't be there you know! They will be using a forward call. What are you going to do about it now Spearing?"

"As I say Wilkins - We have a squad car on the way, but if they are not there then it is more like what are you going to do about it Wilkins?"

"What the hell do you mean? What can I do about it?" Wilkins was beginning to sound hysterical.

"You know who 'They' are Wilkins. If you state who 'They' are we can arrest them and your problem disappears."

"You know they would be out in five minutes. They have already denied they had anything to do with this for Christ sake and dumped us with the blame. We are just criminals who have been caught and they will say we are making it up to get a lighter sentence. Then off they will go."

Andy replied drily; "Well at least your family might stand a chance."

Wilkins retorted with; "That's the whole point of letting me know they have them. The message is if I open my mouth they are dead."

"Well, it is up to you Wilkins, but probably, like you, they will be killed and you are letting them away with it!"

"If I keep my mouth shut at least they will have a chance."

"If I were a gambling man Wilkins I would say the odds are stacked against your family, or you, coming out of this alive."

"I thought you said I would be put in a top security prison?" Wilkins was alarmed.

"Oh, you will be - in Parkhurst Wilkins, but you know that is no guarantee. You and I both know that MI5 can get anyone in and out of prison, so it is only a matter of time before they nail you."

"Well thanks a bunch."

Andy just smiled and replied; "No need to thank me Wilkins. It is only you your family have to thank for getting them into this mess."

Wilkins stood up and made to walk out of the room and said; "I've had enough of this shit. I want to go back to my cell."

I moved over and blocked his path.

Andy raised his voice slightly and said; "You will leave when I say you can leave Wilkins and not before." Andy paused for effect, before adding; "One last point Wilkins! Suppose Jones turns 'Queen's evidence' – Where does that leave you Wilkins – have you thought about that?"

Wilkins eyes betrayed fright and emotion before he replied again with some bravado; "He wouldn't dare."

"According to my colleagues, Jones is ready to talk. I think my colleagues are a bit more reliable than your lot Wilkins. Don't you think? Still – it is up to you, but I would not like to be left holding the baby for this lot and then letting off the guys who kill your family and then will kill you!"

"It is chance I have to take!" Wilkins replied quietly and almost weakly.

"That is quite a gamble Wilkins and the odds are stacked against you!" Andy replied with some sorrow in his voice.

"I don't see what else I can do Spearing!"

"You can stand up and be a man for once in your shitty life and try to at least save your family!" Andy replied with venom.

"As I see it Spearing that's what I am trying to do!"

"I only hope your family see it that way when you are all pushing up the daisies lad! On your way now lad. I do hope it works out for them, but believe me there is not a snowball's chance in hell."

Wilkins got up and walked out slowly and almost reluctantly thinking about what had just been said. I opened the door for him and closed it behind him. I walked over and spoke into the microphone and said; "Interview with Robert Wilkins concluded at 13-30 Hours." I switched off the recorder.

"Kevin - let Kavanagh know we are ready for Jones, but make sure they don't meet each other on the road. And Kevin – I want you to handle this interview – I will act bad copper and you be good copper. Okay?"

"Yes Andy." I replied, taken aback by the sudden proposal and added; "You know, we have to get one of them to break sir? We cannot use 'The Fox' as a witness, even if we knew how to find him!"

"That's for sure Kevin. That is why I thought your psychology degree would come in handy. I got nowhere with Wilkins so we have to try something different!"

I replied swiftly; "Well Andy if you cannot break Wilkins I hope you are not expecting too much with Jones."

"We can only try our best Kevin, but we have got them cold on one major charge!"

I went out and let Kavanagh know the position.

Fifteen minutes later Jones came into the room. He was a small wiry guy about five feet six inches in his mid-thirties, jet black hair swept back in an old fashioned 'teddy boy' style and with a smirk on his face.

I walked over and switched on the tape recorder and spoke into the microphone; "This is the recording of an interview with Mr Michael Jones in Kings Cross Prison on Friday the twenty-first of July 1967 at 13-45 hours. Present are the aforementioned Michael Jones and Detective Inspector Andrew Spearing and Detective Sergeant Kevin Devlin, both from New Scotland Yard."

"Do you find this funny Jones?" I asked with a hint of anger in my voice, again taking out my notepad and pen.

"It won't be funny for you lot when 'The Firm' find out about this!" Jones replied..

I just stared hard at him and shook my head before asking; "Ah yes – 'The Firm' - Are you really as thick as you sound Jones?"

"What the hell are you on about now?" Jones asked still smirking.

"I am DS Devlin and this is DI Spearing who is in charge of this case. We are from New Scotland Yard."

"Good for you two, but why NSY are involved in an MI5 case is beyond me"

"We are not involved in an MI5 case Jones. In fact, as you know, we had arranged for you and a Robert Wilkins to be arrested for the abduction and causing grievous bodily harm to one Thomas Broadbent."

Jones face was again holding a smirk as he replied; "The guy was wanted by MI5 and was involved in a conspiracy against the UK!"

I thinly smiled and replied; "As we were telling your mate Robert Wilkins. The thing is, your boss, Mr. Robert Lambert flatly denies that you were working for 'The Firm,' on this, or on the other murders. So, in other words he is hanging you both out to dry."

Jones turned a whiter shade of pale as the words sank in and he meekly replied; "What other murders?"

I again gave him one of my now infamous hard man stares for one full minute and replied; "Oh didn't we tell you? We have a witness who saw Wilkins and you take a huge box marked 'Sofas' into a Kensington Apartments in London and a short time later we went in there and found the mutilated body of one Joseph Bolger. We also have another witness who saw you and Wilkins with the same Joseph Bolger the last time he was seen alive. Then of course when we arrested you two yesterday we found that same sofa box in the van you were driving and we also found fibres of materials and blood which match up to Joe Bolger's underpants and blood. Not to mention we found an iron bar in the same van which matches the design of the bar you, or Wilkins, used to hit a security guard on the head and the blood matches his blood. The guard is in a coma and is critically ill in hospital and may not survive. So, you two are probably in for at least three life sentences and your bosses are walking away scot free. So, Jones are you really that thick?"

Jones now looked agitated, the smirk was gone and he replied; "I aint taking the fall for anybody that's for sure!"

I quickly interjected and said; "Before you say anything further Mr Jones. In addition to the previous charges, regarding Thomas Broadbent, I am now also charging you with first degree murder of Joseph Bolger and with assault and battery causing the grievous bodily of a Security Guard at the Kensington Apartments. I must warn you that you do not have to say anything. However, it may harm your defence if you do not mention when questioned something which you later rely on in court. Anything you do say may be given in evidence. Do you understand? Do you have anything to say?"

Jones was shaking his head violently silently saying 'no' and suddenly replied; "I have plenty to say, but I want a deal!"

I looked at Andy who smiled and shook his head to indicate 'Yes' and I turned back to Jones before quietly saying; "These are such serious charges Jones, the only deal we can offer you is if you go to 'Queens Evidence.' We will have words with the judge and ensure you get the lightest sentence possible of the lot. How does that sound?"

"If that's what it takes I will do it! I ain't letting them away with dumping it all on me!"

I took a little time before saying; "Okay here is what we will do. We will get you to write out a statement in your own hand writing and sign it. Please ensure you include all the things that happened in Yiewsley within the Falling Lane house and all the people involved, including your bosses. We have fingerprints, blood samples and even penises with testicles. So, we can trace most people who have been held and tortured or killed there!" I knew I was pushing the facts and added; "We will then have it typed up and witnessed!"

Jones looked aghast, probably realizing for the first time that he faced the rest of his life in prison, and muttered; "I aint taking the blame for all of this – I was only doing what I was told."

I replied quietly but firmly: "Yeah that's what the Nazis said after the war! I will get a pen and paper." I left the room and got Kavanagh to find the paper and pen and asked him to get a camera and come in and act as a witness.

I re-entered the room with Kavanagh in tow and said; "Jones this is Officer Kavanagh who is going to act as a witness that your statement was made freely and without duress. He will take a photograph to show you signing the paper without duress. Do you understand?"

"Yes, I fuckin understand. I am not some imbecile."

I recognised the slight change in attitude and decided to ease off and said; "I didn't the law?"

"Yeah right!" Jones replied sullenly.

I passed Jones the A4 sheets of blank paper and pen. He almost immediately started to write, it was as though he was writing fast before he changed his mind. Within fifteen minutes he had written two sheets of paper and he signed his name as Officer Kavanagh took a photo on a Polaroid

I took the two sheets of paper and did a speed read of the statements. I noted he had admitted working for MI5 on six cases in which people had been tortured for information and apparently disappeared or died, including Joe Bolger and Thomas Broadbent. He stated that his boss was Robert Lambert and he had been working under his direct orders, but there was no mention of any other bosses being involved.

I took out my notebook with pen and asked, without much hope of an answer; "We know about Broadbent, who is now in our custody, but can you state in writing what happened to the other five?"

Jones looked hard at me but surprised me by replying; "Yeah, well unfortunately the other five became ill during interrogation and were taken away!"

"Dead or alive?" I asked as a matter of fact.

"Alive when they left us!" Jones replied without hesitation.

I was taken aback for a second with the lies, before replying with a question; "Well that was not the case with Joseph Bolger – now was it Mister Jones? After all he had been dead for several hours before you and Wilkins were seen by our witness dumping the body?"

Jones just nodded matter of fact and replied; "Yeah well Bolger was the exception. – We had left him alive with our boss Lambert and then we got a call that he was dead and we were to dump him in those Kensington Apartments!"

It was obvious Jones was lying, but at least he was admitting to having been involved in the torture, so I decided to hit hard; "It is no wonder he was dead after you two were finished with him. You know even hardened coppers and the coroners were sickened by the sight of Bolger's body? – You know that?"

Jones amazingly just grinned before replying; "Yeah well Bolger was a difficult one! He hung out for a long time and he gave us very little information!"

I just nodded and knew I had an amazed look on my face and I almost stammered with my next question; "So - So - with – with - the exception of Broadbent did all five finish up dead?"

Jones pretended to think before replying; "Don't know, but I think so because they never re-appeared!" He then laughed and made a joke; "I guess none of them were Jesus Christ!"

I shook my head in disbelief before asking; "Did you dispose of the other bodies?"

Jones just shook his head and replied: "Nope! That would be another department's job!"

I shook my head and asked louder than intended; "You really expect us to believe that your Mr. Lambert would involve others who were not involved in these cases of murder?"

Jones again just shook his head and with a thin smile replied; "I cannot comment on what you may or may not believe! I can only state how it was!"

I was again astounded but managed to ask; "Can you add a postscript to your statement and record what happened to all six, including your torture of them? Then sign at the end of the postscript"

Jones looked smug, obviously not realising he was implicating himself enough to get several life sentences as he wrote down the details and signed the postscript. He then handed over the statement as he replied "Sure! - No problem with that. – You do realise these people were all involved in crimes against the state and were wanted by MI5?"

I just smiled as I took the statement and replied with a grin; "You do realise 'Mister' Jones – MI5 have disclaimed anything to do with any of this, therefore, they are saying there were no cases against these people and you and Wilkins were acting as rogue agents?"

Jones sounded agitated but with a certain amount of bravado replied; "Yeah, well we will see about that now – won't we?"

I laughed a little and replied; "Yeah – We sure will 'Mister' Jones!"

I passed the statement to Officer Kavanagh and asked; "Can you sign as witness Officer Kavanagh? Also add that this statement was given freely without coerce? I then added: "And DI Spearing – Can you do the same?"

"Certainly" Both Kavanagh and Andy replied together and signed the statement. Kavanagh handed me the Polaroid photo and I placed the signed statement and the photo in an A4 envelope.

I tried one last time to get one of the other MI5 bosses involved when I asked; "So Mister Jones
- who was Robert Lambert's boss?"

Jones looked amused, but coyly replied; "That is Sir John Dawson. But he was never involved in any of that stuff"

I just nodded my head again as I wrote down the name in my notebook and replied; "You mean he was never seen to be involved! Surely Robert Lambert could not carry that off on his own?"

Jones just laughed and replied; "Don't know about that, but he was never seen around when any of these guys copped it – excuse the pun."

I took the statement and the photo and filed both in my inside jacket pocket.

I had enough of Jones the psycho and reacted quite badly and gruffly said; "Right Jones on your way. I hope they throw the key away! - Officer Kavanagh - Can you get this piece of shit taken back to his toilet?"

Jones just smiled and then asked; "Can I see the company lawyer?"

I replied; "Like we advised your friend Wilkins. Your Mr. Lambert is searching every prison for you two and on the basis that, you are the only ones who can implicate him in these murders, we are certain that he will make arrangements to take you out of the equation in prison! So, we are strongly suggesting to you both that you wait till we can get you into a high security prison. It is up to you, but I would say, while you are here in this prison, your life is in danger."

"What high security prison are you sending me to?"

I smiled ever so slightly as I replied; "Broadmoor!"

Jones looked a bit shocked as he mumbled his reply; "Broadmoor? But that is a Nutters' hospital."

I kept on my smiling face and replied; "Actually, it is a Psychiatric Hospital for the criminally insane which is the ideal place for you!" I turned to Kavanagh and added; "Officer Kavanagh, like I asked before, get someone to take this piece of shit back to his toilet."

I spoke into the microphone; "Interview with Michael Jones concluded at 14-15 hours. I turned the tape recorder off.

Officer Kavanagh took Jones by the arm and led him away closing the room door behind him.

"Well Sergeant – If that was you playing 'good copper' – I would hate to see you playing 'bad copper,' Andy laughed, and slapped my shoulder in a friendly way before adding; "Well done Sergeant – You were brilliant!"

I felt like a million dollars and mumbled my reply; "Thanks sir." I suddenly remembered the tape from the tape recorder and pocketed it.

My walkie-talkie started to ring and I promptly answered; "DS Devlin here! Over."

"This is Duty Sergeant Biddle here at New Scotland Yard Sergeant. Just to let you know – We have been to Wilkin's home and there is no sign of his wife or kids. However, DCI Flash Harry wants an urgent word with DI Spearing – He cannot get through to his walkie-talkie. Over."

I pulled a disappointed face with a grimace and nodded towards Andy before replying; "Okay Sergeant – We didn't expect his wife or kids would be there. The battery was flat on DI Spearings walkie-talkie! Put Flash Harry through on this one Sergeant. Over."

My walkie-talkie crackled and finally I heard Flash Harrys' doleful tones shout; "DI Spearing are you there? Over."

I handed my walkie-talkie Andy who gave an equally good face grimace as he replied; "Yes DCI – What can I do for you?"

"Where the hell are you Spearing? And why are not answering your walkie-talkie? Over."

"I am at Kings Cross Prison DCI (He was now making a point of not saying 'sir') where I have just charged two people with murder and grievous bodily harm. My walkie-talkie is not picking up a signal as usual and it turns out the battery is flat. Where are you DCI? Over" Andy replied sarcastically with a wink at me.

"Oh." Flash Harry replied, obviously taken aback by Andys response before pulling himself together and adding irritably; "What the hell has where I am got to do with it? Now for your information your target man 'The Fox' has been in action again. Except this time, he has taken out one of ours. Over."

Andy sounded concerned as he asked; "One of ours – a policeman? That is not the MO of 'The Fox.' Over." Andy replied with a thin smile and another wink towards me. I understood his laughing at his use of MO again, only a few days ago he did not know the meaning of 'MO.'

Flash Harry again sounded irritated when he replied; "Whatever, but the facts are, we have a witness who has positively identified 'The Fox' as in the building where our man has turned up dead with his throat slit from ear to ear. Just like John Palmer's minder. So, you need to get your asses over
there and take over the case. Over."

Andy just smiled and for the third time winked in my direction and then said; "Excuse me DCI, but London is a very big place! - It would help if you could tell me the address where this body is lying? Over."

Flash Harry sounded exasperated as he replied; "Oh shit! Let me find it." There was a rustle of papers being moved around his desk and then he came back on the line and said; "It is The Penthouse Suite,' Grosvenor House, Kensington High Street, London W14!"

Andy responded with a laugh; "I thought 'flashy' addresses were more your scene DCI?"

Flash Harry sounded as though he was about to blow a gasket when he replied; "Don't give me any more of your lip Spearing. Just get there now! Over and out."

Andy spoke into the dead line and said; "I certainly would not give my lips to you - you moron." He turned back to me and handed me the walkie-talkie just as Officer Kavanagh returned to the room.

Andy turned to Kavanagh and said; "Ah Officer Kavanagh! We have got to get over urgently to Kensington to cover a murder scene. Can you escort us quickly to the Governor's office to finish our business here? Oh, and thank you for your help today."

Officer Kavanagh smiled and replied; "Certainly sir. No problem. - If you would follow me this way." He took the lead and showed us back through the maze of corridors with two feet thick plastered walls which were painted white. We reached a door marked with gold letters as 'The Governor's Office.'

Andy turned to Officer Kavanagh before entering the room and said; "Once again thanks for your help Officer. I wonder if I could ask one last favour of you? We must rush off on this Kensington murder case. Just to let Wilkins know that his wife and kids have been taken and, we at Scotland Yard, are doing all we can to track them down. If he now wants to give us the information we have requested, perhaps you could ring me on the number on this card?" Andy passed Kavanagh a card and added; "I don't hold out much hope he will give us the information, but we can but try."

"Certainly sir." Officer Kavanagh replied and turned away.

We walked into a surprisingly large spacious outer office. The office was furnished with two very modern white pedestal desks. Behind one sat a very prim and proper, but good looking thirty- ish year old lady with a nameplate on the desk which stated; 'Sheila Watson – Secretary.'

There was a single in and out green tray with one piece of A4 paper in it. A white – unusual for the time - telephone was to the right-hand side of the desk.

The other, equally white desk had the three -rawer pedestal to the left and had another desk surface running at right angles with a three drawer pedestals underneath. On top of this desk there was, what looked like a brand-new IBM Selectric typewriter, another white telephone with a copy of the green in and out tray and a Phillips tape recorder, probably used for dictation.

Along one full wall was twelve three-drawer filing cabinets, the tops were all white and there stood a few flower pots. The front of the drawers were very sixties, all the top drawers were painted white, the middle all grey and the bottom drawers all bright yellow.

The chairs were all white basket bucket chairs with bright yellow seats matching the bottom drawers. Each cabinet was fitted with a large padlock.

The walls were covered with paintings of open country scenes containing green, yellow and white colours. The floor was covered with a fitted, thick, bottle green luxurious carpet.

All in it was a surprisingly modern nineteen-sixties designed office full of nice little touches and wonderfully colourful.

"Go right on in gentlemen. He is expecting you!" Sheila said with a rather sexy voice and she pointed to the solid oak panel with a cut out viewing panel which was closed.

We entered the office and yet another surprise. It was huge, painted in pure dazzling white with panoramic viewing windows looking down onto what I thought must be an exercise yard. The Governor sat in a luxurious bottle green leather bucket seat with matching green leather armrests behind a double pedestal pure mahogany desk.

The floor was covered with the same fitted, thick, bottle green luxurious carpet as in the outer office.

The desk had the same single in and out green tray with again one A4 piece of paper and another white telephone, but this time there was also a red phone. It looked like the office rules were, to have at least one piece of paper - just to show you had something to do. There were three bucket chairs matching the seats in the secretary's office, all facing The Governors chair.

The Governor rose from his seat and pointed to the chairs in front of him and said with a smile; "Please be seated gentlemen. How did it go with the pair of them?"

Andy replied; "Thank you Governor. – DS Devlin here got a good statement from Jones confirming guilt to the abduction and torture of Thomas Broadbent and to dumping the body of Joe Bolger last night. Also, he put his hands up to the grievous bodily harm of the security guard. Although he has not admitted to murder, I think we may have enough to make the murder rap stick."

The Governor smiled and asked; "And what about Wilkins?"

Andy shook his head negatively before replying; "Wilkins is a different fish altogether. One of the old school! He thinks if he keeps his mouth shut they will treat him good. We have warned him - and he of all people should know – he will get done in prison. Already they have taken his wife and kids as a warning, so he aint saying nought for now."

The Governor shook his head and asked; "So what is the plan now?"

"I am hoping events will persuade Wilkins to join Jones in going Queens Evidence, but we have a problem Governor! We have just got called out to a murder scene in Kensington. I am afraid we must ask you for another favour. Can you arrange for Wilkins to be transferred to Parkhurst and Jones to Broadmoor, if possible, within the next twenty-four hours?"

"Well yes DI – But it obviously depends on their capacity." The Governor replied with a nod of the head.

"Yeah, but let's make sure they are aware that lives are in danger and they must be in a high security prison. If necessary, we will involve the Home Secretary, and let them know that Governor."

The Governor smiled and stood up and offered his handshake before replying; "I understand DI and I will get straight onto it as soon as you leave. Nice to have met you and you DS Devlin."

I simply nodded and smiled.

Andy accepted the handshake and replied; "Thank you so much for your help Governor." Andy spoke sincerely and paused to take out a card before adding; "If there are any problems Governor please give me a ring on the number on the card."

"Will do." The Governor replied with a smile as Andy and I hurried out of the office to be met by Officer Kavanagh who led us through to the exit.

As Andy and I walked towards the Jag I felt I had to say something and said; "Even with the Jones confession sir, I doubt if we have enough to nail Lambert – not with his prior denial of any involvement."

Andy look to be faraway in thought and very melancholy as he replied; "Tell me about it Sergeant! Still there is more than one way to skin a cat."

I decided to stay quiet on the journey across inner London to Kensington unless Andy opened a conversation. There was no conversation as Andy nodded sleepily.

Chapter 26 - Payback Time

Due to heavy traffic, it still took us thirty minutes to get across inner London from Kings Cross Prison to Kensington, despite going with the 'blues and twos' on the Jag which was a first for me in London.

We arrived outside the reception area at the Grosvenor House Apartments, Kensington High Street, London W14 and found a wooden top sergeant on the front steps. Behind him there was the usual blue and white police crime scene tape strung across the doorway with the message 'Police Do Not Cross' in blue letters repeatedly printed along the length.

Andy got out and walked briskly up the front steps in front of me and with a simple nod to the Sergeant he ducked under the tape quickly followed by me.

We walked in and came face to face with a man who had 'Police' in white bold letters emblazoned across a blue police Kevlar bullet proof vest and he was holding a Sterling Mark 6 semi-automatic gun which was pointing straight at us.

He was around six feet with a weight lifters physique. He had on, what looked like, size twelve rubber soled boots with black trousers and black polo necked sweater.

He nodded and smiled and said; "DI Spearing I presume?"

Andy nodded and replied; "Aye, well it aint David Livingstone – that's for sure. Who are you? – Henry Stanley?"

"Yeah - very good sir." The guy gave a nervous laugh sounding unsure of himself before adding; "No I am afraid I am only Squad Leader Turner from the Armed Response Squad based at Paddington sir!"

Andy laughed and said; "Yes, I am pleased we got over that misunderstanding. By the way I am only a DI too so no need for the sir! Anyway, what have we got here Turner?"

"Murder victim on the sixth floor – 'The Penthouse' throat slit ear to ear. We have a witness who claims he saw a man who fits the description of 'The Fox' coming from the sixth floor – The witness seems okay - sensible like - so he may be right."

"Where is this witness?" Andy asked nonchalantly.

"In the caretaker's room – locked himself in there when he realised it was 'The Fox.'

Andy replied with a ruthful smile; "Sounds like he had the right idea. – A little scared, was he?"

Turner the squad leader replied; "Just a little – wants to be a copper!"

Andy laughed and replied; "Ah that explains it! I will talk to him later – make sure he doesn't leave till I speak to him. We will go up to 'The Penthouse' now. How did you identify the victim?"

Turner replied with a smile; "He had his wallet in his back trousers pocket, so we picked it carefully without smudging any prints."

"Yeah – okay" Andy replied ruefully and suddenly asked; – Has forensics arrived yet?"

"Just a couple of minutes in front of you sir! - A Doctor Harvey and his assistant, a David Arkwright, plus Joe Lacy a photographer.

"Doctor Harvey? The gang leader! It makes a change them being here before us. Thanks DI we will make our way up – are the lifts working?"

"Yeah! – A bit rickety, but it eventually gets you there." Squad Leader Turner replied with a laugh.

Andy suddenly stopped and turned back to DI Turner and asked; "Look

Turner – Could you get on to the Yard and speak to DCI Tomlinson? Ask him to get us some more wooden tops down here. We need them to go door knocking and doing interviews on anyone seeing anything. Use my name - Okay?"

Turner smiled and replied; "Yes sir – no problem!"

We entered the ancient rickety lift. As we emerged on 'The Penthouse' floor, surprisingly we found the corridors covered with wooden 'Parquet' flooring. Usually in hotels and apartments the corridors were always carpeted to keep the noise down for residents in the night. To our right we saw Doctor Harvey, the forensics expert, was kneeling over the victim who was around six feet and lay face down in a pool of what must be his own blood. Doctor Harvey was attempting to turn him onto his back and then David Arkwright knelt-down the other side and helped to ease him onto his back.

Both David Arkwright and I gave an involuntary gasp as we stared at the white and deathly grey mask of what had once been Nigel 'hooray Henry' Worthington.

Andy looked more closely and asked; "Is that your 'hooray Henry' from the Chief's introductions the other day?"

I was still taken aback, and I replied quietly; "Afraid so sir." It was all I could say before adding; "At least he got a quick one!"

Doctor Harvey looked up and acknowledged Andy with a nod before with a ruthful smile saying; "Yes! - DS that's for sure. The killer knew exactly what he was doing. Slit the poor sod's throat from ear to ear and then, before he fell, a knife in the back. He knew exactly where to stab him in the back to reach the heart, so he is an experienced killer!"

Andy and I looked at each other and automatically understood the implications, without saying a word, before Andy turned back to Doctor Harvey and asked; "Has he been dead long Doctor Harvey?"

Doctor Harvey shook his head and replied; "The coroner's department will be more accurate, but I would say no more than two hours or so! – I hear he is one of ours DI?"

Andy was looking grimmer by the minute "Yes a recent recruit – One of the 'Trained Brains' we all met with the Chief on Monday – you remember?"

Doctor Harvey nodded and replied; "Oh yes – now I recognise him. As I recall the 'hooray Henry' – the one who was full of self-importance!"

Andy smiled and replied; "Yes that's the one. Not very important now I am afraid! 'Hooray Henry' and our Glaswegian DS here really sparked from the outset!"

I ignored Andys remarks and started looking around. I noticed the bare marble stairwell which was just before the spot that Nigel Worthington had been attacked. I went over and inspected the wall. There was nothing visible to see but there were some scuffed dirt marks on the two top stairs which suggested someone had been standing there waiting on someone. I looked back at the body, which was only a few yards away – Worthington had obviously been walking towards the lifts when he had been expertly attacked from behind.

I re-joined the party looking down at 'Hooray Henry' as Doctor Harvey moved the body on to its side.

Doctor Harvey smiled, and from his pocket, produced a set of keys and handed them to Andy and quietly said; "These are the keys to The Penthouse. One of the squad took them from the victim to check out 'The Penthouse. 'If you want to, go ahead and have a look inside, but please don't disturb anything!"

Andy smiled and ruefully replied; "I leave disturbances to Forensics every time. You lot always do a good job with that!"

Doctor Harvey looked furious, so I quickly intercepted with a smile and said; "Doctor Harvey – I suggest you look around the top steps in the stairwell and the walls. It looks like our attacker was waiting around there and took our victim from behind as he was heading for the lifts!"

Doctor Harvey looked quizzically at me and then at Andy, but said nothing.

Andy laughed and looking at Doctor Harvey said; "Our DS Devlin studied 'criminology' at Cambridge – don't you know Doctor Harvey?"

Doctor Harvey laughed and sarcastically replied; "Well thanks DS Devlin – It is always good when we have modern techniques being used by 'some' of our detectives." He stared with a blank expression on his face directly towards Andy.

Andy only laughed and replied; "Always happy to help our forensics department on any scene Doctor Harvey!"

I then decided to add a little afterthought; "Our attacker may have been wearing soft soled shoes? Otherwise Nigel here would have heard him coming on these Parquet flooring tiles?

Doctor Harvey nodded; "Good point Sergeant – We will do a scan on the steps and the floor!"

I then decided to go for broke and added; "Besides being a pro, this guy must have been at least six feet plus! He had to be to reach from behind and slit Nigel's throat from ear to ear!"

Doctor Harvey looked quizzically at both Andy and I before replying with a grin; "Can't argue with that Holmes – me - I am only a forensic man!"

Andy and I quickly moved away towards 'The Penthouse' entrance door. We were suddenly met by DS Keene another six-foot young twenty-year old policeman dressed exactly as per Squad Leader Turner, right down to the Sterling Mark 6 semi-automatic gun which was again pointing straight at us.

Andy smiled and pointing to the gun said; "Turn that thing away from us – there's a good lad!"

Keene awkwardly pointed the gun downwards towards the floor and said; "Afraid we have not checked the apartment out yet sir. We were put on hold. We did not want to disturb anything before you lot got here, so we don't know if the killer is still inside."

Andy smiled condescendingly and replied; "I think any self-respecting professional killer would be long gone by now lad – What do you think?"

The young policeman looked unsure, but suddenly smiled and replied; "I guess you are right sir."

Andy laughed again and said; "I'll tell you what lad! – Just in case! – You go in first with that gun out front, but don't fire it unless you have to – Okay?"

Keene nodded with enthusiasm and replied; "Good idea sir. Let's go!" He tried to open the solid oak door and when it did not budge he belted it with his shoulder, grimacing with pain, before aiming the gun at the lock apparently about to fire.

Andy looked at him quizzically and held out the key before saying; "Perhaps it is best to open it with the key lad. What do you think?"

To give Keene some credit he laughed at himself before replying, tongue in cheek; "That's not a bad idea sir." He unlocked the door and did an exaggerated body roll into the front room, which turned out to be the lounge, pointing his gun in several directions.

Andy and I just coolly walked in and Andy, with a straight face, said; "Yes it looks all clear lad – Go check the other rooms. – Sergeant, I think we ought to put on gloves for this. We both need to poke around in here!" We both put on our disposable rubber gloves.

Keene bounded off, gun at the ready and went straight into the main bedroom which was straight off the lounge.

Andy and I began to look around the lounge. I spotted a whip lying on the seat of a Chesterfield green leather chair. There were dark brown marks on the tails. I pointed out the whip to Andy and said; "Looks like blood on the whip tails sir?"

Andy nodded and looked closely at the carpet before saying; "Yeah and I think there are droplets of blood all over the carpet in a circle. Don't know if you noticed that pool of blood as we came in the door – that may have been where our witness saw our 'hooray' Henry smacking a young lad the other day!"

I nodded and replied; "Yeah." Then I noticed the dog lead and collar on the solid oak table. I went over and saw the same dark brown spots, obviously more blood on the collar and added; "By the look of the whip and this dog collar – I would say there has been some kinky sex going on in here sir!"

Andy smiled grimly and replied; "Not that I know anything about kinky sex, but yeah – it looks like it our 'hooray' Henry has some very odd games – I am willing to bet there are other sex toys in the bedroom."

Keene came through from the other rooms looking subdued and simply said; "All clear sir – except for, as you say, some of those disgusting sex toys and things in the main bedroom. I will be outside the door sir - if you need me just yell."

Andy raised his eyebrows and replied; "Yeah right lad and thanks for your help. Let's go through to the main bedroom Sergeant."

We entered the main bedroom and found a super King Size bed surrounded by mirrors on every wall and on the ceiling. The bed was covered in the finest white silk sheets on which there were an abundance of brownish marks – again, by the look of it, dried blood.

There was a pair of opened handcuffs attached to the headboard. At the bottom of the bed there was a pair of small red, silk, boxer shorts and a huge, hard, rubber, imitation penis again with dark brown marks. I gingerly lifted the penis and put it up to my nose.

I screwed up my face and in disgust said; "Shit!"

Andy just laughed and replied; "Two guys in a bed – What do you expect it to smell like Sergeant?"

I put the thing down before replying; "There is blood on the thing as well!"

Andy wandered over to the bedside cabinet on the left and opened the top drawer. He pulled out a huge bundle of fifty pound notes and put them on top of the cabinet. He then went into the middle, followed by the lower drawers and produced another two-huge bundle of notes which he stacked on top of the others.

Andy raised his eyebrows; turned slowly to me and quietly said; "This looks like the fifty grand Mrs Palmer paid to our 'hooray' Henry for that blackmail we heard about." He looked thoughtful before adding; "You know Sergeant, this is untraceable loot! Our 'hooray Henry' cannot claim it now - he is dead, and neither can Mrs Palmer, unless she implicates herself!"

I didn't know how to respond – Was this a test? Or was Andy suggesting we pocket the money? I decided to play safe when I replied; "If it was 'The Fox' who carried out this assassination sir, then this puts Mrs Palmer right back in the centre of the picture for her husband's murder and taking out Worthington?"

Andy responded; "Yeah it sure looks that way Sergeant, but that assumes 'The Fox' was responsible. But - like we said earlier - this assassination of a so called 'policeman' - does not match his 'MO' – does it?"

I looked hard at Andy and shook my head before replying; "That's true sir, but we have to remember we have a witness who, by the sound of it, is very positive it was The Fox."

Andy quickly retorted; "It could be all he is saying is this guy fits the description of 'The Fox' as put out by Flash Harry yesterday."

I immediately saw where he was coming from and replied; "So you are thinking this is a copycat killing?"

"Well it is a possibility, but the only lead we have now is the link between Mrs Palmer and 'The Fox.' Anyway, could you find a box or a carrier bag around the place and count this money into it Sergeant? Also, if you find any bills, bank statements and any videos with that machine in the sitting room, stuff them on top."

I wandered off into the kitchen opened a few drawers and eventually found an extra-large Harrods carrier bag. I headed back into the main bedroom where Andy was still sniffing around and started counting the money from the top of the bedside cabinet placing it into the carrier bag. The money was bundled with elastic bands in one thousand pound batches and there were forty-five bundles.

I shouted across the room to Andy who was now in the main bedrooms en-suite and said; "There is forty-five thousand pounds in that lot sir!"

Andy shouted back; "That's five-grand missing according to our information." as he re-entered the main bedroom

I unconsciously nodded and retorted; "Yeah – Do you think he has blown five grand already?"

"Nothing would surprise me with his lot!" Andy replied with a shake of his head before adding; "There are cotton wool balls with blood and some sort of ointment in the bathroom bin Sergeant. Take a note to make sure Doctor Harvey picks them up and bags them with the other kinky gear!"

I replied; "Yes sir." I took out my notebook and pen before adding; "Do you think what happened here is related to the killing out at the lifts sir?"

Andy looked around the bedroom before replying; "Well, on the basis that our killer has not broken into the 'The Penthouse,' nor did he take the keys, I would say it is unlikely! Unless there is some other connection we have not seen?"

I shook my head and replied; "No I agree sir. This looks like 'hooray' Henry's regular home scene. A strange world they live in these people who are into this Marquis De Sade stuff."

Andy replied quietly; "Yeah it takes all sorts, but this De Sade stuff usually goes too far and somebody finishes up badly hurt or dead. I've seen it so many times. Now go and put any bills, bank statements and videos you can find on top of that money Sergeant."

I felt, and probably looked, a bit bewildered, but I went into the lounge and did what I was told, before re-joining Andy in the bedroom where he was still nosing around.

"Hello, are you there Andy?" A familiar voice called out from the direction of the entrance door.

Andy looked up and having obviously recognised the voice shouted back in response; "In here John!"

DI John Sanderson entered the bedroom.followed by the pratt DS Tony Booth.

Andy laughed and said; "My God – you made it in double quick time John! I've never known you to be so quick."

DI Sanderson looked bewildered and replied; "What do you mean Andy? – I am just following up a lead from an apparent suicide this morning – in fact not far from this place!"

Andy shook his head and replied; "Sorry John – We just telephoned Flash Harry for some assistance in questioning residents on this murder case. Anyway, how is this place connected to your case?"

DI Sanderson was still looking and sounding bewildered as he replied; "Oh the suicide was a young boy only about nineteen to twenty or so. The apartment owner reckoned he was a squatter and he had an old-style suitcase with him. It had a label inside the suitcase with a name and this address on it!"

It was now Andys turn to look bewildered as he replied; "What name was on the suitcase John?"

DI Sanderson took out his notebook and read out; "Mister James Worthington and the address is this place; 'The Penthouse Suite', Grosvenor House, Kensington High Street, London W14."

Andy quickly replied; "Yeah! – The right address John, but the name is the old man who shot his bolt a year or so back. Our murder victim out there is the son Nigel who incidentally is one of ours – started work at New Scotland Yard last Monday with the 'Fraud Squad."

DI Sanderson shook his head in disbelief before replying; "He one of the 'Trained Brains then?" DI Sanderson turned to me and apologised; "Sorry DS."

I replied with a smile; "No problem Sir. I think every copper and ex-copper in 'The Met' has already got the name! – Was the young boy abused?"

DI Sanderson looked bemused and replied with a question; "How do you know that? - He was badly sexually abused to say the least!"

I nodded before explaining; "We have evidence here sir to suggest there was some kinky sex going on which appears to be unconnected to the murder outside. We also have a witness who stated that he saw our Nigel punching a youngish boy in this apartment before slamming the door shut!"

Andy interrupted with a question; "You sounded as if you didn't believe the apartment owner John?"

DI Sanderson quickly replied; "Yeah you are damn right there Andy. – I mean have you ever heard of a squatter, with suicidal tendencies, taking residence in a squat when he has near enough five thousand quid in his back pocket?"

Andy pretended to look down at something on the bed before quietly replying; "Yeah John – it does sound a bit suspicious to say the least. – What does the owner of the apartment look like?"

DI Sanderson smiled as he replied; "He is a big lad all right! Over six feet tall and a strong looking man about fortyish! - An ex-rugby player and looks like one. Owns and runs a big Knightsbridge estate agent under his own name - 'Bridgewater's.' Not stuck for a bob or two" DI Sanderson took out his notebook and added; "His first name is Jonathan.

I asked the next question; "Is he ex-army sir?"

DI Sanderson replied; "No! ex Navy, but Special Projects! Why do you ask?"

Andy and I exchanged glances before Andy replied; "I guess you and I are thinking along the same lines Sergeant. Okay! – Do you have this Bridgewater's home address John?"

DI Sanderson again looked in his notebook before replying; "Ambleside Road, Lightwater that is in Surrey. According to him a cheaper area in Surrey, but developing. I checked and 'cheap' to him is £50,000 for a detached property. - The average for the UK - for those that can afford it - is £30,000. Even London is £60,000 in the best area!"

Andy smiled and replied; "So he has bob or two! – John - do you fancy going out there with us this afternoon to question this guy again?"

DI Sanderson looked quizzically at Andy before replying; "I thought you had 'The Fox' in the picture for this one Andy?"

Andy smiled and replied; "Well that is what we are supposed to believe! We do have a witness who thinks he saw 'The Fox,' but to be honest John – we cannot see this as 'The Fox' – it does not fit his 'MO'!" Andy smiled wickedly at me and winked.

DI Sanderson looked serious and thought for a few seconds before replying; "That may be so Andy. But you have a witness and the kill looks awfully like John Palmer's bouncers kill?"

Andy looked disappointed, probably because DI Sanderson understood straight off what 'MO' meant, then he replied quietly; "Well of course we have not disregarded the possibility of 'The Fox' being the man John, but I am uncomfortable with the whole scenario. Also do you think 'The Fox', we have been chasing for twenty odd years, would go out today in the same disguise as the one that was plastered over the news yesterday? I say, no way!" As you are with your man John - my gut tells me to look at this a lot more John, but at this stage it is only a gut feeling and we have not yet spoken to our witness!"

DI Sanderson replied; "Fair enough Andy – I am only going on a gut feeling with my Mr. Bridgewater! He is a very cool customer although at times he was a bit nervous. So, I will go along with you for the ride!"

Andy rubbed at the stubble on his chin before replying ruefully; "One problem we have John is, straight after we interview your man, we have to go down to Bournemouth to put Mrs Palmer and her kids into protective custody. Is that all right?"

"Bloody hell Andy!" DI Sanderson sounded exasperated before he added a little more coolly; "Bournemouth is hours away! You get an inch and take a mile"

I too was a bit angry as I must admit I saw yet another night slipping away and getting back in the early hours of tomorrow morning. I was already dog tired and could do without, as The Beatles said; 'A Hard Day's Night.'

Andy just grinned and replied; "Well you know what old Gilbert and Sullivan said; 'A Policeman's lot is not a happy one?" Andy paused smiling again before adding; "Anyway it is less than two hours from Lightwater to Bournemouth down the A3 and if we use the 'Blues and Twos' in the Jag we will get there in just over an hour! A woman's life could be at stake here you know John."

DI Sanderson looked flabbergasted and mumbled his reply; "Bang goes another night. They are not even paying overtime Andy!"

Andy just laughed as he replied; "Aye it's a hard life John, but someone has to do it!"

"Yeah, why is it always us on these ones Andy?" DI Sanderson moaned.

Andy was looking at DS TonyBooth when he smiled and ruefully said; "That's the price of not being on the take John. They will get their comeuppance one day. Sooner, rather than later!"

I could not believe Andys amazing statement considering the amount of money he had just told me to hive off, or at least I suspected he had told me to hide! I must have shown my amazement because Andy simply smiled at me and nodded to the Harrods bag signalling for me to pick it up.

"Yeah, I will believe it when I see it. They have been at it for so long it is just a way of life for them. Okay, but you can explain to her indoors Andy."

Andy laughed and replied; "I am not the best of consultants on broken marriages John. My record is not a good one in those matters."

DI Sanderson laughed and replied; "Aye, that is true Andy. The problem is you are all I've got so you will have to do!" He added; "I tell you what! – Why don't we try and catch him in his office before he goes home? It is not too far away from here and it is only four thirty."

Andy looked at his watch and replied; "Good idea John, but if he is not there we have to go straight to his home!"

We all left 'The Penthouse' and stopped off to let Doctor Harvey know about the cotton wool balls and things to look out for and samples to take when DI Sanderson interrupted and added; "Sergeant Arkwright – could you check the fingerprints and blood samples in 'The Penthouse' against the boy suicide victim this morning?"

David Arkwright looked up quizzically and asked; "Do you think there is a connection sir?"

DI Sanderson paused slightly before replying; "Well it could be coincidence, but I don't like coincidences – this was the address in the boy's suitcase if you remember? There are also sex tools and Marquis De-Sade stuff in there with blood marks. Considering the boy's abuse, I would say it is a good chance it happened here!"

David Arkwright smiled and simply replied; "Will do sir."

We were on the lift down when I remembered the witnesses and said; "Just a reminder sir – We have to interview the witnesses, that delivery guy and the caretaker; – they are in the caretaker's apartment."

"Bloody hell your right Sergeant. Let's do that quickly. I don't think they will help much, but it is got to be done!"

As we emerged from the lift into the ground floor we saw several press men some with cameras and another from London Weekend Television with the well-known LWT Crime Reporter Derek Jackson a well-rounded man in front of the camera who spotted Andy and shouted across; "DI Spearing - is it true that this is another killing by 'The Fox?'

"No comment yet Derek. We are still to positively identify the victim, never mind the killer!" Andy shouted back, a lie as we all knew.

Derek Jackson shouted again; "We understood there is a witness who positively identified 'The Fox' within the building

Andy ignored the reporters.and asked; "Who the hell let the vultures know there was a body and 'The Fox'? may be involved?" Andy asked as we went over to the door labelled 'The Caretaker.'

DI Sanderson and I just shook our heads.

Andy rang the doorbell which was almost instantly answered by a guy in blue dungarees faded white shirt and safety boots. He stayed out of sight of the cameras.

"Are you 'The Caretaker' for the building?" Andy asked while producing his ID badge.

"Yes, I am – Harry Wright is my name, will you come in – I don't want to be seen by those cameras in case this 'Fox' fella comes back."

We all followed Mr Wright into the small apartment and closed the door behind us.

"I don't think 'The Fox' will ever come back here Mr Wright – if indeed it was 'The Fox' who was here!" Andy replied with a slight smile.

"This fella here swears blind it was 'The Fox' all right'" Harry Wright pointed over to a man dressed in a City Couriers company uniform.

Andy did not hesitate and asked; "Ah – you must be Pete Baker – the courier who says he saw 'The Fox' here an hour or so ago?"

"That's right sir. It was 'The Fox'- I can swear to that sir!"

"Well you can swear it was a man who fitted the description of 'The Fox' that was in the papers and on television yesterday. – Is that correct Mr Baker?"

"Yes, indeed sir – that is correct." Pete Baker replied hesitantly and now defensively.

"Good – just as long as we all understand – It was a man who fitted the description of 'The Fox!" .Andy nodded in a condescending manner.

"So, you don't think it was 'The Fox' sir?" Pete Baker looked inquisitively at Andy who smiled and replied; "Yes, very good Mr Baker – I can see why you want to be a copper. Quick on the uptake eh?"

Pete Baker smiled happily and replied; "Yes that is my ambition sir!"

Andy suddenly spun around angrily and asked; "Was it you who phoned the press then Mr Baker?"

"No, of course I didn't!" Mr Baker replied indignantly and quickly added defensively; "They were probably listening into your communications system sir!"

I noticed Harry Wright – 'The Caretaker' - shake his head and Andy must have noticed as he retorted; "Just remember, when you speak to the press and television Mr Baker – the man fitted the description of 'The Fox' – It might just save your life later!"

Pete Baker suddenly looked alarmed and replied; "You don't think he would come looking for me do you sir?"

Andy again smiled and replied; "Well put it this way Mr Baker – if I was 'The Fox' and I had been wrongly accused I would want to find out what is going on – You know? He turned away with a wave of the hand indicating we were to follow.

Pete Baker suddenly looked downtrodden and afraid before asking; "Don't you want to take my statement?"

Andy rather nonchalantly replied over his shoulder as he moved quickly to the door; "We will send one of the PC's to get your statement."

As we went out I called over a PC and asked him to take a statement from Mr Bake get him to sign it and forward it to us at NSY.

With that we left the building and got into the Jag.

Andy shouted across to Sergeant Tommy; "We need to go to an office in Knightsbridge Tommy! DI John will give you an address and afterwards we maybe need to head for Lightwater in Surrey. Blues and Twos please Tommy."

"Is it an emergency sir?" Tommy asked.

"Certainly, it is Tommy. Afterwards we must get to Bournemouth, where Mrs Palmer's life may be at risk."

"OK sir." Tommy replied, switching on the blues and twos and moving out into the traffic which immediately gave way to the Jag.

Within fifteen minutes we were sitting outside Bridgewater's Knightsbridge estate agents' swanky modern offices.

We entered the Bridgewater's offices led by Andy and were faced by a stern looking middle age lady with a label stating; 'Kathy Holmes'. She was neither good, nor bad looking, but dressed in a very smart woman's dark blue business suit and lighter blue blouse puffed up at the neck. Her desk to the left of the office had empty 'in' and 'out' filing trays, a telephone and a nameplate stating in gold letters 'Administrator.'

There were another two desks on the right, both with nameplates stating in gold letters

'Sales', but only one was occupied by a slightly built young man with the red tousled hair, dressed in an immaculate black business suit and black tie wearing a name tag stating 'Andrew Watson.'

The desk directly behind Kathy Holmes had a nameplate stating 'Mortgages.' This was also occupied by a twenty-five ish year old good looking small guy with jet black hair, angelic face and brown eyes. He was dressed in a dark brown business suit, white shirt and dark brown tie to match his suit and he had a name tag stating 'James Phillips.'

Kathy Holmes had virtually ignored us and then suddenly spoke in a very posh BBC announcer's voice, without looking up asked; "Yes sirs – What can we do for you today?"

Andy flashed his ID and replied; "Police! I am DI Spearing and these other officers are DI Sanderson and DS Devlin. We are from New Scotland Yard and would like to talk to Mr Jonathan Bridgewater please."

"I am afraid Mr Jonathan has gone for the day sir – about thirty minutes ago!" Kathy replied all prim and proper.

DI Sanderson asked; "Does he usually leave this early?"

"No, he usually leaves around five, or even six sometimes, but he has not been well today! - Had a bit of a shock this morning – a young man found dead – a suicide, in one of our apartments and he has been upset all day. There again I would imagine you lot would know all about that?"

Andy interrupted; "Yes I suppose that would be a shock. Was he in the office all day?"

Kathy looked and sounded annoyed and replied; "Yes of course! At least since he arrived back here at twelve ish! He has of course his own office out the back."

I noticed the young red headed Andrew Watson shaking his head to indicate 'No' but he did not say anything.

Andy smiled nicely and asked; "Can we please take a look at Mister Bridgewater's office Miss Holmes?"

"I am afraid the office is locked up Detective." Kathy replied promptly looking down at her desk.

"I am sure you have a spare key Miss Holmes?"

"Yes, I have, but Mister Jonathan does not like us to go into his office if he is not here!"

Andy was still smiling, but replied sharply; "Miss Holmes I am afraid I do not care what 'Mister Jonathan' likes, or does not like. DI Sanderson here is investigating the suicide of that young boy you mentioned and I am investigating an associated murder. So please open the office and let us and you get on with our jobs."

"Do you have a warrant Detective?" Kathy asked haughtily.

Andy responded sharply and unsmiling said; "No! - We do not have one yet Miss Holmes, but as we are investigating the murder of a NSY employee, which appears to be connected to the apparent suicide of a young boy found in one of Mister Bridgewaters apartments, I am sure we will not have a problem getting one. However, if you insist, then we will have to hold everyone here until it is cleared - which will be a
minimum of four hours. "

Kathy's face showed alarm but she controlled herself before replying; "Why didn't you contact Mister Jonathan in the first place?"

Andy showed anger for the first time as he replied; "Believe me Miss Holmes - we will be going straight to Mister Bridgewater's home after we are finished here. Now, as you may know, the first few hours are vitally important in all murder investigations. Much as I would not like to do it, I will book you for impeding a police murder investigation. Do I make myself clear Miss Holmes?"

Kathy Holmes face again showed alarm and she immediately went to the top drawer in her desk and took out a large key before replying haughtily; "Loud and clear Detective. You are obviously used to bullying people into getting what you want."

Andy smiled again and replied; "I would not say bullying Miss Holmes. It is only persuading you to see common sense and not to waste police time!"

Kathy Holmes got up and walked towards the office and said curtly; "Follow me Detective. I will stay in the office with you!"

Andy just smiled and turned back and shouted to the others; "I would appreciate it if you could wait for a few minutes as we have several questions for each of you."

Andrew Watson and James Phillips nodded their heads in unison.

DI's Spearing, Sanderson and I followed Miss Holmes into the office with the gold lettered nameplate 'Mr Jonathan Bridgewater' and 'Managing Director.' It was an impressive office with a solid oak desk containing empty 'in' and 'out' trays, plus a telephone and three matching large oak chairs. Behind the desk was a brown chesterfield swivel chair with side arms and a matching huge brown chesterfield three seater leather settee was placed along one wall.

Above the settee, on the plain white wall, were several photos mounted in glass frames showing large very expensive Kensington and Knightsbridge Edwardian houses and apartment blocks with nameplates and below each one 'Bridgewater Estate Agents.' We stood on a plush, deep, dark brown carpet and in one corner stood a four drawer oak filing cabinet locked with a padlock. There were no windows, but there was an air conditioner which did both heating and cooling.

There were two doors, one of which led to a private bathroom containing a shower unit, hand basin, a very full toiletries cabinet and a wardrobe containing evening and work suits, shirts, socks, underwear and several pairs of dress and work shoes. There was also racking containing bath and hand towels. The other door was a back-exit door, but it was locked.

"Where are the keys for the door and filing cabinet Miss Holmes?" Andy quietly asked.

"Mister Jonathan has the key!" Miss Holmes replied haughtily.

"But you do have a spare key Miss Holmes?" Andy replied with a nod.

Miss Holmes nodded, but did not reply or move.

Andy asked angrily; "Then can you please fetch the keys Miss Holmes?"

Without replying Miss Holmes turned around and hurriedly walked away.

Andy sat on the bosses' chesterfield swivel chair and asked; "Sergeant - Can you check the shower and sink unit for any signs of blood?"

"Yes sir I replied and went into the bathroom and thought I saw some discolouring around the drains, but it was very difficult to tell if it was blood or not as most of whatever caused it had been washed away and it did smell like bleach had been used recently. There was still water lying around the shower base and the hand basin.

I let Andy know about what appeared to be blood in the shower room.

"Okay Sergeant get on the Walkie - tatkie and get forensics out here.

I went off to make the call just as Miss Holmes re-entered the office carrying a bunch of keys in her hand.

Andy took the keys and handed them to me and said; "Check out the back door Sergeant and make sure you use gloves on the door handles – Okay?

I got the message and asked Miss Holmes; "Which one is for the door and the one for the filing cabinet?" Miss Holmes separated the two keys and handed them back to me without a word and stood there staring.

I opened the rear door, checked the door handles which were clean and walked outside into a clear backyard at the end of which there was a locked gate with a notice attached stating; 'Private Parking - Do NOT park across access.' I came back into the office and opened the filing cabinet. Each drawer had dozens of files with property names and addresses and piles of papers and photographs inside, but nothing personal in any of them. I caught Andys attention and shook my head.

Andy looked very hard at Miss Holmes and said; "Now then Miss Holmes – We have several questions for you. Please take a seat!" He indicated to one of the seats opposite and indicated to DI Sanderson and I to take the other two chairs. I took out my notebook and pen.

"I really cannot see how I can help you detective." Miss Holmes said it in a petulant school mam manner as she sat down.

"I think we are in a better position to know that Miss Holmes don't you think?" Andy replied with a smile and then asked me; "Can you take notes Sergeant and you or DI Sanderson are both welcome to add any questions."

Andy turned to ask; "Now then Miss Holmes – You said that Mr Bridgewater was in his office since he returned – What time was that Miss Holmes?"

"Oh, I was just about to go for lunch so it was around twelve thirty!" Miss Holmes answered promptly as though it had been rehearsed.

"I see and he went straight to his office and did not emerge until forty minutes ago?" Andy asked quizzically.

"No! He first told us what happened with him discovering the body in one of the Kensington apartments. Apparently, the poor boy committed suicide."

"Yes, well that is part of our ongoing investigations. So anyway, he then went to the office and did not come out for the rest of the day?"

"No! Mr Jonathan was so upset he said he would have a lie down for a bit and he asked not to be disturbed by anybody for the afternoon."

I thought as a Special Projects team Bridgewater would not be so hard hit by a death even if it was a boyfriend so decided to interrupt and asked; "Did he lock his office Miss Holmes?"

Miss Holmes replied again haughtily; "I believe so Sergeant."

I asked; "Is that unusual Miss Holmes – I mean locking his door all afternoon?"

"Well I think if you had a shock like finding a dead body in an apartment you too would need to lie down Sergeant!"

"I meant did he often lock the office door Miss Holmes?"

"Yes, quite often Sergeant. He often used to shower and change before he left for an important meeting or an evening out at a London theatre!"

Andy interjected; "Did he shower and change today before he left Miss Holmes."

"I didn't notice detective." Miss Holmes replied, again too promptly.

"You a woman and didn't notice a showered and changed Mr Jonathan?"

"I resent such sexist remarks detective."

Andy looked her up and down before replying sarcastically; "I can understand that Miss Holmes! Did you happen to notice if Bridgewater was carrying anything when he left?"

Miss Holmes smiled very slightly before replying; "Cannot say that I did detective! You see he left via the back door."

I again interjected quickly; "Did Mr Bridgewater have his car parked in the backyard Miss Holmes?"

"Yes Sergeant – That was not unusual"

DI Sanderson asked; "What type of car does he own Miss Holmes?"

"It is a Bentley T1 Saloon detective."

DI Sanderson said; "A very expensive car."

Miss Holmes smirked and replied; "Well one has to live up to one's position in life detective!"

DI Sanderson smiled broadly and replied sarcastically; "Yes, I can see an estate agent is required to put a face on. - Do you have the car registration number Miss Holmes?"

"Mr Jonathan is much more than an estate agent detective. He actually owns many of these properties!" Miss Holmes replied smugly before adding; "I have the car registration number in my filing cabinet."

DI Sanderson sounded irritated when he asked; "Can you fetch it now please Miss Holmes?" She went off almost instantly and when she left the room DI Sanderson added; "Andy I think we ought to put an all points out on Mr Bridgewater's car on the A3. There is an outside chance he doesn't realise we are onto him and he may still have incriminating stuff in the car thinking he has plenty of time to dump it?"

Andy nodded in agreement and said quietly; "I agree John. When she gives you the number, go out the back and get on that Walkie - talkie thing and put out an arrest and detain on him. Also get the car impounded – get him taken to Camberley police station and we can meet him there, or we can chase him to his home."

Miss Holmes re-entered the office with a sheet of paper containing the car registration number which she handed over to DI Sanderson. He read out aloud;

"JB 001 E. - A personalised number plate and a brand-new Bentley T1. Not bad for a guy who said this morning he was not rich, only comfortable." DI Sanderson turned away and went out the door with the Walkie - talkie in his hand.

Andy then said; "Right Miss Holmes can you send the red haired lad in next please?"

"Mr Watson? Miss Holmes sounded incredulous.

"That's the one!" Andy just nodded.

As Miss Holmes exited DI Sanderson returned to the office and said; "We have an all points out on Bridgewater and his bloody Bentley."

Andy laughed and replied; "Sounds like a bit of jealousy in there John."

DI Sandersons reply was interrupted as Andrew Watson rapped on the door and entered the office saying; "You want to talk to me sir?"

Andy waved him in, pointed to a chair and said; "I am DI Spearing – this is DS Devlin and that is DI Sanderson. Take a seat Mr Watson."

Andy continued; "Now Mr Watson I noticed you shaking your head when we were questioning Miss Holmes. What have you to tell us?"

Andrew Watsons pale face went red and he stammered as he replied in an Edinburgh accent; "Yes that was then, and now it is different."

Andy looked angry and retorted with a crisp tone in his voice; "Now lad – let me make it very clear – this is a joint murder and possible suicide investigation. – Now if you have anything which can help this investigation now is the time to tell us. Because if you choose to withhold information Mr Watson I will have your guts for garters! Now then – What do you know?"

"It's all right for you sir – it's not you who will lose their job!"

Andys expression changed as he replied quietly and sympathetically; "Let me assure you Mr Watson – if you are sacked for making a statement, I will arrest Miss Holmes for attempting to pervert the course of justice and I will tell her that before I go. Also, in any case, she will not know a thing about your, or Mister Phillips' statement, or its contents. How is that?"

Andrew Watson looked down and mumbled his reply; "Fair enough detective! I don't know much, but I can tell you a little!"

Andy smiled reassuringly before saying; "Okay lad now speak up so as Sergeant Devlin here can take your statement. Right lad now you can start."

Andrew Watson suddenly brightened up and replied clearly; "Well for starters, Jonathan bloody Bridgewater was not in his office all afternoon, contrary to what Miss 'primly' Holmes said. When she went to lunch at one I went to his office a couple of times, the door was locked, but I knocked the door very loudly both times no answer."

I decided to interrupt with a question; "Mister Watson. Why did you try to get into the office when you were told not to disturb Mr Bridgewater?"

Andrew Watson shook his head before replying; "I had an important enquiry from a Middle East customer and it needed Mister Bridgewater's input! And I was manning the office on my own during lunch"

I asked another question; "Did you manage to see Mr Bridgewater before he left?"

"I did, yes, just before he left!"

DI Sanderson asked; "Mr Watson. Did you see if Mr Bridgewater had changed before he left?"

"Yes, not only had he changed, but he had showered and shaved by the smell."

Andy came back in with an almost sarcastic question; "You recognise Mr Bridgewater's after shave?"

Andrew Watson smiled nervously and his face went red before he replied quietly; "Well that is a different story!"

Andy simply asked; "What story is that Mister Watson?"

Andrew Watson again looked nervous and with a slight stammer replied; "Well you know – well one day he locked the office door and he came up behind me and put his face on my shoulder and touched my bum."

Andy and John Sanderson exchanged knowing glances before Andy asked; "And what did you do Mr Watson?"

Andrew Watson shyly replied, his face still red; "I just removed his hand and said I was not like that!" Andrew Watson smiled and added; "Afterwards I laughed, thinking about how many girls had said that to me, but for me I felt creepy!"

DI Sanderson asked; "And what did Mister Bridgewater say Andrew?"

"At first he was okay and just said 'fair enough'. But then he said quietly into my ear; 'Just remember Andrew – If you want to hold onto your job not a word to nobody about this!"

"And did you? – Have a word with anybody?" DI Sanderson asked.

"No! – No way! He may be a shit shifter, but he has a reputation as a hard man – war soldier - came through Normandy landings and all the way to Berlin! (Andy and Sanderson again exchanged knowing glances) before Andrew Watson added; "Not to mention I wanted to hold onto my job!"

Andy asked; "And how about young Mister Phillips out there - Has he had a problem?"

"You would have to ask him sir."

Andy smiled slyly before replying; "Yeah, we will do that - if you could send him in now Mr Watson."

Andrew Watson got up to walk away when I remembered a question I wanted to ask; "Oh by the way Andrew – did you notice if Mr Bridgewater was carrying anything when he left this afternoon?"

"Yeah – He had a large holdall with him, zipped up, so I could not see what was in it!"

I replied: "Thanks Mr Watson – You have been a great help." Andrew Watson left the office.

Andy smiled and spoke to both of us; "Very interesting – especially the part about his army life – Could be our man eh?" We all nodded as James Phillips entered the office with a nervous smile on his face.'

Andy again took the lead; "Hello Mr Phillips – 'James,' isn't it? - I am DI Spearing (and pointing to each of us) he added; "This is DI Sanderson and DS Devlin. Now the first question is – did you see anything of Mr Bridgewater this afternoon?"

"No, we don't tend to talk too much these days! – Only when it is strictly necessary for the business!"

Andy said; "That sounds a little bit cynical Mr Phillips – Was Mr Bridgewater a shirt ---"

I decided to quickly interject and asked; "Did Mr Bridgewater make any sexual advances towards you James?"

"You could say that Sergeant – we were lovers for a couple of years!"

"I see!" I replied, trying my best not to show surprise and added; "So what happened to you two?"

"He met a younger model - as they say in your world Sergeant – a guy called David! (We all exchanged knowing glances again). James continued, oblivious to our reaction, and added; "So that was that – I don't mind; I moved on and found other people."

I decided I was better placed to ask these types of questions without prejudice so I asked; "Tell me James – Did you ever meet David?"

James replied; "No, but what I gathered from friends was he was eighteen and a rent boy."

"How did you know that James?" I asked as a routine .

"The gay world, even in London, is not that big Sergeant. You soon get to hear about most people!"

I then decided to ask the obvious question; "Was Mr Bridgewater ever violent to you?"

"No, never in fact –the opposite! He was very gentle - never ever violent – always loving!"

I felt a little bit of traditional male chauvinistic revulsion, but held my cool and asked; "So you do not see him mistreating his boyfriends?

"No! No way could he be violent Sergeant!"

"But he had been trained to be violent James? He was in the army during the war!

"He spoke about that, but then he often said he lived in a different world back then."

Andy interjected; "That's for sure James, Anyway thanks for your frankness. We will take it from there, but if Miss Holmes, or anyone else, threatens you with your job security please let us know at New Scotland Yard and we will sort them out – Okay?"

"Yeah thank you – You know it is not easy to be one of 'us' even in the swinging sixties!"

"Yeah I understand" I lied.

James Phillips left the office looking more nervous than ever.

Andy immediately said; "Okay – It looks like we are on the right track. Let's get down to Lightwater and pick him up there, or hopefully we will have him in Camberley"

As we left the offices Andy stopped off and whispered in Miss Holmes ear. She looked bemused and said; "You are no better than a thug detective!"

"You had better believe it Miss Holmes!" Andy replied with a wicked smile.

As we exited the Bridgewater offices Andy turned to me and said as a matter of fact; "Thank you for handling those queer's questions. Afraid I am not too good with that lot!"

I replied with a smile; "Yes, we have noticed sir." I noticed DI Sanderson smiling.

We got back into the Jag. Andy said; "Okay Tommy, 'Blues and Twos' again down to Lightwater – DI Sanderson will give you the address."

Book 1 in the DI Spearing and DS Devlin series

Chapter 27- Times they are a Changing

Sir Mark Wright, the Commissioner for the Metropolitan Police, sat at his desk and decided that at about 5 p.m. on a fine Friday summers evening he was feeling extremely tired. It was about time to think about going home.

For him it had been a very successful, but stressful day, made more so by his meeting with his political boss John Fairley, the government's Home Secretary and George Felts, the Attorney General. After over two year's covert investigations into the alleged corruption throughout The London Met, and in particular New Scotland Yard, at long last he had been given the go ahead to proceed with his plans to get rid of some of the proven corrupt officers.

Sir Mark knew there were more corrupt officers than on his list of thirty plus men, but knowing it and being able to prove it were two entirely different things. George Felts had agreed the list of officers against whom the corruption charges were more likely to be proved, but more importantly he had also agreed a process which would limit the damage to The London Mets reputation. Now it was down to Sir Mark to implement the process.

He suddenly decided that he needed to have one of his 'straight' non-corrupt officers with him on each of the interviews with the corrupt officers and without hesitation he decided to use his old friend DI Andy Spearing. He knew he could not go through Spearing's immediate boss, DCI Tomlinson. He pressed the button on his intercom for his secretary who replied almost instantly with "Yes sir." Sir Mark grinned and replied; "Helen could you arrange for DI Spearing to be paged on his Walkie-talkie and patch it through to me. Oh, and if he is not answering, as is usual, tell them to call DS Devlin. Okay?"

"Yes of course sir." Helen replied and hung up. Five minutes later Sir Mark's phone rang and he immediately answered. "Mark here – Is that you Andy?."

"No sir – It is DS Devlin – Hang on and I will pass it over to him."

Andy took over the Walkie-talkie and said; "Hello sir – What's happening? Over."

Sir Mark smiled at Andy being so formal and grinned as he heard Andy ask what button to hit before replying; "Andy where are you now? Over."

"I am on my way to Lightwater sir - chasing a suspect for the murder of Nigel Worthington this afternoon. Over"

"So, it was not 'The Fox' as the papers have been saying? Over." Sir Mark sounded cheerful.

"We don't believe so sir. However, until we talk to the suspect and get some more evidence we cannot dismiss anything. Anyway, what can I do for you sir? Over."

"Andy I need you in here first thing Monday morning. I cannot afford for you not to be here. We are under the direct orders of the Home Secretary himself."

Andy recognised the urgency in Sir Mark's voice and responded; "Yes sir – No problem at my end. Something important, is it? Over."

"It is very important Andy! I cannot say over the open wires, but you must be here. Over."

"I will be there I promise sir. Over and out."

Sir Mark recognised Andys need to avoid any further questions so he let it go. He cleared the paperwork from his desk putting it into his 'out' and 'in' trays. He then hand- brushed down his uniform, put on his cap and went out to the outer office where he turned to his secretary Helen and said; "Can you get me a car Helen? I am off now - have a good weekend."

"Yes, certainly sir. Thank you and you to - have a good one." Helen replied with a smile as she lifted the 'phone and dialled an internal number.

Sir Mark walked out and seeing the lift arriving and about to open he hurried across not noticing, until it was too late, a young man limping with walking sticks also hurrying for the same lift. They crashed into each other at the lift doors and the young man's right hand stick caught Sir Mark on the left knee. The knee started to buckle and the young man raised the stick apparently trying to catch Sir Mark and caught him at the top of the thigh. Sir Mark felt a ping, but thought nothing more of it.

"So, sorry sir – Are you alright? I am not used to these sticks yet!" The young man looked sheepishly, but directly into Sir Mark's eyes as the lift moved downwards

"No – No son it was my fault didn't see you coming – sorry!" Sir Mark replied, forever the gentleman and asked; "What happened with your legs?"

"Oh, had them broken sir, by a couple of thugs while doing undercover work?" The young man replied almost casually.

"You are not a detective, are you?" Sir Mark asked inquisitively fearing he had missed a report on one of his detectives.

"Oh, no sir – I am with MI5 just visiting one of your officers!"

The lift was, as always, making Sir Mark feel claustrophobic and close proximity of the young man was, he thought, making him a little sweaty almost cold sweat, but he asked politely; "Which officer were you visiting?"

"Oh – I was in DCI Tomlinson's office! Trying to contact his DI Spearing who is apparently holding two of our officers on some charge or other, but even DCI Tomlinson cannot get hold of him"

Sir Mark was immediately suspicious as DCI Tomlinson's office was two floors below and of course Sir Mark had just been speaking to Andy. Of course, he thought, if Andy Spearing did not want to talk to his DCI, he would almost certainly ignore his calls. The lift suddenly bumped on the ground floor reception area when Sir Mark suddenly thought again, but why would the MI5 man be two floors above? This was the senior management's floor along with Detective Superintendents.

As the young man emerged from the lift Sir Mark shouted after him; "Well sorry for bumping into you up there young man – What is your name?"

"Oh David – David Whitfield!" The young man replied just a little bit too quick as the lift doors closed.

Sir Mark had decided to go down to the basement car park, make sure the car was ready to take him home to his town house in Sloane Square SW1, only a few minutes from New Scotland Yard.

On a whim, his curiosity aroused, Sir Mark went back up in the lift to the reception area on ground level. He entered the reception area and went straight up to the young lady with the name label over her ample left breast 'Sandra' and asked; "Sandra can you check your register for a young man David Whitfield who has been visiting DCI Tomlinson?"

"Yes sir" Sandra replied hastily – the first-time Sir Mark had ever spoken to her and she so wanted to please him in a professional manner. Looking at the register she said; "Let me see sir – Yes DCI Tomlinson had a visitor and he just signed out the young guy with the sticks, but his name was Peter Hazlewood?"

Sir Mark's gut feeling had been proved correct and he again felt the cold sweat coming out. He wiped his brow and replied, rather weakly for him; "Look Sandra – report this to Security and get them to investigate immediately - use my name and tell them they have to get back to me within the hour at home. Take note - this man gave me a false name – David Whitfield – and he was on the top floor where he should not have been and he accidentally, or otherwise, bumped into me. Make sure Security know and investigate and keep a detailed report. Tell them to get back to me within the hour – Understood?"

"Yes sir! I will do it straight away!" Sandra replied, noticing one of the security guards quickly walking over, but Sir Mark walked off towards the lifts.

"What was all that about with the boss Sandra?" Sergeant Baxter the security duty officer asked.

Sandra explained and Sergeant Baxter exclaimed; "Shit – Why does it happen on my shift? Okay tell the telephonist to get me put through to MI5 Security ASAP Sandra." With that Sergeant Baxter went off to the little security office in the corner of the reception area.

Twenty minutes later Sergeant Baxter emerged grim faced and looking very pale. He said loudly to all; "Okay folks – It looks like we have had a security breach which has involved Sir Mark our boss. It seems someone has been impersonating an MI5 officer and visited DCI Tomlinson apparently trying to contact DI Spearing, but then this man is found by Sir Mark on the top floor! So, we will now have a tightening up of security and Bill Hastings our Chief of Security will be issuing new procedures in the next few days. In the meantime, before anyone - and we mean ANYONE - gains access to this building - we are all responsible for making sure they have positive identification that says they are who they say they are. If not, get security involved. Okay that's it for now thanks people – Oh and make sure when you are finishing your shift that you pass over this information to the person taking your place."

Sergeant Barker turned to go back to his office when Sandra the receptionist asked; "Oh Sergeant – Did you remember to phone Sir Mark and let him know what happened?"

Sergeant Baxter replied over his shoulder as he continued; "Yes Sandra! Bill Hastings is calling him as we speak thanks!"

"Sergeant – you know that young guy did have an MI5 identification badge which said Peter Hazlewood."

Sergeant Barker turned away and replied; "I am sure you are right Sandra, but MI5 cannot trace him at the moment. Don't worry it was not your fault Sandra."

Sir Mark put the phone down after Bill Hastings' call and turned to Shirley his wife and grimly said; "It looks like we have had a security breach at the Yard love. That young guy who bumped into me was not who he said he was."

Shirley, who was actually Lady Wright, was a distinguished looking middle aged woman; she still retained a very trim figure, only four pounds over what she was as a sixteen-year-old. Her classical high cheek bones and cream white face had little make up. At five feet and ten inches, she had long shapely legs, wearing very tasteful clothes which all added to her distinguished looks.

Sir Mark again came out in a cold sweat which had immediately followed a high temperature sweat and the colour in his face drained away.

"You all right Mark?" Shirley asked

"Not really! – I feel like I have 'flu or something coming on. I think I will have a quiet nap."

"I think I will ring Doctor Bowen just in case!" Shirley said sounding worried.

"I - I - Well I suppose better be safe than sorry." Sir Mark replied wearily as he went into the bedroom.

With that reply, Shirley knew there was something seriously wrong and immediately phoned Doctor Henry Bowen, a family friend, and the 'on call' Doctor for New Scotland Yard. After hearing Shirley's worried voice, he promised he would be there in thirty minutes - traffic permitting.

In any event, it was forty-five minutes when Doctor Bowen hurried into the Wrights' home.

Doctor Bowen was middle age, dressed in his customary formal black suit, impressively white shirt and dark blue tie. The black suit was always worn in an attempt to hide his wide girth. With his rapidly thinning hairline he looked a lot older. He was always a bit blusterous and garrulous, but he used to be a good doctor who had become a bit lazy and had not kept up with the latest techniques. Nowadays he only carried out the yearly required physical checks for the London Met police officers. He was carrying a battered old leather medical case stuffed full of all sorts of medical gear.

"Sorry it took so long Shirley – bloody Friday night traffic! Anyway – How is he?"

"In bed resting Henry – I knew something was wrong when he said it was okay to send for you!"

"I will not take that as offensive Shirley!" Doctor Bowen smiled and added; "Okay let's go see our patient!" They went into the bedroom.

Sir Mark lay spread-eagled on his bed wearing only a pair of light blue boxers. He had been obviously sweating his body still covered in stale sweat and the bed clothes were very damp. He produced a weary looking grin, his face now greyish and he said; "Hello Henry – never thought I would be so glad to see you!"

"Well Mark – What have you been up to this time?" Doctor Bowen was trying to be casual as he crossed the room and looked down on Sir Mark.

"God knows Henry – Just suddenly started feeling a bit rough late this afternoon. I think it maybe this virus that's going around The Yard!"

"Well, it certainly looks like you have got the sweats. Hot and then cold, is it?" Doctor Bowen asked as he took Sir Mark's wrist and felt for his pulse.

"I'll say – very hot and then very cold I had to pull the covers up!" Sir Mark replied with a weak smile.

"Your pulse rate is slow Mark."

"Well - no change there Henry – You know I have always had low pulse rate – all down to the years of gym work and training and playing rugby!"

"Yeah that's true Mark, but it is a bit lower than it usually is. Okay let's take your blood pressure!"

Doctor Bowen set up the blood pressure test and afterwards announced; "Again you have low blood pressure Mark – way below what you were earlier in the year when, if I remember right, it was a bit high!"

"Low is not as bad as high Henry?"

"That's true Mark! But it depends on what else is around – Lets listen to your heart now!"

Doctor Bowen fitted his stethoscope to his ears and he sounded Sir Marks heart. He went around the chest for another couple of more minutes.

"Have you had a stressful day Mark?"

"Well a little bit more than usual – A heavy meeting with the Home Secretary and the Attorney General – the accumulation of two years of very hard work!"

"Any breathing difficulties or cramps Mark?" Doctor Bowen asked returning his stethoscope to his ears and again sounding out Sir Mark's chest.

"A little bit difficulty breathing tonight and some cramp, but I thought it was down to this virus!"

"Have you been drinking plenty of water today Mark?"

"No – No - not really Henry!"

"You know Mark; some of your symptoms could be put down to dehydration? - insufficient water intake."

"Never thought about it Henry– such a busy day."

"Well I suggest you start right now!" Doctor Bowen replied, turned to Shirley and said; "Can you get a litre of water Shirley and put another litre in the fridge and get your man to drink it all within the next hour?"

Shirley replied; "No problem Henry." and rushed off into the kitchen to fetch the water.

Doctor Bowen quietly added; "Also Mark, I think I detect an irregular heart beat in addition to the slow pulse and low blood pressure. I think we ought to get you into hospital for a check-up."

"When will that be Henry? I have a heavy schedule next week!"

"I think your health comes first Mark!"

Shirley re-entered the room and having overheard the end of the conversation said; "That's for sure Henry! – that damn job of his always comes first! She put down the jug of water and a glass before adding; "Well not this time Mister Wright

Doctor Bowen interrupted the quiet banter and said; "I'll tell you what Mark – I will take a blood sample now and rush it through the hospital in the morning and, if there is anything, we will get you in immediately" He quickly took the blood sample and as he was doing it said; "In the meantime to be on the safe side I am going to give you a few days' supply of pills. First there is Warfarin which thins your blood and protects against clots and things. The others are simply Salt Tablets which will help with the low blood pressure and the cramp. Take one Warfarin now and two salt tablets with all that water before you go to sleep.
Understood Mark and Shirley?"

Shirley replied; "He will do Henry and thanks for coming at such short notice!"

"What happened to your knee Mark?" Doctor Bowen suddenly asked looking at the black and blue marks on Sir Marks left knee.

"Oh, I run into a young guy with sticks at the lifts on the top floor. Unfortunately, it turns out it was a security breach!"

"Really? So, you know who it was?"

"Apparently, he claimed at reception to be MI5, but it turns out he was an imposter!"

"My God Mark – did he cause any other injury?"

"No, not really! – Got a twinge in my left thigh as he caught me from falling over!"

Doctor Bowen asked with an incredulous or sarcastic tone to his voice; "What? A young guy who is walking with the aids of sticks saved you at six feet and three inches – weighing fourteen stones - from falling over? That must have been a fantastic balancing act!" and then asked; "Could you turn up the leg of your boxers please Mark – let me see if there is any damage to your thigh!"

Doctor Bowen took out a magnifying glass and closely examined the top of Sir Marks left thigh. He stood up and with urgency in his voice asked; "Was it after the clash with the sticks that you felt tired and not well Mark?"

Sir Mark smiled rather weakly and quietly replied; "I was tired before, but yes, I began to feel unwell afterwards!"

Doctor Bowen looked and sounded astounded as he said; "My God Mark, you knew and was going to let me go off and leave it overnight!"

Sir Mark looked sheepish and again quietly replied; "I only began to realise what it might be when you started giving me the symptoms!"

Shirley asked, sounding slightly hysterical, "Can someone please tell me what is going on? What this 'thing' might be?"

"Well Shirley – it looks like Mark may have been injected with something when he clashed with the sticks man. There is a small pin mark at the top of his left thigh! At the moment it is almost impossible to see with the naked eye."

Shirley's hand shot up to her mouth and again, sounding hysterical, said; "Oh my God – I knew something like this might happen! What are we going to do Henry?"

"Where is your phone Shirley? I will get Mark admitted under emergency procedures to the private ward at The Hammersmith Hospital"

Shirley, still looking shocked, pointed over to the corner cabinet in the lounge.

Doctor Bowen walked into the lounge and went to make the call. Shirley walked over and took Sir Mark's hand and said; "My God Mark – do you think it is our lot, or MI5?"

Sir Mark shifted uncomfortably in his bed and weakly replied; "I don't really know Shirley. Look, if anything happens, make sure you get Andy Spearing or John Sanderson to investigate. Do not trust any of the others no matter what they say! But let Andy know that if it is the crowd from 'The Met 'then it must be hushed up. – We cannot afford to tarnish our reputation anymore"

Shirley shook her head and replied; "You are unbelievable Mark. Even when they poison you – you still want to protect their worthless reputation? You have to be kidding me!"

"Please Shirley! If the public lose complete confidence in 'The Met' there could be anarchy. The Home Secretary is keenly aware!"

"Fuck the Home Secretary Mark! These people have poisoned you and you are going to let them get away with it! Well fuck them all!"

Sir Mark smiled weakly and replied; "I may have been poisoned! AND if you do as I say and get Andy to investigate – he will find a way to at least get them rough justice." Please Shirley?"

There was a cough and Doctor Bowen re-entered the bedroom.

"Ah Henry! – I want you to know too – if this is poison – we must record it as a probable heart attack, especially if 'The Met' is involved. The Home Secretary is aware of the problems."

"I don't think I can do that Mark. If you have been poisoned then it is a police matter!"

"Henry I am the police and don't worry – any problems will be taken care of internally."

Doctor Bowen looked very uncomfortable and quietly replied; "Anyway Mark, the emergency ambulance is on its way – it should be here in a few minutes and you will be in hospital in fifteen minutes or so."

With that there came the noise of sirens and an ambulance pulled up outside the house. It was obvious that the high-profile name of Sir Mark Wright had attracted extraordinary service. Doctor Bowen opened the front door and introduced himself to the ambulance crew who came running into the house pulling a portable gurney stretcher with portable breathing apparatus and hospital bed drip feed bottles.

The ambulance crew immediately fitted the drip feed to Sir Mark's left hand and the portable breathing apparatus strapped across his mouth. The senior of the ambulance crew turned to Doctor Bowen and asked; "Have you given him anything yet Doctor?"

"No, not yet! – I was about to give him Warfarin and Salt Tablets!"

"Is that what you are recommending Doctor?" The senior ambulance man replied.

"Well – Yes! – It was on the basis that he has a heart flutter, low pulse rate and low blood pressure." Doctor Bowen sounded almost defensive.

The senior ambulance man smiled and replied; "Sounds good Doctor – We will go ahead with these injections?"

Doctor Bowen did not like the idea that the ambulance man was putting the onus on him, but just nodded and the senior ambulance man administered the drugs.

"Right, I think we better get our patient into the hospital ASAP. Are you coming with us Doctor?"

"Of course!" Doctor Bowen replied and turning to Shirley asked; "And you Lady Wright are you coming?"

"Try stopping me." Shirley replied, pulling on a cardigan and dusting down her skirt.

"Okay let's get going." The senior ambulance man said.

Within a few minutes, they were all on their way with the blues and twos on to The Hammersmith Hospital.

Book 1 in the DI Spearing and DS Devlin series

Chapter 28 – Pursuits

With the blues and twos blaring we made the twenty–seven-mile journey from central London, during rush hour, to Lightwater, Surrey in thirty minutes.

We arrived outside Jonathan Bridgewater's big Lakeside mansion in Lightwater Road and found the Bentley T1 with the personalised number plate JB 001 E in the driveway.

"So much for our all points on the car" DI Sanderson said with a scowl.

Andy replied with a smile; "I doubt if they have even sorted out the paperwork yet John, never mind actually doing the job!"

We all exited the Jaguar and walked up the driveway. Andy felt the bonnet of the Bentley and said; "Still hot – not long since he arrived!"

DI Sanderson walked on and rang the doorbell.

The door was opened by Jonathan Bridgewater who turned white and looked astounded staring at DI Sanderson as he said; "What the hell are you doing here? You promised me nothing would happen until the trial!" Bridgewater nervously looked over his shoulder to ensure his wife was not listening before quietly adding; "I have not had a chance to tell my wife anything yet – please give me a chance?" He pleaded.

DI Sanderson replied quietly, but firmly; "I am sorry Mister Bridgewater, but I didn't make any promises. In any case, there has been, as you may know, further developments. That is why DI Spearing is here!" DI Sanderson pointed to DI Spearing and then to me before adding; "And this is DS Devlin. We are all based at New Scotland Yard and we need to ask you several questions."

"Can it not wait till later?"

Andy joined us and replied; "Afraid not Mister Bridgewater. Can we come in? – We don't want the neighbours hearing all your business, do we?"

"No – you cannot come in." Jonathan Bridgewater was chalk white, very agitated and blocked the door.

Andy replied with a hint of anger; "In that case I am going to have to ask you to accompany me to Camberley Police."

"What do you mean accompany you? I can come down in my own car!" Jonathan Bridgewater was in a cold sweat, but still managing to force himself to stay cool.

Andy smiled and replied; "Afraid not Mr Bridgewater. We are impounding this car."

"What the fuck are you on about now? Jonathan Bridgewater sounded and acted astonished, but it was a flicker of the eyes that gave the game away, there was a quick flash of fear, before regaining his composure.

Andy sternly replied; "Mr Bridgewater – please mind your language – you are speaking to an officer of the law. Now we believe this car may have been used after a murder in London earlier this afternoon!"

Again, that brief flicker of fear in Bridgewaters eyes but he again collected himself before coolly replying; "Murder? But I am the only one to have driven the car this afternoon!"

Andy again smiled and quietly replied; "Now that is a coincidence Mr Bridgewater. Now please, the car keys, and DS Devlin will accompany you to collect them."

Jonathan Bridgewater stood his ground and replied; "Not without a warrant – neither he nor anyone else is coming in here!"

Andy looked and sounded angry and said; "Okay Mister Bridgewater – we will have to do this the difficult way! If you would step out here please - hands out in front of you!"

"You are making one hell of a mistake Inspector. I will make it my business to ensure you lose that job of yours. Believe me!" Jonathan Bridgewater sounded confident, but again that flicker of fear in his eyes as he stepped out.

Andy replied nonchalantly as he cuffed Jonathan Bridgewater; "Yeah! – Whatever!" and then added; "DS Devlin call Mrs Bridgewater out and get her to bring out the car keys! Come along Mr Bridgewater" Andy guided Mr Bridgewater out to the Jaguar and put him in the back seat in the middle between him and DI Sanderson before calling back to me; "DS drive the Bentley and follow us down to Camberley Police Station. Don't forget to wear gloves and cover any spots before sitting at the wheel."

I just nodded and replied; "Yes sir." And I knocked the open door before shouting; "Mrs Bridgewater."

A really petite youngish looking woman appeared at the door. She had long flowing black hair, wearing a short, but expensive, figure hugging, black satin dress. In the short dress, she showed a fine pair of shapely legs, but she was flat chested hardly a breast in sight.

I produced my ID and said; "Mrs Bridgewater? I am DS Devlin from New Scotland Yard and the two DIs in the car with your husband are Spearing and Sanderson. We are taking your husband to Camberley Police Station for questioning in connection with a couple of incidents in London earlier today. I require the car keys to the Bentley – the car is being impounded!"

"Oh, my God – has he been arrested??" Mrs Bridgewater asked, but sounded very timid.

"No Mrs Bridgewater! He is helping the police with our inquiries into these two incidents" I replied patiently.

"But he has only just got in! He has not had his dinner yet!" Mrs Bridgewater stated, sort of absent mindedly.

I had to smile as I replied; "I can assure you that that is the least of his problems right now Mrs Bridgewater! The car keys please?"

Mrs Bridgewater looked and sounded flustered and said; "Can I go with him?"

I shook my head but had to smile again before replying; "No I am afraid not Mrs Bridgewater. The car keys please?"

"Oh yes, sorry!" Mrs Bridgewater replied and turned around in the porch and produced the car keys which she handed to me with a nod of the head.

I asked; "When Mr. Bridgewater, came home today, did he have his holdall with him, or did he act strange in any way?"

Mrs Bridgewater looked quizzically at me before replying; "No! - He didn't have his holdall with him that's for sure, but he did something very strange! – He came straight in and gave me a big hug!" Mrs Bridgewater wistfully smiled and added; "That's the first time he has done that since before the kids were born! That's why I know he didn't have anything in his hand!"

"Yeah, I can relate to that" I replied and then added; "Thanks for the keys and Mrs Bridgewater – you can ring Camberley Police Station in a couple of hours and find out what is happening. Okay?"

"Yes, thanks Detective." Mrs Bridgewater replied, still sounding confused.

I went over to the Bentley and started it up. The Jag pulled away and I followed. I noticed a smell like interior upholstery cleaning fluid. Also, the steering wheel looked as if it had been washed and polished.

At Camberley Police Station Andy immediately went up to the desk and introduced us all to the Duty Sergeant Watkins. Showing his ID, he said; "I am DI Spearing and this is DI Sanderson and my DS Devlin. We are all based in NSY. We have brought in Mr Jonathan Bridgewater here for questioning in connection with two incidents earlier today in London. You may have heard an all points out on Mr Bridgewater's Bentley earlier this afternoon?"

"Yes, I heard the all points about twenty minutes ago!" Sergeant Watkins replied dead pan.

"Aye – well that sounds about par for the course! Andy replied with a shake of his head and added: "Anyway, we caught up with him in Lightwater and have impounded his car. I would like you to put the car in your compound and keep it locked pending the arrival of our forensics team."

Sergeant Watkins who had started writing details in the Daily Log Book suddenly looked up and with a sarcastic note in his voice said; "We do have our own forensics now sir?"

"I am sure you do Sergeant, but our lads have already collected evidence at both crime scenes this afternoon and we hope they will match a few things!" Andy was as smooth as silk and turned to me to ask; "DS Devlin can you pass the car keys to Sergeant Watkins?"

I went up and handed over the keys before Andy added; "We want to hold Mr Bridgewater in a separate cell for questioning later."

Sergeant Watkins looked up again and asked; "Do you wish to record what you are questioning Mr Bridgewater in connection with sir?"

"No! No Sergeant - At the moment it is sufficient to record it is in connection with two incidents earlier today in London which we believe may be connected through Mr Bridgewater!"

"I want to see my lawyer now!" Bridgewater was now sounding very concerned and agitated.

"That of course is your prerogative Mr Bridgewater. You can of course have your lawyer but not until we start questioning you. So that could be a little later as we have a very important case to clear up!"

"What is more important than this Inspector?" Jonathan Bridgewater asked, sounding kind of desperate.

Andy retorted with more than a little anger; "I tell you what Mr Bridgewater – We have a young middle age woman, who has two lovely kids, whose life may be in danger! Is that more important than your little poxy affair with an under-age boy? Get real man as they say nowadays!"

Sergeant Watkins came around the counter quickly to interrupt; "Okay Mr Bridgewater – Can you please take off your belt and remove your shoe laces please?"

Jonathan Bridgewater shouted back; "This is just ridiculous!" But he did as was asked and went off with Sergeant Watkins to the cell.

Sergeant Watkins returned with a smile on his lips and said; "There goes a very concerned gentleman who is going to wet himself shortly!"

Andy just laughed and replied; "I hope so Sergeant. – Now stick it in your log book and make sure nobody, but nobody, sees that guy until we get back – wife, lawyer – nobody – Okay?"

"Sure – No problem – how long will you be?"

"I don't really know Sergeant – It may be two or three hours - We are off to Bournemouth to try and contact this lady, but who knows? Just make sure he sweats it out until we get back!"

"Sure thing sir!" Sergeant Watkins replied with assurance.

We set off from Camberley and joined the A3 and A31 via Southampton to

Bournemouth. There was no motorway in sixty-seven. Even with the blues and two again flashing, there were a lot of bottlenecks so it was just over one and a half hours by the time we hit Bournemouth at seven thirty.

Andy had radioed ahead to Bob Driscoll, a fellow Detective Inspector, his Bournemouth police contact and arranged for him to meet us at the thirty miles per hour posts by the 'Welcome to Bournemouth' signpost. We met as arranged and he led us to Phil Hickey's address in East Overcliff Drive.

It was arranged it would be a quiet approach and the Bournemouth man would stop off before nearing the address. All went to plan and as we approached the semi-detached, but just before reaching the huge four storey town house, we noticed a youngish looking man in a black Mini Cooper duck down pretending to pick something up from the floor.

All three of us went in and Andy rang the doorbell.

Almost instantly the door was opened by a tough looking man of about sixty, salt and pepper thinning hair and a little bit of a beer belly showing below a tight white T shirt. He had real or developed arm muscles. He grinned showing white teeth and speaking with a thick London East End accent said; "Inspector Spearing – What brings you this far down south?" and looking over DI Spearing's shoulder he added; "And you too Inspector Sanderson – My I am surely honoured! – Two Inspectors in one visit – Oh my God I must have done something big. Andy just smiled and replied; "Phil" and turning to me added; "And this is DS Devlin."

Phil grinned and replied; "And a DS too! – So why am I this honour inspector?"

Andy just kept smiling and replied; "Can we come in Phil?"

"Certainly Inspector – Always willing to help the police in any way I can." Phil Hickey laughed and moved into the house followed by three of us and being the last one in I closed the door..

Andy was still smiling as he replied; "Yeah Phil – you being so helpful was probably the reason we never could quite nab you!"

Phil's eyes flickered with a little anger, before he controlled himself and again smiling replied; "Yeah that was a different life back then Inspector – Now retired and the grandchildren here you know!"

After the small porch, we entered a massive lounge area which had obviously been furnished and decorated to the tastes of a man. A large, chunky, light oak table surrounded by eight oak chairs was in one corner. A dark brown, leather, Chesterfield four seater settee and two matching large chairs faced a massive television set. The set was a nineteen sixty-seven model with a bubble of electronics behind. It was placed on a matching oak table in another corner. Along one wall sat a rather grand, matching, oak sideboard, with a cream telephone on top and lots of photographs of Sarah and the grandkids, but noticeably none with John Palmer. A large oak coffee table completed the furnishings. The floorboards had been sanded and varnished. The décor reminded one of the big London pubs décor.

"Nice place Phil." Andy said with a deadpan expression.

"Yeah, well its home – not easy when your missus has gone – I never thought it was so difficult to pick things and get things done."

"Yeah, I can second that emotion" Andy spoke with some feeling and added; "Sorry to hear about your missus Phil."

Phil reacted emotionally and replied pointing to the Chesterfield settee; "Take a seat gentlemen. Yeah - she died young at sixty – cancer! Anyway - What can I help you with?"

"Yes, well Phil – we really want to talk to your daughter!"

"Sarah? – She is not here – as you know she just lost her husband this week and the kids are here! She is now trying to get the business sorted out!" Phil responded too quickly and defensively.

"Well that's the thing Phil. Your Sarah has done a runner and we have information that her life maybe in danger and that may be why she did a runner?"

"What do you mean Inspector? Who is threatening my girl?"

"I believe Sarah knows that answer Phil! Let's put it this way Phil – it is the same lot who took out your cousin Joe Bolger!"

"But we thought it was 'The Fox'? Under contract from Jo---" Phil replied cutting himself off suddenly and sounding very weak or astonished.

"Afraid not Phil. We have arrested two people for the murder of Joe, but their bosses are still in control. Have you noticed the guy outside in the mini cooper Phil?"

"Yeah - He is impossible to miss! He has been there all afternoon! He must think we are totally blind or idiots! I thought he was one of yours"

"Again, I am afraid not Phil. If it was us we would only do it that way if we wanted you know we were there. Maybe that is what they are doing?"

"Who are 'they' Inspector?"

"Let's put it this way Phil – When this lot come in they will not hesitate to take you out – with or without your information on Sarah. Not to mention what will happen to the grandkids!"

For the first time, there was real fear in Phil Hickeys eyes and the body language showed real doubt.

Andy sounded very concerned when he said; "Look Phil – if you know where Sarah is I suggest you contact her now! We want to take you all into protective custody until we can get these guys put down. Now what do you think?"

Phil Hickey ran his fingers nervously through his thinning hair before replying; "Okay I will ring her!" He moved over to the cream phone on the oak sideboard and dialled zero before saying; "Did you hear all that? What do you think?"

Inspectors Spearing, Sanderson and I exchanged glances.

Phil Hickey nodded to no one and said; "Okay come down then!" He turned to us three and said; "Sarah is coming down!"

"Has she been living here Phil?"

"No! She is living next door! It belongs to me under another name and I have a hidden door between!"

"Very good Phil, but believe me it would last five minutes with these bastards when they come in."

Sarah Palmer entered the room looking rather forlorn.

Andy spoke quietly nodding his acknowledgement; "Mrs Palmer – I assume you heard all of our conversation?"

"Yes, I did." Mrs P replied firmly and added; "So what do you want us to do Inspector?"

"I believe we have to, immediately, get you all out of here, but first Mrs Palmer – can you confirm it was a Mr Lambert who threatened you?"

"How do you know that Inspector?" Mrs P appeared to be genuinely surprised.

Andy replied with a smile; "We are detectives Mam! We have been searching for you for two days. – So, it was Mr Lambert?"

"Well yes Inspector, but it was more subtle than just an outright threat. His words, as I recall, went something like this 'You know Mrs Palmer we would hate to see the same thing happen to you as happened to Mr Palmer' – I think that was the sum and substance!"

Andy shook his head and quietly replied; "Yes as subtle as a sledgehammer, but nothing I am afraid that we could nick him for Mrs Palmer. However, we have doubts he, or 'they,' were behind the murder of your husband!"

"For Gods sake! - Who are 'they' Inspector?" Phil Hickey suddenly interrupted.

Andy looked and sounded very serious when he replied; "Oh 'they' are an MI5 vigilante group who claim to be acting on behalf of national home security, but we believe some of them may have gone beyond their remit and are acting illegally! – But knowing it and proving it are two entirely different things as you know from the past Phil?"

I thought Andy had gone too far and had said too much, but at the same time knew he had to make them aware of the real danger.

"Jesus, that MI5 mob don't mess around! This whole thing is getting out of hand!" Phil Hickey said fearfully.

I thought an odd expression for him to use 'this whole thing is getting out of hand' and I made a mental note to follow up later.

"So, you do know who killed my husband?" Mrs P asked simply as a matter of fact.

"Yes, we believe we do Mrs Palmer, but we are trying to find out who hired him! We believe it was an assassin known as 'The Fox.' But catching him has proved very difficult for over twenty years.

Phil again reacted badly; "Jesus – this goes from bad to worse – MI5 and now 'The Fox' - the odds are being stacked against us!"

Andy replied with a quizzical tone in his voice; "So you know 'The Fox' Phil?"

Phil Hickey hesitated for a very telling second before replying; "Of course we do!" Phil Hickey again hesitated before adding; "At least we don't know him thank God, but everyone in our business knows about him."

"Well yes Phil – That is why we want to immediately move you and your family – in fact – now move you into a safe house."

"Jesus is there a safe house Inspector?" Phil sounded a bit on the desperate side.

"Well this place is certainly not safe with them already outside waiting on reinforcements to arrive -now is it? Now is there another way out of the houses?"

Mrs P replied; "We can go out the back door via next door and walk down to Manor Road - I have my car back there!"

"Not a good idea to use your car Mrs Palmer! They will trace that car in five minutes! If you and the kids and Phil go out the back door from next door we will double back and pick you all up in Manor Road! They will not even know you have gone!"

"Okay – let's do it now! Phil Hickey replied almost meekly.

"I think if you come to the front door and see us off Phil pretending that you are sorry you could not help us. Then let him see you go back into lounge before sneaking back upstairs and away. Remember and lock the front door when we go. - Okay?"

"Yeah Okay I suppose! I would far rather go over there and take him out!" Phil was suddenly sulky.

Andy shook his head as he replied; "I would not advise that Phil. Believe me these people are extremely dangerous and they are loose cannons."

"Why don't you go arrest him?" Phil asked with a little irritation in his voice.

Andy replied firmly; "Because Phil – he will probably flash his ID and supersede me in the name of national security and there is not much I could do about that! So, let's move it before the wild bunch arrive. Have you got stuff to take with you?"

Mrs P smiled and replied; "All packed and ready for any emergency Inspector!"

Andy suddenly looked very serious and quietly said; "You know Mrs Palmer - you are still going to have to answer at least the charges of perverting the course of justice. That rat of a solicitor of yours and the two monkeys have shovelled it all back on you! You understand?"

"Yes Inspector, but I am sure we will be able to enlighten those three later." Mrs P replied confidently and smiled.

Andy looked solemn as he said; "Yes I am sure you can and will, but just make sure it is legal! After all you are contending with a solicitor if you can call that rat Aldrich a solicitor. Now we better get moving!"

Mrs P ran off upstairs and we heard her gather the kids and their suitcases before we went to the door followed by Phil Hickey. We exited as Phil Hickey shouted rather too loud and obviously aiming to be heard; "Sorry I could not help Inspector, but as I say, our Sarah is in London working and getting ready to bury her husband."

Andy replied blandly; "Yeah right Mister Hickey. I am sure we will find her soon."

We got back into the Jaguar and after the doors were closed I said; "I don't know if you noticed sir but the coldness of Mrs Palmer regarding her recently deceased husband? She never even asked when the body would be released!"

Andy nodded and then surprised me with his response' "Yes, very noticeable Sergeant! And did you catch that remark from Phil – 'this whole thing is getting out of control'?"

I was surprised and responded; "Yeah I noticed that and put it to the back of my head to ask him later!"

Andy nodded again and replied; "Yeah most definitely Sergeant." And then turning to Sergeant Tommy our driver, he asked; "Tommy can you pull up at Bob's - our Bournemouth police friend's car?"

"Sure thing Andy!" Tommy replied as he completed a three-point turn and roared off back down East Overcliff Drive before he added; "It was like a comedy show with that guy in the Mini Cooper. Every so often he would stick his head up like Peter the rabbit and duck back down into his hole! I was watching him in the rear-view mirror which I repositioned. He was a joke as a surveillance man!"

He went around a corner and we found Bob's car where we had left him and pulled over beside him. Andy wound down his window and Bob did the same with his driver's window. Andy smiled and said; "Thanks for waiting Bob. We have a problem back there – one of the Mobs lot has turned up and is watching the place. It is only a matter of time till they raid the place. We must get the family out and into a safe place. – Is there any place local?"

Bob laughed aloud and replied; "Afraid we don't have much of a call for 'safe houses' in Bournemouth Andy – The only 'safe' houses you are likely to find here are 'retirement homes' and some of them are not too safe either!" Bob laughed again and then suddenly looked as if he was thinking and added; "Come to think of it Andy – I have just bought my retirement home in Christchurch which I am doing up on my own in my so called spare time. How would that do?"

Andy smiled and replied; "That would be great Bob – Your missus won't mind?"

"No, she is no longer around!"

"The policemen's curse Bob?"

"Aye the usual, but there you go."

"Okay Bob – Can you follow us round into Manor Road and you can pick them up there? Oh, and Bob – can you arrange for a couple of armed wooden tops to be with them for the next few days?"

Bob laughed aloud again before he replied; "Afraid not Andy – our lot would be more likely to shoot themselves in the foot than shoot anybody, or maybe the people they are supposed to be protecting would be in equal danger! I can get a couple of constables armed with truncheons though!"

Andy laughed and replied; Okay Bob – just make sure they know not to say to anyone, including their Sergeants, what they are up to!"

"Okay Andy – I think I can handle that!"

We moved off and swung a first left into Manor Road and fifty yards down we saw Phil Hickey stick his head out from behind some bushes and pull it back in – He must have seen the two cars which he was not expecting. We pulled up and saw the family behind the bush with four suitcases.

Andy got of our car and was joined by Bob. Andy spoke quietly; "Phil this is DI Bob Driscoll from the Bournemouth police."

Phil Hickey nodded his head; "Yes I know him – He has been here before asking after Sarah!"

Andy replied and said; "That's good! Bob here is going to take you to a safe house in Christchurch. I will only contact you through Bob and it will only be Bob who will relay messages! You should not make any calls until we get this sorted! – Is that understood?"

"Yeah - Yeah – Whatever!" Phil Hickey replied sullenly.

Andy "Just you remember Phil – you and your family are in real danger now and these people are deadly serious. I am out on a limb for you lot! Now off you go before our dickhead friend in the mini cooper finally realises you are not there!"

Bob and I helped with the suitcases and managed to squeeze the cases into the boot of Bob's car and off they went without a word of thanks.

Andy got back into the car and sarcastically said; "It reminds me of the bible story when nine of the lepers did not bother to thanks to JC."

I did not think before I laughed and replied; "Then again governor I don't suppose they were lepers. And you, I know, are certainly not the big yin. After all they were only going to be killed that's all."

Thank goodness we all laughed and Andy replied; "You know lad – you Glaswegians have a really weird sense of humour! – You lot can turn anything into a joke." We all laughed and Andy added; "Okay Tommy, let's get back to Camberley Police Station for this interview and don't spare the horses or the blues and twos – I want to be home before midnight."

It was now eight fifteen on a Friday and dusk was beginning to fall on a fine summer's evening.

We discussed our questioning strategy as we travelled. We agreed for now we had very little hard evidence on Jonathan Bridgewater regarding the murder of Nigel 'hooray Henry' Worthington and we were depending on breaking him down through the homosexual charges.

The traffic was not so bad on the way back; most of it was heading in the opposite direction for Bournemouth. We made it to Camberley in just over an hour pulling up in the police station car park at nine twenty-three, just as it was getting dark.

All three of us trudged wearily into the station only to be faced by a tearful Mrs Bridgewater who immediately rushed up to Andy and shouted; "What the hell is going on Inspector? Why can I not see my husband?"

DI Spearing turned angrily towards Mrs Bridgewater and said firmly; "Please sit down Mrs Bridgewater. Your husband is about to be interviewed in connection with a murder of an employee of New Scotland Yard and another item for which he has already been charged. Only when this interview has been completed, will you may be able to talk to him!"

Mrs Bridgewater looked genuinely shocked and distressed as she turned away with tears in her eyes and sat down.

Another expensively dressed, Savile Row three piece blue striped suited, and pompous looking guy immediately came forward. A lawyer was written all over his round middle aged face with the thinning hair and well - rounded girth. With an obvious smirk, he presented his business card with a flourish to Andy and said; "As you know Inspector Spearing I am William Clements representing 'Clements and Beckhams' – We are Mr Bridgewater's barristers! Can I ask you why you are holding Mr Bridgewater?"

I immediately recognised 'William' Clements name as Judith Clements 'Uncle Bill.'

"Sir, I think" I said, before being interrupted by Andy, who coolly said; "Yes I know Sergeant! Okay 'Mr William Clements' – What can I do for you?"

They obviously knew each other, probably from the crime courts, Mr Clements replied; "Inspector Spearing – as I have just said - I wish to know why you are holding my client without questioning or charges for several hours?"

Andy shook his head as he replied; "I think you know the answer to that one Clements! Your client has already been charged with homosexual offences against a minor earlier today and he has admitted these offences! Now we are investigating an associated murder of a man employed by New Scotland Yard and your client will be helping us with our inquires. I have already made it clear to 'your client' that he is entitled to a solicitor after initial questioning, as per the good book, so I will let you know as soon as he requests one."

With that, Andy, John Sanderson and I started to walk through the reception into the police station offices. I then noticed Mrs Bridgewater crying and mumbling with her hand over her mouth. I went back to her, touched her on the shoulder and said quietly; "I am sorry Mam that you had to find out about it this way, but it had to come out sometime!"

Mrs Bridgewater started dabbing her eyes with a handkerchief and replied; "Thank you Sergeant – it was just such a shock. This will ruin us you know."

I was taken aback! Her husband had been charged with a homosexual offence with a minor and was 'helping the police' on a murder enquiry and all she could think to say was 'This will ruin us you know'? I managed to mumble; "Yes, well anyway sorry about that!" I turned away and saw Andy and John had waited for me and had probably overheard the brief conversation.

We walked on through into the station proper and, as soon as we were clear, Andy turned to me and said; "There's nowt queerer than folk – Eh Sergeant?" I shook my head and replied; "Aye that's for sure sir!"

Andy asked a young PC for directions to the interview rooms and asked him to bring Mr Bridgewater through from the cells.

We found our way to the room and we organised three chairs facing two chairs across a table on which there was a Phillips Tape Recorder which I set up to record. Jonathan Bridgewater came in and sat down sulkily I spoke into the microphone; "This is the recording of an interview with Mr Jonathan Bridgewater in Camberley Surrey police station on Friday the twenty-first of July 1967 at 21-50 hours Present are the aforementioned Jonathan Bridgewater with Detective Inspector Andrew Spearing. DI John Sanderson and Detective Sergeant Kevin Devlin - all from New Scotland Yard." I nodded to Andy.

Jonathan Bridgewater said, while pointing at the recorder; "You can forget that thing. I will not be talking until my lawyer gets here."

Andy shook his head and replied; "I am afraid, unless you reply to our initial preliminary questions, you will not be seeing any lawyer! – It is up to you Mr Bridgewater. I don't really care if you stay in that cell."

Jonathan Bridgewater moved uncomfortably in his chair before he asked; "What are these preliminary questions then?""

Andy again shook his head before replying; "There is no negotiation on these questions you either answer them, or you stay in that cell until you do! Now are you going to answer these questions?"

Jonathan Bridgewater mumbled his reply but said; "I suppose so."

Andy continued; "We are here to interview Mr Jonathan Bridgewater who has agreed to assist the police by answering questions in connection with our two investigations. Mr Bridgewater if you would identify yourself."

Jonathan Bridgewater suddenly looked up and said; "I have not agreed to answer any questions without my solicitor being present!"

Andy replied firmly; "Mr Bridgewater, we have already explained to you that you have to answer these preliminary questions before we can call in your solicitor. Now please state your full name and then answer these preliminary questions."

Jonathan Bridgewater again shifted uncomfortably, but replied; "Jonathan Alexander Bridgewater."

Andy asked; "Mr Bridgewater, can you please state your date of birth and current full address?"

Jonathan Bridgewater shook his head and replied; "Twenty-eighth of April nineteen twenty-two. My current address is; 'Lakeside,' Lightwater Road, Lightwater, Surrey."

Andy smiled and asked; "Can you confirm your business and your business address Mr Bridgewater?"

Jonathan Bridgewater was now relaxing and he replied; "My business is a London based Estate Agents and Property Management and we trade under Bridgewater Estate Agents, in Cromwell Road, Knightsbridge, London.

DI Sanderson suddenly interrupted and asked; "Can you confirm Mr Bridgewater that it was at one of your properties in Kensington that you discovered the body of a young man named David Long who had apparently committed suicide earlier today?"

"I think this is now beyond the preliminary questions and so I should have my solicitor present."

DI Sanderson shook his head and asked; "Why do you think you need a solicitor to answer this question Mr Bridgewater? After all - your reporting of finding David Long's body is already the subject of public record and all we are asking you to do is confirm it was you personally who found the body in one of your properties?"

Again, Jonathan Bridgewater looked uncomfortable before he quietly replied; "I suppose so – yes it was one of my company properties."

DI Sanderson replied sharply; "There was no supposition Mr Bridgewater – it was one of your properties?"

Jonathan Bridgewater looked bewildered and sounded agitated when he replied quietly' "Yes."

DI Sanderson smiled but without any humour said; "Okay Mr Bridgewater – earlier today we charged you with having homosexual activity with a minor – A charge you did not deny. Is that correct?"

"I don't know what I said or did not say this morning – I was so stressed out it was not true! I want my lawyer now!"

DI Sanderson simply shook his head and softly said: "Of course Mr Bridgewater – that is your prerogative, but your reluctance to answer a question, that you answered and recognised from only this morning, is noted for any future trial!" DI Sanderson turned to Andy and nodded.

Andy then said; "Okay Mr Bridgewater we will keep the tape running and bring in your solicitor 'Mr William Clements' - a barrister from 'Clements and Beckhams' – Sergeant Devlin – cam you bring him in?"

"Yes sir!" I replied and went out of the room to collect him. On my return, Andy simply recorded on the tape; "We are now joined by Mr William Clements, a barrister from Clements and Beckhams London, representing Mr Jonathan Bridgewater who has admitted and been charged in connection with his homosexual relations with an under-age boy on numerous occasions. We also intend to question Mister Bridgewater, regarding the associated murder of a man working for New Scotland Yard. Mr Clements for the tape can you confirm your identy?"

Mr Clements, with a pompous tone in his voice, immediately said; "I am Mr William Clements from 'Clements and Beckhams' – We are Mr Bridgewater's barristers! He then added; "I hope for your sake Inspectors you have not been questioning my client without my presence?"

Andy again simply smiled and replied; "I can assure you Mr Clements. As required by law we have only been establishing facts under the preliminary questions routine and as soon as Mr Bridgewater asked for his solicitor to be present we called you in. Of course, you are welcome to a copy of the initial tape containing the preliminary questions."

"Yes of course I will require that, no matter what happens now Inspector."

Andy, apparently ignoring Mr Clements' remarks said; "Of course Mr Clements you will have a copy of the initial tape, if and when these cases go to trial.. Now, if you would like to continue your questions DI Sanderson, regarding Mister Bridgewaters admitted homosexual relations with Mr David Long, a minor and Longs subsequent suicide in one of Mr Bridgewater's apartments this morning?

Bill Clements looked aghast at Jonathan Bridgewater who turned away.

DI Sanderson took his cue and sounding confidential said; "Okay Mr Bridgewater – as I understand from my earlier question regarding your arrest by me earlier today for having unlawful homosexual relations with a minor – you now claim you do not know what you said and that you were too stressed out this morning to remember – Is that correct?"

"You are simply twisting my words!"

DI Sanderson shook his head and said; "It is fairly simple Mr Bridgewater – Is that what you said a few minutes ago or not? It was just before you requested your solicitor to be present. We can always play the tape back!"

"Yes, I suppose that is what I said a few minutes ago" Jonathan Bridgewater mumbled his reply with more than a little irritation.

DI Sanderson then took out and referred to his notebook and, staring hard at Jonathan Bridgewater very coldly but calmly said; "I can understand that under the stress this morning you cannot remember your exact words, but I am sure you can remember having samples taken from your body by our forensic experts this morning in the apartment?"

"How can I forget the indignity of all that? The so called 'forensic expert' was not much older than David – I mean the victim."

"I hope you had read him his rights before you did that Inspector Sanderson?" Mr

Clements interrupted.

DI Sanderson just smiled and replied; "I believe Mr Bridgewater volunteered to submit to this examination, which was done with a Doctor Henry present as per the good book. In any case, at that point he was not charged! And Mr Bridgewater - regarding the young forensic expert – I was not aware there was an age limit to becoming an expert in any field – In any case he was at least eight-years older than your – sorry – the very young victim!"

DI Sanderson was now bristling with anger and he waited for a few seconds before adding coolly; "Now to get back to the point Mr Bridgewater – After the forensics' examination this morning you can recall I charged you with having homosexual relations with a minor – that is - a boy under twenty-one?"

"Yes, I remember that." Jonathan Bridgewater responded again with his eyes welling up with tears.

"Do you remember what you replied when I asked, having charged you with these offences- I asked you – Do you understand? DI Spearing asked at the same time finding a page he wanted in his notebook.

"No I cannot recall what I said." Jonathan Bridgewater shook his head and acted sullen.

"Where is all this going Inspectors? You have already charged my client with this offence. My client can bring me up to date on this!" Mr Clements again interrupted.

Andy replied angrily; "I am afraid, with his selective memory, your client may not be able to give you all the facts Mr Clements. As to where we are going with this, we believe this whole business is linked to a murder of a New Scotland Yard employee this afternoon in Kensington and your client may be able to help us with this investigation. Now carry on DI Sanderson."

Upon the mention of the associated murder a flicker of fear crossed Jonathan Bridgewater's eyes. Neither did Mr Clements now look so smug.

DI Sanderson added; "Let me remind you Mr Bridgewater - In response to the charges of having homosexual relations with a minor and my question 'Do you understand?' was – and I quote – "Yes – Yes I understand, but I never beat him up!"

"I don't recall those words Inspector." Jonathan Bridgewater's eyes were welling up again with tears.

DI Sanderson smiled and replied; "Ah yes – that selective memory of yours. Okay can you remember your response when I asked you – 'Why did you have to sexually assault him when he was in that condition Mister Bridgewater'?"

Jonathan Bridgewater had tears flowing down his cheeks and he tried to wipe his tears as he replied; "I think I said something like – I repeat it was not me who beat him up."

"Exactly Mr Bridgewater - your memory is not that bad! But what we all noticed was you never denied that you had sexual relations with David – You only denied that you beat him up is that correct?"

Mr Clements immediately jumped in and said loudly; "You do not have to answer that Mr Bridgewater It is no more than a supposition and a bit of conjecture."

Andy again interjected loudly; "Believe me Mr Clements – We have far more evidence than supposition and conjecture from this investigation!"

Jonathan Bridgewater said nothing but continued crying emotionally.

DI Sanderson decided to continue and gently asked; "Mr Bridgewater - Do you remember throughout our interview this morning you continually denied that you knew David Long the victim?"

Jonathan Bridgewater wiped away some tears and responded; "Yes I did, didn't

I?"

"Mr Bridgewater, do you still deny knowing David Long before today?"

"I don't know what to say!" Jonathan Bridgewater replied tearfully looking directly at Mr Clements.

"Then say nothing." Mr Clements advised with a dismissive wave of his hand.

Andy again interjected; "I would remind both you Mr Clements and Mr Bridgewater – If you are later charged with a crime and you have not mentioned, when questioned, something that you later come to rely on in court, then this may be taken into account when deciding if you are guilty."

Mr Clements shook his head and replied; "I don't think I need instructions on the law thanks Inspector Spearing."

Andy just smiled and said; "That may be so for you Mr Clements, but perhaps Mr Bridgewater was not aware and needed to know?"

DI Sanderson then continued; "Mr Bridgwater, following your constant denial of knowing David Long before this morning – Would it surprise you to learn we have a witnesses who have told us that David Long was a regular visitor to your Kensington apartment over the last few months. Also, another witness who tells us you have had a new young boyfriend named David – a rent boy – or in real terms a boy prostitute! - for the last few months. – What do you say to that Mr Bridgewater?"

"Oh God!" Jonathan Bridgewater exclaimed with anguish in his voice as he raised his hand to his mouth.

Mr Clements interjected again; "I think we have made it clear Inspector Sanderson that Mr Bridgewater has nothing further to add."

Andy shook his head and replied; "I have not heard Mr Bridgewater say he has nothing more to say. In any case, we have more questions to ask Mr Bridgewater in connection with our investigation into an associated murder case which happened this afternoon. We require his help and we require it now"

Mr Clements interjected immediately "Inspector – Mr Bridgewater has the right to remain silent. You know that!"

"What I do know Mr Clements is that if Mr Bridgewater has nothing to hide then he should not mind answering our questions! – Right?"

Mr Clements replied smiling; "My God Inspector Spearing – If you are diving down to that level you must be really low in any real evidence."

"Believe me Mr Clements – we have got a lot of evidence. We just need answers from Mr Bridgewater to several questions, that's all!"

There was a knock on the door and the Desk Sergeant Watkins appeared in the doorway; "DI Spearing I have an important message from your forensics' team."

I spoke into the recorder; "Interview with Mr Bridgewater and his barrister suspended at 22-20"

Andy stood up and said; "Right Gentlemen! We will have fifteen minutes for a nature break. It will give you time Mr Bridgewater to consider if you should reply to our questions."

We all left the interview room and I watched from a distance as Andy spoke to Sergeant Watkins.

Sergeant Watkins quietly said; "Well Inspector – We appear to have good and bad news. First, Mr Bridgewater's car! It had been cleaned very recently and although there were a couple of dark spots, which could have been blood, because of the upholstery cleaning fluid used, it was practically impossible to lift anything. There was nothing in the boot either – It had also been cleaned with the same fluid.

Second, we got a real lucky break – At Camberley Waste Disposal Tip – one of the attendants noticed a guy this afternoon take a black bag from the boot of his Bentley Registration Number JB 001 E – Yes, it is Jonathan Bridgewater's car – The reason our attendant detective noticed – he had never seen anyone with a brand-new Bentley and as he said, 'dressed to the nines', carry his waste to a dump. So, when Mr Bridgewater went off, the attendant grabbed the bag out of the tip, found a suit with what appeared to be dark stains, possibly blood, and then he phoned us. I took your Forensic people over there and in the bag found a holdall and a near brand new Savile row suit!"

Andy interjected with a sarcastic comment; "An intelligent Refuse Tip Attendant? – What is the world coming to?" Then thoughtfully asked' "Nothing else? No knife or disguises?"

Sergeant Watkins replied; "No afraid not, but he had attempted to wash the suit and the holdall but there was a couple of blood stains left and there were a few more left on the inner part of the holdall! They found a Savile Row tailors label and it is traced back to Jonathan Bridgewater. Forensics have taken the lot back for analysis. Oh, and forensics also say that, the pubic hair found on Bridgewater matches the colour and texture of the pubic hair belonging to Nigel Worthington! Oh and David Longs fingerprints are all over your murder crime scene!"

Andy smiled and said; "It gets better and better Sergeant – Okay, any chance of ordering a few cups of Cha for the interview room?"

Sergeant Watkins smiled and replied; "Certainly Inspector – PC Toner – Can you arrange for six cuppas to the interview room?"

"Yes sir!" PC Toner a tall willowy man replied.

Andy said; "Okay, let's get this thing done before I fall down!" and then he noticed DI Sanderson and pulled him over and said; "Nice session John. As we discussed on the way here - You first raise the question of Bridgewater denying he knew David Long and ask him if he knew any other 'Gentlemen' that David worked for as a rent boy. Try to get a connection to Worthington! – We have pubic hair taken from Bridgewater which matches Worthingtons. We also have blood found on Bridgewater clothes which matches Worthingtons! When you are finished we will then move onto the murder case. DS Devlin and I will then take over the questions Okay?"

"Sure thing Andy. I think it is still dodgy on the murder charge!"

"Yeah, but we just got some good news from forensics which may help."

As we made our way back to the interview room I noticed Jonathan Bridgewater and Bill Clements coming from the toilets in an animated conversation.

We three all filed back into the interview room with Mr Bridgewater and Mr Clements on one side of the table and the DIs and I on the other side. I switched on the recorder and simply said; "The interview with Mr Bridgewater and his barrister Mr William Clements and attended by DIs Spearing and Sanderson plus DS Devlin is now recommenced at 22-35 hours on July twenty one, 1967.

DI Sanderson opened the interview by asking a simple question; "Tell me Mr Bridgewater are you still denying you knew David Long before this morning – despite our witnesses who will testify to the contrary?"

Mr Bridgewater again moved uncomfortably in his chair, but this time he appeared calm when he quietly replied: "No! – I knew David Long before this morning. I was only a bit desperate earlier in that, as a married man with two kids, I did not want to admit to having a homosexual affair with a minor. This will destroy me and my family as you well know Inspector."

DI Sanderson did sound sympathetic, but he replied strongly; "Yes - Well maybe you should have thought about that and the consequences before dropping your trousers so easily. Apparently not for the first time with young boys either Mr Bridgewater?"

Mr Bridgewater "Yes, well we live and learn Inspector!"

Mr Clements then broke into the conversation; "Gentlemen let's not forget this is a 'rent boy' we are talking about here – Surely we can come to an amicable agreement?"

Andy flared up and with a challenging tone in his voice asked; "Like what Mr Clements?"

"Well I am sure Mr Bridgewater here can come to a settlement with his parents and everyone else. After all it was not Mr Bridgewater who beat him up was it?"

DI Sanderson responded strongly; "Maybe not Mr Clements, but he certainly enforced sex on a minor when the boy was obviously in dreadful pain. So, you want him to be allowed to bribe his way out of it – Is that it Mr Clements?"

Mr Clements snorted and replied; "I certainly did not mention any bribes Inspector!"

Andy interrupted quickly; "That's good to know Mr Clements. Carry on DI Sanderson."

DI Sanderson calmly stated; "So Mr Bridgewater you now admit you lied this morning! And you now now confirm having had homosexual relation with a minor?"

"Yes I do admit this but I did not know he was only eighteen!" Bridgewater looked very sad and sounded contrite.

DI Sanderson shook his head and said; "Now we can move on." DI Sanderson paused for effect for a few seconds and then asked: "Did you also lie Mr Bridgewater when you said you did not know anyone who could have physically and sexually abused David?"

Jonathan Bridgewater reacted angrily and almost shouted his reply; "No of course not! Do you think I would let anyone get away with that?"

Andy then interjected calm and collected; "You see Mr Bridgewater that is our problem. The man we suspected of beating David up has turned up very dead this afternoon with his throat slit and a knife through his heart from the back – a very ex-military type execution! – You are also a well-trained ex- military man - are you not Mr Bridgewater?"

Jonathan Bridgewater instantly reacted, perhaps a little too quickly, and shouted: "That was nothing to do with me – I was resting in my office all afternoon! The shock of the loss of David finally got to me so I had to rest."

Andy calmly added; "Yes we will come to that in due course Mr Bridgewater." Andy glanced at me for my cue.

I was suddenly glad I had DI Sandersons notes on the case so far. In my most soothing and understanding psychology voice I asked; "Mr Bridgewater, I understand you had an intimate affair with David over quite a few months. Are you sure he never mentioned any of his other clients who could have beaten him up like this?"

Jonathan Bridgewaters' eyes again began to well up and he wiped away a tear rolling down his cheek as he replied; "It could not work like that Sergeant! David – David was as you say a 'rent boy' and believe me most of his clients – yes like me – could not afford to have their names associated with homosexuality nor have publicity – not to mention the fact that most of these boys were under twenty-one. So, David could not breach confidentiality unwritten rules, or David would just not have any business – You see?"

I kept my calm exterior, but held my pent-up fury in check when I smoothly replied: "Yes I can see that Mr Bridgewater even though you said you loved David. However, my problem Mr Bridgewater as a psychologist, I recognise this beating of a young man as the work of a psycho – This was the work of a man who is into all this Marquis De Sade stuff. So, this was not the first time David would have taken a beaten from this man – Was it Mr Bridgewater?"

Jonathan Bridgewater still had tears rolling down his cheeks as he replied; "No, but it was the first for a long time and it was the worst time ever!"

I stayed calm and pushed out the obvious follow up question; "And he still did not tell you who this thug was Mr Bridgewater – Is that what you expect us to believe?"

"No, he would not Sergeant – I even offered to go around and sort him out, but David would have none of it."

"Go around where Mr Bridgewater?"

Jonathan Bridgewater gave a wry little smile and replied; "I have no idea Sergeant. As I say David would not tell me."

I heard myself say; "Not even on the morning of his death? Like he knew he was going to commit suicide, or so we think, and yet he still did not tell you although he didn't have to protect anyone anymore. Is that what you expect us to believe Mr Bridgewater?"

"I believe Sergeant that David, for whatever reason, actually perhaps misguided, he loved this guy whoever he was!"

"So, he did not love you then Mr Bridgewater and instead loved your rival?"

"He was hardly a rival Sergeant! I was, and had accepted a long time ago, that I was an additional pay cheque for David – that's all."

"Yet he turned up at your apartment with a full suitcase and he appeared to want to stay there. What happened between you in the morning session Mr Bridgewater?"

"Nothing happened – I left him to go check into the office and when I came back he was dead!"

"Why do you think he suddenly decided to end it all Mr Bridgewater? Was it something you did? – Like you forcing him to have sex when he was so badly hurt?" I knew I was being very hard with Bridgewater, but I felt it was needed and it was making the first charges watertight!

Jonathan Bridgewater gave an anguished cry and replied through his tears and snot; "I am not proud of doing that! It was only afterwards that I realised what I had done and I came back to apologise, but found him dead."

"So, then you made up this story of a dosser or a squatter breaking into your vacant apartment and lied to the police pretending you did not know him! Is that correct Mr Bridgewater?"

"I was desperate – I didn't know what to do – It was the first thing that came into my head!"

"Did the thought of revenge on David's so called 'lover,' who had beaten him up so badly, just come into your head too Mr Bridgewater?"

"Of course not Sergeant – I didn't know the man or where he was. Anyway, I was already in big enough trouble all on my own!"

"That's for sure Mr Bridgewater." I replied wryly and looked at Andy which was his cue, but he nodded and mouthed to me 'carry on.'

To give me time to think I nodded a couple of times then said; "To revert to the aforementioned suitcase apparently brought by David to your apartment. I understand you were present when the name and address of the owner was read out by DS Booth. Do you recall that Mr Bridgewater?"

"I remember the suitcase being mentioned, but I did not pay much attention as I was too stressed out."

"Ah yes, that selective memory again – Eh Mr Bridgewater?"

"I can only tell you what I remember Sergeant!"

I intentionally drummed my fingers on the table, both to show my irritation and to give me time to think, then I asked; "Okay let's move on to the afternoon and see if your short-term memory gets any better! You have already said you were in your office resting all afternoon from twelve ish Mr Bridgewater - is that correct Mr Bridgewater?"

"Yes, that is correct Sergeant."

"So how come Mr Bridgewater - one of your staff tried to contact you in your office at one pm, one thirty and just before two and never got a reply from you?" I lied.

"As I said before I was resting and when I sleep I am like a zombie!"

"Most people who have just been stressed as much as you claim to have been Mr Bridgewater– would find it almost impossible to sleep!"

"I am obviously not like most people – I do sleep very heavily Sergeant!"

"Even through the loud knocking three times on your office glass door?" I again lied.

"I don't understand, because all of my staff were told not to disturb me!"

"That's irrelevant Mr Bridgewater – The point is one of your staff could not contact you AND there is a rear exit from your office from where you can get into your car and drive off. Is that what happened Mr Bridgewater? – Did you take off to get your revenge on David's lover who was murdered outside of his apartment this afternoon at an address you heard read out this morning? Is that how it was Mr Bridgewater?"

"Don't be so ridiculous Sergeant. Like I said I must have slept right through the knocking!"

"That must have been a terrible thing when you were a soldier eh Mr Bridgewater? You could have slept right through an attack!"

"Lucky I did sleep lighter when I was younger!" Jonathan Bridgewater replied almost with a smile.

Andy just nodded to me which was my cue to give way to him.

Andy spoke with more than a little irritation in his voice; "Right Mr Bridgewater perhaps you can explain when one of your staff used a key to get into your officeat 13-00 you were not there and your car was not in the parking spot at the back of the building?"

Jonathan Bridgewater looked aghast at this revelation. He face turned chalk white as he shook his head but he said nothing.

Andy then continued; "No comment by Mr Bridgewater? Now you can explain why you were observed this afternoon dropping off a black refuse bag at a Camberley Refuse Tip which contained an nearly new Savile Row suit and a holdall. Both items contain spots of human blood?

This time there was a look of sheer terror in Bridgewaters eyes,

"Mr Clements interjected; "I believe Mr Bridgewater has nothing to say on this at this point! However, I would point out that it is likely that any evidence found on a Refuse Tip is likely to be contaminated."

Andy responded: "I note that Mr Bridgewater does not deny that he dumped a nearly new, very expensive, Savile Row suit at the Camberley Refuse Tip. Also, I would point out that the bag was picked up within two minutes, so the likelihood of contamination at the Refuse Tip is unlikely. However, most importantly I must point out that the blood type on Mr Bridgewater's suit and in the holdall within the bag that Mr Bridgewater dumped at the Refuse Tip, matched the blood type of our murder victim. Can you explain that Mr Bridgewater?" Andy was obviously taking a chance because he did not have confirmation on the blood types.

"I don't know – How should I know?"

"Well it was you who dumped these items Mr Bridgewater – You are probably the only one who can explain why you dumped a nearly new Savile Row suit and holdall, on which attempts had been made to clean with upholstery cleaning fluid, but had still blood spots compatible to the blood group of a very recent murder victim. Perhaps you can explain where the blood spots came from Mr Bridgewater?"

Mr Clements interjected; "Like I said earlier Inspector Spearing – At this point Mr Bridgewater has no explanation, therefore remains silent!"

Andy laughed aloud and replied; "Very well Mr Bridgewater! – Perhaps you might like to answer the next question! – Can you explain why our forensics experts found a 'foreign' pubic hair on your body which is also compatible with the pubic hair on our murder victim from this afternoon – the same murder victim with the same blood type found on your dumped Savile Row suit and your holdall."

Mr Clements immediately interjected again: "That is a scandalous assumption – Simply a step too far Inspector and you know it!"

Jonathan Bridgewater suddenly smiled and said; "I know how that could have happened! When I had sex with David I must have picked up this pubic hair from him'"

There was complete silence before Andy spoke; "So you now admit there was an association between David, yourself and the murder victim?"

All hell was suddenly let loose with Jonathan Bridgewater shouting; "I never said that - did I Mr Clements?"

"You certainly did not Mr Bridgewater. Our Inspector Spearing here is again making one of his famous suppositions. It is really time now Inspector to stop all this conjecture and tell us where your proof is?"

DI Spearing put up his hand to signal 'stop' and said very clearly; "Mr Clements – your client Mr Bridgewater has already changed his story several times and has now finally admitted that he had illegal homosexual relations with a minor under twenty-one, namely David Long for which he has already been charged earlier today. Also, during questioning in relation to an associated case of murder - Mr Bridgewater - you have refused to answer any questions related to police evidence associating you to the murder of one Nigel Worthington, through both of your associations with the deceased David Long. I, therefore, have no alternative other than to to advise you that pending the results of the full forensics results we will be charging you with the murder of Nigel Worthington. Do you understand?"

Jonathan Bridgewater raised his hand to his mouth but did answer clearly; "Yes I understand."

Andy replied; "Do you now wish to answer any of our questions Mr Bridgewater?"

Mr Clements replied; "Mr Bridgewater will reserve his answers for his defence."

Andy replied, almost casually, and with surprising sensitivity; "Very good! – I just hope you understand the warning regarding not mentioning something during questioning which you later come to rely on in court! Mr Bridgewater, you will be taken back to your cell tonight. I am sure Mr Clements will be applying for bail for you as soon as possible. To let you and Mr Clements know - the police will object to bail on the basis that you have the means to flee the country! – We will require you or your wife to hand in your passport to this police station. Is that understood?"

Jonathan Bridgewater tearfully replied; "Yes Inspector" He then turned to Bill Clements and asked; "Can they do that Mr Clements?"

"They can do, but believe me that as they are only charging you with having homosexual relations with a minor – You will get bail in the morning!"

I quickly switched off the recorder with the words "Concluded interview at ten forty-five" and I took Jonathan Bridgewater and Mr Clements through to the Duty Sergeant Watkins, explained what had happened and PC Toner escorted him through to his cell.

Mr Clements then asked if he could have a word with his client and Sergeant Watkins escorted him through to the cell. I returned to the interview room and re-joined DIs Spearing and Sanderson and wearily sat down.

Andy said; "I have to say gentlemen, very well done! I personally have never sat in on a better interview with a suspect. I can only say it was a delight! I think we made a very good team! The lesson learned today gentlemen is that we must prepare for questioning and stop flying by the seat of our pants!"

DI Sanderson broke into a smile and said; "Very good Andy – BUT?"

Andy laughed and replied: "Yes, very good John – you know me too well! - I think we have nailed him brilliantly for the homosexual relations with a minor – with the right Judge he will get at least ten years, but one with leanings towards queers he may only get five! Clements and Co are very good – they will probably get him off the murder charge if the DPP even gets us that far!" Andy then turned away before surprisingly adding; "To be honest I somehow feel a little bit sorry for Bridgewater. In a few short hours, he has destroyed a lifetime's work and his family - all over a rent boy. The boy deserved justice, but it seems a hell of a high price!"

"I think we all agree." DI Sanderson replied and I simply nodded.

Andy replied; "Okay let's get home – at this rate we should be in bed for midnight!"

We all got up and began to troop out of the interview room when I suddenly remembered I forgot to take the tape from the machine and exclaimed; "Shit – hang on a minute." I ran back and carefully removed the tape from the machine and decided to pick up an envelope from the desk to keep it clean.

Andy smiled and said; "Well that could have been a disaster Sergeant!"

As I re-joined them I replied; "You are not kidding sir!" I picked up an envelope from the desk Sergeant Watkins and popped the tape into it.

Andy was speaking to Sergeant Wilkins: Can you note down in the Log Book? Note that we are opposing release on bail, which will probably be tomorrow morning, - If he gets bail Bridgewater has to hand in his passport before he is allowed to leave here! Understood?"

"Yes, certainly Inspector." Sergeant Wilkins replied with a wily grin.

"Thanks Sergeant for everything."

I noticed Mrs Bridgewater still sitting with red eyes in reception and I went over to her and gently said; "Your husband is being held in a holding cell probably overnight pending a bail hearing Mrs Bridgewater. He is now with his barrister Mr Clements and I am sure you will be able to see him when Mr Clements is finished. By the way, before your husband can leave on bail, you will have to deposit his passport with the Desk Sergeant Mrs Bridgewater."

"Yes – Yes – thank you again Sergeant – You are most kind."

I didn't know what to say, so I just nodded and as I turned away I saw Mr Clements come hustling past the two DI's and came straight to Mrs Bridgewater and said; "Mrs Bridgewater, your husband would prefer if you did not see him in this place. Can I offer you a lift home?"

Mrs Bridgewater gasped a little and put her hand to her mouth and quietly replied; "I see Mr Clements – Yes I would be grateful for a lift – Thank you." The misery in the lady's eyes was almost touchable.

I thought to myself, at a barrister's hourly rate, it would probably be cheaper to buy a brand new mini to get home than take a lift from him!

The two DI's and I made our way out to the Jag and found Sergeant Tommy nodding in the driver's seat. "Wakey-Wakey-aaaay!" - It's the Scotland Yard band show Tommy." Andy shouted trying his best to impersonate Billy Cottons introduction to his Sunday Band Shows, which certainly startled Tommy. We all laughed.

"Where to now Andy?" Sergeant Tommy asked, yawning.

"Home James and don't spare the horses or the blues and twos. Before you ask – it is an emergency! – We all need our beauty sleep!"

I laughed and said; "I think it is a bit late for you sir!"

"Hoy, you – that's enough of that hurtful, dry, Glaswegian humour for one day thank you very much. Sergeant" Andy replied acting all hurt. Well at least I thought he was acting!

We set off at full speed and Andy suddenly said; "I think we will need to go into work tomorrow – We need to catch up with our reports and bring young Miss Clements up to scratch with our arrests. – Can you do the typing Sergeant and we can all sign – You are ten times quicker than us two!"

"Yeah I suppose so!" I replied acting sullen.

Andy smiled slyly and said; "Well you didn't expect to get away with your beauty comment - now did you lad?"

I had to laugh, then Andy added; "I'll tell you what, as a bonus, when you are finished typing, we will let you liaise with Miss Clements - Get her to come into the office or go visit her at home – Now that would nice now wouldn't it?"

"You are all heart sir!" I replied sarcastically. We all laughed and began to settle down. I realised that bang goes another day without the gym, or any other social life. I was beginning to hurt in all sorts of places. The gentle purring of the Jag soon began to get to me and the next thing I knew I awoke in London's Buckingham Palace Road at around twelve midnight.

It was decided, to save Sergeant Thomson the bother of travelling all the way out to my flat in Palmers Green and back again to Victoria where he lived, I would spend the night again in Andys apartment on the bed settee.

I protested about needing a change of clothing; shirt, socks and underpants plus a shave, but all I got in response from Andy was: "I can do something about everything except the Y fronts, but you can do without them for one day – Can't you?"

I had to smile the man was incorrigible.

I noticed Andy going into the Jag's boot and taking the Harrods bag containing the evidence from Nigel Worthington's Apartment and of course the forty-five thousand pounds.

I once again went straight to the bed settee, but this time took off my suit and shirt before diving in. Again, I was sleeping within five or ten minutes of putting my head down.

Book 1 in the DI Spearing and DS Devlin series

Chapter 29 – Conclusions

I awoke as usual at about seven a.m. but to the unusual smell from the kitchen of bacon, eggs and toast with the background sound of the BBC Light Programme, as it was known in those days, prior to the formation BBC Radios One and Two. I got up and put on my trousers, yesterdays smelly shirt and wandered through to the kitchen in my stocking feet. I must say I could even smell the stale smell of sweat above the bacon and my day-old socks did pong.

Amazingly, I found Andy bright as a button standing at the cooker whistling and turning bacon and he greeted me smiling with; "Morning Sergeant – how do you like your eggs – turned or soft? - No sunny side up in this establishment!"

"Toast will do me Andy!"

"Nonsense – I have already cooked enough bacon and sausages, not to mention French toast, to feed an army! In my married day's this was always my weekend speciality – at least, whenever I was home at weekends! – I promise you, I will not poison you."

"Oh, okay thank you - as long as you promise – I like them turned – I will have a bit of everything!"

"That's better – a man after my own heart! You know, this is the first Saturday morning in a long time that I have actually been sober and it feels good you know!"

I smiled at his almost boyish enthusiasm and could only think to say; "Yeah that's good – You should try and do it more often." I saw a grimace appear on Andys face and wished I had not said it, but Andy suddenly responded with; "Aye Sergeant – You are probably right there!"

We sat down at the kitchen table and started eating breakfast which I had to admit was delicious.

The presenter on the BBC Light Programme announced in very smooth and very posh English; "This is Paul Hollingdale presenting to you 'Music of the Week' here on the BBC Light Programme. Now taking us up to the news on Saturday, July 22 we have the BBC Band of the year 1967 – The Black Dyke Mills Band! - This track is taken from their LP 'The Virtuoso Band' It is March – The Champions." The band came on in full swing.

Andy spoke through a full mouth; "You know, in my Yorkshire – The brass bands are still the backbone of most of our communities – never mind you're Beatles or The Stones – this brass band music is still the heart of Yorkshire!"

"Aye they are very good Andy!" I had to admit it was such a nice change from the pop groups.

"Aye lad they should be - They were runners up in the 1966 National Championship which in my opinion was a travesty of justice, I watched it live, but they will win this year! Mark my words!"

"I didn't know you were into the brass Andy?"

"Yup part of my heritage 'ee by gum lad 'as we Yorkshire lads like to say!" Andy laughed as he said it, but added; "I still prefer the blues and soul with brass!

The Black Dyke Bands music finished and Paul Hollingdale came on and said; "Well that's it for another week folks. I'll talk to you all next week. Here now is the news." There was a second's break and then a voice came on: "This is the BBC News on Saturday, July 22nd. Within the last few minutes it has been announced by The UK Home Secretary's Office that - Sir Mark Wright - the Commissioner for the Metropolitan Police, including New Scotland Yard and The London Metropolitan Area; - has died overnight in the Hammersmith Hospital. He was fifty-eight years old. According to reports he died from a massive heart attack! According to the same reports, a private funeral will take place next week and a Remembrance Service will be held in September. Sir Mark leaves his wife Shirley. – And now for the rest of the news."

Andy and I simply stared in astonishment at each other. He walked over and turned the radio off and exclaimed; "Oh my God! They have done it! I never thought they would carry it out! But they have! He asked me to come in on Monday to nail the bastards, but it is too late! They have only gone and done it"

I asked; "Who are 'they' Andy?"

"I don't know for sure lad – Not yet! You know as well as I do Sergeant we have a lot of 'bent' coppers in 'The Yard' but I intend to can get the bastards. Sir Mark has left the proof to get rid of the bastards even if we cannot get them for his murder because that is what it is! – I don't care what they say- Look lad Andy suddenly paused for thinking and added; "Then again, we have to consider that Lambert guy the rogue MI5 man and maybe his bosses." There was a pause and he continued; "I just don't know! - I'll tell you what Sergeant - You go and get a shower and get changed - Pick out whatever from the drawers in my bedroom cabinets - suggest you keep a tie on same as yesterday all the media will be there! – use whatever after shaves and stuff you want. I will go and call Shirley - Sir Mark's wife! - then we can do whatever is necessary – Okay?"

I trotted off to the double bedroom and found a white shirt two inches around the collar too big, but decided by tightening the tie I might get away with it. A pair of universal size socks which fitted me and decided not to bother with the underpants carrying the dirty ones with me in a plastic bag.

The shower revitalised me and while trying to dry off I could hear Andy on the phone in the lounge as he quietly said; "Hello this is DI Spearing. Could I speak to Lady Wright please? Yes, this is Detective Inspector Spearing from New Scotland Yard. Who am I speaking to?"

"Hello, DI Spearing this is DCS John Sutherland here. I am at Sir Mark's residence in Sloane Square. What can I do for you?"

"I would like to speak to Lady Wright sir – I am a family friend and have just heard the news on the radio about Sir Mark!"

"Yes, DI I do know from past expcrience you are a family friend!" DCS Sutherland reply was almost sarcastic or sneering and he added; "But I am afraid Lady Wright has just been sedated by the doctor – I am afraid she will be non-compose for the next few hours."

"Can you tell me when approximately she will be available sir?"

"Afraid not DI – it really depends on when she comes out of her sedation!"

"Will Sir Mark be going for a post mortem?"

"Well DI – Lady Wright does not want a post mortem carried out on Sir Mark!"

"I am afraid it is not down to Shirley – I mean – Lady Wright – As you well know sir! – It is the law for any sudden deaths in this country there has to be a post mortem - no exceptions!"

"For Gods' sake man! Sir Mark has died in hospital from a massive heart attack! I should think that is enough! The hospital doctors were working on him last evening and practically all night!"

"The hospital doctors know the law sir – A post mortem has to be carried out - no question"

"Why don't you respect Lady Wright's wishes DI? She has spoken to the doctors and made her wishes clear and they under the circumstances have gone along with it because the cause of death is so obvious. So, why can't you DI?"

"Maybe it's because it is unlawful sir? I thought as a DCS for NSY you of all people would understand and support that?"

"Listen to me DI Spearing! – You had better get this straight – We do not want to upset Sir Mark's family any more than we have to. So back off DI and that is an order."

"I am afraid I don't accept orders which tell me to break the law sir." Andy replied and quickly hung up the telephone.

I quickly finished dressing and re-entered the lounge and saw the fury on Andys very red face as he banged the telephone down on the cradle.

I very quietly asked; "Problems Andy?"

"Aye lad – It appears our DCS John bloody Sutherland is trying his best to sweep Sir Mark's death under the carpet. He actually tried to order me to break the law. What an arsehole!"

"What are you going to do Andy?"

"I am going to have to go to James Hall - the city of London coroner – I know him personally – I will get him to sign an order to hold the post mortem. Funny enough he is in Eagle Street just around the corner from Judith Clements place I believe Sergeant?"

"Oh, I see!"

"Well there is no point in us both running around High Holborn and the Temple is there? Anyway, you have to type up those reports and take them over to her. At the same time, you can type out the application for the coroner."

"I thought you were going to come in with us and sign all the reports? You will have to sign the order as well!"

"Well I don't think it would be a good idea for me to go into 'The Yard' for the moment!" Andy again went thoughtful and then continued; "I tell you what – I have to go to Sloane Square to talk to Sir Mark's wife when she is awake in a couple of hours. I can meet you there and sign the stuff then you can jump on the tube at Sloane Square station – take the circle line to Victoria and then the new Victoria Line to Green Park and swop onto the Piccadilly Line to Holborn. It is walking distance from the tube station to Miss Clements place in Red Lion Square – you can always get her to counter sign the order as the representative from DPP before you go down the adjoining Eagle Street where James Hall the coroner's offices are – no problem eh Sergeant?"

"I can see a few. I don't expect the coroner will be around after lunch when I finish these reports and order application will he? I don't know if Judith – Miss Clements - will be around either – she might be off home for the weekend and not working like us idiots!"

"Ah don't worry Sergeant – I will give you time in lieu for all this overtime as soon as we get these cases off our hands. The Coroner's office is open all day – These sudden deaths don't stop for the weekend you know. I will phone the Coroner's office - they will know how to contact him and you can catch up with him wherever."

The phone rang which startled both of us and Andy lifted it and said quietly; "Hello."

"Andy it's me!"

Andy straightened up and signalled for me to stay before replying; "Shirley – is that you? I thought you were sedated?"

"That's what DCS Sutherland thinks. I persuaded Doctor Bowen to give me tablets to take later and I also got him to go to The Yard and await your call – he will explain that part to you Andy – we three - Doctor Bowen and I were with Mark before he died – I think that the so called massive heart attack was brought on by a mysterious injection. Someone who claimed to be from MI5 got ito New Scotland Yard yesterday evening as Mark was leaving. I have not told anyone else yet. Anyway, I listened into your conversation on the upstairs line. I never said I didn't want a post mortem Andy, but I did not push for one until after I had spoken to you!"

Andys face showed anger but he replied very calmly; "Oh I am so sorry to hear about Mark, sorry Shirley I should have said that first! - I was down in Bournemouth on a case last night and didn't get back until midnight!"

Shirley sounded strained when she replied; "I know Andy – You don't need to say it! I know! But Andy - among Mark's last words to me were; 'Trust no one at 'The Yard' – only you Andy and John Sanderson. But he also said that if 'The Yard' was implicated in his death you had to make sure it never comes out! He said it would destroy 'The Yard' and people would never again trust the London police. He said to make sure you understood that Andy. Him and that bloody New Scotland Yard! – He even gave up his life for it!" Shirley was now sounding emotional.

Andy was struggling to keep control as he replied; "I know 'The Yard' and you were his life Shirley and I do understand what he said. He also knew I would never allow 'The Yard' to be implicated and I never will! But if it is the case that 'The Yard' is implicated and I find out who is involved, I will try and find a way to get rough justice if nothing else!"

"You just be careful Andy – These people, whoever they are, obviously take no prisoners and if they can kill the top policeman in the country then they will have no problem with you!"

"Yeah, I know Shirley, but there are ways and means! Listen! - I need to come over and get you to sign a piece of paper - write it out in your own hand writing - saying that you do want to have the post mortem and have never said you do not want to have one. I will be a couple of hours before I can get there - so stay in your room and pretend to be sedated until you hear me at your front door. Okay?"

"Okay and thanks Andy!"

"No problem Shirley - that's what friends in the police are for eh?!" Andy was about to hang up when he heard Shirley shout; "Andy - I almost forgot! Mark also gave me a copy of the files giving the proof he had gathered against forty officers for fraud and being on the take. He said that the Home Secretary and the Attorney General had the originals and agreed the charges, but they also agreed they were all to be offered to resign quietly and be given a redundancy package. But if they were near retirement age they were to be offered full retirement packages. But they all have to sign that they go quietly and it was their decision because they wanted the redundancy or the retirement package! Do you understand it Andy? I just wrote it down and read it out parrot fashion!"

"Yes, I understand it and why it has to be this way, but it sticks in my gullet to think they are going to get away with it, but some may be involved in Sir Mark's death as well" Andy said it with a straight face and with feeling added; "Give me the copy files when I come over Shirley."

"Yes Andy- and one last thing - Mark said he had logged the incident with New Scotland Yard security regarding the MI5 guy, or whoever, on Friday evening. He said for you to check with the Security Log book. I'll have to go now." Shirley hung up rather quickly without a goodbye.

Andy put the phone down slowly and thoughtfully back in the cradle before turning to me saying; "There is more evidence to collect in 'The Yard' Sergeant. You will have to go and see Doctor Henry Bowen. I think he is on the second floor and collect his statement. I will ring him and organise it for you to pick it up. Also, you need to go to Security and take a copy, or at worst a Polaroid photo of their log from Friday evening involving Sir Mark. – It maybe we have MI5 involved again! Bring them both with you to The Coroner's office along with the rest of the stuff. I will ring you at 'The Yard' on what I want to put in the Coroner's Application Form for the post mortem. Oh, and Kevin! - Take the evidence from Worthington's Apartment and put it in his file along with a copy of our report, but leave the money here – we will discuss it later when we have the time. Okay?"

"Aye, okay Andy." I answered, not really knowing what to say! I added; "I had better get going it's going to be another long day by the look of it!"

"Aye – You can say that again lad! Phone me when you are ready with the reports."Andy handed me his business card with his address and phone numbers on it and added – "Hopefully a few hours?"

"Yeah at least that Andy - I will try and get some help when I get there. See you later."

On the way out, I picked up the bits and pieces of 'evidence' from Nigel Worthington's' apartment, leaving the money and re-pocketed the Bridgewater tapes.

As I exited it was around nine and turning into another fine summer morning, so I decided on a bit of exercise and did a forced march down Buckingham Palace Road to NSY. At the end, I was hot and bothered. I then noticed the mass media gathered outside the entrance and muttered under my breath; "Oh fuck." - There were TV crews from BBC, ITV and the American networks ABC and CBS News, not to mention the hordes of press people, men and women, from UK Nationals and locals like the Evening News and Evening Standard, with cameras flashing at anything that moved. They were all being held at bay outside the entrance by a thin blue line of PCs.

Of course, being Saturday morning, there were few police, or workers, going in or coming out. I had to hard shoulder my way through the mob avoiding all the quick-fire questions about 'What happened to Sir Mark?' or 'Was it a heart attack?' etc. I knew better than to answer them so I shouted; "You know as much as I do ladies and gentlemen! I am sure our press office will have released statements and will bring you up to date as and when anything further develops. Now please, I have to get into work!" Amazingly they suddenly made a corridor through, like the parting of the Red Sea for old Moses and as I reached the thin blue line I flashed my ID to one of the PCs and went on through.

I signed in at reception and having decided to give Doctor Bowen a bit of time to write his statement, I went direct to the Security Office in the corner of the reception area to check the log book for yesterday evening for Sir Mark's statement. I went into the small office where I found a Sergeant behind the desk and I again flashed my ID before I said; "DS Devlin Sergeant! – I would like to take a copy or a Polaroid photo of the entry in your log book from yesterday evening regarding Sir Mark and this MI5 guy!"

The Sergeant shook his head and replied in a Scottish lowland, possibly Glaswegian accent; "I am Sergeant Baxter DS - I was the one that recorded that entry, but twenty minutes ago I had DCS Sutherland on the phone and he asked me to drop the Log Book off in his office on the top floor!"

"Isn't that a bit unusual Sergeant?"

"You're telling me DS! I had to go to stationary and get a new book to start and you know what that is like on a Saturday morning! But the DCS said that in view of Sir Mark's death they had to investigate the incident."

"Aye that's right – My DI Spearing has copped the investigation!" I lied.

Sergeant Baxter looked quizzically at me and said; "Funny that, because the DCS said to me he alone would handle this question."

I shifted uneasily from foot to foot and mumbled; "The left hand doesn't know what the right hand is doing again. Is the DCS in?"

"No! - he can't make it in until this afternoon, but he ordered me to get it up to his office and to make sure the office was re-locked!"

"Oh" Was all I could think to say before I stammered to ask; "Would it be possible to go up there and take a Polaroid photo of the entry? Leave the Log Book there, but bring me a photo of the entry?"

Sergeant Baxter looked very serious before he said; "Oh I don't know!" Then he suddenly smiled broadly and winked before saying; "I can do better than that DS Devlin!" He went into his drawer and produced a Polaroid photo of the Log Book entry and then said; "You know us Glaswegians DS Devlin - if a boss tells you to break the rules you automatically cover your arse especially with the English!" He laughed and added; "Even if I hadn't taken it, I would have got it for you! If we cannae help a fellow Scot you know! Anyway, I trust DI Spearing and I, like most Scots me thinks, just naturally don't trust a boss!" He laughed again.

I laughed with him and replied; "Well thanks very much Sergeant – The problem is that around here it's hard to know who to trust – You know what mean?" I looked at the back of the photo and sure enough Sergeant Baxter had signed and dated it, plus he had even recorded the Log Book it had been extracted from.

"Yeah, I know exactly what you mean DS – and don't worry, I won't be saying to anyone about any investigation." Sergeant Baxter smiled and again winked

"Has anyone told you that you are also a devious sod Sergeant?" I smiled.

Sergeant Baxter laughed and replied; "I am sure I don't know what you mean DS! - By the way, you know that our receptionist Sandra reckons that she could identify this MI5 guy? – Said she quite fancied him!"

"Really? – The lovely Sandra who would have thought?" My question trailed off before I added with a little embarrassment; "That would be great if we can ever get our hands on the MI5 man Mr Hazlewood! - Thanks Sergeant – have you any idea where Doctor Bowen is on the second floor?"

"Oh aye! – You turn left when you come out of the lift and his little medical centre and his office are the last two doors on the left before you hit the south facing windows. I thought it was weird him being in on a Saturday?"

I winked and said; "You are not the only devious one around here Sergeant."

That tickled his fancy and he laughed again as I started to leave his office he suddenly said; "Just make sure you do not lose that photo oh devious one!"

"No problem! I usually only mislay things until I need to produce them - you know what I mean?"

"Get on with you!" Sergeant Baxter laughed and waved me away.

On my way to the lifts I thought – How the hell did DCS Sunderland get onto this so quickly? Then I thought he has to be listening in on the phone call from Sir Mark's wife! Thank the Gods that Sergeant Baxter was on duty this morning!

I decided to take more exercise and bounded up the stairs to the second floor which I regretted about three quarters way up. I thought again how amazing that, after years of solid exercise, only a week away and it already feels so difficult.

I was almost breathless, breathing almighty hard, but found Doctor Bowen's office as directed and knocked the door to be greeted by a subdued voice saying; "Come in."

I entered the small office which only contained a metal grey, double pedestal desk with a phone on top and two filing 'In' and 'Out' green plastic trays. There were two uncomfortable, grey, plastic chairs facing each other across the table. Two four-drawer matching grey, padlocked, metal filing cabinets went along one wall with a whirling fan on top – the only ventilation in the office - but in reality, it was only pushing warm air around a very confined space – at nine thirty, or so in the morning it was already stiflingly hot.

"Good morning Doctor Bowen – I am DS Kevin Devlin - I am DI Spearing's DS. He sent me to pick up your statement?" We exchanged hand shakes.

"Ah yes, DI Spearing rang me thirty minutes ago and I have done it!" He went down to the third drawer on the right of the double pedestal desk and produced a hand written single A4 page. I could not decipher most of it!

I looked at Doctor Bowen and asked; "Do I have to get a doctor to act as an interpreter Doctor Bowen?"

Doctor Bowen laughed and replied; "Yeah! - You might, come to think about it! – My hand writing is getting worse!"

"That's putting it politely Doc!"

Doctor Bowen laughed "Yeah! Well! – All you need to remember DS is this! – It says Sir Mark was injected with something in his thigh only hours before his death, which may have contributed to his early and unexpected death. – Only a thorough post mortem can answer that question!

"Well thanks Doctor."

"Let DI Spearing know DS that about fifteen minutes after he called, DCS Sutherland called and asked me to hold any medical reports on the death of Sir Mark. - I told him I had already submitted my report to the next level which I have just done now! What you have is a copy, but Sir Mark asked me to ensure DI Spearing got the first copy." Doctor Bowen smiled.

"Thanks again Doc – This will be in DI Spearing's hands within the next few hours."

"Jolly good DS." Doctor Bowen replied with a very English accent and attitude.

I thought to myself – that is the second time DCS Sutherland has moved to try and shut up this investigation. Once a coincidence, twice a problem and third time smells of a conspiracy!" Never mind we are ahead of his game for now!

"Thanks again Doc – I will let DI Spearing know what is happening!"

I walked back towards the lifts and decided, since my third-floor office was only one floor up, it had to be in for a penny in for a pound and I bounded up the stairs. Again, at the top I was still a bit on the breathless side.

I finally got my breathing under control and exited the door to the stairs. I walked straight over to the message board and picked up two messages for DI Spearing. I noted one from DCI Flash Harry, Tomlinson telling DI Spearing to call him immediately he arrives. The other from DCS Sutherland, saying the same and I stuck both messages in my pocket.

As I walked across the office I noticed that for a Saturday morning it was busy then DI Sanderson called over to me; "Sergeant – Have you got a second please?"

"Yes, sure sir!" As I walked across towards him I noticed DS Booth sitting at the desk opposite to him and there was an old-fashioned typewriter in front of him.

"Yes sir – What can I do for you? I asked politely.

"Sergeant – What tragic news this morning!"

"Yes sir – unbelievable?"

"Yeah it is that Sergeant – Is Andy – DI Spearing - coming in this morning."

"No sir – He is off on something personal! Trying to help an old friend I believe." I almost felt like giving him a nod and a wink.

"Oh, I see Sergeant." DI Sanderson gave a knowing smile and then added; "By the way Sergeant – DS Booth and I have started doing the Case Reports and Interviews with Bridgewater from yesterday morning and the interviews etc. from the office employees, plus I will do the initial report at his home. If you can pick it up from the taped interview onwards and add to the case book. How does that sound?"

"That would be a great help sir! I still have five outstanding case reports for this week. I don't know where to start!"

"Probably best start at the latest and work your way back from yesterday evening! I find it easier that way Sergeant."

"Aye – It's as good a place as any I suppose." I started to wander over to my desk, but suddenly remembered; "Any idea where I can get a recorder to play this tape sir?"

"Yeah, there is one in the interview room downstairs – The one you were in the other day with the rape case!"

"Oh, aye that's right. – It seems like an eternity ago!"

"Yeah - When you are with DI Spearing the days and nights just roll away."

DS Booth interjected with a sarcastic comment that was meant to be funny, but backfired; "More like 'rolling over' with DI Spearing than anything else I would think!"

DI Sanderson stared hard at DS Booth before replying; "That's your trouble DS Booth. You cannot think!" DS Booths face went red, but he did not reply.

I smiled as I went away I said; "I'll snatch a cup of coffee and then go down there."

I wandered over to my desk, noticed some more messages on Andys desk – one from the coroner on the Joseph Bolger case asking Andy to ring back.

I looked up Judith Clements number on my Rotadex and dialled her number. She lifted the phone almost immediately and cheerily replied; "This is the Clements residence."

I replied in my most stern voice; "Good morning The Clements residency – Could I speak to Madam Clements please?"

"There is no 'Madam' in this residency – only Miss Clements – Kemosabe?"

"Ouch! How did you know so quickly?"

"There is no disguising those deep Glaswegian tones my Lone Ranger!"

"Me thinks you are too fast a lady for The Lone Ranger! I am too slow on the draw!"

Judith laughed aloud and replied; "Idiot! – Not what I heard at Cambrige! What can Kemosabe do for you oh Lone Ranger?"

I then tried to get all serious; "You have heard about Sir Mark dying during the night?"

"Oh, my God – NO! - What happened?"

"Apparently, it was from a massive heart attack, but there are some very important questions to be asked! DI Spearing has asked me to drop off an application to a coroner's office which is just around the corner from you and he has also asked me to bring some case reports for you to review! – We have made a few arrests and we need you to back them and take the necessary action as soon as possible."

"Yeah! — sure, but when?" Judith suddenly sounded very unsure almost defensive.

"Well, it is going to be a couple of hours at least before I am ready and I have to go over and see DI Spearing at Sir Mark's residence in Sloane Square en-route to seeing you."

"Oh, yes that's all right!" Judith sounded self - assured again and she added; "It is just I am still in my jimjams and I must have a shower!"

I laughed and said; "Oh that's alright! - You can wait until I come to have that!"

"Kemosabe speaks with a forked tongue again!"

I laughed again and replied; "Damn caught out again! My only excuse Judge is that is the way I was brought up on the Glasgow streets – We were so poor – the homeless guy on the corner offered us handouts!" (I had picked that one up in an American magazine, only because it did apply to our family!). – "Please your honour can you be understanding and lenient! Please Judge!"

"My sentence could not be more severe Mr Devlin. I order you to serve an additional year under the care and guidance of DI Spearing!"

"Oh, my God! – Not that your honour! That is worse than sending me to Siberia!" I laughed and then added; "Actually I am only joking - he turns out to be a very good detective - sober or otherwise –I am beginning to like him."

"Yes, you forget I have heard your Morecambe and Wise routine! I could see and hear the mutual disrespect!"

"I say again – you are too clever by half Miss Clements. Anyway, I will have to go. See you in about two hours. Okay?"

"Yeah no problem. I will be showered, changed and ready!"

"Aw shucks! Never mind! Maybe next time! See you later!" I hung up with a real smile on my lips.

I decided on a coffee to kick start my day as the machine coffee always did. I wandered on over. There I found Bill Brown lurking beside the coffee machine doing as little as possible as usual.

"Why if it isn't our resident 'trained bairn' – still sucking DI Spearing's tit are we?" Bill Brown with his semi - Edinburgh accent.

"It beats licking your bosses arse! Like you Brown" I replied with my usual disarming smile.

Bill Brown moved angrily forward, his purple high pressured face now contorted.

"I wouldn't advise that Mr Brown – unless you want to finish up on your ass among your own shit! It would be kind of embarrassing for you don't you think?"

"You are about to get your come-uppance smart ass!"

"Well it certainly won't be from sleaze bags like you BB! Now move your fat ass Mr Brown and let me get a cup of this poison!"

I put my shilling in the machine and got another cup of the coffee filth, which tasted more of chocolate with a hint of Bovril, - It all came out of the same tubes and mixed. Shit!

I stood and drunk the stuff for a minute and then poured half of the cup back into the machine's overflow grill which was already overflowing with stinking rubbish smells.

I decided to go down to the first floor and collect the tape recorder. I needed to complete my case report.

I waved to DI Sanderson and indicated by sign language that I was going down to the first floor to collect the recorder from the interview room. I again walked down the stairs – the fitness regime again on my mind! Not so bad going downstairs, but still noticeable compared with a couple of short weeks ago.

I reached the conference room on the first floor and got under the table to take out the three-pin plug. When I came back out from under the table and got upright, I was faced by Bill Brown and to his right Tony Booth, both trying their best to look very hard. I was not bothered; even though they were both around six feet and big men they were obviously amateurs at this game! They were not on their toes, not in a position to throw a decent punch without me seeing it coming from a mile off and finally, if they had been any good, they would have ganged up on me - stopping me from being effective with either fists or feet – there again they were probably not expecting the kick boxing!

"Not so tough now are we 'trained bairn'?" Bill Brown almost spat out the words pointing a finger at me.

"I would not go down that path Tweedledee, or you Tweedledum. You will both find out just how hard I really am!"

"All mouth and no substance eh bairn!" Bill Brown responded and I saw he was bunching his fist and I hit him so fast and so hard in the solar plexus he practically shut over like a pen knife and he hit the floor, rather heavily.

I spun and threw a scissor kick – just like the pro footballers do an overhead kick of the football, only this time my right shoe connected with a sickening thud on two balls belonging to Tony Booth whose eyes almost popped out of their sockets and he collapsed towards me – I thought I had better catch him or his head would have been bashed on the table and then the floor. I gently put him down on the floor out cold.

Suddenly I noticed standing in the doorway was DI Sanderson. He looked shocked.

"I am a witness Sergeant – I saw these two attack you and you had to defend yourself, which you certainly have done! I saw them follow you down here from the coffee machine and knew they were up to no good so I tailed them down here. – Probably just as well – They would have made up any cock and bull story!"

"Aye I suppose you are right sir! I smiled and added; "Thanks sir. I don't think I have ever landed two sweeter blows, but I was a bit harder than I intended. I think I had better get Doctor Bowen down here, especially for Booth. I reckon he will be singing soprano parts for the rest of his life!"

Bill Brown, his face a sort of contorted mauve colour, gave a moan and he muttered; "Bastard I think you have broken my ribs!"

"I would not be surprised Tweedledee – but you were warned and DI Sanderson here is a witness."

"Well, we will see about that!" Bill Brown muttered finding breathing difficult.

I knelt down beside him and talked into his ear but loud enough that Tweedledum could hear it - if he had regained his consciousness; "Let me make this very clear to both of you. - If you make any trouble for me you both will think this was just a ticking off!"

Bill Brown was still gasping for breath but just about managed to say; "You heard him DI – He threatened the two of us!"

"Sorry DS, but my hearing is not so good these days. However, I would advise you if DS Devlin is giving you two some advice, then if I were you I would take. After all, you have just witnessed he is a man of his word!" DI Sanderson just smiled and nodded.

"Bastards!" was all Tweedledee could reply, but he did look in pain his face ashen.

I laughed and said; "You are probably quite right Tweedledee and both of you don't forget it!"

I grabbed the tape recorder with the socket and said; "Could you keep an eye on them sir? I will go up via Doctor Bowen and get him down here! I will tell him they seem to have had a bit of a dispute down here. Okay sir?" The adrenaline was beginning to slow down.

DI Sanderson smiled and replied; "Yeah DS – that should do nicely."

I caught Doctor Bowen just as he was on the way out. He was standing awaiting the lift to come up with his doctor's bag in hand. I quickly explained the situation downstairs and with a shake of his head he said he would attend to it before he left.

I carried on using the steps again to the third floor and started to get on with the first report using the taped interview. Progress was a lot quicker than I thought when the telephone on Andys desk rang, I leaned across and picked it up; "DI Spearing' phone- this is DS Devlin speaking."

"Hello DS Devlin can I speak to DI Spearing?" A man, sounding middle age, with a strong London east end accent was on the line. But there was something not quite right about the accent! - Perhaps too heavily put on?

"No sir - afraid not - DI Spearing is not in today. Can I help?"

"I am afraid not DS. The thing is DI Spearing was supposed to speak to me yesterday, about this time and I tried several times but no answer!"

"Yes sir –Well I am afraid yesterday was just mental. We finished up getting back from Bournemouth at twelve o'clock last night. Can I have your name and number and I will get him to ring you?"

"No I am afraid not DS! Just tell him he missed my call - he will know who it is and what it is about!"

"I'll tell you what sir. I will ring him and tell him you called and – if it is all right with him for me to give out his number – you can call back in, say fifteen minute,s and then you can contact him direct. How's that? "

"That's very kind of you DS – I will speak to you in fifteen minutes?" The tough London east end accent had melted down and he hung up.

I immediately dialled Andys home number in the hope that he had not left yet.

He picked it up on the first ring; "DI Spearing here!!"

"Hello Andy – it is Kevin here!"

"Why Sergeant - I think DI Lawler was right about you the other day - about you being a Celtic paranormal! - I was just about to ring you!"

"What was that for Andy?"

"No – No – You first – you rang!"

"Oh right – Well! I have just had a call from a very mysterious gentleman who is putting on a London east end accent. He said you were supposed to speak to him yesterday, about this time, and he tried several times."

"Oh shit! I completely forgot – With all that was happening yesterday!"

"Yes, I explained Andy – I also said I would speak to you and if it was okay with you I would give him your number if he rang back in fifteen minutes?"

"Oh well done Kevin! - I do need to speak to him urgently - so go ahead and give him my number!"

I noticed Andy was not saying who the mystery caller was, but me being a Celtic paranormal detective; I have my suspicions but best kept to myself. I only said; "Oh and by the way - I think Sir Mark's phones are tapped, or there are bugs in the house! DCS Sutherland seems to be a step ahead of us with the security question and Doctor Bowen – The DCS appears to be trying to plug holes!"

Andy laughed again and asked; "Really, bugs under the rugs eh? Oh, did you get the statements from both?"

"Yes, no problems! Both are good people!" I replied and then asked; "And what were you going to call me about Andy?"

"Oh Yeah - bad news I am afraid! – Our MI5 star witness - Jones - has been found dead in his cell this morning. Apparently, it has been made to look like suicide by hanging!"

"Oh fuck – Those MI5 guys are really cleaning up their shit behind themselves!"

Andy laughed and replied; "That is what I like about you Scots! – Such a genteel, but abrupt way of reporting the facts! The problem is, there were only four people who knew Wilkins and Jones were in there and where they were located. That was Mitchell the Governor, Kavanagh the senior officer, you Sergeant and I. Now then - I know you and I are in the clear and Mitchell does not have the build or the muscle to handle Jones, which leaves Kavanagh! – He has the build and the muscle to do it! I have asked the Governor to hold him and anybody else who has been near Jones until we get there."

"Are we sure it is not suicide Andy?"

"Well no, but I am pretty sure that yesterday afternoon he had no intention to commit suicide. He wanted a way out, hence his signed statement! Anyway, I have organised Forensics and a Coroner to get there pronto with a photographer and told the Governor to make sure nobody touches anything, although Kavanagh took him down, claiming he wanted to try reviving him!" There was a pause before he added; "Well it is just as well we got that signed statement and photograph of him signing yesterday. - Have you got them with you Sergeant?"

"Aye – I have just finished putting them in the case book for Judith Clements to look over."

"Look, you had better get off this phone just in case my man rings you back early! Oh by the way, that result means we have to change our schedule today - After you finish your reports get a car – the Jag with Tommy preferably – tell him I have authorised it! Then meet me in an hour or so at Sir Mark's place in Sloane Square. I will wait for this guy's call in a few minutes then head straight over there to pick up Shirley's statement - it will only take a few minutes - and we can swing round Holborn to the Coroner's office etc. then on to Kings Cross Prison – Okay?"

"Yeah okay Andy – see you in an hour or so!" I hung up with the thought that another day was slipping out of my grasp and still no gym work.

After no more than a few minutes, Andys phone rang again. I answered it as usual; "DI Spearing's phone DS Devlin speaking."

"Hello DS Devlin – Do you have DI Spearing's number for me?" It was the 'mysterious' London east ender.

I gave him the number and he hung up pronto, no chance of tracing that number; anyway, it was a public phone box because I heard the coins drop. See, I am a bit of a detective!

I continued with my reports and amazingly got them all done, at least my lot, completed in forty-five minutes and I picked up two more from DI Sanderson who counter signed the lot and said; "By the way Tweedledee and Tweedledum have been taken to hospital. Tweedledee has suspected broken ribs and Tweedledum has two balls the size of footballs!"

"Oh my – I wonder what went on there then. Did they say anything sir?"

"Apparently not a word, but someone heard a soprano singing!" DI Sanderson laughed as he said it.

"Well that was to be expected!" I replied with a sly smile.

I phoned the car pool and asked to speak to Sergeant Tommy Thomson.

"Sergeant Tommy came on the phone and I said; "Hi Tommy – DS Devlin here! DI Spearing has asked me to book the car with you again – We have a round trip around London!"

"It is not another all day and half the night thing again Sergeant?"

"Well you know Andy don't you Tommy."

"Yeah only too well! - Too well! See you in five minutes" He hung up.

Andy walked across Sloane Square toward Sir Mark's residence, saw the TV and

Press crews, ignored them all and their questions and rang the doorbell. It was answered by a grim looking DCS John Sutherland who beckoned him in and hurriedly closed and locked the door behind him.

"What the hell are you doing here? I told you Lady Wright had been sedated!"

"That's all right DCS – I am awake now!" Shirley Wright called from the top of the stairs which went straight up from the entrance hall!" Shirley was on cue and continued; "I would like to see Andy in private DCS! I will be down in a minute Andy - Go through to the lounge."

DCS Sutherland muttered with the side of his mouth; "I warned you DI – On your head be it."

Andy just smiled; "Or in my back eh Brutus? You will not and cannot cause or order me to break the law and not have a post mortem – SIR!"

"The Home Secretary himself has ordered that this be hushed up!"

"Not even God himself can order me sir! Do you remember what we all said when the captured Nazis said; 'We were ordered to do this'?" Andy turned away

"Don't be so ridiculous DI. – That has nothing to do with this! - You know your career will be in tatters."

"I never thought I had a career anyway after you appointed your mate Flash Harry. What a joke he is." Andy replied over his shoulder.

"We have you already for insubordination and disobeying direct orders from DCI Tomlinson – Just remember you no longer have the protection of your friend, DI!"

"Whatever you say DCS." Andy smiled and waved his hand as he went. DCS Sutherland turned away, his face red and furious. He came face to face with Lady Wright who had obviously heard the last part of the conversation and looked disgusted but coolly said; "I would like you and your Police Constable to leave my home now DCS. You are not welcome here!"

"But the Home Secretary ordered us Mam."

"Neither the Home Secretary nor anyone else can tell me who I can, or cannot, have in my home DCS – Now please leave!"

DCS Sutherland looked furious, but rather meekly said; "If I could have time for my PC to raise my car driver?"

"Yes, but both you and the PC, please wait in the front porch – Please do not come anywhere near my lounge." Lady Wright wheeled away carrying two A4 sheets of paper in her hand and walked towards the lounge door where a smiling Andy stood waiting, obviously having heard the confrontation.

As Lady Wright came over Andy held out his arms and kissed Lady Wright on both cheeks and said; "So sorry for your loss Shirley – It must have been an awful shock?"

"For us – Yes Andy – but somebody knew this was going to happen!" Lady Wright turned and stared directly at DCS Sutherland.

"Come along Shirley and we will get this rolling!" Andy replied with a grin directed at DCS Sutherland who shook his head.

Andy closed the lounge door and put his right forefinger to his lips and pointed to the patio doors. Shirley took the cue, went over, unlocked the doors and stepped out into the patio. Andy followed and closed the double-glazed doors behind him.

"Just a precaution Shirley! – My DS thinks they have your phones tapped and/or have bugs around the house for listening in!"

"Well, they are definitely listening into my phone calls I have heard them click after I hung up! That is easy for them - there are extensions in every room! But I don't know about bugs though!"

They heard the front door slam, which they assumed must be DCS Sutherland leaving and heard the shouts of the Press and Television crews as they left.

"Well, it makes it sound like our lot are a load of amateurs. At least MI5 would have had your phones tapped and bugs in your rooms!"

"I thought they needed a court order for that sort of thing and they would never get it for our place, would they?"

"MI5 are a law onto themselves, or so some of them think. Some of their bosses are running amok in the name of internal security. We have just arrested a couple of their operators who have been linked to at least six cases of murder and torture and they have told us their boss, by name, who ordered the tortures and murders. Now within twenty-four hours from making a statement one of them turns up dead this morning in Kings Cross prison no less!" "

Oh, my God Andy – You don't think MI5 are behind Mark's death, do you?"

"At this early stage, I don't really know Shirley. But if Mark was given poison or something to produce a heart attack, then MI5 are in a better place to obtain this kind of stuff, in the correct quantities, from the Government's Porton Down establishment, which I believe involves itself in chemical warfare."

"Oh, my God Andy – You do know that Doctor Bowen believes Mark may have been injected to induce his heart attack?"

"Yes, you told me earlier Shirley. My DS will be here shortly with Doctor Bowen's report. If you don't mind me asking Shirley - Where is Mark's body now?"

"Oh, they have moved him to the Landers Funeral Directors Chapel of Rest in Golders Green Andy. He wanted to be cremated."

"You know Shirley; we cannot allow him to be cremated until after the post mortem has been carried out?"

"Yes, I know Andy - Neither do I want the cremation until he has had the post mortem – not after what you have just told me." Shirley hesitated for a moment then, handing over one of the A4 sheets of paper she had been carrying said; "Here is the statement you wanted Andy – but Andy you know I told you, but I have to make it clear - that it was Mark's dying wish, and supported by the Home Secretary - that if The Yard is implicated in his death then he wants it hushed up. That is all he and the Home Secretary wanted hushed up – Not to have a post mortem, or to the results of a post mortem hushed up was never his, or the Home Secretary's intention - Mark said simply, you would know how to handle it and to only trust you and John Sanderson."

"That was very nice of him Shirley, but all that means is I wonder what DCS Sutherland is up to?" You do know that if I found out who was responsible I would be duty bound to charge him, or her, no matter where they work. However!" - Andy put-up his hands to stop Shirley from protesting and continued; "However, the chances of me proving who was responsible are very thin! I know what Mark is saying; which I think is - If I find out who is responsible, I will find a way to deal with them!"

"Oh, talking about that; this is the list." Lady Wright handed over the second A4 sheet of paper and continued; "I told you about earlier – it is a list of the London Met employees who the Home Secretary, the Attorney General and Mark agreed could prove, from their investigations, had been on the take from organised crime and stuff. As I said earlier they have decided that either that they are going to make them redundant with full redundancy pay, or if they are old enough, then they give them early retirement. But Mark suggested this may be a starting point for your investigation. He also said there are a large number at the bottom of the list for whom, he said; they did not have enough proof. You may be interested to see that our DCS Sutherland is on that list at the bottom."

"My oh my – it gets more and more intriguing. I think I was supposed to work with Mark on these lists and get shot of this lot, first thing Monday morning. I don't know what will happen on Monday now!"

"Mark said it will be down to the new man!"

"Well at least it won't be DCS Sutherland that's for sure – Not now!" Andy said it with some feeling before adding; "I am just waiting for my DS to come and then I am off to the coroners and things. Will you be alright on your own Shirley?"

"Andy, you know Mark and his work! I have been on my own for three quarters of our married life! Anyway, my sister and her husband are coming this afternoon and the maid is a live in. So, no problem, but thanks anyway!"

As if on cue, the doorbell rang and the maid appeared from nowhere to answer.

"DS Devlin, - DI Spearing is expecting me!" I said showing my ID.

The maid turned around and Lady Wright called out; "All right Margaret! DI Spearing is just coming!"

"Thank you again Andy – I won't show myself at the door. Good luck with everything."

"Thank you, Shirley – You take care and I will stay in touch." Andy went out the door and immediately was faced by a barrage of popping cameras and TV crews all shouting questions; "What is happening DI?" and "Did Sir Mark die from a heart attack?" etc. Andy stopped suddenly, as if he had had made his mind up to say something, and replied; "I am sorry lads, but I cannot answer any of your questions until after the post mortem!"

A voice came out of the crowd of reporters; "I believe there was some question of a post mortem being held DI Spearing since Sir Mark's body has been moved out of the hospital?"

Andy did not look at the face or where the sound came from but just replied; "Bill - you know that in a sudden death it is illegal not to have a post mortem." Andy left it like that and went straight over and got into the Jag. Sergeant Tommy pulled out into the traffic and with the blues and twos already going he took off at speed heading for Holborn.

I smiled at Andy and asked; "That would not have been a pre-loaded question on the post mortem – now would it sir?"

"Would I do such a thing?" Andy just smiled and added; "Just to save time we will drop you off at the end of Miss Clements road. You can take care of the business with her while we are sorting out the stuff with the coroner. Give me the papers relevant to the coroner's. We will pick you up from Miss Clements when we are finished and then we head for Kings Cross Prison!"

We appeared to be no time in getting to the end of the Red Lion Square and I got out of the Jag with my Case Reports. I looked at my watch and realized I was at least forty minutes earlier than I had said. I walked around the corner, I don't know why, but I ducked back when I saw what I saw. Judith was standing in her doorway holding hands with Mary Randalll, the girl who had been gang raped a couple of weeks ago. They hugged and kissed full on the lips. Mary Randalll came walking quickly towards me so again, I don't know why; I ducked down an alley out of sight. Mary walked past and so I knew with time marching on I had to hurry to Judith's house.

I rang the bell to her apartment and seconds later it was answered by a bewildered looking Judith.

"Sorry I am a bit early Judith – I am too late for your shower – I can smell!" I smiled, but it must have been a nervous smile.

"You saw us didn't you Kevin?" Judiths face was red and she was certainly flustered.

"I am the Lone Ranger and I cannot tell a lie Kemosabe." I smiled and added thoughtfully; "But hey - who am I to judge you on your preferences? Let's just get you into this stuff - I am going to be picked up in a few minutes!" I realised my response was not great, perhaps it was just the disappointment that I realised the chase for this one was over. Then again, I thought, I really like this girl, she is fun and always up for a laugh, giving as good as she gets, so I added; "Kemosabe?" I put my high five up.

"Kemosabe." Judith replied with a sense of relief and returned the high five.

We went into the apartment and got into work without any joking, in fact it felt, for the first time with Judith, a bit awkward. I knew it would take a little time to adjust to the new situation, but it was just a matter of time. I liked her too much!

Andy entered the coroner's office and asked for James Hall who emerged from the inner office with a smile on his face and his hand extended and said; "DI Spearing – How are you? All on your own?"

Andy shook his hand warmly and replied; "My DS is around the corner visiting one of our DPP people. Then we have to go onto Kings Cross Prison for that apparent suicide I was telling you about on the phone!"

"Keeping you busy then DI? - Shocking this thing with Sir Mark though!"

"Well yes - as I said I would, I have brought the evidence with me to confirm Sir Mark's massive heart attack may have been induced, hence the need for a post mortem, although by law it has to be done!"

"To be honest DI – I don't need any evidence to order a post mortem – a sudden death is sufficient to require a post mortem – especially when it is the death of such an eminent person as Sir Mark. I don't understand why anybody should think a post mortem is not required?"

"I think there may be a number of ulterior motives with undercurrents going on, but at this time we are not sure who is involved. But we do know somebody, or some people are heavily involved."

"Well let's hope you can nail them down. Well come on through to my office DI. I have the order all ready. You can keep your evidence for the inquest DI. - So where do you go from here?"

"Straight over to Landers Funeral Directors Chapel of Rest in Golders Green to stop them doing anything and get them to transfer Sir Mark back to the Hammersmith Hospital for the post mortem."

"What? They have already removed him from the mortuary?"

"Exactly James! I wonder if you could do me a favour? – Could you ring Landers at Golden Green and tell them to do nothing and I will be over within the hour with your order?"

"Certainly DI – No problem. I know the boss over there – a Thomas Bell - take note" James Hall replied as he handed over the order.

"Thomas Bell – I'll remember that! Thanks again James – much appreciated." Andy and James Hall again shook hands and Andy went off. James Hall had not forgotten that as a young coroner DI Spearing had stopped him making an elementary mistake during an autopsy, but had never mentioned it to the powers that be, or anyone else.

Andy got into the Jag and told Sergeant Tommy to go back to Red Lion Square and pick up DS Devlin. Then onwards to Golders Green – Landers in Finchley Road. Sergeant Tommy looked up the London A to Z for the Golders Green address. No Sat Nav in those days!

I heard the Jag horn and got out straight away just saying to Judith hurriedly; "I need to go Judith – I will leave that lot with you and ring you later to see what you think, particularly the Bridgewater's case. They will be after bail today?"

"Yeah, but I would not worry too much, not many Judges around Saturday mornings so it will be Monday before anything can happen and they will not do anything without the DPP input!" Judith appeared to slowly have her self-confidence returning.

"Don't forget it is your Uncle Bill's case Judith."

"Yeah, there is that to it – I will get on to it, but if there is also a murder charge do you think we should be offering bail?"

"I think Andy would like you to go for 'No Bail'– but if there is no murder charge I doubt if we will be able to hold him on a no bail" But the homosexual charges are a done deal. Look I have to go Judith." I turned and hastily made my way out of the apartment and ran down to the Jag.

The Jag took off - blues and twos on again and headed for Golders Green just off in Finchley Road. Amazingly we were there within fifteen minutes.

Andy went into Landers alone and did the business with Thomas Bell the manager. He was quickly assured that Sir Mark's body would be returned to Hammersmith Hospital's mortuary within the hour and he would give them the coroner's order for the post mortem.

Andy gave Thomas Bell his card and asked him to make sure the mortuary people called him to be present at the post mortem. They had to make sure they contacted him before – on his walkie-talkie via New Scotland Yard, or on his office or home phones, but he had to be there for the post mortem! Thomas Bell agreed and said he would ring himself, when he found out, the post mortem date and time.

Andy came back out to the Jag and we were soon speeding with the blues and twos again blaring across to north London and amazingly reached the gates at Kings Cross Prison within twenty minutes, a hairy scary ride. We were checked through very quickly, the Governor having cleared everything in advance.

As we went through the various gates and doors we heard the slam bang and the locking of each one behind us. Unlike the last visit I suddenly realised what it must be like to be incarcerated for the first time. It was not a very pleasant feeling. I could sense the feeling of utter loneliness a prisoner must feel as he walks through. The foreboding of walking through into the unknown and the mind's conjecture, having probably read so many appalling stories of what happens to men and women at the hands of inmates, or the wardens. Even though I was a policeman and only visiting, for the first time I sensed the panic that spread into my body and settled in my mind.

We were led by a burly, middle aged Officer named Burns to Mitchell the Governor's office. We passed through the outer office – no Sheila Watson the secretary – it being Saturday she was probably not working. We went straight into the Governor's office without knocking.

Mitchell was sitting behind his desk today casually, but smartly, dressed in an open necked blue checked slim fitting shirt and when he stood up to greet us he had on causal but smart blue expensive trousers. Perhaps the only surprise was, he had some stubble on his chin, obviously not had time to shave this morning.

"DI Spearing." Governor Mitchell extended his hand and shook Andys hand before adding; "What an awful business!" and then turned around to me and offered his handshake and continued; "DS Devlin! – Please both of you take a seat." He pointed to the chairs. We both acknowledged his greeting and then he added; "Now what do we do?"

"Well, I think we have to establish a few facts sir, perhaps you can take notes Sergeant?" I nodded and took out my pen and notepad and logged the date and time. Andy continued; "First – are the coroner's and the forensics people here along with a photographer?"

"Yes, they are all in the cell now - there are three from the coroner's office, but I think two are ambulance people or from the mortuary – they had a portable trolley with them! There is a young guy from forensics plus a photographer. So, five all together!"

"Oh, that's good – getting a better response today!" Andy smiled and then asked; "What time was 'it' reported sir?"

"Well I got the call from senior officer Kavanagh at eight –o -five!"

"That's a bit late rising for a prison sir?" I asked.

"Well it is a solitary confinement block we sometimes use for people to be isolated, or who are for transfer out shortly. We are a bit more lax in there Sergeant!"

"What about the security in there sir?" Andy asked and his quizzical look said it all.

"We have only three officers covering that small block – they each do eight hour shifts Monday to Saturday morning. The first one starts at eight and so on through the day and night until next morning at eight when the day shift man starts again!"

"And which officer was on last night sir?" DI Spearing asked.

"Oh, senior officer Kavanagh was the overnight officer!"

"Why is that Sir? Officer Kavanagh was on yesterday afternoon so how come he did the night shift?"

"As far as understand it - Officer Martin, who should have been on last night, asked for a swop yesterday morning and will do Officer Kavanaghs shift this afternoon!"

"Can I talk to Officer Martin please sir?"

"I will try his number, but you know, he may be out! - It being Saturday morning and all DI"

"Well if you could try sir, I would be obliged."

While the governor was dialling the number I asked; "Is there anybody else has access sir? – Trustees, cleaners and so on? Oh, and where was Wilkins in relation to Jones?"

The Governor finished dialling and talked while he waited on Office Martin answering, but replied; "Let's see - Yeah the Trustees take the meals over there at eight, one and six, but they cannot get in because there are two doors and the inner door has a security four pin code to get in and that gets changed every week. Trustee cleaners are the same – They cannot get past the inner door! The prisoner's do their own cleaning out and if they don't do it they live in their own squalor!" The Governor suddenly put his hand up to stop our conversation and said; "Is that Officer Martin there? Ah good – It is the Governor here John. I have a DI Spearing from New Scotland Yard here who wants a word." Governor Mitchell stretched the phone across and DI Spearing grabbed it and asked;

"DI Spearing here John – It is really one quick question – Whose idea was it to swop the nightshift last night with Officer Kavanagh?"

"Well actually it was a bit of both! I happened to mention I was going out for my wife Trish's birthday party early on Friday evening, before my shift and Kavanagh said why don't we swop as he said he had things to do on Saturday afternoon and I could do the double shift on Saturday afternoon and night shift."

"Did that sort of thing often happen with Officer Kavanagh John?"

"Well no, not really – I was just saying to the wife – there is a first time for everything! You know what I mean? – Not many people like the graveyard shift so it was nice to get one off once in a while!"

"I think the graveyard shift is a rather unfortunate choice of words John since someone died in the isolation block last night!" Andy replied with a little sarcasm, but regretted it almost instantly.

"Oh, my God I didn't know sir – It is just what we call the night shift! Who died?"

"Well you will hear when you come in John – We don't want to leak it now until we know for definite what happened."

"Oh, okay sir – is that all?"

"Yes John – thanks for your help!" Andy passed the phone back to the governor and said; "Well it looks like Officer Kavanagh asked for the swop sir and not the opposite way around, as he said, which brings up several questions!"

"Look I have known Officer Kavanagh for several years Inspector and I am sure there is nothing untoward about this!" Governor Mitchell sounded very sincere.

"Yes, I am sure you may be right sir, but when MI5 get involved anything can happen to very normal people!"

I interjected with another question; "Is there any way prisoner Wilkins could communicate or get through to Jones sir?"

"No, not at all Sergeant – There is another double door between them and the inner door has a pin number, known only to the guard, and it is changed every week. Plus, there is a six-inch wall on both sides of the thick oak doors, so I doubt it!"

"But I suppose the guards could turn a blind eye sir?" I knew I was pushing it a bit, but I had to ask the question.

"Yeah, I suppose that could happen, but I doubt if Officer Kavanagh would be into doing such a thing!"

"Or maybe he could be up to doing it himself – I mean making it look like suicide?"

"I very much doubt it Sergeant!"

"Where is Officer Kavanagh just now sir?"

"He is waiting outside the lawyer's interview room you used last night Sergeant."

"Tell me sir – How often are the guards supposed to check these prisoners are okay?"

"Every two hours and they log each visit in the day book Sergeant! Oh, by the way we transferred Wilkins to Parkhurst this morning"

Andy broke into the conversation; "That's good for Wilkins! Well, I think we must first establish if it is a suicide or not. We had better get up there and have a word with the Forensics and Coroner's people before they go."

"Certainly DI – Officer Burns is waiting outside to take you up – Let me know what is happening before you go."

"Certainly sir - If we have time before we go or I will give you a ring later – Do you have your card?"

"I do DI somewhere in here." Governor Mitchell looked around the top drawer and, eventually finding a card, passed it to Andy and said; "My home number is on it as well – You are welcome to use it, if it is after business hours."

"Thank you for your help sir – We had better 'Move It' as Cliff Richard used to sing!"

"Yeah – It was not a bad rock and roll song for a British performer!" Governor Mitchell's response was surprising.

We exchanged pleasantries and joined Officer Burns who took us up to the cell where Jones had met his end.

As we entered, we saw David Arkwright, the photographer Joe Lacey and somebody else – presumably the doctor, another youngish, good looking guy from the Coroner's office – they were all examining the back of the victim's head and Joe Lacey was taking some flash photographs. Two of the mortuary people were hanging around in the background awaiting instructions.

"Hello David, Joe" I said before adding; "How is it going?"

"It's cool man!" - It is going very well thanks!" David Arkwright replied.

"No Doctor Harvey?" Andy asked.

"No sir – Like I said to DI Sanderson yesterday – It was reported as a suicide so you get the lackey!"

"According to what I heard from DI Sanderson – you are not a bad lackey lad!" Andy replied with a smile.

"One can only do what one can do sir!" David Arkwright replied with his tight, little, shy smile.

"Okay David what do you see so far?"

"Well sir – Jones appears to have tried to hang himself from the light fitting! I don't think even for an idiot and a light weight it would have been possible" David then continued; "Of course the light socket has ripped out and he may have fell and hit the back of his head heavily on the floor. But to be honest - I cannot see him damaging the back of his head that much because he had to land on his feet and topple or even wobble over – and to hit the back of his head that hard would have to be almost impossible! On top of that, there is nothing in the cell for him to jump from to hang himself. He is six feet plus sir and the only thing he could jump from is the bed over there and that has not been moved in years! On top of that, I cannot see a guy with that damage to his head getting up again and within an hour managing to hang himself from a six-feet six cell door – there is not even a stool in this cell to launch himself from! And even then, there is only a maximum of a six-inches drop. In certain instances, I suppose a six-inch gap would be enough, but it is an estimate and I just don't think it would be enough. Also, the point is, the bed sheet is not even tied to the top bar in the cell door – it is lower - so it looks like he only had a six foot drop and he is slightly over six feet - so how in his condition could he get back up and kill himself?"

"I see David" Andy replied and turned to the other guy and said; "I am afraid I don't know you lad? I assume you are from the Coroner's office?" What says you?"

"Yes sir, I am Doctor Cairns – A pathologist with the Coroner's office. I go along with David's analysis, but until I get this guy to the lab. I cannot say for sure, but like David I would question suicide at this stage based on the evidence so far!"

"Fair enough – so you both think we have a put-up job here?"

"It looks that way sir, but not easy to prove in court." David Arkwright replied without delay. "It will be a tetchy argument – One consultant against the other! But the big question is- it is almost impossible to damage the head to that extent with a fall of only a few inches."

"But you would be prepared to stick to your guns in court?"

"Oh, yes sir – No question - this head injury is unexplainable!"

"That's fair enough lads – now one last question – the time of death for Mr Jones – approximately?"

"Well I will know better when I get back to base. But I estimate, according to how the rigor mortis is setting, it would have to be around six to six thirty this morning, but not easy to gauge at this stage!"

"Okay lads - We have to go and question the officer in charge last night - Officer

Kavanagh me thinks he has a bit of explaining to do! Great job you lot many thanks!"

The guys all looked very pleased as we left. One thing Andy knew how to do was to motivate people and get them on his side! He handed out his card to both guys and said; "Let me know if there are any changes to what you just told me!"

We met up with Officer Burns again outside the block doors and made our way back to the interview rooms we had used yesterday. Andy asked him to stay outside the room as we may need him again in a few minutes.

Officer Kavanagh was sitting outside the room, rather nervously smoking a cigarette! No law against that at work in those days! No mention of cancer sticks or secondary smoking back then! It was fashionable to smoke!

Andy walked past Kavanagh and opened the door to the Interview Room before calling over his shoulder; "Ah Mr Kavanagh please come in!"

"I want to know why I have been waiting here for three hours and more DI?" Officer Kavanagh asked sounding very nervous, as we switched on the lights in the dismal interview room.

"Well, maybe it is because one of your prisoners died on your overnight watch? What do you think Kavanagh?" Andys reply was ultra-sarcastic.

"Well it is not my fault." Kavanagh replied curtly.

"Well Mr Kavanagh – For the moment that may be a matter of opinion?" Andy was right in there on the button.

"It is a matter of fact DI!" Kavanagh was certainly starting off cool, calm and collected.

Inside the room, the Tape Recorder and the Golf Ball Typewriter from yesterday's interviews were still on the table, but with a new tape in the machine. There were now four chairs around the table.

"Take a seat Kavanagh." Andy pointed to the same seat as Jones yesterday. Andy and I took the same seats opposite. I thought that was rather pointed.

"Sergeant - Could you please take notes and turn on the tape recorder?"

I did as I was told and Andy continued speaking into the microphone; "This is an interview with Officer Kavanagh, a Senior Prison Officer in Kings Cross Prison, North London. The interview is held in Kings Cross Prison on Saturday, July the 22nd at eleven a.m. Present are; Officer Kavanagh, Detective Sergeant Devlin Detective Inspector Spearing – both detectives from New Scotland Yard and we are investigating the death of prisoner Jones in his cell in Kings Cross Prison. The death occurred overnight between Friday, July21 and Saturday July 22 nineteen sixty-seven."

"I would like to have my solicitor present." Kavanagh said it very slowly and precisely.

"I wonder why you feel you need a solicitor Officer Kavanagh when you are only here to answer questions on the death of a prisoner on your watch last night?" Andy said it with a sly smile on his face.

"Because, just like that – you lot just turn and twist everything one says!"

"I merely asked a question Officer Kavanagh as to why you think you need a solicitor now? I don't see how I can twist anything! - By 'You Lot' - I assume you mean the British police Officer Kavanagh?"

"Yes! Who else is in the room?"

I felt a prickling on the back of my neck and my basic instincts, or gut feelings, started to switch on.

"Well – Just to let you know Officer Kavanagh - in fact until basic questioning is done - and or we charge you with something - you do not have an automatic right to a solicitor. However," (Andy held up his right hand to stop Kavanagh from saying anything) and he then continued; "In the interests of fair play I can allow a fellow prison officer to be present to ensure nothing untoward happens although the tape recorder will record all. How does that suit you Officer Kavanagh?"

"We all know these tapes can be altered after the event. However, I suppose a fellow officer as a witness will have to do!"

"Okay – Sergeant could you bring in Officer Burns? He is just outside!"

"Yes sir!" I replied into the tape and went out and fetched in Officer Burns.

"And by the way Officer Kavanagh, any time you, or your lawyers, can have the tape inspected to see if it has been altered."

"That as you well know can be copied over to another tape deleting what you don't want to go through and there would be no signs of alteration to the tape!"

"I do believe Officer Kavanagh there are experts who can categorically say if a tape is the original or a copy. Did you know that?"

No reply came from Kavanagh as Officer Burns entered the room.

"Ah Officer Burns – your Senior Officer Kavanagh here has requested a fellow officer be present to ensure fair play during this interview. Are you prepared to act as an independent witness as to this interview being fair?"

"Yes sir. I am no expert on fair play though!"

"You don't have to be an expert Officer Burns! Only witness that we do not abuse Officer Kavanagh and we are fair and reasonable - while you must realise we will have to ask some difficult and searching questions – Is that understood Officer Burns?"

"Yes, I'll give it go!" Officer Burns replied cheerily.

"Yes well! Okay – Take a seat please - For the sake of the recording – Officer Burns has joined this interview to act as an independent witness as to fair play. You will not ask nor will you be expected to answer any questions Officer Burns is that understood?"

"Yes sir." Officer Burns gave the quick reply.

"Now then - We can get started at last! Now Mr Kavanagh – I understand you reported Jones' death at around eight-o-five – Is that correct?" Andy asked.

"Yes, it must have been thereabouts!" Kavanagh was still very cool.

I knew instinctively it was my turn to ask a question and try to throw him out of his comfort zone so I asked; "So, when did you last look in on the prisoner Mr Kavanagh when he was alive?"

"I suppose it was about six!" – He was sleeping then!"

"Oh, catching up on his beauty sleep then? Before deciding to suddenly commit suicide – is that it Mr Kavanagh?" I asked with a weary sarcastic expression.

"I can only say how it was Sergeant!" Kavanagh was still cool man as we used to say in those days.

Andy interrupted; "We are told you were the only one on duty last night Mr Kavanagh?"

"Yes DI, that is correct!"

"So, no one else had access to the prisoner Jones last night – Is that correct Mr Kavanagh?"

"To my knowledge that is correct DI."

"Our forensic team and our pathologist don't reckon it possible that the injury to the back of Jones' head was caused by a fall. What do you make of that Mr Kavanagh?"

"I am not a forensic man, but what I hear, that lot can make two and two make five. A bit of dust from there and a bit from here and we suddenly have a hill to climb!"

"Yes, modern day science is wonderful Officer Kavanagh don't you think?" Andy said it with a straight face and continued; "Well the other thing which is obvious,

357

even to us lesser mortals Officer Kavanagh, is this! – A man with those head injuries - having just failed to apparently hang himself from a seven foot high light ceiling fixture - without a stool or anything to get up there or jump from?– He will not recover sufficiently for several hours far less somehow reaching the top of a six feet six inches high cell and again without anything – again not a stool or anything in sight – He still manages to somehow tie a sheet and then somehow manages to throw himself out and hang himself – All by himself with no help!"

"Well I really don't know how I can help you DI – I only found the body – How he managed to do it I am not qualified to even guess!" Kavanagh was certainly a very cool customer.

"I can tell you how you can help Mr Kavanagh! A man who is badly injured cannot do what he has supposedly done! He has to have had help – at least if it was suicide! – There is only one other person there who could help him to die and that is you Mr Kavanagh. So, explain that Mr Kavanagh."

"I cannot explain DI because as I say – I only found the body!"

I knew it was my turn to have a go, I knew I had to deviate, again try to throw him out of his comfort zone, so I went back to my gut reaction of a few minutes ago and asked; "What are your first names Mr Kavanagh?

Kavanagh moved uncomfortably in his chair before answering; "Patrick Joseph."

"Of Irish descent then, - with a name like Patrick Kavanagh are you?" I watched his eyes very carefully and sure enough just that little flicker of fear.

"Um - yes! All my Dads people came from Donegal and on my mother's side both came from Killarney.

"Real republican stock then - Is that how they got to you Mr Kavanagh?" Again, there was another flicker of fear across the eyes.

"Who got to me? What are you on about now Sergeant?"

"Come now Mr Kavanagh – You were part of the interview with the prisoner Jones yesterday and you signed the statement. You heard our warning to prisoner Jones that he was now a danger to his former bosses MI5 and that he had to be held in a high security prison. Did you not?"

"Yeah, I heard all that sure, but how does it apply to me Sergeant?"

"Well let's just say for a minute that you had been hanging out with some of those Irish lads up Camden way. Let's assume you got into things against the UK government like some of those Irish lads are doing – We know MI5 have their stool pigeons all around Camden and they caught you in one of their snares – but although they could have nailed you they didn't but now they use you – How about that Mr Kavanagh?"

"That's an awful lot of guess work Sergeant?"

I was watching those eyes and now it was more than a flicker of fear.

"Well, just humour me for another minute Mr Kavanagh – Suppose you were forced to help MI5 out and you did help Jones to commit 'suicide,' so to speak, although we now know it was no suicide. However, just suppose you did help MI5 out – What do you think happens now Mr Kavanagh?"

"I wouldn't have a clue Sergeant. You tell me."

"Well you see Mr Kavanagh – You are no longer useful to them, and in fact, you are a very real danger to them and look what happened to our Mr Jones when he became a danger! You know all about that, now don't you?"

"I can see what you are doing Sergeant."

"Oh, can you? – That is good, because I can tell you now what happened to your other prisoner Wilkins yesterday. It order to stop him from talking they kidnapped his wife and family. They have disappeared; probably will not be seen again! Now, if they can do that to two employees who have worked with them loyally for years – what do you think they are going to do to you and yours Mr Kavanagh?"

Now it was not just fear in his eyes but outright panic.

Kavanagh shifted uneasily in his seat and said in a panic-stricken voice; "I didn't know they had done it before! They cannot kill them all, can they?"

"They can and they will Mr Kavanagh! What we have here is a rogue element near the top in MI5 who are running amok. We already have a whole family in protective custody because they have been targeted."

"But my whole family – my wife and three kids - they have them you know!" Kavanagh was now tearful to the point of breaking down. I was about to move in when I was shocked by an interruption from Andy.

"Okay Mr Kavanagh, this is the point when I have to inform you that you can now have your solicitor present if you so wish!" Andy then turned around and turned the tape recorder off. He then got up and said to me; "Sergeant - can I have a quiet word outside please? And turning to Officer Burns asked; "Could you watch him for a couple of minutes Burns?" He replied; "Yes sir."

I spoke into the tape recorders microphone and said; "Interview suspended at 11-20. I turned off the machine. I was puzzled but got up and followed Andy out the door closing it behind us and down the corridor away from earshot of the interview room.

Andy offered his handshake which I took and he said; "Congratulations Sergeant! That was a brilliant grilling. Where the hell did you dig up that Irish angle?"

"It was after he said something about 'you lot' meaning the police I just got this gut feeling!"

"Some gut feeling – I reckon that was just another of your paranormal trips Sergeant?"

"No, don't forget I come from Glasgow and half the population of Scotland have Irish blood there somewhere. – Me included! - All my grandparents were Irish - men and women! We have that big Catholic and Protestant divide in Scotland and the Protestants still unbelievably hold their Orange walk on July the twelfth - It is probably bigger in Scotland than it is in Ireland! Anyway, I just recognised that sort of embittered talk coming from Kavanagh and my gut feeling took it from there!"

"I still feel there must have been some of that paranormal stuff there, but your interview technique was brilliant!"

"Thank you, Andy." It was all I could think to say.

"Anyway, I suppose you are wondering why I stopped you just at the point of him admitting to it?"

"Yes, I must admit Andy I was a bit puzzled?"

"Well the thing is, as soon as I realised they were holding his family – I reckoned if we arrest him and take him with us they will know he will talk or has talked and the family are a goner – they will not hesitate! I don't want another family on my conscience!"

"Yeah, I can see that Andy, but what can we do? - We know he has killed Jones!"

"Yeah - a useless piece of shit - who has tortured and killed at least six – probably more."

"Even so Andy – He still deserves justice!"

"Even if on top of all this, there is the killing of an innocent wife and three kids who are about to join the list of casualties?"

"Aye I suppose there is that to it. Can we delay charging him until we know the wife and kids are safe?"

"Well that's along the lines I was thinking. We need to make it look like we have accepted it as a suicide and therefore accepted Kavanaghs version of events and so give the wife and kids a chance. In any case, according to the pathologist, we would only finish up having technical arguments in the court by consultants and any good lawyer will play on any doubts!"

"Not if we have Kavanaghs confession!"

"If we have that then we condemn the wife and three kids – is it worth it to give justice to a multiple murderer who has effectively escaped justice by getting himself hanged in jail?"

"I see where you are coming from Andy – but it is rough justice!"

"Better than no justice at all – Eh Sergeant?"

I intentionally did not agree when I replied; "So what do you want to do Andy?"

"Well let's get Officer Burns out of there first and then have a nice friendly chat with Kavanagh – see what we can come up with – shall we?" Andy turned and walked smartly back to the interview room followed by me trotting behind.

We entered the room and saw Burns smoking and chatting with Kavanagh. Andy interrupted without apology and said; "Officer Burns – for obvious reasons we cannot have any of this repeated to anyone – not even the Governor - not anyone - you understand, for the safety of Officer Kavanaghs family?"

"Yeah I understand sir – listening to all this I don't want to know a thing. No way am I getting involved with that lot!"

"Good man – and go tell the Governor we believe Jones death is suicide and Officer Kavanagh will be over to talk to him shortly, before he goes home as his shift is finished. Okay?"

"Yes sir."

"Oh Burns – Could you come back in fifteen minutes to take us straight out? – We have to be on another case very shortly!"

"Yes sir." Burns replied over his shoulder as he left the room.

"I would rather not talk to the Governor." Kavanagh mumbled.

"I am afraid you are going to have to Mr Kavanagh – Part of the charade to save your family!"

I decided on the spur of the moment to ask; "Why don't you want to talk to the Governor Mr Kavanagh?"

"Because I have been thinking Sergeant – The only person – besides you two and me – who knew those two were in that block and I was there in charge, and knew how to contact me in there, was the Governor. Yet I get a call in there from an MI5 man who knew the two prisoners were in there and knew I was in charge of them. - Don't you think it very strange?"

Andy and I looked at each other, rather astonished, before Andy replied; "Well yes! We can see that - Now you have pointed it out! We will have to tackle that problem later when your family are safe. However, we must keep up the charade that you have convinced us you are not guilty, although you have admitted to the offence. But we must convince everybody, that on the evidence, we have to go along with the 'suicide' theme."

"I have not admitted to nothing Detective Inspector!" Kavanagh was suddenly very sultry!

Andy reacted very angrily; "Well Mr Kavanagh – You know DS Devlin and I have gone way out on a limb and bent the rules. In fact, we have broken the rules, to accommodate you, because you and your family are in real danger! Now, if that is the way you want to go, then so be it! But let me tell you - if that is the way you want to go

– then we have no problem in throwing you and your family to the wolves! So, as they say in Thailand mate – it's up to you?"

"Okay! Okay! I am not prepared to put my family at risk! I want to make a deal please let's start again!"

"Okay that's fine Mr Kavanagh. I do understand the pressure you are under, but we have got to make this look good to whoever is watching. Now we must get your written and signed statement as to admitting to the murder of Jones and the reasons why you were forced to do it. Sergeant Devlin here will type it out for you and we will sign it. Okay?"

"Why am I signing? – I mean, I thought you were" Kavanagh stopped talking abruptly when he saw the expression on Andys face.

"You Mr Kavanagh have just denied it and only came around when you realised that your family are still at risk! What is to stop you doing the same again when - and if - your family is safe?" Andy finished and just smiled his little sly smile.

"Okay! Okay – just get on with it!" Kavanagh was getting panicky again.

I turned on the tape recorder and spoke into the microphone: "Interview with Mr Kavanagh and DI Spearing and DS Devlin recommenced at 11-30." I then asked:; "For the statement I need to know what they had on you from your Irish connections in Camden Mr Kavanagh?"

"They had very little, but of course they exaggerated it just to snare me. Look - I was brought up on stories by my grandparents of the 1916 Easter rebellion and the massacre of the, so called, leaders who were mostly poets and non-fighting men – The fighting Irishmen - almost 200,000 of them - were fighting with the British and American armies in the trenches during the First World War."

Andy interrupted and said; "Look Mr Kavanagh we do not have the time to have a history lesson on the Irish troubles!"

"I am only trying to explain how I got involved!"

"Well get on with it without the history bit."

Kavanagh ignored Andy and continued; "Anyway, I used to enjoy talking about it and researching the whole thing through - from The Home Rule act of 1914, which gave Ireland independence, but which was suspended till the end of the war and then the British Government broke their word which caused the Irish War of Independence in 1919 until 1922."

"Oh, come on Mr Kavanagh get to the point." DI Spearing irritated now.

"Yes – the British people still don't know or don't care what actually went on in their name!" Kavanagh coolly replied and continued; "Anyway, I only went up to Camden Square with a mate, because we heard there were people there who had actually been in Dublin in 1916 when the Easter Rising happened and so they were there. Anyway, it was only a talking shop at first these older Irish guys reminiscing, but a few weeks later some younger guys came along and started talking about guns and stuff. They were talking about starting the troubles again, but in London. A few days later I got a visit at home from a couple of MI5 guys. I think one of them was a boss and they were trying to lay some charges of treason. To say I was shitting myself was to put it mildly. I said I had nothing to do with those young guys; I was only doing some research for a book. Anyway, they wanted me to keep going and act as their spy so I agreed and that was that until yesterday."

I asked; "Did you get any names from these MI5 guys?"

"I got a flash of their ID's I think the boss man his name was Lampard or something!"

"Could it have been Lambert?"

"Yeah it could have been, but they were so quick just flashed their ID's."

Andy and I yet again exchanged knowing glances.

"Okay – So what happened yesterday?"

"Well they came onto the Irish thing again threatening me with the treason thing again if I didn't do what they wanted? I said fuckoff go ahead and then they brought up the wife and kids and they threatened me with their lives! – I had no alternative, did I?!"

Andy again interrupted again sympathetically and said; "We do understand your predicament Mr Kavanagh - we really do - which is why we are talking to you and not charging you yet! - Let's get the statement done Sergeant and then we can move on!"

"Okay I will sign a statement and do it!" Kavanagh was almost on the point of crying.

Andy then turned back to Kavanagh, nodded and said; "I am afraid we have to become formal now Mr Kavanagh. It is my duty to inform you that I am arresting you for the murder of a prisoner Michael Jones - here in Kings Cross Prison- between Friday, July twenty-first and Saturday, July twenty-second - nineteen sixty-seven. It is your right to remain silent, but it may harm your defence, if you fail to mention now something which you may later rely on in court. Anything you do say may be given in evidence. Do you understand?"

"It is a bit late now to be reading me my rights eh? Anyway – 'Yes' I understand I just want my family protected!"

"It is for the record Mr Kavanagh. We can now turn off the recorder Sergeant."

"Yes sir." I replied and spoke into the microphone; "Interview with Mr Kavanagh concluded at 11-45" and I turned off the machine and started typing the statement.

Andy continued angrily; "Now Mr Kavanagh – off – the - record – We do not intend to pursue you on these charges of murder. - Believe me, Sergeant Devlin and I are way out on a limb because of the danger to your family! However, if you as much as sneeze at your Irish friends again, or appear to be involved in anything like this again, you will not have time to sneeze before you are behind bars again and for a lifetime. Do you understand Mr Kavanagh?"

"I can only say thank you to you both. – Believe me I will never, ever, get involved with anything like this again." The look of sheer relief on Kavanaghs face was worth a million pounds!

"Thank you both. You have been so kind and understanding!"

I finished typing the statement and asked; "Your home telephone number and full address Mr Kavanagh?" He gave them to me and I finished the statement. We all signed it.

Andy was again all sympathetic when he said; "Okay Mr Kavanagh off you go and convince the Governor you are in the clear and hopefully your family will be back tonight. Here, take my card and phone me at home tonight and we will move you all into protective custody for a few days until we can fix our rogue MI5 friends!"

"Okay!" Officer Kavanagh got up wearily and went to go out the door when Andy Spearing shouted after him; "Remember Mr Kavanagh your family's lives may depend on your performance with the Governor."

"Don't worry Inspector – I will give the performance of my life!"

I said; "Just remember the body language as well Mr Kavanagh. It tells people a lot more than words. Look perky and confident!"

"Yeah! - Right!" Mr Kavanagh shouted back. But not sounding too confident.

I closed the door and turned around to face Andy and said; "You know Andy – Kavanagh and the Governor plus Mrs Palmer, besides the deceased Jones and our non-cooperative Wilkins, all give us a direct link to Robert Lambert. If we can see that, so can Lambert. So, he is going to break those link's, isn't he?"

"Yes, that has occurred to me too - he has to - that's for sure - except we are going after Lambert to arrest him as soon as we know Kavanaghs wife and kids are safe!"

"But Andy he may - and probably will - cut his losses. He gets shot of Kavanagh and the Governor now and our connections have gone."

"Well Kevin - We still have the statements from both Kavanagh and Jones which implicate Lambert. Also, our Mrs Palmer has already given us her statement that she was threatened by Lambert. So, we have a good case and, when he is out of the way, I am sure Wilkins will talk. We must check up on his family! Do you have Wilkins' house number with you to check if his family are back?"

"I have it in my notebook" I replied, opening the book before adding; "Are you really throwing them - Kavanagh and Mitchell - to the wolves and hoping they won't attack until you pick up their leader?"

"Look Sergeant – I have no intention of letting Kavanagh off with murder, nor Mitchell off as an accessory! As soon as his family are safe I will be re-arresting him. Then we go interview Mr Mitchell and try to pin the accessory charge on him!"

"You know you are a devious sod Andy! – You think like a criminal!"

"It is the one thing you have to learn Kevin If you don't think like them you have no chance of catching them! Kavanagh and that Irish mob were right about one thing though – they should never trust the English – We are by nature very devious people!"

"Aye Andy - We Scots can also vouch for that in our history! Oh, I have got the Wilkins home number – shall I give them a ring?"

"Yeah do that! – It will give us a better idea if they are trading the families."

I rang and the phone was answered almost immediately.

"Hello?" A mature lady's voice!

"Hello, is that Mrs Wilkins?"

"Eh Yes! Who is this calling?"

"I am Detective Sergeant Devlin from New Scotland Yard."

"Oh, my God! Has something happened to Bobby?"

"No – No Mrs Wilkins he is okay! At least – I am afraid your husband is in prison Mrs Wilkins. - He negotiated you and your families release by refusing to talk to us or making a statement."

"When can I see him?"

"I am afraid he has been moved to a high security prison for his own protection. – His life is in danger! When he is safely installed today we will let you know"

"My God who are these people?"

"Best you don't know Mrs Wilkins – just count your blessings you and your family got away from them. When were you all get released?"

"Oh, this morning we were all blindfolded throughout for practically twenty-four hours. I think we were brought back to the house in the middle of the night but not released until this morning. - It was frightening."

"I am sure it was, but good to hear you are all okay Mrs Wilkins. We will be in touch about your husband's prison later in the day." I hung up quickly to stop any further questions and said to Andy; "well - it looks like the Wilkins family are okay."

"There you go! They are dealing!" Andy sounded almost relieved and added; "Right Sergeant let's get packed up here – don't forget the tape and the statements. I think we can go back to 'The Yard' now."

Officer Burns escorted us all the way back to the prison yard where the Jag was parked and we were met by a rather bored looking Sergeant Thomson, who immediately rushed into the Jag and said; "I have had Flash Harry on the Walkie-talkie at least four times – Going berserk – wants you back at 'The Yard' immediately Andy!"

"Now there is a surprise Tommy – I suppose we had better go in and face the music." Andy laughed and added; "Don't bother with blues and twos Tommy just take your own, good, slow time."

"Want me to go via Bournemouth Andy?" Sergeant Tommy asked as we pulled out of the prison gates and went down Kings Cross Prison Road.

"Via Scotland would be better Tommy!" Andy barely smiled and then turned to me and taking out his badge from the wallet cover he handed it to me and said; "Take care of this Sergeant - remind me to pick it up when I get out from Flash Harrys!"

"You think it is as serious as taking your badge sir?"

"Well they think it is, but a lot of them have a hell of a shock coming Sergeant?"

"How is that?" I asked out of curiosity.

"Well Sergeant, they all underrated Sir Mark and part of his last will and testament is with The Home Secretary and The Attorney General and a lot of their little ships, including Flash Harrys, are going to be sunk!"

"Well there will be no grieving for their lost souls! But if he asks you for your badge?"

"Oh, I will just put my watch here" (taking off his watch and putting it into the badge wallet); "Now it is about the same weight and I will hand him the empty wallet. He is so incompetent he will not even look inside."

"Are they going to sack you?"

"No, they cannot do that straight away – They have to go through The Police Federation to do that! – No - they will, at most, suspend me pending a disciplinary hearing?"

"Bloody hell what about the cases we are on – they are reaching the climax."

"The last thing they are interested in is solving crime Sergeant. They are only interested in building their little castles in the air! Anyway, I will stay in contact with you via my home phone. They will probably take my walkie-talkie, but before I go into Flash Harrys office I will get a spare one set-up with my favourite Sergeant Thomson and pick it up from him on the way out. Okay Tommy?"

"No problem Andy – It will be my pleasure!" Sergeant Thomson replied.

In no time at all we were swinging into the NSY entrance to the car park. It was noticeably quiet – the Press and TV crews had disappeared like a whiff of wind in the air. Already Sir Mark was yesterdays news! But I thought perhaps the repercussions will roll on for a long time.

Our office floor was now practically empty, but within a minute of sitting down, Andys 'phone rang.

"DI Spearing." He answered non-chantily.

"Spearing where have you been all day?" Flash Harry was sounding agitated.

"Well DCI – It is my day off! However, like the good little detective I am – I have been trying to catch criminals! What have you been doing all day DCI?"

"Don't be the smart ass with me any more Spearing. You no longer have your friend to protect you. Get your smart ass in my office now!"

"It is not really difficult to play the smart ass with you DCI. But now you mention it - I do want to question you regarding a visitor you had in your office on Friday evening who bumped into Sir Mark with a needle!"

"How dare you? Get up to my office now?" Flash Harry threw the phone down.

"Oh dear, our petulant little schoolboy has thrown his dummy out of the pram!" Andy simply said and added; "Oh well I suppose I have to go up and try to give him some bottle!" He trudged off towards the lifts.

I shouted after him; "The stairs would be good exercise sir!"

"Not if I want to be able to talk to our beloved leader when I get there." Andy replied over his shoulder and gave a wave of his hand.

I had to smile, the man was incorrigible.

Andy intentionally knocked very loudly and heard the voice of Flash Harry roar; "Come in you idiot!"

Andy entered the office and saw Flash Harry and another man dressed in a dark blue suit, dazzling white shirt and a red, white and blue silk tie. He was middle aged with greying thinning hair and beefy. Andy thought he recognised him, but could not put a name to the face. Flash Harry introduced him; "This is Jason Day from the Police Federation who will be representing you in this dispute.

Andy then recognised Jason Day from another dispute with a fellow DI several years ago. He was a very fair and honest man; at least he was back then and a highly experienced ex-copper. He also knew the score around The Met.

Andy was intentionally slow in replying: "Hello Jason nice to see you again!" He turned back to Flash Harry and said; "Sorry DCI you were saying about a dispute. What dispute?"

"You know very well DCI Spearing!" Flash Harry was a bit shaken by the fact that Andy knew Jason Day, the London area senior representative for police inspectors.

"No sorry 'sir' – Have you something in writing regarding this dispute between us DCI?"

"No, I don't have written warnings, but you have also have been verbally warned several times regarding your conduct and disobeying direct orders. Also for being impertinent to your senior officers which is also in writing!"

"Oh yes! - The impertinent charges – I believe the Chief Constable threw that one out with the cryptic message of 'Stop wasting my time DCI Tomlinson' or words to that effect – Is that correct?"

Jason Day turned away with a smile on his face.

"That was only because the ex-chief constable was a close friend of yours."

Andy shook his head and decided to ignore that remark and said; "These - what you call 'verbal warnings' – Did you put any of these in writing to me DCI? because I do not recall any such warnings – I remember threats yes, but not any warnings?"

"Oh, you do have a selective memory Spearing."

"Well DCI you must be paranoid."

Jason Day interrupted; "Gentlemen please – DCI Tomlinson – do you or don't you have any copies of written warnings to DI Spearing?"

"Yes, I do have, but I cannot lay my hands on them right now. I have been redoing my filing system and my clerk has been sorting it!"

"You do realise DCI, that if DI Spearing has not been given written warnings, then it is pointless to go through with the disciplinary procedure?"

"Yes, I am aware of these procedures Mr Day. I suppose Spearing you have even forgotten the warning just this morning?"

"Oh Yes! – I did forget about that one. Remind me again what it was about DCI?"

Jason Day raised his eyebrows.

"It was a direct order to stop interfering in the arrangements for Sir Mark's funeral and get on with your own job!" Flash Harry was almost smiling, thinking he had caught Andy out.

"Oh, as I recall, it was a DCS Sutherland who gave me a warning. Are you now saying you are taking responsibility for that warning DCI?"

"Yes, I am your supervising officer!"

"Well you do realise that they are hanging you out to dry DCI?!"

"What the hell are you on about now Spearing?"

"Well you do know that the DCS was trying to order me to break the law in relation to Sir Mark's sudden death DCI, but since you are now taking responsibility, it is all down to you – bang goes your career!"

Flash Harrys face went red - the blood pressure building. Jason Day could not hide his smile.

"I don't care what you pretend smart ass! I am now formally suspending you until a disciplinary hearing can be held. Can I have your badge and your Walkie-talkie?"

Andy acted shocked and turned to Jason Day and asked; "Can he do that?"

"Yes, he can DI, but he has thirty days to produce these written warnings. Now let me warn you DCI - If these written warnings are not counter signed as having been received by DI Spearing there will be no disciplinary hearing. The Disciplinary Board will then advise you that you will be held to account for your actions and statements today. Incidentally, I have also noted for The Disciplinary Board your abusive behaviour both on the telephone and during this meeting towards a senior police officer and I will ensure this is advised to 'The Board' who will be able to take separate action on this issue."

The colour was now draining from Flash Harrys face and he meekly replied; "You – You - union types are all the same – You didn't hear my telephone conversation Mr Day!"

"DCI - You forget I was waiting in the outer office and everybody could clearly hear your abusive language towards the DI by name!"

Andy just smiled and handed over his badge which Flash Harry put straight into his drawer. Andy then quietly said; "My walkie-talkie is on my desk – the battery is flat again!"

"You are out of this police force Spearing!" Flash Harry said it with venom.

"I think I can promise you DCI – You will be long gone before me!"

"I will get security to escort you from the premises Spearing!" Flash Harry went to lift the phone.

Jason Day stood up and said; "I am afraid that too is against the disciplinary procedure DCI. As a senior police officer, DI Spearing is allowed to clear his desk of his personal effects and sign out with Security provided he does not take any longer than sixty minutes."

Flash Harry threw the phone hard back down onto his cradle and sat there scowling

DI Spearing went over and shook Jason Day's hand and said; "Thank you Jason for a very fair hearing – It is much appreciated!"

"Don't mention it DI – That is what I am here for. I'll walk with you to the lifts and let you know how this thing works."

They both pointedly walked out without reference to Flash Harry who was left raging.

On the way to the lifts Andy asked; "Was that thing true about me being given an hour to clear my desk?"

"I don't know, but it sounded good and fair. I also took my cue from you knowing he didn't have a clue!"

"Nice one Jason – Thanks a lot!"

"Don't mention it DI – This case will go nowhere!"

"Yeah I know! The only thing going anywhere is Flash Harry out the door – and it will be sooner rather than later.

"Really is that a fact? It would help morale around here!"

Andy smiled and said; "No question – He is out!"

They both shook hands when the lift stopped at the third floor and Andy got off and went into his office area.

Andy came to his desk and started taking out his personal effects which amounted to a few photographs and his shaving gear.

"It was as expected Andy?" I asked as I went around the desk and quickly palmed him his badge.

"Yep it sure did Sergeant, but hopefully no more than thirty days. We will stay in contact, as arranged, but don't tell anyone in this lot you are in contact as officially I am suspended. Only DI Sanderson should know but on the QT."

"Okay sure thing Andy."

The phone on DI Spearing's desk rang and he answered; "DI Spearing here!"

"This is Hammersmith Hospital mortuary here sir." A man with a very young voice obviously a junior added; "We were asked to inform you when we would be ready to start the post mortem on Sir Mark Wright?"

"Yes, that's right."

"Well it is going to start at three p.m. today Sir!"

"God that was quick."

"Yes, well the powers that be pushed it. I suppose it being a high-profile case!"

"Yes, that's good anyway. Who is leading the post mortem lad?"

"Professor John Stokes is leading!"

"My we are getting the top brass out – Who ordered Prof Stokes?"

"I believe it came from the Home Secretary himself sir!"

"Oh really – well now we are getting it from the top boys. Inform them they must not start until I, as the police representative from New Scotland Yard, am present."

"I am afraid Professor Stokes waits for no man sir."

"Just tell him it is me and he will wait, I assure you! I should be on time anyway, traffic permitting!"

"Very well Sir I will inform him and run for my life!"

"You are going to have to be quick lad as the Prof used to be quite an athlete in his time – one hundred yards in less than eleven seconds I heard!"

"That was a long time ago back in Roger Banister's day sir!"

"Aye very good lad – I'll see you shortly, but I have to take a taxi for a hundred yards' sprint lad!"

"I think you might need the blues and twos today Sir." The lad hung up.

Andy put down the phone with a smile and a shake of the head and said; "I do like this 'cheeky chappie' sense of humour these days – Bloody Jimmy Tarbuck was never in it! I am off to the morgue Kevin - don't want you there Kevin – One suspension a day is more than sufficient! I'll let you know how it goes. I better take a taxi over there."

"Okay Andy – don't forget pick up your Walkie–talkie from Sergeant Tommy."

"Oh yes – I almost forgot - I will get it on the way out – That is my old one on my desk give that to Security when they come looking!"

"Okay Andy – I'll give you a call at home tonight. – Okay?"

"If I am not there call me on the Walkie-talkie thing – via 'The Yard' – See you later."

Andy was not looking forward to this post mortem. He didn't like any post mortems, mostly boring and cringing as they used electronic saw cutters to get through bones. But this time it was his old friend and former boss Sir Mark Wrights post mortem, so that made this one extremely different and all the harder to witness.

The taxi arrived at two forty-five and dropped him alongside the mortuary department at Hammersmith Hospital. Having witnessed quite a few post mortems in this mortuary department, he knew the way through to the rooms where they carried them out and he hurried through to ensure he did not delay Professor Stokes.

He heard voices from Room Number One so he knocked the door and heard the unmistakeable voice of Professor John Stokes call; "Come In."

As Andy entered the room and closed the door behind him he was startled to see Doctor John Harvey was the other voice he had heard.

Professor Stokes nodded to Doctor Harvey who added; "I assume you already know Doctor Harvey 'The Yards' Forensics expert? He is also a pathologist!"

Andy smiled and replied; "Yes of course I do" He nodded and added; "Doctor Harvey – Surprised to see you. - How did you find out about the post mortem?

Doctor Harvey raised an eyebrow and replied; "The Home Secretary himself contacted me direct and asked if I would assist Professor Stone as it is such a high-profile case."

Andy thought to himself, how very interesting, since it was only enforced only a few hours ago how did the Home Secretary get the word? It could only have come from James Hall, the Coroner, probably protecting his own back side.

Andy then noticed Sir Mark's nude body lying on the slab in the centre of the room with a table alongside containing electronic saws, a variety of scalpels and strange tools. There was also a Philips tape recorder with a trailing wire to a microphone which was positioned on the slab alongside the body. A young chap stood by the tape recorder ready to turn it on and off as necessary.

"Now we are all here gentlemen, shall we get on with it?" Prof Stones moved over to the body and added; "By the way gentlemen this (pointing to the young chap) is my assistant Tommy Hardgrieves who you both probably spoke to earlier."

"Sirs – It is nice to be of assistance today, even if it is only to manage the tape recorder." Tommy Hardgrieves smiled mischievously.

Andy recognised the Cheeky Chappie voice from earlier and replied; "Well it's a better job than these two have to do today Tommy."

"Yeah there is that to it, but when you are studying forensic pathology, like I am Inspector, then it comes with the territory!"

"Right Tommy, machine on for this first bit." Prof. Stokes said as he bent over and looked with a magnifying glass at Sir Mark's left thigh and said; "As suggested in Doctor Bowen's report, I would agree that Sir Mark appears to have had an injection into his thigh, which is still slightly discoloured around the area. Would you agree Doctor Harvey?" He handed the magnifying glass to Doctor Harvey who closely inspected the area.

"Almost certainly this appears to be an injection - I would say with something larger than a syringe, it looks more like the size of a darning needle!"

"I agree Doctor Harvey!" Prof Stones said it for effect and added; "Right let's get on and look at the heart. Tommy turn off the recorder while we cut through the rib cage."

This was the start of the part which DI Spearing hated - the saw cutting through the breast bone and the parting of the rib cage. He looked away, pretending to rub his head, as the electronic saw did its work in the hands of Prof Stones. It appeared to take a long time of that horrible grinding noise before finally Prof Stones stopped and picked up a bigger magnifying glass which had adjustments for zooming in close.

"Tommy turn the tape on again!" Prof Stones ordered, and after Tommy nodded to indicate it was back on, said; "It would appear that there is damage to the heart tissue and I am now going to take a blood sample to check." Prof Stokes immediately took a blood sample from the body and added; "I think we ought to check this out before we proceed Doctor Harvey – Agreed?"

"Yes, I agree Professor – That will answer many of our questions. I think we should also look at the hospital doctor's report on Sir Mark's condition when he was admitted last night!"

"Do we have a copy of that report Tommy?" Prof Stones asked.

"Yes sir – I have left it in the mortuary office!"

"Go fetch it please Tommy – And turn off the tape machine until you get back." Tommy did as he was told.

Prof Stokes and Doctor Harvey then sat down at microscopes with the blood samples and began to work with them.

Tommy came back and first turned the tape recorder back on and from a single sheet of A4 paper he read; "Sirs – it appears that when Sir Mark was admitted he had tachycardia" Tommy looked at DI Spearing and added; "A racing - fast heartbeat.- he also had shortness of breath – had the sweats – hot and then cold and light headedness."

Tommy looked at everyone and added; "Despite being given the standard drugs to combat a possible heart attack, his position got worse as the evening wore on. So - as the symptoms showed, the faster heart beat was causing low blood pressure - supraventricular tachycardiaand ventricular tachycardia- the heart specialist Mr Keith Matheson then decided that Cardioversion was necessary" Tommy again looked at DI Spearing and added; "Electronic shock treatment! – For a time, the abnormal heart rhythm moved back to allow a normal rhythm, but then the abnormal rhythm returned. Eventually they lost the fight and Sir Mark died 22-15 last night."

Andy felt the cold analysis very disconcerting, but realised that is how doctors just give the cold facts. Suddenly Tommy was no longer the cheeky chappie – maybe that was his cover up for his job?

"Okay thanks Tommy – Well it looks like we do have unusually large amounts of potassium in the bloodstream – Would you agree Doctor Harvey?"

"Most definitely, but as you know Professor – It is not that unusual, after the heart is damaged, large amounts of potassium are usually released into the bloodstream!"

"Yes, I agree Doctor!"

DI Spearing interrupted and angrily said; "Hang on a minute – You are saying that we have a body here which you both agree has been injected with something and yet you are saying that these high levels of potassium are the usual?"

Prof Stones shook his head and for the first time appeared to be unsure when he replied; "Well yes and no Inspector. – The thing is, it would be difficult – if not impossible – for either of us to stand up in a court and state categorically that the fatal heart attack was caused by whatever poison. If it was a trial the defence lawyer would be able to have a clear counter argument, because it is very difficult to prove conclusively with potassium, because it appears naturally in large doses after any heart attack!"

"Bloody hell! So, we know he has been poisoned, but cannot prove it conclusively! – Is that what you are telling me gentlemen?"

"In a nutshell Inspector that is the problem! Whoever did this knew exactly what they were doing and although, we know what they did, proving it would be nearly impossible without a confession!" Professor Stones sounded apologetic, but that did not help.

"So, we have a murder and two very eminent doctors are not prepared to put their reputations on the line. That is the bottom line gentlemen – is it not?"

"That is very unfair Inspector." Doctor Harvey was the only one to respond.

"No Doctor Harvey – the only thing that is unfair is that somebody, or some people, are getting away with the murder of Sir Mark Wright and to protect your reputations you are allowing them to get away with it! Now that is unfair. Gentlemen! Let me know if you come up with anything useful that we can use!" Andy spun around and walked out of the mortuary.

As he walked down Du Cane Road he picked up a copy of The London Evening Standard from a street vendor's newspaper stand - The headline read; '**Sir Mark Wright Dies.**' It was a nicely written piece with a glowing tribute from The Home Secretary for the tremendous work Sir Mark had done, particularly in the organisation of the move to New Scotland Yard.

Then a sub headline caught Andys eyes; '**Prisoner escapes during transfer to Parkhurst.**' The story went on give details of a police Black Maria vehicle at around one p.m. being rerouted by a road block near Southampton Docks. The vehicle was later found with three policemen bound and gagged. The prisoner, Bobby Wilkins – on charges of multiple murders - had escaped. The story went on to warn the public not to approach Wilkins as he is considered highly dangerous.

'Not bloody likely to ever surface again! – a walking dead man' Andy thought to himself as he took out his Walkie-talkie and got patched through to DS Devlin which was answered almost immediately.

"Have you seen the news Kevin? Over."

"No Andy – I am still in the office doing the reports from today! Over."

"Well it looks like our man Wilkins has escaped, but escaped to what? I reckon he is probably a dead man walking! Over."

"Bloody hell Andy! – This does not look good for Kavanagh, or Mitchell the Governor? Over."

"Oh yes! I think you had better ring Kavanaghs home number! I think we also got Mitchell's home number as well did we? Over'"

"Yes, Andy I have both numbers – I will ring them now and find out where they are. I'll give you a ring back in ten! Over"

I thought to myself, I reckon he knew this was going to happen, but I let it go!

"Okay Kevin, let us see where we are! Over and Out."

Ten minutes or so later I phoned back to Andy and said; "Hello Andy – Nobody answering either of their phones. Over."

"Okay Kevin! Get some of the PC Plods over to both addresses and check them out Kevin. I think we may have problems! Over."

I could not help but have a gut feeling he knew there was going to be a problem, but I tamely replied; "Affirmative Andy! Over and out."

I got onto Paddington Street Police station and asked for Kavanaghs addresses to be urgently checked out.

I then phoned through to Southgate Police Station, which was a stone's throw away from where I lived in Palmers Green off Aldermans Hill. I gave the desk Sergeant Governor Mitchell's address in Broad Avenue, Winchmore Hill. It was a very select area with huge detached houses in North London, again not too far from where I lived. The desk Sergeant agreed, after a little reluctance, to get a couple of his Constables to go check out the address. I hung up and waited.

After an hour, I again got on the phone and rang Kavanaghs home number. After a couple of rings a male voice answered by repeating the phone number. I asked; "Is that Mr Kavanagh?"

"No! – Can I ask who is calling please?"

"I am Detective Sergeant Devlin from New Scotland Yard! Now can you please identify yourself?"

"How do I know you are who you say you are sir?"

"Well you can phone New Scotland Yard and ask to be put through to me! How will that do? Now can you tell me who you are?"

"I am DI Rawlings – I am attached to Paddington Green police station DS. Who is your DI, Sergeant?"

"DI Spearing sir!"

"Okay – yes I know you DS Devlin! You were in our station the other day with DI Spearing, so no need to phone you. Why did you want to speak to Mr Kavanagh?"

"He was involved in a case which my DI and I are on. It involves two mass murderers. I asked your station to check out his address an hour ago"

"Oh, thats okay Sergeant. That the one with the prisoner who committed suicide?"

"Yes sir, that's the one!"

"Well DS, sorry to have to tell you that the Kavanagh family returned this afternoon and found the place had been burgled. Then they found Mr Kavanagh in a pool of blood by the bedroom door with what appears to be a knife wound to his heart. The knife appears to have been twisted on entry. It looks like a burglary which has gone terribly wrong!"

"We do have information which may suggest that this may not be the case sir! Where did the family say they were sir?

"Well Sergeant - They said they were away for a few days for family reasons!"

"I suggest you question them more closely about that sir! We have information that they were held as hostages in an elaborate scheme to persuade Mr Kavanagh – a prison officer – to do something in prison for them."

"Do you know who 'them' are DS?"

"Oh, yes sir – we know who, but proving it may prove to be too difficult. We were going to pull the guy in for questioning, based on two signed statements, but now both these people have turned up dead."

"Oh dear – I think I can see where this is going DS. I will give you a ring back as soon as I have talked to the family! Okay?"

"Yes sir – Thanks." I hung up.

I then rang Governor Mitchell's home number and it rang continually, but no reply.

I rang Andy on the Walkie-talkie. He surprised me by answering almost instantly' "DI Spearing. Over."

"It is me Andy. The shit is certainly now hit the fan. Patrick Kavanagh has turned up dead. It was made to look like a burglary gone wrong, knife in the heart. His wife and kids found him when they returned, but have not said where they were! Also, Governor Mitchell is not answering his 'phone! I have asked Southgate Police Station to also check Governor Mitchells address. Over."

"Oh shit! They really are running amok again! Probably the wife and kids have been warned they will be back if they say anything and finding Kavanagh dead will just emphasise the point. So, they will stay silent and who can blame them? Who is in charge of the Kavanagh case? Over."

"DI Rawlings – Paddington Green is in charge Andy! Over."

"Oh, I know Bob Rawlings – a good man, but you had better let him know not to push the family too much. As far as Governor Mitchell is concerned – it is Saturday – he may be out shopping! Still better play it safe - Let me know if there is a problem Sergeant! I think it's time to pull in our friend Mr Lambert. I will get a warrant for his arrest and put out an all points for him. Over."

"How are you going to do that Andy? You being suspended and all and where is your evidence? Over"

"Whoops you have a point there – Okay – I will need copies of the Jones and Kavanagh statements – Those implicate him in the murder of Jones himself and in the multiple murders which Jones and Wilkins committed. We also have Sir Mark's statement that he was injected with someone who claimed to be from MI5 and he – Sir Mark – was dead a few hours later! - It is enough to allow me, with a good judge, to pull him in for questioning. Can you get them to me? – meet me in about an hour in 'The Bag of Nails' pub at Number 6 Buckingham Palace Road – Do you know it? Over."

"Yeah I think I can find it!" I really thought Andy was still holding back information

"Will do Andy. What are you up to this evening? Over."

"I am probably going back to see Sir Mark's widow – I am afraid the post mortem was inconclusive and our eminent Pathologists and Forensics consultants are not willing to put their reputations on the line. Shitbags! Then I must go to Harpenden something not right with my ex-wife. So, I may be out of range this evening. Over."

"That's bad news about the post mortem Andy! Okay, if I hear anything in the meantime on Mitchell I will let you know when we meet. Over and out."

Less than half an hour or so later, just as I was finishing my week's reports, I received a return call from the desk sergeant in Southgate Police Station who told me they found the front door open at Governor Mitchell's house. Inside, the house was immaculate. In the main bedroom, they found the body of Mitchell, with a suicide note and a double barrel shotgun in hand apparently shooting his heart to pieces.

I thanked the desk sergeant and hung up. I thought to myself this is like an epidemic of slayings; these MI5 guys are definitely running amok. I thought it was just as well Andy had decided on the arrest warrant for Robert Lambert. He had somehow to be stopped. I went off and copied the two statements on the Xerox 813 desk top copier. I tried Andys Walkie-talkie and then his home number, but got no reply from either. He was obviously on his way to our meet in 'The Bag of Nails.'

I placed the copy statements in a large A4 brown envelope and put the originals in my desk drawer and carefully locked the drawers.

I decided to walk along to "The Bag of Nails" to meet Andy and make some excuse that I was feeling a bit sick or something and I was going to call it a day and head home for some sleep.

I need not have worried about Andy – He could hardly wait to get away. He appeared to barely listen when I reported the apparent suicide of Governor Mitchell. He hardly even acted surprised.

I handed him the envelopes containing the copy statements and with a simple "Thanks" he bustled out of the pub leaving half a glass of lemonade undrunk. He was obviously very serious about cutting out the demon drink. He shouted back to me; "I am running late to meet the judge – Catch up with you in the morning!"

Robert Lambert, one of the MI5 bosses, emerged from The Olympia Grands nineteen sixty-seven Architecture Design Exhibition in Kensington London at six-thirty. He was dressed casually, as would be expected on a fine warm summer evening, in an open necked white silk shirt, black trousers with a black leather belt. He headed towards 'The Olympia Pub' in Olympia Way. He thought to himself he deserved a celebration drink or two!

He had no interest whatsoever in Architecture Design, but the exhibition had served its purpose. The place, with its magnificent Victorian glass dome, reminded him so much of St Pancras railway station. He had to have an alibi for the afternoon from one p.m. onwards and he now had the stubs of the entrance tickets tucked away in his wallet.

From Robert Lambert's point of view, it had been a highly satisfactory day. There had been two very difficult days when his partner in crime had become – quite rightly - very shaky indeed! The partner had also quite rightly accused Robert Lambert of losing control of the situation. Now he thought smugly to himself, everything was back under his control, so he deserved a celebration drink.

He entered the old Victorian building which housed 'The Olympia Pub.' It came complete with a superb solid oak horseshoe bar and traditional swivel brown leather bar stools. He ordered a pint of Old Speckled Hen beer from the affable Scottish barman with the name label 'James.' He took his pint over and sat in one of the large fan wooden backed oak chairs with the comfy soft brown cushions supping the pint slowly, on his own, at the traditional oak tables which surrounded the bar. He lit a Senior Service cigarette and slowly puffed smoke rings. The huge old pub was almost deserted. Either it was too early for the regular's, or it was just not a good catchment area for customer's on a Saturday evening.

Robert Lambert knew in his own mind that the last couple of days had been a challenge – the first for a long time. He simply had to move into action a lot quicker than he normally liked, but he had to be decisive. He had been decisive and he had, as usual, loved the feeling of ultimate power.

This afternoon he had taken care of Wilkins to ensure he would not talk ever again. During last night, he had taken care of the talkative Jones. That had left the loose ends of Kavanagh and the Kings Cross Prison Governor Mitchell. It had been a pity – they had been two good servants, but they had been links back to him and his partner and those links had to be cut!

All the bases had been covered and taken care off. They were highly satisfactory actions, all within the last twenty-four-hours. - Now see what you can make of that DI Spearing! As was always the case, policemen had to follow the rules, whereas MI5 were allowed 'in the interest of the countries security' to make their own rules.

One drink led to another. He felt quite tipsy, which was the norm after a few pints of the rather strong Old Speckled Hen. It was suddenly nine p.m. and getting dark. He called it a night and headed back to The Olympia multi-story car park. He had arrived around one p.m. and being a Saturday afternoon the car park had been nearly full so he had finished up on the top floor. The lifts were again not working so he struggled up the concrete stairway to the seventh floor.

He found his car, drunkenly inserted the keys and opened the door. Suddenly a very strong arm like a vice was across his throat restricting his windpipe. He almost instantly began to feel faint. As he was passing out, his legs thrashing out behind him trying to kick whoever, he felt a strap tying his legs together.

Eventually Lambert came to with a rasping voice in his ears saying; "Okay Mr Lambert – You tell me – Who is your partner?"

"I don't know what you are talking about!" Lambert replied his voice screeching.

"Okay Mr Lambert – have it your way!"

Lambert felt the guy grab his belt at the back of his trousers and he was suddenly lifted off the ground with tremendous force and projected horizontally towards the open space and hung out seven floors, about eighty feet above the concrete ground.

Lambert screamed and shouted; "Okay – Okay!"

The guy pulled him back and stood him on the ground. Lambert whispered a name to the guy who responded with: "I don't believe you!" With that the guy again lifted him and again hung him out horizontally across the eighty feet precipice.

Lambert again screamed and shouted; "I am telling you the truth mate – that is who it is!"

'The Fox' nodded and replied; "That's good Mr Lambert. – Now this is for my friend Joe Cole and from me for daring to try to frame me with John Palmer! – Goodbye Mr Lambert – I will meet you in hell someday!" With that 'The Fox' yanked off the belt holding Lamberts legs and threw him out into space from eighty feet up.

The last thought of Robert Lambert, as the concrete pavement rushed up to meet his head was; "Shit! – I did not cover all the bases."

'The Fox,' alias Sam Aldridge, alias Eric Liddell was dressed all in black, even his boots were black and with black gloved hands opened Robert Lambert's car door and threw in a type written suicide note with the perfectly forged signature of Robert Lambert. He relocked the car door and threw the car keys after the body.

He then got into his own car and leisurely drove off well before the sound of sirens shattered the peaceful night around The Olympia.

Later that same evening I decided I needed to talk to Andy about the case against Robert Lambert so I gave his London home number a ring from our call box. No reply only an answering machine so I left a message for him to ring me.

Then I tried the Walkie-talkie and again no reply. So, I phoned 'Directory of Enquires' and got his Harpenden home number which was still listed under the Spearing family name. It took only two rings for it to be answered by a rather snooty sounding woman complete with the BBC Home Counties accent; "Ms Spearing speaking. Who is calling?"

I hesitated for a second and with my best posh voice replied; "Mrs Spearing – I am Detective Sergeant Devlin from New Scotland Yard – Your husband is my DI. Can I speak to DI Spearing please?"

"Well Sergeant Devlin – It is Ms Spearing – DI Spearing is no longer my husband! And 'No' – you cannot talk to him because he is not here – He has gone to his hotel earlier this afternoon?"

"Sorry Ms Spearing – Could you tell me which hotel is staying at?"

Yes, I can Sergeant – He is in 'The Grove' just outside Harpenden in the country – Very nice too – I don't know how he can afford to stay there."

I resisted the temptation to reply 'Especially after you and the boyfriend were finished fleecing his pockets' instead I asked nicely; "I don't suppose you have a telephone number for it Ms Spearing?"

"I have Sergeant, but I am sure you can get it from inquiries!" Ms Spearing immediately hung up. "Cow" I replied into the dead line.

I phoned inquiries and got put straight through to 'The Groves' reception desk where another rather snooty sounding woman answered with; "Good afternoon. 'The Grove' Harpenden – How can I help you?"

"Hello, I am Detective Sergeant Devlin from New Scotland Yard. I am trying to contact my boss Detective Inspector Spearing who I believe is staying at the hotel just now. - If I could speak to him please?"

"I am sorry, but I am afraid Mr Spearing is no longer with us." The receptionist replied, but she must have heard my sharp intake of breath before she quickly added; "What I mean is – Mr Spearing checked in this afternoon and apparently came back later, but has not been seen since then. We don't know if he is spending the night, but he has not checked out and his case is still here. I don't suppose you know his whereabouts sir?"

"I am afraid not Miss, I am looking for him. I am sure he will be back soon so ask him to ring DS Devlin on my home number." I hung up quickly to avoid any more akward questions.

. Now I was really wondering what the hell was going on,

The mysterious call came about two hours or so before darkness on Saturday evening. The voice was in a thick East London accent said; "I am told that you hired 'The Fox' last week to kill your husband. I know you have been frightened off by Robert Lambert from MI5 I have been sent here to get you sorted out – I want fifty thousand quid to shut me up."

"Don't be so ridiculous! Why are you doing this?"

"Like I said, I am getting out of this business. So, you will meet me tonight in The Upper Gardens with fifty thousand quid. You will come on your own – If anybody else shows up – you are dead! You know I am deadly if you cross me! I will meet you on the bench in The Upper Gardens just before the tree trail starts heading northwards. Make no mistake, if you do not appear, I will come looking for you and I can assure you – you will not like that! So be there at nine p.m." The line went dead.

At nine p.m., he watched from the trees directly behind the bench. He watched very carefully as his subject made her way up the little hill to the bench carrying a stuffed full paper bag, a hand bag on her arm and took her seat. She was dressed sexily in a loose fitting, white summer top and tight fitted skirt which showed off her tan and her figure to best effect. He watched for a few minutes to ensure that nobody was following, then silently came out of the trees directly behind her, pulling out a gun, with the silencer fitted, and held it tight to her bare neck.

"Now Mrs Palmer – First, give me your handbag, without turning around, or you will be dead before you turn!"

Mrs Palmer sucked in a deep breath, but passed the handbag over her shoulder without turning around as ordered.

He looked into the bag and picked out a Smith and Wesson Model 36 Revolver gun with a silencer fitted and said; "My oh my Mrs Palmer – you are indeed untrustworthy." As be tucked the gun into his belt he added; "Now the paper bag! – The same way without turning around Mrs Palmer."

Mrs Palmer again did as she was told and he looked into the bag which was indeed stuffed with twenty-pound notes.

"Okay Mrs Palmer, stand up and take one step forward, legs apart and do not turn around no matter what!"

Mrs Palmer did as she was told. He came around the bench, his hand still holding his gun, and stood behind her. He frisked her down the front, his hands dwelling for a moment between her breasts. He then frisked her all the way down her back and then suddenly lifted up the skirt of her dress and frisked her between her legs in front plus behind her white panties. He found a knife in the front of her panties which he removed and said; "Tut - Tut - Mrs Palmer you are really carrying dangerous weapons aren't you?"

"Enjoying yourself? – Getting a hard on are we?" Mrs Palmer said it coolly with a smile.

"Not my type I am afraid Mrs Palmer!"

"You like little boys better then Mr Fox?"

"Not at all Mrs Palmer, but I don't like brazen women who arrange to murder their husbands."

"What do you know about anything?"

"Ah, yes but I do know a little Mrs Palmer – I had a very interesting conversation with Mr Robert Lambert. You know what you started Mrs Palmer by arranging the murder of your husband, has already resulted in six people dying"

"My husband was a wife beater and womaniser Mr Fox! I don't suppose you knew that?" Mrs Palmer replied without feeling.

"Nothing like the venom of a woman scorned eh Mrs Palmer?" He sounded sarcastic and added; "Yes I suppose that another few dead people mean nothing when you are killing and maiming so many with the drugs selling company you are trying so hard to relaunch?"

"My so called 'husband' arranged for the murder of my Uncle Joe Bolger.

"I am afraid you are wrong about that too Mrs Palmer. You see Mr Robert Lambert and his MI5 colleagues were responsible for that! You see, that is how he snared you into his little web!"

"No, it can't be – He assured us! He got out of control with those later killings!"

"Don't worry; Mr Lambert won't be bothering us anymore. He has had a very big fall from grace!"

Mrs Palmer went to turn around to her right, but the gun was quickly put to her right ear. "Now don't be silly Mrs Palmer do not turn around." He moved behind her back carrying the gun in one hand and the bag of money in the other and added; "Now go to the right towards the trees Mrs Palmers."

"So, you do want a bit then?"

"Don't flatter yourself Mrs Palmer just move there and don't turn around. We have to get out of here without being seen."

They got into the trees which made it darker as it was now after nine p.m. They walked into the deeper trees at the side of the trail.

He pulled out Mrs Palmer's gun with the fitted silencer and tapped her on the shoulder. She turned around and faced him and said; "But you are not 'The Fox' – you are that Detective---."

"Yes, that's right Mrs Palmer. This is rough justice! We are taking over your company." He replied with a grin and pushed her gun into her mouth pulling the trigger at the same time. There was a pop and the back of Mrs Palmer's skull blew out, brain matter spewing out like a fountain behind her.

He placed the gun in her hand making sure her fingerprints were all over it. He had on gloves.

Carrying the bag of money in his hand he made his way to the back gate of the upper gardens in Bournemouth Central Park and disappeared into the misty night.

Book 1 in the DI Spearing and DS Devlin series

Epilogue

I awoke on Sunday morning at eight a.m. I was wide awake as usual every day at that time. It was another lovely morning in London during July of nineteen sixty-seven.

I decided to jog half - heartedly down Aldermans Hill to the newspaper shop at Palmers Green triangle. I picked up the Sunday Express and read the main headline which read; **'Were these cases connected?' By John Fisher** I remembered the name as a reporter with 'The London Evening Standard 'who had given a staged question to Andy Spearing. I then remembered at that time The Express Group owned The Evening Standard.'

The main storyline quoted insiders within New Scotland Yard who had said many of the cases quoted on this front page were sensationally being linked to rogue personnel within MI5.

There were four sub headlines under the headline story, one to the right of the main story. The other three sub headlines were below the main story, to the left, centre and the right of the front page.

The sub headline to the right of the main story read; **'Sir Mark Wright was injected.'**

The story had a photograph of Sir Mark and reported sensationally that; "hours before his death Sir Mark had apparently bumped into a man going into a lift within New Scotland Yard and had been injected in his thigh with an undefined substance which *may* have later caused his massive heart attack. The mystery man had booked into NSY stating that he was a representative of MI5 and had a meeting with a Senior NSY Officer DCI Harry Tomlinson."

The final paragraph stated that Sir Mark's funeral service would be a private affair and would be held at Golders Green Crematorium next Friday. July 28.

Under the main story, the sub headline to the left read; **'Jones & Wilkins worked for MI5.'** The storyline was all about the arrest, charges and imprisonment of the two MI5 officers for the murder of Joseph (Joe) Bolger and their implication in the torture of many people, some of whom have disappeared and would likely be presumed dead.

It went on to say that statements had been taken by New Scotland Yard and charges had been admitted. Also, a senior officer in MI5, a Mr Robert Lambert, had been implicated and NSY has issued a warrant for the arrest of Mr Lambert.

Towards the end of the story there was a report that Michael Jones had been found hanged in his cell apparently, a questionable suicide. Later a Senior Prison Officer Kavanagh (See other Headline story) was charged with the murder of Jones.

The final paragraph stated that Bobby Wilkins, who having been charged with the same offences as Jones, had escaped from custody while being transported from Kings Cross Prison to Parkhurst on the Isle of Wight. He was currently being sought and was considered a dangerous criminal and should not be approached.'

The centre sub headline read; **'MI5 Deputy Chief wanted!'** The storyline basically read; 'MI5 Deputy Chief Robert Lambert is being sought by NSY in connection with being implicated in murders and torture carried out by his officers Jones and Wilkins. Statements have made it clear that Lambert has been involved.

The sub headline to the right read; **'Governor Mitchell and Officer Kavanagh implicated.'**

The storyline read; 'Governor Mitchell and Senior Prisoner Officer Kavanagh from Kings Cross Prison both of whom had been implicated in the murder of prisoner Michael Jones have been found dead.

Officer Kavanagh was murdered in his home apparently following a burgarly which went wrong.

Governor Mitchell was also found dead in his home, apparently, a suicide.

Senior Prisoner Officer Kavanagh had signed a statement which has implicated himself and Governor Mitchell in the murder (and not suicide!) of the prisoner Michael Jones. Officer Kavanaghs statement has also implicated MI5's Mr Robert Lambert, in the murder of Michael Jones in the prison.

I decided to try to phone Andy Spearing again and jogged back to the flat in Old Park Road. I first tried the Harpenden Grove hotel again and was politely informed that Andy had returned in the afternoon but had disappeared and had not checked out though he had paid in advance. Then I rang the rather posh Mrs Spearing at home and was told frostily that 'HE' had gone off in a temper and went to his hotel. Then I tried his London home number and the Walkie-talkie, but no reply so I left a message on his London home number to call me as soon as possible. I did not like my stray thoughts on what Andy may have been up to yesterday afternoon and evening, so I tried to put them to the back of my mind.

I decided, since it was Sunday, I would have a day off, rest and sod everything else that was going on. Just cool down and let whatever happen!

An hour later I was lying dozing on the settee when my Walkie - talkie rang. I hit the reply button and said; "DS Devlin here. How can I help? Over."

"Hello Sergeant DI Sanderson here! I have been trying to ring Andy but no reply! Any idea where he is? Over."

I immediately decided in view of my earlier stray thoughts to keep it short and simple when I replied; "I suppose you know he was suspended on Friday sir? The last I knew he was going to Harpenden something about his divorce, but I have been unable to raise him this morning either at home or in Harpenden. – You know what he is like with the Walkie-talkie sir!."

"Yes, I do know all about him and the Walkie-talkie things!" DI Sanderson replied with a short laugh, but there was hesitation in his voice. "I have been trying to raise him as well but no joy! Anyway, you are on the same cases so I suppose you should know - I was called out last night to an apparent suicide – The only reason I was called out is the diver was a high-profile MI5 man that we want to question. Over."

I was visibly shaken and stammered my replied; "Oh shit! – Its not Robert Lambert, is it?" Over.

"Right first time Sergeant! Splattered all over the road under The Olympia car park. Jumped from the seventh floor. Left a suicide note, admitting his involvement in murders and things. Over."

"Does it look like suicide sir? "

"Why do you ask that Sergeant? Do you know something I should know?" Over." DI Sanderson sounded irritated, not like him.

"No not at all sir! I just thought Lambert was not the type to commit suicide. The truth is we probably did not have enough to convict him especially with the other deaths – and he knew it - So why commit suicide? Is it cut and dried suicide sir? Over."

"Well not exactly Sergeant. There are a few scrapes on the body around his belly and his fingers are cut and along the ledge of the seventh floor there is what appears to be matching skin. Also, the suicide note is too precise, it is also typed which is unusual, although it is signed and as you say suicide does not make sense. However, it may be difficult, if not impossible, to prove anything except suicide. Sorry my phone is ringing Sergeant – I will have to ring you back. Over and Out."

I sat staring at the Walkie-talkie for a few minutes, my thoughts running over all sorts of scenarios when the thing suddenly started buzzing again. I switched it on and again stated; "DS Devlin here. How can I help? Over."

"Hello Sergeant – it is me again! It was DI John Sanderson and he continued; "That was Bob Thornton from Bournemouth CID on the phone! I am afraid he has just given me more bad news – another suicide in one of your cases!""

I found myself stammering again as I replied; "Oh my God. It is getting like London buses. Who is it this time – Mrs Palmer?"

"Spot on again Sergeant. I reckon you are truly paranormal. It appears she blew off her head in Bournemouths Upper Gardens and she was found this morning. Apparently Bob Thornton have been trying to get Andy this morning, but like us he could not get him. He remembered my name and got patched through to me."

"I just don't believe it sir! - She was not the type! She has, or I should say had, a couple of kids who were relying on her. No way would she have done that! She was too cool a customer for that! "

"That is exactly what Bob Thornton said. But he also said her Dad said she received a call from a public phone box and, against his advice, went off with a bag of money to meet someone about her business. She also took the gun with her."

"There we go – There was somebody else involved! It must be the MI5 mob again!"

"Why does it have to be just MI5 Sergeant? It could be anybody wanting to take over her business and Bob does say there are no signs of a struggle – No evidence of anything but a suicide."

I found myself shaking with anger when I replied; "Oh come on sir! – We already knew MI5 were after her and previously found her in Bournemouth! With their resources, it would not take much for them to refind her." I was having those bad thoughts again about Andy Spearing.

"That is for sure Sergeant. Always assuming it was them. There is one thing her Dad reported that he seen the same guy who had been outside their home was now hanging around their hideaway and some young copper caught him on Friday early evening, but he flashed his badge. He was a MI5 guy by the name of Peter Hazlewood. The one query we have is the only person other than Bob Thornton who knew that telephone number was Andy Spearing."

I ignored the part about Andy and replied; "Oh my God sir – that Peter Hazlewood is the guy we are after for injecting Sir Mark with that poison! Over."

"Really? – Oh, my goodness this is getting to be a proper who done it! If MI5 are involved we are going to have to escalate this through our bosses and the Home Secretary."

"I suggest we hang fire and give it to our new boss sir. As it stands some of our bosses will probably sit on it and cover up."

"Yes, I agree Sergeant – Lets hope that happens sooner rather than later. Look Sergeant – I know that this may sound awful, but I think we should say nothing to anubody, including Andy, until we speak to the new boss and get this escalated."

I was taken aback by the statement, but that is where my earlier stray thoughts had been leading to so I repled; "Yes sir – I agree – It makes sense – We will see what tomorrow brings."

"Good well done Sergeant – Hopefully we are being over cautious, but better be safe than sorry. See you tomorrow. Over and Out"

I was suddenly sure if Andy phoned me back I would stay quiet - it was time to shut up and go along with whatever. Somethings are better left unsaid, but there again he has to know about Mrs Palmers 'suicide.'

I did not receive any further calls on the Sunday, either from Andy or anyone else.

Monday morning came and to me - DS Devlin - it had been one hell of a start on the job with NSY. More like a month! Everything that had happened now appeared to be like a nightmare! Yet it was true! It had happened!

Our cases were falling apart as one after another suspects and prisoners died off.

I went into NSY on the Monday morning at eight thirty a.m. and there was a buzz about the place. Everyone was talking about the announcement that was going to be made this morning. I honestly didn't have a clue what they were talking about, but I acted real cool. In nineteen sixty-seven that was more important than anything else!

I did notice Tweedledee and Tweedledum alias Bill Brown and Tony Booth glaring at me, but when I returned their stare with my angry 'hard man' glare they quickly averted their eyes.

I set about updating the case files with the latest information, including the deaths. As I recorded the details I began to realise most of our cases could be closed; probably the only three that could remain open were the charges against Jonathan Bridgewater and the case against the bouncers Tommy Smith and Bobby Cosgrove with the solicitor Aldrich. Even that case, with the death of Mrs Palmer, maybe now a non-starter, but I knew Andy would not drop it because of his snaring of the solicitor Aldrich.

Then of course there was the tracing of Peter Hazlewood from MI5 who had almost certainly injected Sir Mark with the poison and I hoped may have been responsible for Mrs Palmers 'suicide.'

At ten a.m. I decided to take the revised cases to my Kemosabe Judith up on the tenth floor. Feeling a bit lazy I decided on the lift. After a minute or so waiting time a lift appeared on the way up. There were three people already in the lift and as I stepped in I recognised all three of them. There was DCS Sutherland, the Home Secretary John Fairly and finally my former boss - the Central Glasgow City Police Chief Inspector - Ian Johnstone. The only difference was he was now dressed in the brand-new uniform of The Commissioner of Police of the London Met. I recognised it because of the pips with the insignia of rank - a crown above a Bath Star. As I got into the lift I hit the number ten button and the doors closed.

Ian Johnstone smiled broadly at me and offered me his handshake and said; "Fancy meeting you here Sergeant Devlin. How are you?"

I took his handshake and smiled in return before replying; "I am very good sir, but a rather hectic first couple of weeks. I see you are our new chief sir?"

I noticed DCS Sutherland looking rather grumpy.

"Yes – It was quite a surprise Sergeant – Never thought I would be following you down here! I have heard good reports about you already."

I looked surprised and replied; "Really? That is good to know sir."

The lift came to a stop on the tenth floor and, as I waited for the doors to open, the new boss suddenly said; "I would like to have a word with you Sergeant. Can you come up to my office at two p.m.?"

I smiled as I replied; "Certainly sir. I will see you at two." I stepped out of the lift and caught DCS Sutherland looking gloomier than ever. I thought to myself I bet he thought he might get the big job. Thank God he did not get it.

I got to Kemosabes office and saw Judith was on her own so I knocked the door, strode in and cheerily said; "Peace be with you Kemosabe!"

Judith smiled broadly and replied; "And to you my Lone Ranger!"She looked thoughtful for a moment then said; "I hear you really are the' Lone Ranger' again! What has happened?" I heard DI Spearing is suspended."

"The infamous rumour control is still working then! – Yeah, he has been suspended for disobeying an order! The only problem was he was ordered to break the law, so I can't see it sticking, but he is not allowed in the office until his disciplinary hearing, whenever that will be."

"Anyway, what can I do for you my 'Lone Ranger'? I have been ordered to be upstairs to meet our new boss at ten thirty, so I can only give you a few minutes!"

"That is all I usually need!"

"Bragging again are we Lone Ranger?"

"I never brag Kemosabe! Anyway, I have just met our new boss in the lift and I have been invited to his office for a meeting at two!"

"Don't tell me - you know him?"

"Yep! – He was my boss in Glasgow – he recommended me for this job!"

"You know my Lone Ranger - if you fell into a pigsty you would come up smelling of roses. – Now very quickly what can I do for you?"

"Oh, I have brought our cases up to date. There has been a drastic change in our cases. No less than five of the people involved with our investigations have turned up dead and one other is missing."

"Yeah I got to read all about it in The Sunday Express yesterday! I hear that MI5 are going ape shit about it! They are threatening to sue New Scotland Yard. Who the hell fed that story to The Sunday Express?"

I chose to ignore the story feed question and replied; "I bet they will withdraw that now, since their Deputy Chief, Robert Lambert nose-dived from the top floor of 'The Olympia' car park last night and left a suicide note admitting to his involvement with Jones and Wilkins. We also have two signed statements from, now very dead people, who also named Lambert as the man behind the murders and torture."

"Bloody hell! But even so, it should not have been leaked to the press."

"That is the point Kemosabe! If it had been kept behind closed doors – as always with 'The Establishment,' it would have been swept under the carpet. Believe me I did not leak any information, but it was very necessary!"

"So, it was DI Spearing then?"

"I really don't know, and that's the truth, but it had to be published!"

"Yes well – if you say so, but five people dead and one missing, that is carnage in my book!"

"You are so right Kemosabe, but just remember it was not who released this to the press, it was who did the murders. And that was, in the main MI5, probably led by Mr Robert Lambert."

"Okay I get the gist! Okay, I will read through these cases and get back to you late afternoon. Now I must go to this meeting. See you later."

At two on the dot I was outside our new Chief's office and was ushered straight through by his secretary Miss Rutledge, a middle age spinster who apparently had been Sir Mark's secretary.

Ian Johnstone was, as always, straight to the point and said; "Well Sergeant – I won't beat about the bush – I only arrived this morning and I have the MI5 chief on my back. I told them even I could not believe what I read in 'The Sunday Express.' I am told that DI Spearing and you as his DS are on these cases. What is going on Sergeant?"

"I don't really know how the Express got the stories sir, I read them the same as everybody else on Sunday morning, but as I was just telling Judith Clements - our DPP representative - this morning, - If it had been kept behind closed door – as always with

The Establishment and this place, it would have been swept under the carpet. Believe me I did not leak any information, but it was very necessary!"

"So, it was DI Spearing then?"

"I really don't know and that's the truth sir - As you will probably know - DI Spearing is suspended on some put up charge!" I paused and then added; "I happen to think sir - we should all remember it is not a question who released this to the press; it is a question of who did the murders. And that was, in the main, a rogue element in MI5, probably led by a Mr Robert Lambert. We do have signed statements from two of the victims implicating Robert Lambert. Also of course, I just heard this morning from DI Sanderson that Lambert has committed suicide in The Olympia car park and left a suicide note admitting his involvement! Also, Kings Cross Prison Officer Kavanagh has made a statement implicating MI5 and Governor Mitchell in the murder of Mr Jones a prisoner and an MI5 Operative who was on murder charges. He has also in a signed statement implicated MI5. We are also looking for an MI5 Operative Peter Hazlewood in connection with the deaths of Sir Mark and a Mrs Palmer who was murdered - made to look like a suicide - last night. We need you to escalate this Sir to the MI5 boss and the Home Secretary?"

"Really? Now that is a game changer! I can now tell MI5 where to go! I will certainly escalate this today."

"Thank you, Sir." I rose to go.

"By the way Sergeant, I tried to get a hold of DI Spearing this morning. He is not answering phones or the Walkie-Talkie. - Any ideas how I can catch up with him?"

"Well as I said sir DI Spearing is suspended. I know he went home to Harpenden on Saturday afternoon - something about his divorce. I tried to get him yesterday and this morning but could not get a hold of him! – I am a little worried with all these murders, disappearances and put up suicides." I decided on minimum information again.

"Yes, well it has only been a couple of days. Leave it till tomorrow and then put an alert call and ring round the usual places. Anyway, it is this suspension that I want to talk to him about – A load of crap! - But it seems he intends to take retirement."

"Who said that Sir?"

"DI Sanderson said he was upset with the suspension!"

"He must have been drunk. I can assure you sir – DI Spearing will never give up the force until they force him out, or he is carried out in a box!"

"Well he sounded very serious to DI Sanderson Sergeant,"

"I think that will last until tonight sir. As you say he is probably very sore about being suspended."

"Well maybe Sergeant! But within the week we will be removing most of the scum from these offices. I can promise you that! Have you seen the list of our people involved?"

"No sir, but DI Spearing told me the names of a couple of people on the list. It is not before time!"

"Yes Sergeant, but at least we are now moving in the right direction!"

"Yes Sir – but from what I hear we are not nailing all the guilty parties?"

"That's true Sergeant, we could only go for the ones we can prove! However, we know quite a few of the others and their careers will go nowhere! We will be watching them for snatching if we get a chance. Anyway, thanks for coming up and, when you get a chance, send me up your case files on these MI5 people – I want to bring myself up to date before I formally reply to MI5."

"Yes Sir!" I replied and got out quick.

At three in the afternoon Judith turned up at my desk laden with the case files I had given her earlier. She was smiling so that was a good sign.

"Well my Lone Ranger it looks like you are left with only three possible cases. The first one you must trace Peter Hazlewood from MI5, but even if you do you will have great difficulty in getting enough proof! The second case is the charges against Aldrich and the two bodyguards. The absence of the deceased Mrs Palmer will make it more difficult, but there is enough evidence left to make the charges stick. The third one is the Bridgewater case – the charges of homosexual relations with a minor is I think watertight, even my Uncle Bill can't get him off on that one, but the charge of murder well, that is dodgy. I think we need more forensic evidence."

"I am on that one Kemosabe – I am just waiting on for our forensic people to get back to me. I am hoping that the foreign pubic hair found on Bridgewater will match our victim Worthington's as well as the blood and fingerprints on the case carried by the boy, which had the Worthington address, will also match."

"Well I would say that would be the minimum Lone Ranger! The problem is, if we proceed with the murder charge, it could hinder the homosexual charge."

"Can we not go for separate trials?"

"Too expensive and the publicity from the first one would probably make the second one unfair!"

"Could we not drop the murder charge on insufficient evidence for now and after we have him jailed for the homosexual things, then recharge him with murder on the basis of new evidence?"

"You know my Lone Ranger you are becoming as devious as your DI Spearing!"

"Is that a 'yes'?"

"Only if you do not bring any 'new' evidence forward until the homosexual trial is underway and you do not tell me anything about it until then. – Agreed?"

"Agreed Kemosabe!" – Could you do me a favour? Take the MI5 cases upstairs to the Chief and leave a message from yourself that some of these cases will now be quietly closed."

"What's wrong with your legs my Lone Ranger?"

"Nothing is wrong as far as I know Kemosabe. I just don't want to be asked any more awkward questions at the moment!"

"Oh, okay – See you later." Judith turned away with a twirl of her black and white mini dress. It gave a very nice show of her fabulous legs and lower thighs.

"Thanks!" I shouted after her as she headed towards the lift. She gave a little wave of her right hand without turning around and those swaying hips still looked sexy.

Well, the start of week three in my New Scotland Yard career was up and running with so many balls still in the air and new ones about to be shot at me.

Book 1 in the DI Spearing and DS Devlin series

About the Author

I was born and bred in Fauldhouse, then a mining village in central Scotland.

I got involved with the music business in Scotland in nineteen-sixty with a couple of my best mates from my schooldays; Jimmy Young and John Carty. We started running 'Record Hops,' which for the uninformed were the forerunner of the far more successful 'Discos.'

Then I got involved with a band named 'The Premiers' that my brother Harry, a drummer, who later became internationally well known, had joined.

Later in the sixties I became a promoter of Dancing and Concerts throughout central Scotland and presented lots of big 'names' (e.g. Stevie Winwood and 'The Spencer Davies' group, 'Them' with Van Morrison, The Bay City Rollers (before they hit the big time!), Johnny Kidd and The Pirates, Alex Harvey etc).

I later joined up in London with my brother Harrys new band 1-2-3 which was formed from the remnants of 'The Premiers' with Ian Ellis and Billy Ritchie.

!-2-3 went on to sign for the world famous Brian Epstein and his NEMS empire which included of course 'The Beatles,' The Bee Gees' and 'Cream' – Guess who did not make it? At this time, the group were resident in the world famous 'Marquee Club' in the Soho district of London. They also got involved with David Bowie who was a friend and 1-2-3 played on his early demos.

There were gigs with Jimi Hendrix at the Savile Theatre and jamming sessions with Hendrix and Eric Burden of The Animals in London's club land.

There followed other world famous agencies which included famous names like; 'Rod Stewart and The Faces,' 'Ten Years After' and 'Jethro Tull.'

I was also editor, writer and chief bottle washer for an entertainment newspaper in Scotland titled 'Nightlife.' During this time, we interviewed Billy Connelly, Gerry Rafferty (Just before they made the big time) and Status Quo in addition to hundreds of 'On Stage' reviews etc.

I have used my experiences and observations on the perimeter of the sixties and seventies entertainment business, plus some friends who worked in New Scotland Yard, as material for this series of novels.

I now live in Northampton, England and holiday abroad in Asia every year, usually writing and having a good time during the dreary cold UK winter months.

I am still in contact with the surviving members of the original group and we meet up every year, particularly with my best mate Shammy singing and dancing across Asia.

P. S. If you would like to catch up with my current writing and news or to offer reviews on this novel go to my Web Site; WWW.Paul-Hughes-Author.com

Two of my friends and I from the nineteen sixties UK groups; Shammy Lafferty and George Nash have got together and written a couple of new songs based on the 60's

Book 1 in the DI Spearing and DS Devlin series
era you can have a view and listen on YouTube at; https://youtu.be/MDFBCazd-ug

Printed in Great Britain
by Amazon